MW01135684

Presence of
Mine Enemies

Stephen England

Also by Stephen England

Sword of Neamha
Lion of God: A Shadow Warriors Prequel Trilogy

Shadow Warriors Series
NIGHTSHADE
Pandora's Grave
Day of Reckoning
TALISMAN
LODESTONE
Embrace the Fire
QUICKSAND
ARKHANGEL
Presence of Mine Enemies

Copyright © 2019 by Stephen England
Cover design by Louis Vaney
Formatting by Polgarus Studio

All rights reserved. No part of this publication may be reproduced, stored in a retrieval system, or transmitted in any form or by any means—electronic, mechanical, photocopy, recording, or any other—without the prior written permission of the author.

This is a work of fiction. Names, characters, places, and incidents either are the product of the author's imagination or are used fictitiously, and any resemblance to actual persons, living or dead, business establishments, events, or locales is entirely coincidental. Views expressed by the characters in this novel are their own, and do not necessarily reflect the views of the author.

To all those, in the spheres of both law enforcement and intelligence, who have gone undercover, risking their lives—and their very souls—in the pursuit of justice, this book is respectfully dedicated.

"Thou preparest a table before me, in the
presence of mine enemies. . ."

– The Twenty-third Psalm

"We have done with Hope and Honour, we are lost to Love and Truth, we are dropping down the ladder rung by rung. . ."

– Rudyard Kipling, "Gentlemen-Rankers"

Prologue

5:43 A.M. Central European Summer Time, June 11th
An apartment
Sint-Jans-Molenbeek, Belgium

Lights, flashing through the darkness of the night. Red, white, and blue. The colors of a flag, waving in the salt breeze over a destroyer's fantail.

The colors of death this night. The wailing of sirens filling the air, mournful and grim. Blood staining his hands as he cradled her body in his arms, looking down at her face—lifeless eyes staring back into his own. "Don't give up on me. Don't you dare give up."

The sound of his own voice, somehow alien to his ears. Distant and faraway. Filled with grief.

Then the ground seemed to crumble from around him, her face melting away to be replaced by that of another, an older woman, her dark hair shot with silver.

Tears of grief and despair shining in her dark eyes. Her voice trembling with anger. "You just turn your back and walk away from everything you've done—the lives you've destroyed. As if they never existed, as if they weren't even real."

A pistol coming up in her hand, aimed straight at him even as fire blossomed from its muzzle. Bullets tearing through flesh and muscle. And then he was falling. Falling. Falling—

The man came awake suddenly, his head coming off the folded jacket he was using for a rude pillow—his bare chest glistening with sweat, his entire body trembling as if caught in the grip of a fever.

It was a dream. Only a dream.

Except that it *wasn't*, he thought, his breathing slowly returning to normal

1

as he pushed himself aright, leaning back into the threadbare cushions of the couch. Glancing down to see the dark, discolored pockmarks on his lower abdomen still marking the place where the pair of .45-caliber bullets had ripped their way through his torso.

Like all which had gone before it. . .*all too real.* Death coming for him, only to be turned away once again at the door. A welcome visitor, now long overdue.

He pushed himself to his feet, feeling a dull pain shoot through his body as he rose, padding barefoot across the grungy, cigarette-stained carpet toward the washbasin. The hot, humid air of the Belgian mid-summer already pervading the apartment, the noise of the city street without clearly audible through the open window.

Over two months, and a full recovery seemed yet beyond his grasp.

The face of a stranger staring back at him from the mirror as he leaned heavily against the sink, drawn and haggard—a ghost of his former self. Only the thick stubble of his beard serving to hide the stark pallor of his cheeks. Eyes the color of blued steel gazing out from deep, hollow sockets.

Eyes which had seen so much of life. Of *death.*

"*Bismillah,*" he said, his lips moving ever so slightly as he turned on the faucet on full blast, water splashing into the basin. *In the name of God.*

He used his left hand to wash his right, cold water running between his fingers as he washed up to the wrist before repeating the familiar ritual with the other hand—taking water into his mouth and swishing it around before spitting it back out into the basin.

Purity. Ever the desire of the believer—purity in the eyes of one's fellow man. And of God.

God. Harry Nichols shook his head, running dripping hands up over his face and through his dark black hair. Stooping to wash his feet.

He had spent a lifetime at war. Fighting *evil.* And yet somehow. . .he'd misplaced his own faith along the way.

Lost somewhere amidst the mocking echo of unanswerable questions.

He caught a glimpse of movement behind him as he straightened—the figure of his roommate just visible in the early morning twilight as he raised his right index finger toward the ceiling, beginning to recite the *takbir.*

"There is no God but God," he whispered, a shadow seeming to pass across his face, "and Muhammad is His Prophet. . ."

Part I

Chapter 1

*3:27 P.M., June 19*th
Alliance Base
Paris, France

The conference room was cool—almost cold, Anaïs Brunet thought, folding her arms as she stared down the table at the man in French military uniform sitting at the opposite end.

Windowless and soundproof, buried deep within the nondescript, heavily-secured office building in the fifteenth arrondissement which had played host to the joint French-American counterterrorist intelligence center for the last five years—three of which she had spent overseeing its activities as the head of General Directorate for External Security, or DGSE, as it was commonly referred to in the media.

"He's only been under for three weeks, Lucien," she said finally, clearing her throat. "It's far too early to expect results."

If they came at all, she didn't add. Attempting to insert an intelligence asset into an Islamist terror network was a hazardous venture at best. Particularly when the target was a community as insular and tight-knit as that of Molenbeek, Belgium.

"I know, I know," General Lucien Gauthier responded quickly, shaking his head. Himself a former Legionnaire, Gauthier had only a few years before been commanding troops in north Mali, rooting out jihadist strongholds there as part of what had been known as Operation Serval—and the switch from counter-insurgency to pure intelligence work as he took command of Alliance Base hadn't been without its challenges for him. "But shouldn't he have at least made *contact* by now?"

Brunet shrugged. Their man had been in place for longer than the three weeks she had referenced, but it was only with his increasing proximity to their suspected targets that communications protocols had changed. "What would you rather LYSANDER be doing, *mon general*? Making contact with us, or making new friends among the Islamists? Armand has been able to confirm that he's still alive—at least as of forty-eight hours ago—so I don't see that we have a problem. . ."

"We don't, Anaïs," Gauthier said finally, his voice trembling with intensity as he raised his head to look at her down the conference table. "We don't—not *yet*. But the next time a bomb goes off in this city—in Marseilles—in Nice. . .you've seen what's going on in the United Kingdom, the riots in the streets. You've seen the protests outside the American Embassy here in Paris since last week's drone strikes in the Sinai."

He took a deep breath before continuing, tapping his index finger into the oak of the table with each successive word. "We are living on borrowed *time*."

That much was hard to dispute, much as Brunet would have preferred to. She opened her mouth to respond, but the conference room's door opened at that moment, admitting a middle-aged man a few years her senior in a dark, somewhat rumpled suit, his tie loosened at the throat—no doubt in an effort to beat the Paris heat.

"Daniel," she said, rising to her feet to greet the CIA's Chief of Station Paris, Daniel Vukovic—a careerist from the Agency's Intelligence Directorate who had spent the last several years in France. "Please, have a seat—we were just discussing LYSANDER."

4:13 P.M., Eastern Daylight Time, June 23rd
The Russell Senate Office Building
Washington, D.C.

". . .raising serious questions as more details continue to emerge regarding last Thursday's drone strike in the Sinai Peninsula, which killed upwards of thirty civilians in what appears to have been a failed attempt to take out prominent Islamic State cleric Umar ibn Hassan. Here to weigh in on the controversy surrounding this, is privacy rights activist Claire Zmirak. Claire, welcome—

could you lay out for us the situation as you see it?"

"Of course, Matt, thank you for the opportunity. I want first to make clear that. . ."

Senator Roy Coftey grimaced at the sound of the woman's voice, turning his attention back to the draft legislation on his desk as the CNN broadcast continued. The feeding frenzy hadn't stopped since news of the disaster in the Sinai had first broken three days earlier, filling up cable news and spreading across social media at the speed of light.

And on Capitol Hill, people were running scared.

As they could be counted upon to do, the former Green Beret mused wryly, shaking his massive head. All the way back to the days when he'd led a Special Forces A-team into the jungles of a place its survivors remembered only as 'Nam.

A long, bitter war which he and his brothers had won, only for the politicians to lose. *All of it for nothing.*

He'd come to Washington to change all that. To set things *right*. Three decades later, and what had changed?

Perhaps he had.

The drone strike had been a CIA operation, knowledge he was privy to as Chairman of the Senate Select Committee on Intelligence. The kind of operation he'd fought hard for the Agency to maintain control over. Conducted in complete coordination down to the last moments of targeting with the Egyptian military—something Cairo was now denying, exploiting its moment of sanctimonious moral outrage to the fullest.

But despite all the safeguards, despite every last ounce of oversight, something had gone wrong out there in the desert. And now the usual suspects were howling for blood.

". . .I really think people like Mr. Carr are missing the big picture of this story," Claire Zmirak said on-screen, her voice drawing his attention back to the television. "It's not merely that this strike failed—that innocent civilians were killed, that Hassan was not among the dead—but that it was ever attempted in the first place. Umar ibn Hassan is an American citizen, born in Duluth, Minnesota, not thirty miles from my own hometown."

And he chose to wage war upon the land of his birth. Sic semper proditores. . .

So always to traitors.

But she wasn't done, continuing on over an unintelligible interjection from her fellow guest, "And as an American citizen, he deserves his day in court—not to be murdered in a foreign land by his government. President Norton has to be held to account—this kind of indiscriminate murder by remote is what characterized the Hancock years and he *campaigned* on bringing it to an end, not perpetuating it."

But like all Presidents, upon arriving in the Oval Office, Norton had found reality to be something. . .different than he'd imagined, Coftey thought, muting the television as he prepared to get back to his work. *Realpolitik.* The province of those tasked with actually making the world work, far from the ivory tower.

The senator's cellphone rang a few moments later, his face growing longer by the moment as he listened to the voice on the other end. "Ellis is saying *what?*"

He shook his head, tucking the phone between his ear and shoulder as he stood, reaching for his suit jacket. This wasn't good—wasn't good at all.

"He and I—we had a deal."

6:24 A.M., Central European Summer Time, June 24th
The apartment
Sint-Jans-Molenbeek, Belgium

". . .the American government has yet to offer a thorough explanation of the role it played in the strikes, which claimed the lives of innocent civilians in the Sinai last week. They. . ."

The voice of the French newshost continued as Harry Nichols entered the apartment's small kitchen, the story out of the Sinai growing bleaker with every passing day. A failed Agency operation. *Like more than a few he'd himself known over the years.*

"They're killing us, man," he heard a voice say, looking over to see his flatmate standing there by the refrigerator, a half-eaten, jam-smeared bagel in his hands as he stared at the small television. "All over the world—every day—*they* murder more of the faithful."

Yassin Harrak. One of the two brothers he shared the apartment with—both of them, second-generation immigrants from Morocco. The younger brother, Reza, was attending the University of Brussels—studying to become an engineer. Yassin. . .well, Yassin was working, or rather, looking for it.

He hadn't had a job in the time Harry had known them—it wouldn't have surprised him to have learned that he hadn't had one since leaving school. Many young Belgians didn't, and those numbers got worse if you were Muslim. *Much worse.*

It was hard to even say whether Reza's degree would make that much of a difference.

"They don't care, none of them do," the young man continued, shaking his head—a mixture of anger and despair written across his swarthy face. "They drop bombs on innocent women and children and they don't *care*— so long as they're safe. As long as it doesn't touch *them*. And this won't end until it does—until it touches them where they live. In the neighborhoods where they live, where their children play."

"*Insh'allah,*" Harry breathed, placing a hand on Yassin's shoulder in a sympathetic gesture as he moved past him to the refrigerator, withdrawing a carton of orange juice. As God wills it.

It was a familiar refrain, and one that had grown more so over the passing weeks, fueled by the escalating situation in the Middle East—the young man's angst becoming more vocal. Along with his desire to strike back.

Harry took a sip of the juice, setting it aside on the card table in the middle of the kitchen as he took a knife and began to spread jam across his own bagel. He had known of the Islamist sympathies of his hosts—it was, after all, why they had chosen to shelter him. And yet. . .

"You were dreaming last night, brother," Yassin's voice began again from behind him, Harry's breath catching in his throat—his blood seeming to freeze at the words. His knuckles whitening around the hilt of the butter knife. *Turn and stab, high—deep into the throat. The blade wasn't sharp, but it didn't need to be. Drive the blade home and—*

"It was Syria again, wasn't it?" the young man asked, turning off the television as he moved back to the table.

The tension slowly beginning to flow out of Harry's body at the question—his fingers trembling ever so slightly as he finished, laying the knife to one side. *Calm down.*

"Yeah, it was," he lied, glancing over at Yassin to find nothing but sympathy in the young man's eyes. "It was like being back there all over again. It was like. . ."

He shook his head, as if feeling something he couldn't quite put into words. "There's no way for me to explain it, to put it in a way you would understand. I—"

Yassin smiled, putting a hand up to cut him off. "It's all right, bro, it's all right. I don't need to. The part you played in the struggle of God, the wounds you received in the jihad against the apostate tyrant in Damascus. . .would that more of us had been granted such an opportunity."

"I saw men cut down by machine-gun fire trying to take regime strongpoints," Harry said suddenly, as though he was unable to stop himself. Not looking at Yassin as he continued. "Tracers flying through the night. Men I had known, men I'd shared bread with just a few hours before—blown to shreds by artillery shells."

"Ushered into paradise as a reward for their bravery," Yassin intoned reverently, something of a perverse excitement glowing in the young man's eyes.

"*Alhamdullilah*," Harry responded, pausing for a moment before he went on. *Praise be to God.* "But out there in the night, when brave men are dying all around you, you can't *see* paradise—you can't hear the singing of the women who welcome a martyr to their bosom. All you hear is the screams."

2:07 P.M.
Alliance Base
Paris, France

". . .and of course, I will count on you to keep me apprised of any developments, Lucien," Anaïs Brunet said, smoothing her skirt as she rose from the chair.

"*Certainement, madame le directeur*," Gauthier responded, looking for a moment as if he might revert to his military training and offer a salute as she turned to leave, the door of his office closing behind her as she walked quickly down the long corridor toward the elevator.

It was a dark place, Alliance Base, or so she had always found it. Something about the very structure, full of foreboding. Its head offices—Gauthier's among them—located in the center of the building, as far away as possible from any exterior walls.

Every window in the building replaced with thick, one-way ballistic glass. Allowing only light to enter. . .and nothing to escape. *A black hole.*

A far cry from the corporate offices she had known a decade earlier as a chief executive in the French aerospace industry, Brunet mused, the elevator doors closing on her as she pressed the button for the ground floor—reaching up to brush a strand of jet-black hair back from her eyes as she leaned back against the wall of the elevator.

Her transition from the private to the public sector had been relatively seamless—an extension of having handled Astrium's contracts with the French military for years before her early retirement from the company.

Acclimating herself to the shadowy world that was the intelligence business had taken far, far longer. And now, confronting the Islamist threat like this, in her own country. . .

The doors of the elevator opened and she walked out into what an American intelligence officer stationed there had, years before, informally termed "the bullpen"—a large, open space filled with workstations—large flat-screen televisions mounted on the northern wall, tuned into cable news networks from around the world, dominantly the United States and Europe.

Brunet overheard snatches of conversation from analysts huddled around their desks as she passed through on her way to the exit—all of it in French, which was the working language of the center. A convenient fig leaf, considering that the majority of their operational budget came courtesy of the CIA.

And then she saw it, the empty desk sitting there amidst the commotion surrounding it, its chair pushed in—the screen of its monitor dark, powered off.

Her face twisted into a grimace, remembering the funeral as if it had been just the previous day. *Victor Mandel.* Forty-one—over a decade her junior—a husband and a father of two. Prior military and a veteran DGSE analyst, one of her finest.

Killed over a month earlier, shot to death aboard the train returning to Paris from Caen, where he'd spent an early summer holiday with his family.

A young Algerian man had stood up in the middle of the crowded train car—screaming *"Allahu akbar!"* as he pulled a Glock from within his jacket.

And Mandel had rushed him, like the soldier he was—like he had been to the very end—taking a bullet to the chest and still grappling desperately with him for the weapon. Until two more rounds entered his body.

He'd died fifteen minutes later, his head in his teenage daughter's lap—his blood flecking her white blouse.

An attack that had, like so many before it, originated in Brussels. More specifically, in the district of Sint-Jans-Molenbeek.

It couldn't be allowed to continue. Brunet pursed her lips together, shaking her head as she turned reluctantly to leave. Far more was riding on LYSANDER's success than she cared to admit.

Everything. . .

6:33 P.M. British Summer Time
A terraced house
Abbey Road, London

". . .facing more unrest in the streets of London as the investigation continues into the murder of prominent right-wing publisher Arthur Colville and the coalition government in Westminster struggles to consolidate power in the wake of Labour's fall. Here to discuss the ongoing situation with us is UK political analyst Naveen Bhargava. Naveen, could you. . ."

The voice of the BBC presenter droned on from the flat-screen television mounted on a stand in the corner of the den as the man came back into the darkened room. Slight and of medium stature, he was just passing middle-age, the sleeves of his white dress shirt rolled past his elbows—a single malt poised delicately between his long fingers, crystal glittering in the light from the television's screen.

He paused by the bookshelf before returning to his armchair, his eyes flickering across the haphazardly-arranged books—gilt-bound volumes of Shelley, Byron, and Kipling mixed in with Rousseau and Solhenitsyn—a ragged paperback of the first volume of *Das Kapital*, half-concealed behind the old photograph propped up in front of it.

Three men, standing on a street corner in West Berlin—two Americans and an Englishman.

*Frank Beecher, David Lay. . .*and a much younger version of himself, so very many years ago.

We three spies, Julian Marsh thought, a wry smile tugging at his lips as he retrieved the photograph from the shelf, turning it over in a weathered hand.

The bad old days of the Cold War—out on the front lines where East had once met West.

An age gone by, just like so much else, the director-general of the UK Security Service reflected, returning the photograph to its place on the shelf as he walked back over to his chair—sinking into its comfortable depths as he placed the crystal tumbler on the end table beside it, retrieving his reading glasses.

Former director-general, that is, he corrected, catching himself as he had so many times over the past few weeks. For that too was in the past—his career just another casualty of the political unrest that had engulfed the UK since the terrorist attack targeting the Royal Family two months before.

Since the Security Service had been implicated in the murder of Arthur Colville, a newspaper publisher who, in the wake of the attacks, had begun to release hundreds of classified documents outlining the Service's failure to stop the plot as it unfolded.

He'd been found four days later, shot to death in his house in the Midlands, along with three members of his security team. *Executed,* the lot of them.

There'd been no evidence of his killer, but in the wake of the revelations. . .the media's finger of blame had been left pointing directly at MI-5.

Marsh sighed, adjusting his glasses as he picked up the remote, switching off the BBC newscast. The news, the security of the realm, none of it was his concern. Not anymore.

He'd been forced to resign by the Home Office in the midst of the media firestorm, a last desperate flailing move to avert disaster by a government whose own days were numbered, with MP Daniel Pearson calling for a vote of no confidence in the House of Commons only three days after he'd left the Service.

We all fall down. The vote had passed by an overwhelming margin, toppling the government. Leaving chaos behind as rival parties scrambled to consolidate power.

To bring *order* to a country that seemed increasingly hellbent on tearing itself apart.

And that had been Colville's plan all along, the former intelligence officer mused, the publisher accomplishing in death so much of what he had failed to in his life.

Marsh shook his head, nursing his scotch as he leaned back into the chair. And none of that was his concern, as he kept telling himself. Again and again—an impulse, a force of habit almost as difficult to turn off as that which still made him take a dress shirt out of the closet every morning. *An addiction.* Powerful as any narcotic.

He turned on the light beside his chair and retrieved his copy of Dostoyevsky's *The Possessed* from the end table with a restless sigh, flipping it open to the piece of scrap paper serving as his marker.

He'd been educated as a young man as a classicist at Cambridge, where MI-5 had first recruited him—if this forced retirement was going to be good for anything, perhaps it would permit him to return to the passions of his youth.

Some of them, anyway.

He'd been reading five minutes when his mobile rang, an unfamiliar number displayed on its screen as he reached for it, answering with a cautious, "Yes?"

"Julian, something's come up," a man began, Marsh instantly recognizing his voice. *Phillip Greer.* The head of the Security Service's D Branch—Counterintelligence. "Is it possible for us to meet?"

Marsh let out a deep breath, staring for a long moment at the ceiling of the den. "Whatever this is about. . .I can't help you, Phillip. My clearance is no longer what it was, as we both know full well."

"This concerns our friend in the Midlands," Greer responded after a moment's pause. *Arthur Colville.* "The bookshop, Julian—five tomorrow evening?"

The former director-general swore beneath his breath, shaking his head. *All right.* "Five tomorrow."

7:03 P.M. Central European Summer Time
Parc du Cinquentenaire
Brussels, Belgium

It was a beautiful evening to take one's family to the park, the man thought, a wistful smile flitting across his dark, weathered face.

Clear and fair—the bright rays of the setting sun casting a long shadow before him as he walked across the grounds toward the *Arcade du Cinquentenaire*, the massive triple arch which anchored the center of the U-shaped complex of the building, weaving his way through the clustered groups of people gathered upon the green with a deceptively aimless purpose.

If anyone was following him—and no one was, he was quite certain of that after the previous two hours he'd spent doubling back upon himself— they were going to have trouble marking his position amidst the throng of tourists and holiday-goers—a group of them clustered around a young woman's easel to one side of the walk.

His own children, well. . .he smiled. They were far beyond such simple pleasures. Grown and gone, scattered across the face of the earth.

His son, a day trader in Hong Kong. His daughter—in Toronto, working as a climate change activist.

Only he remained. He and Claire, together as always throughout the decades.

He glanced up as he approached the arch, the greenish bronze of the sculpture surmounting it looming high above him, a female charioteer representing Brabant itself forming the centerpiece of the quadriga—standing erect in the chariot, the Belgian flag held aloft in her hand.

His gaze flickering away from the statuary to search the face of the nearby wall for the tell, the single, unobtrusive line of chalk that would serve to alert him that a drop had been made.

The photo ID in the man's wallet identified him as Armand Césaire, an officer of the French diplomatic service, headquartered in Quai d'Orsay in Paris—here in Brussels these last few months as a part of the staff of the Ambassade de France, a half-dozen kilometers to the west of the park.

The name was his own, given to him by his parents nearly sixty years prior, in his birthplace on the West Indies island of Guadeloupe. As for his place of employment, it lay further to the east in Paris, along the Boulevard Mortier—the imposing building which served as the headquarters of the DGSE.

He'd spent more than three decades as a case officer of his country's foreign intelligence service—the majority of it in Africa, the color of his skin giving him an advantage in recruiting local assets on the continent as France struggled through the final throes of a dying colonialism.

And now. . .he found himself here, as the seeds of those years began to bear the bitterest of fruits. Defending his country, as ever before.

The wall was naked and bare, his eyes failing to find the slightest trace of what he was looking for as he passed on without pausing beneath the arch—giving no outwardly visible sign of his interest.

LYSANDER had yet to make contact. . .

Chapter 2

8:09 A.M., June 25th
Brussels, Belgium

Fear. A nameless panic seeming to wash over him, his leg muscles protesting from long disuse as he pedaled on, the wheels of the bike a blur as it careened down the shaded Brussels street and across an intersection. *Faster and faster.* As if trying to escape the demons, the ghosts of the past crowding into his mind—drowning out all thought of anything else.

Screaming out for attention. For *redress* that would no longer be denied.

The haze cleared just long enough for Harry Nichols to glimpse a group of tourists paused on the crosswalk ahead, his hand squeezing the bell to sound a warning as he leaned right, guiding his bike around them at the last minute.

Curses in three languages floating out after him as he picked up speed once again, going. . .he knew not where.

Escape.

He stopped only when exhaustion overtook him, on the outskirts of the Cinquentenaire—a large, spacious park in Brussels not more than a few kilometers from their dingy Molenbeek apartment.

Leaning the bike against a tree as he collapsed onto a park bench—nearly doubled over, his legs burning from the exertion. Biting his tongue to keep from crying out from the pain in his side, the wounds in his abdomen still healing and reminding him of it every time he subjected them to strain, as he struggled to get himself back into condition—the limitations imposing a keen awareness that he was no longer what he once had been.

That what had been so *simple* almost two decades earlier, making his way through CIA training at The Farm in Camp Peary, Virginia was no longer nearly as effortless now, as he found himself nearing forty.

But he had no other choice. Not if he wanted to stay alive.

But is that really what you want? A haunting voice from somewhere deep within asked—no, *demanded. Insistent, unanswerable.*

He'd spent a career staying alive—fifteen years as a paramilitary operations officer for the US Central Intelligence Agency, the euphemistically-named "Special Activities Division." Fighting for a flag, all over the world.

Fighting. Surviving, where other—*better*—men had died, all through the years. The guilt of the survivor, that most crushing of burdens. The moment when your own humanity was brought back into stark focus and you realized you couldn't save the world. *You couldn't even save the ones you loved.*

His own faith left in ashes, setting him adrift. *At the end of all dreams.*

The face of a woman, staring back at him from a photograph as flames licked at the paper, circling around and around her face until she vanished from sight, only the charred embers remaining. The embers of what might have been.

But that was all in the past. . .or was it?

Harry leaned back against the park bench, drinking in great gulps of air—his sides heaving as he reflected on Yassin's words from the previous day.

He had known the danger, coming here to Brussels—to Molenbeek. And he had come all the same, for he'd had no other choice. A wounded animal, on its last legs—seeking refuge from the hunters.

And that's what Molenbeek was. A *refuge.* The last place those who had once employed him would ever think to look—that he would be hiding, not in plain sight, but among the very people he'd made a career of tracking down. *Hunting.*

But now. . .he closed his eyes, fighting back the pain—his right hand balling into a fist, the knuckles of his left whitening around the arm of the bench.

Now he found himself coming to the inescapable conclusion that he had gravely miscalculated. *Flown too close to the flame.*

Echoes of his past, come back to haunt him. And this time, there was no team. No fallback. No support network. *No extraction.*

The pain seemed to pass over him and he opened his eyes to scan the park—searching, as ever, for threats. Overcome by the irony of it all.

He'd spent years on his own, out far beyond the edge—

prosecuting the "war on terror" in the dark shadows of the world.

But he'd never been truly *alone*. . .until now.

He shook his head, a bitter ghost of a smile passing across his face. *Eloi, Eloi, lama sabachthani. . .*

My God, my God, why hast thou forsaken me. . .

4:53 P.M. British Summer Time
A bookshop
Central London

He'd been coming to Cyril's for something near thirty years, Julian Marsh thought, the bell ringing as he pushed open the door to the small bookshop—tucked down an obscure side street on the outskirts of London's West End.

Thirty years, and so very little had changed—the interior uncertainly lit, towering bookshelves extending back into the depths of the Edwardian building, creating caverns of shadow. Stacks of books spilling over the counter and onto the floor. In recent years, Cyril's grandson had succeeded in expanding the business onto the Internet, but the shop remained, if for no other reason than that Cyril himself was the only one who knew where each of his thousands of rare volumes were actually located.

He heard the sound of footsteps from somewhere in the back, and then a voice booming out, "Julian!" as the proprietor himself appeared from around a bookshelf.

He'd imagined Cyril to have been an old man when he had first darkened the door of the bookshop so many years before, but now, like his store. . .he seemed little changed.

Eternally bald, only the thick mustache on his upper lip marking his passage through the seasons of life as it changed from brown to silver and finally the whiteness of snow.

Or perhaps he had simply become more forgiving in his assessments of age as he found himself growing old.

"It's been too long," Cyril said, greeting him warmly. "I'd begun to think you might have found another source for your collection."

"Never," the former director-general smiled. The older man was one of his few genuine friends, a relationship which had taken root in their mutual love of rare literature—and one that had afforded him rare solace throughout the lonely years as an intelligence officer with Five.

"Ah!" Cyril exclaimed, his face suddenly lighting up. "Your timing is, as ever, impeccable, Julian—I was about to e-mail you. Last week. . .I found *it*."

There was only one thing "it" could be referring to, and Marsh found himself nearly carried away by his friend's exuberance. "The Pushkin?"

"Yes! Or *da*, perhaps I should say," the bookseller corrected himself, his old eyes twinkling with amusement. "*Puteshestvie v Arzrum*. The first edition."

Journey to Arzrum, Marsh thought. The nineteenth-century Russian novelist's account of his travels to the Caucacus in the late 1820s. A volume he'd been in search of for over a decade.

"I have it in the back, saved for you—if you'd like to see it," his friend went on, as eager as a child.

And he did, more than anything else in the world. A treasure, found after so long—but Marsh found it impossible to get Greer's voice out of his head. Dark and ominous. *This concerns our friend in the Midlands.*

"I think I'd like to browse for a bit, if you don't mind," the former DG said, patting his old friend on the shoulder as he pushed past him, making his way toward the winding staircase leading to the shop's second story, where he expected to find the counter-intel spook waiting for him. "I'll see it before I leave."

"Are you sure you wouldn't rather look at it first?" the old man's voice called after him, something strange in his tone arresting Marsh where he stood. *Could it be?*

He and Greer. . .they both knew Cyril, from years before. And his employment with Five was hardly the secret it once would have been—particularly now, in the wake of a departure that couldn't have been more public.

"On second thought," he replied, turning, "I rather think I will."

Cyril disappeared into the back with one of his characteristically enigmatic smiles as Marsh stood by the counter, glancing distractedly through a stack of books balanced on the edge. Disraeli's *Sybil* tucked in among Stevenson's *Kidnapped* and a novel by Thomas Hardy. A late 19th-Century edition of *Wuthering Heights* perched atop the pile as if by the most careless of afterthoughts.

"Here we are," the bookseller's voice announced a few minutes later, reappearing with a small volume in his hands. His voice trembling with genuine excitement as he passed it over to Marsh. "A first edition *Puteshestvie v Arzrum*. So very rare."

The former Security Service officer took the book from Cyril, opening its thin, weathered pages with a gentle reverence. And there it was. . .nestled just within the frontispiece. A scrap of very modern paper, folded in half—and within, an address.

Phillip, you clever sod.

6:16 P.M. Central European Summer Time
Embassy of the United States
Paris, France

". . .to end the campaign of murder by remote which has characterized American foreign policy abroad over the latter half of the last decade. It must—it *will*—end here. We—"

The door of the chancery closed behind Daniel Vukovic even as the crowd of protesters without erupted into chants of "Drones kill kids! Drones kill kids!"

God, what a disaster, the CIA chief of station thought, handing his briefcase over to a kid in the uniform of a Marine lance corporal. Taking a step back to drop his keys and phone into the basket as he prepared to go through the final metal detector.

He'd been on overseas duty when the news of Abu Ghraib first broke, and this furor over the Sinai was becoming far too reminiscent of those days for his liking. *Blowback.* Ever the bane of direct action.

He shook his head, picking up his briefcase on the other side of the x-ray machine as he adjusted his identification badge—making his way deeper into the embassy, down the corridors toward the heavily secured wing known as Paris Station.

And all of it so *avoidable*. If the Agency had only remained focused on its original mandate—intelligence *collection*—as it had been when he'd first joined the Intelligence Directorate as a young man in the early '90s, instead of reshaping itself into the quasi-paramilitary organization it had become in the years following 9/11.

But the Cold War had been over for a decade and the Agency had been an organization in search of a mission.

All of it understandable, looking back—justifiable, even. Like the drone program itself, a natural reaction against the years of media controversy surrounding the treatment of captured terrorists.

Somewhere along the line, no one could quite say where, it had just become way easier to kill than to capture. Less noise, less drama—at least, when things went right.

He could understand it. Didn't mean he had to like it.

Or accept his role in having to clean up after it any more gracefully.

And now with this operation with the French consuming his attention. . .he wasn't any less aware of the pitfalls of human intelligence operations than he had ever been, but even he had to concede that SIGINT was giving them nothing—had *done* nothing to stop the previous five attacks in France.

The only solution was to get a man on the inside, and pray he stayed alive.

LYSANDER. Vukovic badged himself into the station past another uniformed Marine. *An ironic choice of codename*. The Westland Lysander had been a British light monoplane during the Second World War, tasked with inserting SOE officers into occupied France to liaise with the Resistance.

Many of them snatched up by the Gestapo not long after landing— betrayed by double agents and themselves turned back against their handlers in London.

One could only hope its present-day namesake would fare better. With luck. . .

5:29 P.M. British Summer Time
"The Nell"
The Strand, London

The visage of Nell Gwynne stared down at Marsh from a portrait over the bar as the former director-general pushed his way through the crowded pub.

A beautiful woman, he thought absently—his eyes scanning the booths for Greer, the faintest of smiles touching his lips as he recalled the history. A fairly scandalous London actress of the late 1600s, Gwynne was perhaps best known for having been the mistress of King Charles II—a king whom Nell, with her characteristically irreverent wit, had styled "Charles the Third", as he was the third of her lovers named Charles.

He caught sight of the counter-intelligence officer then, sitting in the darkest corner of the pub, his back to the wall. The remnants of a nearly-demolished lunch on the plate before him, a pint of beer sitting just to one side.

"Julian," Greer said as he approached, sliding into the booth across from him. "It's good to see you once again."

Marsh just sat there for a moment, regarding his old comrade with a wary eye. He was a tall man, tall and thin—frail, almost, to appearances—a smoker's rasp tinging his every syllable, thick glasses perched atop an aquiline nose.

But appearances were deceitful, as the former director-general knew all too well. And whatever other adjectives one could have applied to Phillip Greer, "frail" wasn't among them.

"What's with all the cloak and dagger, Phillip?" Marsh asked finally, breaking the silence. "First Cyril's, now here. . .what are you going to tell me next, that you had people running countersurveillance on me all the way here?"

"I did, as a matter of fact," Greer announced calmly, plucking a stray crisp from among the wreckage on his plate. "Two of my men—officers I trust personally."

He shrugged, popping the crisp into his mouth and dusting the salt from his fingertips. "You're still a person of considerable interest to people in high places, Julian. And I'd just as soon they not take undue note of this meeting today."

Fair enough.

"Ashworth among them?" the former director-general asked coolly, his eyes never leaving Greer's face. Patrick Ashworth was the former chief of the Joint Terrorism Analysis Centre, or "JTAC" as it was commonly referred to in the community—now the acting director-general of the Service following Marsh's forced resignation.

Greer just looked at him. "Patrick is. . ."

"A good man," Marsh interjected when the counter-intelligence officer paused, appearing to search for words. "A good man, and a competent officer with a long career in the Service. I shan't allow my personal dislike for the man to color my assessment of his abilities. The PM could have done far worse."

"He's a good man whose 'long career' began in the late '90s," Greer retorted bitingly, seeming finally to find the words he'd been looking for. "He's spent his entire career focused on terrorism, it's all he knows—the world we knew, Julian, it's a stranger to him."

And the world moves on without us. As it ever has.

Marsh shook his head, smiling at the heat in his colleague's tone. "As it is to most of our fellow officers today. Don't waste time in mourning the *ancien régime*, Phillip—it's not going to do any of us any good. So why *did* you ask me to come here today?"

Greer looked for a moment as if he intended to continue, but then he shook his head, reaching for his pint. "The investigation into Arthur Colville's murder is now essentially. . .closed. It will be kept up for another few months for the sake of the media, but we have our man."

"Are you serious?"

He nodded, extracting a tri-folded piece of paper from the briefcase by his side and sliding it across the table toward the former director-general.

"Should you be showing me this?" Marsh asked, hesitating—his fingertips resting on the very edge of the paper. "You're aware that my clearance was—"

"Sod your clearance, Julian. You being out doesn't change the reality that you're still one of the only men I trust. We picked this up off CCTV at a retail park nine miles east of Colville's estate," Greer continued as Marsh unfolded the paper to reveal a screengrab from a surveillance camera, "three hours after the established time of death. It's Harold Nichols."

6:59 P.M. Central European Summer Time
The apartment
Sint-Jans-Molenbeek, Belgium

"When one stretches forth his hand, he can hardly see it," Harry breathed, reading aloud in Arabic from the Qur'an spread before him on the table as he sat alone in the apartment, "for any to whom Allah hath not granted light—there is no light."

He pushed back his chair, dropping to the floor and beginning a series of push-ups, reciting the next verse from memory even as he did so, his arm muscles rigid with tension as he struggled to push himself aloft. The words of the recitation coming out between gasps for breath. "Seest thou not that it is God whose praises all beings in the heavens and on earth do celebrate, and the birds with wings outspread?"

Down and back up again. Down and up, down and up. Sweat beading on his bare chest as he pressed on, forcing himself to ignore the pain from his side. "Yea, to Allah belongs dominion of the heavens and the earth, and to Allah is the final destination of all."

He heard a key in the lock just then, holding his position for another long moment as the door opened, Reza's voice calling out in greeting.

"Ah, there you are, Ibrahim," he heard a moment later, rolling over onto his back to see the younger of the two brothers enter the kitchen. "*Salaam alaikum*, my brother."

"*Wa' alaikum as-salaam*," Harry responded, pushing himself to his feet and reaching out to clasp the younger man's hand, drawing him in for a brief embrace. "Where's Yassin?"

"At the boxing club," Reza said, placing his laptop case on the chair as he turned to the refrigerator, pulling out a can of Pepsi.

Again, Harry thought, wiping the sweat from his forehead with his undershirt as he walked back to the table. The boxing gym had become Yassin's nightly haunt in recent weeks—the place he seemed to spend every waking hour he wasn't searching for work, helping someone in the neighborhood out for extra cash, or attending prayers at the masjid.

"I'm headed over there in a few minutes myself," the young Moroccan continued earnestly, popping the top of his soda and tilting it back, "why don't you join us?"

He gestured toward the floor where Harry had so recently been doing his push-ups. "You're trying to get back into condition, bro—you can do it way faster there."

No. If he was to have any chance of staying off the radar of Western intelligence long-term, it was going to mean keeping his head down. He started to shake his head "no", but Reza's next words arrested him.

"You really should come tonight, man. Some of the brothers train there, and they meet for prayers afterwards. It's a good time—I think you'd enjoy meeting them."

"Would that more of us had been granted such an opportunity." Yassin's words, coming back to him from the previous day. The fire in the young man's eyes when he had spoken of jihad. If there was something there. . .

"Praise be to the name of God, *subhanahu wa ta'ala*," Harry said, forcing a smile to his face as he turned toward the young man. *The most glorified, the most high.* "Let me get my shirt—I'll join you."

6:03 P.M. British Summer Time
The Nell
The Strand, London

Nichols, Marsh thought—the sound of Greer's voice and the noise of the pub around them seeming to fade away as he stared at the figure of the tall, dark-haired man in the image.

The former CIA officer who had arrived in the UK several months earlier, on his own—acting without sanction. *Gone rogue.*

In search of Tarik Abdul Muhammad, the Pakistani-born terrorist who was alleged to have been responsible for the Christmas Eve attacks on Las Vegas, Nevada.

And now the attack on Her Majesty herself, he mused, for by the time Nichols had located his target, the attack was already underway. Good men, already dead.

Marsh shook his head, his finger tracing over the surveillance photo— grainy and indistinct, but clear in the message it told.

The deathly pallor of the American's face, the way he was leaning heavily against the counter of the mini-mart, as if using it for support.

As if wounded—which he had been, according to their best intelligence.

Wounded desperately, and yet somehow he had managed to make it from the docks of Aberdeen all the way to Colville's estate in the Midlands. Targeting the man who had financed the attack on the Queen, who had hoped to plunge England into civil war.

And, in killing him. . .making him into the kind of martyr for his cause that Colville had always dreamed of becoming. *Accomplishing more by his death than his life.*

"My *God*. . .what have you done?" the former director-general murmured quietly to the image, glancing back up at Greer. "Are you *sure*?"

"Quite sure," the spook replied, his voice cold and certain. "The man who murdered Arthur Colville and took out his security team left quite a bit of his own blood behind. We sent DNA samples to the cousins over a month ago, and they came back with a positive match. It's him."

A formidable man. As demonstrated by their own failure to find him.

He'd tortured and killed a British citizen in order to get the information that had led him to his target. Co-opted not one, but two former officers of the Security Service for his own purposes. A bloody quest for vengeance which had ended that night in Aberdeen, a bomb killing Tarik Abdul Muhammad and his bodyguards—turning his vehicle into flaming wreckage.

"So," he began, re-folding the paper and sliding it back across to the table toward his colleague, "that settles it, doesn't it? We weren't involved in his death, no matter how damning the circumstantial evidence may have first appeared. The witch hunt in the press can be brought to a close, and the Service can get back to work."

"I wish it were that simple, Julian," Greer responded, tucking the surveillance photograph back into his briefcase, "but none of this is ever going to see the light of day. We—"

"For the love of God, *why*?" Marsh demanded, his dark eyes flashing as he leaned forward across the table. His own career was over, he knew that—but the *Service,* that was what mattered. All that had *ever* mattered.

"Think about it," the counter-intelligence officer responded calmly, seeming to rummage in his briefcase for a moment before retrieving a slim folder. "Releasing it is to no one's benefit—not ours, certainly. And the Americans are not overeager for the media to explore the role their officer played. What difference would it make, after all? The relationship between the Service and the Agency is well-documented—if it were known that an American paramilitary officer had been responsible for Colville's death, the media would simply pivot to the belief that Five had contracted out its dirty work. That the Americans had taken care of our 'problem' for us."

He was right, that was the worst of it. The narrative in the media, in the on-line blogosphere, was already too deeply embedded to be rooted out. They could only batten down the hatches and hope to ride out the storm.

"Then I'm going to have to ask you again, Phillip—what does any of this have to do with me?"

Greer paused for a moment, regarding him keenly across the booth.

"Because," he began, pushing the folder across the tabletop, "I think there's more to this than either of us know to date. Look at this."

The former director-general took the folder from him, flipping it open to the first page. It took him a moment to realize what he was reading, and when he did he snapped the folder closed—his head coming up to meet Greer's gaze, his voice coming out in a low hiss.

"Are you out of your sodding mind?"

7:20 P.M. Central European Summer Time
The boxing club
Brussels, Belgium

The interior of the gym was cool and dimly lit, fans working overtime to dispel the summer heat as Harry followed Reza's lead into the building—his dark eyes flickering back and forth, searching out every shadow.

Knowing just how much danger he could be walking into. *From all sides.*

Loud rock music was pulsating off the walls, drowning out nearly all else as they passed small knots of men gathered around the rings. An African man wearing a *kufi*—a traditional Islamic skullcap—atop his greying hair as boys in their teens, presumably his students, clustered around him.

Young men, stripped to the waist, their chests gleaming with sweat as they danced beneath the lights—pummeling each other with gloved fists. And then he saw Yassin, in a ring near the back of the building—sparring with another young Arab, the two of them circling 'round each other like cats, waiting an opportunity to pounce.

He wasn't very good, Harry realized, watching as Yassin seized an opening—only to find it *wasn't* one, rocked back as his lithe opponent landed a gloved hook to the side of his helmet. At least not yet—everyone had to start somewhere.

But he recovered, darting forward with a flurry of blows buffeting his opponent's arms and shoulders. Forcing him to give ground.

"Go Yassin!" Harry shouted, forcing enthusiasm into his voice as he clapped Reza on the shoulder, the two of them standing there on the edge of the ring.

Looking on as the boxers circled, feinting in and out. Trading blows which seemed to build in intensity until a buzzer sounded from a phone laying to one side of the ring, both boxers dropping their gloved fists as if recognizing an agreed-upon signal, the Arab cuffing Yassin playfully on the shoulder. "Another time, man—you're getting better."

"Ibrahim!" Yassin called out, vaulting over the ropes of the ring as he came forward to greet Harry, embracing him fiercely. "I didn't expect to see you here tonight."

"I dragged him along," Reza said, grinning. "Screaming and kicking."

"Marwan," Yassin said, glancing back over his shoulder as his sparring partner came up behind him, mopping sweat from his forehead and shoulders with a towel. "I'd like you to meet a friend of mine. . .Ibrahim Abu Musab al-Almani."

"*Salaam alaikum,*" the young man smiled, extending his hand to Harry. "It's good to finally meet you."

Finally? An alarm flashed somewhere in Harry's brain, his eyes narrowing—watching the boxer carefully as he forced out the expected response. "*Wa' alaikum as-salaam,* brother."

"It's good to have you join us tonight," Marwan went on without seeming to notice the hesitation. "From what Yassin tells me, I understand you fought in Syria?"

Syria. His words struck Harry like a blow to the face, his mind racing. *Just how much had they said? Who else had they told?*

He found himself incapable of stopping his eyes from darting to Yassin's face—a look of accusation. Of *warning.*

The young Moroccan laughed, shaking his head. "Relax, man—Marwan's a brother. You're among friends."

You're in no position to judge, Harry wanted to say, but didn't, glaring at Yassin for another long moment. There would be time enough to deal with him later.

"Yes, I did," he responded finally, turning back toward Marwan. "Once the bombings started. . .I couldn't stand by and watch anymore. I had to do *something*—had to go to the aid of my fellow believers."

"*Subhanallah*," Marwan exclaimed softly, his dark eyes gleaming at Harry's admission. *Glory be to God.* "A man I trained with here at this very club when I first started boxing went to fight against the apostate in Damascus."

He paused a moment, his voice changing ever so slightly. "He was killed three weeks later, in an airstrike shortly after he arrived."

"*Mash'allah.*" Harry smiled, reaching out to grip the young man's shoulder firmly. *As God has desired.* "The blood of the martyrs, it is a beautiful thing in the sight of God."

"*Allahu akbar*," he heard Reza breathe from behind him, an exclamation of praise echoed softly by the other two young men.

Time to move on.

"You're a good fighter," he said, nodding toward the ring over Marwan's shoulder as he changed the subject. "I used to spar myself, once—when I was in *Gymnasium* back in Germany."

"Were you any good?"

"I liked to think that I was," Harry smiled in answer to Yassin's question. "I was a very proud young man in those days. And very far from the truth, as are all who are filled with such pride."

"You up for joining me for a round?" Marwan asked, throwing his towel over onto a duffel bag piled in the corner. "I'm just getting warmed up."

It took Harry a moment to realize the invitation was being directed at him, and then he shook his head, chuckling as he met the young man's eyes. "The last time I put on the gloves, I doubt you had left your mother's breast."

He saw something flash in Marwan's eyes, as if he had taken the reference to age as a slight—Reza's voice distracting him in that moment. "But you fought bravely against the *safawi* in Syria."

"I fought in the way of Allah, yes," Harry replied, turning to his friend. "But that was actual *fighting*, not this. . .child's play, as different from the real thing as night is from day. And once you've tasted the reality, it's very hard to ever go back."

6:26 P.M. British Summer Time
The Nell
London

"So the wife tells me, now and again," Phillip Greer replied, seemingly unperturbed by Marsh's outburst. He took a long sip of his beer before continuing, pausing to wipe the foam from his lips.

"I can't be looking at this kind of thing, Phillip," the former director-general went on without waiting for him. "I am under suspicion of having ordered his *death*, and these are—"

"Arthur Colville's financial records," Greer interjected calmly, adjusting his glasses as he leaned forward, tapping the folder with a long forefinger. "And if you'll turn to page 11, you will see something very interesting."

Marsh obeyed grudgingly, his eyes running down the long columns of figures displayed on the page. Hundreds of transactions, incoming and outgoing. "What am I looking at here?" he asked finally, glancing up.

"Eight years ago, the *Daily Standard* was on the brink of insolvency," the counterintelligence officer responded, using the name of Colville's paper, "and then, Colville began receiving money from right-wing groups in the United States. First a few thousand pounds a month, then more. 'Donations' in the tens of thousands, pouring in almost every month from over three dozen organizations."

Marsh shook his head. "He was telling them what they wanted to hear. Confirming their apocalyptic vision of 'Eurabia' as they wished to see it, and they chose to finance the furtherance of their narrative. I don't see how any of this involves us."

"It involves us, Julian," Greer said, his eyes narrowing behind the glasses, "because from what I've seen thus far, I can state with measured confidence that most of these groups simply don't *exist*."

"Then where is the money coming from?"

Greer raised a suggestive eyebrow. "Where do *you* think? Who's spent the last decade steadily building up right-wing elements all across Europe, picking out the most extreme voices and ensuring they had the funding to drown out all the rest?"

Russia, Marsh thought, a sudden chill seeming to wash over him, knowing all too well to what Greer referred. No one had ever done influence operations like the Russians, and these last few years. . .he caught himself suddenly, looking sharply across the table at his colleague. "What exactly are you saying, Phillip? My God. . .you're not trying to tell me that Russian money was *behind* the terrorist attack on Her Majesty? It's—"

"Too early to say," the counter-intelligence officer said cautiously. "Earlier still to say whether such was by design. Colville's money was, we know that much. And we now know that his money was not his own. Everything else is speculation, and will remain such until we can gather more intelligence. I think you can now see why I asked for this meet, Julian. I need your help."

"No, you don't," Marsh responded, shaking his head. "You need far more than I'm in any position to provide, Phillip—this needs to go straight to the DG. You're in a position to do so, and he can—"

"No, Julian, I can't."

"In the name of God, why *not?*"

"The Colville affair," Greer began slowly, seeming to weigh his words with more than usual care, "is one which Ashworth is desirous to put behind the Service—permanently. He would prefer that his own tenure not be. . .tarnished, by any association with the mistakes of his predecessor."

My mistakes. Marsh drew a deep breath, only too aware of how his career had ended. And yet, Ashworth's instincts weren't wrong—in this brave new world of relative public transparency, the Service needed good press. Needed it fast.

And they weren't going to get it by re-opening their investigation of a man *they* were suspected of having assassinated.

But Greer wasn't done. "When I came across the first evidence that the source of this money might not be as represented, I went to Ashworth with my concerns. And was ordered to leave it alone."

"And you didn't, did you?"

A quiet smile. "You've known me for more than twenty years, Julian. You know I follow my own lights."

Chapter 3

9:42 P.M. Central European Summer Time
The apartment
Sint-Jans-Molenbeek, Belgium

". . .she asked me to spar with her the other day, bro, honest. Right there in the club."

"And?"

"And I told her 'no', of course," Harry heard Yassin respond, the two brothers bantering ahead of him as they ascended the stairs to their third-floor apartment. "I'm not fighting a woman! She was a beauty, though—"

"As beautiful as Nora?" Reza asked, naming his girlfriend—a young French college student whom Harry had met a few weeks before at the mosque. She had, Reza had told him, converted to Islam the previous year. "I doubt it."

He shook his head at the folly of it all, feeling anger build within him as the three of them moved down the dimly lit corridor, pausing outside the door as Reza fumbled with his key in the latch.

He'd managed to keep his head down for two months, stay off the radar. All of that, potentially blown by the loose lips of these *fools*. It was possible that he would have to leave Brussels, to go on the run. *Again.*

Go black.

". . .isn't that right, Ibrahim?" he heard Yassin ask, glancing back at him as they entered the flat. "You've been quiet, man, is—"

"And you've been talking far too much," Harry hissed, something seeming to snap within him as the door *clicked* shut behind them, the anger boiling over.

He turned on Yassin before the younger man could react, his forearm driving into the young Moroccan's throat as he forced him back against the thin wall of the apartment, the drywall seeming to shudder from the impact. "Who else have you *told*?"

"Easy, man, easy," he heard Reza protest, placing a hand on his shoulder, but he shook him off—his blue eyes boring fiercely into Yassin's own as he pressed harder.

"Answer me now! Who have you been telling about me?"

Yassin shook his head desperately, taken completely off-guard by the sudden outburst of violence. "Mar-Marwan," he stammered out in a near panic, "and a couple more of the brothers I know from the mosque. No one else, no one I couldn't trust."

"Ibrahim, my brother—let him go!" Reza exclaimed again, this time pulling Harry away from his brother. "What's gotten into you?"

"No one you couldn't trust?" Harry demanded, ignoring Reza as he moved back toward where Yassin still leaned against the wall, rubbing his sore throat—jabbing out a long forefinger toward his young friend. "And just who are you to make that decision, tell me that? Who are *you*?"

"Ibrahim, just calm down," Reza attempted to interpose, "there's no need for this. We can—"

"This Marwan," Harry spat, cutting him off as he turned to glare at the younger brother, "how long have you known him?"

"A month and a half, two—I think," Reza replied, shaking his head in incomprehension. "Why does any of that matter?"

"How do you know he's not an agent of the *Sûreté de l'État*?" Harry shot back, using the French name for the Belgian intelligence service otherwise known as the VSSE. "Of the French secret service?"

He saw Reza flinch at his words and pressed them home, his anger fully real. If they realized he was here. . .

It would only be a matter of time before the Agency came after their own. And after all that he had done in the UK—there could be no redemption.

"But neither of you ever even thought about any of that, did you?" Harry swore, turning his back on both of them as he stormed into the kitchen. "I went to fight in the jihad in Syria, I sacrificed *everything* in the cause of Allah. But if I am arrested now, if the secret police come through that door because you just *had* to talk, it's all for nothing. My usefulness, at an end. An *end*, do you understand that?"

He shook his head, his hands closing around the curved back of the lone wooden chair at the table as he forced himself to calm down. *Message sent.*

He didn't know what the odds were of them having spoken to an actual intelligence service asset were, didn't care to find out. He'd give it a couple days, then make his excuses and leave them—move on, he knew not where.

No sense in trusting to fate. As many times as it had betrayed him before.

He looked up to see Reza standing in the doorway of the kitchen, his dark eyes regarding him carefully.

"Ibrahim. . ." the engineering student began slowly, almost apologetically. As if shamed by the knowledge that what he had said was all too true. "There was a reason we told Marwan. . .and the others, of the part you played in Syria. We've been wanting to strike a blow ourselves in the struggle of God. *Here.*"

4:51 P.M. Eastern Daylight Time
Russell Senate Office Building
Washington, D.C.

"You will lower your voice, Roy," Scott Ellis announced firmly, leaning back in his chair, "or you will leave. If I wanted to be yelled at, I'd go on talk radio. I'm not going to sit and take it here in my own office."

"We had a deal," Roy Coftey repeated for the second time in as many minutes, his voice lower this time—his eyes blazing as he glared across the desk at the Senate Majority Leader. The man he had *made* the Majority Leader.

Gratitude is a disease of dogs.

"The operative word there, Roy," Ellis responded, seemingly unmoved, "is 'had.' We *had* a deal. The political realities have changed."

Coftey shook his head, as if incapable of believing what he was hearing. "The *realities* are unchanged. Our nation was attacked not seven months ago, Scott—our allies continue to suffer these 'lone wolf' attacks on what seems like a weekly basis. We've never needed a robust intelligence capability more than we do at this very moment. *Those* are the realities."

Ellis let out a heavy sigh. "Look, Roy. . .I get it. You and I have both spent a long time in this town, and on this issue—we're not so very far apart."

Here it comes, Coftey thought cynically, recognizing the majority leader's tone of voice.

The one the former prosecutor reserved for cajoling influential donors and the despised "electorate." Equal parts flattery and empathy—the way he would have stroked a chicken right before popping its head off growing up on the farm in Oklahoma. It wasn't going to work on him.

"I was glad to kill SB286 for you," Ellis continued, "not just because our deal and your resulting change of party affiliation secured the Republican majority in the Senate, but because, between you and I—I genuinely felt that the President's allies in the Senate were taking things too far. You can make the argument that the intelligence community has needed to be reined in, but they were going to gut it. They—"

"So now we're gutting it," Coftey said flatly, not giving an inch. He saw Ellis raise a hand in protest and plowed on, ignoring him. "I'm not one of your donors, so don't sit there and condescend to me, Scott. I've been in this town too long for that. You're telling me that we're going to do the wrong thing, because we don't have the backbone to do the right one."

"I'm telling you that we aren't going to have the votes to do what I'd like to do, Roy," the New Mexico senator responded, letting out a deep sigh as he reached for the smartphone laying in front of him on his desk. His thumb moving across the screen for a long moment before he extended it toward Coftey. "You've seen this, I'm sure."

A nod. It was the kind of thing he hadn't seen since Vietnam, the former Green Beret realized, staring at the photograph displayed on-screen. The lifeless, partially-charred bodies of men and women strewn across a desolate courtyard—the strangely perfect visage of a young boy laying half-buried in rubble.

"Images like this one, of the civilian casualties from our drone strike in the Sinai, have been going viral for almost a week now," Ellis said quietly when he looked back up. "I doubt there's anyone in the world with Internet access who hasn't seen them or at least heard about them. They're shifting public opinion, Roy, and there's nothing we can do about it. This is Abu Ghraib all over again."

"Can we even be sure this is really them?" Coftey asked, leaning back in his chair as he stared coldly across the desk at the Senate Majority Leader. "Who's to say this picture isn't from one of Bashar Assad's bombing raids on civilians in Syria? Or even the last time the IDF rolled into Gaza?"

"God, you're such a cynic," Ellis exclaimed in seeming disbelief, shaking his head. "You just don't get it, do you? Whether the picture is real or not—whether it's from the Sinai or not—doesn't matter. What matters is that people out there *believe* it to be real. And they believe that we did it."

Unbelievable. Coftey bit back a contemptuous laugh as he looked away from Ellis, out the window—the dome of the Capitol itself visible through the trees, just across Constitution Avenue to the southwest. "So what you're telling me is that our national security stance is now governed by what people *think* on the Internet."

"No, I'm telling you that circumstances have changed, Roy," Ellis snapped, his patience seeming to reach an end. "Don't be obtuse. We both know what we would have once liked to have accomplished, but public opinion is no longer on our side. So you can either get onboard, or get run over. Those are our—your—choices."

"With respect, Scott," Coftey began, a dangerous light glittering in his eyes as he rose to his feet, buttoning his suit jacket, "I've heard that song before."

He turned and began walking toward the door of the Majority Leader's office, Ellis' voice calling out after him as he went. "You've already changed parties once, Roy. You've alienated every ally you've ever made in this town. Where are you going to go now?"

Coftey paused with his hand on the doorknob, a curious smile playing across his lips as he looked back at the Senate Majority Leader. "Home, for starters."

1:08 A.M., Central European Summer Time, June 26th
The apartment
Sint-Jans Molenbeek, Belgium

Leave. That single word, repeating itself over and over again through his mind as he lay there, flat on his back—staring up through the darkness to the ceiling above.

Just turn and walk away, Harry thought, shifting restlessly on the couch. *Walk away. Just like he had so very many times before.*

It was the first lesson you learned working for the Agency, that you couldn't save the world. That even trying to. . .wasn't in your job description.

Your job was to carry out your orders, to the best of your ability. Get the intel you were sent to collect. Keep your people alive. And try to make it through with some fragment of your soul still intact. That last part, entirely optional.

But now. . .there were no orders. No one to collect for. No one to report back to. No one to keep alive. No one at all, except *himself*, his own survival all that hung in the balances.

Weighed and found wanting. Every part of him worth living for, already dead. Back in Las Vegas on that hellish December night.

On the docks of Aberdeen.

He closed his eyes, seeing Carol standing there once more before him as she had that night in the Bellagio, so much of her father's determination visible in her in that moment. Fierce and raw. *Everything he'd loved about her.*

"You thought I was going to leave you?"

And yet leave him she had, even as the air around them became tinged with the smell of camphor—soman nerve gas—the two of them stepping out the doors of the resort. . .and into the abyss awaiting them just beyond.

A rifle bullet, piercing the night. *And his own heart.* The future, shattered with a single shot. *What might have been.*

And even as he watched, her face seemed to fade away, becoming more indistinct by the moment until it was gone, beyond hope of recovery. Replaced by that of another. A woman's dark eyes gazing at him through the steam rising off a cup of Darjeeling. Regarding him with suspicion. *Fear.*

Mehreen's voice echoing in his ears, the way it had sounded on that fateful night he'd found himself sitting in her flat there in London—the photograph of her dead husband on the end table just a few feet away, bearing mute witness to all that was to come. The *betrayal* of all once held sacred.

"You're here to kill a man, aren't you, Harry?"

And she was right, as she had so often been. His quest for vengeance upon the man who had attacked Vegas—*killed* Carol—ensnaring them both, dragging them down into the abyss.

"Those who seek to take that which belongs to the Lord of Worlds. . .do so at their peril."

The voice of a man he had killed, as surely as if he had pulled the trigger himself. Words of a truth he'd chosen to blind himself to, until it was all far too late. Lives shattered, all about him, worlds in ashes.

It was said that one who set out to take vengeance must dig two graves, one for his enemy and one for himself—but for him, two graves had been nowhere near enough. *To cover his sins.*

The moment when you glimpsed a murderer through the mist, moved to stop him. Unsuspecting that he would turn at the last, revealing his face to be your own.

Driving home the realization that to strike him down would be to end yourself. Survival itself, cold and primal, all that stayed your hand.

He'd been lying awake for hours, unable to get Reza's words out of his head. *"I tried to go to Syria, a year ago—but was turned back at the Turkish border. And I was discouraged, I thought that somehow Allah had rejected me, that I was unfit for His struggle. When I saw the caliphate begin to crumble, I wept, fearing that I had missed my opportunity. That I had* failed. *And then you entered our lives, and I began to believe once again. . ."*

All his worst fears, confirmed in that instant. Confirmed? *No.* Revealed to be breathtakingly insufficient.

And now here he was again, trapped in a snare of his own making, searching for an exit that would allow him to escape. . .without damning all those left behind to certain destruction. *Innocent blood, once more staining his hands.*

No way out.

12:48 A.M. British Summer Time
A pub
Central London

Russia. It still seemed impossible, Marsh thought, staring across the table into the empty chair across from him. More so with each passing drink.

He'd spent his last few years at Five watching it. The tentacles of Russian influence, spreading across the continent with the plodding inevitability of a glacier—infiltrating groups across the political spectrum, elevating voices from far beyond the mainstream. Subverting Western democracy from within.

Sowing the seeds of chaos, to be reaped at a later date. The gradual return of an old familiar enemy—once thought vanquished.

Perhaps men like himself had always known better. Too jaded, too cynical to have harbored any faith in the narratives which had permeated the West's political leadership after the fall of the Wall. The idea that the Iron Curtain had been ripped away to reveal an eager world just *waiting* for freedom on the other side. *A new Russia.*

He and his colleagues had known the truth, watching with mounting concern as political pressure and constricting budgets inexorably forced the Western intelligence community to avert its eyes from its oldest foe.

The truth that for every student out in the streets, eager for liberty—whatever that meant in reality—and rapprochement with the West, there was someone else, older and wiser, behind the scenes. Someone who had benefited from the old system and wasn't about to let go of their hard-won power. The grim recognition of which of those forces was going to win out, in the end.

The truth that Russia was far too old to change.

But this. . .the idea that Russian money could have been behind the attack on Her Majesty, it seemed absurd. So alien a departure from all that which had characterized their efforts at direct action in the past.

And what part was Greer himself really playing in all of this, the former director-general found himself musing, the question forcing its way to the fore. The counter-intel officer's words playing on repeat in his head as he filtered through them again and again, searching for nuance, subtext—anything left hidden, just below the surface.

"Sod your clearance, Julian. You being out doesn't change the reality that you're still one of the only men I trust."

But whom could you trust, *really?* He'd known Phillip for decades, but the man's loyalties—like his own—were first and foremost to the Service.

"You still have contacts, Julian—from the old days. I need you to shake the tree, see what reaction that gets us. Find me something to go on."

Was it all a lie? Meant to force him into the open, expose his own network? Reveal whom he had maintained contact with, even after his resignation from Five?

Perhaps. Marsh shook his head, hearing approaching footsteps from off to the side—the back of the pub near the lavatory. It was a risk he was just going to have to take, the threat to the Service if Greer's suspicions were true. . .far too serious to be ignored.

The footsteps halted at his table, a woman near his own age sliding wordlessly into the booth across from him—her face half-veiled in shadow, but no less recognizable for all that.

"Thanks for agreeing to come meet with me, Margaret," Marsh said, the faintest of smiles touching his lips. "My apologies for the hour."

2:13 A.M. Eastern Daylight Time
Vienna, Virginia

"You're still up?" Coftey heard a woman's voice ask, somewhere in the darkness behind him, the glowing screen of the laptop perched on his knees providing the den's only illumination.

He clicked "end turn" on the strategy game he was playing before answering her, watching the AI cycle through its calculations, acting and reacting to his own decisions as he placed the laptop on the end table—leaning back in his recliner. "Yeah, couldn't even begin to think about sleeping."

"Ellis?" his secretary Melody asked, moving into the circle of light. Her blonde hair tousled hopelessly around her face, sleep still visible in her eyes, her pajamas rumpled as if she had just gotten out of bed.

She was young enough to have been his daughter, something that probably should have bothered him more than it did. The latest—and longest—of the string of relationships with young women on the Hill he'd formed in the years since his wife had passed away from Lou Gehrig's, nine years into his career in the Senate.

Jessie. He'd married her right before leaving for Vietnam—a war bride in the truest sense of the word, in an era when marrying a soldier wasn't the most popular thing to do. Even in rural Oklahoma.

And she'd stayed true to him, all through the years at war. And all that followed, as he uprooted both of them from the place of their birth and moved to D.C. to pursue his career. Until she'd been slowly stolen away from him in the end, piece by piece—bit by bit—by a disease whose very name he had come to hate.

Burying her back in that cemetery in Oklahoma, five miles from where he'd been born, he'd sworn he would never love again.

And he never had. *Until now.* Melody's arrival in his life, changing so much. Different, somehow, than all the women who had come and gone before.

He smiled, shaking his head in answer to her question—shifting his weight to one side of the recliner as she slid in beside him, her warm body molding itself against his. *Leave the politics at work.*

That had always been their pact, ever since the first night—perhaps the secret of why their relationship had worked when all the others had failed.

Their bed, a sanctuary against all that lay without—the treachery and double-dealing that characterized Washington. *A haven.*

"A storm is coming," he said softly, her head nestled against his chest—his arm wrapped around her body, holding her close. "And it's going to break upon us all too soon. I want to get away from. . .all this, before it does. Get myself grounded, once more, back where I belong. I want to go home."

"Oklahoma?" she asked, her voice a murmur in the semi-darkness.

He nodded. "I plan to leave Monday—spend a week on the old homestead, back in Chandler. And I want you to come with me."

8:04 A.M. Central European Summer Time
The apartment
Sint-Jans Molenbeek, Belgium

"Sit down," Harry ordered, hearing Yassin enter the kitchen of the small apartment behind him, a draft of cold air washing across the room as he pulled open the refrigerator.

"I have to get going, Ibrahim—there's a possibility of work at a bakery just a few blocks from here. I don't want to be late, and miss the chance—"

"Money?" Harry turned to look at him then, his blue eyes flashing fire as he cut him off. "That's what is important to you? Sit down."

Yassin hesitated for only a moment, then did as he was told—likely knowing what Harry did, that for one job there would be several dozen applicants, many better qualified than himself. *Hopeless.* The chair scraping against the floor as he pulled it out, taking his seat across from Harry.

Reflexively rubbing his throat even as he did so, as if remembering the night before. The fire burning in Harry's eyes as he'd shoved him up against the wall.

When his fingers came away from his throat to rest on the table top, Harry saw that they were trembling. *Good.*

He didn't acknowledge it, didn't speak—just sat there, his eyes locked with Yassin's. The silence growing, building—swelling between them. *Don't blink first.*

"What did you want?" the young man asked finally, his Adam's apple bobbing as he swallowed hard, seemingly unable to bear the tension for another moment.

Harry waited another long moment before replying, his eyes never moving. People couldn't take silence—he'd learned that years before, interrogating enemy combatants on the battlefields of Iraq and Afghanistan. The emotional pressure far too strong for the untrained to resist without cracking. Without giving themselves away.

"I want to know," he said finally, tapping a long forefinger against the table, "who proposed the idea for this attack. Was it you and Reza? Or was it this boxer. . .this Marwan fellow?"

Yassin shifted uncomfortably in his seat, not meeting Harry's eyes. His body language giving Harry the answer, as plainly as if he had spoken the words. "I don't remember, I—"

"It was Marwan, wasn't it?" Harry pressed, knowing the answer and forcing him to say it. To *confront* the reality of what he had done. They were in danger here, they all were.

"Fine, it was Marwan, I think," he spat, shaking his head in frustration and anger, "but I don't see how any of this matters, Ibrahim. It doesn't—"

"It matters because this is exactly how they *work*!"

7:09 A.M. British Summer Time
The terraced house
London, England

It had been some time since he'd woken up with a hangover this bad, a blinding headache pounding against the inside of Julian Marsh's skull as he rummaged in the cupboard—finding his canisters of salt and sugar and dumping roughly equal amounts of each into a tall glass of water.

Years. Perhaps not even since Berlin—alcohol had been a staple back then, pushing one's way through the dark German winter. Trying to stay one step ahead of the Stasi and seeming to fail more than one succeeded.

"You can call me 'Maggie', Julian, you know that. The way you all did back then."

Back then. He smiled despite himself, so many of the old memories coming back. Margaret Forster—'Maggie', as they'd called her back in the day—had always been a formidable woman, a highly successful M.I.-6 case officer in an era when that field had been dominated almost exclusively by men.

Operating in the denied space that had been Moscow in the '80s, running assets under the nose of an enemy which dismissed her as a secretary, a functionary—unworthy of their notice. An underestimation they'd made at their peril.

Maggie Forster had handled some of Six's most valuable assets behind the Iron Curtain in those days—could have gone far in the Service herself, had she chosen to.

But the Cold War had come to an end, the old enemy vanquished—or at least so everyone wanted to believe at the time—and she'd wanted a husband, a family.

A life beyond the Service. And she'd been smart enough to know that you couldn't have them both.

Unlike him, Marsh thought morosely, glancing around the starkly appointed kitchen of the flat. At least for her, the first half had come true.

"'Maggie', then," he'd said, smiling sheepishly at her in the dim light of the bar, her greying hair framing a weathered, weary face. The years hadn't been kind to either of them. *"I regret getting you out at this hour."*

"Don't, Julian. I wouldn't have been asleep anyway," she'd replied, dismissing his apology with a wave of her hand. *"As Richard's. . .illness has*

worsened, he's up at all hours, more at night than during the day. I left him in front of the telly."

Early onset Alzheimer's, which had begun to claim her husband seven years earlier at the far too young age of fifty-six.

"I'm sorry," he'd said, wincing despite himself. *"Will he—"*

She'd shaken her head, reaching forward to cover his hand in hers. *"He'll be fine, Jules. He's not going to go anywhere or hurt himself—we're not at that place yet, even if he does sometimes think that I'm the housekeeper. So tell me, why did you ask me here tonight?"*

It had been a long moment before Marsh replied, weighing his words as if he somehow thought the decision hadn't already been made. The moment he picked up the phone.

"There are forces which have been set in motion in this country, Maggie," he'd said finally, his eyes locking with hers as she raised her drink to her lips. *"You can see their effects every night on the telly. But who set them in motion, and why, those are questions I don't have the answer to. Yet. I need someone with contacts in Moscow, from back in the old days—people who can tell me who's at the levers of power now. Who's pulling them."*

She hadn't reacted, not at first. Not perceptibly. Taking another long sip of her drink before responding, her fingers trembling ever so slightly as she set the glass back down. *"Those questions, Julian. . .just how sure are you that you want them answered?"*

He hadn't known what to tell her, and even now, this morning—as he drained the last of his water, grimacing at the mixture of sugar and salt, he didn't have a better answer.

But he suspected it was one Rubicon which had already been crossed. No way back—for either of them, now.

Alea iacta est.

8:11 A.M. Central European Summer Time
The flat
Sint-Jans-Molenbeek, Belgium

"This is how *they* entrap young Muslims all across the West," Harry said, seemingly struggling to control his voice as he rose to his feet, the anger boiling over. "Seeking out the faithful, those receptive to the call of God's struggle. Luring them in, to a web of their own design, imprisoning them for their beliefs."

The way the FBI had done so successfully in the States, in the years since 9/11. Controversial as all the rest, but since when had defending one's country ever been simple? Or morally clear.

"It isn't that way," Yassin said, looking up at him—denial written across his face. "I *know* Marwan—I've prayed beside him, I know his heart. He would never betray us, would never turn his back on the faithful."

Harry shook his head at the absurdity of it all.

"You know *nothing*," he said, his voice sinking ever lower as he continued, a menacing intensity pervading every syllable. "In the jihad in Syria, I served beside a man who could have been my brother. We fought together by day and ate bread together by night. We talked of the homes we had left behind, of all we had abandoned—how all of it counted as *nothing* to us anymore compared to the joy of serving a single day in Allah's struggle. And then one day, I learned he had been executed—as a *spy*. An informer for the *nusayri* regime."

He could see the shock in Yassin's eyes at the story, the growing self-doubt—knew to press his advantage.

"Only God can know the heart of each man, and separate his truth from his falsehood," he went on, spinning the elaborate web of his own lie. "That is the reality, whether you choose to acknowledge it or not."

"So what are you asking of me?" Yassin demanded, his own face flushing with anger as he rose from the table. The anger of youth, of knowing one was wrong and being too proud to admit it. "That I sit here and do *nothing*? That I go back to my life and pretend that none of this ever happened? I can't do that—*you* didn't do that."

"No," Harry said, shaking his head. "Far be it from God that I would suggest such a thing—to turn back from the path of jihad once your feet have been set upon it would be a sin. But the holy struggle is not a game, and—"

"I've never thought that it was, I—"

"And those who would take part in it," he said calmly, talking over Yassin without raising his voice, "must be prepared to make sacrifices for the security of their brethren."

"What kind of 'sacrifices' are you talking about?" Yassin asked, the uncertainty only too visible in his eyes. He was out of his depth and he knew it, somewhere deep down.

"I want you and Reza to sever your ties with Marwan and the others at the club," Harry replied, placing a gentle hand on the young man's shoulder. Looking him directly in the eye. *Isolate, spread distrust. Manipulate.* The tools of any good social engineer, equally those of the case officer. "Do that, and I will ensure that you both get to Mindanao, to join our brothers who still fight under the black banners there."

"You can do that?"

"I can," he nodded, a smile of calm assurance crossing his face as he squeezed Yassin's shoulder. "I swear before God."

8:47 A.M.
Parc du Cinquentenaire
Brussels, Belgium

"Come along, Pierre," Armand Césaire said, clucking his tongue as he gently tugged at his recalcitrant dog's leash, forcing him to follow along as he moved toward the *arcade*—shaking his head at the small French bulldog's distraction.

Being invisible. That had always been his talent, whether it was in Cote D'Ivoire—or here on the streets of Brussels. Fading into the background, unnoticed as he went about his work. Corrupting people, convincing them to betray their country. *Their God.*

The work of the case officer, as old as time itself. And all people saw was a man, walking his dog.

LYSANDER was different, though, from so many of the agents he had run through the decades. A fellow intelligence officer, not a recruited asset. Which only made him more concerned by the silence.

Four weeks, and *nothing* from his asset. That wasn't normal, and it was bringing old fears back to the surface. Demons he'd once thought buried beneath the tough skin he'd been forced to develop over the years.

Memories. Ghosts of long ago.

He'd woken up in the middle of the night two days ago, rousing his wife from her own slumber—paralyzed by a premonition of evil. Of something having gone *wrong.*

Get a grip, he told himself. This wasn't like him at all, but then again, he was getting old. As his wife never missed an opportunity to remind him, her own hair white as snow.

And then he saw it, the single streak of white chalk against the stone at the base of the arch itself, barely two inches long—hardly noticeable and yet too deliberate to have been left by accident. *The tell.*

His breath caught in his throat, struggling not to betray the emotion on his face as he reached down scooping up Pierre into his arms, the little bulldog attempting to lick his face as the case officer strode from beneath the arch, his pace quickening as he made his way toward the dead drop.

LYSANDER had made contact.

7:49 A.M. Eastern Daylight Time
The Yellow Line
Washington, D.C.

She could still feel his hands on her body, his breath hot against her neck—the warmth of his bulk against her, holding her close long after he'd finished. The two of them huddled together in the chair in his den, nothing to break the silence but the rhythmic sound of his breathing and the monotonous ticking of the old clock on the mantel above the fireplace.

The pendulum swinging back and forth, back and forth until the sound nearly drove her insane.

Melody Lawlor leaned into the pole just inside the door of the metro car, the floor gently moving beneath her feet with the motion of the train, a weary sigh escaping her lips as she tried to shut it all out. Lose herself in the bustle and clamor of the crowded car, packed with her fellow denizens of the Beltway. Knowing she would be seeing him again, all too soon—as soon as she arrived on Capitol Hill.

It had all been a mistake, her affair with Roy Coftey. Though it hadn't seemed like it at the time, so soon after her arrival in D.C.

She'd wanted a job on the Hill, access and connections to people in power—and Roy Coftey had both, along with an unabashed appetite for young women that was the stuff of legend around Washington.

They'd used each other from the beginning, him for her body—her for his connections. A pretty even trade, or so she'd thought. And the sex hadn't even been that bad, a tender patience about Coftey that she'd never been able to find among men her own age in D.C.

But she had never dreamed that it would ever be about anything more than that, the growing depth of his affection for her taking her completely off-guard.

She'd nearly walked away from it all then, left him the moment she realized that, for the senator, things had become serious. But by that time. . .other considerations had already injected themselves into the situation.

Melody felt a body press into her from behind, not an uncommon experience on the Metro during rush, but she knew instinctively that it was *him*.

"What have you been able to find out for me?" A voice asked, low, almost lost in the noise filling the car.

The reason she had stayed with Coftey, despite it all. Betraying him even as she shared his bed. Because there were some things even he couldn't offer.

"He had a meeting with Ellis yesterday," she replied in the same low tone, not looking back. "It didn't go well."

"How about something I don't already know?" came Ian Cahill's irritated rasp, only inches from her ear.

"I'm sorry," she said, struggling to keep her face neutral, "but that's all I know. As I've told you from the beginning, he doesn't like bringing that kind of thing home."

"And you assured me back then that you could find a way around that," the man responded, not giving an inch. Cahill was a legend in D.C., a street-savvy political operative who'd managed to accumulate more power than almost anyone else in town without ever once holding elected office. A former ally of Coftey's, but time. . .and something else, she knew not what—had turned them into the bitterest of foes.

Melody shook her head, looking away from him. "I can and I have, you know that. You knew about his plan to change party affiliation ahead of time, and that was only because of me. It's not my fault that you weren't able to do anything with it."

"Old news," Cahill said dismissively, refusing to give her the point. "If you want to continue to justify our arrangement, I need something fresh."

"He's going out to Oklahoma next week," she replied finally, even as the train slowed, an automated voice announcing "Capitol South" as the stop. "And he wants me to go with him."

"Then make it count."

2:05 P.M., Central European Summer Time
Palais de l'Élysée
Paris, France

". . .as the security situation in the migrant camps there has become more tedious in recent weeks."

Anaïs Brunet leaned back in her stiff, high-backed chair, looking around her as Raoul Dubois, her counterpart at the DGSI—France's internal intelligence service—continued speaking.

Struck as always by the elegance of the meeting room, painstakingly restored—like the rest of the Élysée Palace—to its Enlightenment splendor.

How a palace for the kings of the earth had come to be named after the resting place of the blessed dead in Greek mythology was a mystery to her that a decade in government hadn't served to parse. But it was from these very windows that the Bourbons had once looked out upon their dominion, upon the masses in the streets of Paris. *Apres moi le deluge. . .*

"Just how concerned should we be?" President Denis Albéric asked, a worried frown on his face as he glanced down the table toward her. Re-elected scarcely four months before, Albéric had won victory by only the narrowest of margins over his National Front opponent.

And that was before events in the UK—and the attack on the Caen-Paris train—had brought the issue of terrorism surging back to the foreground. He had every reason to be worried.

"I think there is cause to be very concerned, *mon presidente*," she replied, choosing her words carefully. "You've seen the unrest, the protests outside the American Embassy here in Paris. We're in the middle of a very volatile period, and it would not be at all difficult for extremists to take advantage of the cover provided by legitimate protests to launch an attack."

She saw Dubois shake his head out of the corner of her eye, a disapproving look on the older man's face. The two of them had crossed swords more than a few times over the years since he'd taken over the DGSI—something she suspected had far more to do with her background than her gender.

Dubois was a career intelligence officer, having come up through the ranks of the DGSI, and the idea of having someone from outside the community serving as his opposite number clearly rankled him.

"I think we have to be careful not to conflate legitimate political protest with the threat posed by extremists. It would be unwise to—"

"I am not conflating anything," Brunet replied, keeping her attention focused on the president, her voice studiously neutral. "But we cannot ignore the potential for danger. I—"

Her phone began to vibrate in her purse at that moment, distracting her just as Dubois broke in once more. A furtive glance at the screen revealing that it was from Alliance Base.

Gauthier.

"*S'il vous plait excusez-moi, mon presidente,*" she said, holding up the phone. "I really must take this."

"*Bien sûr.*"

"This needs to have been important, Lucien," Brunet announced, the door of the conference room closing behind her as she slipped into the corridor without, an ornate portrait of one of the palace's former residents . "You've pulled me out of a meeting with the President."

"I assure you it is," General Gauthier responded, his voice tight. "LYSANDER made contact, earlier this morning."

Finally. "And?"

"We just finished decoding the contents of the dead drop thirty minutes ago, and the intelligence LYSANDER has provided will require further—"

"I understand that your analysts haven't had time to parse every sentence, Lucien," Brunet interrupted, cutting his explanation short. Intelligence work had made the general cautious, sometimes painfully so. And this was one of those times. "Just give me the raw assessment—what was he able to provide?"

"He believes he's made contact with an active cell, or at least a cell in the process of going active, a group of young Muslim men at a boxing club there in Molenbeek. University-age, most of them."

The demographic drawn upon by terrorist groups, revolutionaries, and armies themselves for centuries. Too young to have developed anything approaching a nuanced view of the world. Too young to fear death. But Gauthier wasn't done.

"The leader of the cell, though, assuming LYSANDER's intelligence is accurate, is an older man—a convert to Islam who reputedly spent time as a foreign fighter in Syria. His name is Ibrahim Abu Musab al-Almani. . ."

Chapter 4

7:04 P.M., Central European Summer Time, July 3rd
The apartment
Sint-Jans-Molenbeek, Belgium

"*Mashallah*," Harry breathed, breaking his bread into rough pieces before dipping one of the larger hunks into the bowl of *za'atar* sitting on the table only a few inches from his elbow. "I have good news."

"Oh?" Reza looked up from his food, a large engineering textbook propped open beside him. Yassin turning back from the refrigerator, a soda in his hand, the same question clearly written in his eyes.

"I succeeded in making contact this morning," he continued, smiling at them both, "with a brother I fought beside in *Sham*, a fellow German who left to continue the fight in the Philippines. And he gave me the name of a man in Dubai, a man who has served as a conduit for the faithful seeking to join the Emir in Mindanao."

He reached into the back of his jeans, withdrawing a computer print-out and smoothing it out on the table as Yassin took his seat. "I've booked both of you on an Emirates flight departing from Brussels next Saturday. *Insh'allah*, you'll arrive in Dubai less than seven hours later."

Where you'll promptly be detained on suspicion of terrorism by Emirati police who will have been alerted to your arrival, he didn't add, looking Yassin in the eye.

The two of them, no longer his problem at that point.

"Our brother will meet you there," he went on, the smile never wavering—his voice, utter conviction, "and look after you during the overnight layover, after which you will fly directly to Manila the following day."

"Next Saturday?" Reza demanded, finally seeming to find his voice. "That's not very far away, I'm not sure—"

"Is there anything which could be more important than answering the call of God?" Harry asked, his eyes meeting Reza's and holding them fast. "You have sought to take part in Allah's struggle, and now that you have been shown the way, you would hesitate from following it?"

"No, no," the young man said, shaking his head, "by no means. It's just—"

"Good," he replied, his face breaking into a wide smile. "Then it is settled. Once in Manila, you'll make contact with my brother and he will ensure that you reach Mindanao to join the fight."

"*Alhamdullilah,*" Yassin exclaimed, enthusiasm on his face as he rose— clasping Harry's hand in his own as the two of them embraced there in the middle of the kitchen, tears of joy shining in the younger man's eyes. "Thank you."

Harry shook his head, fighting to repress the feelings which rose within him in this moment. *Anger. Fear.*

Striving for the mastery.

"Give all the thanks to God, my brother," he said finally, his face betraying nothing of his true feelings as he held his friend close. "I am nothing but a conduit for His will."

He smiled, meeting Reza's eyes over Yassin's shoulder. "Just to think of it, brothers—in another week, you will have joined the ranks of those defending our religion. *Allahu akbar.*"

"*Allahu akbar!*"

12:47 P.M. Mountain Time
Bell Cow Lake
Chandler, Oklahoma

No rest for the wicked, Roy Coftey thought, wiping sweat from his forehead as the senator picked up his hammer once more—stripped to his shirtsleeves as he drove another ten-penny nail into the scaffolding of the main stage from which the dignitaries of Chandler would oversee the small town's annual

Independence Day 5K run at noon on the morrow.

"Nothing's changed, Ben," he said with a laugh, reaching for a nearly-empty bottle of water as a man approaching his age crawled out from beneath the scaffolding, dusting off his blue jeans and dirty t-shirt. "Growing up, I remember the Fourth was always hotter than hell."

The man chuckled, accepting the water bottle as Coftey passed it over.

"That it was, Roy. That it was. There's better fishing now, though," he added, nodding toward the lake as he unscrewed the cap of the bottle, taking a long drink. "Ever since we put the lake in. Mikey Farnum caught a ten-pound bass during the tournament last year."

"He's still around?" Coftey asked, looking over at his old friend.

A nod.

"He moved into assisted living up in Stillwater back last December after his stroke—but his son still makes sure he gets down for the tournaments." The man paused, screwing the cap back on the empty bottle. "I appreciate you lending a hand today, Roy. I mean that."

"It's the least I could do," he replied, taken somewhat off-guard by the man's earnestness. "It's good to bring back the old times, even if it's just for a day or two."

"You've changed," his old friend went on, looking him in the eye.

"I don't know what you mean."

The man seemed to hesitate for a moment before going on, his gaze shifting from Coftey's face out across the waters of Bell Cow Lake. "I'm going to be honest, Roy. . .I didn't vote for you in the last election. I didn't like what you'd become, what that town had done to you. But when you came back to Chandler this past January—as I see you now—it's like seeing the man I saw get off that plane when we both came back from the 'Nam. The old Roy, back again. Full of piss and vinegar, and spoiling for a fight."

At what cost, Coftey asked himself, following the man's gaze out to the water. Reflecting on the events of the last seven months, everything that had happened since he'd helped take down the Hancock administration. Spoiling for a fight, indeed. . .

"I nearly lost myself, Ben," he said finally, turning to face his old friend. "I let it all get to me, just like I swore I'd never do—and nearly lost everything I truly valued in the process."

A nod, as if the man knew all too well what he was saying. Had predicted it, had *seen* it, long before he himself had.

"But you're right," Coftey said, placing his hand on his friend's shoulder and squeezing it firmly as he moved past, picking up the hammer once again. "I'm back."

6:54 P.M. British Summer Time
Regent's Park
London

Be at Regent's, her text message had read. *The concert tonight.*

And so here he was, Julian Marsh thought, leaning awkwardly back into his rented deckchair, trying to relax—sunglasses shielding his eyes as he stared ahead at the bandstand, where the uniformed members of the Scots' Guards jazz ensemble were arranging themselves in their positions.

The last time he'd been to a concert in the park like this. . .it had been years. With Janet, most likely—his second wife.

His dress shirt had been discarded at last for a short-sleeved polo, but the sharp crease of his khakis gave him away in a moment.

He *wasn't* a man given to relaxation. Never had been.

"Julian!" he heard a woman's voice call out suddenly, startling him as he glanced up to see Maggie Forster standing there just a few feet away, paused artlessly as if she had just caught sight of him, a pair of sunglasses in her hand. "Fancy seeing you here tonight."

Indeed. Chance had never been a part of their lives. Not then, and not now.

"Julian," she went on, calling his attention in that moment to the middle-aged, heavyset man at her side, "I'd like you to meet my husband Richard. Richard, this is Julian Marsh—an old colleague of mine."

My husband. He accepted the proffered hand, finding himself searching the man's eyes for any sign of the disease which had begun to so slowly steal him away from her.

"Julian Marsh," the man repeated with the utmost of clarity, his bluff, honest face breaking into a warm smile, "why you'd be the former head of Five, wouldn't you?"

Nothing wrong with the man's memory.

"One and the same," Marsh replied uncomfortably, wondering instinctively if they could be overheard. He needn't have worried—their fellow concert-goers were, as ever, absorbed in their own lives, the first notes of a saxophone being tuned up on-stage drifting out over the park.

"Quite right," her husband smiled, as if rather pleased with himself for the recollection. "I've seen a lot of you recently on the telly."

That was something of an understatement. The former director-general glanced helplessly at Maggie—salvation appearing just then in the form of a younger copy of her husband, a little girl in the young man's arms as he approached them. Her husband turning, distracted by the new arrival, the little girl holding out her arms for him with a high-pitched shriek of joy.

"My son and granddaughter," Maggie said softly, moving away from her family toward Julian as they began talking.

"My stepson," she added, seeing his look, opening the large purse around her neck to withdraw a slender folder. "Richard had children before we met."

A ready-made family, imagine that. It was difficult not to envy her, hard though her life must have been. But there had been something. . .normal, about it all. Something he'd never known—or ever would know.

"Is this it, Maggie?" he asked, forcing his attention back to the present, the reason for them all being here. Opening the folder just far enough to glimpse an official dossier photo nestled within, stapled to the cover sheet—blue eyes staring back at him from a face lined and weathered by the decades. The face of a man somewhere near his own age, not even the passage of time serving to soften his sharply-chiseled Slavic features—thinning silver hair swept back from his brow in a manner that almost struck one as rakish. *Defiant.*

"It is," she nodded, something of a shadow passing across her face as the jazz ensemble struck up behind them, the music of Duke Ellington washing out across the park. "Be careful, Julian. Be *very* careful. My contacts are limited, now more than ever, but they were able to give me a name. The name of the man in that folder."

"And?"

"He's a former KGB officer, a man they say has been involved in spear-heading the Directorate's active measures against the West in recent years. It's said that as of last year he was posted to the *rezidentura* in Los Angeles. After that, everyone seems to have lost track of him—but my source was confident that if anything of the kind you describe was going on, you would find him somewhere near the bottom of it."

Former KGB. Marsh rolled the folder small in his hand. But that was an oxymoron, and they both knew it. There was no such thing as a "former" member of the *siloviki,* the old adversaries against whom they'd once played the great—the eternal—game across the streets of a divided Berlin.

"Come on, my dear," her husband said, his voice breaking in upon them once more. "The concert is beginning."

"Be careful," she repeated urgently, even as her husband flashed a genial smile at Julian, reaching forward to grip his hand once more, something that almost seemed like confusion flickering across his face for the space of a second.

"A pleasure meeting you. . .Henry."

1:26 P.M. Mountain Time
Bell Cow Lake
Chandler, Oklahoma

"You're working too hard," Coftey heard a worried voice say behind him, looking back over his shoulder to see Melody standing there, having traded in her customary Beltway office attire for shorts and a tank top.

Looking good as ever. "So how are the good people of Chandler?" he asked, deliberately ignoring her observation. She reminded him of Jessie in moments like these—attempting to mother him, despite the gulf in their ages. What he loved about her.

She shook her head, glancing back to where a flurry of people were hustling around near another stage, setting up microphones and speakers for an amateur singing competition. "Have yet to hear anyone who can carry a tune."

"Well that much hasn't changed."

She looked at him, only too aware he was trying to lead her astray. "Sweetheart, I'm serious. This heat. . .at your age, it's not—"

He wrapped his arm around her back, drawing her in close to him and silencing her protest with a kiss. He grinned, enjoying the moment—the feel of her body against him. "You've never had cause to worry about my age before."

"I know," she said, pulling away from him, "but this is different. This—"

He started to answer her, but just then he felt his phone vibrate in his front pants pocket. *The burner*, he thought, turning away from her as he pulled out the cheap disposable phone, flipping it open—a single line of text displayed across the screen.

Flying into Tulsa tonight, will see you in the morning. We need to talk, away from the circus. Away from the eyes.

"Roy, what is it?" he heard Melody ask behind him—the noonday sun still beating down hot on his forehead, but it felt as though the sweat had frozen to his back. A cold chill creeping down his spine.

"It would appear," he began, forcing a smile as he turned back to face her, "that we're going to have company."

7:41 P.M.
The Richmond Footbridge
Central London

"You can let me out right here," Julian Marsh said, reaching forward to tap his Pakistani cab driver on the shoulder—the black London cab pulling over to the side of the city street. The turgid waters of the Thames not fifty feet away, rolling on toward the sea. As they had for eternity.

He pressed a handful of pound notes into the man's palm, retrieving his light jacket before stepping out onto the cobblestones, his eyes flickering toward the footbridge just down the street, its arches spanning the river as they had over a century.

It seemed as though just yesterday that he had stood there himself, meeting with Arthur Colville on a chill spring morning—in the aftermath of a terrorist attack.

Attempting to pull them all back from a brink over which, as it turned out, one of them had been all too ready—no, eager—to plunge.

The bridge had been deserted then, just the two of them—standing there together in the early morning mist, but now it was choked with foot traffic, a flood of tourists passing across it in the growing twilight.

And in the center of the span, a solitary figure somehow apart from the crowd—standing there looking out over the Thames like a gargoyle perched in the eaves of some ancient cathedral.

Greer.

It was a mark of his faith in Maggie's abilities that he'd set up the meet with the counter-intel spook before making contact with her at the park. Secure in the assurance that, if she were reaching out, it could only mean she had something for him.

And so she had.

"So what do you have for me, Julian?" Greer asked softly as Marsh joined him in the center of the span, his hands shoved into the pockets of his windbreaker.

"A name," Marsh replied, not looking at his former colleague. He'd made the decision on the way over not to give Greer the folder itself—anything that could compromise Maggie as his source. Digging up information was what people like Greer did best. . .let them dig. "Alexei Vasiliev."

He saw Greer flinch out of the corner of his eye, the intensity of the response taking him off-guard.

"*Who* did you say?" the counter-intel spook demanded, his hand on the balustrade as he turned toward Marsh—his dark eyes flashing.

"Alexei Mikhailovich Vasiliev," Marsh responded. "He's a former KGB officer, was part of—"

"I know *who* he is," Greer interrupted, a sharp edge in his voice as he looked back out over the Thames. "He's here, Julian. In London. As of two days ago."

The former director-general shook his head, scarce able to believe his ears. "My God, Phillip. . .you're serious."

"Deadly so. Came into Heathrow on an Air France flight from Trieste the other night."

"Where is he now?"

"God knows." Greer saw Marsh's look and shook his head bitterly. "Don't give me that, Julian. The Service's budget goes to monitoring AQ and Islamic State affiliates here in the UK, you know that as well as I do. I no longer have the money or the manpower in my branch to go chasing after stray Russians."

He was right, that was the worst of it, Marsh thought. This wasn't the

Cold War, even if it was looking more reminiscent of it by the day. The powers that be. . .had moved on.

"Your source's intelligence," Greer went on after a long moment, "how good is it?"

"Very good," Marsh replied without hesitation, watching as Greer's face grew pale in the twilight. He let out a deep breath finally, shaking his head as if in resignation.

"That's what I was afraid of."

8:51 P.M. Central European Summer Time
The flat
Sint-Jans-Molenbeek, Belgium

A week. That's all that remained, Harry told himself, lifting his face into the stream from the shower head as steaming hot water cascaded down his naked body, puddling endlessly around his feet.

A week, and this would all be over—this, this ghastly *charade* he'd found himself swept up in. Yassin and Reza, on a plane to Dubai—flying straight into the arms of the Emirati authorities.

Himself, disappearing into the night.

He would take what money he still had remaining from what he'd managed to withdraw from the Korsakov accounts—take it and run, as he had before.

It wasn't enough to disappear, not completely, but he could stay off the radar. Keep moving among the refugee population, keep his head down. With his wounds healing, slowly but surely, he'd soon be able to drop the foreign fighter pose he had been forced to adopt here in Molenbeek.

Minimize his risk of falling in with more radicals.

Make it to Eastern Europe, if he could, fading farther and farther away from the prying eyes of Western intelligence. *Go dark.*

He reached up and shut the water off, sinking slowly back into the side of the shower stall as he stared out through the steam, catching a ghostly glimpse of himself in the mirror across the small bathroom.

Hollow eyes staring back at him through the mist, something of reproach in their depths. *Loathing.*

This *needed* to be over.

7:58 P.M. British Summer Time
Bai Wei Restaurant
Chinatown, London

The night was off to a promising start, Simon Norris thought, wiping the last traces of sauce from his lips as he returned his fork to its place beside the demolished plate of pork slivers—checking his phone quickly to make sure there was nothing from the office.

Nothing. The analyst shook his head, the mild heat of the savory Chinese food still lingering in his mouth. It would be just like Thames House to disrupt his evening, a date with a young London accounts manager he'd met on the Internet.

A date that was going rather well, in his opinion. He was only waiting for her to return from the restroom before proposing their next move. Off to a local club for after-dinner drinks, music—then, hopefully, back to his flat. With luck—

"Have you ever been to China, Mr. Norris?" a faintly accented voice asked, interrupting his thoughts as a man slid into the booth across from him—an older man, his silver hair glinting in the lights of the restaurant, ice-blue eyes transfixing Norris as he favored him with an assured smile.

"Who are you?" he demanded, finding his voice then. Every alarm bell in his head screaming a warning. *Something was wrong.*

"I was in China once," his visitor went on, as if he hadn't spoken. "For six months, back in the 1980s. Beijing, where spies go die—or so the saying goes."

Another smile touched his thin, almost bloodless lips. "But I didn't die."

"I'm going to ask you to leave," Norris said, struggling to keep his voice even as he stared into the man's eyes. "*Now.*"

The smile never faded, his mind finally registering the accent as the man began to speak once more. *Russian.*

"Are you sure you aren't making a mistake here, Simon?" the stranger asked quietly, his eyes cold and hard—a long, thin index finger tapping gently against the tabletop as he continued. "I was certain you'd want to hear me out, to hear what I had to say. We know, you see."

No. He felt a wave of panic break over him, his throat seeming to constrict to the point where he could hardly breathe. All thoughts of his date, of the evening he'd planned, forgotten in that moment.

"What? Who are you? *What* do you know?"

"I thought you would come to see reason," the man said, leaning back into the booth as he regarded Norris calmly. "Who I am, doesn't really matter. You can call me 'Alexei.' As for what we know. . .why, I think that should be obvious. Your relationship to the late Arthur Colville, Simon. We know *everything*."

9:57 P.M. Central European Summer Time
Neukölln, Berlin
Germany

"You're sure we can trust him," Anas Bukhari asked his older friend once again as they walked briskly across the darkened Berlin street.

Two years out from Syria—his parents killed in a regime bombing raid, his older brother seized and forced to fight by one of the rebel militias—it seemed impossible for the Syrian teenager to imagine that you could trust anyone. Least of all someone here in the West.

Two years, and he'd watched as the government in Damascus continued to slaughter his people by the hundreds of thousands. Bombing them, gassing them—executing them in cold blood.

All while Western governments just stood by and did *nothing*—no, even nothing would have been preferable to what they'd done, as they turned the might of their militaries against the brave *mujahideen* of the Islamic State. The only ones who, in their pursuit of the true path, had accomplished anything genuine against the regime.

The West spoke out against the Assad government, they called for an end to the violence against the innocent, but their actions. . .their actions put the lie to their words.

And now it was time for them to be called to account for their sins.

His friend turned back on him, pausing a foot from the sidewalk. "Of course we can," Yusuf said impatiently, his eyes hidden in shadow. "Come on, we've been over this before, bro—a hundred times. He came recommended to me by the brothers. He's not a plant."

"*Insh'allah*," he responded softly, shaking his head as they both moved down the sidewalk, toward the small Lebanese-owned café on the street corner.

It was well-nigh deserted, the bell jangling loudly as Yusuf led the way in—Anas following behind him. His eyes falling upon a single man sitting in the back of the café, clean-shaven, built like an athlete—perhaps in his mid-thirties, no older. A small laptop open on the table before him.

"*Salaam alaikum*," he greeted them, closing the laptop as they approached and gesturing for them to take a seat.

"You're not a believer," Anas responded, his eyes full of suspicion as they scanned the man's face, searching for any sign of treachery.

"No, I am not," the man replied calmly, seeming unruffled by the teenager's tone. "But I show respect. Please, sit."

"*Wa' alaikum as-salaam*," Yusuf added hastily as they took their seats across from him. "Do you have a location?"

The man nodded, pulling a piece of paper from his pocket and unfolding it to reveal a printed-out map.

"At noon tomorrow, your target will be here—at the Adlon—meeting for lunch with a counterpart from the *Bundeswehr*. That's when you'll strike." He smiled then. "How is it the Americans say? 'Two birds, one rock'?"

There was something wrong about all of this, Anas thought, staring across the table at the man, Yusuf's reassurances still ringing hollow in his ears.

"How can you *possibly* know all this?" he demanded, his dark eyes flashing with suspicion. "Who are you?"

"Anas, this is absurd. You're being—"

"No, it's a fair question," the man said, putting up a hand to cut Yusuf's outburst off. "Were I to be the one sacrificing myself in martyrdom, I would want to know."

He turned back toward Anas, his face still utterly neutral. *Expressionless.* "You ask who I am, and I can only tell you that I am a man with no more love for the West than you. The enemies of my people for even longer than they have been yours. My father and mother lived the prime of their lives believing that any day the sky could open and nuclear fire rain down upon us. *American* fire. That can *never* be again. As for how I know what I know, I am a facilitator. I have sources. And the Americans are nowhere near as secure as they think."

"*Allahu akbar*," Yusuf breathed, his face breaking into a wide smile.

"You will find the car in the parking garage at this address," the man continued, indicating a handwritten scrawl at the bottom of the map as he slid a set of keys across the table. "The trunk has been welded shut to hinder any efforts to disarm the device, and the detonator is a mobile phone in the center console of the vehicle."

"Sounds good," Yusuf nodded, placing his hand on Anas' shoulder and squeezing it affectionately. "We know what to do."

The man acknowledged his words with a quiet smile. "Then may your god smile upon your efforts."

He sat there for a long while after the two Arabs left the café, staring at the screen of his laptop as he finished up his tea. Marking the clock on the opposite wall, its hands creeping slowly onward.

Fifteen minutes, and the man dug a mobile phone from the pocket of his jeans, tapping in a number from memory and waiting until it was picked up on the other end.

"*Da*," he replied after a moment, listening as his contact went on. "*Delo sdelano.*"

It is done.

9:48 P.M. British Summer Time
A flat
London

"*We know you were his man on the inside, Simon,*" the Russian had said, continuing in the same, maddeningly even voice, "*the man who provided Colville with classified intelligence on the Service's surveillance of Tarik Abdul Muhammad. On the Queen's security arrangements at Balmoral Castle.*"

It seemed impossible. Simon Norris fell to his knees on the bathroom floor, retching uncontrollably—panic once more overwhelming him. *How?*

An unanswerable question. His sweaty fingers dug into the rim of the toilet, struggling to hold himself aright as his stomach emptied itself into the bowl, the foul taste of bile searing his throat. His date, all the plans he'd once had for this night—all forgotten.

"How?" he'd asked back there at the restaurant, sitting there frozen, looking into the Russian's eyes like a snake hypnotized by its charmer.

"You were not the only one who had a. . .'relationship' with Arthur Colville," the man replied. *"He was an asset of ours for many years, if an unwitting one. A useful fool. Or so we thought."*

Norris leaned back against the wall of the small bathroom, his hand trembling as he wiped vomit away from his lips—his knees drawn up to his chest as he huddled there.

"We underestimated Colville, I confess. A nearly fatal mistake on our part. Fomenting unrest, he was good at—a good return on our investment, what there was of it. But our analysts failed to predict that he would take the next step, to direct action. An attempt to kill the Queen herself. . ."

"It wasn't an attempt to kill her," he'd protested, struggling to keep his voice down in the restaurant. *"We had ensured that, we—"*

"You really didn't know, did you?" the Russian had asked, a trace of amusement flickering across his lips. His words striking fear to Norris' heart. *"Your Queen* was *to die that night, along with her family—the Crown Prince and his lovely wife and children. All of them a sacrifice on the altar of Colville's ambitions—his* war."

"That's not possible. That's not—"

"Colville was a fool," the Russian replied flatly, cutting him off. *"He went far beyond anything we had expected—anything we were* prepared *for. And that, Mr. Norris, is where you come in."*

Norris closed his eyes, the darkness of the bathroom seeming to enfold him—his right hand balling into a trembling fist, tears of anger and rage streaming down his cheeks as the Russian's words played over and again through his head.

This had all seemed so very simple once. So. . .*right.* It was hard to even remember what "right" had looked like now.

He only knew that his nightmare was only beginning.

Chapter 5

2:05 A.M. British Summer Time, July 4th
A terraced house
Richmond, London

Out in the hall, the old grandfather clock struck the hour, its sonorous tones filling the house as it had done for the better part of a century.

Five minutes late, as usual, Phillip Greer thought, an ironic smile playing at the corners of his mouth as the counter-intelligence officer nursed the last of his gin.

His wife had gone to bed hours before, but he had yet to join her—sitting alone in the parlor in silence, the ambient light of the muted telly casting flickering shadows across his face.

Alexei Vasiliev.

That name, running over and again through his head—as it had ever since Marsh had spoken it there on the bridge over the Thames. Driving sleep from him as effectively as a shot of caffeine to the veins.

Spending a career in counter-intelligence lent itself particularly well to paranoia, and one had to be careful to place a check upon it—to keep oneself from plummeting over the edge. *There lies madness.*

But this. . .this was different. Shades of the past, returned to haunt them once more.

He'd never encountered the man in person, but he'd seen his file more than enough times to be able to conjure up his face.

The face of a young man in the full dress uniform of a KGB officer from the mid '80s, eyes as cold as ice staring out from beneath the visor of his uniform cap, a cornflower-blue band running beneath the khaki crown.

Only years before all that had come crashing down, disintegrating into dust and ash. Or so everyone had told themselves.

But the men like Vasiliev, those who had come up defending the old order—they'd never gone away. They'd simply faded into the shadows, to await a better day.

A day which seemed as though it had now arrived. But what did it all *mean?*

"What in God's name," Greer began aloud, staring out into the darkness of the room as if he thought he could summon the man up before him, "are you doing *here?*"

7:31 A.M. Central European Summer Time
Diplomatic Residential Housing
Berlin, Germany

It had been another one of *those* nights. Thomas Dwyer looked into the bathroom mirror as he did up the cuffs of his uniform shirt, straightening his collar.

Flashbacks to Iraq. Filling his dreams once again—memories of their convoy coming under attack that day outside Ramadi.

A massive IED disabling the convoy's lead Stryker, rifle fire drumming against the shell of his up-armored Humvee as they struggled to react. *To fight back.*

They'd lost three men on the highway that day. *Frank, Colton, and Obed.* Good soldiers all, some of the finest men he'd ever served with.

Gone in an instant, amidst a hellish clangor of small-arms fire and explosions. He hadn't even realized that Obed had been killed until later on, arriving back at their base. Seeing the sergeant's body carried out of a bullet-pocked Humvee.

No time to mourn, not for them or any of the others they'd lost on that deployment, the bloodiest of his three. No time to do anything except keep moving, keep fighting. Try to stay alive yourself.

And yet—he shook his head, a shadow passing across his dark face. In some perverse way. . .*he missed it.*

He'd never intended to make a career of the military, walking into that recruiter's office back in Atlanta at the age of 18 in the summer of '95. Serve out a hitch, and move on—he had other things to do with his life.

Then 9/11 had happened, and he'd been called back up. . .and after that, there was no going back.

So now here he was, a wife and two kids later, a bird colonel—serving his country as defense attache at the US Embassy. Chained to a desk, liaising with his German counterparts in the *Bundeswehr*.

Somehow wishing he was back in combat. Like that made any sense, he smiled ruefully at his reflection in the mirror—hearing his wife stir in the bedroom behind him.

At least the shift had been good for his marriage, if nothing else. If he had been deployed once more. . .

He felt her hand on his shoulder and reached up to clasp it in his, meeting her eyes in the mirror.

"They were back last night, weren't they?" she asked, her dark eyes seeming to search his face.

"Yeah, they were," he responded finally, leaning heavily against the counter. *The nightmares.* It had been a few months, longer than ever before. Long enough to make him think they might be gone for good. "I'm good now, though."

"Thomas, are you sure—"

"I don't want to talk about it," he snapped, pulling away from her hand and regretting it almost as soon as he'd done so. "I'm sorry, I just. . .it had been so long, I. . ."

"You don't have to." She shook her head, her face unreadable. Moving past it. *Changing the subject.* Like they had so many times before. "A busy day?"

"Not really, not until this afternoon, the fireworks celebration at Tempelhofer Feld. You'll bring the kids for that, won't you?"

"Of course."

"Good," he replied, relieved to have managed to avoid the conversation, at least for the moment. Retrieving his uniform jacket from the closet as he moved back into the bedroom—draping it over one arm. "I'll be over mid-afternoon. I'm meeting General Müller at the Hotel Adlon for lunch. . ."

7:42 A.M.
An apartment
Paris, France

Ibrahim Abu Musab al-Almani. Anaïs Brunet frowned, reaching behind her to zip up the back of her dark blue dress, standing alone before the mirror in the bedroom of her Paris apartment. She rarely saw her chateau in Aquitaine these days, or so it seemed. It had been a couple months since she'd been able to spend the weekend there.

A week had passed since the first contact from LYSANDER, the dead-drop conveying his message. A week in which open-source intelligence had enabled them to identify most of the members of the "cell", if that's truly what it was.

Everyone except for al-Almani—"the German"—to translate his *kunya* from the Arabic. The man was a ghost, and a dangerous one, if he had been to Syria. *And returned.*

She picked up her necklace, a single strand of pearls she had inherited from her grandmother, looking into the mirror as she adjusted them around her neck.

Her eyes were bloodshot, foundation serving to obscure the dark circles which had formed around them. The product of long nights at the office, poring over intelligence reports. Trying to hold things together, to make *sense* of it all.

Brunet retrieved her laptop case from beside the bed and left the room, hearing the television on in the kitchen—still on from when she had eaten breakfast, an hour before. The female newshost's voice becoming more distinct as she entered, retrieving the remote from the table.

". . .ahead of more protests planned at American embassies around the globe today as the United States prepares to celebrate the anniversary of its independence. Here with us to discuss the ramifications of these protests—"

She turned the television off and set the remote to one side, standing in the doorway of the kitchen for a long moment, just staring at the blackened screen.

It promised to be another very long day.

2:01 A.M. Mountain Time
Tulsa International Airport
Tulsa, Oklahoma

The heartland. Dark eyes the color of obsidian betrayed no expression as the middle-aged man gazed out the window of the Boeing 737 toward the terminal building, its lights blazing brightly in the darkness of the night.

Flyover country. The kind of place people back in Washington liked to pretend no longer existed, or perhaps never had.

It reminded him of home, growing up on the plains of Kansas. Flat, as far as the eye could see. Simple people, simple faith.

The kind of place he'd turned his back upon, decades before. He'd joined the military right out of high school, a career that had taken him around the world and into the ranks of the Army's most elite unit, the 1st Special Forces Operational Detachment-Delta.

Somalia. Kosovo. Iraq.

Bloody waypoints along the path which had let him here this night. Now, as then, looking out for his men. *Protecting them.*

"Sir, do you need help?" he heard a woman's voice ask, looking up to see a flight attendant standing over him.

It took him a moment to process what she meant, and then he pulled himself aright, propping himself against the back of the seat in front of him, his empty right pant leg flopping limp and useless beneath him even as he did so.

The rest of his right leg—everything below the knee—left somewhere back in a place in Iraq called "Tikrit." An IED blast, well over a decade previous.

He smiled at the young woman, a smile that never touched his dark eyes—his voice edged with steel as he shook his head, replying softly, "I've got this."

Balancing himself against the back of the seat as she disappeared down the aisle, he turned back, reaching up to unlatch the overheard compartment to pull down his carry-on. Unzipping the bag to reveal a prosthetic leg.

More than a decade, and somehow this never got any easier, he thought grimly, raising his stump in one hand to fit it into the socket of the prosthesis—pushing it home until he heard the pins click into place.

But all those years at war—at Delta—there'd never been anything "easy" about any of it. And for him, it was a war that had never ended.

Which was why he was here this night.

He extended his prosthetic leg, feeling the floor solid once more beneath him as he stood erect, hoisting his carry-on over his shoulder as he made his way down the aisle, pushing his way past other passengers as he went.

Time to do this.

7:48 A.M. Central European Summer Time
Neukölln, Berlin
Germany

"All right, you understand what you're supposed to do, don't you?"

Anas nodded silently, his mind running back over it once more. The plan was very simple, as straightforward as one's death could ever be. Take public transit to the parking garage and retrieve the sedan. Then drive it to the Unter den Linden, the tree-shaded boulevard leading to the Brandenburg Gate. Less than five miles.

The boulevard was closed to automobile traffic, but that shouldn't matter, not in the time it would take to reach the café.

As for the rest. . .well, it would all be over in an instant. As God willed it.

"I do," he said finally, meeting Yusuf's eyes in that moment. Feeling nothing but coldness within, the gnawing darkness which had haunted him ever since the death of his parents, now reaching out to embrace him. "I do."

"*Mash'allah,*" his friend breathed, his eyes shining with fervor, a nervous excitement pervading his body. "Would that I could join you in this hour of sacrifice."

Yusuf reached out to embrace him then, his beard rough against Anas' cheek as he held him close. "May the angels welcome you to paradise, little brother."

11:45 A.M.
Masjid Al-Rahma
Sint-Jans-Molenbeek, Belgium

The Fourth of July. It had been years since he'd celebrated it in the land of his birth, Harry thought, the noonday sun beating down upon him. *The land of the free.*

He could remember having spent the Fourth in Iraq—more than once. Afghanistan, the same. Celebrations at war, in an alien land. Incoming mortar rounds, their only fireworks—RPK tracers streaming through the night.

Immersing himself in the culture, the people. Until everything once alien became familiar. . .and everything once familiar, somehow alien. Until going back home seemed more foreign than what he had known overseas.

The hem of his long white linen *thawb* fluttered about his ankles as he paused at the door of the mosque, a nondescript former factory building which had become a center of the Islamic community in Molenbeek.

There was no going home, not for him. Nothing there for him, anyway. *No one.*

"Are you coming, Ibrahim?" he heard Yassin's voice ask from the doorway, shattering his reverie even as a woman in a brightly-colored hijab pushed past him, a little boy in her arms.

"Of course," Harry replied quickly, entering behind her—his eyes adjusting to the dimly lit atrium as he stooped to remove his shoes, placing them reverently in the rack provided for the purpose.

"Are you all right, man?" Reza asked as he turned back to join them, genuine concern in the young Moroccan's eyes.

"I'm fine," he lied, meeting his gaze, "just thinking."

Thoughts of home. Just because he couldn't go back, didn't mean there weren't times he didn't hunger for it. Like the hunger for a woman you could never have.

"Come, my brothers," he said, forcing a smile to his face as he put a hand on each of their shoulders. "It is time for us to pray."

12:02 P.M.
Hotel Adlon
Berlin, Germany

"Gerhardt," Thomas Dwyer greeted warmly, rising from his seat as his counterpart came up to the table. "Thanks for joining me today. I haven't yet had opportunity to congratulate you on your promotion."

"You are too kind, Thomas," General Gerhardt Müller smiled, doffing the grey *Bergmütze* denoting his prior service with the alpine *Gebirgsjäger* as he took the offered seat. "I fear my brother Andreas is not so pleased. He's grown far too accustomed to outranking me, you see."

Dwyer laughed. Müller had been a colonel like himself when he'd first arrived in Berlin two years earlier, serving on the command staff of the USAEUR—the United States Army Europe.

His primary liaison point with the Germans, Müller had done much to show him the ropes of the *Bundeswehr* command structure in his first months as defense attache.

Now he'd been promoted from *Oberst* to *Brigade-General*, serving at the *Kommando Heer*, the Germany Army Command in Strausberg.

"So tell me, Thomas," Müller began, leaning back in his seat. "What's the purpose of our meeting here today? You ask me here, on the day of your national holiday. . .why?"

12:09 P.M.
Mitte District
Berlin

I seek refuge in Allah from Satan the accursed, Anas thought, murmuring the words of the *dua* beneath his breath as the sedan crept forward in the heavy traffic choking the city center—his eyes flickering to the bridge just ahead, a seventy-three meter span crossing the Spree.

The car had been just where the man had told them they'd find it, the trunk welded shut. *Just as he'd said.*

"*Insh'allah,*" he whispered, his palms slick with sweat, his knuckles white around the steering wheel. Not as that *man* had said—that unbeliever—but as *God* Himself had willed.

He swore angrily, willing the traffic ahead to move faster, feeling as though the walls of the car itself were closing in around him. Trapping him within, *crushing* him.

He had to remain calm, had to get hold of himself. If the *Polizei* saw any reason to stop him. . .

Just a few more miles.

He'd only just been learning to drive when the civil war broke out in Syria, driving the car of his father—a dentist—around the streets of their town.

But he could do this. He was but a tool, in the hand of God. He could do this.

12:09 P.M.
Masjid Al-Rahma
Sint-Jans-Molenbeek, Belgium

"O our Lord," Harry breathed, raising his hands as he straightened, repeating the words of the *salat* in unison with his fellow worshipers. "All praise is for you. *Allahu akbar!*"

God is greatest. A hundred voices in Arabic swelling in the sound of the *takbir*, resounding through the prayer hall. A rough, yet somehow melodious sound.

He couldn't remember the first time he had attended prayers at a mosque, but it had been before 9/11. Before he'd joined the CIA.

Just a student of the Middle East, back then. Seeking a deeper understanding of his subject. There was something of peace in the ritual, he had found, a calm that remained even in this moment—despite all that the intervening years had brought.

Despite his present reality, he thought, catching a glimpse of Yassin at his side out of the corner of his eye as he sank to his knees, prostrating himself toward Mecca.

The darkness which lurked in the midst of these who had gathered here for prayer.

"Glory to my Lord, the Most High," he whispered, his forehead touching the prayer rug, the Arabic rolling freely from his tongue, "the Most Praiseworthy. *Allahu akbar!*"

12:15 P.M.
Hotel Adlon
Berlin, Germany

"...our intelligence reports concur with those of your agencies," Müller nodded, seeming to mull over Dwyer's words. "The Russians moved yet another motorized rifle brigade into Kaliningrad a month ago, the 5th Guards *Tamanskaya*."

Crack troops, the American officer thought—a reconstituted unit which had taken on the name of a legendary Soviet-era division awarded the Order of the Red Banner during the Second World War. The Russians were building up their presence in the Kaliningrad salient, that narrow spit of former German land between Poland and Lithuania. That much couldn't be disputed. But *why*?

The question that all their intelligence reports couldn't answer to anyone's satisfaction.

"Why?" he asked, choosing to give voice to his uncertainty. His eyes never leaving his counterpart's face. "What is their purpose in doing so?"

Müller smiled, shaking his head.

"Thomas, Thomas...you can hardly think me so rash as to attempt to discern the secret will of the Kremlin. However, I will say this. Königsberg," he continued, pointedly using the old German name for Kaliningrad like the Prussian he was, "was, in the days of the USSR, the most heavily fortified piece of land in all of Europe, even surpassing our own preparations at the Fulda Gap. It cannot have escaped either of us how reminiscent this build-up is of those dark days, even if the purpose is now more opaque. If the Federation should choose to move against one of their former client states, the, how would you put it...'escalatory advantage' will be all on one side. *Theirs*."

Everyone's worst fear. And a legitimate one, as strange as that would have seemed a mere five years before. Dwyer hesitated a moment before replying, picking at the food on his plate. "And if something of that nature should happen—what will be the stance of the *Bundeswehr*?"

The smile was long gone.

"Officially," the general began, his voice tight, "Germany stands ready to support its NATO allies, as it has always. And I would like to observe that, despite the murmuring insinuations of your political leadership regarding the one-sidedness of the alliance, in actual historical practice, it has been us coming to *your* aid—not the other way around."

"I understand that, Gerhardt, I simply—"

"Unofficially," Müller continued, going on as if he hadn't spoken, "any chancellor who committed the force of the *Bundeswehr* to armed conflict against the Russian Federation would be forced from the office."

12:17 P.M.

Almost there. Anas caught a glimpse of the Brandenburg Gate ahead through the cover of the trees overshadowing the boulevard as he accelerated around a slower car, the monument seeming strangely small amidst the more modern buildings surrounding it. As well it should.

A godless monument to victory past.

Now to bear mute witness to a defeat. A blow against the governments which had enabled the slaughter of his people.

It seemed strange, knowing he was about to die, and yet. . .was that not itself a gift from Allah? The ability to choose the time, the place of his death. To *know.*

The bus in front of him turned, and he turned with it—catching sight of the restaurant even as he did so. *It was time.*

His hands clenched tight around the steering wheel as he accelerated, his eyes shining with tears as he repeated the *takbir* beneath his breath.

God is greatest.

12:18 P.M.
Hotel Adlon

Müller leaned back in his seat, his eyes growing cold, distant as he regarded his American colleague. "We are both veterans of your 'war on terror', you and I. . .let us be honest with the realities. When your nation invoked Article V following 9/11, Germany did not hesitate to step to your side, but our country never truly accepted the idea that we were at *war.* Coming home from Afghanistan, I found that our people far preferred to think that I had spent my time digging wells—teaching schoolchildren to read—not killing terrorists, hunting guerrillas through the mountains. That was something they were simply not prepared to accept—and the distance enabled them not to have to. Choosing to engage in a conflict on our very borders, against one of our most powerful neighbors? That's not our reality. Germany will not sacrifice her young men and women to defend the sovereignty of the Slavs. It's not going to happen, Thomas."

The cold, brutal reality no one wanted to face. Whether in Berlin or Washington. That the alliance which had protected Europe's eastern front for sixty-odd years now effectively remained only on paper.

"But Lithuania and Estonia are NATO allies," Dwyer said, offering what he could in way of protest. "A failure to defend them would shatter the alliance, permanently. We cannot allow—"

It took the American officer a moment to realize Müller was no longer listening to him, the general's eyes fixed on a space behind his head—out the window onto the boulevard, even as his brain registered the sounds of people screaming, the squeal of automobile tires against the pavement.

A dark, nameless fear seizing hold of him. *Memories of Iraq, flooding back.*

Colonel Thomas Dwyer made it to his feet, even as the building shuddered from the impact of the vehicle slamming into the wall twenty feet to their rear.

His mouth opened to shout a warning, but it was too late—far too late—his voice drowned out as the world erupted around him, the café suddenly drowned in flame and flying rubble.

And everything went black.

Chapter 6

12:27 P.M.
DGSE Headquarters
Paris, France

". . .make sure you collate those reports and get them to my desk as soon as possible," Anaïs Brunet ordered, handing the folder back to one of her threat analysts. "I want to be kept apprised of anything the DGSI should develop from Marseilles."

Another day, and as ever, more potential threats than one could keep track of, she thought, suddenly distracted by a low murmur running through the room—her eyes coming up just in time to see first one, then another and another of the television screens on the opposite wall cut away from their coverage of the protests outside the American Embassy to reveal footage from a helicopter circling over a city—a black, deathly pall of fire and smoke rising from the devastated facade of an ornate building.

". . .now breaking from Berlin, where a massive explosion has taken place at the Hotel Adlon. *Das Erste* news cameras are live from the scene as we endeavor to learn. . ."

My God, she breathed—seemingly frozen in place for a few seconds. It was happening. *Now.*

Her shock lasted only a few seconds and then she reached out, grabbing the arm of her deputy director, Nicolas Murat, as he walked by.

"I want you to reach out to Heinrich Köhler," she ordered crisply, referencing the director of the BND, the *Bundesnachrichtendienst,* Germany's principal intelligence service. Forcing herself to focus, to distance herself from the tragedy of what was unfolding. "Offer him our condolences and any support he may require. And have our people scour the 'Net, look for chatter—anything we might have that might indicate a similar attack in progress here. *Do it now.*"

12:36 P.M.
Masjid Al-Rahma
Sint-Jans-Molenbeek, Belgium

". . .have to go to class right now, but I'll catch you later, man," Reza said, clasping Harry's hand as they left the prayer hall together, joining in the crowd of worshippers flowing from the mosque as the *zhuhr* ended.

"*Insh'allah*, brother," he responded, forcing a smile as his young friend turned away, a young woman in a hijab approaching from behind them. *Nora*, Harry thought, recognizing her despite the covering. Reza's girl. He shook his head. This was all going to be over, soon enough. Just had to get through the next week. Just had to—

"Look at this," he heard Yassin exclaim suddenly, his voice trembling with excitement as he extended his phone toward Harry. "There was a blast at a hotel—in Berlin."

It was a terrorist attack, Harry realized, struggling to control his face as he scanned the news alert, Yassin's cry of exultation ringing hollowly in his ears—Reza pressing forward beside him. Assessing the damage with an all-too-practiced eye, the flames billowing from the destroyed façade of the hotel, smoke obscuring the scene. It had to have been a VBIED, and a sizable one. There was no other way to account for it.

He'd spent his life trying to *stop* such attacks, trying to hunt down those responsible. Tracking them through the dark shadows of the world, losing so much of himself in the process. His country, his faith. . .his very *soul*.

For what is a man profited. . .

"*Alhamdulillah*," he whispered fiercely, clapping Reza on the shoulder as he handed the phone back to Yassin. *May God be praised.*

"*Allahu akbar*," the young man replied, his eyes burning with a zealous fervor. "As they have bombed, so they will *be* bombed—so God will revisit their sins upon their heads, bring violence to *their* streets."

"Keep your voice down," Harry spat urgently, glancing past Yassin's shoulder to see a middle-aged Muslim man standing there glaring at them as if he had heard, seeming on the point of speaking—anger distorting his features.

He met the man's eyes, staring unflinchingly into them until the man quailed, spitting out a single word as he turned away.

"Kwarijite."

The apostates of prophesy. Those who had risen in rebellion in the days of the Prophet, declaring *takfir* on their fellow Muslims and setting themselves up as the arbiters of God's will. The spiritual ancestors of al-Qaeda, of the Islamic State, accursed themselves of their Prophet.

"No," Harry said, placing his hand on Yassin's arm as he moved to go after the man, "let him go."

"But he is a blasphemer, and he must—"

"Be dealt with," he replied gently, his voice low, "and he will be, but in Allah's time. Not before. He—"

"Yassin!" he heard another voice exclaim, turning to find Marwan and one of the other young men from the boxing club standing there in the hall, only a few feet away.

"It's been too long, man," the young Arab said, clasping Yassin's hand as he came up to them. His eyes met Harry's briefly, acknowledging him with a murmured *"Salaam alaikum"* before turning back to his friend. "Haven't seen you at the club these last few days. Have you heard? Have you seen the news?"

"Just now," came the excited response from Reza's lips. "It's a beautiful thing, isn't it?"

"They say there are over a hundred dead," Marwan went on, his face radiant as Harry searched his eyes for any sign of duplicity—any hint that he might be an informer—and found nothing.

Even worse. It meant he was either very well-trained, beyond his years—or a true believer.

It was hard to say which of those he feared more.

"Mash'allah," Yassin breathed in reply, sharing in his friend's enthusiasm. *How beautiful.*

The slaughter of the innocent.

Harry caught his eye then, shooting him a meaningful look. *Remember.*

"You two stopping by the club later on?" Marwan asked, placing his hand on Reza's shoulder as he turned to leave.

Yassin hesitated a moment too long, looking over as Harry gave him an imperceptible nod. "Yeah. . .yeah, we should be able to. *Insh'allah.*"

"*Insh'allah,*" the young Arab repeated, smiling. "*Salaam alaikum.*"

They were three blocks from the mosque before Yassin spoke, turning toward Harry as they paused before a crosswalk, traffic flashing past them on the street. As if nothing had happened, as if it were just. . .a normal day.

"I thought you said—" he began, stopping short as Harry held up a hand to cut him off.

"I know what I *said*. And if we could have avoided crossing paths with him again until you were safely on your way to the Philippines," Harry continued, turning to his young friend, "it would have been far better. But Allah has not so willed, and it would be best not to rouse his suspicions."

Another car went by, and then the symbol above the crosswalk changed. *Walk.*

Time for them to part ways.

Yassin to the house of a friend, him to. . .well, elsewhere. He reached out, placing a hand on the young man's arm as he turned to leave.

"Go," he said, his fingers digging into yielding flesh—hard enough to leave marks. His eyes flashing a warning. "But be *careful.*"

7:04 A.M. Eastern Daylight Time
CIA Headquarters
Washington, D.C.

Looking at the footage streaming out of Berlin—the images of dazed and bloodied survivors staggering away from the devastated Hotel Adlon. . .it brought everything back. All the memories of watching television of the attack in Vegas that dark night.

Not knowing then that his own daughter was among the dead.

"Please accept my most heartfelt condolences, Heinrich," David Lay said, clearing his throat as he stared at the photo sitting on his desk. A beautiful young woman, with azure-blue eyes the color of the sea. *Just like her mother's.*

"On behalf of myself and my country, please know that our thoughts and prayers are with you in the wake of this attack. My agency and I stand ready to do. . .whatever we can to assist you."

"Thank you," came Köhler's reply finally, following a pause so long that the CIA director almost thought he'd been disconnected from his German counterpart. "You have known such tragic loss of your own, David—I know your sympathy to be genuine. And I accept your offer of help. We are following up what leads we have, though details remain few."

"I will be on the phone with my Chief of Station in Berlin within the hour," Lay promised, his eyes never leaving his daughter's face. "He'll be instructed to give you whatever cooperation you require."

Within reason, he thought, a caveat both men were professional enough to know went without saying. No intelligence agency was ever going to be completely open with another, not even an ally. *Especially* not an ally.

"It will be most welcome, David. We're working to establish the provenance of the vehicle now, see if we can tie it to any known actors. We—"

Lay's computer *dinged* with an incoming alert in that moment, distracting him as he looked over to see a message pop up on the screen. *Ron Carter.* One of the Clandestine Service's top analysts, a man he'd known for many years.

The message was terse, which was like Ron. And as chilling as it was terse. *One of ours is believed to be among the dead.*

Heinrich Köhler's voice still in his ear, Lay clicked on the attachment, a personnel file opening in his browser. The face of a middle-aged African-American colonel in full dress uniform gazing back at him, his eyes flickering down to read the text.

The defense attaché. And what was more. . .

"Excuse me, Heinrich," he said, staring into the dead man's eyes. "I'm going to have to call you back. Something's come up."

2:33 P.M. Central European Summer Time
A café
Sint-Jans-Molenbeek, Belgium

It was like reliving the worst moments of his life, all over again. Every misstep. Every *failure*.

Playing on repeat through his brain. Like a series of bodies hitting the ground, again and again. *Davood. Aydin. Ismail Bessimi.* Carol *herself.*

Only the latest, the most personal, in a list that was far too long.

Harry sat there in the café, his eyes glued to the television mounted on the far wall—his tea now growing cold, forgotten on the table before him.

The confirmed death toll was thirty now, with the potential to rise, even yet. Video uploaded by a young Japanese college student who had been filming the boulevard on her smartphone at the moment of impact had hit the Internet and was going viral—showing a brown sedan coming into frame from the left, ostensibly just making the turn, but coming too fast for that.

And just seconds later, the shockwave of an explosion hammering the boulevard—debris raining down upon the young woman as she struggled to get away. Her screams filling the microphone.

Terror.

Like that which his young "friends" wanted to sow. They were too young to truly understand the world, the consequences of their actions.

His face hardened. *Not too young to* pay *them.*

8:32 A.M. Mountain Daylight Time
A ranch house
Chandler, Oklahoma

". . .attack upon the Adlon Hotel, which stands only two blocks from the United States Embassy in Berlin. Counterterrorism experts speculate that the attack may have been an attempt on the embassy itself, which was deterred by security measures in place. There has currently been no claim of responsibility from the Islamic State, however, and. . ."

Talking to fill up space, Roy Coftey thought, staring out the kitchen window of the ranch house to the east, the last of his coffee in his hand. That's all cable news hosts ever did–worthless, the lot of them.

There wouldn't be anything worth hearing for days, not in open sources at least. God only knew what the folks in the intelligence community were coming up with—and could, so long as the lights weren't switched out on them.

He heard movement behind him and turned to see Melody enter the kitchen, her long blonde hair still wet from the shower—a towel wrapped around her body.

"There's been a terrorist attack," he announced brusquely, "in Berlin."

"I saw," she replied, a grimace crossing her face. "It's all over Twitter. Some of the images. . .you have e-mail one of us needs to answer—CNN and Fox News reaching out for comment."

Speak of the devil. Coftey shook his head, placing his empty cup in the sink as he gathered up his wallet and keys. "Think something up and send it before you come out to the parade route—you know me well enough to know what I'd say."

There wasn't time to deal with it himself, not with all that remained in the offing for this day.

"You're leaving already?" she asked, pulling a carton of orange juice from the refrigerator. "The parade's still hours away."

He smiled, the first genuine one he'd allowed himself since the text message had landed on his burner phone the previous afternoon. "You don't know towns like this. They always find a way to fill up the time. And I'd be well advised to be in the thick of it, pressing flesh."

"I'll get something written up," she replied, not looking up from her phone. "Should I send it your way for approval?"

"Don't bother. I won't have time to read it. And Melody," he hesitated choosing his words carefully. "If anyone stops by the house before you leave, *call* me. Right away."

3:41 P.M. Central European Summer Time
The apartment
Sint-Jans-Molenbeek, Belgium

Forty-three dead. Another eighty injured. Harry paused for a moment on the stairs leading to their second-floor flat, his fingers digging into the rail until his knuckles whitened.

He'd left the café when he could take it no more, the death toll climbing steadily with each passing hour since the attack.

Remembering the reaction of his young "friends", of the *joy* filling their faces at the news. He could have killed them both in that moment.

And perhaps that would still be his best way out of all this, he thought, a darkness overshadowing him—steal a car and drive out, the three of them, into the countryside. Three out, one back.

He'd killed better men in his life. Men who'd seen him coming, been ready for him. And he'd killed them all the same.

It wouldn't be difficult.

But somehow, for some reason he struggled to define, he found that he didn't want their blood on his hands.

He knew who they were, *what* they were, and yet. . .they had taken him in, given him shelter when there'd been nowhere left for him to run.

Nowhere else to hide.

It was hard not to feel something of kinship after all of that. *Was it a form of Stockholm?* It was hard to know, and perhaps it didn't matter—not in the end.

Not so long as he could get them on that plane.

Harry inserted his key into the lock, attempting to push all such thoughts from his head as he pushed the door open, entering the small flat. Reza was at his classes, and Yassin was out, helping an elderly Muslim widow two floors down with her shopping—both of them, gone for hours. It should give him enough time alone to begin pulling things together for the Emiratis.

A mixture of genuine history and fabrication, like any good lie. Enough to ensure they were stopped—watchlisted. Put away for long enough for him to get clear.

And then he heard it, a strange, indistinguishable sound coming from somewhere deeper in the apartment—every fiber of his body tensing as he froze, rooted in place.

His ears straining for the slightest sound, any repetition of what he had heard. His eyes flickering across the apartment in the dim light, struggling to place it.

Another moment, and then it came again, this time from the bedroom—still unrecognizable, something between a grunt and a moan—but human all the same. *He wasn't alone.*

He crossed the kitchen with quick, noiseless steps, wrenching a steak knife from the cutting block and flipping it over, reversed in his hand as he moved, cat-like, toward the bedroom door.

The sounds growing ever clearer and more distinct as he approached. Bringing the knife back, out of sight along the flowing white sleeve of his *thawb* as he pushed the door open.

"*Reza!*"

2:45 P.M. British Summer Time
Thames House
Millbank, London

". . .I understand, I'll get right on that," Simon Norris said impatiently, responding to the person on the other end of the phone. "Of course. As soon I have anything, you'll be the first to receive it."

He signed off with a heavy sigh, replacing the phone in its cradle on his office desk. *Finally.*

His day hadn't gone anything remotely according to plan, the MI-5 analyst thought, running his fingers through his hair. The bombing in Berlin, throwing everything off.

None of which changed what he had to do.

He'd drunk himself to sleep, waking up this morning with a pounding headache, the worst hangover he could remember in his life—even surpassing those he'd known in college. The events of the previous night—the *Russian*— seeming distant, somehow. Little more than a bad dream.

And yet, as the effects of the alcohol had worn off, everything had come flooding back. All the horror of what was now his life.

"*Arthur Colville really wasn't*—shouldn't—*have been that important,*" the Russian had said there in the restaurant, something of regret in his voice. As if the miscalculation had been his own. "*Just one of scores of such agents of influence*—polezniye duraki—*across Europe.*"

Useful idiots. A Russian term that dated back at least to the first half of the 20th Century, serving as reminder that Russia's intelligence services had been relying upon unwitting dupes as far back as Stalin.

Was that what he was, now? Perhaps.

"*Given the West's endearing fetishization of free speech,*" Alexei had gone on, "*it was assumed that, as a newspaper publisher, Colville was relatively safe from scrutiny. As a result—*"

He'd interrupted, unable to take it any longer. *"What does any of this have to do with me?"*

"As a result," the Russian had continued imperturbably, *"his handlers were not as cautious as they should have been. They left us exposed. And that, Mr. Norris—is where you come in. You're going to help me mend their errors."*

"And if I refuse?" It had seemed silly—cliched—to have asked. And yet he'd done so anyway, unable to stop himself.

The Russian had just looked at him, favoring him with the kind of indulgent smile one might give a wayward child. *"I think we both know the answer to that, Simon. And it's not a road either of us would wish to travel down."*

3:49 P.M. Central European Summer Time
The apartment
Sint-Jans-Molenbeek, Belgium

It was as though a bomb had been set off in the bed at the sound of his voice, white limbs flashing in the semi-darkness as Reza rolled off the body of the young woman lying beneath him.

Her scream filling the small confines of the bedroom, mingled with the sound of cursing in French as Reza grabbed for his pants—stumbling into the wall and nearly going down as he struggled to pull them on.

"What's going on here?" Harry demanded, forcing righteous anger into his voice as he descended on the couple, the answer to his question only too obvious—Reza still naked from the waist down despite his best efforts, the girl struggling to cover herself.

"Ibrahim, I'm sorry—I-I thought you'd be gone the rest of the afternoon, I thought—"

"You thought it was a good opportunity to come back here and bed your slut," Harry stormed angrily, finishing his sentence for him. He heard the girl start to speak up in their defense and turned on her, a long forefinger jabbing out in her direction. *"Enough.* Get dressed and get *out."*

"Ibrahim, this isn't necessary," Reza protested weakly, looking more than faintly ridiculous standing there against the wall, finally having managed to pull up his boxers. "This—"

"You're in no position to decide," came Harry's furious retort, his eyes flashing fire as he transfixed the college student with a hard stare. "What were you *thinking*? You know what the Prophet said should be done with fornicators, you know—"

"I know, I know," Reza said, putting up a hand as if he expected Harry to strike him—tears shining in the boy's eyes. "But Nora. . .I love her, and—and this was the last time I'd be able to be with her before I leave, and I didn't want to die a virgin. I just had to—"

Harry began to respond and then he froze, a cold chill running through his body.

"Did you tell *her* that?" he demanded, the question coming out as a low hiss. *"Did you?"*

"I told her I was leaving, yes," Reza choked out, clearly taken off-guard by the shift in questioning. "But I didn't tell her where, I swear before God, I—"

"Stay here," Harry ordered, a murderous look in his eyes as he turned away from the young man, moving purposefully to the door—Reza's voice calling out after him as he went.

"Ibrahim!"

2:52 P.M. British Summer Time
Thames House
Millbank, London

The Royal Bank of Scotland, Simon Norris thought, staring at the browser window open on his computer screen. It made sense that Arthur Colville would have kept his accounts there—the Colville family name dating back to Scotland in the 13th Century.

Accounts filled with Russian rubles. Or dollars—whatever their equivalent had been after filtering through the Russians' proxy organizations in the United States.

Norris shook his head.

Had Colville ever known—ever suspected—that he was being used?

No, he decided, after a moment's further thought. The publisher would never have been capable of that kind of self-questioning. That *doubt*. His unswerving moral certitude—his belief in the righteousness of their cause—the very thing which had drawn Norris to him in the beginning.

Started him down the road to treason. To betraying everything he'd once sworn to defend. And, if he could believe anything the Russian had said. . .to nearly causing the death of his Queen.

"England confides that every man will do his duty."

Nelson's signal to his ships at the outset of Trafalgar. Colville's words to him that night on London Bridge, on the eve of something far more terrible.

But all that, was now in the past. Decisions, which could never be unmade.

All that remained now was to *survive*. He swallowed hard, looking at the screen.

Making the Russian money trail vanish wasn't going to be easy, not without getting caught. He'd successfully pinned the leak of the PERSEPHONE files—the leak which had brought down the government—on his former branch head, but arranging that had taken months.

He no longer had months. Not even weeks. And there was no longer any turning back. . .

3:55 P.M. Central European Summer Time
The apartment
Sint-Jans-Molenbeek, Belgium

Nora was still standing in the kitchen of the small apartment when Harry emerged from the bedroom, buttoning up her blouse with trembling fingers as he approached. Tears streaking her face, her hijab—the symbol of her modesty—wildly askew, as if in mockery of the pretense. Loose strands of blonde hair hanging in her eyes.

She trembled as Harry put a hand on her shoulder, her small frame wracked with silent sobs.

"*Salaam*, little sister," he whispered, gently helping her adjust the hijab until it covered her head, worn as a true *Muslima* should wear it. "Dry your tears."

"I-I'm sorry," she managed, her voice on the verge of cracking. Unable to look him in the face.

"It is not to me that you should repent," he said tenderly, turning her to face him, "but to Allah, whose laws you have violated. You have not been a Muslim long, have you?"

"N-no," the young Frenchwoman managed, wiping at her eyes as she tried to pull herself together. She was a pretty girl, that much he had to admit. It wasn't hard to see why Reza had fallen for her. "Just last year—after I met Reza at university."

"May God be praised," Harry smiled disarmingly, "for it is never too late to turn to the truth. But that is no excuse for doing what you knew clearly to be sin."

"I know," she said, biting at her lip—fresh tears welling in her eyes. "I knew it was wrong, but Reza said that I might never see him again and he insisted—"

His hand came up without warning, back-handing her across the cheek, the slap ringing out like a pistol shot in the confines of the small apartment. Nora cried out in fear and sudden pain—stumbling away as he closed in on her, pressing her back against the counter.

"Do *not*," he hissed, his face only inches away from hers— summoning up all the anger he had felt earlier, at the mosque, "tempt God by blaming another for your own sins. You slid back into your old ways and nearly dragged a brother down with you. *That* is the sin of which you are guilty."

She shrank away from him as if she would have tried to escape, tears streaming down her cheeks, weeping uncontrollably. *Terrified.*

Good, Harry thought—his face dark as he pinned her to the counter. *Fly, little bird. It may just save your life. There's no place for you here.*

"Reza said you might never see him again," he said, suddenly releasing her and taking a few steps away, his voice shifting back to a normal conversational tone as though nothing in the world were wrong, "what else did he tell you?"

She just stared at him, her cheek still bearing the bright red imprint of his hand, taken completely off-guard by the transformation. "N-nothing, I swear it before God. I *swear.*"

Whatever that was worth. His eyes searched her face. "You're sure."

"I *am*," she protested, almost seeming angry at his doubting her. "He's talked for months of wanting to take part in God's struggle, li-like any good Muslim should, but nothing more than that—he never told me any details. I promise you."

She was telling the truth.

"*Mash'allah*," he smiled, pushing away the sense of disquiet rising within him at her words. There would be time to deal with that later, if it came to that. He wrapped an arm around her trembling shoulders, leading her to the door of the apartment and showing her out. "*Wa' alaikum as-salaam*, sister."

Blessings and peace be upon you. . .

11:05 A.M. Eastern Daylight Time
CIA Headquarters
Langley, Virginia

"We were using a defense attache as a backchannel intelligence conduit to the German military?" David Lay asked, looking over the top of his glasses at the analyst seated in front of his desk. "Why?"

Ron Carter shifted uneasily in his chair, seeming to hesitate for a long moment before replying. "We have grown. . .concerned, over the course of the last couple years. That the BND may itself be compromised by Russian intelligence. Following the re-unification of East and West Germany and the subsequent fall of the Soviet Union, the Russian services retained a lot of assets in the former Democratic Republic. Former Stasi and otherwise, a whole network of contacts across the now-unified country. The German government has always struggled to filter them out from their security establishment, and we've come to believe that their influence in the BND has grown rather than diminished over the years. Agents recruiting agents and the like. I believe mention of this has been made in reports which ended up on your desk."

It had, the CIA director thought—and he'd taken special note of it. Berlin Station had been his beat, back in the day, running agents into East Germany. He knew the ground well.

"That still doesn't explain why we had to reach out to DIA resources to run it for us," he pressed, his eyes never leaving Carter's face. The analyst had spent time in Air Force intelligence prior to joining the Agency, working first for the Intelligence Directorate before being shanghaied over to the 'Dark Side.' *The Clandestine Service.*

"I don't know all the details," Carter replied, still seeming ill at ease with the discussion. "You'd have to speak to Director Kranemeyer to get the full picture. What I know is that we wanted a direct conduit to the *Bundeswehr*, and following his promotion, General Müller was in a position to provide us with an accurate portrait of the mindset of the Command Council regarding Russian activities in their near-abroad."

"And now he's dead," Lay observed flatly, feeling as if a dark shadow had passed over them. *Was it coincidence?* "Along with our officer."

It was hazardous to believe in coincidence in this business—equally so to connect dots where none existed.

"Speaking of Kranemeyer," he went on after a moment, "where is the director? I haven't seen him today."

Carter didn't look up, studiously shuffling his notes in the folder on his lap. "Kranemeyer? He took the holiday."

5:11 P.M. Central European Summer Time
The apartment
Sint-Jans-Molenbeek, Belgium

Maintaining a cover, it was the hardest thing he had ever done in all his years with the CIA. Staying alive, accomplishing your mission. Trying not to lose yourself in the process. That line between who you were supposed to be, and who you *were*—so easily blurred.

So hard to reclaim.

"Put her out of your mind, brother. She's only a distraction to you now," Harry said, squeezing Reza's shoulder as he passed behind him, circling around the table until he was facing the college student. He smiled at him, his face betraying none of his inner revulsion. "You'll find far more beautiful women when you reach your destination. Sisters who have joined the struggle, and *ghanima* alike."

Ghanima. The spoils of war. *Slaves.*

"I know," the young man said, as if trying to convince himself. "I still shouldn't just. . .*leave* like that. I should talk with her, try to get her to see—"

"No," Harry shook his head. Another time with her, and he would spill everything he knew—that much he could read in the kid's eyes. "It is regrettable that things should come about as they did, but what's done is done. And it *had* to be done, you know that."

"I know, I just—"

93

"Once you are there, my brother, all this will seem a distant memory—paling in comparison to the joy, the brotherhood you will know among your fellow *mujahideen* in the Philippines. Trust me on this, it is not something you can understand without actually *being* there—as soon you will be. I only wish that I could join you there, to be with you in that moment when you first—"

Harry heard his mobile phone vibrate against the table top, his voice breaking off as he reached over, sliding his finger across the screen to reveal a text message. *Yassin.*

"Is everything all right?" he heard Reza ask, his sudden movement jarring the college student from his own thoughts.

It took Harry a long moment to respond, his eyes focused on Yassin's text—a cold chill seeming to wash over him in that moment. *A premonition of evil.*

"Come to the boxing club as soon as you can. We need to talk."

Chapter 7

Independence Day. Roy Coftey smiled despite himself, watching a red Chevelle drive by the reviewing stand as the parade began, slowly but surely, to take shape—a smooth-cheeked drum major standing perhaps thirty feet away, high-schoolers in marching uniform shuffling slowly into formation in the July sun. National Guard soldiers in front of them, clustered around a desert-tan Humvee from the armory in Tulsa.

It reminded the senator of the parades he remembered as a kid, through the center of a small town which hadn't gotten that much bigger in the decades since. *Americana.*

"It's a beautiful sight, isn't it?" he heard a voice ask—his head coming round to see Bernard Kranemeyer standing there a few feet behind him. No sound having betrayed his arrival. *Not bad for a man with one leg.* "The good old US of A."

A faintly ironic smile touched the lips of the Director of the Clandestine Service as he spoke the words, coming forward to stand at Coftey's side. A pair of dark sunglasses masking eyes the color of anthracite.

And just as unreadable.

"This right here—this is what they tell us we're defending, Roy," he continued quietly, his voice not audible more than a few feet away. "That for which we both once volunteered to lay down our lives. Places like this little town. *America.* A nostalgic vision of a past that never was. The red, white, and blue—fireworks in the park on the Fourth of July. The Star-Spangled

Banner, sung by a off-key debutante who's been told she'll 'make it big' some day. The *ritual*."

5:34 P.M. Central European Summer Time
The boxing club
Sint-Jans-Molenbeek, Belgium

There were moments in an operation when you sensed that everything had begun to fall apart—that the ground had shifted irrevocably beneath you.

A sixth sense warning you of danger. Warning you to run, far and fast. *Get away.*

That moment was now, Harry thought, forcing his pace to slow as he approached the gym, his eyes flickering from one side of the street to the next.

But running wasn't an option, not with all that now hung in the balance. There were innocent lives enough on his conscience as it was, enough for a lifetime. Far more than any man should ever have to bear. Any honorable man. . .and perhaps that was the heart of it, wasn't it?

The choices we make.

Never so clear as in hindsight, the choice already made—the damage, already done. Perhaps it was all a mirage, looking back upon your past—thinking you could have gone any other way. Choice itself, an illusion. Fate, forcing your hand.

Perhaps. . .

He took a final look around the street as he reached the door, looking for any signs of surveillance. Any sign that he might be walking into a trap. *Nothing.*

Which didn't mean a thing, as he knew far too well.

Harry pushed open the door of the boxing club, peeling a few euros off the roll in the back pocket of his jeans and handing them to the attendant as he went in.

He'd changed into Western clothes before leaving the apartment—less likely to attract attention in this setting. To be noticed, if something went wrong.

If. Something already had, after all, or he wouldn't be here.

The locker room they had used for prayers the previous week was at the very back of the building and he made his way toward it, moving like a ghost in the semi-darkness.

The insistent, throbbing sound of the ventilation fans masking the sounds of his movement, a vibrant hum mingled with the sound of men sparring, of gloves impacting sweat-soaked flesh. Cheers of exultation, ringing distantly in his ears. *So very far away.*

His world narrowing to the space just ahead of him, his eyes burning with a fierce intensity as he approached the door to the lockers, putting his hand up against it.

Hesitating only a second before pushing it open. *The moment of truth.*

"*Salaam alaikum,* my brother," he heard Yassin's voice announce, looking up to see his friend there, in the center of the room, flanked by a half-dozen young men his own age. Just standing there, waiting.

Marwan, a few feet away.

"*Wa' alaikum as-salaam,*" he responded, forcing a smile to his face. Every fiber of his body on alert as he met Yassin's eyes—feeling the boy quail under his gaze. "So. . .who is going to tell me what's going on here?"

9:26 A.M. Mountain Daylight Time
Chandler, Oklahoma

"There's nothing wrong with ritual," Coftey said, gazing at his old friend. They shared a kinship, based in their mutual service of their country—Coftey in Vietnam, Kranemeyer in Iraq, where he'd left the lower half of his right leg.

But he'd never seen him like this before.

"No," the CIA man went on after a long reflective pause, "nothing wrong with ritual, save what it represents. The empty form of a nation which has lost its way, the jealously-guarded husk of that which has perished long before, quietly and without alarm. It's been true of all the great empires, all through the ages, and we'd be fools to think ourselves any different."

He smiled again, a bitter edge creeping into his voice. "We've both seen it, you and I, going to war—realizing our nation hadn't followed us there. That for everyone back home, *nothing* had changed. Your generation was shunned, mine feted—but the end result. . .might as well have been the same.

These people out here, they don't understand what's going on out there, half a world away, and they don't care to. It's enough to call everyone who's been there a 'hero' and go on about their lives as if it wasn't real."

Plus ça change, Coftey thought, hearing echoes of himself in the former Delta Force sergeant. Their wars, so very different. . .yet so very much the same.

"It isn't real," he said after a moment, "not really, not for them."

"Isn't that the truth?" Kranemeyer shook his head, his eyes still focused upon the marchers. "I didn't give my leg—all these years of my life—for a ritual, a *husk*."

"And yet here we both are, all the same."

"I'm still *here*," Kranemeyer said, pulling his sunglasses off as he turned to face Coftey, his eyes flashing like dark coals of fire, "for one reason, and one reason alone. Not for the flag, not for this country, but because there are still men out there, men just like you and I—doing what we did. And they deserve to know that there's someone back here who *gets* it—who's going to be standing there, ready, when these people decide that a 'thank you for your service' entitles them to tell them how to do their jobs."

"Like they have now," Coftey observed grimly, looking away out toward the waters of the lake. They'd been down this road together before, plunging them both into the kind of darkness to which he would far rather have not returned. The catastrophe which his change of party affiliation had been intended to avert.

"Like they have now," Kranemeyer repeated, looking him steadfastly in the face. "So, what's the plan?"

5:47 P.M.
The boxing club
Sint-Jans-Molenbeek, Belgium

"No," Harry heard himself say, his mind racing as he struggled to process what he'd just been told. To find a way *out*.

"But Ibrahim, you have to understand—"

"No," he repeated, his eyes blazing as he turned back on Yassin, "*you* have to understand. Once the caliphate was established in *Sham*, that changed *everything.* And now, as in the days of the Prophet, the faithful have an obligation to rally to its defense, something you cannot do here."

"The caliphate is in ruins," Marwan observed flatly, his gaze seeming to pierce Harry through and through. "The time for its defense has come and gone. We—"

"Raqqa has fallen, but those who pledged *bayah* to its banners still fight on. And we must join them, to lend our strength to their struggle. God has not given us this glimpse of paradise only for it to be taken away, like this." He paused, his attention shifting once more to Yassin. "Your tickets are already purchased, and I have already reached out to our brothers in Mindanao to be expecting your arrival. There will be no further discussion of this."

He glanced around at the young men standing around them, knowing in that moment just how hopeless this all was. The mark of any good operator was the ability to stay one step ahead of a rapidly-evolving situation, stay aright even as the ground crumbled from around you. *Be careful where you put your feet.*

Manipulate the chaos to your will. *Control it.*

But this was already escalating far beyond his control. And he'd put more than one foot wrong.

"Given time and money—I may be able to secure safe passage for the rest of you to fight beside your brothers," he said as he met the gaze of the younger men. *Lying through his teeth.* This had been meant to be a one-off, get them on a plane and leave town. But that wasn't going to work, not now—and deep down he knew it. "But you and Reza must go *now*. There can be no—"

"Why?" Marwan demanded, the young Arab's dark eyes flashing as he cut Harry off. "Why should Yassin—why should any of us—leave, when we can take part in Allah's struggle right where we are? We can travel anywhere, strike at will. Why would we give all of that up?"

Stay in control, an inner voice warned Harry, recognizing the threat even as it rose. The young wolf, challenging the leader of the pack for dominance.

"What is this truly about?" he demanded, taking a step into the younger man—dangerously close, watching his eyes for any signal of danger. "Is this about your own glory? Are you too good to give your life alongside your brothers, as so many brave mujahideen already have? Are you too proud to

99

die as just another one of the nameless *shaheed* on the battlefield?"

A telling blow, and it struck home—Marwan flinching before the accusation. "No, that's not true, that's—"

"If you are to martyr yourself, you want it to be here, don't you?" Harry continued, pressing his advantage. "Here where it will make you famous, where your name will be repeated on the lips of every *kaffir* newshost for weeks to come. Is that what is important to you? *Is it?*"

"No!" the young man spat in exasperation and anger, turning away from Harry—moving back toward the wall, trying to give himself space as he found his voice.

He turned, his gaze flickering from Harry to his brothers and back again, his finger stabbing out in a gesture of indignation. "Those men you fought beside in Syria—the men who died, do you think anyone here noticed? Do you think anyone cared? No, because the West *doesn't* care, not unless it comes to them—to their door. On their *streets.*"

A low rumbling murmur of approbation rippled through the small group in response to his retort, making it clear. *The pack had chosen.*

Perhaps it had been a foregone conclusion, from the very beginning. Perhaps he had known better than to think he could handle this so effortlessly. *Absolve his sins.*

"And just how do you propose to do that?" Harry demanded, his gaze never leaving Marwan. His voice still slightly mocking. *Change tactics.*

The young man's dark face flushed with an angry heat, a curse escaping his lips as he half-turned away, his hand slipping into the duffel bag on the footlocker behind him. Coming back out with something in it—a dark, deathly shape Harry recognized all too well.

"With *this.*"

Gun.

9:50 A.M. Mountain Time
Chandler, Oklahoma

"You don't have a plan," Kranemeyer went on after a long, painful moment, staring earnestly into Coftey's eyes. "Do you, Roy?"

It was an accusation, not a question. He'd known Kranemeyer long enough to tell the difference.

"I'm doing what I can," he responded, a sharp, defensive edge creeping into his voice. "The intelligence community has few friends in Washington these days, all the old enemies are coming right back out of the woodwork. The President has never been a fan of the Agency, and now after the firestorm which has embroiled the administration following the debacle in the Sinai, it's all become personal. You're being backed into a corner."

"That much is obvious. The question is, are you *in* our corner?"

"Of course I am, Barney," Coftey shot back, swearing softly beneath his breath. *This was what D.C. did to people, sooner or later.* Sowed suspicion, turned friends and allies upon each other. As inevitable as the rising of the sun. "Always have been—you know that."

"I know we're running out of time."

"I'm working on it, I don't know what else to tell you. It's going to be a close thing, that I can promise you. We're going to have a fight just to—"

His voice broke off suddenly as Kranemeyer shot him a warning look, glancing over his shoulder even as Melody approached the two of them, her blonde hair falling in waves over her bare shoulders as she came across the street.

"I'll see you later on, Roy," the CIA man said softly, replacing his sunglasses as he turned away. "At the farm."

"Who was that?" he heard Melody ask as she came up to him, her hand sliding around his waist. Her voice sounding distant, somehow. Far away.

"A friend," he replied after a long, hesitant moment. He *thought*.

5:54 P.M.
The boxing club

Death. Coming to meet him once again, as it had on those docks of Aberdeen. As so many times before.

Harry stood there, rooted in place—watching the gun come up in Marwan's hand. Describing that familiar, inexorable arc through the air.

Certain as the grave.

He could still see Mehreen standing there in the mist of the docks, the Heckler & Koch leveled in her hand, smoke curling from its barrel as he collapsed backward.

Death returning now to claim the due of which it had been cheated that night. *So many times before.*

But hard as he might look, there was nothing of death to be found in the young man's eyes. Only uncertainty and. . .*fear*—the barrel of the pistol continuing upward until its muzzle was pointing at the ceiling.

Trembling in Marwan's hand as he swore in Arabic, his face distorted in anger, knuckles whitening around the grip. "*This* is how I will bring the struggle of God to the *kuffar*. *Here*. Where they *live*."

Harry just looked at him, taking his measure in that moment. A young man, full of passion and zeal. A dangerous opponent, not to be underestimated—but far out of his depth.

"Have you ever used one of those, boy?" he asked softly, his voice barely above a whisper, his eyes locked with Marwan's. "Do you know what it feels like to kill a man?"

There was no answer, just an angry curse as the student stood there, seething with anger. Harry shook his head, his gaze sweeping the rest of the young men as he turned away from Marwan. "Have *any* of you?"

They looked as if he had slapped them across the face, no one seeming to dare respond, most of them refusing to meet his eyes.

"Children," he said, shaking his head once again, "children, led by a child, playing at war. This is not the way of Allah, this—"

"We are not—"

"Is folly," Harry finished, cutting Marwan off—his eyes searching the faces before him. "And I will have no part of any of this. You've chosen your leader, now let him lead. Go *play*."

"But Ibrahim," Yassin burst out, finally seeming to find his voice as he stepped forth from the circle, "if we are to be successful, we *need* your knowledge, your experience, we—"

"No you don't," Harry responded bluntly, meeting his young friend's eyes. "You've made your choice, and now it's time for me to leave. If you want to continue playing these games, go ahead—follow this proud fool. If you want to fight in the way of Allah, then follow me."

Walk away. The most critical tool of any salesman, equally that of the intelligence officer. He turned, placing his hand on the shoulder of the young man standing behind him and pushing him aside as he began to make his way to the door.

"*No.*" Marwan's voice, arresting him in his steps. "You're not going anywhere."

Harry looked back to see the muzzle of the Beretta aimed now at his head, just a few feet away, a black hole in the dim light of the locker room. The barrel wavering back and forth, clutched in an outstretched, trembling hand. He smiled, despite himself.

"So you're going to shoot me now, are you?" he demanded, a baleful glint entering his eyes as he stared at the young man. "A fellow Muslim, a *mujahid*?"

"If I have to, yes, by Allah," Marwan swore loudly, moving a step closer.

Another smile, as Harry spread out his hands to the rest of the cell. "So you see the kind of man you have chosen for your leader? A child who would kill one of the faithful, who would bring the *politie* down upon all your heads with the discharge of his weapon—bring all your plans to nothing—all to soothe his own injured pride. Truly it is as the Prophet has spoken, 'he who harbors in his heart the weight of a mustard seed of pride shall not enter Paradise.'"

"Go ahead and shoot, boy," he continued, turning his back on Marwan as he headed once more for the door, "shoot a *mujahid* in the back."

Eight steps to the door, a half-dozen sets of eyes boring into his back as he went.

Hearing in his mind's ear the crash of a pistol shot ringing out, over and again—a bullet mushrooming through his body, tearing apart muscle and tissue.

Harry's hand hit the door of the locker room, pushing it open as he walked out into the common area of the boxing club. No gunshot shattering the air, no bullet pursuing him as the door closed behind him.

He let out a deep breath he didn't know he'd been holding, realizing only then that his heart was beating like a trip-hammer—his legs suddenly as heavy as if he'd run a marathon, the pain in his side jolting through him with every step.

His mind racing as he forced himself to push ahead, moving past boxing rings as he made his way toward the entrance. Walking away was a last resort—a desperate gambler's throw of the die.

If they landed wrong. . .

And then he heard it, Yassin's voice calling out after him. "*Ibrahim!*"

5:15 P.M.
The United States Embassy
Paris, France

"I understand, Anaïs," Daniel Vukovic said after a moment's pause from the other end of the line, the receiver of the Secure Telephone Unit tucked tight to his ear as he kneaded his forehead between his fingers. "I truly do."

All too well, he thought, letting out a heavy sigh as he glanced around his small Paris Station office. This was the danger of human intelligence—of trying to run assets deep inside your enemy's network—at its most fundamental.

What happened when the policy makers got cold feet? When they realized that the intel wasn't going to come quickly enough to save them.

And just whose life did you place in jeopardy then, when the pressure came down from on high?

He'd been against the LYSANDER operation from the beginning, from the time the DGSE had first placed the idea of infiltrating an asset—no, not an asset, but one of their own trained intelligence officers—into Molenbeek on the table.

"What happened in Berlin today can't be allowed to happen here, Daniel," Brunet replied, a hard edge creeping into the Frenchwoman's voice. Witness to the corporate executive she had once been. "That is not negotiable—we will not, we *can*not run such a risk. President Albéric has made that clear."

Oh, yes. *Albéric.* The narrowly re-elected president, whose government would be hanging by a thread if there was any repetition of Berlin. French administrations had been brought down by far less.

Vukovic shook his head. The talking heads liked to prattle on about the "politicization of intelligence," and associated dangers. What they lacked the knowledge to understand was that intelligence was *inherently* political. Ever at the mercy of those who made policy, who had been elected to carry out their vision of how things should be.

The nature of the beast.

"I understand," he repeated. "And the Agency will stand ready to help with whatever resources we are capable of providing, as ever. Just be careful, Anaïs, whatever you do. Very careful."

He listened for a couple more moments before signing off, replacing the phone in its cradle with a heavy sigh.

The casters of his office chair squeaked loudly in the stillness of the room as he pushed it back, walking over to the window and staring out over the boulevard, into the declining sun. The American flag, stirred restlessly by the warm summer breeze. *The Fourth of July.*

The protesters outside the embassy had dissipated earlier in the afternoon, dispersed by fears of a similar attack to the one in Berlin—and the resultant appearance of heavily-armed Marines deploying with M4 carbines.

But they'd be back. He swore to himself, rubbing the back of his neck under the loosened collar of his sweat-stained dress shirt as he turned back to his desk.

Six months. He just had to hold it together for six more months before he rotated back to the States, his three years as chief of station coming to an end. Up finally, after all these years, for a promotion to the Senior Intelligence Service, a flag officer-level position. All the problems of Station Paris, becoming those of someone else.

The last few kilometers of a marathon, the finish line almost in sight. *So close you could* taste *it.*

But try as he might, he couldn't shake the premonition that it was going to feel like an eternity. . .

6:03 P.M.
The boxing club

Harry pulled up short, turning to find the young man hurrying up behind him. *Breathless.* Flushed with excitement.

Glancing around them as if to see if anyone was watching as he reached out, pressing something cold and hard into Harry's hand.

The gun.

Suppressing a sharp intake of breath, he shoved the Beretta quickly into the waistband of his jeans—seizing Yassin by the shoulder and drawing him in close.

"What is this? What's going on?"

"Marwan, he—he wanted to come after you, to kill you," Yassin gasped, the words spilling unstoppably from his lips. His dark eyes burning with a passionate fire. "Driss and I—we took the gun away from him."

"*Alhamdullilah*," Harry responded, putting his arm around his friend's shoulders—embracing him fiercely. *May God be praised.*

Feeling something of a shudder run through his body as he stared into the blank, vacant wall of the gym past the young man's shoulder, his eyes filling with sadness.

Yassin had risked his life for his own, a bond forming between them in that moment. A *debt* of blood.

A bond he intended to exploit. A debt. . .which would only be betrayed.

His knuckles whitened as his fingers dug into Yassin's back, summoning up every last reserve of his strength, fighting against the raw surge of emotion. Don't give in. Don't *weaken*.

He closed his eyes, conjuring up an image of Berlin, of the bombing earlier. Men and women, running in terror. *Fear.*

His face, hardening into an implacable mask. There could be nothing but death at the end of this road, for any of them.

Himself included.

He smiled, clapping Yassin on the shoulder as he took a step backward, releasing his young friend.

"Let's go back in, shall we?"

A residence
Brussels, Belgium

Nights like this had been so rare over the years, Armand Césaire thought, scooping the crisp rice of *bhel puri* onto his spoon as the sound of slow '50s jazz drifted through the small apartment from a small vintage gramophone in the corner of the living room, a relic of his childhood. Nights at home.

He'd spent far too many of them sitting in a parked car, all alone. Waiting for an asset. Conducting surveillance. Far from his home, his bed. *His wife.*

"You're quiet tonight, Armand," she said after a long moment, his head coming up from his food to meet her eyes. *Devastatingly blue.* "Is everything all right?"

He smiled. Claire's once-blonde hair had turned to silver, like what little remained of his own, but she still reminded him of the day they'd first met.

Her, the only daughter of an army captain, from an old French family and a veteran of Indochina. Him, a young officer with what was then still being informally called the "*Deuxième Bureau*," the SDECE. A spy, to put it more baldly.

And a negro.

Their affair had been a scandal, their marriage more so. But neither of them had cared—it had been an age of rebellion, after all.

"Of course, *ma cherie*," he replied, dabbing his lips with a napkin. "This food is delicious. Forgive me. . .there's just been a lot on my mind of late."

LYSANDER. Another week, and no further contact from his agent. And now, with the bombing in Berlin, he was growing worried.

"Let me put something else on," he smiled then, rising from his seat as the record shifted to its final song. "Something more cheerful, perhaps?"

The intelligence officer felt his wife's eyes on him as he went, disappearing out of view into the living room. She was accustomed to this by now after four decades of marriage, the life of secrets, those parts of his life which could never be disclosed or discussed.

He was sorting through the stack of records beside the gramophone when his mobile rang, a jarring, discordant sound in place of the music which had so recently filled the apartment.

Alliance Base, he realized, looking at the number—running a dark thumb across the screen as he raised the phone to his ear.

He listened to the voice on the other end for a few moments, finally responding with a simple, "*Oui*."

It was the call he'd been expecting, ever since watching the footage streaming from the Adlon in Berlin, hours before. As certain as fate.

He knew them, a knowledge borne of decades of hard, bitter experience. Had known how they'd react.

"What is it?" Claire asked as he returned to take his place at the table—the silence hanging over them like a pall.

"I have to go to Paris in the morning," he replied, picking at his food. It went without saying who was calling him away—the same force which had separated them so very many times through the years.

She simply nodded her acceptance, her eyes searching his face. "But we have tonight?"

"We have tonight."

6:05 P.M.
The boxing club

Tension. Harry could feel it, pervading the air as he and Yassin re-entered the locker room—dark eyes flickering in his direction. Hushed murmurs rippling around the room.

Marwan, sitting off to himself, his head in his hand. Blood trickling from a nasty gash in his left temple. The young Moroccan—the one Yassin had called "Driss"—standing a few feet away, his tense, poised stance that of a man who had delivered the blow and stood ready to do so again.

"*Salaam alaikum*, my brothers," Harry smiled, spreading his open hands as he stepped to the center of the room, the members of the cell slowly gathering around him. Curiosity, not unmixed with suspicion, filling their faces. "A great many rash words have been said this night, but we need not dwell upon them any longer. To allow such things to continue to divide us would only play into the hands of the *kuffar*."

He paused a moment, hearing Yassin's whispered "*ameen*" behind him. Knowing just how thin the ice upon which he was about to tread was. His eyes shifting from face to face. *Was one of them, as he had warned Yassin and Reza, an informer? In the pay of a Western intelligence service?*

All questions whose relevance had passed—his decision made for him from the moment he'd stepped into the room. *Choice*, as before, itself an illusion.

"But our brother," he continued, gesturing briefly to Marwan, "despite his rashness. . .is not entirely wrong."

Harry saw the young Arab glance up in surprise, something of disbelief in those dark eyes. *He had his attention.*

"It surprises you that I would say this?" Harry asked, turning to address Marwan directly. "That I would admit my fault?"

He smiled. "When you first set foot upon the path of the *mujahideen*, you must lay aside your pride like a garment, never to be worn again. We are all but weapons, you and I—*tools* in the hands of God. Instruments of His will. Nothing more."

That was all he had ever really been, Harry thought, a shadow passing across his face at the memory. In all those years at the CIA. Nothing but a weapon. A *tool*, in the hands of another.

"We are the instruments, not the architects, of policy." The oft-repeated refrain of the Agency over the years. Accepted, as an article of faith.

To find himself in his own hands, after so long. It was a strange feeling.

"And you were right," he went on after a long moment, his eyes locking with Marwan's for a brief moment before he stepped back, addressing the rest. "It is the will of God that you are all gathered together here, in this place—that I was brought back from the battlefields of *Sham* to be your leader. And so that is where we will strike. *Here*, in the House of War. *Allahu akbar!*"

"*Allahu akbar!*"

Chapter 8

11:49 P.M. Mountain Time
Chandler, Oklahoma

Silence. Only the ticking of the old grandfather clock from out in the hall of the old farmhouse, the tapping of a single finger against the oak of the kitchen table.

Roy Coftey leaned forward, encircling the neck of the half-empty bottle of bourbon in his big hand. Pouring a couple fingers into the glass before him, the amber liquid glistening in the dim light of the kitchen. Smoke curling upward from the tip of the thick *Romeo y Julieta* clenched between his teeth.

A scrape of glass against wood breaking the stillness as Kranemeyer pushed his glass over. The tapping stopped.

It reminded him of nights back in 'Nam, the former Green Beret thought, obliging the silent request before returning the bottle to its place on the side of the table.

Hard men, drinking together back at base following a mission. A brotherhood. *In vino veritas.*

Simpler times, looking back—hard as that would have seemed to imagine at the time. Perhaps that was always the way.

They'd been talking for hours, as the sun slid down across the plains, as night fell over the Oklahoma prairie. *Questions without answers.*

Kranemeyer cleared his throat, setting aside his empty glass and reaching forward, deftly flicking the ash from his cigarette into the ashtray on the table between them.

"Tell me you can do this, Roy," he said finally, taking a long draw on the cigarette as he leaned back in the rough wooden chair. Smoke obscuring his face for a moment as he exhaled.

Coftey drained the last of his bourbon, feeling the fire race down his throat as he shook his head. "It's all going to depend on the kind of coalition I can pull together—you know that. As long as I had Ellis, I could—"

"Tell me you can do this," Kranemeyer repeated in that same cold, flat voice, the smoke drifting away to reveal hard dark eyes staring across the table, sna `ping like coals of fire.

The unspoken alternative, only too clear. Like a concealed dagger, just beneath the surface of the table.

"No," he responded firmly, punctuating his words with a shake of his head. "No, we're not going there again, Barney. We can never—"

"We will do what is *necessary*," came the unbending answer, Kranemeyer's gaze never wavering.

"No," Coftey swore angrily, his voice rising. "The kind of thing we did with Haskel, with Shapiro, we can't—"

The chair scraped back over the wood of the farmhouse floor as Kranemeyer came to his feet, a long finger jabbing out toward the senator. "We do not discuss that. *Ever.*"

"It's just you and I here, Barney," Coftey said, looking up at his old friend. Seeing in him the man who had stood before him that dark December night in Foxstone Park, blood already on his hands. On *both* their hands, for there was no way for the senator to extricate himself from the responsibility for what had been done that night. Two of the highest officials in the American intelligence bureaucracy dead—one murdered, the other driven to suicide, a header off the Key Bridge.

So always to traitors. But they could never go down that road again, not like *that*. . .

"The only other person for miles is Melody," he continued, collecting himself after a moment, "and I'd trust her with my life."

Kranemeyer stabbed his cigarette into the ashtray, a faint burst of flame flickering in the semi-darkness as he extinguished it with a savage gesture.

"That's your choice, Roy. Just don't trust her with mine."

8:04 A.M. Central European Summer Time, July 5th
Sint-Jans-Molenbeek
Belgium

Fired up, fired up. Feels good.

Harry could feel the sweat beading on his forehead as he ran down the sidewalk, the early morning sun beating down on him from above. The words of the old cadence running through his mind, the way they had during Jump School at Benning, so many years before.

A deep-throated drill sergeant, bellowing out commands, leading he and his fellow CIA trainees on a run every morning. Young men and women, fresh from the Farm, running in the hot Georgia sun. *Fired up. Feels good.*

Just keep putting one foot in front of the other, he kept hearing a voice say, driving him onward—his legs burning, his lungs feeling as though they might explode. It was what had gotten him through Jump School, through all that had followed. A dogged, obstinate refusal to quit.

One of these days, it was going to get him killed.

"So tell me, this attack of yours. . .what have you been planning?" Echoes of the night before, running over and over through his mind as he collapsed to his knees, leaning back into the wall of the building behind him—at the point of exhaustion, his breath coming in great gasps. Struggling to collect himself.

Marwan, recalcitrant as ever, hadn't wanted to answer the question—but Driss, the young Moroccan who'd helped disarm him, had been more than ready to fill the void.

"There's a police officer in Koekelberg. . ." he'd begun, referencing the tiny Brussels municipality just to the north of Molenbeek. Just a few miles away, really. *"The man is former military—a member of the Western crusade in Afghanistan."*

He'd had photos of their target and his family on his phone, a montage cobbled together from social media, police websites. . .and a few that appeared to have been taken on the street. By *them*, presumably.

Their plan, so very straightforward. Ambush the man outside his house—kill him, his wife and children. Burn the house. *Send a message.*

Simple. Devastatingly simple, Harry thought, wiping the sweat from his forehead with the front of his stained t-shirt as his breathing slowed—feeling the hard concrete of the storefront against his back. He felt a shadow fall across him and looked up to see a middle-aged *Muslima* standing there, her head swathed in a dark, drab *hijab*.

She met his gaze for a half-second before averting her eyes hastily—hurrying on by down the street toward the corner market.

Simple, and almost impossible to thwart. They'd clearly had the officer under surveillance for several weeks—amateur though it might have been, he couldn't allow himself to underestimate them.

That most dangerous of mistakes.

There was no way to warn him without them noticing the shift in routine, without them *suspecting*. And what if that's all this was anyway—a dangle? A ploy to flush him out, force him to show his hand.

Was one life—a handful, even—worth the consequences of that? The loss of life which could follow, if he lost control.

That damnable *math*, the calculations which had governed his life. As cold and brutal as ever before.

And yet he could still see those photographs—the faces of the officer's family. A man in combat gear, standing outside Kandahar Airport. The same man, playing with his children in the grass of the Cinquantenaire.

Stop it. Harry closed his eyes, remembering his own words to Mehreen, the two of them there in Leeds—not so long after he'd been responsible for the death of another soldier. A former comrade in arms.

"They all have families."

If you once allowed that to factor into it, where would you stop? The paralysis of indecision, seizing hold.

And yet. . .he put a hand back against the concrete, forcing himself to his feet. To continue on. There had to be another way.

If only he could find it. . .

9:35 A.M.
DGSE Headquarters
Paris, France

"Merci beaucoup," Armand Césaire acknowledged, closing the door of the taxicab behind him as he stepped to the curb, taking a deep breath as he

paused for a moment—looking up at the DSGE Headquarters building, its massive façade nearly shrouded from view from the street, a low wall topped with barbed wire surrounding the perimeter immediately before him.

He was already on camera, and he knew it, Claire's final words to him still echoing in his mind—her hands reaching up to straighten his tie as he'd left their Brussels apartment. Her lips meeting his.

"Be careful."

But it wasn't for himself that he feared.

"Non," he heard himself say, the single word seeming to reverberate through the small conference room, every eye around the table suddenly focused on him.

Nothing like putting yourself on the spot, mon ami, he thought uncomfortably, suppressing a wry smile.

"Excuse me?" he heard Director Brunet ask, her dark eyes meeting his as she glanced down the conference table from her place at its head. Cold and emotionless, the way he had always seen her in the years since she had assumed control of the intelligence agency—though he had only found himself together in a room with her like this on a handful of occasions. Something about her demeanor that made her come across detached. *Clinical.*

Perfect for the job.

"The risk you are proposing," he began, glancing around the table in search of support for what he was about to say, "is simply unacceptable. After all that we have put on the line to—"

She never let him finish, her voice slicing across the conference room like a knife.

"What happened in Berlin—*that* is 'unacceptable.' Anything short of that, anything we need to sacrifice to ensure that we don't all end up having to watch similar video streamed live from the streets of France, is not only acceptable, it is what we will *do.*"

"And with all due respect, *madame le directeur,*" he began, biting back the first response which came to mind, "it is my professional opinion that the most effective way of ensuring that is to continue on the course we have already been pursuing in this operation."

He was too old to lose his temper—had sat in far too many meetings just like this one over the years. Few of them this high-level, but the fundamentals never changed.

Men and women sitting around a table, gambling with human lives.

"It's already been weeks since he made contact with this cell, Armand," she said after a long moment, her eyes never leaving his face. "And thus far, all LYSANDER has been able to give us is a *name*. The name of a man who could even now be preparing to carry out an attack against this country. We have to push him harder."

"In my days in Africa," Césaire replied, his voice neutral, "it was considered nothing short of miraculous if an asset began to pay dividends *months* following a recruitment."

Brunet shook her head. "And in your days in Africa, France wasn't facing an imminent threat from the targets of your intelligence collection. This man—Al-Almani—is, if we assume LYSANDER's intelligence to be correct, a veteran of the fighting in Syria. If he's been sent back here, we have to assume an attack is being planned. And we have to know the nature of it. Circumstances have changed."

They were both right, that was the worst of it, he mused—feeling his supervisor glare an unspoken warning from just across the table. *Stand down.*

But he couldn't. Not and live with himself.

"The circumstances may have changed, *madame*," he began, steeling himself for what he needed to say, "but the realities of human intelligence have not. Infiltrating a hostile network takes time—and any attempt to accelerate that process risks not only the life of our asset, but the entire operation. One chance is *all* we get to penetrate a cell like Al-Almani's, that's it. If LYSANDER is compromised because we forced him to push too hard, too fast—it all goes dark. *Everything* goes dark."

8:51 A.M. British Summer Time
A terraced house
Abbey Road, London

". . .cameras provided this image of an as-yet-unidentified young man, believed to be responsible for driving the car into the café of the Hotel Adlon moments later."

It was maddening, Marsh thought, staring across the room at the telly as he finished his tea. The helpless feeling of *inaction*.

He'd never known anything like it. The reality of being forced to sit back, to take the news as it came—unable to do anything but watch, like any other common citizen. It was an unsettling awareness.

A few months before, such an attack would have meant long hours at Thames House—sleeping on the couch in his office. The hours and days following spent working feverishly to coordinate the UK response, to liaise with their allies, to ensure that terror abroad did not serve as a trigger for similar attacks at home.

He wondered if that was what Patrick Ashworth was doing now, his mind returning to Phillip Greer's words at the pub.

There was no doubt in his mind that Patrick was doing exactly what he believed to be in the best interests of the Security Service—to say nothing of his own. But the consequences of all this, if he were wrong, were staggering.

If something wasn't done to avert them—but he was in no better position to do so than he was to stop another attack like the one in Berlin.

Marsh swore angrily, turning the television off as he reached for the burner phone Greer had given him two nights before. He'd heard nothing from the counter-intel spook since, and. . .there was nothing now, he realized—sliding his thumb clumsily across the screen.

Another curse exploding from his lips as he tucked it into his pocket, angry at everything and nothing at the same time.

Helpless.

10:13 A.M. Central European Summer Time
DGSE Headquarters
Paris, France

". . .of course, any information you can obtain," Armand Césaire responded, smiling as he clasped the analyst's hand. "Fore-warned is fore-armed, *non?*"

His smile faded as he caught sight of his supervisor, Albert Godard, approaching from down the hall toward the conference room they'd all left just minutes earlier. A dark cloud written across the bureaucrat's countenance.

"*Merci*," he said by way of acknowledgment, dismissing the analyst even as Godard reached him.

"What in God's name were you thinking, Armand?" the man demanded, taking him by the arm as they both moved toward the corner. "*Mon Dieu. . .challenging Brunet like that? Have you lost your mind?*"

"Not that I am aware of," he replied mildly, keeping his voice even with an effort. Nearly twenty years his junior, Godard had spent most his career in the DGSE behind a desk—first at embassy postings overseas, then back here in Paris, working his way up the ladder with relentless zeal.

It tended to make for someone who was. . .how would the Americans put it? "Risk-averse." And that had been his perception of the man, from their first time working together, two years before. Little had served to alter it since.

"I was thinking of the success of the operation," he continued, choosing his words carefully. "Of the security of our asset."

"That doesn't mean you can just rebuke the director in front of everyone—in front of the Americans." Godard shook his head. "There are ways to handle this, Armand—but that was not one of them."

And there are things in this dark, shadowy world of ours more important than saving face for those appointed above us, the old intelligence officer thought, staring unflinchingly at his younger colleague. "It had to be said. Someone had to say it to *her*, and no one else in that room was going to."

Certainly not you.

Not that it had done any good in the end. *"Duly noted, Armand,"* Brunet had replied, her voice perfectly even. *"But we have to move this forward. And we have a plan. . ."*

Godard gestured with his finger, seeming on the verge of saying something when Brunet herself emerged from the conference room barely thirty feet away, accompanied by the American station chief, Vukovic.

"You've made your point, Armand," he said finally, apparently reconsidering his words. "And now you have your instructions. Make sure you communicate them to your asset."

"Of course," Césaire nodded. He knew how this was done—knew the only alternative to executing his orders was to resign in protest. And that would only serve to imperil his asset even further.

Brunet's plan was nothing if not a high risk/high reward gambit. If it worked, LYSANDER's credibility within the Molenbeek cell would be cemented, giving him—and them—the kind of access they so desperately needed. If it failed. . .

He looked over his shoulder as Brunet walked past, the American still at her side—unable to escape the feeling that his warning had fallen on deaf ears.

8:34 A.M. Mountain Daylight Time
The farmhouse
Chandler, Oklahoma

The sun was already high above the horizon by the time she felt the mattress shift beneath them, the smell of whiskey thick on Coftey's breath as he leaned over to kiss her cheek.

Melody didn't open her eyes, stirring ever so slightly as if still in sleep—willing him to go away. To leave her alone.

She felt him turn away, sitting on the side of the bed for a long moment before rising, disappearing into the bathroom. A few moments later, she heard the shower come on and only then did she release the breath she'd been holding—her body trembling despite the summer warmth as she hugged the sheets closer to her.

He was lying to her, she knew that much—for the first time since their relationship had begun, all those months ago, in a hotel room following the symphony. It was strange, she found, how much that bothered her. She'd been lying to him, almost since the beginning. But to find the roles reversed. . .

An old friend from the Army. That's how he had described the man who had spent the night in the guest bedroom, but she didn't believe it for a moment.

He wasn't old enough to have served with the senator, and there was something about his eyes—she felt another chill shudder through her body at the memory of the way he'd looked at her when he first arrived at the farm.

The two men had talked and drunk late into the night, their voices rising and falling through the thin walls of the old farmhouse. She'd risen at one point, planning to get a drink from the kitchen, only to be arrested by the sound of Coftey's voice.

"The kind of thing we did with Haskel, with Shapiro—"

His friend, cutting him off, his voice like ice. *"We do not discuss that. Ever."*

"It's just you and I here, Barney. The only other person for miles is Melody,

and I'd trust her with my life."

Eric Haskel, she thought, feeling herself tremble once again. The director of the Federal Bureau of Investigation. *Mike Shapiro*. The deputy director of the CIA. Both of them dead, in a single December night just days before Christmas—the talk of D.C. for months.

Shapiro's body had washed up on the banks of the Potomac following an apparent suicide—commuters on the Key Bridge having reported a man preparing to jump. Haskel, found dead in his D.C.-area home, the victim of what the coroner had determined was a massive stroke.

But what if that wasn't what had happened at all? What if Coftey—

She hardly dared allow herself to finish the thought. And if it were true. . .

Melody reached for her phone, cursing beneath her breath as her trembling fingers fumbled with the lockscreen, opening her last text to Cahill. The screen lit up in the semi-darkness of the bedroom and she lay there for a long moment, chewing her lip as she stared at the message, weighing her options.

He was the only one who could help her now, but even so—could it possibly be enough?

We need to meet, she began finally, her nails tapping against the screen, *as soon as I get back to the city. It's urgent.*

3:58 P.M. British Summer Time
Thames House
London

The eyes were just as he remembered them, Philip Greer thought, staring at the old photo clutched in his right hand as he leaned back in his office chair. Hard and cold, startlingly blue—shadowed by the visor of the KGB officer's cap.

Something almost. . .insolent in the expression. The insolence of a young man, of someone at the top of their game, their entire life yet ahead of them. *The confidence of youth.*

Greer laid the photo aside to shuffle through the contents of the "Eyes-Only" jacket he had retrieved from the Registry three hours before, picking out another, newer, photo—only a couple years old.

The ash-gray clouds of Moscow in the background exchanged for the sunshine of Los Angeles, a man exiting from the back seat of a taxicab. He was a young man no longer, the full dress Russian uniform he'd worn in the '80s now replaced by a business suit—his hair turned silver, tousled rebelliously in the breeze.

And yet. . .the insolence remained. The insolence of a *survivor*. Far more dangerous.

It was unsettling just how little they knew about Alexei Vasiliev, for a man who had spent more than three decades on the radar of the "Five Eyes."

And there was precious little in what they did know that gave Greer any comfort with the thought of him having entered the UK.

In the old days, they would have had a team on him from the moment he landed at Heathrow. Stayed with him till he left the country, no matter how long it took.

But those days were no more, and now, under the budgetary pressures imposed by the "war on terror" Greer's CI shop had found itself in a vise, squeezed thin. He couldn't have pulled together the resources for that kind of operation if his life had depended on it.

As well it might, he told himself, laying aside the Vasiliev jacket to reveal the one lying just beneath it.

The face of the SVR deputy *rezident* in London staring back at him as he peeled away the cover sheet.

Hello there, Dmitri, Greer mused, the faintest of smiles creasing his weathered face. He sat there for a long moment, lost in thought—in *memory*—silence filling his office as he gazed at the photo.

Intelligence work was full of moments just like this one. . .moments of desperate, lonely indecision. Keenly aware that you wouldn't know what the right choice would be until it was already made.

The Rubicon crossed.

Greer snapped the jacket shut with a sudden, decisive motion, replacing the cover sheet as he stacked both folders neatly atop each other—rising from his seat.

A stray phrase from his grammar school days running over and again through his head as he made his way to the door, locking it behind him—striding purposefully down the halls of Thames House on his way out.

Alea iacta est.

The die was cast. . .

9:01 A.M.
The farmhouse
Chandler, Oklahoma

The morning sun struck Roy Coftey full in the face as he stepped out onto the porch of the farmhouse, looking out over the open prairie toward the east, past the barn—the corral which had once held his father's herd of cattle.

He could still remember when the barn had been built—an event which had filled him with wonder at the age of nine.

"God's country," he heard himself say, scarce realizing he had spoken aloud—his head still pounding from the night before.

It had been years since he'd gotten that drunk. Vietnam, maybe? Perhaps when Jessie had died. . .those dark nights, far too many of them, spent asking *"Why?"*

"Are you sure you won't join us for breakfast?" he asked, turning as the screen door slammed shut behind him, the CIA man joining him on the porch.

"No, Roy," Kranemeyer replied, coming to stand beside him at the top of the steps, the scruff of a five o'clock shadow on his usually clean-shaven face. "You've seen the news, everything coming out of Germany. D.C. beckons."

Indeed he had. He'd be back there soon enough himself, as distant as it had seemed these last few days.

"About last night," he began heavily, following a few steps behind Kranemeyer as the latter made his way out to his rental, parked in the driveway. "We were drunk. We both said things we didn't mean—things that. . .are best left forgotten."

Kranemeyer just looked at him, his hand on the door of the rental, those dark eyes as unreadable as ever. "I wasn't drunk, Roy. And I said nothing I didn't mean."

Darkness. Coftey shook his head, taking a step toward his friend. "You don't understand, Barney. No matter what happens, no matter what comes down through Congress, what I can or cannot stop—we *can't* go down that road again."

"We did once before, you and I," Kranemeyer responded, all too clearly unmoved, his eyes holding the senator's in an unwavering gaze.

"That was different." The senator looked away, then, taking a deep breath before he went on. *It was like looking into an abyss.* "The President was guilty of treason, had been responsible for the deaths of CIA officers overseas."

"And these *people* will be responsible for the deaths of more. You can see that, can't you, Roy?" Kranemeyer demanded, a raw edge creeping into his voice. "Just like they have, over and again, all through the years, your war, mine—God only knows how many others in between. Men who have never set foot outside that wire, attempting to cuff the hands of those who do. And sooner or later, it's going to get people killed. I end up burying my people either way, so you tell me. . .what's the difference, really?"

The pain of loss, Coftey thought, looking out over the Oklahoma prairie. They'd both buried far too many comrades over the decades. The lot of the soldier, the one they'd accepted for themselves, so many years ago.

"It's not treason to be wrong," he said finally, "not even when it comes at the cost of human life. We all—you and I, the Congress, the President himself—serve at the pleasure of the people. We exist only to carry out their will, and in this democracy, they're entitled to be wrong. But God help us when they are."

It was a long moment before the CIA man responded, a shadow seeming to pass across his saturnine countenance. "Frankly, Roy, I'd just as soon we helped ourselves."

6:39 P.M. British Summer Time
High Street Kensington Underground Station
London

Philip Greer could feel his pulse quicken as he heard the train approach, the peculiar rushing sound filling the tube station—a woman jostling against him as she moved closer to the edge of the platform.

The moment of truth.

He was gambling here, and he knew it. Gambling with stakes impossible to even quantify, let alone weigh properly—his eyes scanning the crowd as the train pulled in, its doors opening.

Come on. . .where are you?

It had been years since he'd done this, and yet it all came rushing back—memories of Vienna back in the '80s, running counter-intelligence for Six back in the day.

Seconds ticking by as the crowd of evening commuters flooded onto the cars, filling the train. *Still no sign.*

It made sense that he would wait until the last moment—lessen the time anyone following him would have to board, deny them the cover of the crowd.

Force them to—*there.* And then he saw him, moving hurriedly toward the train—a short, middle-aged man in a business suit like so many of his fellow commuters, his thinning hair cropped short to the scalp, emphasizing sharply Slavic features. *Dmitri Pavlovich Litvinov.*

Got you.

Glancing around him to make sure no one else was with him, Greer moved swiftly into his wake—murmuring a soft "pardon me" to a woman holding a child in her arms as he pushed past her, the three of them making it onto the train only seconds before the doors closed.

He felt the train lurch into motion as he cast his eyes about the car, searching for his quarry—his gaze finally falling on a familiar head, barely ten feet down the car.

"Pardon me, is this seat taken?" he inquired quietly, the Russian's face blanching as he looked up.

"My God," he heard the man exclaim, swearing beneath his breath as he sat down beside him.

Greer never looked at him, his eyes fixed impassively forward. "Now, now, Dmitri. . .let's not have a scene, shall we? Neither of us can well afford that, can we?"

The SVR deputy *rezident* shook his head, his face a study in anger and surprise. "Just tell me what you're doing here."

"We have a problem. . ."

7:54 P.M. Central European Summer Time
Transavia Flight 389
Paris, France

". . .are now on final approach to Charles de Gaulle Airport. Please make sure your seatbelt is fastened. . ."

The man glanced out the window of the Boeing 737 as the voice droned on over the PA system, looking out over the sprawling landscape below. *France.*

He'd been here so many times over the last thirteen years, but he never wearied of returning—which was not to say he'd ever had any choice in the matter. A beautiful country, which never lost its ability to delight and surprise.

A beautiful country which had spent the last seven decades of its storied history sheltered behind the might of American armored divisions, he thought, his face hardening. Prospering, while his people suffered.

No more.

His flight from Vienna had been as uneventful as his drive across the border from Germany to Austria had been two nights previous. And judging by the continuing reports flooding out of Berlin, his time in-country had been an unmitigated success.

There would be no problem with his Hungarian passport upon landing, any more than there had been crossing any border during these last five weeks in Europe. Freedom of movement, one of the chief ideals of the EU.

Such a beautiful thing.

A smile touched the man's lips at the thought, a hard smile that never reached his eyes. One had to wonder how long such ideals would last, once the real violence started.

Once Berlin became only a footnote.

But that was none of his concern. His was only to pour gasoline over the heaping piles of kindling. It would be left to someone else to throw the match.

Burn it all down.

Chapter 9

The apartment
Sint-Jans-Molenbeek, Belgium

". . .not a chance, man. *Les Rouches* will be back on top next week, you just watch."

"After the way Club Brugge spanked them last night?" Reza asked, turning back from the refrigerator with an amused smile creasing his swarthy face. "Their team's no good this season, I keep telling you that."

"And you've been wrong every time," Driss returned stubbornly, subsiding into silence as he cut into an orange with his pocketknife.

Harry felt himself smile despite himself, spreading butter across his toast with a knife. If one closed one's eyes, it could all seem so. . .*normal*. University students, or at least no older, the five of them sharing breakfast around a table. Talking trash about sports, about their friends, their professors. Like anywhere in the world.

This is what people meant when they talked about the "banality of evil." *This.*

Thou preparest a table before me, in the presence of mine enemies. . .

A fragment of Scripture, drifting unbidden through his mind as he glanced across the table, his eyes meeting Marwan's. *Surely goodness and mercy. . .*

No. He pushed it away, suppressing an involuntary shudder. There was nothing of "goodness" to be found here. And there could be nothing of mercy at the end of this road.

"So," he began, brushing crumbs from his dark, close-cropped beard as he

125

crammed the last of his toast in his mouth, "this police officer of yours. . .how soon do we leave?"

6:49 A.M. British Summer Time
The Bakerloo Line
London Underground

"I have no idea what you're talking about, Phillip. None. I need you to leave, now. Approaching me like this, in public—*this is madness."*

Perhaps so. That was always hard to determine in this business, the line blurring between the insane and the all too real. Phillip Greer leaned back in his seat, lost in thought as the train picked up speed once more, heading out of the Piccadilly Circus station toward Charing Cross. Remembering Litvinov's words from the night before, the way the man had looked at him when he had dropped Vasiliev's name.

The look of utter, unfeigned surprise. *Or was it?*

He'd known the man for a very long time, back to those days in Vienna— those dark, uncertain days as the Soviet system collapsed under its own weight and the world teetered on the brink of a precipice, holding its collective breath.

He had been running CI operations against Russian penetration efforts there at the time—efforts which Litvinov, himself a young KGB field officer, had been a part of spear-heading.

A few years before, one might have foreseen a promising career for Litvinov. He was competent, ambitious, and running and recruiting assets aggressively in one of Europe's premier spy capitals.

But it wasn't a few years before, and in those turbulent months, the ground was ever shifting beneath one's feet—the old edifice of Lenin and Trotsky now shuddering from repeated blows. Threatening to come down and crush all beneath it.

Dark days of the soul, full of fear and doubt.

Litvinov, a communist to the very end—suffering the fate of every true believer who finds his gods to be false, his fellow worshipers. . .frauds. *Devastation.*

"I believed." Those two words, stark in their very simplicity, printed in the

file Litvinov's case officer had given Greer following the first meet which had led to the Russian's eventual recruitment by Six.

Two words, summing up why Dmitri Pavlovich Litvinov had chosen to betray his country.

It had been a short-lived recruitment, as it turned out. As Soviet republics began to break away and soldiers marched into Red Square—with Boris Yeltsin facing down the last Communist hard-liners from atop a tank, the West had begun to let out the breath it had been holding for so very many years.

And in the wake of the USSR's final collapse, the war "won", the decision had been made—somewhere high above them all—that paying former Soviet assets was not a worthwhile use of Her Majesty's exchequer.

Scores of men and women just like Litvinov, simply. . .cut loose. Years of potential insight into the wounded animal that had been Russia in those troubled years throughout the '90s, squandered.

It was no wonder that he'd been surprised by Greer's reappearance—an unsettling apparition from a past he'd no doubt long tried to convince himself was permanently behind him.

But betrayal was never something one left in the past.

And that brought him back to the fundamental question which had been troubling him ever since the previous night—was Dmitri telling the *truth*?

Greer shook his head, his face drawing up in a tight grimace as he stared out the windows of the train into the stygian darkness of the Underground. If he was—if the SVR's deputy *rezident* really wasn't aware of Alexei Vasiliev's presence in-country—then this had the potential to be far bigger than even he'd imagined. Far more dangerous.

And the Rubicon was already at his back.

9:09 A.M. Central European Summer Time
Sint-Jans-Molenbeek
Belgium

"Aryn said he'd be ready by the time we got here," Reza observed, staring at his phone as if expecting that it would provide the answers he sought. He held it up, displaying the last text—nine minutes old, his own unanswered response just below it.

Harry shifted his weight from one foot to the other, the broken concrete of the sidewalk rough beneath his feet as he glanced up at the side of the apartment building.

Aryn Younes. He closed his eyes, visualizing the young man as he had met him at the boxing club on the night of his showdown with Marwan—quiet and reserved, several years older than the other members of the cell. No leader, but *dependable* in a way the younger men simply weren't.

Or at least that had been his impression, he thought, glancing at his wristwatch. Because this morning, Aryn's dependability was nowhere to be found. *Where was he?*

They were due to meet up with Yassin and the others, soon.

"I'll go up, see if I can find him," Reza said after another long, awkward moment. "He lives with his mother–I've been to their flat before."

Indeed. "I'll come with you."

"Oh, it's you," Aryn said, looking out at them through the cracked door. He reached up to undo the chain blocking their entrance, pulling it open. "I'm sorry, I know I said I'd be ready when you got here, but things with mother since her last treatment. . ."

"*Salaam alaikum,* brother," Harry replied gently, placing his hand on the young Moroccan's shoulder. "Is she unwell?"

A quick, reflexive nod, as if he scarce trusted himself to speak. "Cancer. Of the liver. Last year, the doctors gave her six months."

Harry winced, surprised at the surge of emotion that welled up within him at Aryn's words. "I'm sorry, *habibi.*"

And he *was*, despite himself. He knew all too well what it was like to have no one—to be alone in the world. *Adrift.*

"Is there nothing that can be done for her?"

"The doctors are trying," Aryn replied with a short, bitter shake of the head, "or they say they are. It was discovered late—Stage Four. She's. . .been growing weaker these last few weeks, I've had to take care of her, I'm all she has."

"As well you should," Harry said, squeezing Aryn's shoulder firmly. "Are you able to join us this morning?"

A nod. "Yes, I just need to change—she'll be fine for the next few hours."

"Aryn?" Harry heard a woman ask from the adjoining room. "Do you have visitors?"

"Yes, mother," the young man replied over his shoulder, his eyes returning to Harry. "Would you sit with her for a moment—while I get ready? She sees so few people these days. . ."

There was a strange, imploring earnestness in his voice—hard to reconcile with what he knew of Aryn. The way he'd seen him, just a few nights before, listening to Marwan in the club. Hanging onto every last radical word.

Yet here they were. *They all have families.* His own words to Mehreen, a few short months before. *And yet. . .*

"Of course."

"So tell me, why did you leave Germany to come here, to Belgium?"

"Work," Harry lied, looking into the eyes of the older woman, her face weary—prematurely aged far beyond her years, her skin yellowed grotesquely by jaundice. "The company I work for is considering opening up offices here."

It didn't matter that it was as far from the story he had told Yassin, Reza, and the others as it was from the truth. He'd known from the first few moments talking with her that she knew nothing of her son's activities.

"Good, good," she replied, her eyes shadowed by the cloth of the hijab loosely—hastily—draped about her face. He had little doubt she'd put it on just before he'd entered the room, struggling to arrange it with what feeble strength remained in her body. *A pious woman.* And a stubborn one. "It can be hard for Muslims to find work in these days. Aryn has. . .struggled. But of course, you're European."

And that makes all the difference, she didn't go on to say, but she didn't need to. And she wasn't wrong. The accusation, barely veiled in her voice.

You're not one of us, not really.

He knew all too well that without the claim of having fought in Syria, he would never have been accepted by his "friends" here, by the young men who now surrounded him. *Sheltered him.* Without that. . .he would have been just another white convert—revert, rather—kept at arms' length.

Viewed with suspicion.

But there was a bond there, in war—a bond of faith, and of blood. Perhaps the Prophet had truly been on to something. *Peace be upon him.*

129

"I'm glad that Aryn has found such a friend," the woman went on, closing her eyes as she leaned wearily back into the threadbare armchair. "Someone who can help him. . .move on, when I am gone. It won't be long, now."

"May Allah raise you up," Harry murmured reverently, his hands folded in front of him. Knowing it was a futile prayer—knowing she was right.

"You're a good man," she announced suddenly—earnestly–looking up at him once more. "I can see it in your eyes. You will help him, won't you?"

What did she think she saw? For he wasn't a good man, far from it—all illusion of that lost long before, forever tarnished by the years.

A part of him wanted desperately to ask her, but Reza and Aryn returned in that moment. Ready to go. Ready to show him the man they were all now intending to kill.

And the moment passed. "Of course," he replied, favoring her with a quiet smile as he rose. "I'll do everything I can."

9:31 A.M. British Summer Time
Thames House
Millbank, London

". . .yes, thank you, that's all I needed. Thank you very much." Simon Norris replaced the phone in its cradle on his desk, his fingers trembling ever so slightly as he leaned back in his chair, staring into space.

That settled that. He'd spent the last three days trying to find a way to establish remote access to the Royal Bank of Scotland's databases, to wipe the files "Alexei" had ordered him to destroy.

And, as he had suspected, once the initial panic from the Russian's approach in the restaurant had subsided—there wasn't one.

The bank's security was simply too good—like that of most financial institutions these days. Which left him with the most dangerous resort of all: accessing their databases in person, armed with his Service credentials.

But once he did that—there would be no road back. He'd be burned, as surely as if he had just gone ahead and turned himself in to the authorities.

Unless. . .he shook his head, scarcely able to believe he was countenancing the thought. Of burning down everything he had worked for, everything he had *built* since he'd been recruited back in college—in one final blinding act of treason.

And yet, that decision had already been made, hadn't it? Made without knowing it, trapped in a box of his own design. *No way out. . .*

Except one.

10:33 A.M.
Koekelberg, Belgium

"It's just up ahead," Yassin announced, moving at Harry's shoulder as the four of them made their way down the sidewalk, with him setting the pace.

Slow and easy. Don't attract attention. It was difficult to run surveillance under these circumstances, he thought—his gaze sweeping across the broad, open boulevard. A pair of one-way streets split by a green median bordered by low hedges.

On foot, in small, confined neighborhoods where strangers could be easily picked out—where it would be almost impossible to find a place to park a vehicle and surveil a target over the long-term. It was a bad operational environment, to put it mildly.

Made him question just how much surveillance Marwan's little cell had actually done. Whether they might have managed to already alert their target.

"There!" he heard Yassin say, his left arm—forefinger outstretched—coming up, visible out of the corner of Harry's eye.

His hand flashed out like a striking snake, seizing his friend's wrist in a steely grip—his blue eyes boring into Yassin's startled face.

"Don't *point*," Harry warned, his voice full of quiet menace as he held the stare, finally letting go of the young man's wrist after a painfully long pause. "Now tell me, quietly—as though we were friends having a conversation—which building it is that I am supposed to be looking at?"

7:35 A.M. Eastern Time
Manassas National Battlefield Park
Prince William County, Virginia

Head east from the visitor center. The stone bridge will be on the first trail to your right.

Melody felt the gravel shift beneath her low heel, cursing softly as she continued down the trail, the park ranger's words still ringing in her ears.

Her heart pounding against her chest—her eyes scanning the trees nervously. She didn't know why she had asked for this, why she had agreed to come.

Why she hadn't just packed all of her belongings and moved back to Seattle. *Run.*

And then she saw him, standing off to one side of the bridge itself, the former chief of staff's short, stocky figure nearly shrouded in the early morning shadow.

"Why did you ask me to come out here?" she demanded, struggling to keep a tremor out of her voice as she came up to him. "You said you wanted to meet somewhere outside the city," Ian Cahill replied evenly, not turning to look at her, "somewhere away from anyone who might recognize us. I couldn't think of a better place."

That made sense, she thought, glancing about them. An old battlefield certainly wasn't someplace she would have ever thought to come.

"My great-grandfather was here at the first battle of Bull Run," Cahill went on after a moment, his eyes shadowed as he gazed out over the slow-flowing waters of the creek. "Eamon Cahill, a private in the 69th New York. He was only twenty-two when the war broke out, had been in this country—a country that hated he and his kind worse than the blacks—for barely nine months. Yet on that hot July day, he and his fellow Irishmen went charging up that hill into a hail of grape—trying to hold off the Southern advance from the creek as the Union army disintegrated around them, the flower of Washington society fleeing for their lives. When they carried him back down, his left leg was gone below the knee, smashed into a bloody pulp by a ball. But he didn't give up."

Cahill's body seemed to shudder as if in the grip of some powerful emotion, a moment or two passing in complete silence before he continued, turning toward her. "And in the months and years that followed, he learned what every Irishman had to learn back then. What we've had to remember, all the years since. That only fighters *survive.* That in this world, no one's going to give you a thing. All that you have, is what you *take.* What you're willing to fight and scrap for, like the beasts we all are."

There was something in his eyes in that moment that frightened her, something akin to that which she had seen in Coftey, in his *friend*.

"So tell me," Cahill went on, leaning in close to her until she could feel his breath against her cheek, "just what did you uncover in Oklahoma?"

12:51 P.M. Central European Summer Time
The apartment
Sint-Jans-Molenbeek, Belgium

"No," Harry heard himself say as the apartment door closed behind them, the street noise still audible through the open windows—a light breeze offering no respite from the oppressive midday heat. "It's not going to work."

"How can you know?" Marwan demanded, turning back on him.

Because I've done this before, Harry thought, knowing he couldn't say it. *So many times.*

So many people, all through the years. And no matter where you went, no matter whom you targeted—the fundamentals remained the same.

The target apartment was three stories up in an old European rowhouse, just down the boulevard from a roundabout—at least two traffic cameras nearby that he'd been able to count, maybe more. People everywhere.

It was a one-way trip, even assuming you *got* your target in the first place.

"You'd all be arrested within two hours of killing him," he replied coolly, meeting the young man's eyes. "Maybe less."

"I wouldn't," came the confident, brash response. "I'm not afraid to die."

The implication, the challenge—all too clear. *You may have won the battle, but the war is not yet over.*

"Nor am I," Harry responded, glancing from Marwan to Yassin and back again, "as I have proven. But dying is not enough—if we are to *win* our war against the *kuffar*, we can ill afford recklessness."

"This is not—"

"There are seven of you—seven of the faithful. Will you trade all your lives for this *one* man? For the lives of his family?" He shook his head. "We don't have those numbers to throw away, brother."

Stall. Delay. Disrupt. Force them to discard a carefully laid plan in favor of an undefined goal.

Keep it simple, stupid. Their plan was simple—as impossible to stop as it would have been for them to exfiltrate. That had to change.

"If there were only one or two of you," he went on, forcing a smile to his face, "I could commend no superior plan of action. As it is, it would be nothing more than a waste of the opportunity Allah has granted us."

"So. . .what?" Marwan demanded skeptically. "You have a better plan?"

Harry nodded, his face hardening into a mask—his eyes betraying no hint of the emotions roiling just below the surface. "I do. But we're going to need more in the way of weapons."

7:34 P.M. British Summer Time
A hotel room
London

"Of course. . .I understand." Alexei Vasiliev pressed the burner phone tight to his ear as he walked across the darkened hotel room to the window, his dress shoes sinking into the rich carpet—his bright blue eyes hooded as he stared out over the city.

It was always difficult to analyze an asset's motivations in the early stages of a recruitment—particularly an asset induced through coercion, one of the reasons he had always preferred 'other' incentives during his years with the KGB. *And since.*

But in this case, they had been left with no choice. And that made handling Norris all the more delicate, he thought, listening to the British officer's voice on the other end of the phone.

He wanted to meet, but *why*? Had he elected to take his chances with the Security Service, given up his contact from the Russians? Vasiliev shook his head. If he had, well. . .he had gravely misjudged the man's courage.

"Do you jog, my friend?" he asked after another moment, a cold resolution entering into his eyes as he reached his decision. In the field, you dared not hesitate, you had to make a decision and stick to it. Trust your instincts to carry you through. "No? Well, I do. And tomorrow morning, you will. . ."

2:51 P.M. Eastern Daylight Time
The Russell Senate Office Building
Washington, D.C.

". . .but, Senator, wouldn't you acknowledge that events like the tragedy in Berlin Friday, which claimed the life of an American serviceman, demonstrate the clear need for the very kind of intelligence collection which the president's proposed reforms would be aimed at rolling back?"

Roy Coftey glared at the television mounted on the far wall of his office, scowling as the face of Daniel Acosta appeared on-screen, nodding in response to the CNN anchor's question. He had once courted the young Republican as a potential ally in the fight to stave off Norton's original push months earlier with SB286, the so-called "NSA bill."

But in the days and weeks that followed, Acosta had demonstrated where his real loyalties lay. With a constituency that knew little about national security and understood less—making up for that lack of understanding with a self-righteous zeal worthy of religion.

"To be honest, I think your question answers itself, Karen," he heard his colleague respond, displaying all the calm self-possession that had turned the son of Cuban immigrants into an ascending political rockstar in a few short years. "We've allowed this kind of governmental intrusion into our lives for years now—ever since the attacks of 9/11—all in the name of this so-called 'security.' And what have we gotten in return, really? Attacks like Berlin still happen all the same, and the actions of the American intelligence community continue to not only intrude into the lives of private citizens at home, but to blacken our name abroad, through incidents the like of which took place in the Sinai. We have crowds of protesters outside our embassies all across Europe and the Middle East, Karen—they've been there for weeks. And they're there because of US policy. We have—"

"But don't you think it's fair to point out that—"

"We have," Acosta continued, cutting her off firmly, "as Franklin warned in the days of our founding, sacrificed essential liberty for a little temporary safety, with the result that we have lost both liberty and safety. It is essential to rein in the actions of agencies which have, under the malfeasance of previous administrations, been allowed to run—"

Coftey shook his head, thumbing the mute button savagely as he tossed the remote aside, returning to the papers on his desk. People like Acosta adored that Franklin quote. . .never realizing it had been written on behalf of a colonial assembly to a recalcitrant governor—the "essential liberty" in question being that of the government, not the individual.

But since when had anyone in the American political sphere let context, truth, or history stand in the way of a good narrative? *The way the game was played.*

The way *he* was going to have to play it, if he wanted to win. Acosta's CNN appearance told him everything he needed to know. The administration wasn't going to treat Berlin as anything more than a speedbump in the way of their legislative agenda.

And he had to find a way to get out in front. *Or* make *one.*

"Here's the report on SB 367 you asked for, sir," he heard a staffer announce, placing a folder on his desk as the senator acknowledged it with an absent nod.

He was missing something here. Some piece, some *lever* he could use. He glimpsed Melody in the outer office as the door closed once more behind the young man, the sight of her distracting him from his thoughts. She'd only arrived a couple hours before, having taken the first half of the day off—for some reason, she hadn't explained it to him.

She had seemed. . .different, somehow, these last few days—particularly in bed together last night, he mused, lost in reflection.

After all these months, he knew her body almost as well as he knew his own, and there had been a tension, a *reluctance* there that he didn't recognize from the countless times before.

He only knew that something was wrong.

7:21 P.M. British Summer Time
Thames House
London

The numbers were beginning to blur together after so many hours, the seemingly endless web of accounts on Greer's screen stretching back from the UK to the United States to Singapore to Eastern Europe. *Russia?*

That was the logical conclusion, but he was going to need more. Far more.

The intelligence officer removed his glasses, digging a handkerchief from a trouser pocket and wiping the dust from their thick lenses. It would have made more sense to have assigned a junior officer to this task, but he was doing his utmost to keep the circle of knowledge small. Even here in D Branch.

With this kind of money being spread around, there was no telling who might be compromised.

He was missing something here—he knew that. But *what*? That was the question, as yet unanswerable.

He'd gambled on Litvinov in an effort to find that missing piece. But so far. . .nothing.

It was early yet.

He replaced his glasses on his face, adjusting them on the bridge of his nose. And then it hit him. *Of course.*

The missing piece—one of them, at least–was Arthur Colville himself, the beneficiary of all this. . .largesse.

A vital witness, or at least he would have been—had he not been forever silenced by Nichols' rash action.

Greer shook his head, a frown furrowing the officer's brow. But that was the American way of war, was it not?

Rash, decisive. Youthful. *Fools rush in. . .*

He'd seen it so many times, working with them back during those closing years of the Cold War. The Americans, supremely confident in their power, their technology. No problem that couldn't be solved with money, tech, or the swift application of overwhelming force.

His own, older, service forced to do more with less. And often succeeding—because espionage wasn't about technology. *Or force.*

And even with Colville dead, there was one card left to play.

He minimized the account windows, searching through files for a few brief moments until he found what he was looking for—picking up the phone from its cradle on his desk.

"Belmarsh," he began when the other end was picked up, "this is Phillip Greer. Thames House. . ."

8:04 P.M. Central European Summer Time
The boxing club
Sint-Jans-Molenbeek, Belgium

I know a man. Harry unscrewed the cap of the water bottle in his hand, watching with unseeing eyes as Marwan and another member of the Molenbeek cell, a young man named Mohammed, pummeled each other with gloved fists in the ring a few feet away, the pent-up aggression of the last two days seemingly unleashed in their breathless, sweating bodies.

His mind far removed from this moment—Marwan's words still running over and again through his mind.

There were dangers in this—in every choice spread out before him. Dangers within dangers. *Yea, though I walk. . .*

He might well be the shadow in this valley of death. But he wasn't the only one.

Marwan had a name. And a number. The contact information of an Algerian man known to the Islamists of Molenbeek. A man who could provide the weapons they sought. The weapons they would need to carry out a larger, more complex attack.

An attack. He'd been gambling on the kind of weapons they needed being difficult, if not impossible, to obtain.

A ploy to buy time—increase the cell's odds of failure.

He tilted back the bottle, feeling the lukewarm water cascade down his parched throat—his eyes hooded as he gazed out, past the fighters, across the semi-darkness of the boxing club. A haunting voice from somewhere deep within asking him just how far he was going to take this—how many more of these gambles he was prepared to lose. . .

Questions, more of them. And all of them, without answers. He turned away, picking up a towel and wiping the sweat from his forehead.

Marwan's man had been contacted. And there was a meeting set up for the morrow.

Chapter 10

Fado's
Washington, D.C.

". . .if they've actually done *this, Ian. . ."* Her voice had trailed off, a shake of her blond head as she stood beside him on the bridge, looking down into the gurgling waters of Bull Run Creek. *"I'm afraid."*

Cahill took a deep breath, leaning back into his booth as he stared out into the darkness of the pub. Noticing how his fingers trembled as he reached out for his pint.

He was too. He had to admit that much—afraid that the rules had changed, somehow, when he wasn't looking. More, that rules. . .no longer existed.

He could still remember standing beside Coftey on that crisp late December morning at Camp David—not even six months before.

Smoke curling from the open breech of the senator's double-barreled Krieghoff, the smell of gunpowder in the morning air.

"I do what's necessary. You've always known that."

And so he had. But it hadn't begun to occur to him just what Coftey might have come to consider *necessary.*

Murder.

And the murder, no less, of two of D.C.'s most powerful and connected bureaucrats. The head of the FBI and the acting director of the CIA.

There was a power in this knowledge, a value to the right people—if it were true, of course. But there had been no doubting the conviction in the

139

young woman's voice. And the fear.

But there was a danger here as well, a danger to himself—if he chose to act upon this knowledge. He had underestimated his old friend, that much was clear. *Miscalculated.*

He couldn't afford to do so again. It might well be as much as his life was worth.

More than anything, he needed to find out who was backing Coftey—he'd never had any doubt that the powerful senator from Oklahoma had developed close relationships with the spies during his time chairing the Intelligence Committee.

What he didn't know was just how far it had gone. . .or who this man in Chandler had been. But he intended to find out.

He glanced down at the business card in his hand, its logo just visible through his fingers. *A shield, standing before the sun.*

"A shield for the shining god," a female voice announced ironically, his head coming up suddenly as a woman dressed in a dark pantsuit slid into the booth across from him. "Good evening, Mr. Cahill."

She was somewhere in her late thirties—her hair dark, cropped closer than he found attractive in most women. A look of cool appraisal in her eyes as she leaned back into the booth.

The hard eyes of a woman who wasn't impressed by his power for a moment—who had seen all the darkness that life had to offer.

"I'm glad we could arrange a meeting," he replied, leaning forward, his elbows resting on the table between them. He didn't use her name—wished she hadn't used his, but that bridge was crossed. No sense in making it worse. "I know it's short notice, and–"

"I'm leaving on a flight for Amman tonight," she interjected in a voice as cold as ice, cutting him off. "I value my time, as well as my sleep, so I'd appreciate you just getting to the point."

An angry reply rose within him, but he choked it back, a masterful effort born of years of working around people in this town. You couldn't always say what you thought.

And he *needed* her.

"I need to identify a man," he began again, clearing his throat as he stared across the table into her eyes. "If my information is correct, I believe he works for your former employers."

She didn't react, not a trace of emotion showing in her face—holding his eyes for a long moment as a couple passed their table on their way out the door.

Then, "Give me what you have."

6:26 A.M. British Summer Time
Hampstead Heath
London

"You'll come in on the 210 Bus to the Prospect Hill gate. Head south."

The sun was just beginning to rise over the commons as Norris made his way down the footpath, his heart seeming to beat audibly against his chest— his eyes darting nervously from side to side.

He should be jogging, he knew that—it was what the Russian had instructed him to do, along with the detailed list of bus changes to make on his way to Hampstead Heath. But his feet seemed heavy, glued to the earth even as he moved.

As if he expected Special Branch to materialize from the surrounding trees, weapons leveled. *Shouts breaking the dawn.*

They shouldn't have anything on him, he kept telling himself. Not *yet.* Not yet.

But that was all going to change, soon enough. Unless—

"Keep walking," he heard Alexei announce suddenly, the Russian appearing at his shoulder without warning, a black-clad figure in the early morning twilight.

The man had to be in his early sixties, but only his silver hair and the lines of his weathered face betrayed his age—his form lithe and trim, the powerfully muscled legs of a runner visible beneath his jogging shorts.

"You weren't followed," he went on, as if in answer to Norris' unspoken question, prodding him to pick up the pace. The two of them jogging down the path past the still, tranquil waters of the pond on their right, the path curving to the west as they entered the woods.

"At least," he added, casting a curious smile back over his shoulder, "not by your employers."

Of course they *were.* And he hadn't seen them, Norris thought, shaking his head as he ran—his nostrils filled with the smell of his own sweat. *Fear*. So consumed with his own thoughts that he barely noticed when Alexei pulled up short ahead of him, bent over with his hands resting briefly on his knees.

"Why are we stopping?" the analyst demanded, glancing about him in the semi-darkness, the tall trees towering overhead nearly shutting out the dawn's rays. They were standing in a wide, open area—very nearly a perfect square—surrounded by the same kind of low, wooden fence that had marked the path in. "What is this place?"

"This?" the Russian asked, spreading his hands as he straightened, turning to face him with that same enigmatic smile written across his face. "Why this is the dueling grounds, Mr. Norris. Where men of honor once came to 'settle' their affairs. To avenge insults, right fancied wrongs."

He stretched forth his right arm with a grin, his index finger pointing directly at Norris' face.

"Bang, you're dead," he said, laughing as his arm recoiled, pantomiming a gunshot. A harsh, guttural laugh, devoid of mirth. A razor's edge, buried just beneath the surface. "But then, neither you or I are men of honor, are we? So we have nothing to fear."

He smiled then, a smile as insincere as his laugh. "It's been days now, Simon. So what do you have for me?"

6:39 A.M.
A terraced house
Hounslow, West London

The relentless ticking of the clock on the nightstand, its luminous dial shining in the darkness of the bedroom. His wife's breathing, slow and rhythmic, still lost in the depths of sleep. The noise of motor vehicles passing on the street below.

The sounds that had formed the background of Dmitri Litvinov's sleepless night.

He lay there, gazing up at the ceiling as he had for hours—his skin clammy with sweat, his mind steadfastly refusing to shut itself off, despite its exhaustion.

He hadn't slept in two nights—not since the approach on the train. Since he'd looked up to find himself confronted by a ghost from his past. A past he'd somehow deluded himself into thinking was behind him.

You were such a fool, he thought, a whispered curse in his native language escaping his lips. Somehow uncertain even in his own mind whether he meant his betrayal of his country in those years of disillusionment so long ago or his decision to remain in the employ of Russian intelligence after the British had cut him loose.

He should have taken what money he'd had remaining and fled—left the country for. . .America, perhaps?

A bitter smile twisted his lips at the irony of the thought. He might have ended up a manager at Wal-mart, on the outskirts of a small town. Dealing with panhandlers and prostitutes, but beyond the reach of both those he had betrayed, and those to whom he had betrayed them.

Peace.

The middle-aged man rose, glancing back at his still-sleeping wife as he padded barefoot across the carpet to the bathroom of the flat—turning on the light only after he closed the door.

A weary face staring back at him from the mirror. Weary. . .and afraid, he realized, unsure what scared him more. The possibility of exposure after all these years, or. . .

He could still see the look in Greer's eyes on the train—the tension in the man's voice, palpable even through his own panic.

"You're the deputy rezident, Dmitri. Vasiliev's running an operation in this country, and you honestly expect me to believe you have no knowledge of it?"

But he didn't. He was in the dark. And that, Litvinov thought, was possibly the most frightening feeling he had ever had.

6:41 A.M.
Hampstead Heath
London

It was a long moment before Norris responded, his eyes searching the Russian's face through the gloom.

"I can get into the banking system, I can erase all the evidence that could link Colville's accounts to you. But I can't do that without being compromised—without exposing myself in the process. I'll be burned."

"That sounds like a problem you'll want to solve," Alexei responded as he knelt, beginning to stretch—his face serene, as if he had not a care in the world.

Norris shook his head, feeling anger build within him. "No, it's a problem *you* will need to solve, or else I won't do this."

"Won't you?" the Russian asked, finishing his stretching before rising, his cold blue eyes meeting Norris'.

The analyst swallowed hard, feeling himself waver. Forcing himself to hold his ground. This had seemed so easy, rehearsing it in his head last night—so straightforward.

"No, I won't. If I'm going to just turn myself in to Five in the end, then that's what I'll do. No need to add to the list of my treasons. If I do your job for you, I want you to get me out. Safe passage out of the country."

"To Russia?" Alexei shook his head, seeming to find something in the idea amusing.

"To a country of my choosing. Along with a new identity. I want a new life."

"A new life. . .none of us get that, Simon." The Russian smiled, the shadows playing strangely across his face. "Not here, not in skies above us, like so many poor fools want so desperately to believe. The 'opiate of the masses', as Marx put it. Heaven, hell—it's all right here on this earth, and all of our own making. We are who we are, and there is no escaping from ourselves."

Norris swore, his face twisted in a grimace. "It wasn't supposed to be like this."

Not like this, not *treason* against his country. He had never intended. . .

"It never is," Alexei responded, the smile vanishing once more. "But betrayal is what it is. Even so—what you're asking is far too much. To—"

"I'm pulling you out of the *fire*—ensuring you don't risk a diplomatic incident like nothing your country has seen in thirty years. And I'm asking too much?"

"To justify such an expense," the Russian continued imperturbably, "this job isn't nearly enough, Simon. I'd need you to give me something more."

The morning air was warm, but Norris felt a shiver run through his body all the same. The question he had been expecting, had *feared*.

The question he'd spent the previous day finding an answer to. He looked down and away, swallowing hard, his mouth feeling suddenly dry. *There was no way back from this. No* redemption.

He looked up once more, meeting the Russian's eyes. "I'm prepared to do just that."

"I'm listening."

3:23 A.M. Eastern Daylight Time
A townhouse
Georgetown, Washington, D.C.

"Do you know who I am? Do you know what having me for a friend in this town could mean for you—for your company going forward?" He'd lost control in that moment, and he realized it now, looking back—his voice rising, his reserve crumbling under the stress and fatigue of the night. *Careless.*

Ian Cahill flicked the switch, light filling up the room as he closed the door behind him.

Throwing his suit jacket over the back of a chair as he made his way into the bedroom, fingers working at the knot of his tie. Exhaustion filling every motion.

Remembering the look of thinly-veiled contempt in the woman's eyes as she'd replied, *"I do. But you're out of your league here, Ian. And there's no amount of 'friendship' that could make this worth my while."*

She *knew*. He'd been able to see it in her eyes. She didn't have to make inquiries—the name he wanted was right there, behind her sealed lips.

The implications of her silence washing over him like an incoming tide.

"Then I'm right, aren't I? This is real. They did *this."*

A shake of the head. *"I don't know the answers to your questions, Ian, and I don't intend to find them. This meeting never happened—we never spoke. But if you still want the advice you asked for over the phone, it would be this: go back to politics, where you belong. This isn't your world."*

"But it is *yours,"* he'd responded angrily. *"And they* burned *you. I know your background. Don't you want the opportunity to make them pay for that?"*

A faint smile, crossing her face as she'd risen to her feet. *"Of course I do.*

But that's the thing about being burned. You learn to stop flying so close to the flame. . ."

8:43 A.M. Central European Summer Time
The apartment
Sint-Jans-Molenbeek, Belgium

The Beretta hadn't been in need of cleaning, but it lay field-stripped on the table before him nonetheless, the slide cradled in Harry's hand as he scrubbed it with an old toothbrush, searching for nonexistent dirt.

It was a ritual—a way to calm himself, focus his thoughts going into an op.

An op.

It was unsettling to realize that he was letting himself think of it that way, as though this was no different than all that had gone before.

A psychological trap, so easy to fall into. So very *dangerous*. And yet that mindset was the only thing keeping him alive. The skillsets from a past life. That ability to analyze threats.

And there was no lack of threats—this so-called "arms dealer" named Said now ranked chief among them. It was impossible to conceive a more perfect set-up for a sting, whether or not Marwan was a mole or a dupe.

That would resolve one problem, he thought wryly, daubing the excess oil away from the slide with a paper towel as he reached for the Beretta, preparing to reassemble it. Imagining the consequences of French or Belgian intelligence being behind this man. The Molenbeek cell disemboweled at a stroke, the remaining members scattered to the winds. The threat, stopped.

And himself, thrown into prison for extradition back to the United States. That last, the only certainty in any of this.

He was under no illusions of what awaited him after his actions in the UK. There were rules, even in this world, and he hadn't left a one unbroken in his single-minded pursuit of Tarik Abdul Muhammad.

Don't make that mistake again, a voice inside him warned, seeming to ignore that he already had. That bridge, already crossed.

And now here he was, walking straight into a trap, eyes wide open. Nothing to be done for it. *Unless. . .*

He pulled the Beretta's slide back until it locked, reaching for the loaded magazine which lay a few inches from his hand. There might just be a way out, if he moved carefully. Quickly.

Cut the knot.

10:08 A.M.
Alliance Base
Paris

"So we're actually going to let this happen," Daniel Vukovic announced quietly, looking up from his notes. The gravity of what was at hand seeming to settle on his shoulders, weighing him down.

Anaïs Brunet simply nodded. "This was the plan, Daniel. You know that."

"I do," he responded, gesturing to the folder in front of him. That latest communique from their asset in Molenbeek, barely an hour old. "And it was a plan I warned you against. As did your case officer."

"It's a risk," she acknowledged, putting her hands together, her fingers tented before her as she caught General Gauthier's look. "But we can't afford further delay. If there was to be an attack in France while we sit here, deliberating. . ."

Her voice trailed off for a moment, the implications clear to all of them. "LYSANDER's credibility needs to be firmly established within the network, as soon as possible. This was a way to do that."

"If it succeeds," Vukovic interjected, the skepticism still clearly audible in the CIA station chief's voice. "That's anything but certain."

Brunet shook her head, steel entering her voice. "Nothing is certain in this business, Daniel. You know that, I know that. But this is the decision I have made."

"I hope you know what you're doing, Anaïs," the American said wearily, closing the folder and handing it back to her. "Have you at least read in the Belgians on these developments?"

Another shake of the head, and Vukovic swore softly under his breath.

"This is a matter of extreme sensitivity," Brunet retorted. "The circle *must* be kept small. Less than thirty people in this building even know of LYSANDER's existence—what, another ten at CIA? We're not reading in a third intelligence service until we have no other choice."

Vukovic threw up his hands in a gesture of surrender, pushing back his chair and rising from the conference table. "How long until the meeting in Liège goes down?"

"Five hours."

10:23 A.M.
The apartment
Sint-Jans-Molenbeek, Belgium

It would be just possible, Harry realized, staring at the images on the screen of the laptop in front of him. *With the right amount of explosives. . .*

He shook his head, jarred by where his mind had gone.

That he had allowed himself, even for a moment, to approach this with the same clinical detachment that had carried him through so many missions in the past. *Assess the requirements of the mission. Adapt to the realities on the ground. Overcome all obstacles.*

As ever before. But this. . .this was an act of terrorism.

But if he was going to pull this off, in the next few hours, everyone around him was going to have to *believe*. That his commitment to this had been total. That he'd had a plan, been prepared to see it through. *To the bitter end.*

And if they were to believe, then he had to believe the lie as well. That line between reality and cover, ever so difficult to maintain.

In an actual undercover operation, it would be the job of the other officers to help the UC maintain his perspective. His *distance*. Keep him from getting too close.

But there was no one to play that part here. He was on his own. And the line was blurring.

A knock at the door of the apartment disturbed his thoughts and he rose, closing the lid of the laptop and picking up the Beretta beside it, thumbing off the pistol's safety.

Holding it behind him as he moved to the door, his hand on the latch. "Yes?"

"Ibrahim, it's me." *Aryn's voice.*

He unlatched the door, safing the Beretta as he opened it. "*Salaam alaikum*, brother. You're here early."

"Is that all right?" Aryn asked, following him into the small apartment. "If you want, I can come back. I was just. . .embarrassed by yesterday."

"Why?" Harry asked, glancing over his shoulder at the younger man as he reached down, re-opening the laptop. The images of the viaduct coming back up on-screen, a high series of arches above fields of grain.

"I had promised my brothers that I would be ready, and I was not. It's not the first time."

Harry just looked at him for a long moment, then slowly shook his head. "There is nothing to be apologized for—your mother required your care, and you were there for her. As you should have been."

"Yes, I know. I love my mother, she's always been there for me, even when I disappointed her—even when I went to jail—but I had hoped to go to Syria, to fight with the brothers there, but this has prevented me, and now that opportunity has passed."

"Allah knows best," he admonished, smiling gently as he began to recite the *ayat* from memory, "'Now among the best of the deeds which We have enjoined upon man is goodness towards his parents. In pain did his mother bear him, and in pain did she give him birth. . .' It is your responsibility to be there for her now, in her pain. There is no higher duty."

"Not even the jihad?"

"Allah will provide a way. Until then, your responsibility to your mother is clear."

A slow, reluctant nod. Then, "You have a beautiful Quranic voice."

"*Mash'allah*," Harry replied humbly, spreading his hands. "I am only a vessel. The words are God's."

"*Ameen*." Aryn's eyes fell upon the laptop in that moment, lighting up at the sight of the pictures. "What is that, brother?"

"The viaduct near Verberie, forty kilometers northwest of Paris—it carries the LGV Nord rail line across the Oise River Valley." Harry leaned down, tapping a command into the laptop to bring up more pictures. "Trains are traveling at nearly two hundred kilometers an hour as they cross the bridge."

Aryn's eyes lit up. "If we could derail one. . ."

"*Oui*," he nodded. "At that speed, a derailed train would smash through the parapet and fall to the valley below. It's more than a thirty-meter drop.

There would be few survivors from the wreckage."

"*Alhamdullilah*," was the reverent, almost breathless response, a fire glowing in the young man's dark eyes. *Praise God.*

"However," Harry continued, mastering himself with an effort, "there are nearly thirty trains crossing this bridge every day. There's no way we can displace the rails manually, not in the intervals between trains. It will require explosives."

"The kind of explosives Marwan's contact can provide us?"

"*Insh'allah.*"

11:37 A.M. British Summer Time
The Russian Embassy
Kensington Palace Gardens, London

Over the years, you allowed yourself to forget what it felt like to be a traitor, Litvinov thought, staring past his computer at the blank wall of his small office. You let yourself *relax.*

He hadn't felt this keyed up in nearly thirty years. Since those first months following recruitment—looking behind him everywhere he went. Fearing at every moment that he would feel a hand on his shoulder.

But he'd been young then. Young and disillusioned, with nothing to lose. Betrayal, his way of lashing back at a crumbling system which had betrayed *him.*

And now he was old, and had everything to lose, he realized, his gaze drifting to the picture of his daughter sitting on his desk, a candid shot taken last summer at a resort on the northern shores of the Caspian—her own little girl holding her hand as they walked through the sand.

She was married now, and expecting—again. And he knew his own employers too well to be assured that retribution would end with him, if they knew.

If.

Greer could well be lying, as well he knew—spreading *dezinformatsiya* of his own for an as-yet-unknown purpose. Sowing seeds of distrust.

And yet the potential for it being the truth. . .his fingers trembling at the very thought, was far too dangerous to ignore. *As Greer would know.*

If his countrymen were running operations of this magnitude in the UK without reading him in—it could only mean one thing.

They knew.

1:09 P.M.
Thames House
London

Calm down. Focus. Simon Norris forced another crisp into his mouth as he finished typing up yet another report, his entire body seeming to tremble with a kind of nervous energy. Half of his sandwich still lying neglected on his desk.

He'd been possessed by a mad desire to run away, after parting with the Russian in the park. Get on a plane and leave the country—leave everything behind.

Anything to avoid committing the ultimate betrayal.

But running took money—*hiding* more so, and at the end of the day, he was a civil servant.

It wasn't the line of work you went into out of a desire to get rich. You did it to serve your country, as he supposed he himself had, once upon a time.

There was a bitter irony in the realization. If he had never set out to serve his country, he would never have been led to betray it.

Because that's what this would be—he could allow himself no illusions about that. No more hiding behind the kind of justifications he'd used in his dealings with Colville. The rationalizations he'd used in pinning his crimes on his former supervisor, Alec MacCallum.

No, it was all out in the open now—naked and ugly. This was about *him*. About not having to pay the price for his sins.

Because that price. . .was far higher than he'd ever dreamed. He was going to have to give the Russian what he wanted, he thought, glancing around the floor of the Security Service's Operations Centre. As if expecting that his fellow officers could see his guilt already written on his face.

He had no other *choice*. . .

2:37 P.M. Central European Summer Time
Belgium

Harry leaned back into the seat, glancing out the window of the Flixbus as it sped down the highway toward Liège, feeling naked without his gun. The Beretta, cleaned and loaded, left back in Molenbeek—tucked beneath the cushions of the couch on which he slept.

It was better that way, he thought. A gun couldn't save him now.

Not with what he had planned. His eyes growing reflective as he stared out the window—the landscape a blur as it sped by. The farm fields of Belgium, their grain slowly ripening in the summer sun, just visible through the gaps in the dense screen of trees lining the road.

Liège. A century earlier, these fields had borne silent witness to the advance of young men clad in the muted *feldgrau* of the Kaiser, the bare-knuckled fist of a massive right hook aimed at France's flank.

Erich Ludendorff had been here then, long, bloody years before his name would ever become associated with the rise of national socialism. *Of Hitler.* Leading his men against the massive forts guarding Liège, his personal bravery responsible for the capture of the city.

A recipient of the *Pour le Mérite* for that action, distinguished for courage, even in that last great twilight age of heroes. But he hadn't known when to quit.

Did you? A voice within him asked, surprising him with the question. So many times, so many places over the years he could have turned aside—gone another way. Left it all behind him.

And his life would have been so very different.

But you only recognized those moments looking back—those choices you could have made little more than an illusion, a mocking ghost. *Fate.*

Nothing for it but to keep moving forward, as he always had. One foot in front of the other.

He was calm now, an icy chill pervading his body despite the humid warmth of the bus. The road, once more plain before him. And it was time.

He cast a brief glance over at Yassin before leaning forward over the back of the seat in front of them, putting a hand on Marwan's shoulder, his voice low as he asked, "How much farther?"

There was a brief flicker of surprise before the young man recovered his composure. *A tell?* Harry wondered, ever aware that he could be playing them all.

"About eight minutes out from the city. We're to get off at the second stop within its limits—his shop is less than a ten-minute walk from there."

"We're not going to his shop," Harry announced, feeling the sudden tension in Marwan's body, hearing the gasp of surprise as Yassin looked up. He gestured to the phone in the young man's hand. "Send him the message."

"What do you mean? This has been set up, this is–"

"Send him the message. If he wants to meet, he can find us at the Parc de la Boverie. On the River Meuse."

Chapter 11

3:01 P.M.
Parc de la Boverie
Liège, Belgium

"This was a mistake," Marwan swore angrily, pacing back and forth on the grass. "We had an agreement—everything was arranged. These are not the kind of men you mess with, brother. We need–"

"And neither am I," Harry responded coolly, breaking apart the last fragments of his slice of bread as he rose from his squat by the riverbank, tossing them toward a nearby duck. "I don't know your friends, and I don't trust them."

He cast another glance past the imposing aviary toward the bridge as he turned back toward the young men. The island of Outremeuse was a scant three kilometers in length, with the park occupying its southernmost third.

If this was a sting, he'd forced an abrupt shift to their base of operations, off the ground they had chosen—into an area too tight for an intelligence team of any significant size to operate in without making themselves conspicuous. Particularly in the rush of relocation.

And even yet, enough of a crowd of tourists to lose oneself in, if you knew what you were doing. He'd get away, even if his young friends didn't.

All that mattered.

"For that matter," he began, his gaze flickering between Yassin and Driss before finally settling on Marwan, "why are you so nervous, brother? What was waiting for us at that shop that you were so intent on us going there?"

He saw surprise, anger flash in the young Algerian's eyes, an angry retort

154

forming on his lips. Knew he was walking a dangerous line, but safety was an illusion in this world. And if he was to maintain control, he needed to take every opportunity to drive the wedge in deeper, separate Marwan from his friends. *Isolate. Manipulate.*

Destroy. Eventually, inevitably. The only possible end to this, for one of them or the other.

The phone buzzed in Marwan's hand just then, before he could respond, and he handed it over so that Harry could see the screen—the brief message in French. "They'll be here in five minutes."

"Good," Harry smiled—casually pitching the phone over his shoulder into the flowing waters of the Meuse as Marwan regarded him in stunned disbelief. "Now we can be certain the *kuffar* will not be listening in."

2:07 P.M. British Summer Time
HMP Belmarsh
Thamesmead, Southeast London

He could still remember when this facility had been part of the Royal Arsenal, Phillip Greer reflected, the heels of his wing-tipped dress shoes ringing out sharply against the tile as he followed the uniformed HMPPS officer down one long, sterile corridor after another. A briefcase held easily in his right hand.

Back during the Cold War, in the twilight years of what had once been known as the "Secret City", a sprawling complex which had employed more than a hundred thousand Londoners at its peak.

And now it was a prison. One of only nine Category A facilities in the country, housing the worst of the worst. Murderers, rapists, terrorists, and. . .traitors.

That last, his reason for coming here now.

"Right in here, sir," the woman announced, opening the door ahead of them and gesturing for him to enter the small, brightly-lit room off to one side of the corridor. "You'll have thirty minutes with the prisoner."

I'll have as long as I need, the intelligence officer thought, choosing instead to acknowledge her words with a nod. She was just doing her job, too low on the ladder to even warrant pulling rank on.

The Security Service credentials in the inner pocket of his grey suit jacket giving him all the authority he needed here.

He stepped through the door, his eyes adjusting to bright, cold light. Settling on the figure sitting behind the low table in the center of the room—clothed in a baggy, ill-fitting grey sweatshirt and grey jogging bottoms, his hands manacled before him, one ankle shackled to the table.

How have the mighty fallen.

Greer nodded briefly at the man standing a few feet away in the corner of the small room—the man's attorney, by the look of him–before taking the seat opposite the prisoner. Setting his briefcase down by the table's leg.

Sinking wordlessly back into the cold metal of the chair—regarding the bowed head of the man across from him with a look of contempt.

"It's been a while, Alec."

3:11 P.M. Central European Summer Time
Parc de la Boverie
Liège, Belgium

". . .they could just walk away after this, you know that. After all the work I did setting this up. After everything–"

"You talk too much, has anyone ever told you that?" Harry asked quietly, watching out of the corner of his eye as a small knot of men approached through the crowd of afternoon tourists. Five of them, with the exception of one older man, swarthy young men in their late twenties—older than his cell members. Casual clothes, if dressed a little heavy for the July heat. *Their contacts.*

He was sure of it—had seen them several minutes before. They were out of place here, off-balance, out of their element. Exactly as he'd intended.

"*Salaam alaikum,*" he announced, turning as the men came up, halting a few meters away. "My brothers."

The men traded awkward glances for a long moment, until finally the older man—Harry would have put him somewhere around his own age, perhaps a year or two older, swarthy and heavy-set—took a step forward from those flanking him.

"*Wa' alaikum as-salaam,*" he acknowledged, grudgingly, no trace of a smile in his dark eyes. *Nothing of peace.* "What is the meaning of this?"

"As I told my young friend," Harry began, his lips creasing into a smile which never reached his eyes. "I do not know you. And it is dangerous, in these times, for the servants of the Prophet—peace be upon him—to trust those whom they do not know."

"Ibrahim," he heard Marwan begin behind him, but neither he nor the older man paid him any mind, regarding each other silently over the intervening couple meters of ground. Then:

"You are the German?"

"So I am called of my brothers," Harry replied evenly, his gaze never leaving the man's eyes, "but it has been many years since I considered that apostate land my home."

There was something in the man's eyes—*was it a flash of approval?* But he merely nodded. "You may call me Said. It is said that you were in Syria?"

Harry smiled. "Many things are said. And if a man is wise, he is careful whose ears they reach. You understand?"

A nod, but Said's body language hadn't relaxed a bit, tension still pervading his form. Clearly waiting for Harry to make the first move. To ask the *question.*

Was it a trap? It was difficult to tell whether Said's caution was that of a jihadist fearing apprehension by the law if he was the first one to broach the subject of the weapons. . .or an undercover officer not wishing his "sting" to be compromised by a defense of "entrapment." It could be either.

And he had to be *certain*, if he was to carry out his plan. If he was to see this through.

"We should talk," he said finally, gesturing over his shoulder through the trees toward the large building housing the island's aviary. "Away from your men—and mine. The two of us. And perhaps we will come to trust one another."

A long moment, as Said seemed to consider the proposition from every side. "Very well then. After you."

2:13 P.M. British Summer Time
HMP Belmarsh
Thamesmead, Southeast London

"It certainly has, Phillip," the prisoner responded, meeting his eyes for the first time. A bitter smile ghosting across his face. "Have to say, you're the last person I expected to visit."

The man had aged in two months of confinement, Greer thought—his eyes ringed by dark circles, his face worn and pale. Two months, and his trial was yet in the offing. He almost felt pity for the man—*almost.*

He was a traitor, after all.

"I'm afraid this isn't a personal visit, Alec," Greer said coldly, stooping to retrieve his briefcase. "I'm here on official business—from Thames House."

A nod. "I imagined as much. I–"

"Mr. MacCallum," his lawyer interjected, cutting him off, "as your legal counsel, I have to warn you that this is a conversation you should not be having. Anything you say here, to this man, could be used as evidence against you in your trial. We–"

"Thank you, Mr. Dakyns," MacCallum said, mustering up some remaining measure of dignity. "But I will talk with him."

"He's not wrong, Alec," Greer announced calmly. "On the other hand, any cooperation you would be able to offer would be taken into account as well."

"My client would need that in writing," the lawyer stated, interrupting once more.

Greer shook his head. It was a promise he had absolutely no intention of keeping—there was no sentence which even could be handed down which would begin to atone for the harm this man had done to his country. To his *service.*

"I'm afraid that's not possible," he replied, the chill re-entering his voice. "And I will have to ask you to leave, Mr. . .Dakyns. You are not cleared for the materials I need to discuss with your client."

"But I am his legal representative," the man responded, shaking his head. "It is imperative that I–"

"You can leave," MacCallum announced, looking up at his lawyer. "Please."

He looked between the two of them again before acquiescing in exasperation—the door closing behind him with an audible *click*.

Leaving the two men alone, looking at each other over the table.

"What's this about, Phillip?" MacCallum asked after a long, awkward moment. The former Security Service branch head looking gaunt in the harsh glare of the overhead light. *Haggard*.

They had been equals once. Before the fall.

"It's about your employer," Greer responded, unlatching his briefcase and retrieving a folder. "Arthur Colville."

MacCallum shook his head in disbelief. "You won't believe me, will you? I had *nothing* to do with that man—with his attack on the service."

"You're right, Alec," the counterintelligence officer replied, not looking up as he leafed through the folder for the file he was looking for. "I won't believe you. Because every traitor says they're innocent—and the evidence says you're as guilty as Cain."

He extracted a single printed sheet of banking information, adjusting his glasses on the bridge of his nose as he slid it across the smooth surface of the table. "So what can you tell me about this. . ."

3:18 P.M. Central European Summer Time
Parc de la Boverie
Liège, Belgium

"It feels strange," Harry mused, looking around him as the two men walked through the gardens to the south of the park's aviary.

"What does?"

"All of this. . .the *peace* that fills a place like this," he responded, gesturing around at the roses, blossoming in the summer sun. The trees, shading the verdant grass to the west. "One could almost allow oneself to forget that our world is at war. That the faithful are under assault by the Zionists and their crusader allies, wherever one looks. That this is, itself, the *Dar al-Harb*."

The House of War. The only existing alternative to the *Dar al-Islam*, in the Manichean worldview of the jihadists.

With us or against us.

"Almost," Said replied, something of a smile touching the man's lips for the first time. "But we must never allow ourselves to forget the plight of the

Ummah, no matter how comfortable our own lives may have become."

"*Ameen*," Harry nodded as the two of them moved into the shade of the trees, truly alone for the first time. The nearest passerby, nearly fifty feet away. Their men, out of sight on the other side of the gardens. "That was how I came to leave Germany the first time."

"For Syria?"

A nod. It was minor enough of an admission, given the stakes. He had to draw Said out. *Draw him out, and. . .*he left the thought unfinished as the man spoke once again.

"Our hopes were once so bright." Regret in that voice—regret at opportunities lost and passed by. Dreams now in ashes as the remnants of the caliphate reeled under repeated body blows.

"*Insh'allah*, they will burn brightly once more," Harry whispered, watching the man's face. His remorse. . .it wasn't feigned. He wasn't that good of an actor. "And with them, the lands of the crusaders."

"*Insh'allah*," his companion assented, looking over at him as they stood now on the riverbank, stone lining the water's edge. "That's why you returned, is it not?"

Another nod. "The fight in Syria is over, even if the young men don't know it, just yet. But the war continues, here, as ever before. Marwan tells me you can assist us."

It was Said's turn to nod, gazing intently at Harry. "I can. Rifles, ammunition, explosives. . .whatever you need. For the right price, I might even be able to find an RPG or two, though that has become difficult."

A chill ran through Harry's body at the words, the confirmation of all he had suspected. *Feared*, even. This was no sting. This was real.

"*Alhamdullilah*," he breathed, controlling his emotion with a mighty effort as he glanced around them. The trees failed to provide much of a screen, but the nearest tourist was more than seventy feet away, and she appeared to be asleep, stretched out on a blanket, sunbathing. Traffic, passing on the far bank of the Meuse, a hundred meters to their west. A city at peace. "It is clear to me that our meeting was ordained of God."

And the hilt of the knife was cold in his hand, the switchblade flicking into position with a faint metallic *snick* as he turned, plunging the blade into Said's ribs, razor-sharp metal slicing through fabric and flesh. . .

2:21 P.M. British Summer Time
HMP Belmarsh
Thamesmead, Southeast London

Alec MacCallum's eyes flicked over the sheets before him—looking from one entry to the next as he shuffled the papers between manacled hands, the shrewd glance of the analyst he once had been still visible in their depths. *Once.*

Greer's lips compressed into a thin, bloodless line beneath the hawk nose. Once, and nevermore. It was a risk, even showing him these, but it was one he had calculated carefully.

The value of what he could *learn*, far greater than any damage MacCallum could yet do from behind these walls.

"This is Russia," the former branch head announced suddenly, a sharp edge in his voice as he looked up from the papers. "Their fingerprints are all over this."

Greer nodded.

"If they were behind Arthur Colville," MacCallum went on, his mind seeming to turn over the possibilities, considering each in turn, "behind, even, the terrorist attacks, you have a problem—far larger than we could have begun to grasp. But you know that, don't you. . .that's why you're here."

Another nod. "Did you ever stop to ask yourself where the money to finance the publication of the PERSEPHONE papers was coming from, Alec?"

He let the question hang there, watching as the analytical glint vanished from MacCallum's eyes, replaced by an angry heat. "Or were such details simply none of your concern?"

The prisoner swore, loudly, his manacled fists crashing into the surface of the table, sheets scattering. "How can you believe this, Phillip? Any of this? I served my country for *years*."

"Until one day you believed that the only way to continue to serve it was to betray it," Greer observed calmly. "I can understand how you saw it."

He couldn't, really, but that was beside the point. Getting someone to open up to you required them to think that you believed in their justifications. That you *understood*.

And that, he was good at.

"But you *don't* understand," MacCallum spat, "because I never betrayed my country. And if I didn't, that means someone else did."

He paused, his eyes burning with a furious intensity as they met Greer's in an unwavering gaze. "Someone you haven't found yet. And if any of this is true. . .they're likely working for the Russians."

3:22 P.M. Central European Summer Time
Parc de la Boverie
Liège, Belgium

There was a look of reproach in Said's lifeless eyes as he lay there, staring up into the summer sun as Harry removed his hand from over the man's mouth, wincing in pain as he glanced at the teeth marks in his palm. Breathing heavily as he rose from his crouch straddling the body.

The exertion had been more than he'd been prepared for, he realized, wiping the bloody blade of his knife against his black jeans before folding the blade back in on itself, its hilt barely protruding from his clenched fist.

And it wasn't over yet.

His shirt was sodden with the man's blood, a damp, barely noticeable stain against the dark fabric as Harry reached into his other pocket for the small packet containing the pair of Bluetooth earbuds he had purchased the previous day.

He stooped once more, one of the earbuds in his hand as he groped for Said's left ear, cooling flesh beneath his fingers as he pressed it into the dead man's ear canal, seating it firmly.

Cupping the other in his hand as he rose—turning back from the bank of the Meuse. Leaving the body where it lay.

No time to waste.

He pushed his way past a family of four as he made his way once more through the rose gardens, past the entwined, sculptured forms of a woman and a faun cast in bronze there, amidst the flowers.

His eyes meeting briefly those of the little girl being pushed in her stroller—innocent, full of peace. Feeling like the shadow of death in that moment. *The destroyer in the garden of Eden.*

He looked up to see an oblivious smile on her father's face, only then aware that blood still flecked his knuckles.

The blood of the man he had murdered, not fifty meters away—holding him down as he tried to scream, to fight. *To escape.* The rhythmic stab of the knife into yielding flesh, again and again, blood staining the grass.

Paradise lost.

Said's men were gathered in a small knot beneath the trees, their backs to him as he approached, quickening his pace.

Driss saw him coming, recognition in the Moroccan's eyes—recognition and bewilderment, opening his mouth to speak.

"Ibrahim, what's–"

Harry put a hand on the shoulder of one of Said's men as he came up, spinning him around—shoving the remaining earbud beneath his nose. "He was wearing a *wire*!"

He saw confusion in the younger man's eyes, heard Marwan call out. "Ibrahim, come on, brother–what are you talking about? What–"

"You *knew a man*," Harry spat, his eyes the color of blued steel as he wheeled on Marwan. *Implacable.* "Did you also *know* that he was a police informer? That they would be listening in?"

He hurled the wireless earbud onto the turf between them, his index finger jabbing out toward it. "They heard *everything*."

"Where is Said?" one of the Algerian's men asked, anger creeping into his voice as he began to grasp the truth. *But not all of it.*

"He's dead," Harry shot back, feeling the switchblade cold between his fingers. Ready for use.

"You killed him?" Marwan again, disbelief—horror in the young voice. "What have you *done*?"

"Of course I killed him–as I would any such *puppet* of the Zionists," he replied, eyes flashing fire. "Driss, Yassin—with me. We're leaving."

The bus station wasn't far. Just over the bridges—get there, and they'd be home free. Just. . .

"No, you're not," another of the Algerians said, finding his voice at last. "Not until you give us some answers."

His hand groping in his waistband—coming back out, fingers clenched around a pistol butt.

You fool, Harry thought, willing him not to draw, not to–

Gun.

The switchblade came out, its blade glistening in the sun as it described an arc toward the man's belly, slashing across the veins of his exposed wrist, the gun half-way drawn.

The man screamed, a wild, primal sound, ringing out across the park— blood spurting from his wrist as he collapsed to the turf, trying in vain to staunch the flow with his other hand.

It was time to go. Past time, another pistol coming out—a shot ringing out across the park, a bullet searing the air past Harry's head.

He found Driss at his elbow, put his hand on the Moroccan's shoulder, shoving him forward, out of the line of fire. "*Run!*"

2:35 P.M. British Summer Time
HMP Belmarsh
Thamesmead, Southeast London

A light summer rain was falling by the time Greer exited the prison, dismal gray clouds hanging low over the city, shutting out the sun.

MacCallum's parting words still ringing in his ears as he made his way through the carpark, stopping by his own nondescript silver Vauxhall Corsa. "*You think you need to guard yourself against paranoia, Phillip—the eternal bane of men in your trade. But the truth is that you haven't been nearly paranoid enough. Your traitor isn't here, sitting before you in this chair. In prison. He's still walking, among you. There at Thames House.*"

He opened the door of the Vauxhall, sliding in behind the steering wheel—just sitting there, leaning back against the seat as the rain continued to fall without, spattering against the windshield.

It was misdirection, he told himself. It had to be. The efforts of a doomed man to pin his crimes on someone else. *The oldest story in the world.*

"*The woman whom thou gavest to be with me, she gave me of the tree. . .*"

And yet, there had been such *conviction* in his voice. Greer had spent a lifetime listening to men lie, and there was something different about this.

A nagging doubt deep within him—persistent as the tapping of the rain. If this were true. . .but *no*, it couldn't be.

The idea that there could still be a mole, in the Security Service, still doing damage—still undermining them from within, it was almost more than he could bring himself to face.

He stopped short—chilled to the bone by the thought. *Is that it?*

Had he ignored a threat because it was easier—*simpler*–to believe that one no longer existed?

Because he didn't want to confront the possibility that he could have been wrong?

That most deadly of mistakes for a counterintelligence officer. *Hubris.* But was that it?

Impossible to know—shadows within shadows. *The wilderness of mirrors.* Ever so lethal.

Greer shook his head, inserting his key into the car's ignition, listening as the engine hummed to life.

One way or the other, he was going to have to find his way out of the wilderness.

3:37 P.M. Central European Summer Time
Rue Varin
Liège, Belgium

Breathe, Harry told himself—forcing himself to calm, resisting the urge to pace. Hands shoved into the pockets of his jeans as he glanced across the street toward the looming white facade of the Liège-Guillemins railway station. There wouldn't be another bus for ten minutes. And he had no choice now but to wait.

As the crow flies, it was less than a kilometer from the island to the Rue Varin, but he'd had to cross the Meuse three times in the process, first to the east over the footbridge from Outremeuse, scattered gunshots echoing behind him. Then south, he'd contemplated pitching the switchblade into the river from the walk, before deciding against it—turning back west—working his way through the maze of streets leading to the station. Sirens wailing in the distance, off toward the island.

But it was done. He'd gambled—gambled and. . .the result was yet to be seen, he realized, only too well. The dice, still in the air. Yet to land on the table.

The roulette wheel, still spinning in the hands of the croupier. *Fate.*

But he'd bought time, whatever else he'd done. Bought time and sowed suspicion. Marwan's supplier was dead, and after this—no one else would be doing business with Marwan. If he had even made it off the island alive, Harry thought—realizing that he had no idea if any of them had gotten away.

Not that it mattered, just now. There would be time enough to concern himself with that later. They would find him, or he would find them. If the police didn't first.

He closed his eyes, shutting out the world around him—his fellow commuters—remembering the look on Said's face as the knife had gone in, burying itself in his flesh. Shock. Pain. Betrayal.

Agony.

He removed his right hand from his pocket, staring at the outstretched fingers. Realizing that they were trembling, ever so slightly.

Get a grip.

Killing a man was different up close—when your blood was cold, when you could look into his eyes. When you had no other *choice*, but to do so.

He hadn't taken a life in nearly two months—since that dark afternoon, standing in Arthur Colville's study. Blood and brains dripping off the painting of Trafalgar on the wall.

Perhaps he had even dared to believe that might be the end. That life, forever behind him—at long last.

But wherever he went, Death pursued him like a shadow. Echoes of Samuel Han's voice, that night in Vegas.

He hadn't been wrong.

Harry checked his watch once more. *Five minutes.* And then he'd be on the bus. *Away.*

Buying more time, for himself. And for everyone his young "friends" had intended to harm.

"Ibrahim!" he heard someone call out—his head snapping up to see Driss hurrying toward him, off the street. The Belgian businesswoman at his side looking up from her phone at the hail.

It took everything within him to keep his face from betraying him in that moment—his mind warning him of danger. *Threat.*

"My brother," he greeted, embracing his friend fiercely. Drawing him close.

"I wasn't sure I'd find you here," the young man began, the words spilling out of him. *Nerves.* "Marwan and Yassin, they–"

Harry cut him off with a look, glancing at the woman before consulting his watch. "The bus will be here in three minutes—there will be time enough to talk when we're aboard."

"A bus—we're going back to Brussels?"

"No," Harry replied, shaking his head. "France."

4:03 P.M. British Summer Time
Trafalgar Square
London

"Lord Horatio Nelson," Alexei Vasiliev intoned solemnly, staring up at the sandstone statue surmounting the column more than fifty meters above him—a representation of the admiral in his Royal Navy uniform, his empty sleeve pinned to the front of his jacket. He didn't turn, didn't acknowledge the man standing behind him as he continued, "Our man was obsessed with him. England's one-armed, one-eyed hero. You know, it is said that at the Battle of Copenhagen, Nelson raised his spyglass to his blind eye to defy an order, saying he 'had a right to be blind sometimes.' Interesting concept, that. . .a right to be blind. One would think–"

"I didn't come here for a history lesson, Alexei Mikhailovich," the man behind him rasped impatiently. His English, faintly accented—echoes of their mother country in his voice. *The Rodina.*

"I know you didn't, Valeriy," Alexei replied, turning then, a peculiar smile playing across his thin lips as he faced Valeriy Kudrin, the SVR *rezident* in London. The summer breeze toying with his silver hair. "Perhaps by the time you are my age, you will have learned that the only effective way to fight one's enemies is to understand them. And one does not understand a people without learning their history."

"You had some reason for requesting this meeting, I trust?" Kudrin went on, as if he hadn't heard. Or simply refused to, Alexei thought, gazing at the younger man critically. Kudrin was at least twenty years his junior, the next generation of Russian intelligence officer.

The first too young to have been a part of the service during those dark years at the end of the Cold War.

And yet here he was—the London *rezident*. And to the extent that Vasiliev answered to anyone in this country, it was to him.

He held Kudrin's gaze for another long moment before nodding. "I met with our asset this morning, in Hampstead Heath."

"So I was informed," the *rezident* responded, still unsmiling—his eyes hidden behind his sunglasses. "What does he want?"

"A new life," Vasiliev said, his voice rich with irony. "Safe passage out of the country, to a destination of his choosing. A new identity."

Kudrin laughed for the first time, shaking his head. "That's ridiculous. You told him 'no', of course?"

Another smile.

"You would so easily throw away a valuable asset, would you, Valera?" Vasiliev asked, purposefully using the diminutive of the man's name. "There is so very much you have yet to learn. I asked, instead, what he had to offer us."

That got Kudrin's attention.

"And?" he demanded, visibly biting back his anger at Vasiliev's insolence.

"And he's prepared to give us the UK's network in Moscow. Nearly three dozen names—names of the men and women who have betrayed the *Rodina*. *If* we get him out."

"Then let's get him out."

"I have already begun making the arrangements with Moscow," Vasiliev responded, watching Kudrin's face fall at the words. *You didn't actually think, Valera, that I was going to allow you to steal the credit for something this big, did you? So young, so foolish.* "And they have instructed you to place your personnel at my disposal."

"Good," Kudrin said, mastering himself with an effort. Nearly choking on the sentence which followed. "You have done well, Alexei Mikhailovich. Once we have him out of the UK, we'll be prepared to shutter British operations in Moscow—permanently. *Smert shpionam.*"

Vasiliev smiled, nodding.

Death to spies. . .

5:09 P.M. Central European Summer Time
The United States Embassy
Paris, France

". . .of course, Cara," Daniel Vukovic responded, his cellphone tucked against his ear as he sifted through the papers on his desk. "I should be home in another hour—those reservations are fine. Yes, it will be good to see Greg and Jess again—it's been years. That was when we were still living in Herndon, wasn't it?"

A *ding* from his computer struck the station chief's ear and he shifted the phone to his other hand, listening to his wife absently as he reached over to open the incoming e-mail.

It was Brunet. There was nothing in the body of the e-mail except a link, to a news article in Dutch. He opened it in his browser, a chill running through his body—recognizing the first word. Liège.

"I'm going to have to call you back, honey," he said, cutting his wife off in mid-sentence. "Yes, yes–keep the reservations—I'll join you as soon as I can."

He pocketed his cellphone, pasting the news article into Google Translate as he reached for the secure line—dialing a number.

"What am I looking at here, Anaïs?" he asked when the other end of the line was picked up.

"There was a shooting earlier this afternoon on the Outremeuse," she replied, her voice brittle. "It's an island in the Meuse River, in the heart of Liège. One man is dead—another two are in police custody. Local news is reporting that they are 'Middle Eastern'."

Vukovic swore softly, staring at the windowless wall of his office. *This was how it always went.*

Control was a pretense in field operations—an illusion, nothing more. If you believed anything else, you were lying to yourself.

He took a deep breath. "Do we believe this to be connected to our operation?"

"We're reaching out to our counterparts in the VSSE," Brunet replied, referencing the Belgian security service. "We'll see what they're able—or willing–to give us. But the timing is right. We have to assume the worst."

The worst. The station chief shook his head. And that was very bad indeed.

"Then there's been no contact from LYSANDER?"

"None."

8:05 P.M.
Residence ULB – Nelson Mandela
Solbosch Campus, Brussels

"Leave the apartment—leave Molenbeek at once. We have been compromised. You have to get out."

Reza ran his hand anxiously over the bearded lower half of his face, Ibrahim's words running on repeat through his mind as he paced back and forth on the sidewalk, glancing up at the *Universite Libre de Bruxelles'* dormitory rising above him, the rays of the fading sun still glinting off its upper stories.

Come on, he thought, cursing softly beneath his breath as he checked his phone once again for the fifth time in as many minutes. *Where was she?*

There had been genuine alarm in the older man's voice. Alarm and. . .*anger,* Reza realized, remembering his own next words. *"Yassin—is my brother all right?"*

"Just get out, Reza. Get out now," had been al-Almani's only answer—the call ending without another word.

Panicked, he'd found himself staring at an empty screen—redialing immediately only to hear it ring. And ring. *And ring.*

Dead.

He'd tried Yassin's mobile then, only to hear it buzzing against the kitchen counter—left behind when he'd departed for Liège.

No way to contact any of them. Cut off. No way to do anything but run. As Ibrahim had warned.

But he wouldn't do so alone.

He heard the door open behind him, *finally*—turned to see Nora coming toward him, dressed in jeans and a loose-fitting top, her *hijab* arranged haphazardly around her head, as if she had thrown it on just before coming out.

"What's going on, Reza?" she asked, her face shadowed in the glow of the streetlight above their heads.

"I don't know," he confessed, looking helplessly around him—the cars passing them on the street, headlights washing over the two of them as they stood together in the gathering gloom. "I just know that I need to leave Brussels."

"When?"

"Tonight. *Now.*"

"Are you in trouble, Reza?"

"I don't know," he said again, honestly enough, taking a step closer to her, wrapping his arm around her waist—pulling her to him. Looking down into her eyes, her lips only inches from his own. "I only know that I want you to come with me. I *need* you to come with me."

"But I can't do that," she protested, shaking her head, "I have classes this week—an exam I have to prepare for."

"And what will that matter, Nora? What will any of that matter at the end of your life, when what you have done is weighed in the balances? And what we have done in Allah's struggle will be all that matters."

His face softened as he reached down, cupping her face in his hands—their lips meeting in a desperate, passionate kiss. "*Please* come with me. . ."

7:26 P.M. British Summer Time
Wembley Central Station
London Underground

The train's doors shut behind Phillip Greer as he stepped onto the platform, checking his phone for messages as he glanced down toward the open end of the above-ground station—glimpsing the light rain still falling without.

His wife had taken to the technology more readily than he had, but with one child now married and another still in university, it was a necessary evil.

Nothing. He returned the phone to the pocket of his jacket, even as a form materialized at his shoulder through the crowd.

"Keep walking," Litvinov's voice admonished unexpectedly, startling him. *Had he been on the train?* "We don't have much time."

He hadn't seen the SVR man in the carriage, but if he had been *waiting*. . .it would mean the Russians knew more about his personal habits

171

than he cared for them to. *Far more.*

"What are you doing here, Dmitri?" It took all of his training to keep him from looking at the Russian as the two men walked together down the platform toward the exit—commuters moving with the flow of the foot traffic.

"*If* what you said is true," the Russian officer began, placing a heavy stress on the first word, "then I too am in danger."

"In what manner?" Greer asked, his eyes scanning the station—looking everywhere except at his newfound companion. Searching for other officers, for any sign that he might be walking into a trap.

Attempting to reactivate an asset was not without with attendant risks. And with Vasiliev involved, all the normal rules were off the table.

"If I am being locked out of an operation of this magnitude," the Russian continued, his voice low, "it can only mean that I am no longer trusted. That my own betrayal is known. . .or suspected. I want out."

Greer winced. The man might be right—and it might just as easily be explained by Moscow's desire for compartmentalization. But a quick, sidelong glance at Dmitri's face told him there would be no convincing him of that. The Russian had made up his mind.

And there was the danger of HUMINT. . .you could never forget that you were dealing with *people*, not pieces. People with their own fears and dreams. If you were clever, a good case officer could make use of those elements—attempt to mold them to their will.

But the results were nothing if not unpredictable.

"I'm afraid that's not on the table, Dmitri," he responded, telling the Russian officer only what he surely already knew. "You're no longer our asset—not officially. We would need something more."

A brief, barely perceptible nod as the two men moved out into the open, the crowd beginning to part its separate ways now—droplets of rain falling on Greer's bare head. *Not much time left.*

"And that's why I'm here. I am willing to make. . .inquiries, regarding the presence of Alexei Mikhailovich. But I need a reason for doing so, a source. I need an asset—inside British intelligence."

Chapter 12

5:38 A.M. Central European Summer Time, July 8th
A hostel
Reims, France

The sun was just beginning to come up as Harry stepped out onto the patio of the youth hostel, its rays striking him in the face as he turned, facing deliberately southeast, toward Mecca. Nearly three thousand miles away.

Never closer than in this moment.

He stooped, laying out a bath towel on the brick of the patio to serve as his prayer mat, his lips moving silently as he recited the words of the *sura* beneath his breath.

"It is not righteousness that ye turn your faces towards east or west; but it is righteousness—to believe in God and the Last Day, and the Angels, and the Book, and the Messengers. . ."

Righteousness. That had so little to do with him, Harry thought, straightening—the brick already warm beneath his bare feet. *Far too much blood, all through the years, staining his hands.*

As it had the previous day. His own belief. . .washed away in its crimson tide.

He closed his eyes, raising his open hands above his shoulders, palms forward, reciting the words of the *takbir.*

God is the greatest.

He had been the only one prepared for the chaos of the previous day—the only one who *knew* what was coming, his decision made back in the kitchen of the Harraks' Molenbeek apartment.

But just because you knew, didn't mean you were ready—didn't mean you could *ever* truly prepare for that moment, when you reached out your hand. . .and extinguished another life.

He lowered his arms, crossing them in front of his stomach, his right hand over his left, eyes fixed in front of him as he began to recite the opening chapter of the Qur'an from memory. *"Bismillaahir rahmaanir raheem, Alhamdullilah. . ."*

Now all that remained was to deal with the aftermath. *Phase V.* Ever the most unpredictable aspect of any op.

Marwan had gotten away from the island clean, more was the pity. Or at least so Driss had thought, relaying the story to him on the bus. The two young men, pushing their way together through the panicked crowd of tourists streaming over the bridges from the island.

But Yassin. . .Yassin had been wounded, struck by a bullet in the flurry of fire as they'd tried to break contact. His lips continued to move in the words of the *du'a*, but he never heard them, gazing forward with unseeing eyes.

Yassin. He could still remember the look in the young man's eyes, that night in the club. *"He wanted to come after you—to kill you. We took the gun away from him."*

The boy had saved his life that night—there was no getting around it. No escaping the *burden* of that.

No matter how much he might want to. No matter how desperately he knew what needed to be done.

His focus returned to his prayers, gun-metal blue eyes staring impassively into the dawn as he repeated the *takbir* once more.

"Allahu akbar."

6:14 A.M.
DGSE Headquarters
Paris

All the king's horses, Anaïs Brunet thought, looking around the conference table at her team, a pen poised delicately between the fingers of her right hand, just above a notepad already half covered. *All the king's men.*

That was what every morning at this job felt like—trying to put the world back together again.

Knowing that it would have fallen apart once more by the next morning. And this morning was worse than normal—whatever that was, anymore.

". . .and that wraps up what we've learned from Berlin," one of her analysts concluded. "The Germans are moving cautiously—doing their best to navigate the delicate political balance while investigating the attack—but they haven't gotten far."

"*Merci*, Henri," she said, acknowledging the analyst with a nod as she glanced around the room from her position at the head of the conference table. "And what read are we getting from local authorities on yesterday afternoon's incident in Liège?"

She'd checked for messages from Armand just moments before coming into this meeting. *Nothing*. They'd heard exactly nothing from LYSANDER since his last communication with his handler the previous morning.

It was an ominous silence.

"That continues to be. . .problematic," one of the female analysts responded. "For more than a few reasons, not the least of which the reality that we knew the dead man."

"Knew?" Brunet asked, knowing that she had to be careful here. No one else in this room was read in on LYSANDER, or the operation in Molenbeek. She hadn't exaggerated to Vukovic—this *was* a tightly compartmentalized operation.

"The dead man was Said bin Muhammad Lahcen, a forty-four-year-old French citizen—of Algerian extraction," the woman added. "And a known arms trafficker with ties to the Islamic State. We'd had him under surveillance, in coordination with the Belgians, for months—were hoping that he might lead us to someone of more importance."

"And now he's been eliminated," Brunet said flatly. *Eliminated* seemed the most. . .anesthetized way of putting it. She'd seen the pictures. The man had been butchered. At least half a dozen stab wounds to the lower chest and stomach—his throat gashed open.

An attack made chilling by its brutal savagery. It might not have been an uncommon sight in the Middle East, but. . .this was Europe. Just on the other side of their very own border.

And their asset had, most likely, been involved.

A nod from the woman. "With him dead, our task of identifying his suppliers just became that much harder. We're starting from the beginning, all over again."

"If we'd had him under surveillance," Brunet asked, a steely glint entering her eyes, "do we know why he was there on the Outremeuse yesterday afternoon?"

"We have an idea," the analyst replied, shuffling through her papers, "courtesy of a memo from the Belgians an hour ago. Apparently, Lahcen was contacted yesterday by this young man, a student at *Universite Libre de Bruxelles.*"

She passed a photo down the table to Brunet, clearly printed off the Internet. "Marwan Abdellaoui, 25, also of Algerian extraction. Also a French citizen."

Brunet picked it up, the dark eyes of the young man staring back at her from the paper. A strange chill running down her spine.

"The conversation between the two was guarded, but we believe that Abdellaoui was seeking to acquire weapons from Lahcen."

No doubt. Brunet took a deep breath, focusing her attention on the analyst. "Do the Belgians have any leads on Abdellaoui's location?"

"*Non.* Not that they've shared."

6:32 A.M.
The apartment building
Sint-Jans-Molenbeek
Belgium

Destruction. Dark eyes glinted from beneath the black balaclava ski mask as the man looked around him at the remains of the flat—the door taken off its hinges, shattered by the impact of a ram. A hot, burnt smell still hanging thick in the air.

Sergeant Benoît Renier stooped down, the stock of his Heckler & Koch MP-5 still pressed against his shoulder, retrieving the casing of the stun grenade from where it lay on the scorched carpet. Handing it back to the officer behind him.

The unit patch on the shoulder of his uniform visible as he did so—an image of Diana, the divine huntress, against a field of blue.

The emblem of the *Directie van de speciale eenheden*, the former *Group Diane*, the tactical arm of the Belgian Federal Police.

A fitting symbol for hunters.

Hunters without their quarry this morning, Renier realized, looking once more around the empty flat, the images of their targets–a pair of second-generation Moroccan immigrants known to the Belgian police as Yassin and Reza Harrak–flashing across his mind.

They were brothers, reportedly. Known associates of Marwan Abdellaoui, the principal "person of interest" in the investigation now swirling around the Outremeuse murder.

Suspected terrorists, in other words. Because that was what you sent *Group Diane* in for.

Renier plucked his radio off his belt with his free hand, bringing it up to his lips as he keyed the mike. "This was a dry hole," he announced quietly. "They're not here—haven't been here for hours, at least."

With luck, the other elements had known better success. . .

8:39 A.M. British Summer Time
Thames House
London

He was still in the wilderness, Phillip Greer mused, gazing at the folder before him—retrieved just hours before from the Registry. The complete jacket on Dmitri Pavlovich Litvinov, every scrap of information they'd obtained on him back in the day. Back when they had first recruited him in Vienna.

Still in the wilderness, and going deeper with each passing step, he feared—mirrors casting a thousand reflections about him, distorting reality. MacCallum's warning, still ringing in his ears.

Litvinov's request was reasonable enough. . .but *was it?* Or was it a ploy? Had he doubled on them—sold out to his employers in the hopes that the sins of his past would be forgiven him?

Surely Dmitri wasn't that stupid. But desperate men did stupid things.

And discerning the truth was going to require taking risks. More specifically, was going to require someone *else* to take risks.

"Please, Mr. Roth, have a seat," he announced, glancing up as the door opened, admitting a short, stocky black man in jeans and a black polo, the overhead light glistening off his shaved scalp. "I'll be with you in just a moment."

He turned his attention back to the folder as the man took his seat, going over the details of the psychological profile. Litvinov had been characterized as a fundamentally loyal individual, a man whose loyalty had been betrayed by his superiors. *So to whom was he loyal* now?

"You've just returned to duty this past week, is that correct?" Greer asked, lifting his head to meet Darren Roth's eyes across his desk. "After a two-month suspension stemming from. . .actions surrounding the attempt on the life of Her Majesty."

"That's correct, sir," Roth responded, his voice even, professional. His bearing still that of the Royal Marine warrant officer he had been, in a previous life. Only a brief flicker of emotion in his dark eyes betrayed his discomfort with the question. With being *here*, in the office of the head of the Service's counter-intelligence branch.

"How did you feel about that?"

"What do you mean, sir?" There was a wary edge to the question. Roth was no man's fool.

Greer shrugged, spreading his hands. "I've read the file. You did your duty as you saw it. You helped *save* the life of the Queen, when no one else could aid her. And you were very nearly sacked over it. It seems. . .ungrateful, wouldn't you say?"

Roth shook his head, looking briefly away from him. "I don't know what you're driving at, sir. *Yes*, I helped rescue Her Majesty in the middle of the attack on Balmoral—but in so doing, I went against protocol, allowed myself to be co-opted by a foreign intelligence officer. The result was the death of a man we had sought to take into custody."

"The *Shaikh*?"

"Yes, sir. My suspension was nothing if not justified, given the attendant circumstances."

Ever the soldier, the CI officer thought, suppressing a smile with an effort. Adjusting his glasses on the bridge of his nose. "That's a commendable spirit, Mr. Roth. Still, you can understand how someone unacquainted with your outlook, someone from a foreign intelligence service, perhaps, could view you as. . .a vulnerable target for a recruitment."

Roth's eyes flashed, a barely audible curse escaping his lips. "Sir, I assure you that—"

"You can save your assurances, Mr. Roth. You're not under suspicion. In fact, that's exactly how I want you to be viewed. Because you are going to become an asset for Russian intelligence, here in London. And this," he said, picking up Litvinov's folder and passing it over, "is the man who will recruit you."

9:39 A.M.
Reims, France

"Do you really believe that Marwan betrayed us?"

It was a question he had been expecting for hours, Harry thought, the morning sun shining down on both men as they made their way through the streets of the ancient French city toward an Internet café not far from the hostel.

He glanced over at Driss, his eyes veiled by the tint of his sunglasses. *Hidden.*

"I don't know what to believe," he replied, unsure why he had chosen to profess uncertainty. It did him small good for Marwan to remain in play. *But he was committed now.* "I know that I discovered the wire on Lahcen. Whether Marwan knew he was a tool of the Zionists. . .only Allah knows."

The young man shook his head. "It is so hard to believe. If it was a sting— how did we get away? Why weren't they there, waiting to arrest us?"

"Because we weren't where they expected us to be," Harry responded calmly, turning to face his companion, his hand on the café's door. Watching the light dawn in his eyes.

"You mean, the island. You knew. . ."

A nod. "I suspected."

10:03 A.M.
A hotel room
Paris, France

It was the fourth time he had read the news story, the latest reporting out of Liège, but somehow it still didn't feel real. He had spoken to him only a day and a half before, a few hours after his flight from Germany had landed. *And now. . .*

The man closed the lid of his laptop, taking a deep breath as he ran a hand through the stubble of his close-cropped hair.

Knowing he had to collect himself.

Adjust himself to the new reality, to the uncertainties that came along with it. Find a way to yet manipulate this situation to his advantage.

This is what he was trained for—all those long months he'd spent in Michurinsky Prospekt, so many years ago. Training for *this*.

But before he could move forward, he would need to contact his superiors. Apprise them of. . .developments.

He stood and moved over to the bed, opening his suitcase and retrieving the satellite phone stored in one of its internal compartments.

The sun struck him full in the face as he walked out onto the balcony of the hotel, briefly gazing out over Paris—the Eiffel Tower visible in the distance—before turning back to face the side of the hotel.

One could never tell who might be watching. And most intelligence services employed lip readers.

He powered the phone on, waiting a long moment before dialing a number from memory.

Another moment, then two—the familiar tone of an encryption sequence engaging. *The line was secure.*

And then, finally a voice. "You were instructed to use this number only in the event of an emergency, Grigoriy Stepanovich. I trust this qualifies as one."

"It does," the man replied, taking a deep breath. "The man I was sent to contact is. . .dead."

10:07 A.M.
The Internet café
Reims, France

"Police Raids in Brussels Net Suspects", the website headline read, confirming his expectations. The fruits of the chaos he had sown the previous day.

Dragon's teeth, springing up armed men.

Harry lifted his eyes from the computer screen before him, glancing carefully around the small, cramped room, toward the door of the café.

A pair of French teens were crammed into the station beside him—one looking over the other's shoulder as they played some kind of on-line game. Across from him, he could see the harried face of a woman in her early fifties, chewing nervously on a fingernail as she browsed.

No one was visibly paying attention to him—or to Driss, positioned a few computers away.

With any luck, it would stay that way.

He ran a hand over the scruff of his beard, working to mask his relief at the headline. If the Belgian news reports were correct, then the Molenbeek cell had been gutted in an early morning series of raids by police tactical units. No names were being published at this time, but he knew the locations all too well. They had *known* where to go.

Harry shook his head. That was, in itself, problematic. It might simply mean that they had all already been on the radar of the Belgian police. *Or. . .*

He could scarce bring himself to finish the thought. It might mean that his accusations had come far closer to the mark than he could have dreamed. That Marwan really *was* a plant—that the man he had killed. . .*no.*

He closed his eyes, the chatter of the teenagers beside him fading away as he blanked it all out, remembering the look in the arms trafficker's eyes. The passion with which he had spoken of the jihad—of the shattered dreams of the caliphate. There was no way that had been faked.

And yet even as he thought it, he knew he was lying to himself. *He* had been able to fake it, had been able to live this lie for weeks now. Thinking that no one else could do so was an absurd conceit.

What if he had stabbed an undercover officer?

He glanced down at his hands as if expecting to see them covered once more in blood—his fist clenching and unclenching spasmodically.

Wanting to run from the café, never to return. But he had to see this through. To the end.

Not much further now.

11:07 A.M.
Parc du Cinquentenaire
Brussels, Belgium

The calls had begun the previous afternoon, late, and they hadn't stopped coming. Godard. Gauthier. Brunet herself, even. Desperate inquiries bordering on panic, demands for answers.

Answers he didn't have, Armand Césaire thought, staring up the massive arch above him as he approached, dark hands shoved into the pockets of his worn jeans. Remembering his own words to Brunet—the warning he had given only days before.

"If LYSANDER is compromised because we forced him to push too hard, too fast. . ."

And now, everything had gone dark, just as he'd feared.

He'd been to the arch twice since the first call, each time looking for some signal, some. . .sign of life. Nothing.

There was no pleasure to be found in being right, not under these circumstances. He could still remember that last night before LYSANDER had gone under, dining together with the younger officer in a quiet Paris restaurant—going over their plans one final time.

He'd known the stakes. They both had. But he'd shown no misgivings, no hesitation that night—his decision already made, long before. He'd volunteered for this mission, knowing the realities of what must be done to safeguard their country.

And now he was gone—perhaps dead, for all they knew. This operation, spinning far out of their control. Beyond their ability to—Armand's thoughts came to an abrupt halt, his eyes focusing on a single, rude line of chalk scratched against the base of the arch, waist-high. *Yellow chalk.*

The agreed-upon signal for emergency contact.

Armand turned on heel, nearly bumping into a Belgian woman pushing a stroller as he walked rapidly away from the arch, digging his mobile phone from his pocket and dialing a number from memory. Listening impatiently as it rang. *Come on. . .*

It was picked up on the fifth ring, a familiar voice answering. *LYSANDER.*

"Are you all right?" Armand spat out, overcome by a mixture of anxiety and relief. His own responsibility for the young man's safety, a heavy burden, weighing him down.

"We need to meet," LYSANDER responded, the stress only too audible in the young man's voice. "At the old place. A half hour."

11:13 A.M.
Reims, France

"How could they have known?" Harry looked over to see the young man shaking his head as they exited the Internet café together, walking down the busy French street.

"They had to have been watching us," he replied, his eyes scanning the street—the cars passing by. Wondering if what he was saying was true. What it meant if it was. *Could they have seen his face?* "They are always watching the faithful, you know that. You've experienced it. The suspicion, the hostility."

Driss nodded, his eyes betraying his understanding of an experience far too common for young Muslims in Belgium. An experience even Harry couldn't deny, however much he might want to. "What now?"

What indeed? It was so easy to lose oneself in these moments—to forget that one's true sympathies lay far more with the hunters than the hunted.

If only there were a way for himself to escape their nets.

"Right now," he responded, putting a hand on the younger man's shoulder, "we go to ground and wait. Reza knows how to contact us once it is safe."

Reza. Had he gotten clear in time? He had to hope that he had taken the warning seriously—that he had left the city without delay.

If he hadn't. . .he shook his head, disturbed by his own concern. *Why had he even warned Reza?*

He knew the reason he had given himself, before placing the call the previous night.

But was it a lie?

11:39 A.M.
Clinique St. Jean
Boulevard du Jardin Botanique
Brussels

The lights were turned down in the hospital room, the sunlight coming through the shades at one end of the room casting strange shadows over the worn, jaundiced face of the woman who lay in the bed—the yellowish cast of her skin somehow darker now than ever before.

The doctor shook her head, casting one final glance at the heart monitor—its measured lines tracking the faintest of pulses–before Marike Beel slipped from the room, closing the door behind her.

A pair of men in dark-gray uniforms and tactical vests stood without, holstered pistols on their hips, flanking a third man dressed in a worn business suit. The bureaucrat was a few years older than her, well into middle age, his hair graying, his blue tie draped over a slight paunch.

A question all too visible in his eyes as he took a step toward her.

Marike shook her head, brushing a strand of dark hair out of her face as she drew herself up to face the man.

"I'm sorry, *Meneer* Kuyper. It is evident from the medical records I was able to obtain for *Mevrouw* Younes that she has suffered from a heart condition for the better part of a decade. The strain of this morning's. . .events," she settled upon finally, "have precipitated a crisis."

She didn't know what had happened, not exactly, but she could guess, from the posture of the armed men, the emblems of the goddess Diana on the sleeves of their uniforms—the news reports flooding over Belgian media since the early hours of the morning.

There had been raids—all across the city–and somehow, this aged, sickly woman had been swept up in them. *Swept up*. . .likely scared out of her mind by the descent of the federal police upon her apartment.

"She won't last the week," she went on, registering the dismay in the commissioner's eyes. "Perhaps not the day, barring a miracle, and I'm not expecting one. A heart attack this massive, coupled with her debilitation from months of battling the cancer—she doesn't have the strength to fight this. Her family should be notified."

"As far as we know," Kuyper said, shooting a significant look at one of the uniformed officers, "there is only the son."

And in that moment, she knew. *The son had been their target. . .*

3:03 P.M.
Alliance Base
Paris, France

"'Why didn't you tell me he was one of ours?'" The silence hung heavy in the conference room following the question. "Those were his exact words?"

Armand Césaire nodded in answer to Brunet's inquiry, his eyes never leaving her face. Searching for any sign of duplicity, any "tell" which would indicate she was concealing the truth from him here. "He insisted that Lahcen was an asset—that he was wearing a wire—that he had *seen* the wire."

Brunet traded a look with Gauthier, her surprise seeming completely genuine in that moment. "But he *wasn't*. That's impossible—we would have known—Daniel, do you know anything about this?"

From the other side of the table, the American station chief shook his head, spreading his hands in a gesture of helplessness. "What are you asking, Anaïs? He wasn't on our payroll, certainly. And we'd confirmed his links to the Islamic State through multiple sources."

"Then why was he murdered? By al-Almani, of all people?" Gauthier demanded. "That makes no sense."

"We don't know what actually happened between them when they were alone," Vukovic observed, taking a deep breath. "We don't. Your undercover doesn't. But I think it's long past time we had a talk with the Belgians."

"You mean. . .?" Brunet's voice trailed off for a long moment, her eyes transfixing the American. "You think he's one of their people."

"I think we can't rule that out. And I think we should have read them in on this long ago."

"You've expressed that concern, Daniel," the director observed, her voice cold. "But before we take the risk of that exposure, we should ensure that we are acting on the best intelligence available to us."

Her focus returned to Césaire then, their eyes locking briefly across the length of the table. "What was your assessment of LYSANDER, psychologically speaking?"

He had known the question was coming—had been preparing himself for it. But that didn't mean he was truly *ready*. The look of desperation in the young man's eyes, still haunting him.

Fear.

"He's a good man. A fine officer. He–"

"That's not an answer, Armand."

And it wasn't. He let out a heavy sigh, lifting his face to meet her gaze. "It is my firm belief that his intelligence product remains reliable."

"But?" There had been a *but* there, and she knew it.

"But he doesn't want to go back under—doesn't believe he *can* go back under." He saw the look on Brunet's face and ignored it, pressing on. "Al-Almani has changed the parameters of what we're dealing with here. The risks of this assignment. He's not a disaffected youth, a petty criminal with dreams of jihad—someone we can subvert and co-op. He's been to war and he's brought that war back *with* him—as his willingness to murder Lahcen in broad daylight demonstrates. And LYSANDER knows as well as you do that we can provide no assurances of his safety."

"And that's all the more reason we need him to remain on the inside. The capabilities of the Molenbeek cell are no longer a matter of speculation—not when they have a man like this at their head. Aborting the mission now, after this—it isn't an option."

"I know," Armand replied, a distant look in his eyes. "That's what I told him."

4:37 P.M.
The hostel
Reims, France

Back and forth, back and forth. The rhythmic, restless sound of feet against the floor. Steady, continuous. *Irritating.*

"Stop pacing," Harry announced coolly, glancing up at Driss from where he sat on the edge of the bed. They were alone in the room, the rest of the hostel's occupants gone—scattered across the city, doing whatever they had come to Reims to do. "It's not getting you anywhere."

The young Moroccan shook his head. "We've been here for hours—there's nothing to do."

No phones, no TV, no Internet access since leaving the café. *A desolate waste, surely.* Harry smiled within, freshly aware of the age difference between the two of them. Age. . .and a life of training. Of *rigor.*

"And we'll be here for hours more," he replied, concealing his amusement. "Do what I am doing to pass the time—recite the verses of the Qur'an to yourself. Look to the words of the Prophet for your strength."

Driss seemed to hesitate, a flush spreading across his swarthy face. "I. . .I have never memorized any."

"Then perhaps it is time you learned. 'Fighting is prescribed for you, and you dislike it," Harry quoted, his eyes never leaving his companion's face, "But it is possible that you dislike a thing which is good for you, and that you love a thing which is bad for you. But Allah knows, and you do not."

"*Ameen,*" Driss whispered.

"*Ameen,* my brother. Tell me," he began, changing directions without preamble, without warning, "do you have any family, anyone that the police could reach in order to find you? To find *us.*"

"My parents live in the city," Driss replied, with seeming reluctance. "My brother and his wife are in America, with their family. But I have not spoken with any of them in over a year."

"Why is that?"

The young man began to respond, hesitating as if embarrassed by his answer. "My father did not approve of the friends I had made—wanted me to leave with my brother. Go to America. He said I would be unable to find work if I stayed."

"And?"

"And he was right. But you've seen how it is, Ibrahim," Driss exclaimed, a desperate edge in his voice, "trying to get a job as a Muslim in that city."

So he had. And for Moroccans like Driss, in particular. There was a place for everyone in Belgian society and slowly but surely, over the decades, Moroccan Muslims had found theirs. At the bottom.

"You were right not to allow him to turn you from the path," he replied after a moment. "There was nothing for you in America."

Nor for him, anymore. It was a bitter, empty feeling, a sense of loss. And yet all that had been already lost, so long before.

"America believes that it has offered the world so much," he went on, "and yet of what worth have any of its gifts been? Dry, lifeless—like dust in the mouth, serving only to choke those who consume it. We–"

His phone began to ring in that moment, and he grabbed it off the bed, bringing it to his ear. *Reza's voice.* Low and urgent.

He took a deep breath, steadying himself. Preparing for what lay ahead. "*Salaam alaikum*, brother. . ."

6:27 P.M. British Summer Time
Edgware Road, London

One moment Simon Norris was alone, standing on the kerb at the edge of the crosswalk, waiting for the light to change—surrounded by a crowd of commuters whom, like him, had just exited from the tube station a couple hundred meters to the west. The next. . .

He could feel something change, as it were in the very air surrounding him—like a cloud passing across the face of the sun. A chill running down his spine.

He glanced up to see the Russian standing at his shoulder in the crowd, the strange, cold ghost of a smile passing across the man's face—the fading light of day glinting off his silver hair.

Alexei.

Then, before he could say a word, the light changed and the crowd began to move—the two of them moving with it, the Russian keeping pace.

"I had begun to think you weren't coming," he managed, struggling to keep his voice level. *Low.* The man was just behind him now, just close enough for their voices to carry.

"You doubted my word?" It was an absurd question, and the touch of irony in the Russian's voice told him he knew it. He couldn't see the man's face, but he could envision what it looked like in this moment—that familiar smile of a man in control. *Supremely arrogant.* "I keep my promises, Mr. Norris, you must understand this. Now—are you prepared to keep yours?"

A nod. The thumb drive was already in his hand, clutched between sweat-slick fingers—reaching back.

"Two names, just as we agreed—with their accompanying files, as proof of my access. SIS assets in Moscow." He felt a terrible chill wrap its icy fingers around his heart as he felt the drive leave his hand. *What have I done?*

It was a question he knew the answer to all too well. But he was committed—*now*, if never before. "I'll give you the rest once I'm out—have you found a way?"

"Of course, Mr. Norris." He felt a slip of paper, pressed into the sweaty palm of his hand. "If your information proves accurate, be at the address on this paper on the night of the 13th. If it doesn't. . .well, if I were you, I would make plans to be very far away."

"You can't just threaten me like that," Norris exclaimed, a strange mixture of fear, indignation, and anger playing across his features. "You need to understand that I can still—"

The words died in his throat as he turned to confront the man, finding himself suddenly face-to-face with a middle-aged businesswoman on her mobile, her eyes wide as she collided with him—his abrupt halt bringing them both up short.

He mumbled an apology, ignoring her wrath as he pushed on past her—shoving people aside as he struggled to make his way back down the street to the corner—eyes wildly scanning the passerby.

But Alexei was nowhere to be found.

7:03 P.M.
A pub
London

The scrape of a pint glass against the wood of the tabletop, seeming unnaturally loud, even against the background noise of the soccer match on the television over the bar—the low hum of voices.

Dmitri Pavlovich Litvinov looked across the table into the eyes of the black man, then back down at the pint of beer he had pushed over to him, shaking his head. "No."

A shrug of the shoulders, and the man reached over, pulling the glass back beside his own. "Have it your way, mate—might as well drink both of them myself. I don't want to be here any more than you do."

That was true enough, Litvinov thought, staring the younger man in the face. But he had no *choice*.

Not if he wished to escape from the web weaving itself around him.

"Greer explained the situation to you."

A nod as the man leaned back into the shadows of the booth, wiping the foam of the beer off his lips with the back of a dark hand. "He did. And I'd suggest that that's the last time either of us speak his name."

The edge in the British officer's voice nettled him, but Litvinov bit back the instinctive response, instead nodding. "Of course, Mr. Roth. What do you have for me?"

Roth replaced his pint on the tabletop, a small USB thumb drive appearing in his hand as he extended it toward Litvinov. "A sample, of the intelligence I am prepared to provide should my recruitment go through."

The Russian took the drive, turning it over and over in his hand. "This information, it's real?"

A nod. "All of it. This is to establish my *bona fides*. And yours."

"Vasiliev?" he demanded, a sharp edge entering his voice—a raw, unspoken fear.

"No," Roth replied, shaking his head, "we're not going to broach that just yet. They'll think I'm a dangle, at first. Bringing up Vasiliev can help us work past that, if we play it right. But we can't lead with it."

Litvinov let out a heavy sigh. At least the British weren't being completely stupid here. He could work with this.

Roth reached into an inner pocket of his blazer, extracting a small folder and sliding it across the table.

"What's this?"

"Our story," the British officer responded. "I need you to memorize everything in that folder before we go our separate ways—make sure we're both singing off the same sheet music. It doesn't leave my possession."

Litvinov nodded his understanding, opening the folder as Roth began to speak. "Two nights ago, I approached you on the Tube. . ."

Chapter 13

"You asked me to come in early, Dmitri—to meet with you alone, before our regular morning meetings." Valeriy Kudrin leaned back in his chair, his eyes narrowing as he stared across the cluttered surface of his desk in the office of the *rezident*. "So tell me, what is this all about?"

Litvinov took a deep breath, looking the younger Russian intelligence officer in the eye as he reached into the inner pocket of his suit jacket.

"Three nights ago, I was approached on the Tube. By an officer of the British security services, a man named Darren Roth. He gave me this," he continued, extracting a USB thumb drive and placing it on the desk in front of Kudrin, "as a way of establishing his bona fides."

Kudrin stared at the drive as though a poisonous snake had suddenly appeared in front of him.

"You. . .haven't put this into any computer here at the *rezidentura*, have you?"

Litvinov snorted, shaking his head. "Do you think I was born yesterday, Valeriy Antonovich? This isn't even the same drive I was given. One of our technicians processed it for me at a secure computer off-site last night."

It was true, all of it. At the end of the day, he had no reason to trust Greer and Roth, not enough to believe they wouldn't try to play him. *Use* him to try to further penetrate Russian operations in London.

That was farther than he was willing to go, more than he was willing to risk.

At least not without something more in return.

"He claims to have access to the Security Service's counter-intel branch. There are more than a dozen files on this stick on our influence operations against members of Parliament—*specific* intelligence, everything they know about them, including the officers we've tasked, in some cases. And he claims he can get more. Much more."

"Do you believe him?" The wariness was still there, in Kudrin's eyes. As well it should have been. They were both familiar with this kind of approach—a "dangle", as Roth had referred to it in the pub.

Waiting for a fish to bite.

"In my professional opinion," he began slowly, following through with the script he and Roth had rehearsed, "this kind of intelligence—limited though it is at this moment—is too valuable for the British to jeopardize by such a gambit."

It wasn't even a lie. He'd been shocked by the details of just what Greer was willing to put on the line. But considering the prize. . .

"But there's no way to *know* for certain," Kudrin observed, leaning back in his chair—his fingers tented before him. "Not without continuing to. . .develop him."

He shook his head. "No there isn't. And that's why I'm bringing it to you."

A nod of understanding. "Were you able to ascertain this man's motivations for approaching us—you?"

"He was angry, that much was clear," Litvinov replied, his eyes never leaving the *rezident*'s face. "He wouldn't say why, but I did some digging. He was involved in saving the life of the Queen during the attack on Balmoral this spring—what, exactly, happened is unclear, but he was very nearly sacked for it. He's an embittered man."

There was a long pause, and then Kudrin nodded once more. "Good. Bitterness is something we can use. Run him."

Litvinov rose to his feet, realizing from Kudrin's tone of dismissal that the meeting had come to an end. He was half-way to the door of the office when the *rezident*'s voice arrested him once more, a sudden fear gripping hold of him at the words.

"But have someone else step in to manage him—you're the deputy *rezident*, not some case officer. I can't have you taking this kind of risk."

9:13 A.M.
DGSE Headquarters
Paris, France

". . .based on the intelligence we received from *Commissariat-Général* Kuyper, these materials were found in the internet history of the laptop computer seized in the raid on the Harrak apartment."

Anaïs Brunet leaned back in her chair at the head of the table, hands folded in her lap as the analyst brought the images up on the big screen.

It was a railway bridge, she realized—a high viaduct above a fertile valley. "Where is this?"

"It's the bridge over the Oise River Valley—the LGV Nord line."

The high-speed line between Brussels and Paris. Brunet closed her eyes, forcing herself to take a deep breath. The scope of the envisioned carnage only too clear.

"So this is what they intended to do with the materials acquired from Lahcen," she observed, trading a look with Gauthier.

"It would appear to have at least been the beginnings of a targets list, yes," the analyst replied. "And this would be a difficult one to defend against. Hard to attack, given the pace of traffic on the line—but harder to defend against. Short of posting *gendarmes* on every bridge in the country, setting up cameras. . ."

"Make it public," Brunet announced suddenly, looking up from the notes in front of her.

"What?"

"Let's go public with the plot—headline it on every news program in the country. Let them know what we know. Force them to recalculate—buy us *time*."

"There are risks to that approach, Anaïs," Gauthier cautioned. "What if they believe the information came from one of their own? We could be jeopardizing LYSANDER even further—he's already under suspicion, according to Armand."

"*Everything* comes with risks, Lucien," Brunet retorted, a steely edge in her voice. "The raids have been no secret and even so, they can't pin this on LYSANDER, because he didn't know about this. If he had, he would have told us, *non?*"

10:24 A.M.
Parc de Champagne
Reims, France

It was the eyes, Harry thought. *Not the hands.* It was ever the eyes that signaled the moment your opponent would strike.

He bent forward, shifting his weight easily from one foot to the other. His eyes never leaving Driss' face, the rhythmic sound of the basketball against the pavement—dribbled back and forth between the young Moroccan's hands—drumming in his ears.

There. He saw the flicker in those dark orbs, felt—rather than saw—the hands shift right. *But the eyes said "left."*

He shifted left as Driss moved, the ball a blur as Harry's hand flicked out, making contact with the surface of the spinning orb.

It wasn't a solid strike, just enough to send Driss recoiling back, surprise in the younger man's eyes as he clawed to keep control of the ball, pulling it back and up—snapping off a quick, panicked shot over Harry's head.

It hit the backboard, too hard, caroming off uselessly to one side, a laugh escaping Driss' lips as it fell to the pavement.

"Good one, *habibi*—thought I had you there for a second."

Harry shook his head, bent forward, his hands on his knees—struggling to catch his breath, The pain from his side reawakened by the exertion. *He had to push through this.*

"It's been too long," he replied, smiling through the pain as he straightened—glancing over at the young man. "I haven't played since I was a kid, back in Bonn. I was decent, then, but that's been a long time."

"With your height, I'm sure," Driss observed, stooping to scoop up the ball—holding it up with a challenge in his eyes. "Re-match?"

Another shake of the head, Harry's hand pressed against his side as he retrieved his phone from the back pocket of his jeans, checking the time. "Sorry, brother—another time, maybe. Reza should be here soon. Then we can start sorting out what's happened—who he's heard from, who's been swept up."

"Nothing from Aryn?"

"No," Harry replied. Neither of them mentioned Yassin—an unspoken fear hanging there in the air between them. He'd been wounded, that much they both knew. Since then. . .*nothing*.

That meant that his young friend was either dead or taken–and it was hard to know which of the two he considered preferable.

Dead, most likely. One less life he would himself have to take, at the end of this road.

Or so he kept telling himself.

He knew already how hard that was going to be, he thought—turning away to glance out through the trees surrounding the court as Driss pulled out his own phone, another of the cheap burners they'd bought the previous night.

The dangers surrounding him in this, the farther he went along. The peril of no longer being able to disassociate himself from the role—one life blurring into another until all was lost. Until–

A curse from Driss got his attention and he looked over to see the young man focused on his phone.

"What's going on?" he asked, walking over to peer over his friend's shoulder, seeing a French news headline at the top of the screen. *"Brussels Raids Uncover Train Plot."*

Well that was fast. Some detached part of himself admired the speed at which the Belgian (French?) intelligence services were moving. Barely twenty-four hours from intelligence collection to its dissemination across the media. *Just as he'd hoped.*

"It had to be my laptop," he said slowly, as if just then realizing the truth. "I'd deleted the browser history. . .but they must have found a way to restore it. I wasn't careful enough, may Allah forgive me."

"There was no way you could have known," Driss responded, looking back at him. "No way any of us could have known, have–"

"That's not good enough," Harry spat, his face twisted into a grimace. "We have to *anticipate* them, brother, or we'll all end up in a dark cell somewhere. Our mission *over*. There's no use trying to hit the bridges now—they'll be watching them too closely–we'll have to come up with something else. We–"

His voice broke off suddenly as he saw a familiar figure walking toward them through the trees. *Reza.*

And behind him. . .the form of a woman.

9:38 A.M. British Summer Time
Embassy of the Russian Federation
Kensington Palace Gardens, London

"I'm concerned, Valeriy Antonovich. What you are proposing is reasonable—protocol, even, and yet. . ."

The stacks of paperwork on Dmitri Litvinov's desk were undiminished from his arrival hours before—reports which should have been filed with Moscow an hour before, his official summary of the Roth recruitment still existing as only a blank document on the screen of his computer. A half-eaten beigel seeking refuge beneath a five-page report on drilling in the North Sea.

He ran a hand through the graying stubble of his close-cropped hair, replaying once again his conversation with the *rezident.* Like he'd been doing for hours, ever since the meeting ended. Hoping against hope that he had. . .what was the expression for it here in the West. . ."sold it."

How typical of the West. Of the entire world, these days. Buying and selling. Things. People. *Lies.*

Like he'd sold his very self, so many years before.

Such a contrast to the values he'd once believed in—the common ownership of property, the universal brotherhood of man. Ideals he once would have given his life for.

But there had been no brotherhood. Not then, anymore than now. And the worker was ever the servant of his "betters"–it made no difference whether they wore a business suit or a Party uniform.

It was simply how the world *was.* And now, his very life depended on his abilities as a salesman.

"Roth may be bitter, but he is also wary. He clearly knows the risks of what he's doing. Bringing in another officer to run him at this critical juncture. . .I am concerned that this could break down whatever level of trust I've been able to establish."

"You feel that this could jeopardize the success of the recruitment?"

"Da, I do."

It had been a long moment before Kudrin had responded—an agonizingly lengthy pause as he waited, praying his emotions did not betray themselves on his face.

Then: *"Very well, Dmitri Pavlovich. We'll do this your way—for now."*

Time. It was all he could have asked for—just long enough to get the information the British needed, to prove himself to Greer.

If Kudrin did not suspect him. *If.*

He retrieved the beigel from its hiding place with a deft movement, cramming it into his mouth as he shuffled the papers into order. There was nothing to be done except go about his daily life as he always had. . .somehow.

And await Greer's signal to begin the next phase.

10:42 A.M. Central European Summer Time
Parc de Champagne
Reims, France

"So you've heard nothing from Aryn or Marwan?" Harry asked, resting back on his haunches as he looked up into Reza's eyes—watching as the college student shook his head. "What about Mohammed and the others?"

They'd all been instructed to check in if anything happened—leaving brief messages in the Drafts folder of the e-mail address Harry had set up. No details—just brief, innocuous messages, their first initial in the subject line.

And there had been nothing. It was almost more than he dared hope, and yet. . .he couldn't help but think that nearly half the cell might well have been taken out by the raids.

Thrown into Belgian jail cells on suspicion of terrorism—taken out of circulation, at least for the time being. *Long enough.*

"No," Reza responded, his gaze seeming to shift nervously between Harry and Driss, "not a word. Once I got your message, I left the city immediately."

"Except you didn't," Harry observed pointedly, a low menace in his voice as he rose to his feet—his eyes locking with Reza's, his meaning only too clear. He felt the college student shrink away him, nearly colliding with the veiled figure of the woman sheltering in his shadow. "I'd ask you what you were thinking, but it's all too clear—you weren't. Not with your brain."

"But Ibrahim, I–"

"Our brothers have been scattered to the winds," Harry continued, cutting him off, "Yassin is wounded and missing or *dead*—yet more of the faithful have been thrown into prison, and all you can think of is endangering us all

197

still *more* for the sake of your woman."

Reza flushed hotly, his eyes flashing as his voice rose in angry retort. "I didn't want to leave her to be taken by the police. Tortured for information about *us*. If you think—"

His voice broke off suddenly, as if Harry's words had just sunk in. The color seeming to drain from his swarthy, youthful face, his voice trembling. "Yassin is. . .*dead?*"

"We don't know," Harry responded coldly, glancing from Reza to his woman. "We don't know anything. And now we need to find a place to lay low. . .with a woman."

11:17 A.M. Eastern Daylight Time
CIA Headquarters
Langley, Virginia

". . .they're still eight klicks out from the objective, and Krahling's reporting heavy resistance," the analyst said, looking up from his workstation. "Estimate platoon-strength, maybe more—forty to fifty fighters. The Afghans are taking casualties."

Kranemeyer shook his head, casting a critical glance at the screens mounted on the walls above them, streaming footage from an RQ-4 Global Hawk in orbit high above Afghanistan's Nangarhar Province.

The mission planning had been simple, a fairly straight-forward raid on a compound north of Jalalabad believed to be acting as the headquarters for a regional Khorasan field commander.

American SF acting as advisors to the ANA troops providing the muscle for the operation, Josiah Krahling and another CIA paramilitary tasked with SE—site exploitation. Capture or kill the commander. . .scarf up any and all available intel.

It was as clear-cut as operations in Afghanistan got, over a decade and a half into a war with no endgame yet in sight.

Except it was all going sideways, the DCS thought, like so very many operations before it, the Afghan force bogged down in heavy fighting well short of their objective.

Everything and everyone of value was going to be gone by the time they got to the compound. *If* they got to the compound, he corrected himself, an increasingly dour look spreading across his saturnine countenance.

"I'll be in my office," Kranemeyer said after a moment. "Keep me updated."

The noise of the operations center without faded away as he closed the door of his office, his eyes falling on the framed photograph sitting, as ever, on the edge of his desk. Seven men posed, arms around each other's shoulders, on a ridgeline somewhere in northern Afghanistan, in the early months of the war.

Every face but his was blacked out, but he remembered each one as well as if it were his own. *Brothers.*

He sank into the leather of his desk chair, eyes still on the photograph—memories of those days filling his mind. Things had seemed so. . .simple back then, in the wake of that dark September morning. So *righteous.*

So many years later, it was hard to remember what that had felt like.

The phone on his desk rang just then, breaking in upon his thoughts with its discordant clatter.

"Kranemeyer," he answered shortly, sitting up straighter in his chair as he recognized Coftey's voice on the other end of the line, his face darkening. "This isn't a good time, Roy."

4:23 P.M. Central European Summer Time
Place Poelart
Brussels, Belgium

Ash-gray clouds traversed the heavens above, carrying the threat of rain as Armand Césaire crossed the street, casting a critical glance up at the extensive scaffolding spiderwebbing the facade of the massive building on his left.

As it had for so very many years, he observed ironically. An edifice larger than St. Peter's in Rome, the *Palais de Justice* had been under renovation for nearly as long as this. . ."war on terror" had been going on. So long that, a few years prior, the scaffolding itself had proven to be in need of renovation.

No end in sight, for either the renovation—or the war. And the latter was why he was here.

He waited for a light tan sedan to pass before crossing the street once more, his objective ahead. The familiar sight of the Infantry Memorial, a granite column towering into the afternoon sky, dwarfing the pedestrians passing by—a collection of bronze figures at its base representing the fallen of the Great War, haggard, yet stalwart Belgian infantrymen gathered under the sheltering wings of an angel.

Césaire paused beneath their shadow, looking up into each war-weary visage. Wondering if they could have known that it was all a lie.

That there would be no end to war.

A figure materialized at his side, startling him even though he'd expected it. "So," the young man began, "what was their answer?"

The intelligence officer turned, looking LYSANDER in the face. "You know their answer."

11:26 A.M. Eastern Daylight Time
The Russell Senate Office Building
Washington, D.C.

"Is it ever?" Coftey asked ironically, looking out the window of his office, toward the white dome of the Capitol building, glistening in the noonday sun. "But I'm afraid this can't wait. There's going to be a congressional investigation into the Sinai incident, Barney. Public hearings, on the Hill. Live on C-Span."

He heard an exasperated curse from his old friend and shook his head. "And it gets better. I've seen the subpoena list, just within the last hour. Your name is on it. You're going to be required to testify."

This time there was only silence on the other end of the line, a long, deadly silence. He could almost hear the gears turning in Kranemeyer's head as the man went through his options, considering and rejecting each one of them in turn.

Then, "What can you do about this?"

As expected.

"Not a thing," the senator replied reluctantly, returning to his desk. "I wish I could tell you otherwise."

"This is all coming from HPSCI," he continued, referencing the House Permanent Select Committee on Intelligence, "with Antonio Tamariz leading the charge. He's out for blood, Barney."

He leaned back into his desk chair, conjuring up an image of the Arizona congressman. Short and wiry, with a full head of jet-black hair, as of yet untouched by age. Still in his early forties, and already in politics for over a decade and a half, Tamariz had used his position as HPSCI chairman to run point for the President earlier in the year, driving the intel bill through the House and all the way to the Senate where it had died. . .thanks to Coftey's own change of allegiance.

Except this was Washington, where bad bills never stayed dead. And this one was already back, in no small part thanks to the Agency's blunders in the Sinai.

"You can't reach Tamariz," Kranemeyer said after another long silence. "I know that. But what about his opposite number—the ranking member?"

"Hank Imler?" Coftey shook his head, suppressing a wry laugh. Nothing about this was particularly funny. "If Tony wants to take down the intelligence community, Hank sees this as an equally good chance to take a President he despises and nail him to the wall in front of the whole country. They both want this, if for entirely different reasons. And they're not going to entertain any suggestion of stopping."

"This isn't about politics. It can't be." The exasperation was clear in Kranemeyer's voice, exasperation and barely-repressed fury.

"It is for them." The senator shrugged, only too aware of the stakes. And the fact that his own hands were tied. "It's the people's House, Barney. Don't look for reason in it. Just prepare to go in front of the cameras."

4:31 P.M. Central European Summer Time
Place Poelart
Brussels, Belgium

"That's an easy decision for them," LYSANDER observed, a trace of bitterness in his voice. "They're not having to deal with *him*."

"Al-Almani?" Césaire asked quietly, his eyes never leaving the younger officer's face. Seeing the fire flashing just behind those dark eyes.

A hurried nod. "He's far beyond anything we expected when we initiated this operation. The other members of the cell. . .they're wannabes. Even

Lahcen, whatever else he was, was little more than a criminal using religion as a cover for his own activities. But Al-Almani—he's the real thing. He has *killed* for his faith, in Syria, perhaps elsewhere. You know what he did to Lahcen, and he only *thought* he was a threat. It's something in his eyes, it's just. . ."

"And that's all the more reason we need you to go back under, Daniel," he pressed, the officer's real name sounding strange on his lips. *The roles they all played.* "Because the threat *is* greater than we knew. I need you to do this. Your country needs–"

"But you don't have to face him either, do you?" the younger man spat, fear and anger playing across his features. He was scared, Armand realized. *Very* scared. "It's easy for you to say what needs to be done, just like it is for them—but none of you actually have to *do* it."

"I'm an old man, Daniel," Césaire replied, transfixing his fellow officer with a hard look—his voice losing none of its calm. "Don't allow that to lead you to make the mistake of thinking that I haven't stood exactly where you stand today. We've both risked our lives in the service of a country that had marginalized us, viewed us as something less than citizens of France, each in our own time—in the belief that one day, that would change. That we could, by our sacrifice, *bring* such change. That day has come for my people, and it yet will for yours."

He paused, watching Daniel's face, watching the younger man flush. "Do you really believe that?" he asked finally, recovering himself.

Césaire nodded, summoning up every ounce of conviction in his being. "I do. And you do too—I've seen it in your eyes, heard it in your voice. That last night in Paris. . .why did you tell me you were doing this? Do you remember?"

Daniel seemed to deflate, the anger going out of him in that moment. A nod. "I told you that I was doing this for my son. That I wanted him to one day live in a world—a *France*-where he could be proud of his faith. Where he could hold his head up and tell the world that he was a Muslim without fear. Without *shame*."

"Do you still want that?"

"Of *course,*" came the anguished reply, the look in his eyes haunting Césaire. His conscience reproaching him for having asked the question. For using *this*. And yet, it had been necessary. "More than anything else in this world."

"Then we both know what must be done."

Another slow, reluctant nod. "Is it possible to call my wife? To speak with her, before I make contact with. . .*him*."

To say good-bye, the older man thought, but he only nodded in reply. "Of course."

Chapter 14

6:13 P.M.
Reims, France

It would be hours before the sun set, but the interior of the office building was dark, the beam of the flashlight in Harry's hand pointing upward at the ceiling as he tested yet another door, the knob giving way beneath his hand.

Empty, just like the rest.

These were the corporate offices, he realized—or at least that had been the intention when the building had been first constructed, years before. Constructed, but never occupied—the economic downturn taking its toll.

And now it was left abandoned like so many other buildings across the country, abandoned and already decaying—the province of vagrants and squatters, the myriad homeless of France. People like *them*.

Except this one seemed deserted, he thought, walking out into the open second-floor office area, his flashlight's beam probing toward a worn bedroll tucked in one corner—a few cans of food scattered about. The cans were rusty, dust and cobwebs covering the bedroll.

No one had been here in some time.

He heard a footstep behind him and turned on heel, finding Reza standing there, apparently having followed him up from where he'd left the others on the ground floor.

Their eyes meeting in the semi-darkness, seeing the uncertainty, the unease written across the young man's face.

"She'll be of use to us, brother," he said finally, earnestly, breaking the silence between them. "I *promise* you that. Having a woman will be of value to our mission—the Westerners will never suspect, they will never–"

"Stop talking." There was no emotion in Harry's voice, just a cold, pitiless warning. "You've found a way to justify this to yourself, that's all your words mean. Nothing more. You haven't stopped thinking about her body long enough to seriously ask whether she is with us or against us."

"That's not true, I–"

"Do you even know what it was that caused her to revert to Islam?" Harry asked quietly, watching the confusion in Reza's eyes as he stammered to produce an answer. "You don't, do you? And if you don't even know that. . .how can you *possibly* know whether she has even begun to understand the sacrifices demanded of us by God's struggle?"

"I'm sorry, brother, if you want me to send her back to Brussels, I can put her on a bus. I only wanted–"

Harry shook his head dismissively. "What's done is done. To send her back now would be worse than to never have brought her here at all. There will be a time for her to be tested, as we all must be. But not today. Keep her close to you—ensure that she behaves modestly, that she does not become the cause of jealousy among the brothers. We're going to be staying here a while."

"How long?"

"Until we can move freely once more," Harry replied, turning away from the younger man, his flashlight playing once more around the corners of the expansive room. "Until we learn what's become of the others. Allah knows."

"Do you think Yassin is all right?"

It was a moment before Harry spoke, the shadows playing strangely across his face. Yassin had made contact thirty minutes before, in the Drafts folder of the e-mail account they were all using. Just the same, simple message—no explanation, no detail, nothing for law enforcement to pick up.

But he was alive. *For now.*

"Allah knows," he repeated finally. "If he does as I've instructed, he'll be calling soon. Until then, we can only wait."

6:03 P.M. British Summer Time
A terraced house
Hounslow, West London

". . .Irina sent me a video of Katya this morning—they're on holiday in Baku, and she was building a castle in the sand of the shore. . ."

The signal had been set, Dmitri Litvinov thought, sipping absently at his wine, his food still nearly untouched on his plate. Knowing he should eat, knowing he should be focusing on his wife's words, but unable to do either.

It was a careless mark on the wall of the Tube station—just below waist-level. White chalk. Almost invisible, unless you were looking for it.

And Roth would be. The signal that everything was proceeding according to plan—so far.

He'd found himself checking for a tail in the Underground—convinced somehow that Valeriy would have sent someone to follow him. That–

". . .is everything all right, Dima?" he heard his wife ask, his head coming up suddenly. "You haven't eaten, and you seem to be somewhere else tonight. Are you okay?"

"Of course, of course," he nodded quickly, emptying his glass in a final swallow, his hand trembling noticeably as he replaced it on the table. "Just a rather. . .difficult day at the *rezidentura.* You were saying about Irina–more wine?"

She nodded and he rose, retreating into the kitchen to retrieve the bottle. Letting out a long, shuddering sigh as soon as he was out of sight. *Get hold of yourself.*

How would she take it, if she knew? It was an impossible question, as he was all too well aware. His betrayal had been years behind him when they'd met in the mid-'90s. Him, a rising officer in the newly-minted SVR, her a financial analyst in Russia's burgeoning private sector, a job she still held—remotely, from their home here in London. *A capitalist.*

The embodiment of everything he had hated in the old days—but that hadn't mattered to him, then. Perhaps his embrace of her had in some unconscious sense been a final act of repudiation. Of all which had gone before.

Yet she was a Russian, for all that. Fiercely patriotic, and proud of the

Rodina's rebirth over the last decade. He knew he would have to tell her, at some point.

But something within him feared that moment almost more than he feared Valeriy Kudrin. . .

7:13 P.M. Central European Summer Time
The abandoned office building
Reims, France

"I understand," Harry said, feeling Reza's eyes on him as he went on. "It is good to hear your voice, my brother. We had grown. . .concerned."

But Yassin's voice was strained, Harry realized, subsiding once more into silence as he listened. *Weak.*

A frail shadow of its former self.

Clearly, Driss had been right—his young friend had been shot, there in the park. Injured badly, by the sound of his voice. By the painful subtext there in between his guarded words. It raised questions as to how he had survived at all. How he had *escaped*. . .

Or if he had.

"Of course," he responded finally, glancing at his watch. He would have to move quickly, but what Yassin wanted was possible.

Possible. And preferable to the alternative—leaving him out there, twisting in the wind. Vulnerable, exposed. A danger to them all. To *him*. "You know it, brother. . .I'll come for you. *Insh'allah*, I'll be there soon. *Salaam alaikum.*"

Harry ended the call without another word, turning off the phone and turning it over to remove the back of the case and the battery, his weathered hands moving in quick, efficient motions.

"Is he all right?" he heard Reza blurt out, unable to stand the silence any longer. *Impetuous as ever.*

A shake of the head. "He was injured, as you feared," Harry said, inclining his head toward Driss. "He has found refuge among brothers in Liège, but he needs to leave the city. He wants me to come for him. Tonight, if it is possible. There should still be a bus. . ."

"I'll go with you." There was no mistaking the determination in Reza's voice, but Harry shook his head.

"Together, we would draw attention to ourselves," he responded firmly, his eyes flickering past Reza to where his girlfriend stood, her face shadowed by the glare of the emergency light—her expression impossible to read. "I'll do this myself."

She hadn't said much, over the last few hours, since she and Reza had joined them. He couldn't tell whether it was simply an acceptation of her role—her *place*—as a Muslim woman in the company of fundamentalists. . .or something else.

It would bear watching.

"If anyone is going to go, it should be me," Reza protested, taking a step away from her and toward Harry, into the glare of the light. "I'm his brother."

"As am I," was Harry's quiet reply. "We are all brothers, in the sight of God, we who have pledged our lives to Allah's struggle—and the ties of faith are no less than those of blood. And unlike you, I helped treat casualties on the battlefields of Sham. If his injuries are severe. . ."

"Can we be sure he hasn't been taken?" Driss asked, surprising Harry with his perception. Of course he had thought it, but he hadn't expected. . . "You could be walking into a trap."

Reza swore, his face distorting with sudden rage. "My brother would *never* betray us!"

"We can't be sure," Harry replied, ignoring the outburst, his eyes locked with Driss' across the vacant room. "But it's a risk I will have to take. Because we are brothers."

2:57 P.M. Eastern Daylight Time
Liberty Crossing Intelligence Campus
McLean, Virginia

"Word travels fast," Lawrence Bell observed, a wary glint in the eyes of the Director of National Intelligence as he gestured for Kranemeyer to take a seat. "I only learned of the hearings myself a few minutes before noon. Your secretary's call had come five minutes earlier."

"I have my sources," Kranemeyer replied, taking his seat on the sofa against the wall on the left side—glancing over to where Bell sat behind his desk.

"Domestically?" There was a trace of humor in the DNI's voice, but Kranemeyer didn't join in the laugh. There was nothing funny about the situation they found themselves in. Or the road that had brought them here.

"Mine. Not the Agency's," he replied, favoring Bell with a hard stare. "I keep my ear to the ground."

The older man nodded, a weary look passing across his face. He looked even worse than he had the day of the strike in the Sinai, Kranemeyer thought—the last time the two of them had been in the same room together. "This is a bad business, Barney. We don't have a lot of friends on the Hill these days—particularly not in the House. And those we might have. . .are no friends of the President. They'll go through us to get at him. Without thinking twice. And they now have all the ammunition they need."

Thanks to you. The DNI might never say the words, but Kranemeyer knew he had thought them, the unspoken reproach all too audible in Bell's voice.

And he wasn't wrong. It had been his call, his decision to execute the strike on his own authority, taking advantage of the absence of the DNI.

It had been what the situation required of any leader worthy of the name—the willingness to act, decisively, when lives hung in the balance and time was slipping away.

So he'd acted. And it had been the wrong call, in the end—an incredibly public failure of intelligence the like of which the Agency had rarely known.

And taking responsibility for one's failures was also a part of leadership. *With all that entailed.*

"They're going to find a scapegoat for this mess," Bell continued heavily, clearing his throat as he stared across his desk at Kranemeyer. "Sooner or later. Someone's going to have to take the fall. Do you understand what I'm saying?"

Kranemeyer nodded, a distant memory from his childhood coming unbidden to his mind. An image from a Sunday School lesson, long ago. A priest, placing his hands on the head of a goat, to be led away into the wilderness. *Carrying away the sins of the people.*

As a child, it had seemed silly—an absurd relic of an ancient religion he had never himself believed in. Not even then.

But sitting here now. . .there was no longer anything silly about it.

"I do."

10:57 P.M. Central European Summer Time
The Luxembourg/Belgium Border

The border was a ghost in the night, nothing more than a sign, flickering past in the lights of the Flixbus. The word *Belgique* against a blue field, surrounded by the gold stars of the European Union, arranged in that familiar unbreakable, unending circle. One Europe, together. It was a beautiful dream.

Unity. Fraternity. Brotherhood.

"We are brothers," Harry remembered, gazing out the window of the darkened bus at the Belgian countryside, reflecting on his own words to Reza. Knowing that they had been a lie—that there had been another, far different reason for this journey tonight.

Knowing that before morning, he would need to kill his brother. *Because there was no other way.*

The raids hadn't been enough, hadn't taken out the core of the cell. He had to begin removing pieces from the board, one by one.

Starting with Yassin.

But he saved your life, a voice deep within him whispered, reminding him painfully of the debt. The remnants of his conscience, torn and tattered by the years?

No. For surely his conscience would recognize the *necessity* of this, as ever before.

Yassin was alone, isolated. *Weakened.* There would be no difficulty in eliminating him.

No difficulty. . .except in finding the will to do it, Harry thought, forcing himself to confront his own vulnerability.

He'd been desperately weak when he'd arrived in Brussels in search of shelter, a hiding-place. Raw holes still marking the places where Mehreen's bullets had ripped into his flesh.

And in the weeks of convalescence which had followed, the brothers had nursed him back to health—sharing their home and their table, encouraging him at each step of the way.

It was as close as he had come to family in a very long time, as perverse as that was.

A family he now had to destroy. *If he could.*

And as the bus rolled deeper into the Ardennes, through the sleepy Walloon town of Bastogne, it was a question Harry still had no answer to.

5:09 P.M. Eastern Daylight Time
CIA Headquarters
Langley, Virginia

"I don't think you do, Barney." Kranemeyer leaned back in his chair, attempting to refocus on the post-mission briefing—the video feed coming in from half a world away in Jalalabad—the DNI's words still running through his mind. As they had ever since leaving his office, an hour before. *"This situation can still be managed, if we're careful. They want blood, the higher the better. So? We give them blood."*

". . .but were finally brought to a halt, five klicks out from the target compound, when the ANA force refused to advance further, after suffering heavy casualties." The satellite uplink from Afghanistan was choppy, but Kranemeyer could see the fatigue in Josiah Krahling's eyes as the paramilitary officer continued, "We lost three of them on the way back—couldn't stabilize them in time. The whole force was pretty shot up."

Another failed operation, the DCS thought. But at least this one wasn't going to be ending up on CNN. Some small consolation.

Bell's plan had taken him by surprise—he hadn't thought the long-time Washington bureaucrat had it in him. But life had a way of changing a man. Even near the end.

"In your opinion," Kranemeyer began, lifting his eyes to look into the camera, "could the mission have been accomplished if the ANA forces had chosen to press on to the objective?"

There was a long moment's pause, and then he saw Krahling slowly shake his head. "I don't believe so, no—not with the forces we had at our disposal. The ISIS-K presence was far stronger than we'd been led to believe—we were up against eighty to ninety fighters at one point, minimum."

The gambit Bell was proposing was not without its own risks. To perjure oneself before Congress. . .at one point, he would have considered it unthinkable. *Now?* After last December?

Lying was the least of his sins.

"Thank you," he replied, his eyes never wavering from the camera. "You did good work today, Mr. Krahling. We win some, and we lose some. I look forward to your full report."

2:30 A.M. Central European Summer Time, July 10ᵗʰ
Liège Rue Lairesse Bus Station
Liège, Belgium

Returning to the scene of the crime. That's what it felt like, Harry thought, dismounting the steps of the bus—casting a glance back toward the island of the Outremeuse, just visible in the glow of the streetlights, off in the distance.

The place he had murdered a man, just three days before. And now here he was, again, prepared to commit another murder.

Or at least he thought he was. He crossed the street, his eyes flickering back and forth between the shadows. Only too aware of just how exposed he'd been, getting off the bus. One of only four passengers.

If Driss was right—if it was a trap—they could have been waiting. Watching for him.

But he'd seen no one, and he struggled to credit Lahcen's organization with the ability to pull off surveillance on the level it would take for him to be unable to detect it.

The Belgian security services? The French? They were another question entirely, and he forced himself to slow as he made his way down the street, past darkened storefronts. *Look casual.*

He had four and a half miles to cover before arriving at the address Yassin had given him—there had been another bus station, closer, but he'd rejected it as too obvious. Too likely to be watched.

But if they had the resources of the VSSE or the DGSE. . .anything was on the table. The risks, far too difficult to calculate.

Harry caught a glimpse of his reflection in the plate glass of a store window, a haggard, bearded face, eyes staring out from deep, shadowed sockets.

What are you doing here? They seemed to ask. Another question he had no answer for.

Fate.

3:05 A.M.
An apartment
Paris, France

It was happening. Anaïs Brunet lay back against the pillow, the sheets pushed away from her body—staring up into the rhythmically revolving blades of the ceiling fan above her head, stirring the humid air of the apartment.

She hadn't been able to sleep at all, and it had little to do with the onset of the summer heat. Armand's last message, still weighing heavily on her mind.

He'd done it. All the skills that had made him one of the DGSE's most successful case officers over the years, used to convince LYSANDER to go back under. After the younger officer placed one more call to his wife. His young son.

One final call, was the way Césaire had put it in his report, the reproach clearly audible even in the written words. His opinion of her handling of this operation, still clearly unchanged.

She'd read his file prior to this operation—knew he had lost assets before. One in particular, back during the collapse of Zaire in the mid-'90s, a highly-placed Tutsi lieutenant of Laurent-Désiré Kabila. He had provided the French with intelligence from within the burgeoning civil war for five months—up until the day Césaire had gone to the regular dead drop to find the man's severed head there, staring sightlessly back at him.

And now, this was no ordinary asset, but a fellow intelligence officer. The stakes, that much higher. The cost of failure, so much the greater.

Brunet swore softly under her breath, cursing the sleep that would not come. If everything had proceeded on schedule, LYSANDER would have already made contact.

By morning, perhaps sooner, he'd be face-to-face once more with Ibrahim Abu Musab al-Almani. Back on the inside.

Their operation, underway once again. For better or worse. . .

4:19 A.M.
Liège, Belgium

There was nothing to be learned from without. Harry had come to that conclusion over the course of an hour of examining the Liège apartment building from the outside.

It was ten stories tall, stark and modern, just another faceless one in a long row of such structures, stretching on down the street, looming dark against the night—a scattered light visible here and there, as though the inhabitants were waking.

"Did Yassin have friends in Liège?" he'd asked Reza, just before parting. *"People he could seek out in an emergency?"*

There had been a long, reflective pause before the kid shook his head. *"Not that I know of."*

All of which increased the likelihood that this was some kind of trap, Harry thought, making his way across the street toward the main access door—one he'd already seen several people use during his time of surveillance.

But he was committed now. Yassin was a loose end—he couldn't afford to leave him out here.

Not alive.

The door gave noiselessly under his hand and he was inside, his eyes re-adjusting to the low light as he glanced up and down the corridors—finding his way to the stairs.

Six stories up. He worked his way up, pausing at each landing to look. *Listen.* Nerves alert for any sign of danger, any hint that an ambush lay ahead.

But there was nothing out of the ordinary—just the usual sounds of a tower slowly waking to greet the morn.

It reminded him of the tower block in Leeds that night with Mehreen. Looking for her nephew.

A quest that had gone. . .*badly*, ending with a pair of broken bodies lying crumpled in the gravel of an empty lot. *Shots ringing out through the dawn.*

A good man, and a messed-up kid, caught up in events far beyond their control. Both of them, dead.

His failure.

But there was no time to dwell on the past, not now—the rasping sound

214

of a door opening coming from above as he rounded the landing to the final flight of stairs, his breath quickening at the noise.

He palmed the switchblade in his left hand, its blade extended back along the underside of his forearm as he mounted the stairs, head down–his pace slow, unhurried.

A figure, descending the stairs toward him. A brief glimpse of a man's face in the semi-darkness.

Young, swarthy—Middle Eastern or North African, by the look of him. *Familiar.* One of Lahcen's men in the park, Harry realized suddenly—every fiber of his body coming alive, alert to the presence of danger. *If he had been recognized. . .*

Another moment, another three steps further up and he heard it—a voice raised in sudden challenge. "Hold up there."

He kept moving, the same stolid pace—his face now fully obscured in shadow. Hearing the young man begin to re-ascend the stairs behind him, repeating the challenge in first French and then Arabic—punctuating the words with an aggravated curse.

He knew that he had been betrayed, that Yassin had—somehow–been forced to give him up, but there was no time to think of that. Not now.

His grip tightening on the knife—gauging the man's approach by sound, by feel. *Just a few more steps.*

4:26 A.M.
Clinique St. Jean
Boulevard du Jardin Botanique
Brussels

The hospital room was quiet—the only sounds that familiar, insistent beep of the heartbeat monitor, seeming to falter now and again, the murmur of nurses' voices in the corridor without.

The form of the woman in the bed, deathly still, her eyes closed in the semi-darkness—the glow of the monitors reflecting strangely off her jaundiced, sickly skin.

Her breathing, increasingly shallow.

I'll see you Tuesday nite, right? The young police officer's thumbs flew over his phone's keyboard. *Drinks after I get off?*

He pressed Send, letting the phone rest on his knee as he looked up from his seat in the corner, scanning the dark room once more. Just another hour and he'd be relieved—another officer coming in to take his place. Another tiresome night of this duty, over.

His superiors had been sure that this woman's son—the wannabe terrorist they seemed to believe was out there–would try to come see her, one final time before the end.

After two nights, he wasn't so sure.

His phone buzzed with an incoming text and he opened it to see his girlfriend's reply—his thumb scrolling down the screen.

And then he heard it, a sudden chill gripping his heart—the monitor's beep replaced by a loud, flat tone.

The phone fell from his hands to crash against the floor of the hospital room as he raced to the bed, calling out for the nurse.

But it was already too late. *Far too late.*

4:27 A.M.
The apartment buildings
Liège, Belgium

"Can't you hear me, you idiot? I asked you–"

Harry felt the young man's hand descend roughly on his shoulder, his left arm suddenly whipping out and back, all its force behind the blade of the knife as it plunged into the man's ribs, going in deep—puncturing a lung.

In. A wild scream echoing off the hollow confines of the stairwell. An anguished, animal sound.

And back out, the blade ripping through reluctant flesh and muscle as Harry tore it from the Algerian's body, bringing it up and across his throat in a single, smooth motion—blood spraying over Harry's shirt as he pushed his opponent back against the railing.

Bending him back over the rail, his knife hand entwined in the bloody collar of the man's shirt, groping for the gun in his waistband.

There was fear in his eyes—a desperate, panicked strength filling his weakening body as he pushed back against Harry, trying to throw him off—

regain the upper hand. But he was already off-balance, his fate. . .already sealed.

Harry's fingers closed around the grip of the small semiautomatic, pulling it from the man's waistband even as he released his grip on his collar.

A strange gurgling cry escaped from the man's slashed throat as he toppled backward over the railing, hurtling six stories down through the darkness to smash against the concrete floor below.

Harry heard the impact, only then letting out the breath he'd been holding ever since the fight had begun. . .what, sixty seconds before? *Even that?*

He didn't think so. He looked down at the blood on his hands, struggling to catch his breath as he folded the knife back in on itself and replaced it in a pocket of his jeans. There wasn't much time. If the alarm was raised. . .

Harry brought the compact CZ up in his hand, quickly brass-checking the chamber in the dim light. *Loaded.*

One in the chamber, another nine in the mag. Little enough, he mused, manually cocking the hammer.

A few more steps upward, and he was on the sixth floor landing, pausing only briefly before moving out into the corridor—covering the distance to the apartment door in a handful of strides, the pistol tucked just out of sight, against the back of his leg.

He glanced briefly up and down the corridor before knocking, a hard, insistent rap.

"Hakim, is that you?" he heard a voice in French ask from within. A young man's voice, by the sound of it—perhaps the age of the man he had just killed in the stairwell.

"*Certainement*," he replied, standing well back and to the side—out of the line of the door's peephole. "Don't keep me standing out here."

A rattle of a chain being undone, and the door slid open—revealing a swarthy face silhouetted against the room light. Surprise filling its features. "You're not–"

They were the last words to leave his mouth, the door slamming into him as Harry's foot lashed out, connecting with the thin plywood—sending him staggering back against the wall.

He hardly had time to react before Harry was on him—wrapping an arm around his throat and pulling him back into his chest. The muzzle of the CZ grinding into his temple, even as another man emerged from the back, a pistol carried loosely in his hand, his eyes widening at the sight of Harry.

"Drop the weapon," Harry ordered brusquely, his finger caressing the CZ's trigger. "Or I put a bullet in your friend's head. *Do it now.*"

"Ibrahim!" he heard Yassin call out—turning his head to see his young friend standing in the open doorway of the apartment's kitchen, a rough, bloody bandage wrapped around his mid-section, just visible beneath his open shirt. "Don't do this, brother—they're on our side."

They'd gotten to him. But there was no time to reconcile himself to that, not now. He had to extricate them both from this, before it was too late.

"Then why," Harry began, his words coming out from between clenched teeth, returning his focus to the man with the gun, "was their *boss* wearing a wire? Why did they use you to lure me here? Put down the gun!"

"Go ahead," he replied, looking him in the eye. Still holding the pistol. "Kill him. He will die in the cause of Allah, as must we all."

He wasn't bluffing, Harry thought, reading cold resolution in the set of the man's face. Hearing Yassin's voice, pleading with him, "They're with us, brother. Just lower your weapon. We can talk this out."

"I don't know what they've told you," he replied, rounding once more on Yassin, "or what you've chosen to believe. But I know what I saw. And I–"

He heard it, just a second too late, a footstep on the thin carpet behind him. Started to turn, to bring his weapon to bear.

The next moment, something heavy crashed into the side of Harry's head and everything went black. . .

Chapter 15

11:37 A.M.
Commissariat Wallonie Liège
Liège, Belgium

"It's not him," Anaïs Brunet announced finally, a long, shuddering sigh escaping her lips as she stared down at the naked body lying there on the cold slab before them—the corpse's flesh deathly pale in the bright lights of the police station's mortuarium, the back of his skull caved in by the impact.

He'd fallen more than fifty feet to smash against the concrete floor, according to the police report. But he'd been dying well before the fall, as the long, ragged gash across his throat bore witness—the stab wound to his chest.

So familiar.

"Do you have any idea who he is?" a voice asked, and Brunet glanced up into the eyes of Christian Danloy, the administrator general of the Belgian State Security Service, the VSSE.

"No," she replied, looking her counterpart in the eye, "but he's not our asset. And that's what matters."

"To you," Danloy acknowledged grudgingly, issuing a brusque command to the Liège police officer standing nearby as they both turned away from the body, with him falling in step behind her as they made their way back to the elevator. "We still have an unexplained murder to solve. And even more questions that need answering. At precisely what point, Anaïs, were you planning to read in my service on your operation here in this country?"

"We weren't," she responded bluntly, turning to face him as they entered

219

the elevator together. Deciding that, in Danloy's case, honesty was the only viable approach.

He would have seen through anything else.

Danloy shook his head, a flash of anger passing across the Walloon's bluff countenance. He was a big man, only a couple years her senior, but a career intelligence officer. They'd worked together closely more than once over the years, but he'd never lost his skepticism of her. Danloy, Dubois. . .it was the theme of her career.

"It was an operational decision, Christian," she replied, ignoring his anger. "We've kept the circle of knowledge on this exceedingly small. Fewer than fifty people, total, between my service and the CIA."

Danloy swore, shaking his head once more in disbelief. "The *Americans?*"

"They're funding the operation," Brunet returned coolly, watching him subside. They both knew how that worked. "Through Alliance Base, as part of the ongoing fight against the Islamic State."

"And you believe that both this murder and that of Lahcen were committed by this German you're tracking? Ibrahim Abu Musab al-Almani?"

"That's why I'm here." Why the news of the murder had precipitated her early morning flight out of De Gaulle. It had been time to read the Belgians in—*past* time, Vukovic likely right in his misgivings from the start. That the corpse hadn't proved to be their asset after all, didn't really matter. This was a conversation that needed to happen, face-to-face. "The style of the killing is almost identical, and the apartment building where that. . .young man was found lies only a few miles from the Outremeuse. Our asset had been set to re-establish contact with al-Almani overnight. When word came of this killing. . ."

"But of course," the VSSE head replied, nodding his understanding. He reached out, holding the elevator doors closed a moment longer. "Tell me, Anaïs—do you have any pictures of this 'ringleader' of yours?"

"No, we do not—not as of yet."

"That seems unusual."

There was something there in his voice—something beyond his usual skepticism. "You don't believe me?"

Danloy shrugged. "Last night I wouldn't have believed that the DGSE would run an operation on our soil without apprising us of it. So now—I don't know just what to believe. Why don't you tell me, Anais? What am I to believe? Or perhaps better, let me tell you what is going to happen. You're going to give my service full access to your files on this operation, with your officers coordinating their activities with mine—or else I will bring pressure to bear to have it shuttered. Permanently."

11:52 A.M.
An unknown location

Footsteps against the floor. The low murmur of voices, somewhere. Out there. Coming toward him.

Harry shifted his weight as he lay there on his back, wincing as the concrete bit into the flesh of his wrists, bound beneath him. He had no idea how long he had been here—darkness enfolding him, the rough fabric of the hood clinging close to his face—but he hadn't been moved since he'd come to.

Hadn't heard any voices, till now.

It was a large room by the echo of the voices, he thought, struggling to process—to analyze his surroundings. Large room—concrete floor. *A warehouse?* Perhaps one Lahcen had used to conduct his illicit trade.

Hard to tell.

His head was still pounding from the force of the blow that had been delivered hours before—felt as though it could split open at the slightest impact. The smell of urine filling his nostrils.

"I seek refuge in Allah," he whispered, his mouth dry and pasty, "from the outcast Satan. They plan, and God plans–"

"Shut up," he heard a voice respond, punctuating the words with a curse. Rough hands, more than one pair of them, grabbing him by the shoulders and heaving him to his feet. He felt the concrete scrape painfully against his bare feet as he was dragged across the floor, gritting his teeth to keep from crying out.

And surely God is the best of planners, Harry murmured, repeating the words of the *sura* to himself as he was thrust suddenly into a chair. Seeking strength for all that was to come. The role that he was committed to. *Play the part.*

And then the hood was ripped away. . .

11:07 A.M. British Summer Time
Thames House
Millbank, London

"All right then," Phillip Greer nodded, turning away from the young woman at his side as they reached the door of his office. "Did he elaborate on the nature of the compromise?"

"No, not yet."

Could be any number of things, Greer thought. A politician's peccadilloes knew few limits. Some took longer to catch up with them than others.

"See what else he's willing to give you—what he wants for it. And, Dara, do your best to validate everything you can. This may require us to pay a visit to our friend in Parliament, inform her that she needs to clean her house. If we take that step, we must be certain."

"Of course, sir." His officer nodded, a certain note of surprise in her voice that he'd even felt the need to say it. Asset validation was elementary in this business, and Dara wasn't a novice at her trade.

He didn't know why he'd said it either, he realized, watching her back as she disappeared down the hallway. Stress, most likely. There was so much at stake just now—things were still so fragile in the UK, following the attack on the Queen, the collapse of the government which had followed.

The last thing they needed was another compromised politician in White Hall. Particularly one who had been an ally.

His secretary looked up at his entry, inclining her head toward the figure of Darren Roth, occupying a chair not far from her desk in the outer office. "Mr. Roth is here to see you, sir, as per your schedule."

"Of course." Greer forced a smile to his face, reaching out to grasp Roth's hand. "I regret making you wait, Darren. My office?"

Not another word was said until the door of the inner office had closed behind them—until Greer had rounded the back of his desk, gesturing for Roth to take a seat in front of him.

"It's on for tonight?"

A nod. "I left the signal—he'll know to take it from there."

There was something uneasy in Roth's demeanor, Greer noticed, watching him closely. Something troubling him.

"Are you sure it's wise to move this quickly?" the younger officer asked finally, meeting his gaze.

Greer shook his head. "I'm sure we don't have another choice."

12:47 P.M. Central European Summer Time
An unknown location

Pain. Shooting like liquid fire through his veins as the cosh slammed once more into his naked body, ripping a tortured scream from his lips as the chair rocked, nearly tipping over and taking him with it.

Unendurable pain never lasts, Harry thought, gasping through the pain—the words of some ancient maxim filtering unbidden through his mind. *If it lasts, it can be endured.* He wondered if the philosopher had ever known torture. . .

It was strange, the absurdities that occurred to a man in extremis—the mind seeking some desperate refuge from a body pushed past its very limits. Had Hashim Rahman known such thoughts, he wondered absently, remembering how he'd tortured Rahman in Leeds—seeking information, seeking *truth*—dealing out the brutality which had once been dealt to him.

And now here he was again, the bloody cycle repeating—feeding on itself. *Consuming*, both the perpetrator and the victim.

Another blow slammed into his ribs, reawakening the fire once more, and this time he felt strong hands descend on his bare shoulders, anchoring him in place. *An unwelcome salvation.*

"Who was your field commander in Syria?" he heard a man's voice demand—fingers sinking deep into his matted black hair, jerking his head back and up.

Harry stared into the man's eyes—dark and black, boring into his own, set in an angular, bearded face. His own age, perhaps slightly older—a harsh, cruel visage.

"Abu Omar al-Shishani," he whispered, a bloody froth moistening his lips. Struggling to process the questions through the pain—knowing that his life depended on these answers.

"Abu Omar is dead," another of his interrogators spat, moving into his line of vision from the right. "Who was your unit leader?"

"Tariq ibn Hamza al-Libi."

He sensed the men exchange glances. "Tariq ibn Hamza is dead. Is everyone you fought beside in Syria dead?"

"Many of them," Harry replied, every word coming out with an effort—his eyes locked with his principal interrogator. "Many of the brothers died in the land of Sham. Many more, scattered to the winds. In Allah's struggle. Had more answered the call of jihad, perhaps their deaths would not have been necessary."

It was a deliberate provocation, but the accusation was a natural one. Exactly what al-Almani would have said, if he'd been real.

And that was itself a dangerous thought, he realized, reeling as one of the men backhanded him across the face, a rough slap that echoed across the empty void of the warehouse. *Al-Almani needed to* be *real*. To himself, most of all—the man he once had been, buried. Deep within.

"Can't you see?" he heard Yassin ask, somewhere behind him—his body coming alert at the voice. He hadn't known the kid was in the room. "He's one of us, just as I told you. He is *committed* to the cause."

"If so, why did he kill Lahcen?"

Harry lifted his head once again, forcing himself to look the man in the eye. "The man was a spy, as I told you once before. I saw the wire."

"He wasn't," a new voice announced from behind him—another man walking into his line of vision. Older than the rest of Harry's captors, a touch of silver in his beard. There was an aura of authority about him, visible in the way the other interrogators took a step back, deferring to him. *Here was the power in this room.* The power of life and death. "Said was many things, but he was not a traitor. We would have known—he would not have been able to hide it from us. He was not a subtle man."

There was no hubris in the statement, just a quiet confidence. Harry just sat there in silence, looking at the man—blood trickling down his cheek from a cut just below his left eye.

"My son Ismail was in Syria," the older man continued after a long moment, reaching into the pocket of his trousers—retrieving a small photo from an inner sleeve of his wallet. "He died fighting among the *mujahideen* of Tariq ibn Hamza. Perhaps you would remember him?"

1:02 P.M.
A Dassault Falcon 50
Over northern France

"Danloy isn't going to be bought off with partial disclosure," Anaïs Brunet replied, a flush of anger coloring her cheeks as she leaned forward in her seat, taking a sip of her Perrier. "Not now. Not with his blood up this way—we're going to have to give him everything, or very nearly."

She swore softly to herself, glancing out the window of the business jet. White cirrus clouds surrounding them at this altitude, wisps of cotton against the sun. "This is why I was concerned about reading the Belgians in from the very beginning—we're now going to have a third agency with nearly unfettered access, and we can't control who Danloy briefs on it."

"And this is why I counseled reading them in from the beginning, Anaïs," Vukovic's voice responded over the secure commlink. "I know Christian—if I had approached him at the outset–"

"What's done is done, Daniel," Brunet responded sharply. She had enough of her own recriminations without listening to his. "There's no profit in revisiting the decisions of the past. There were reasons for them, but now we must adjust—find a way to deal with our new reality."

"Which means reading in the Belgians," Gauthier observed, rejoining the discussion.

"*Oui.* Or else President Albéric will be receiving a call from Brussels." She hesitated, weighing the realities of their situation once again. Then, "Have a copy prepared, Lucien, of everything LYSANDER has given us over the course of the operation to date. Redact anything which could be used to identify our officer. Once I've reviewed the file, we will send it to Brussels via courier. For Danloy's eyes only."

1:03 P.M.
The warehouse

It was a youthful face that stared back at Harry from the photograph—a dark-haired young man in his early twenties, tall and lean—struggling to grow a beard. Just the right age to have fallen victim to the siren call of the caliphate. *And he was dead.*

There could be no danger that a dead man could contradict whatever story he chose to tell, and yet. . .

There was something wrong. A sudden awareness of his danger filtering through to him past the throbbing pain consuming his body.

It was too easy.

Harry kept his eyes focused on the photo for a moment more, as if endeavoring to memorize the face. Then, lifting his face to look the older man in the eye, "No, I would remember his face if he had. He did not fight with us."

Out of the corner of his eye, he saw one of the interrogators move in, the cosh already drawn back—his battered body bracing for the blow.

But the older man's hand was raised in a restraining gesture, a curious smile playing across his features. He gestured to the man with the cosh. "Untie him, and get him some water. He's telling the truth, this one."

Harry held the man's gaze until the interrogator forced him to lean forward—sawing through the ropes with a long knife—keeping the relief from his face with a mighty effort. His instincts had saved him, once again.

For now.

"A man intent on deceiving us," the older man began once more as Harry's wrists came free, "would have seen claiming my dead son as his dearest comrade as his surest path of salvation. And I would have known he was lying, for my son did not die in Syria. He died here, in a motorway accident outside Lille five years ago."

"I am sorry," Harry said, his voice hoarse—rubbing his raw wrists in an effort to restore circulation. Every inch of his body throbbed with pain, the beating leaving him bruised and bloody—reawakening old wounds.

The older man shook his head dismissively. "Don't be. He was a sorrow to me while he was alive."

Contempt was the only emotion in the man's voice when he spoke of his son—cold and remorseless.

He smiled, reaching out a hand to lift Harry from the blood-spattered chair—wrapping his other arm around Harry's shoulders to steady him, drawing him into a warm, almost gentle, embrace. The man's lips, only inches from his ear. "*Salaam alaikum*, my brother. You may call me Gamal. Gamal Belkaïd."

8:04 A.M. Eastern Daylight Time
The Old Ebbitt Grill
Washington, D.C.

". . .if you could bring it up in conversation with the Minority Leader, it would be. . .most appreciated." An expression of unusual earnestness crept over the lobbyist's florid countenance. "It is very, very important that this passes the House, Ian."

"Of course it is, Robert," Ian Cahill responded, struggling to keep the boredom out of his voice as he picked at his omelet—skewering a stray bit of andouille sausage with his fork.

Everything in this town was "very important." Everyone consumed with their own petty little agendas. Each of them, more important than the last.

Cahill tuned out the lobbyist's soft, importunate, almost whining voice with an effort—nodding as though he were still listening as he set about cleaning up the remnants of his omelet with a diligence that spoke of his own humble beginnings.

He'd known what it was not to have all this—once.

Now people came to him, not because he had a vote, but because he had something far more important. The ear of the people with the votes.

Power.

And yet, when it truly *mattered*. . .he was powerless, he thought, still reflecting on his dilemma with Melody Lawlor. More particularly, with what she had overheard. There had to be a way to get to the bottom of it. To find out the truth.

He might have even thought she'd imagined it all—he'd always been plagued by doubts about her reliability as a source—if not for his own meeting in Fado's, just a few nights before. There had been fear in the woman's eyes as she listened to what he had to say, and that told him much.

She had served in some of the world's worst places, if even half of what was said about her was true—wasn't the type of woman to scare easily.

Which meant that Melody's story was far more. . .*plausible*, at the very least, than he ever would have wanted to believe.

Now he just had to figure out what to do about it.

2:21 P.M. Central European Summer Time
The warehouse
Liège, Belgium

"You ask how I can be so sure that Said did not betray us," Gamal Belkaïd observed, turning back toward the rude wooden table that sat in the middle of the warehouse's small office.

He set a mug of steaming hot tea down in front of Harry, returning to the seat across from him—his long fingers delicately cupping a second mug as he lifted it to his lips, his visage briefly obscured by the rising steam. "How I can be sure, for example, that you are not, even now, a plant of a Western security service?"

Harry remained silent, drawing the man out, feeling pain shoot through his body once more as he took a sip of the tea—his tortured body had been cleaned and bandaged after he had been released from the chair, fresh, if ill-fitting clothes had been given to him, but it was going to take a few days for the bruises to fade. *Perhaps longer.*

"Are you not even curious?"

A shake of the head. "Allah preserves me here, as He did in Sham. I take no other protectors to myself—I would not be of those who build for themselves the house of the spider."

Gamal smiled, clearly recognizing the Qur'anic reference. "You are a bold man, Ibrahim. I like that about you. But I will tell you, anyway."

He set his cup aside, the smile unwavering as he looked at Harry across the wooden table. "I am a businessman, to speak of my affairs as I see them. A criminal, to describe myself through the eyes of others. Some men try to bring down the West with guns and bombs. I do so through women. Drugs. Anything else a decadent society requires and men will pay a premium for. Selling them the rope to hang themselves, as I believe is the Western idiom. And when I am able, I help the men with guns and bombs."

His eyes narrowed, watching Harry's face for any signs of a reaction. "You do not approve?"

It was an old line, Harry thought, holding the man's gaze steadily. The Taliban had used a similar rationale for their own opium trafficking during his years in Afghanistan—in those rare moments when any of them had bothered with a rationale. Trafficking that had done much to alienate the conservative Muslim populace they worked amongst. A smarter counter-insurgency strategy might have been able to exploit the fissures there, if only they had been understood. *If.* . .

"It's war," he replied finally, shrugging his shoulders. "There are many things we do which would be *haram* in normal times. To normal men. But we do not live in normal times, you and I."

The older man laughed, a harsh laugh with an edge of steel in it. "Nor are we normal men."

2:31 P.M.
Alliance Base
Paris, France

This was a mistake, Anaïs Brunet realized, staring down at the folder spread out on the desk before her. The details of LYSANDER's mission, laid out in cold, sterile text. *Black and white.*

Seeing, in her mind's eye, the man behind the words. The young officer they had sent into harm's way—had asked to return, even against his better judgment.

And now they were endangering him once again. But her hand was being forced.

She shook her head, closing the folder. There was nothing black and white about this world. Nothing clear.

Only deals one made with oneself—trading off one interest against another. Hoping against hope that you'd made the right call.

Trying to learn to live with yourself, even when you hadn't.

Brunet took a deep breath, reaching for her pen. The cover page, awaiting her signature, staring back at her like a warrant of death.

Another moment, and she scrawled her signature across the sheet with a brusque motion, taking the folder and handing it off to the waiting courier.

"See that this gets to Brussels. Before nightfall."

2:33 P.M.
The warehouse
Liège, Belgium

Gamal paused, taking another sip of his tea before going on—a wary light entering Harry's eyes as he realized the man was getting to his point.

"And as a businessman, I. . .'employ' people to keep me informed of all that might concern my business. One of those men is a functionary in the security services of this country, the VSSE. And he knew nothing at all of Lahcen."

Harry shook his head. "That means little—I'm sure the French take an interest in the affairs of the faithful in this country, after the blows our brothers have struck in the last few years. He could as easily have been an asset for the DGSE."

"And the same could be said for you," Gamal returned sharply, his eyes locking with Harry's for a brief moment before he started laughing again, that same, harsh sound. "But if it were true, you wouldn't have ventured to say it. As for Lahcen. . .he was a man of expensive tastes. If he had been receiving money from a Western service, he would not have been able to conceal it from us. He lacked. . .self-control, much like my son. So I do not weep for either of them."

Gamal paused, running a hand over the scruff of his trimmed, greying beard. A shrewd look passing across the older man's face. "You, on the other hand—you sought weapons from Said, yes? To carry out an attack?"

Harry inclined his head in an almost imperceptible nod.

"I may be able to help, if you can help me. But first," the older man drew a small mobile phone from his pocket and slid it across the table to Harry, "call your people. Assure them that you're all right. Tell them we should join our forces."

All right? That hardly seemed an accurate way to describe his bruised and battered body. He just sat there, looking from him to the phone and back again. Gamal laughed. "You still do not trust me, do you? I've had the number for days—Yassin gave it to us—but it would be better if it came from you. They are your men, after all."

And a woman, Harry thought but didn't say, reaching slowly for the phone and dialing the number from memory.

Wincing in pain as he lifted it to his ear. Waiting as it rang—one, twice, three times. And then a voice answered—so familiar, but so unexpected.

Marwan.

Chapter 16

4:17 P.M. British Summer Time
Embassy of the Russian Federation
Kensington Palace Gardens, London

There was a long silence after Dmitri Litvinov took his seat in the *rezident*'s office, across from Kudrin's massive desk. Waiting as the *rezident* finished up the last of his paperwork. The summer heat palpable even in the air conditioning of the *rezidentura*.

Climate control. It would have been a luxury in the old days, back in Russia. Perhaps the capitalists had something to offer, after all. *But was it worth the cost?* That was the question he couldn't answer, even after all these years.

At length, Kudrin closed the folder—setting his pen aside as he looked up. "My apologies, Dmitri Pavlovich. I regret detaining you—I know you must want to get home. But Moscow is very pleased—they've validated the intelligence your new asset has provided, and they want us to continue cultivating him, as we had planned. See where it leads."

"Good," Litvinov responded, suppressing a laugh which would have been ill-advised. Leave it to Kudrin to make a premature report to the Centre in the endeavor to take the credit for an intelligence coup. "Because I have another meeting with him—tonight."

The insincere smile vanished from the *rezident*'s face, replaced by a look of concern. "So soon?"

A shrug. "I thought the same thing, but he left the signal this morning. He will, no doubt, make contact with me on the Tube."

"Do you think it could be a trap?" The concern was more genuine than the smile, Litvinov thought—the *resident* clearly now wondering if he had overreached himself. "If you are arrested in the act of receiving classified documents, you could be deported."

Litvinov shook his head. "What would the British gain from such an action? I am a functionary, Valeriy, we both know that. If they declare me *persona non grata*, Moscow has a hundred more to take my place. A thousand? We must remain wary, of course, but the intelligence value of what we have already received. . .it would not be risked in such a gambit."

"*Da*," Kudrin assented after thinking it over for a moment. "You are right, no doubt. Do you desire security for tonight's meeting—a couple men from here at the *rezidentura* to shadow you, make sure the British do not have their own watchers?"

It was a loaded question, and Litvinov knew it. But that was the reality of being a double agent—a perilous course, and one which often relied upon one being as "open" with both sides as possible. Dispelling suspicion with honesty, or the closest counterfeit of it possible. Allowing people to interpret what they saw, through a lens of your own design.

"Of course, as long as they can be discreet. The back-up would be welcome."

5:44 P.M. Central European Summer Time
A flat
Liège, Belgium

Harry stared down into the water pooling and eddying between his feet as it circled the drain—dark, rust-brown water stained with blood. The hot water pulsating into his naked, tortured back, a raw, indescribable sensation somewhere between pleasure and torture.

But he stayed under its hard, insistent stream, feeling it wash away the blood of the morning's beatings, cleansing the fresh scars.

Scars. His body was covered with them—the physical evidence of mistakes of the past. Moments when he'd. . .*miscalculated.*

Like he had the previous night.

Belkaïd would have found them anyway, of that he was now certain—

Yassin's cooperation had made that a foregone conclusion, but he should never have come for the kid. Risked everything to. . .*what*—save him? *Kill him?*

Looking back, his actions didn't make sense. Even to him. He'd been running on little save emotion since Vegas—a dangerous mental state for an operator—and if he couldn't get it under control, it was going to be the death of him. *If he was lucky.*

If he wasn't, it would involve far more than just his own death.

He wasn't alone, even now, as he leaned back against the wall of the shower stall—water beating down upon his upturned face and chest. Three of Belkaïd's men had taken him from the warehouse to this apartment. . .somewhere, he'd been hooded for the trip—fresh proof that the Algerian wasn't ready to trust him, not yet, all his talk of cooperation aside.

Belkaïd was a dangerous man, of that much Harry was certain—but he'd met a lot of dangerous men over the years, and he'd been able to get a fairly solid read of the Algerian in the course of those moments together in the warehouse.

There was more to his claim of being a businessman than one might think, strange as it had sounded coming from his lips.

He was devout enough to have despised a son who strayed from the path, but the business would come before the jihad. *Always.*

It didn't mean he was any less of a threat, but the threat he presented was different than that posed by the young men of the Molenbeek cell.

By. . .*Marwan*, Harry thought, remembering the shock of hearing his voice once more on the other end of the line. Their exchange had been necessarily guarded, over the open line, but the young man was clearly back in circulation.

He'd hoped against hope that he had been swept up in the raids.

Maybe he was, a dark voice suggested from somewhere deep within as Harry pushed himself away from the wall, reaching forward to shut off the water.

Swept up and turned, laying a trap for them all.

No. He might have believed it of Yassin, but Marwan was too far gone—a "true believer", in every sense of the word.

And he would have to be dealt with, sooner or later.

Harry stepped from the shower, catching a glimpse of his battered body in the mirror as he wrapped a towel around his torso, biting back a cry of pain as the cloth pressed against the raw flesh. Running a hand through his dripping black hair.

They would all have to be dealt with.

7:32 P.M. Central European Summer Time
A residence
Brussels, Belgium

The TV was on in the other room, but Armand Césaire paid it no heed, staring straight ahead into empty space as the light faded without, the evening sun casting declining shadows down the streets of Brussels.

Recalling his meeting with Daniel, just the day before, standing in the shadow of the monument to fallen men.

"I need you to do this. Your country *needs you to do this."*

The words with which he'd consigned a man to a danger far beyond any he should have ever been expected to face. They felt like a betrayal now.

Paris had made contact two hours earlier, delivering word of the decision which had been made to read the Belgians in on the operation.

His operation. He'd lodged a vehement protest, but it was too late for any of that. The decision, already made—handed down like a decree from Mount Olympus.

It would have been different, using a recruited asset, Armand told himself for what seemed like the hundredth time since this operation had began. Far less reliable, and even so. . .far easier on the conscience.

As it was, Daniel would have to be told, sooner or later. He deserved to know the risks, all of them. Even if it meant that he chose to walk away.

But for the moment, he had no way of reaching out to him. No way to warn him.

He could only hope that the Belgians would, themselves, keep the circle close.

Hope. Such a fragile thing.

8:35 P.M. Moscow Time
An apartment building near the Belorusskaya Metro
Central Moscow

Smoke drifted away from the tip of Gennady Ivanovich Natashkin's cigarette into the fading twilight as he leaned back into the outside wall of the Stalin-era apartment building, listening to the traffic pass on the street, forty feet or more below his balcony.

All these years, almost half a century, since he had come to the city—a teenaged Young Pioneer from the banks of the Dnieper, in Smolensk Oblast.

He frowned, taking another long drag of the cigarette—the dying rays of sunlight reflecting off his balding head. He felt exposed out here, as he always did, old instincts from his days as an intelligence officer, refusing to die.

But Maryana wouldn't hear of him smoking indoors, and even now—with her out of the country, visiting their son in Los Angeles, he dared not violate her prohibition.

A smile touched the older man's lips at the thought of his wife. She was a good woman—the two of them had been together for nearly forty years, through the good times, and the very bad. And he'd known she was formidable from the moment he'd laid eyes on her—even after all the time they'd been married, he rather feared the thought of crossing her.

She'd been working as a typist at the Lubyanka when they had first met, both of them employed by the famous—or infamous, depending on one's perspective—Committee for State Security. *The KGB.*

A service he had alternately served, and betrayed, over the course of a twenty-five, almost twenty-six-year career. It was curious, the absence of regret he felt at his actions.

Perhaps he had known, all along, that the old system he had been a part of had not been worthy—of the country it had claimed to serve, or his own loyalties. Maryana knew nothing of all that, of course, nor could she. *Ever.*

No point in thinking about all that now. His business affairs wrapped up, he was due to fly out of Sheremetyevo at the end of the week, to join her. It would be good to see Michael again, after all these years.

And it would also be good to get out of the country, Gennady thought, his face darkening as he reached over to stub out the cigarette against the metal railing—glancing briefly down to the sidewalk below.

Hearing from Margaret Forster—the woman he had known simply as "Teresa" back in those dark days of betrayal—a week prior had been as unexpected as it was unwelcome.

He'd given her what she wanted—even in his retirement, he retained certain contacts inside the security services—but he'd known even as he did so that it was a mistake. The risk of her exposing him weighed against the risks of discovery. *And found wanting.*

He flicked the cigarette away, watching it arc out into the gathering darkness, a faintly flickering ember still visible as it fell, winking through the night.

The door opened behind him even as he started to turn to go inside, a rush of feet against the surface of the balcony—a glimpse of hard eyes behind balaclava masks. Rough hands, descending onto his shoulders.

A brief, desperate struggle, and then Gennady Ivanovich followed the cigarette down to the street. . .

6:45 P.M.
The Circle Line
London Underground

Alexei Vasiliev. Litvinov crushed the folded piece of paper in his hand, willing his fingers to stop trembling. He had known this was coming, but somehow he hadn't expected Greer to move this fast. *And yet. . .*

He glanced back into the British officer's eyes—the two of them crushed together in the standing-room-only press of the car, the flood of commuters making their daily exodus from the city. His eyes radiating an unspoken question.

Are you sure?

The only response was a barely perceptible nod, not even significant enough to be picked up by the closest of the *rezident*'s men, just on the other side of the carriage, near the door—an unwavering certainty in the black man's eyes. But of course *they* were sure.

He was the one that had to make this work—*sell* it to Kudrin. His life, on the line, if he failed.

There was only one way to play this, he thought, clutching tighter hold of the strap above his head as the train slowed, lurching to a stop as it came into Blackfriars. And he would have to do so with the utmost of care.

When he looked back around, neither Roth nor Kudrin's man were anywhere to be seen.

Darren Roth came out of the tube station onto Queen Victoria Street on the north bank of the Thames, his eyes flickering up and down the street in the fading light—every muscle alert, his body poised for action.

He was being followed, he knew that much—a man, hanging about thirty feet back. Average height, perhaps a few years younger than himself—a distinctly Slavic face.

Litvinov had had watchers, on the train. Someone from the embassy, watching him—watching Roth, it was hard to say.

Had the Russian been burned? Roth glanced in the window of an idling taxi as he began to cross, catching sight of his tail in its reflection, still behind him—closer now.

Just as importantly, what did it mean if he *wasn't?* If he'd known the surveillance was going to be in place on the meet, and yet made no sign?

If he hadn't made both of them—at least he thought there had been only two—within minutes of boarding the train. . .things could have gone very badly.

Roth swore under his breath, digging in the pocket of his jeans for his phone—dialing a number from memory as he moved down the far side of Queen Victoria Street, working his way west.

He waited until Greer picked up, a moment later, then, "You still at the office?"

"Yes." The CI spook's voice was instantly alert. *Cautious.*

"Stay there," Roth advised, his dark face grim and drawn. "I'm inbound."

11:08 P.M. Central European Summer Time
A hotel room
Paris, France

The man was a criminal. That much was clear after reviewing his file. That. . .and so much more.

Grigoriy Stepanovich Kolesnikov leaned back against the headboard of the hotel bed, running a hand over the lower half of his face as he stared at the sheets of paper scattered across the duvet.

The sordid story of a life—deposited for him, eleven hours before, in a dead drop not far from the Seine. The life of the man his superiors in Moscow now expected him to do business with.

Gamal Belkaïd.

Kolesnikov shook his head, his lip curling in an expression of disgust. It wasn't the man's criminality that bothered him—criminals were ever useful in his chosen profession.

It was the nature of it. Counterfeit electronics, prostitution, and drugs— that last most of all. A scourge which had touched even his own family.

He put a hand to his chest, a reflective look entering his blue eyes as his fingers touched the pendant hanging from a golden chain about his neck, its raised surface just visible beneath the fabric of his athletic shirt.

An icon of Our Lady of Vladimir, the Christ Child cradled in her arms— an image he knew almost as well as he knew his own face. *The protectress of Russia.*

His older brother Sasha had fallen prey to drug addiction in those dark years following the collapse of the Soviet Union—heroin flooding the streets of a once-proud nation now humbled, brought to its knees, by the West.

Heroin trafficked by the *mafiya*. By criminals, just like Belkaïd.

Grigoriy had never known his father, a Red Army veteran whose body had never come home from Afghanistan, but Sasha, nearly eight years his senior, had filled the role as well as any teenager could. Already nearing adulthood at the time of their country's collapse, he'd been a talented hockey player, with dreams of one day, perhaps, even representing the *Rodina* abroad. *The Olympics?*

Anything had seemed possible, then, even after their father's death. Youth was invincible like that. He could still remember those afternoons after school, watching his older brother move across the ice—looking up to him. *Idolizing him.*

Then everything had begun to collapse, the ground giving way all around them as the USSR entered freefall. First they had lost their apartment, such as it was—then Sasha had lost his job. And as the impotence sank home, he'd watched his brother change.

Slowly, at first, then more rapidly as the months and years went by—addiction, an avalanche gathering momentum as it raced downhill. Threatening to crush everything in its path. *All the dreams.*

His brother had spent more of the '90s in prison than out, a record of addiction and arrest which had very nearly jeopardized Grigori's own dreams of becoming an FSB officer.

They hadn't spoken in more than a decade.

And yet here he was, all the same. Kolesnikov leaned back into the plush pillows, picking up the surveillance photo of Gamal Belkaïd and holding it up to the light.

Said bin Muhammad Lahcen had been a known entity—someone they could do business with. Someone happy to accept help, without asking too many questions of the hand that fed him.

This man. . .was an unknown.

But that didn't change the job he had come here to do.

10:37 P.M. British Summer Time
Thames House
Millbank, London

It was quiet in Phillip Greer's office, almost painfully so—the outer office long since deserted, the building nearly so, save for the night watch manning Five's operations center on another floor, the armed security personnel making their rounds.

That left the two men alone, sitting there in the quiet. Each lost in his respective thoughts.

There simply wasn't much more to be said. Greer glanced over to where Darren Roth sat in a chair facing the desk—the former Royal Marine's fingers tented before him as he gazed off into space.

Roth had arrived at Thames House nearly two hours before, having run a ninety-minute surveillance detection run through the twilit streets of London, losing his Russian friends in the process.

It hadn't been that much of a surveillance team—only two operatives that Roth had made. Possibly three.

Fairly small-scale. *Or conversely, very large,* Greer thought dubiously—

knowing all too well that the more people you could put on the ground, the fewer of them your target was likely to see.

But Roth would know that as well, and the man was good at his craft.

The phone on Greer's desk began ringing abruptly just then, its harsh jangle shattering the silence.

Greer picked up the receiver, listening for a few moments before answering with a curt, "Thank you."

"We'll have access in five minutes," he announced, turning toward an expectant Roth. "And then we'll know."

"If the cameras can tell us."

"They will," Greer replied quietly. Cameras covered London like a blanket, and nowhere was thicker with them than the Underground. "We need to see who the target of the surveillance operation was—him, or you."

What the cameras couldn't tell them was what any of that would actually *mean*—whether Litvinov had chosen to play them false, or was simply running his own game, covering his tracks with his own side, best he could.

Greer leaned back in his chair, running endless scenarios through his head, examining them from every angle.

As one of the original officers from those years in Vienna, he knew Dmitri Pavlovich better than probably anyone else still remaining in the Service.

But that had been very many years ago, and life changed men, for better or worse. *Often both.*

Had he pushed the man too hard? Asked him for too much, too fast? More questions, with no more answers than any of the rest.

A message popped up on his computer's center screen, giving him the access he had requested, and he typed in the password, waving Roth over to look as he began pulling up CCTV footage from the Circle Line.

Hours' worth of it, streaming over the screens, beginning at Blackfriars and working from that point, forward and back. Pausing as Roth identified faces, as they searched for repeated sightings in the crowd. Anomalies. *Patterns.*

An hour later, Greer leaned back from the computer, his eyes grave, his glasses riding low on the bridge of his nose. The conclusion, by now, inescapable.

"They were there for you."

Chapter 17

7:51 A.M. British Summer Time, July 11th
Embassy of the Russian Federation
Kensington Palace Gardens, London

"Your message sounded. . .urgent, Dmitri," Valeriy Kudrin said, waving Litvinov to a seat in front of his desk. The remnants of the *rezident*'s breakfast were still scattered on a plate to one side of his computer keyboard, a rather large piece of a muffin distending his cheek. "Did something happen with your asset? My men reported no problems that they were able to observe."

Did something happen? Litvinov found himself unable to respond for a moment, remembering the cold shudder that had gone through him, unfolding that piece of paper to see Vasiliev's name printed thereon.

He had wanted to run, wanted to leave the train and vanish, into the night. But he had known, even then, what he knew now. That there was only one way to handle this. Only one way out.

"He's a dangle."

8:53 A.M.
A terraced house
Islington, North London

"Hold still, Richard, you're spilling it on yourself." Maggie Forster sighed heavily, noting the look of bewildered disbelief on her husband's face as she reached over to wipe the spilled porridge from his shirtfront.

He'd always detested porridge, his whole life—said it brought back bad memories of his childhood, growing up the son of working-class parents in Sheffield.

This past year, as he slipped deeper into the grip of Alzheimer's. . .it was the only thing he would eat for breakfast. And now, the last few days, he seemed incapable of holding his spoon level as he brought it to his mouth.

Maggie daubed away the mess, suppressing another weary sigh as she rose to wash the cloth in the sink. The screen of the phone charging on the counter lighting up with an incoming message.

No name, a blocked number—but she knew who it was, a chill running through her body as she glanced at the preview text. *Have you seen the news?*

She glanced back at her husband as she swiped her thumb over the screen, tapping in a brief, one-word response. *No.*

What did it mean? It seemed as though an eternity came and went in the forty seconds that passed before the mobile vibrated once more in her hand, the second message just as brief as the first. *BBC One. Now.*

A small television sat in one corner of the kitchen, and she reached for the controller on the counter, a dark fear clawing at her heart. *A premonition of evil.*

She filtered through the channels until she found BBC One, turning up the volume just in time to hear the newshost say, ". . .where securities trader Gennady Natashkin was found dead last night after an apparent fall from the balcony of his Moscow apartment. Police are investigating the incident, but there are no reports of. . ."

The blood seemed to freeze in her veins, her fingers trembling around the controller as she muted the telly once more. She'd heard all she needed to.

"Richard, dear," she began, forcing an unfelt calm into her voice, "I may need to go out this morning. Will you be all right?"

He looked up at the sound of her voice, an utterly baffled expression on his face—porridge dripping once more from his chin onto the stained shirt. "I've met you before, somewhere. . .haven't I?"

Maggie swore softly under her breath as she turned away, too distracted to feel the sorrow those words normally brought. Her mobile was in her purse, hanging behind her coat on a hook at the top of the steps, and she retrieved it, dialing a number from memory.

"Julian," she announced as the other end was picked up, "we need to meet. This morning."

7:55 A.M. British Summer Time
Embassy of the Russian Federation
Kensington Palace Gardens, London

Kudrin stopped chewing, his face frozen in an expression of surprise and disbelief. "What did you say?"

Good. That had gotten his attention. Litvinov took a deep breath, steadying himself. "I'm saying that there is another agenda at play with this purported 'walk-in'—some effort at *provokatsiya* on the part of the British security services. This man Roth is not as he seemed, at first glance, or even the second."

The expression of dismay on the *rezident's* face would have been comical, had the situation not been so serious. His own danger, so very great. *You shouldn't have been so quick to take credit with Moscow, Valeriy. . .*

"B-b-but the intelligence—the *documents* you were given. That all checked out, it was all legitimate, it—"

"Was clearly something the British were willing to sacrifice to advance their interests, whatever those might be," Litvinov finished grimly, his gaze never wavering. "But last night, the information he gave me was patently false, and could only have been designed to trigger a reaction from our service—that's the only logical interpretation that can be placed upon it."

So close to the truth. And yet so very far.

"What was it?" Kudrin demanded, his voice a harsh, almost desperate rasp.

The moment of truth. *Or rather, of lies.*

"It was some nonsense about an illegal operation we are purportedly running in this country, involving one of our officers. A man named Alexei Vasiliev."

Even as he watched, the color seemed to drain from the *rezident's* face. He reached out, clawing wordlessly for the receiver of the phone on his desk, calling his receptionist in the outer office. "Ensure that Dmitri Pavlovich and myself are undisturbed for the next hour. No interruptions—*none,* for any reason. *Spasiba.*"

Kudrin replaced the phone in its cradle, seeming to consider his next words very carefully. "There is something you need to understand. . ."

9:36 A.M. Central European Summer Time
The warehouse
Liège, Belgium

He could still see flecks of his own blood, staining the warehouse floor beneath where the chair had sat. A grim reminder of the cause of the pain that still wracked his body—purplish bruises discoloring the flesh.

And a suggestion that Belkaïd's men could be careless. *Worth knowing.*

But this morning, there was little other hint of what had gone before, Harry thought, moving across the warehouse at Belkaïd's side—the two of them flanked by a pair of the trafficker's men, armed, presumably. As near as he could tell, Belkaïd himself carried no weapon.

The massive doors at the eastern end of the warehouse were open, the bright rays of the morning sun spilling inside around the bulk of a box truck backed into the building, its rear door lifted. Men clustered around like bees swarming a hive, off-loading boxes and stacking them off to one side.

"Consumer electronics," Belkaïd announced proudly, gesturing to one of his bodyguards to slash open the nearest box. He reached inside the ripped cardboard, retrieving a slim white phone and handing it to Harry.

"The newest iPhone. Or rather, a counterfeit so close that not even an Apple executive could tell the difference." He waved a hand to the truck. "A thousand of them—just arrived from China. On the streets of Brussels, of Paris, of Marseilles, they'll bring three to four hundred euros apiece. What do you think?"

Harry looked up, his gaze drifting idly over the truck, the boxes full of counterfeit phones being off-loaded for storage.

"I think that I see here being piled up the good things of this world."

He heard an audible gasp from one of the bodyguards, saw Belkaïd's face color at the accusation implicit in the words. The timeless warning of the Prophet, in one of the Makkan *surahs*, that such "good things" would divert the faithful from the true path.

The path of jihad, as a man like al-Almani would interpret that particular passage.

"Everything in its time, brother," Belkaïd replied, bridling his temper with a visible effort.

"Time?" Harry demanded, knowing that he was treading on dangerous ground—knowing all the same that he must *sell* this. His cover *must* be believed. And this was the only way. "We had a *caliphate*—for the first time in a century, we had a place that the *ummah* could truly call their own, a place where God's laws were enforced on earth as they are in heaven. We *had* it, and we *lost* it, because some still believed it wasn't *time*."

The older man met his gaze, their eyes locking across the few feet of warehouse floor. "And yet here you stand, among us."

His glance flickered to his bodyguards, standing there a few feet away on either side. "Perhaps my men were not wrong to ask—how *is* it that you are still alive, when everyone around you died back in *Sham*? Whatever the dream of caliphate meant to you, you don't seem to have been willing to die for it."

"It was not my choice," Harry returned steadily, his eyes never leaving Belkaïd's face. "Abu Omar always believed that those of the faithful in Europe should have been returned to the West to continue the war as soon as they were trained—not expended on the battlefields of Syria. I was to be *sent* back, even before I was wounded. Once that happened, I was no longer able to protest the decision."

"And so you've returned, alone," Belkaïd said, a touch of irony in his voice, "to carry on the war."

"*Insh'allah*," Harry replied, hearing the sound of voices from the rear of the warehouse behind them—turning to see a blindfolded Marwan and Reza being led into the building. The girl, just visible behind them. "And here are the soldiers Allah has seen fit to give me."

9:05 A.M. British Summer Time
Embassy of the Russian Federation
Kensington Palace Gardens, London

". . .so you understand, then, why it is imperative that you continue to develop this asset."

Litvinov nodded, still struggling to process everything that he had been told in the space of the previous hour. *The enormity of it all.*

Influence operations were nothing new, of course—he was as familiar with them as any career Russian intelligence officer. But this. . .someone had, somehow, put their foot into it, in a major way. He wondered idly if they remained in the employ of the service.

Or if they were still alive.

"Of course, Valeriy," he replied, mastering himself with an effort. "I will make every effort to learn whatever else Mr. Roth can provide us related to what the British know about our operations."

"Make this a priority," Kudrin warned sharply, glancing across the desk. "I was wrong to suggest that you should hand your contact off to another officer at the earliest opportunity. We must not—we *dare not*—run that risk. If the British are watching this operation Vasiliev is running, if his contact inside the Security Service is already under surveillance—it could destroy everything. We need to know, one way or the other. As soon as possible."

"I understand," Litvinov responded, rising from his chair, the meeting clearly reaching its end. "I'll set up another meet with him as soon as it's safe to do so. . .we must be careful not to cross paths too often. If he has himself somehow fallen under suspicion, the digital trail we both leave behind, wherever we go, could give them a dangerous amount of insight."

Kudrin's voice arrested him where he stood. "Some risks are unavoidable, Dmitri Pavlovich. Find out what he knows."

10:23 A.M. Central European Summer Time
The warehouse
Liège, Belgium

". . .and Aryn, have you heard from him?" Harry asked, his eyes fixed on Marwan's face as their small group stood off in one corner of the warehouse. Alone, for the moment, but still under the watchful eye of Belkaïd's men.

A nod. "Late last night," the young man replied, seeming ill at ease. *Unsure of himself.* It was an unfamiliar look on him, but perhaps he was still sorting out where he fit into the hierarchy, now that Belkaïd dominated the picture. Perhaps they all were. "After you made contact. He should be arriving here in Liège soon, on the bus."

"His mother is dead," he added, after an awkward pause.

Shock and unfeigned sorrow flickered across Harry's face. "I am sorry. She was a righteous woman."

Belkaïd appeared at his elbow before he could say another word, a curious smile playing across the trafficker's face as he looked from one to another.

"I'm glad to see the *mujahideen* reunited," he said, a mocking edge to his voice, "though I understand there yet remains one more?"

Another nod from Marwan. "He'll be here on the noon bus."

"Good," Belkaïd replied. "Then Ibrahim can go to meet him. And then we can discuss what it is that I need you all to do. . .for me."

9:27 A.M. British Summer Time
Embassy of the Russian Federation
Kensington Palace Gardens, London

"Make sure you have those reports to me by the weekend," Litvinov admonished, turning away from the young SVR analyst as they parted in the corridor. "Make it a priority—we need to understand what the British are doing if we're to find a way to counter them."

He pushed open the door of his office as the analyst's footsteps retreated down the hall, favoring his own secretary with a perfunctory nod as he crossed the outer office.

It was only after the door of the inner office closed behind him that Litvinov let out the breath he'd been holding, seemingly, ever since his meeting with the *rezident* had begun.

It was simply. . .unfathomable, all of it. He knew the Kremlin had become audacious in recent years—there were times when it even seemed as though the Centre was using the UK as a test bed, to see just how far the West would allow them to prosecute their operations with impunity.

But even so, this was. . .*unfathomable* remained the only word he could think to describe it.

Arthur Colville. That the Service could, somehow, be linked—however loosely—to an attempt on the life of the *Queen*.

And now, this effort to cover it up. . .and to unmask the UK's remaining assets in Russia itself.

The career intelligence officer within him realized that this was how the game was played. Legitimate espionage, all of it—at least, if they *hadn't* been involved in the attack on Balmoral.

But the traitor inside feared that his own name was on that list. That's what he was—a *traitor*, now more than ever. No escaping it.

And only further treason would save him now.

10:57 A.M.
Parliament Hill
London

She stood alone on the crest of the hill as Marsh approached, a solitary figure silhouetted against the sky—the summer breeze playing with her greying hair.

There had been fear in her voice when she called, the former director-general thought, trudging up the steep slope of what archaeologists believed had once been a burial barrow, back during the Bronze Age. *Back before there was an England.*

"You left your mobile at home?" she asked, glancing quickly up into his face as he reached her side.

A nod, as he turned to stand beside her, looking out over the city. "As you requested, Maggie."

Even that was a move that could rouse suspicion in this age of ubiquitous tech, but there was no way around it. And she had insisted.

He leaned back, feeling the breeze wash across his face, hands shoved into the pockets of his trousers. Waiting for her to speak.

When he'd been a lad, you could stand on this hill and see the Houses of Parliament, nearly ten kilometers to the south. The heart of a nation, spread out before you. Or so it had seemed, in those youthful days.

Now the view was obscured by new construction—buildings growing up like weeds all around the city. And somehow, the nation he'd served seemed to have become obscured, right along with them.

Perhaps so it ever was. *The clarity of youth.* That firm, unshakeable sense of right, becoming murkier with the years.

"Who did you tell, Julian?" she asked suddenly, turning to face him—transfixing him with a hard gaze, her voice earnest. Trembling ever so slightly. "I need to know. . .that folder on Alexei Vasiliev, who did you give it to?"

"A friend."

"*Who*, Julian?" She swore loudly, the profanity sounding strange on her lips. Her eyes flashing anger. "Give me a *name*."

"Philip Greer—the head of D Branch, counterintel. Why? What's going on, Maggie?"

"My contact," she replied, taking a deep breath, "was a former KGB officer named Gennady Natashkin. I hadn't spoken to him in years—to my knowledge, *no one had*. Until last week. For you. And last night, Julian, someone threw him off the balcony of his Moscow apartment."

12:03 P.M. Central European Summer Time
The bus stop
Liège, Belgium

It was a fierce, desperate embrace—the young man holding on as if to life itself.

"I'm sorry, brother," Harry whispered, his hand on the back of Aryn's neck, holding him close. His blue eyes staring out over his friend's shoulder, across the busy Belgian street—knowing that they needed to move, that Belkaïd's people would be getting impatient. Finding himself unable to press—the genuineness of the emotion he felt, nearly overwhelming him.

The humanity of your enemy couldn't be denied—not this close. Not in a war this intimate.

He'd known case officers who had retired from the Agency early, unable to take it any more—day by day forced to find empathy with men they would, in any other life, have rather killed. Because you had to have empathy to be able to *work* with such men—and working with them was your job.

And what happened when your support network was gone. . .and those men were all you had left?

"They killed her," Aryn whispered, choking back an angry sob, his fingers digging into Harry's back, into the fresh scars left by Belkaïd's men.

Pain. His due in life, the price of his sins. He bore it in silence, taking the younger man gently by the shoulders and steering him back toward the waiting car.

At the end of the day, it was just another question he didn't have an answer to. *One he dared not face.*

2:30 P.M. British Summer Time
A terraced house
Abbey Road, London

It was raining by the time Julian Marsh returned home, a distant rumble of thunder far-off in the summer sky.

He'd taken the long way back from his meeting with Maggie Forster—criss-crossing the city in an effort to see if anyone had been following him. He was sure she had done the same.

"I'm afraid, Julian." Those words meant something, coming from Maggie. But she had reason to be. *"They've killed British citizens already, you know that as well as I. Here in this country. And nothing's been done to them, so they'll do it again."*

"Is there any way you could leave the city, even for the weekend? Just get out until we can get this sorted."

He was being optimistic in thinking things could be worked through that fast, and they had both known it. But she'd shook her head. *"We could go to my stepson's, but I wouldn't think of putting him in this danger. To go anywhere else. . .the break in routine would only upset Richard. And money isn't the easiest to come by these days."*

"I can give you the money, Maggie, that's not a problem. I feel as though I am responsible for this."

"You likely are, Julian. But keep your money—there's few places I could go that they can't follow. Just find who did *this. Promise me that."*

A promise easier made than kept, Marsh thought, running a hand through his rain-slick, greying hair. Huge drops of water coming away on his fingers. *Greer.*

It *couldn't* be, and yet he could see few alternatives—knowing how close Philip would have kept such information. Hard to believe that his old colleague could have been turned—and yet who better?

The ultimate recruitment—to make a spy out of the spycatcher.

He would have to find a way to confront him about it. . .some way to do so without further jeopardizing Maggie—and whatever other sources she might still be harboring.

A resolution that, like his promise, was easier made than kept. *Far easier.*

6:01 P.M.
New Southgate Cemetery
East Barnet, London

He felt as if he were going to vomit—his breath coming fast, his body possessed with a restless energy as he paced back and forth across the red carpeting of the small chapel.

It couldn't be true—couldn't be. None of this was actually happening. No, no, no. . .it wasn't real. None of it.

Except it was, something within Simon Norris reminded him. It all was. *So very real.*

His eyes settled on the cross at the front of the chapel, a mad desire to rip it from where it hung seizing hold of him.

But he dared not leave such trace of his presence. Not even here.

When the door opened behind him, his heart nearly died within him, turning on heel to see the Russian standing there in the opening, regarding him calmly.

"What were you *thinking*?" Norris fairly screamed at him, his body trembling with fury, the pent-up rage breaking free like water through a broken dam.

Alexei simply shut the door without a word, walking past him down the length of the chapel, checking the side rooms off the sanctuary to ensure that they were alone. The fury building up within the analyst more with every passing moment.

"Were you even thinking?" he demanded, unable to maintain his silence for a moment longer. "Tell me that, hey? Were any of you precious bloody sods even *thinking*?"

"We are alone, Mr. Norris," Alexei observed, gesturing to the adjacent rooms. "Had you even checked?"

"Of course I had," Norris lied angrily, knowing all too well that the Russian could see right through him. "But you're not *answering* me!"

The faintly contemptuous smile was proof enough that Alexei hadn't believed the lie. "We weren't supposed to meet again, Mr. Norris—not until you were set to leave the country. But you demanded this meeting. So it falls to you to tell me what has precipitated all *this*. Without shouting, if you please. We are not alone in this cemetery, even if the chapel itself is vacant."

"You *know*," Norris spat, struggling to calm down. Lower his voice. "One of those *names* I gave you, Alexei. He's dead. You *killed* him."

"*Smert shpionam*," was the Russian's casual, almost off-hand reply. *Death to spies.* "What did you think was going to happen, Simon? That we were going to deliver vodka and caviar?"

Of course he knew, even if he'd been lying to himself, deep down.

"But to do it while I'm still *here*, in Britain?" he demanded, feeling the panic rise once more within him. That primal instinct for survival moving, as ever, to the fore. "Are you all insane? You've placed everything in jeopardy, Alexei. *Everything.* If I fall under suspicion now, you lose it all—everything I'm prepared to give you."

"And yet you still asked to meet once again, in person," the Russian mused, "putting yourself in further jeopardy. Did you even think that through, Simon?"

"Answer my question!"

Alexei just looked at him, something of pity—or was it condescension—written in those ice-blue eyes. "He was due to leave the country, or so I was told. We had to act, or let him escape. Perhaps he suspected something, I don't know. Either way. . .you still have a deal to uphold, Mr. Norris. Don't be late."

Alexei Vasiliev passed through the wrought-iron gates of the cemetery, glancing briefly at the red brick of the building on his right before turning left—heading down the wooded street toward where he'd left the car, two blocks away.

The trees adding to the gloom of the gathering twilight as he dug the pieces of his mobile phone from his pocket, replacing the battery and SIM card with practiced ease, tapping in a familiar number.

A tiny smart car skittered past him down the street as he raised the mobile to his ear, bringing a cold, contemptuous smile to his face.

"I've just been to see about the house," he announced when the other end connected. "The seller is anxious to move—he gives the impression that he would rather be out sooner than later. Is that possible, do you think?"

It was a moment before Kudrin replied, a curious hesitancy in the *rezident's* voice when he did so. "Possible. . .but inadvisable. There are others interested in the property, and they know about you. Possibly him, as well."

Chapter 18

"You're certain?" Roth asked, his voice low as the train rumbled once more out of the tube station, the carriage around them packed with passengers.

A quick, almost imperceptible nod from Litvinov as Roth studied him. "Kudrin was taken off-guard—I could see it in his eyes. He wasn't lying to me."

But are you to me? That was ever the question, wasn't it, the British officer thought—aware of Greer's uncertainty. *Still. . .*this wasn't something any of them could afford to ignore.

The best dezinformatsiya *never was.*

"But you weren't able to learn the name of their source?" he asked cautiously, carefully scanning the car. No sign of the watchers this morning. *Interesting.*

"No," the Russian replied. "I don't believe Kudrin himself is privy to that information. And if he isn't. . .there's no way I can obtain it, either."

"I understand," he heard a voice—presumably that of the British officer—respond. "Just stay alert, and make sure you don't expose yourself to any unnecessary risks. If anything can be developed on our end. . .I'll set up a meet to pass it along."

"Of course." *Dmitri Pavlovich Litvinov.* "I'll keep an eye open around the *rezidentura*—relay anything I can that pertains to the case."

And then both men fell silent, as if they had parted. The voices gone, replaced only by the low hum of the voices on the train.

Alexei Vasiliev pulled the earbuds from his ears, leaning back against the seat of the carriage—his face expressionless, his tablet neglected on his lap.

The micro-transmitter he'd slipped into a pocket of Litvinov's suit jacket in a deft brush-pass as they boarded the train would continue broadcasting for another twenty minutes, but he had what he needed. Knew, everything he needed to know. *Treason.*

He'd encountered many traitors to the *Rodina* over his decades in intelligence work, but it was something you never got used to. The sense of *betrayal*, ever fresh.

And there was only ever one remedy, to such a cancer. *Cut it out.*

Smert shpionam. . .

7:49 A.M. Central European Summer Time
The Ardennes Forest, near Malmedy
Belgium

"It's a job," Harry thought, remembering Gamal Belkaïd's words the previous night as the box truck sped along the quiet roadway, dappled sunlight flickering across his face as its morning rays filtered through the woods of the Ardennes—tall trees lining the road on both sides for as far as the eye could see.

Miles upon miles. During the Second World War, Allied commanders had made the mistake of believing that these forested mountains were impenetrable, the terrain far too difficult to allow for any kind of major armored offensive.

The Germans had proven them wrong—*twice.* A mistake for which over eighty young American artillerymen had paid with their lives, taken prisoner and gunned down by the machine guns of the *Waffen-SS* in a field not too far from this very road. Broken bodies, crumpled in the crimson snow.

And now, here was Belkaïd, sending them into the same terrain. It was a test of some kind, he knew that much—not believing the trafficker's excuse of simply needing extra men on the job for a moment. The man was a cipher. . .his motives much harder to parse than the straightforward black/white religious ideology driving his young companions.

That Belkaïd wished to advance the Islamist cause seemed without doubt, but it rang false somehow—a discordant hubris, something. It might be a weakness, even, but something about the man spoke of someone to be underestimated at one's own peril.

Harry let his arm hang outside the window, feeling the slipstream rush by—casting a glance over at the driver.

The man had spoken perhaps five words since they'd set out from Liège, an impassive, unmoveable entity in the driver's seat. A short, dark-haired Arab—Algerian, presumably, like Belkaïd.

There were four other trucks, just like this one—fanning out through the Ardennes by different roads toward a singular goal. A rendezvous with smugglers from over the "border" with Germany, presumably trafficking cargo from points further east.

Much further.

And that's all Belkaïd had chosen to reveal. The shipment could be anything. Drugs. Guns. More counterfeit phones like the ones he'd shown off at the warehouse.

Women, even. Harry's face tightening at that last, a brief, almost imperceptible grimace before the mask fell back in place.

He'd seen them in the windows of the Gare du Nord in his early weeks in Brussels—red-lipped and beckoning, a haunting illusion. It had almost been enough to tempt him to seek some solace in their arms, a comfort as counterfeit as Belkaïd's phones. . .but there were some lines he could never bring himself to cross.

Even if he no longer knew what they were.

7:31 A.M. British Summer Time
Thames House
Millbank, London

"He was clear that this. . .'contact' of Arthur Colville's was still at large," Phillip Greer observed, his mind still racing as he sorted through everything Roth had just laid out before him.

A nod.

The counter-intel spook swore beneath his breath, suddenly remembering MacCallum's words, sitting there in the small interview room in HMP Belmarsh.

"I never betrayed my country. And if I didn't, that means someone else did. Someone you haven't found yet."

He might even have been telling the truth, Greer realized, the wilderness of mirrors in which he walked suddenly distorting once again, projecting back crazed images of oneself, of one's surroundings.

Madness.

"There has to be someone else," he said finally, glancing quickly over at Roth. "Perhaps someone in MacCallum's old branch, someone close enough to. . .you're sure that Litvinov can't get us the name?"

"He seemed quite sure," the former Royal Marine replied, his dark fingers interlaced as he leaned back into the chair, his eyes thoughtful. Reflective. "If he's telling the truth—if he's not, himself, being played—that's something that's being kept compartmented from the *rezidentura*."

It made sense, Greer thought. And insisting that Litvinov probe further was foolhardy—the risks of compromise, far too great.

Even if it made the job they had to do that much harder.

Greer picked up the receiver of the phone on his desk, connecting him to his secretary in the outer office.

"Rhona," he began, "I'm going to need access records for the Registry, as soon as you can obtain them for me. And personnel files for G Branch. Thank you."

He set the phone back down, glancing through his thick glasses at Roth as he began to undo the cuffs of his dress shirt, rolling the sleeves back to the elbows. "You and I, are going to be in for a long day."

8:46 A.M. Central European Summer Time
Alliance Base
Paris, France

"Bonjour, messieurs," Anaïs Brunet announced, glancing up from her seat at the head of the table as a uniformed security officer ushered Christian Danloy and his deputy into the conference room. "I'm glad you were both able to join us this morning."

The cold, flat tone of her voice made it clear that she wasn't as she gestured for them to take a seat, continuing on with the introductions. "I believe you already know my counterpart here at the Base, General Gauthier."

She watched as the men exchanged greetings, her eyes never leaving Danloy's face. "I trust you've had time to review the information we sent over, Christian?"

A nod, as the VSSE head took his seat, his hand resting on one of the folders which had been distributed around the room—one in front of each principal. "*Oui.*"

"As you will see from the folder in front of you. . .there have been developments." Brunet paused, scanning the faces of the men before her. "According to intelligence received last night from LYSANDER, we have a new player. An Algerian-born Belgian national, named Gamal Belkaïd."

She saw a flash of recognition pass across Danloy's face, and turned her attention on her Belgian counterpart. "You know him, Christian?"

"*Certainement.* He's a well-known figure in the world of organized crime in Belgium—our counterparts in the *Police Fédérale* have been trying to put him in prison for years on charges of conspiracy, murder, and drug trafficking, but evidence has always been hard to come by. And despite his connections to Algeria, there's never been anything linking him to terrorism."

"Well now there is."

9:01 A.M.
The Ardennes Forest, near Vielsalm
Belgium

Drugs. That's what it had turned out to be, Harry thought, watching as Reza leaned down from the open back of the Isuzu in the middle of the wooded clearing, taking a bag of mushroom soil from Aryn's outstretched arms—stacking it with the others in the back of the truck. Mushroom soil—and buried in the dirt, bricks of heroin.

The street value of what was being loaded into these trucks was. . .difficult to even calculate. Millions upon millions of euros. Enough to fund a small war, if that was the use one proposed to put them to.

His instincts had been right. Gamal Belkaïd was a very dangerous man.

He felt a presence behind him and turned to find the Algerian standing there, regarding him with a peculiar smile. "You see, Ibrahim? The beauty of it all? You remember the years before the war, before the crusader invasion of Afghanistan?"

A nod. "I was far from God in those days, before I found the true faith. But yes, I remember."

"Mullah Omar had banned the growing of poppies the year before, declaring them *haram*. Cracking down, like he and other Taliban leaders had on so many sinful things throughout the previous decade. And it was working—supplies of opium and hashish began to dry up, all across the world." The older man smiled. "Even the *kaffir* were forced to admit that it was one of the most successful anti-drug campaigns in history, far more effective than anything they could have accomplished in their own decadent societies."

There was pride in the man's voice at the memory, a strange, incongruous pride considering his own trade.

"And then the war came, and the crusaders devastated Afghanistan—left its people in poverty. Forced the leaders of the Taliban into hiding. In the midst of such devastation, the poppy became people's only recourse— blooming once more all through the fields of Afghanistan. And once more, the tide of heroin began to roll West, corrupting a society on the brink of collapse." Belkaïd paused, a curious intensity creeping into his voice as he continued. "They are *paying* us to destroy them, brother—willingly funding our own war against them. Is that not a beautiful thing?"

"*Mash'allah*," Harry responded, a grim smile creasing his lips. "They plan, and God plans. And God is the best of planners."

He turned, scanning the trucks—the last of them, now being loaded. Prepped for departure. "It does surprise me, though, Gamal."

"What?"

"That you would risk yourself like this. . .out here, with the trucks. Surely someone else could do this for you, ensure that you were not compromised if anything went wrong."

"Were you expecting something to go wrong, Ibrahim?"

8:09 A.M. British Summer Time
Thames House
Millbank, London

It had taken everything in him just to come into work, his brain still screaming with the awareness of his danger—his meeting with the Russian doing nothing to allay any of those fears.

Simon Norris reached for the cup of coffeee on his desk, watching his fingers tremble even as he did so. He was already keyed-up, on edge. Feeling as if the word "Traitor" was already tattooed on his forehead. *A scarlet letter.*

How had it all come to this? He wondered, for the thousandth time since it had all begun. Knowing the answer all too well. *One step at a time.*

And now he was so far past redemption that he could barely even remember what it once had looked like.

But staying away from Thames House, wasn't an option. Not if tomorrow was going to work. They had to be expecting him.

And he could only pray that it wouldn't set off any tripwires. . .

He reached for the phone on his desk, his mouth suddenly dry as he dialed the number on his screen, waiting as it rang. *Once. Twice.* Then:

"Royal Bank of Scotland."

"Yes, this is Simon Norris. . .Security Service. I need to submit an official request. . ."

9:10 A.M. Central European Summer Time
The clearing
Ardennes Forest, Belgium

Suspicion dripped from every word, the edge of hostility in Belkaïd's voice only too clear. *Thin ice.*

He looked back, keeping his face neutral as he shook his head. "Syria taught me nothing if not that things can always go wrong. And caution is ever warranted."

"But of course." It was impossible to read the Algerian's expression, the filtered sunlight playing across his features. "But today, there are things that no man can do for me. And I am never in any danger."

He took a step past Harry, gesturing for him to follow as the two of them walked across the clearing toward the trucks.

"Another shipment successfully delivered, Umar," Belkaïd began, addressing the short, slight man leaning against the hood of the white Peugeot, smoking a cigarette. The sole remaining representative of "points east", as Harry had mentally labeled the smugglers delivering the heroin to Belkaïd.

The money man, presumably, a suspicion confirmed as Belkaïd gestured for one of his men to approach, bearing a pair of briefcases. "The remaining money, as we agreed."

Half up front, half on delivery? It was hard to tell what sort of arrangement Belkaïd might have in place—given the amount of heroin he'd just seen transferred, the two briefcases would be hard-pressed to even cover a third of its value.

"And about the other matter?" the money man asked, looking from Belkaïd to the man with the briefcases. He dropped his cigarette butt to the grass, grinding it into the dirt with a peculiarly savage gesture.

"Ah, yes," Belkaïd said, as if he'd forgotten—turning to the man with the briefcases. "Ahmed, you had something to add, didn't you?"

There was something wrong here, Harry realized, his own body tensing, every muscle alert. Watching the man's swarthy face take on an inexplicable pallor—his knuckles whitening around the briefcase handles.

"Something about the last shipment, Ahmed. . .a couple bricks of the product went missing, and you under-reported the tally." *Full-blown panic, now.* Eyes wide as the man glanced wildly about him at the rough semi-circle of men gathered round, looking for a way of escape. "Tried to convince me that our friends had short-changed us. But that wasn't the truth, was it?"

"N-n-no. . .please, Gamal, it wasn't that way," the man stammered, guilt written in every feature. The suitcases, falling to the earth of the clearing as he raised his hands in protest. "I would never try to deceive you, I would never—"

"*Enough!*" Belkaïd snapped, the gun out in his hand almost before Harry even saw the movement—a compact Walther P99. "I've heard far too much from you already."

He turned, the gun now outstretched in his open hand, butt-first—his eyes locking with Harry's.

"Take this. And kill him."

8:13 A.M. British Summer Time
Thames House
Millbank, London

"What about her?" Darren Roth, passing a file folder across the desk to Greer, a dark index finger indicating the name in question. *Nicola Spelman.* "She potentially has the right access—transferred over to us from Six, where she worked Eastern Europe. Divorced five years ago, appears to have a rather. . .significant mortgage, has fallen behind on it at least once in the last three years. Might be indicative of some financial vulnerability, something that could be exploited."

Greer shook his head. "She only transferred over in the last nine weeks. She might have access to the Russia files, but she wouldn't have had the necessary access to PERSEPHONE, or to MacCallum if we're still working off the theory that his access was somehow used without his knowledge."

"None of this makes sense," Roth observed, his eyes scanning the mess of papers spread out before him.

"What doesn't?"

"All this is in Six's territory, not ours. And it's supposed be broken down—compartmentalized. Access, heavily restricted. How does one of our officers even *get* this list?"

"You're talking about a system," Greer replied, looking up from his own, hand-scrawled notes. "Systems break."

The phone on the CI spook's desk began ringing a moment later, and he shuffled the folders aside to answer it, listening for a couple moments before replying, "Thank you, Henry. I appreciate you making an opening. Yes, I'll be there soon."

He replaced the receiver, reaching for his suit jacket as he stood. "Vauxhall Cross," he replied, answering Roth's unspoken question. He nodded toward the folders. "Keep at it while I'm gone—perhaps between the two of us, we'll find some answers yet."

Perhaps.

9:16 A.M. Central European Summer Time
The clearing
Ardennes Forest, Belgium

Time itself seemed to slow down, the clearing a frozen tableau—every eye suddenly focused on Belkaïd. On *Harry.*

So this was it, Harry realized, his mind strangely detached—as though he were himself nothing more than an observer to this scene. Belkaïd's motive, in bringing them here. All of it, a test.

That ultimate test of an undercover. *Murder.*

The act through which he could finally *prove* himself to Belkaïd. *At the cost of a human life.*

He glanced from the gun in Belkaïd's outstretched hand to Ahmed, a glance curiously devoid of pity—seeing him cower there, half-shrinking away, eyes darting back and forth like an animal in a trap.

How many times had this man stood in this very same place, staring down the barrel of the gun at someone else? Enforcing Belkaïd's will. This was no innocent here before him.

Who of us is? A passage of Scripture, flickering back across his mind's eye. *Let him who is without sin. . .*

"If he has stolen from you," he responded, returning his focus to Belkaïd, "take his hand, not his life. That is *shari'a*—those are the bounds prescribed by Allah."

Belkaïd took a step into him, shoving the Walther into his hand—moving in until the two men's bodies nearly touched—the Algerian's face only inches from Harry's, a baleful gleam in his eyes as he looked up into Harry's own. His voice barely above a whisper. "He stole from *me.*"

And that made all the difference, Harry thought, glimpsing the trafficker's hubris in that moment. Feeling the hard, textured polymer of the Walther in his hand.

"You have the gun," Belkaïd continued, not backing down. "*Use it.* Kill him—or *me.*"

The challenge was there, clear in the Algerian's eyes. The temptation, so very strong. To end it all. *Right here.* With Belkaïd's death and his own—two lives, extinguished in a storm of gunfire.

Leaving behind them, a better world.

Harry took a step back, the Walther coming up in a single, fluid, dream-like motion, a fleeting vision of a face through the pistol's rear sights as the trigger broke beneath his finger—once, twice, the shots reverberating out from the clearing to awaken the echoes of the forest.

The bullets smashed through Ahmed's forehead and out the back of his head, blood and brains spattering over the grass as the thief crumpled to the forest floor. *Dead before he hit the ground.*

His ears still ringing with the blasts, Harry shoved the Walther back into Belkaïd's hands—taking a step away from him, off to the side, toward Marwan and the rest of his people.

"Let Allah be witness," he spat, his eyes flashing with a cold fire, "that his blood is on your hands. Not mine."

Chapter 19

10:03 A.M. British Summer Time
Secret Intelligence Service Headquarters
Vauxhall Cross, London

"I don't know what to tell you, Phillip," Henry Brise said finally, turning back from his office window overlooking the Thames, the river glistening in the morning sun, far down the ziggurat-like stories of the MI-6 Headquarters Building.

Hands resting on his hips as the SIS counter-intel chief faced Greer. "Everything you've just laid out for me—it all just seems highly. . .improbable."

It was to the man's credit that he had refrained from using the word "impossible."

There were no impossibilities in their world—only betrayals you hadn't prepared yourself for.

Greer leaned back in his chair, regarding his colleague with an appraising look. Brise was at least ten years his junior—heavy-set, his dress shirt already wrinkled at this early hour of the day, a black tie with stripes of Eton blue extending insufficiently out over his belly.

An utterly unprepossessing picture of a bureaucrat—but Brise had a solid reputation within the relatively small world of British intelligence. A reputation he'd spent twenty years building, since joining the SIS after graduating with honors from Eton. A classicist—*like Marsh*—Greer mused, a shadow of a smile crossing his face at the thought of his friend.

"Even with the pivot we've all made away from Russia and Eastern Europe in the years since the dissolution of the USSR—since the rise of the Islamist threat—the list of our assets, both current and former, in Russia remains one of Six's most closely-guarded secrets. Or at least it should be." Brise paused. "How reliable is your source?"

Greer thought about it for a moment. "Quite reliable, I believe. I was involved in his recruitment myself."

That brought raised eyebrows from Brise. "You? I didn't know that you were running assets out of your CI shop, Phillip."

A shake of the head. "Years ago. Back in the old days."

"I see," Brise replied slowly, the skepticism still clearly visible in his eyes. As well there might have been—he'd have considered it warranted if someone brought something this fantastical to him. But this time. . .*it was real.* He could feel it, somewhere down deep within him—all the instincts of a career in this world crying out.

"I'll do what I can, Phillip," the SIS man went on after a long moment. "You understand, of course, that sorting all this out may take a few days. A week, even."

"I do," Greer acknowledged, rising to his feet—Brise's body language implying that the meeting was nearing its end. "And you appreciate that this needs to be prioritized. If my source's intelligence is accurate, this information could be handed off in a matter of days."

"Of course, I'll attend to it personally. But my shop's even smaller than yours, and we're stretched thin." Brise shrugged, gesturing around him, at the office—at the lower levels of the Headquarters building visible through the window. "You know it yourself, Phillip. We may have a more imposing headquarters, but we don't have the staff you do there at Thames House. It's a limiting thing."

He reached out, clasping Greer's hand. "But I'll do everything in my power. I give you my word."

But would that be enough?

Greer was halfway across Vauxhall Bridge when the mobile in his jacket began to ring. He paused, hand resting on the squat, faded red parapet—bringing the phone up to his ear even as one of London's iconic double-decker buses crossed the bridge just behind him, drowning out the sound of all else.

"Yes?" he asked, putting a hand up to his other ear to block the noise. *Marsh's voice.*

"We need to meet, Phillip. As soon as possible."

"This is a bad time," Greer responded, gazing out over the Thames—the river choked with traffic on this bright summer day. An idyllic scene, almost. *Full of life.* "Perhaps later this week?"

"It has to be today," came Marsh's reply. Cold and assured. "I have word of our friend."

Alexei Mikhailovich. Then he had no other choice. "All right then—two hours? The usual place?"

"You'll find me there. And, Phillip. . ."

"Yes?"

"Lose the phone."

10:24 A.M.
The terraced house
Abbey Road, London

That should bring him, Julian Marsh thought, staring down at the phone in his hand. It was a dangerous game he was playing, and he knew it.

If Greer had played him false. . .

But he couldn't bring himself to believe that—that his old colleague could have betrayed their service. Anymore than that he himself would have.

But even if he was innocent, Greer needed to understand the forces that were now in motion. A desperate hope that they could somehow head this off, before it got completely out of control. Before anyone else ended up dead.

The former director-general laid his phone on top of his chest of drawers, briefly glancing at his own reflection in the mirror before opening the top drawer, pulling away a pair of folded shirts to reveal the holstered Sig-Sauer P320 subcompact nestled beneath.

He started to reach for it, then stopped himself—grim resolution playing across his features.

As ever in his career, if it came down to guns. . .the situation was too far gone to be salvaged with one.

The drawer slid shut with a click as Marsh turned away, plucking his sports jacket from where it hung on the door.

He would just have to take his chances. *As always before.*

11:56 A.M. Central European Summer Time
The Ardennes Forest
Belgium

A pair of shots, crashing out through the forest—their echoes returning to him, again and again. The echoes of death.

Harry closed his eyes, and he could see—*feel*—it all again, the Walther recoiling into his hand.

The condemned man, dropping like a marionette whose strings have been cut—blood and brains exploding from the back of his skull. Staining the grass.

It had been the wrong choice, he knew that now, gazing out the heavily-tinted windows of the BMW as the forests of the Ardennes flashed past. Knowing that he should have turned the gun on Belkaïd.

Accepted his fate, ended it all—right then and there.

But that seemed to be the one thing he was incapable of doing, strange as it seemed. Capable of ending any life. . .except his own.

He could feel Belkaïd's eyes on him—sitting across from him in the backseat of the SUV—but his own gaze remained fixed out the window. The forest was so *peaceful* at this time of year.

A forest that had just borne witness to violent death. Belkaïd's men had been tasked with disposing of the body, somewhere, he knew not where. He—

"You're still angry with me, aren't you?" He heard the Algerian ask quietly.

"It was wrong," Harry responded, his own voice barely above a whisper.

"Perhaps it was." He could hear the shrug in Belkaïd's tone. "It was also necessary. He needed to be punished—and I needed to know that I could trust you. You weren't wrong about Said."

It felt as though Belkaïd had just dropped a bomb on the vehicle, Harry's head whipping around to face the trafficker. "*What?*"

"His apartment is still crawling with police, but he had another place—in Antwerp—under a false name. My men finished searching it last night—took his computers. He was receiving money from someone."

"So he *was* a spy!" Harry exclaimed, channeling all the fear of this moment into an angry hiss. *Was it possible, even yet. . .?*

That he could have killed a man working for Western intelligence. . .

"We don't know. Not yet—haven't been able to trace the money back far enough. If that proves fruitless, we'll simply respond using the contact information provided. Request a meeting." A quiet, knowing smile creased Belkaïd's lips. "See who shows up."

12:41 P.M. British Summer Time
"The Nell"
The Strand, London

"My God." There was no mistaking the surprise in Greer's eyes—the look of disbelief telling Marsh everything he needed to know. Whatever had transpired, his colleague wasn't involved. *Not knowingly.* "Are you *sure* about this, Julian?"

"That he was one of ours, back in the day?" A nod. "I talked with his handler. They were the source for the files I gave you, Phillip. More specifically, Natashkin himself was. And now he's dead. I struggle to think of that as coincidence."

"You would, of course," Greer acknowledged slowly, a light seeming to dawn in his eyes behind the thick glasses—his fingers toying idly with the toothpick which had skewered the as-yet-untouched sandwich on the plate before him. "But there are other things going on here, Julian—things you're not aware of."

Marsh leaned back into the booth, his eyes never leaving Greer's face. Alert once more for any sign of duplicity. "Tell me about them."

"We have a mole."

Neither man had yet touched their food by the time Greer finished, Marsh's sandwich grown cold on his plate, unnoticed.

"So Alec was innocent after all," he mused, his mind struggling to comprehend everything he had just been told.

"Potentially, yes," was Greer's cautious reply. "Or at least he wasn't alone—though a pair of moles together seems unlikely."

A pause, before the counter-intel spook went on. "He tried to warn me—last week, when I visited him in Belmarsh. Confronted him with the evidence of Colville's financial. . .entanglements. He warned me that we were looking in all the wrong directions—that, if what I was showing him was true, we still had someone under our very noses. Working for the Russians. He was *right*, Julian, and I couldn't see it."

Such were the recriminations that came with this line of work. Those endless moments of realization that, despite your best efforts, you'd missed something along the way. *Something vital.*

"And you still don't know who it could be?"

A shake of the head. "No, I don't. When you called, I'd just left Vauxhall Cross—asked them to begin digging into connections. But that's going to take far too long. And if your intel on Natashkin is accurate. . .Moscow already has the names."

"Some of them, at least," Marsh observed quietly. "Likely not all."

"What do you mean?"

"Think about it, Phillip. According to your man, the Russians haven't extracted their asset yet. He's still here, in this country—waiting for them to get him out. If you were him, would you give up your leverage before you were safe?"

"No." Greer shook his head once again. "No, I wouldn't. But if I were the Russians, I would need some proof that the intelligence was real—some way to verify that the asset could deliver what he promised."

Of course. That's the way this game was played. Marsh saw the realization in his colleague's eyes as he reached the conclusion Marsh had drawn him to. "Natashkin was the verification."

"I believe so, yes. At least part of it. But the rest of the list is likely safe, at least so long as your mole remains on British soil."

Greer picked up his sandwich, turning it around between his fingers before replacing it on the plate, as if something had struck him. "I'm going to need you to talk to Ashworth."

Marsh's eyes narrowed, taken aback by the proposition. "Are you *sure*? Why?"

"I need more cooperation from Six than I can secure on my own. If he could be convinced to place an official request with C, it might just do it."

"And when he finds out that you've kept the investigation open, counter to his explicit instructions? That you've confided the results in *me*, despite my fall from grace?"

"It's a risk we're going to have to take." Greer's voice brooked no disagreement. "We don't have a lot of time, Julian—perhaps even less than we think."

"All right, then. Why me? Why not confront Patrick with this yourself? Your admissions to me don't have to enter into it, then."

"I'm a branch head. You were his chief. That gives you influence with him that I don't have."

Marsh's eyes grew distant. "Patrick has never been as. . .open to my influence as you might imagine. But I'll do what I can, Phillip. You know that."

1:59 P.M.
Embassy of the Russian Federation
Kensington Palace Gardens, London

"Really? *Today?*" Dmitri Litvinov exclaimed, aware that his voice was too sharp almost as soon as the words left his mouth. Still struggling to process his wife's words. "I mean—that's wonderful, Natalia. It will be good to see her again. And she's bringing Katya with her?"

"Of course," he heard his wife reply. "That's what she said in the message. Is everything all right, Dima?"

"*Da, da,*" he lied absently, his mind racing. "It will be wonderful to see her again."

It shouldn't have surprised him. Flights between Moscow and London were a matter of routine these days, more than half-a-dozen every single day. Nothing could be more natural than that his daughter would come for a visit. It was only the timing.

But the timing could be perfect, he realized, if only Greer could be convinced to cooperate. To *extract* he and his family from this situation.

All of them, here in the UK. . .with the exception of Yuri, he thought, a cloud passing across his face at the thought of his son-in-law. But that was a chance he was prepared to take. *If only. . .*

His train of thought broke off abruptly, realizing only then that his wife was still speaking. ". . .I'm to pick them up from Heathrow at seven, so I won't be here when you get home. But the chicken from last night is still in the refrigerator."

271

"*Spasiba,*" he smiled, feeling a sense of peace wash over him for the first time in days. *This was all going to work out.* "I will see you soon, darling."

2:31 P.M.
Thames House
Millbank, London

"But of course, Julian." Patrick Ashworth leaned back in his desk chair, the phone's receiver held against his ear. "I'd be happy to meet. Today? Why, is it a matter of some importance?"

His brow furrowed as he listened to his predecessor on the other end of the line. *What was Marsh up to now?* He'd never trusted the man, not even when he'd worked under him. The man was a relic of an earlier age—someone who couldn't bring himself to admit that the world had *changed.* Moved on past him. Because the costs of such an admission. . .were more than he could face. The structure upon which one had built one's life, crashing down all around. "I understand. Drinks at my club this evening, then? Around 7. My wife is away, visiting her parents in Cornwall. Good. It will be my pleasure, Julian."

He hung up the phone with a grunt, eyeing the receiver with suspicion for a moment longer.

Whatever else drinks with Julian Marsh might prove to entail, he was fairly certain that "pleasure" wouldn't enter into it.

6:43 P.M.
High Street Kensington Underground Station
London

And so here he was again, Litvinov thought—walking out onto the station platform, dusting his hands to remove faint traces of the chalk he'd just dropped in a rubbish bin in the corridor.

The signal placed.

It had been on this very night—in this very station—a week ago, that Phillip Greer had come walking back into his life. Up-ending it. Ripping it asunder.

Only a week? It felt like a lifetime. A part of him hated the man for it—but deep inside, he knew that, in Greer's position, he would have done exactly the same thing.

And now Greer would know to send Roth in for another meet—tomorrow morning, likely, where they could discuss extracting him from all of this. He and his family, both.

Irina's arrival was fortuitous, he thought, filing onto the carriage along with the crowd of businessmen and women leaving the city for the night. *Providential*, even, though he had never subscribed to his wife's faith. Believed in her God.

Perhaps that, too, should change. *In their new life.*

And the carriage doors closed.

On the platform, a young man in a blue tracksuit—apparently arrived just too late for the departing train—turned, retracing his steps back down the tiled corridor toward the exit. Touching a finger to his Bluetooth headset as he moved.

"*Da, h*e's on the train," he announced after a moment. "Headed your way."

6:59 P.M.
The Rag
Pall Mall, London

Somehow, it just felt right that this should be Ashworth's club, Julian Marsh thought, following the uniformed back of a butler through the club's carpeted hallways.

The Army & Navy Club—referred to colloquially as "The Rag" by its intimates for generations upon generations—occupied a starkly modern building on a street corner in Mayfair, just off St. James's Square.

The staff were doing yeoman's work to preserve the atmosphere of the traditional English gentlemen's club, but the contrast with the Old World antiquity of Brooks's—Marsh's own club—couldn't have been more striking, for all that.

"This way, sir," the butler instructed, bowing almost imperceptibly as he ushered Marsh into the Smoking Room.

The bar was directly in front of the former intelligence officer as he entered, its attendant acknowledging him with a polite nod as his gaze swept across the room. Taking in the sight of Henry Pilleau's 1879 oil canvas "Elephants in a Dust Storm" hanging on the far wall before falling on the figure of Patrick Ashworth, sitting in a red leather armchair just to the right of the room's fireplace.

The acting director-general rose at his approach, a broad smile creasing his face as he extended a hand. "It's good to see you again, Julian. I'm so glad you were able to join me this evening."

But it wasn't, and he wasn't, as they both knew perfectly well. Marsh murmured a polite reply before taking his seat on the sofa opposite Ashworth. Neither of them were suffering under any delusion that this was a social affair.

"Your pleasure, sir?" a waiter asked, materializing at Marsh's elbow.

"Your sixteen-year Lagavulin, if you please," Marsh replied, his eyes never leaving Ashworth's face.

"So what do you think of my club, Julian?" the acting DG inquired, sinking back into his chair. "It's quite a place, isn't it?"

"Quite," Marsh replied noncommittally. "I spoke to Lord Robertson for a moment on the way in."

The former NATO secretary-general was getting on in years, Marsh reflected, looking into the fresh, far more youthful face across him. As were they all—a generation, on its way out. Soon to be replaced. By men like Ashworth.

May God defend the realm. "I didn't realize you had served in the military, Patrick."

A laugh, harsh and grating on Marsh's nerves. "Oh, I didn't. I was sponsored for membership soon after taking over at JTAC. We all serve in our own way, I suppose."

"Indeed." There was something to be said for tradition. And for those who dispensed with it.

"So tell me, Julian. . .your call, what's this all about?"

"Unfinished business," Marsh replied, taking the measure of the man across from him. "Pertaining to the late Arthur Colville."

7:23 P.M.
The terraced house
Hounslow, West London

The house was dark as Litvinov made his way toward it, pausing for a moment with his hand on his own front gate, scanning the lengthening shadows of the street—the weakening rays of sunlight glancing off the windscreens of parked automobiles. *Quiet.*

There was a peace he had always loved about this neighborhood, and yet it made him feel alien, somehow. As though he remained an intruder in it. He. . .and everything he represented.

London was the home away from home for the *nouveau riche* of Moscow—hundreds and thousands of Russians, scattered all across the city. Scarce a day had gone by in his three years in this city that he hadn't heard his native language spoken on the Tube.

It should have been a comfort, but Russia wasn't that way. *Perhaps it never had been.*

He unlocked his front door, shrugging off his suit jacket and draping it over the tree in the entry hall, glancing briefly up the stairs to the flat's second level. His briefcase still in hand as he made his way into the first floor kitchen, setting it on the table as he turned on the light.

And then he felt it, a *presence* there in the room with him—standing in the kitchen doorway through which he had just entered—his blood running ice-cold.

Fingers trembling as though seized by a sudden fever, Litvinov turned to look into a face he knew only from file photos. A face he had hoped *never* to see in person.

Hard eyes, a startling shade of ice blue, staring out from a lined, weathered face, surmounted by a rough, disheveled shock of silver hair.

Cruel, bloodless lips, distorted into an insolent caricature of a smile.

"Welcome home, Dmitri Pavlovich."

7:26 P.M.
The Rag
Pall Mall, London

"And do you believe him?"

"I have not seen the raw intelligence," Julian Marsh replied, measuring his words carefully, the single malt half-raised to his lips. "People at our level rarely do—you know that, Patrick. But Greer has given me his professional assessment, and I'm inclined to agree with it. He knows his business."

"Greer. . ." Ashworth put his head back, a skeptical light glinting in his eyes as he seemed to search for words. "Is a good man."

But. Marsh smiled, unable to escape the irony of it all, the mirror image of his own words to Greer, at the meeting which had set all this into motion. *Concerning Ashworth.*

His gaze drifted over to his right, his eyes falling on the nude portrait of Nell Gwynne which hung on the opposite wall, Peter Lely's 17th Century masterpiece—the half-amused eyes of the royal mistress gazing down upon the two of them from the canvas.

It was strange how Charles the Second's paramour seemed to dog his steps in recent days—a mocking presence. No doubt she had borne witness to many such scenes in her own life. The palace intrigue, men and women scheming for power. For *survival.* But had the stakes then been this high?

No doubt they had seemed so, in the moment. They always did. But Ashworth was speaking again.

"He's a good man," the acting director-general repeated, the unnecessary emphasis sounding somehow even more damning. "Good at his job—which is finding threats against this country, rooting out enemies from within. We both know where that can lead, Julian. To seeing enemies in every shadow—to finding threats even where none exist."

Ah, yes. Spycatcher. The grim specter of Peter Wright, still menacing them all, even all these decades later. He somehow wasn't surprised that Ashworth had chosen this tack. *But Greer was no Peter Wright.*

"But what if they do exist?" he asked quietly, draining the remnants of the Lagavulin in a single draught. "What then?"

Ashworth just stared at him, incredulously. "You're asking me to believe that *Russia* financed the man who orchestrated a terrorist attack on Her Majesty, Julian. Do you have any idea of just how absurd that sounds? Any idea at all?"

Marsh shrugged. "It would fit into the recognized Russian *modus operandi* of funneling money to fringe groups across Europe and the United States, both right and left. That's not to say they *knew* what Arthur Colville was planning, but I don't believe we can dismiss this out of hand."

"You don't believe. . ." Ashworth looked at him helplessly. "This whole business with Russia, it's an obsession with people like you and Greer. You still want to see the world as you always saw it, back in the old days. Black and white. Spy versus spy, East versus West, the Warsaw Pact facing off against NATO. Face *reality*, Julian—that world is dead."

Marsh shook his head, smiling ever so faintly. "No, you're wrong. So very wrong. That world was *dying*. . .so it faked its own death. Because no one ever bothers to kill that which is already dead, now do they?"

7:30 P.M.
The terraced house
Hounslow, West London

Every man's sins caught up with him, in the end. The choices of that dark spring so long ago, returned to haunt him at the last.

Inescapable. Litvinov just sat there, gazing across the table into the eyes of Alexei Mikhailovich Vasiliev—a thousand voices within screaming for him to move, to run, to get *away*.

But he lacked the will to do so, somehow—something gluing him to his seat. Resignation, perhaps. The knowledge that this had been the inevitable end, all along.

"I'm not going to ask you why you did it," Vasiliev went on, after a moment, the mocking glint still there in his cold blue eyes. "I really don't care. I've listened to so many men justify their treason over the years, they all just seem to run together after a while. All of them, so. . .unimaginative."

The older man paused, smiling.

"Valera would probably want me to ask how long you've been an asset of British intelligence," he said, using the diminutive of the *rezident*'s name with palpable contempt, "but I'm content for you to take that to your grave, just to spite him. As long as we're agreed that that's where this ends—with your death."

That brought Litvinov to his feet finally, the chair scraping backward across the kitchen floor, his body trembling with fear and anger as he stared at Vasiliev. "You aren't just going to *kill* me."

It was an assurance he didn't feel, a desperate grasping in the torrent for some scrap of wreckage that could bear his weight.

"No, I'm not," the older man conceded, the smile never wavering. "You're going to do that, Dmitri Pavlovich."

He felt a cold sweat break out on his palms, something terrifying in the man's calm assurance. The inescapable feeling that Vasiliev was toying with him, like a cat would play with its victims. "N-n-no, I won't do *that*, and you can't force me to. I'm going to walk out of here, right now, and if you want to stop me, you're going to have to kill me. *Yourself.*"

The older man spread his hands. "Be my guest. I'm not going to stop you. I don't even have a gun."

Come on. *Move,* Litvinov's mind screamed at him, taking the first of several faltering steps to the door. *Almost there.* Just a few more feet and he'd be in the hall, headed for the door. And then—

Vasiliev's voice arrested him where he stood. "Just understand, Dmitri Pavlovich, that *someone* will pay the price for your betrayal of the *Rodina.* If not you, someone else. A substitute will be found. And don't forget that your family remains in Russia. Where we can reach them, so very easily."

But that wasn't true—not as of tonight. They were safe, or at least as safe as he was. He just needed to find a way to warn Natalia. . .

"No, you can't," he replied, feeling the first burst of genuine confidence he'd felt since he'd turned to find Alexei Mikhailovich standing in his kitchen.

A puzzled look flickered briefly across Vasiliev's countenance, and then he laughed, a harsh sound that chilled Litvinov to the very bone. Something almost akin to pity in his voice when he spoke again.

"Oh, I'm sorry. . .you believed that, didn't you, Dmitri Pavlovich? That your daughter and grandchild were come for a visit? Our way of getting your wife out of the house for the evening, I'm afraid. Irina and her husband— little Katya—remain at their home in Smolensk Oblast. Irina herself arrived home from work," he made a show of checking his watch, "two hours ago," according to the officers assigned to her surveillance."

NO. Something snapped inside Litvinov and he hurled himself against Vasiliev, a red mist seeming to descend across his vision, his hands reaching out for the man's throat—his mind consumed by a single imperative: *Kill.*

He never made it—the older man reacting with unexpected speed—catching him off-balance and pivoting, slamming him hard into the wooden floor. His knee, grinding into Litvinov's chest. Cold, expressionless eyes, staring down from above.

"Don't be a fool," he whispered. "Kill me, and you only delay the inevitable. Kill yourself. . .and the debt is paid."

He held Litvinov's gaze for a long moment more before releasing him—an audible sigh escaping from the older Russian's lips as he rose to his feet. He turned away, leaving Litvinov laying there on the floor, still struggling to recover his wind—pulling a chair out from the table.

"Get up," he instructed, gesturing to the chair, "and have a seat. We don't have much time."

7:36 P.M.
The Rag
Pall Mall, London

"No." Ashworth's tone was utterly uncompromising, his eyes betraying exasperation as he leaned toward Marsh, the remains of his drink long-since forgotten at his feet. "That's absolutely out of the question, Julian. I'll talk to C, find out what information he can provide about the possibility of this, this. . .mole, but the other is totally out of the question. We're not going to be making provisions for the 'defection' of the SVR's No. 2 in London, for God's sake!"

"Why not?"

The acting director-general swore softly, tapping the ends of his fingers together. An angry, insistent gesture. "That you have to *ask*, Julian. . .illustrates just why you're no longer behind that desk at Thames House. And I am. It is not in our national *interest* to antagonize Moscow at this moment in history, for a myriad reasons. The Russians are our principal source of intelligence on Chechen militants as the Syrian diaspora continues—if they close their doors to us, we lose our ability to screen those fighters out before they get *here*. And they are coming, make no mistake. And those considerations don't even begin to factor in our increasing reliance on Russian natural gas. We take the wrong step, and the British winter grows very cold indeed."

"It was not in our 'national interest' for England to respond when the Germans violated the neutrality of Belgium in 1914," Julian Marsh responded quietly, eyeing the man who had replaced him. *Out with the old, in with the new*. Perhaps he had been the wrong messenger for this, all along. "But this nation understood more than mere *interest*, back then. It understood the principle of the thing—understood that to yield in that hour would only encourage further aggression in the months and years to come, once we had been revealed as faithless. *Weak*. And so, England went to war."

"And an entire generation didn't come home from that war," Ashworth responded, shaking his head, "all because some old men were afraid that they might be perceived as 'weak.' Is that what you want, Julian? Is that what you want to see happen again? Because that's where your schoolboy ethics would take us."

Schoolboy ethics, Marsh thought ironically. His own hands, far more soiled through the years, than he expected those of the man before him would ever be. But you had to maintain some kind of hold on your *self* if you were to come out the other side. If anything was to survive.

"You've seen the rhetoric coming out of the administration in Washington," the acting DG continued, rising to his feet as if to signal that their meeting was at an end, "you know how Norton feels about the NATO alliance. This isn't 1914. If Britain stands this time, she will stand *alone*."

He started to speak, but Ashworth cut him off, holding up a hand. "We're done here, Julian. You and I wouldn't even be having this discussion if Phillip Greer hadn't gone far outside his remit—in probable violation of the Official Secrets Act—to read you in on matters you no longer have any legitimate reason to be privy to."

Marsh cleared his throat, suppressing his own mounting anger with an effort. "Greer did what he felt was appropriate."

"That wasn't his decision to make, Julian—you know that. Anymore than it's yours, any longer." He shook his head. "We may have a Shadow Cabinet, but we don't have a Shadow Security Service. Nor will we, as long as I'm DG."

9:07 P.M.
The terraced house
Hounslow, West London

There was no explaining it, Natalia Nikolayevna Litvinov thought, closing the door of her Nissan with a shove as she stepped out onto the kerb. Her daughter had been nowhere to be found—no record of her or Katya on any of the inbound flights from Russia. As if they had never *existed*.

Yet there were the messages she had exchanged with Irina earlier, right there before her in black and white. She'd showed them to security officials there at the airport, but there had been nothing they could do.

And for some reason, she hadn't seemed to be able to reach Irina since. Dmitri would know what to do, she assured herself, fumbling in her purse for her key as she reached the door. He was SVR, after all—the deputy *rezident* of one of the most important foreign postings in the world. A powerful man.

And of what use was power if you couldn't use it to help your family?

The door gave beneath her hand, letting her into the dark entry hall, a strange smell pervading her nostrils.

"Dima," she called out, reaching for the light as she moved toward the kitchen, "I'm home. There was no one at the airport, and I haven't—"

Her voice broke off suddenly, the light revealing a pair of trouser-clad legs, hanging down from the stairs above her. A macabre sight, swaying ever so slightly in the draft from the door.

She looked up, her eyes catching sight of the familiar face, twisted grotesquely to one side, and began to scream, helplessly. Incoherently.

Again and again. And again. . .

Chapter 20

7:30 A.M. British Summer Time, July 13ʰ
Thames House
Millbank, London

Roth was already there by the time Phillip Greer arrived, poring diligently over a mass of folders and files in the conference room that Greer had finally appropriated for their purpose late the previous afternoon.

They needed more manpower on this, but the circle had to be kept so small—at least until they could narrow down more precisely what they were looking at. Perhaps Litvinov could yet help in that regard.

And still nothing from Six.

He knew it was far too early to reasonably expect any such fruit. . .and yet, something deep within warned him that they were running out of time. That they needed results. *Now.*

Before it was forever too late.

"I think I have something," Roth announced as Greer entered the conference room, closing the door behind him to wall off the world without. "Have a look at this."

Greer took the Registry jacket from his hands, opening it to find a pale, youthful face staring back at him. *Simon Norris.*

"An analyst from G Branch?"

A nod. "MacCallum's right hand during his time there—one of his best analysts, focused on the homegrown jihadist threat. And two years ago. . .he was seconded to Six for nine months. It was barely mentioned in his file—as you can see, the whole thing is rather thin—and I missed it in my initial search yesterday. But he was there, and could potentially have had the access."

"Yes, but. . ." Greer flipped through the loose pages of the file, scanning for anything of note. "We've flagged any number of officers who *could* have had access—never mind that if mere access to Six means access to their assets in Russia, something is badly broken—what did you find to cause you to single out this Norris fellow?"

Roth nodded, shuffling through the mass of papers spread out before him. "I did some digging. Went through the archive of his social media postings from before he joined the Service—found pictures. From a BDC rally he attended back in '09."

The British Defence Coalition, Greer thought, the realization dawning upon him. The connection Roth was making. But it wasn't enough. "By itself, that's not—"

The former Royal Marine held up a hand. "Delivering the keynote of the rally, was Arthur Colville. His praise for the publisher, both in the initial post and subsequent comments to friends was. . .effusive."

It all made sense. The pieces, falling into place. "Mr. Norris is working today?"

"Should be."

"Have me notified as soon as he enters the building. You've done good work here, Darren. We'll need to make sure that we can—"

Greer's voice broke off suddenly as the phone on the conference table began to ring—reaching over to bring the receiver up to his ear.

"Greer." He went silent, an ashen look creeping over his weathered countenance the longer he listened. Shock and horror, mixing with a profound resignation.

Then, "Thank you, Rhona. Please keep me apprised of any further developments."

He replaced the phone, his shoulders sagging. Leaning with both hands on the table—whitened knuckles pressed into the wood. All the life seeming to have gone out of him in that moment.

"What is it?"

The old counter-intel spook raised his head to look Roth in the eye, his every movement weary—suddenly old beyond his years.

"The Met received a 999 call last night from a residence in Hounslow. A woman, incoherent—raving, crying, distraught. Responding officers arrived on the scene to find her clasping the lifeless body of her husband. He'd hung himself."

"The woman?" And Roth knew, the haunting realization of their mistake—of the *consequences* of their mistake—slamming into him even before Greer spoke the words.

"Natalia Nikolayevna Litvinov. . ."

7:45 A.M.
A flat
Edgware, London

He should have gone to work, Simon Norris told himself, peering through the curtains of his small studio flat out at the street—as if he suddenly expected to see Met police cars coming swarming down upon him. Kept everything routine—*normal.*

But he'd called in sick instead, unable to face them on this last of all days. Certain that his guilt would betray itself on his very face.

He wasn't even sure it was a lie—the pallor of his own face matching his dress shirt. Frightening him when he caught side of his reflection in the mirror, a desperate, bloodless white relieved only by the dark circles under his eyes. The detritus of nights without sleep.

He hadn't been eating or sleeping regularly since that night. . .ten days ago, was it? *It felt like a lifetime.*

That fateful moment when the Russian had slid into the booth opposite from him at the restaurant in Chinatown. Everything changing, in that heartbeat.

But that wasn't true, was it? The restaurant wasn't where everything had changed—so far past that fateful point of decision that one couldn't even see it from there.

His course, irrevocably set, long before. Years, even. Back to that first time he'd ever laid eyes on Arthur Colville—heard the charismatic publisher speak, in person.

Everything else, a consequence of that moment—a long line of dominoes, cascading into one another, down through the years. *Until they all fell down.*

He couldn't stay here, Norris thought, gripped by sudden resolution. His meeting with the Royal Bank of Scotland at their Fleet Street branch wasn't scheduled until four o'clock in the afternoon, but he couldn't wait here, in this flat, where someone might know to find him.

And there was so little to take, he realized, looking around his flat for the last time. An entirety of a life, left behind him.

Even his phone—abandoned here to keep his employers from tracking him.

He palmed the final burner the Russian had given him, sliding it into the pocket of his dress slacks—moving into the kitchen and taking down a box of dry cereal from on top of the refrigerator. Opening it up and shaking it until the flakes parted to reveal the USB thumb drive he'd concealed there days before, ever since securing the files from Six. A list he never should have been able to access, even with his clearances—the list of Britain's assets in Moscow. Current and former.

He'd expected to be arrested every single minute he'd spent there at the SIS Headquarters in Vauxhall Cross. Every hour since, waiting for the knock on the door—the uniformed security officers, making their way through the sea of cubicles toward his desk.

But nothing.

No one was going to intervene—to restrain him from doing what he had set out to do. To pull him back from the brink.

And he lacked the willpower to do so himself.

He shoved it into his pocket after another long moment, along with the burner—picking up his keys and the small pouch containing the larger portable drive the Russian had given him.

The door of his flat, closing behind him, one final time.

And somewhere, off in the distance, another domino began to topple. . .

7:59 A.M.
Roof of the World
Mayfair, London

The sign on the door indicated that the club had closed—finally—two hours before, after another hard night of raucous partying from London's youthful emigre elite, but signs had never meant a great deal to Alexei Vasiliev.

Nor did they to the two men flanking him as the three of them swept into the desolate club, brushing past security and the loose knots of staff working to clean up the detritus from the previous night's bacchanal.

His companions were hard, muscled figures—dwarfing Vasiliev's own slight frame. *Mafiya* types, former military, most likely.

But there was no question, looking at them, of who was in charge—the easy confidence written in Vasiliev's features, the smile in his cold eyes. A confidence that, in Russia, was the sole proprietorship of the security services.

As for the men, they had no official links to Moscow—beyond their admittedly dubious immigration status—which made them perfect for Vasiliev's purposes.

"Roman Igorevich!" Vasiliev bellowed, pausing in the middle of the club's deserted dance floor. "Where are you, you young idiot?"

Every soul in the place seemed to freeze at the sound of his blasphemy, wide eyes staring at him from all across the open space of the club.

He smiled at the reaction, a hard cruel smile—wheeling on a young woman in a housekeeping uniform, standing a few feet away from him. "Where is Roman Igorevich?"

"H-h-he's upstairs," she stammered, clearly torn between her fear for her employer's son, and fear for the man who now stood before her. "In the lounge. But he's not to be disturbed."

Not to be disturbed, the intelligence officer thought, feeling something catch the tip of his dress shoes as he turned away from her—looking down to see a discarded pair of women's underwear wrapped around the polished wingtip. He kicked it away with a snarled curse, his companions falling in step behind him as he moved toward the stairs. *We'll see about that. . .*

The women—most of them still half-naked, their reactions dulled by the after-effects of the night's revel—scattered like a covey of flushed quail at the entrance of Vasiliev and his retinue, recognizing in their arrival a greater threat than anything their. . .patron could have ever mustered.

Their patron. The room stank of sweat, alcohol, vomit, and urine, Roman Igorevich Zakirov's lanky body—naked except for an incongruous pair of socks—draped bizarrely over a white couch stained with his own vomit, a contortion made comfortable only by his own unconsciousness.

Expensive bottles of champagne, knocked carelessly on their side, and drug paraphernalia littered the low wooden table in front of the couch—white powder turned to muck in the spilled liquor, soaking a rolled-up fifty-pound note bearing the image of Queen Elizabeth II.

How far have we fallen, Vasiliev mused, his gaze drifting over the young man's face, the dissolution—the *weakness*—already indelibly inscribed in his features. He could remember the older Zakirov at this very age, so very many years ago.

So very different than his son.

It was enough to make Vasiliev glad he'd never had children of his own. Not that anyone had ever told him about, at least.

Old age was difficult enough without your legacy being marred by such. . .*failures*.

It was more than enough to have a protégé, he reminded himself, stooping down at the side of Roman Igorevich, pressing two fingers to the side of his neck. And he was fortunate enough to have that.

There it was. A pulse, still beating strong. The young man's heart still beat, fortunately or unfortunately—but it was enough for his purposes this morning.

"Get me a bucket of water," Vasiliev barked, his eyes flickering toward the young employee hovering in the entrance of the lounge, watching them nervously.

His face blanched, fear and indecision playing across his countenance—but fear of Vasiliev won out under the FSB officer's cold, unyielding stare, and the young man disappeared, returning a few minutes later with the kind of bucket a hotel might use to deliver champagne, filled to near the brim with cold, clear water.

"*Spasiba bolshoi*," Vasiliev murmured, dismissing the employee without another word as he took the bucket in his own weathered hands—emptying it over Roman Igorevich's upturned face and upper body.

The young man moaned and spat reflexively, his eyes fluttering open ever so briefly. Vasiliev stooped down once more, taking the boy's jaw in his hand, holding it firmly as he slapped him viciously across the cheek, leaving a red handprint against the pale flesh.

"Come now, Roman. . .did you forget what day this is?"

10:44 A.M.
Thames House
Millbank, London

"I saw the news. Am I right to presume that that was him?"

"You are, Julian," Phillip Greer replied, leaning back in his office chair, his office phone cupped against his ear. The coroner's photos of Dmitri Pavlovich Litvinov spread out before him on his desk. "They got to him, *somehow.*"

"I'm sorry." From most men, the sympathy would have struck Greer as meaningless, but Julian Marsh knew the realities of this world as few others. He knew, keenly, how this felt.

"How did things go with Patrick?" Greer knew the answer before he even asked it—knowing that if Marsh had been successful, the call would have come much earlier. *Last night, even.*

"About as well as you might expect." There was a long, awkward pause. "I was the wrong messenger, Phillip. Too much bad blood there, all through the years."

"You were the only messenger," the old counter-intel spook replied. He had known it was a lost cause from the beginning. . .there was no convincing someone of Ashworth's background that history had made its inevitable return. That the world order was nowhere near as stable as he believed. "Let me guess. . .he compared me to Peter Wright?"

"You know him well. I wish I could have done more."

"There's little else that anyone could do, Julian." *Except for what we've uncovered on MacCallum's analyst,* Greer thought, but he wasn't about to discuss that over an open line. The dangers, after last night, all too clear. "I appreciate your call."

He hung up, waiting a second before ringing his secretary. "Rhona, has Mr. Norris arrived for work yet?"

"No, sir—I just checked with Security five minutes ago. He hasn't entered the building."

Strange. Had he been warned—had something happened to scare him away? Or was this simply moving forward. . .*already.* The thought chilled Greer to the bone, and he almost missed his secretary's next words.

". . .just received a call from the acting DG a moment ago, sir. He wants you to meet with him in his office at three o'clock."

11:07 A.M.
Biggin Hill Airport
Bromley, UK

There were at least a dozen business jets and other assorted light private aircraft scattered around the small general aviation airport as the blacked-out Mercedes pulled into the carpark, wings glistening in the morning sun.

The playthings of the rich and famous. Alexei Vasiliev shoved open the door of the SUV almost as soon as it stopped moving. Men far wealthier than he could ever hope to be. *More powerful?* That remained to be seen.

It was ironic, he thought, turning to pull open the rear door of the Mercedes—a still hung-over, slightly high Roman Igorevich stumbling out, nearly falling before Vasiliev wrapped an arm around his shoulders.

He was only hours away from shattering the UK's intelligence network in Russia, and it would all happen *here*. Here, where once British pilots had risen into the sky to defend their country against another, far different, threat.

Men and women in the operations room, moving countless counters across the great map tables—tracking their efforts to intercept Luftwaffe bombers.

Their finest hour. They had passed a small RAF chapel on the way in—a vintage Hawker Hurricane and Supermarine Spitfire mounted out front, testament to the England that once was.

And was no more.

Vasiliev turned to find a short, middle-aged man hustling across the burning macadam toward them—sweat beading on his forehead from the exertion in the summer heat, staining the armpits of his dress shirt.

"Mr. Zakirov!" he exclaimed, unnatural cheer in his voice as he reached out, pumping the young oligarch's hand vigorously. "Richard Carrick, Spectrum Flight Support station manager here at Biggin Hill. It's so good to have you with us again."

And that was England today, Vasiliev thought with a smile—eyes masked by his aviators as he listened to Roman's almost incoherent, fumbling reply.

A dying country, prostrating itself before anyone with enough money to ensure its survival for another day.

Gulf sheikhs with ties to terror, corrupt oligarchs responsible for more butchery than most English kings. . .it didn't matter, so long as the money kept flowing in.

Hastening its death would almost be a mercy. *Almost.*

Vasiliev took a step forward, placing his hand on the short Englishman's shoulder—looking down at him. "What Roman Igorevich is trying to ask is, have all the preparations been made for his personal jet to depart from this airport this evening?"

"Of course, of course," Carrick replied, the ebullience draining from his voice, flinching away from Vasiliev's hand. "You'll depart here at 1800 hours according to the filed flight plan. Destination: St. Petersburg."

"Good, good," Vasiliev smiled, glancing at Roman. "His father will be glad to have him home."

12:35 P.M.
Thames House
Millbank, London

"There he is," Greer said quietly, his hand on the shoulder of the young technician sitting in front of them—his finger pointing at the screen.

Obediently, the technician hit pause, freezing the CCTV footage on-screen, the face of the indicated figure, clearly identifiable.

"That's Norris," Darren Roth confirmed, running a hand absently over his dark chin—his eyes narrowing as he stared at the screen. "What does he think he's doing?"

The footage was two hours old, taken from cameras at the Piccadilly Circus tube station. They'd first picked up the analyst leaving his Edgware flat hours before, the web of cameras thrown out across London and blanketing the Underground, enabling them to track his seemingly aimless progress through the streets to board the Tube at Baker Street, staying on the Metropolitan Line as he crossed London before switching over to Northern at Moorgate and finally to Bakerloo at Elephant & Castle south of the Thames.

And now here he was. . .pacing randomly back and forth across the platform at Piccadilly Circus, approaching the very edge at moments.

As if he intended to hurl himself from it, Roth thought, a sudden chill passing through him. "Is he. . ."

On-screen, Norris moved back from the tracks before he could finish the sentence—disappearing in the crowds of commuters—presumably in the direction of the escalators leading up to the station's famed circular concourse.

"Switching over to the next camera," the technician announced, glancing up at Greer in the semi-darkness of the room as he tapped in the command to cycle forward. But Norris wasn't there, the analyst's slight figure lost in the crush of people flooding through the station, as they did every day at the Circus.

Simply. . .nowhere to be found.

Roth looked over, his eyes meeting Greer's. "Should we alert Special Branch?"

"Not at this point." Greer picked up his jacket, throwing it over his arm—preparing to leave. "We don't have enough to go on, not yet. Just stay here, do what you can to re-acquire him. And let me know the moment he's found."

2:43 P.M.
Temple Church
Temple, London

I should have done it. Simon Norris shuddered, cursing himself, thinking of just how close he had come, moving onto the platform there at the Circus.

Just another step—two, maybe, as the train came rushing into the station. And it would have all been over—the thumb drive crushed beneath the wheels, along with his own mangled body.

But he'd quailed, at the last moment, like he had at every critical moment in his life. He swore, his knuckles whitening as his hands balled into fists—his eyes opening to look down into the mailed visage of William Marshal, lying there eternally in stone effigy on the floor of the old Round Church, as he had ever since the 13th Century. *The best knight who ever lived. . .*

"You would have done it, wouldn't you?" he demanded aloud, startling a young Korean woman who stood a few paces away, studying the architecture of the nave. *Fallen on his sword.*

But of course he would have—for in Marshal's world, honor had been worth far more than life. A brittle, desperate smile crossed the analyst's face, never reaching his eyes.

In his own, life was all—brief and fleeting, though it was, and honor? A name, scarce ever spoken.

In another hour, he would leave this church and walk the few blocks northwest to 1 Fleet Street, the old Child & Co., now the London headquarters of the Royal Bank of Scotland.

A short walk, that's all it was. And then his betrayal would be complete—his course irrevocable, once he'd uploaded the Russian's worm into their network.

But even that was self-deception—his course had been set, long before this. *No choice.*

Or maybe that *was the lie.* He felt like he was going mad, the room swimming around him, his eyes flickering up to find more stone faces gazing down upon him, grotesque, horribly distorted visages. *Mocking him.*

He fell to his knees, his shoulder brushing against the chain which held tourists back from the ancient effigies—feeling as if he was going to retch. *Or scream.* But finding himself as incapable of doing either as he had been of throwing himself in front of that train.

No way out.

3:24 P.M.
Thames House
Millbank, London

It felt like being summoned before the headmaster, Phillip Greer reflected, waiting in the DG's outer office. Ashworth was delayed—apparently on the phone with some opposite number in the United States. Perhaps the DCIA, even. Whoever they were, they were more important than Greer, and so he sat—cooling his heels.

There had been no further sightings of Norris on CCTV—not even after feeding his file photos into the OSIRIS network. *It shouldn't be this hard.*

The man was an analyst, not a trained field officer, there was no reason that he should be having this much success staying ahead of them. *And yet he was.*

Greer shook his head. If nothing else, his behavior was serving to confirm that he *was* their man. Now if they only had time to act upon it. . .

"You can go on in," Ashworth's secretary announced suddenly, gesturing to the door. "The DG will see you now."

With a brief word of thanks, Greer rose, crossing to the door of the inner office and opening it.

"Please, Phillip, have a seat," Ashworth announced, gesturing to a chair in front of the desk—not looking up from his papers, his pen moving furiously.

Greer took the indicated chair, glancing around the office as he did so. He'd been in this room so many times before, mostly during Julian Marsh's tenure, but it seemed different, somehow. *Changed.*

Toward the far end of the room, beyond the bookshelves, Marsh had hung a canvas of George Romney's *Cassandra,* the mad prophetess of Troy—granted the gift of seeing the future, yet forever doomed to be disbelieved.

It was no longer there—no doubt taken down by the former DG when he'd been forced out. Carried home, its prophecy fulfilled at the last. In its place hung another piece of. . .art, Greer supposed, a few abstract splashes of red and black paint against the stark white of the bare canvas.

No doubt Ashworth's selection, he thought, turning his attention back to the acting director-general. *Novus homo.*

A new man, indeed.

Even as he watched, Ashworth finished signing the documents, dropping the pen into a golf mug that sat on the desk to the right of his computer. "I had drinks with Julian Marsh last night," he began at long last, looking up to meet Greer's eyes. "At The Rag. But you know this, don't you?"

Greer just stared at him, inclining his head almost imperceptibly forward. "I do."

"And perhaps you are also aware of the outcome of that meeting?"

Another cautious nod.

Ashworth leaned forward, his fingers tented before him. His eyes taking on a hard cast. "What were you even *thinking*, Phillip? Showing classified intelligence of this nature to someone outside the community, someone *not* authorized to receive it. . .I'd be within my rights to cashier you, here and now. Probably should, even."

"Julian Marsh has served this country for longer than almost anyone in this building," Greer observed quietly. It was true—Five was known for the youth of its workforce. "My trust in him is implicit."

Ashworth shook his head. "That doesn't matter, it wasn't your decision to make. The rules are very clear, and your breach of them equally so."

And that was what mattered, in Ashworth's world, Greer realized, his face an impassive mask. Rules. *Order.* Results, far less so, as long as the inquiry would show that the procedure followed had been blameless. *By the book.*

"I knew I needed more evidence before I could make my case to you," Greer responded after a moment, the silence in the room becoming awkward. "But. . .events forced my hand. So I enlisted the help of a peer. Someone you might be more inclined to take seriously. Someone—"

"Who refuses to accept that the world has changed," Ashworth retorted, cutting him off. "Who somehow can't accept that we're not still in West Berlin in the bad old days. An old Russia hand, like yourself. That's why you approached Julian—there aren't so very many of you left."

"No," the old counter-intel spook replied simply, bridling his anger with an effort, a strange sadness hidden behind the thick glasses. "There are not."

He went on after a pause. "He's dead now, you know? The asset Marsh told you about—the man we were trying to extract. His wife found him last night, in their Hounslow flat."

"I know." The words came out flat, emotionless. Utterly unsurprised. He wasn't sure what reaction he had expected from Ashworth, but this wasn't it. The acting DG reached over to one side, picking up a manila envelope from where it lay on one side of his desk.

He half-stood, leaning across the desk to hand it to Greer. "Have you seen these?"

3:39 P.M.
1 Fleet Street
City of London

"Simon Norris, Security Service. I believe you're expecting me?" Norris asked, struggling to maintain his composure, to keep his voice from wavering as he glanced around the interior of the bank, taking in the white globes of lights hanging down from the ceiling above, a small knot of businessmen clustered together around the yellow sofas in the center of the room. Unable to meet the secretary's eyes.

Half-expecting her to press some button beneath her desk, a signal for Special Branch—the jaws of a trap, snapping shut about his neck.

Somehow, a part of him almost hoped it was. . .

But she smiled instead, a warm, genuine smile that seemed to mock the desperation his own masked. "But of course, Mr. Norris. We received your call from Thames House yesterday. You're early, but one of our associates will be with you in a few moments."

3:41 P.M.
Biggin Hill Airport
Bromley, UK

Twenty minutes, Alexei Vasiliev thought, glancing critically at the sky as he stepped out of the air-conditioned Mercedes into the heat radiating off the airport tarmac. *Give or take.*

The heat was building up to a breaking point, if the clouds moving down from the north were any gauge. Great thunderheads, towering into the sky, darkening the horizon with the promise of rain.

It might cause them some problems, getting off the ground—even if their pilot *had* cut his teeth flying Su-27s in the Russian Federation's air force.

But for the moment, getting off the ground wasn't Vasiliev's principal concern.

If Simon Norris was on schedule, he'd be arriving at the bank in twenty minutes or less. In less than thirty, the thumb drive Vasiliev had given him would be inserted into the bank's network. And the Royal Bank of Scotland's seven hundred *billion* pounds' worth of assets would lie exposed, to the worm.

It would be the most devastating cyber-attack in history, an entire bank's holdings wiped out in the space of a few heartbeats. Or as good as wiped out—the records of who owed what to whom, erased beyond restoration.

The records of whom had paid what to Arthur Colville. . .lost in the shuffle.

The fallout would destroy the British economy, bring down this government, like the last one before it. The shockwaves of the public crisis of confidence would ripple around the world, tearing apart the West at its very heart. *Money.*

And with their network inside the *Rodina* practically disemboweled, the British would be unable to retaliate, even if they could muster the will to do so.

All of it resting upon the shoulders of Simon Norris. *The man of the hour.*

A shadow passed across Vasiliev's face at the thought, dark as the gathering clouds. The analyst couldn't be counted upon, and he knew it, perhaps more keenly than Moscow.

But there was no one else.

3:43 P.M.
1 Fleet Street
City of London

"Your people have taken quite an interest in the late Mr. Colville's financial matters, haven't you?" His interlocutor was an Indian woman in her early thirties, dressed professionally in a navy blue pantsuit. *Rani Sherawat, a senior associate with RBS.* The look on her face half-serious as she glanced back at him along the corridor leading to the underground room that housed the electronic heart of the Royal Bank of Scotland's London operations. *His target.* "There's no truth in what the media has been speculating, is there? That the security services were responsible for his death?"

"No, no, that's ridiculous," Norris replied distractedly, still focused on her earlier comment. *Quite an interest.* "There have been other officers?"

"Oh, yes," she replied, brushing a strand of dark hair back from her face as she moved into the door, placing her eye close to the eyepiece and waiting as the machine scanned her retina. Both he and their accompanying security officer drawing up short to wait for her. "A Mr. Greer, I believe. You didn't know?"

The spy-hunter. He shuddered involuntarily, glad she wasn't watching his face. Remembering that day, only a few months before, when that very man had swept into the heart of G Branch's operations centre, Special Branch in tow. He'd known that they were coming for him, known then that it was all over.

He couldn't have suspected that that would have been a mercy, that he had so much farther yet to fall.

But Greer had taken away MacCallum instead, an innocent man sacrificed for the guilty—his misdirection successful, at the last.

And so here he was. With the spy-hunter's footsteps echoing close behind him once more. "No," he replied finally, mastering himself as she turned to face him—forcing a smile. "Compartmentalization, I suppose. We've never learned to share."

"Well then perhaps I shouldn't have told you," she said, seemingly embarrassed, opening the door. "This way, Mr. Norris."

"Don't worry," he said, following her into the cold, semi-darkness of the room. "I know how to keep a secret."

Did he ever. The irony of the words tasted bitter on his tongue, his gaze flickering around the room, taking in the dozens of glowing terminals—the faint chill in the air seemed to penetrate to his very bones.

His escort led the way to one of the computer terminals, typing in her access code and taking a step back. "There you go, Mr. Norris. This computer has full access to our network. You can bring up Arthur Colville's account history—all of his transactions, deposits, all the business he did with RBS over the years. Everything."

"Excellent, thank you," Norris acknowledged, withdrawing the thumb drive from his pocket, his eyes quickly scanning for a port. *There.* "I will need to make a copy for our Registry at Thames House."

"Hold on, hold on. . .wait just a minute," the bank associate interjected, bringing him up short. The security officer a few feet away, visibly stiffening at the sight of the drive in his hand. "This is a secure facility, you can't just come in here with a foreign drive and insert it into our systems—that would compromise the security of our networks."

"Ms. Sherawat," Norris began, struggling to keep his voice level—his palms slick with sweat, even in the chill of the room. He resisted the urge to wipe them against his pants. "I am only doing what I was sent here to do, and I'm sure I don't need to remind you that the Royal Bank of Scotland has agreed to cooperate fully with the Security Service in this investigation, in the interests of national security."

She just looked at him, not giving an inch. "That's all very well, Mr.

Norris, but I'm responsible for your actions while in this building, and what you're proposing violates every protocol we have on the books. I can't permit it."

The security officer cleared his throat, stepping forward. "With your permission, sir, I can take your drive and scan it on an air-gapped terminal. Should only take ten minutes, and then you'll be clear to proceed."

There was no help for it. Norris glanced from the associate to the security officer and back again, seeing no way out of handing it over. No way to talk his way through this.

And once they had scanned the drive. . .

He could sense the walls closing in once more, all around. The suffocating feeling of fingers, interlacing themselves about his throat.

"All right," he conceded finally, handing the drive over to the officer, "but while you're doing that, I'm going to need to go back upstairs. Place a call to Thames House."

He met her eyes, mustering up the courage for a Parthian shot. "It *is* Sherawat, isn't it? Rani Sherawat?"

3:47 P.M.
Thames House
Millbank, London

The story was there, written clear in the 4x6 prints scattered across Phillip Greer's lap. The story of their undoing.

Of a man's death.

"That *is* one of our officers, isn't it?" Ashworth asked after a long moment, his tone acidic.

A nod. "Yes, it is. Darren Roth, a G Branch field officer. The man I assigned to handle Dmitri Pavlovich."

And there the two of them were. Standing together in the middle of an Underground carriage, clearly under surveillance. Had this been the night that Roth had detected the Russian officers?

Or had this been another meeting, some other time that he *hadn't?* They had been rumbled somehow, that much was clear.

"Where did you get these?"

"They were delivered earlier this morning," Ashworth replied, his voice losing none of its edge, "by a courier from the Russian Embassy. They are claiming, Phillip, that Litvinov committed suicide after our Security Service discovered his embezzlement of Russian government funds and used it in an attempt to blackmail him into betraying his country."

"That's nonsense!" Greer exclaimed, recognizing, even as he spoke the words, the mastery of the plan. The net that surrounded them, closing fast.

"Is it?" The acting DG just looked at him. "The suicide note the Met recovered from Litvinov's kitchen table corroborates the money angle, and the Russian ambassador is preparing to lodge a formal protest of the Security Service's behavior with the PM."

"Listen to me, Patrick," Greer began, shaking his head, "Litvinov did not commit suicide. They *killed* him. They had him under surveillance—these *photos* prove *that*—and they killed him for it. I know that, you know that—anyone who examines this critically has to come to the same conclusion. They *murdered* a man on British soil, and they want us to answer for it."

"*You* know that, Phillip," Ashworth said quietly. "So far, you're right, but no further. You and Julian Marsh, perhaps. But otherwise. . .you're alone, and you can't prove it. I couldn't prove it, either, even presuming I was willing to stake the reputation of an embattled Service on what you 'know.'"

A knock came at the door before Greer could reply, Ashworth's secretary's head appearing around the door. "There is a call for Mr. Greer. A Darren Roth, G Branch—he says it's urgent."

"Excuse me," Greer said, rising from the chair. "I must take this."

"Tread carefully, Phillip," Ashworth warned, his voice hard and cold, his eyes boring into Greer as he paused at the door. "The potential diplomatic fallout of what has already been done. . .is well-nigh incalculable. I won't hear of you antagonizing the Russians further."

Greer turned without a word, closing the door of the inner office behind him as he moved over to the secretary's desk, accepting the phone from her hand. "Darren?"

"We got a call from Fleet Street a few minutes ago," his officer replied, the words coming rapidly, his voice breathless with excitement. "Simon Norris showed up at the RBS branch less than a half hour ago, claiming to be on official business from Thames House and requesting access to Arthur Colville's financial records."

Got you. "And?"

"And it's not clear just what happened next. He wasn't given access, and left the bank to head back out on the street where we were able to acquire him on CCTV being picked up by someone driving a black Passat a few moments later. They're headed south-east, near as we can tell—we're working to track them now."

"Leave that to the techs," Greer snapped, "and get us a car from the motor pool. I'll meet you on the street in a few moments. And alert CO-19—have them mobilize a team."

"Yes sir."

4:02 P.M.
London

Failure. That was all that filled Norris' mind as he sat in the back of the car, rain pelting down on the roof to the accompaniment of the rumble of thunder, glancing out through the heavily-tinted windows as London flashed past. *One final time.*

He would never see this city again, so long as he lived, he realized—and that was the best case, assuming that the Russian would overlook his inability to fulfill the original conditions. The request—the *order*, really—which had been Vasiliev's central focus from the beginning of their relationship.

"The people handling him were careless. . .you can make this go away for us, can't you? Find a way."

And he had found the way, and lost it. . .all in the space of an afternoon. A moment's indecision.

But he still had the list, Norris thought, glancing forward to where Vasiliev's man sat in the driver's seat of the Passat, an impassive, silent figure. Didn't seem like the intelligence type, for some reason. *A criminal, most likely.*

It was strange how discordant that judgment seemed to him in this moment, even as he prepared to exchange so very many lives, in exchange for his own.

Outside the car, the rain continued to fall—lightning streaking across the sky back toward the Thames, the crack of thunder penetrating into the interior of the Passat.

He could only hope it would be enough. . .

4:06 P.M.
Thames House
Millbank, London

The heavens had let loose by the time Phillip Greer emerged from the vaulted archway of Thames House out into the street, passing uniformed guards with slung Heckler & Koch MP-5s as he made his way to the waiting car.

Fifteen steps. *Less.* But he was soaked to the skin in the time it took to cross the street, rain running in rivulets through his thinning gray hair—his suit jacket sodden, shirt uncomfortably plastered to his chest.

Lightning rent the sky above them, the peal of thunder following behind it just as Greer slammed the door of the Audi shut.

"Where are they now?" he demanded brusquely, offering no greeting or preamble as the car jerked into motion, an intense, focused look on Roth's face as he guided it away from the kerb, the windscreen wipers offering up a rhythmic drumbeat.

"Passing through Herne Hill now," was the reply. "Cameras picked them up on the roundabout, merging southbound on the A2199."

"Already?" Greer swore, looking out the window as Roth merged with traffic heading out over Lambeth Bridge. London's legendary congestion wasn't cooperating with them this day—Norris was already further out of the city than he would have expected. Soon passing out of London's CCTV blanket.

Where were they headed?

Out of the country, little doubt about that. But. . .what? Sea? Air? *Was there still time to head them off?*

Time? Too much of it, for them to have any hope of making it to the coast. And the Russians would have to know that. Whatever Norris' gambit at the bank had been, they would have been prepared for it to result in his compromise.

And if he had yet to hand over the list. . .

301

They wouldn't want to give Thames House time to react, to mobilize a response. Get him out of the country, and fast. Beyond UK jurisdiction.

Air.

The conclusion reached him with startling certainty. It was only thing that made sense. Only realizing then that Roth was still talking.

". . .if they stay on the A2199, they should lose time in the traffic around Crystal Palace Park—we may be able to gain on them there."

It wouldn't be enough. "Biggin Hill," Greer announced simply, cutting Roth off. "We need CO-19 meet us there—lock down the airport. No one in or out."

The former Royal Marine looked over at him, taking his eyes briefly off the road. "Are you sure?"

"Think about it," Greer returned, taking off his glasses and fishing for a handkerchief to wipe the raindrops from them. "On their current heading, it's the closest general aviation airport to the city. Business jets depart from it all the time—many of them owned by Russian oligarchs with ties to the Kremlin."

And Ashworth's warning echoed once more in his ears. *Tread carefully, Phillip.*

But there was no time to consider that now, not with stakes this high. He saw the realization dawn across Roth's face. "What's one more Russian jet among so many?"

A nod. "Lock it down." Then, "Do you have a gun?"

"No." There was surprise in Roth's eyes. "Of course not."

4:37 P.M.
Biggin Hill Airport
Bromley, UK

"What do you mean?" Vasiliev demanded, taking a step off the stairs of the Embraer Legacy 450 business jet—his eyes boring in on the station manager.

"Exactly what I said," Carrick replied, seeming about to wring his hands in despair, the man's entire demeanor craven. *The attitude of a dog, seeking approval from his master.* He turned toward Roman Igorevich, leaning heavily there against the door of the nearby Mercedes SUV. The young man had been drinking again, but hadn't mixed them with any more drugs. Or at least Vasiliev was relatively sure. "I am *deeply* sorry that this has happened, Mr. Zakirov. I can't begin to express how truly I regret that you're being subjected to this inconvenience. I realize you must want to return to Russia as soon as possible."

The oligarch's son shrugged, his words slurring ever so slightly. "Hey, man, it's really not—"

"'Not acceptable,' I believe you were about to say, Roman Igorevich," Vasiliev interjected, transfixing the station manager with a cold look. "What *is* the meaning of this, Mr. Carrick? If it's the approaching storm, I assure you that there's no need to concern yourself on our account. Our pilot is one of the best—if he wasn't, he wouldn't remain in the employ of Igor Petrovich."

Roman's father. Vasiliev smiled, the unspoken subtext only too clear. *Those who fail Igor Petrovich don't remain long in any employ whatsoever.*

"No, no, no, it's not that," Carrick stammered, abject dismay spreading across his face. *The dog, once more, feeling the sting of his master's rebuke.* An endearing trait in an animal, perhaps. Not in a man. "It's not our decision whatsoever, I *assure* you—and it's not just us. All general aviation airports within a fifty-mile radius of London are being closed down, orders of the Civil Aviation Authority. No flights, in or out."

"Why?"

"National security—the nature of the threat wasn't specified."

And there it was. Vasiliev's smile vanished as quickly as it had come. "Thank you, Mr. Carrick. That will be all. Please, let us know when the restrictions are lifted."

It could only be the Security Service, he thought, tuning out the station manager's continued obsequies. Reacting to the devastation he had unleashed upon them.

Too little, too late.

Still, this presented a problem, their course now set. *Unalterable.*

He found himself touching the front of his sports jacket unconsciously, feeling the outline of the passport in its inner pocket. Kudrin had come through for him, at the last.

If only it would be enough.

His eyes drifted up to the northern sky, the towering cumulo-nimbus clouds now bearing down upon them like a slow-moving freight train, the rain line visible in the distance.

More than one storm was coming for them.

"I'm going to need you to go ahead and board the plane, Roman Igorevich," Vasiliev announced, brushing the Englishman brusquely to one side as he took his friend's son by the shoulder, steering him toward the Embraer's stairs.

"But, he said—"

"I know what he said," Vasiliev continued patiently, his grip on Roman's shoulder brooking no disagreement. "The police will be here soon, and we need to be ready."

"Police!?!" He thought the young man's eyes were going to come out of his skull, the panic almost comical. *How was it even possible that this was Igor's spawn?* The contrast between father and son, never more dramatic "What have you *done?* But that can't happen, that—what about the drugs, the cocaine in the jet? I need to get away from here, Alexei, you fool, I need—"

"To be a man," Vasiliev responded icily, his tone dripping with contempt. His fingers, sinking deeper into the flesh of the young man's shoulder—smiling as he began to whimper in pain. "Now shut up and listen to me. No one is going to arrest you—no one is going to touch you—as long as you do exactly what I tell you to do."

4:51 P.M.
Hayes, Bromley
UK

Ten minutes out, Phillip Greer thought, wincing slightly as Roth whipped the Audi into the small village roundabout, cutting off a box truck about to enter—water spraying up from beneath their wheels, the truck driver laying on the horn behind them as the pool car swept south, the little Kent village of Hayes a blur outside the window.

"CO-19 is eight minutes behind us," he announced, looking up from his phone.

"That far?"

A nod. "They're plowing through the same traffic we faced—rolling with the pair of ARVs and a Guardian."

A full CT-SFO team. A sergeant and fifteen constables, all of them heavily armed. Greer glanced out the window at the rain, cursing the storm for the hundredth time. *If CO-19 had been able to utilize the heliport at Battersea. . .*

But there was no point in wasting regret on the unavoidable. Only time to do what needed to be done.

He looked over at Roth. "We're not going to wait for them. When we reach the airport, we're heading straight in."

4:56 P.M.
Biggin Hill Airport
Bromley, UK

Vasiliev was standing at the foot of the business jet's stairs as the Passat rolled to a stop less than forty feet away, the gathering wind whipping at the hem of the Russian's sports jacket.

The sky black as ink behind him, dark and lowering over the hangars to the northwest—the first few heavy, massive droplets of rain spattering against the Passat's windows. Harbinger of the storm following on their heels.

The storm.

Norris just sat there for a long moment, seemingly frozen to his seat—unwilling to face the reality of what stepping out of this vehicle would mean. The final step in his long path of betrayal. As though he were something less than a traitor, as long as he stayed *here.* A desperate illusion.

"You get out here, *da*?" his driver asked, glancing disinterestedly back at him. It wasn't a question, the look in his eyes that of a man who would kill without a second thought.

Fate. Norris shoved open the door, stepping out onto the tarmac, glimpsing Vasiliev moving to meet him even as he did so—a cruel caricature of a smile playing on the Russian's lips.

"It's good to see you, Mr. Norris. Things went well in London, I trust?"

He wanted to lie, to tell him that it had—but somehow he feared the consequences of lying to this man, more than anything else in his life.

Norris shook his head slowly. "They stopped me before I could get the drive into their system—I had no choice but to get out there."

The smile vanished, an angry curse escaping the Russian's lips as he shook his head. "Then why did you bother coming here, Simon? The task with which I'd entrusted you, still undone?"

"I had no other *choice!*" Norris fairly screamed, his voice cracking with panic. "I would have been arrested by the end of the day, and you would have lost the list!"

"You have it?"

"Of course." There was hope there, and Norris seized it like a drowning man clasping a scrap of flotsam.

"Then let's see it," the Russian declared, gesturing to a laptop computer set up in the open back of the Mercedes SUV parked a few meters away.

"No, I'll show you once we're airborne—once we're out of this country. Then you can have the list."

Vasiliev smiled indulgently, the sort of smile one would reserve for a small child. The wind tousling his silver hair, raindrops falling all around them now. "What sort of fool do you take me for, *tovarisch?* You've failed me once already, why should I trust you again? Pull up the list."

5:00 P.M.
Bromley, UK

The trees beside the roadway bent and swayed in the wind as the storm bore down upon them, quiet country residences flashing past as the Audi sped down the road, seeming hellbent on out-running the storm.

But it would catch up with them, sooner or later. *All of this would,* Greer thought, overcome by a sense of foreboding as dark as the storm.

His phone rang even as he glimpsed the signs for the airport, indicating the turn-off for the Passenger & Executive Terminal.

Almost there. It was a bad time for a call.

"Yes?"

"Mr. Greer?" a woman asked, a trace of Cockney tingeing her voice. "Sergeant Kate Thomas, CO-19. We're seven minutes out from the airport— my team will deploy to secure the facility once we arrive on site."

Good. There was a moment's pause before the CO-19 team lead continued, hesitation in her tone. "Our brief mentioned a rogue Security Service officer believed to be at the airport, sir. Are we anticipating armed resistance?"

Greer shook his head as Roth took the turn into the airport hard and fast—the red brick control tower already visible ahead of them, silhouetted against the sky. Lightning carving a wicked streak across the darkness to the north, followed almost instantaneously by the tearing sound of thunder.

The storm was here.

"Truthfully, Sergeant. . .I have no idea."

5:01 P.M.
Biggin Hill Airport
Bromley, UK

Norris flinched at the clap of thunder, feeling unnaturally exposed standing here on the tarmac at the back of the Mercedes. *Naked.*

"Very good," Alexei Vasiliev announced, looking up from the laptop—using the trackpad to scroll through the list displayed there on the screen. No doubt already memorizing names, but there was nothing Norris could do about that.

Nothing he could do about any of this, now—his own powerlessness striking home, as never before. He closed his eyes, envisioning the platform of the Circus once again, the onrushing train. *Oblivion.*

If only.

"Pack it up," he heard the Russian say, closing the laptop lid with a sharp click. The thumb drive disappearing into the man's hand.

"I want that back," Norris exclaimed, feeling a surge of panic rise from deep within. "I've proven to you that I've kept my word, now I want you to keep yours."

"And I will, *tovarisch*," Vasiliev smiled. "And the drive, for safekeeping. *Trust* me."

"It won't do you any good! I've encrypted the files—you don't have the pass, unless you take me with you."

Another smile, as Vasiliev handed the drive off to one of his men, reaching up to close the rear door of the Mercedes. "I wouldn't think of leaving you behind, Simon. A man who has performed such service to the *Rodina*? Perish the thought."

Norris heard a faint, far-off drumming in that moment, looking up to see the rain line sweeping across the runway to where they stood near the hangars, steam billowing off the macadam as it came.

There was no time to seek shelter as it hit, drenching Norris to the skin in seconds—plastering his wet hair to his scalp. He stumbled to one side of the Mercedes, nearly blinded, struggling to wipe the water from his eyes just in time to see a dark navy blue Audi swing in toward the hangars, coming to a stop not more than forty feet away.

An all-too-familiar figure emerging from within as the door opened, walking across the tarmac toward them as the rain continued to fall all around. *Phillip Greer.*

The storm had arrived.

5:03 P.M.

Greer drew himself up fifteen feet short of the Mercedes, favoring the man cowering there against its side with a cold, hard glance.

"Simon Norris, I believe," he announced, raising his voice above yet another peal of thunder—rain trickling down his weathered cheeks.

A nod, as the man seemed to flinch at the sound of his own name—unwilling to meet his eyes. A pathetic sight, but Greer could find no sympathy for him in this moment.

"Get in the car and we'll go back to Thames House together." He paused for a moment, sensing the hesitation in the man's body language. "I'm giving you a chance, Simon—a chance not be taken back to London in chains. It's the only chance you're going to get."

"But what if he doesn't want to go back?" an unfamiliar voice demanded—its accents unmistakably Muscovite. Greer swiveled, his dress shoes scraping against the wet macadam—finding himself face-to-face with a man somewhere near his own age, slight, almost frail of build. Thinning silver hair matted against his skull. But the *eyes*. . .the eyes were the same eyes which had stared out of the jacket photos he had spent so long studying.

"Alexei Mikhailovich," Greer breathed. He saw the flicker of surprise in those ice-blue depths, but the man recovered quickly—a smile creasing his face.

A hard, cruel thing, that smile.

"Perhaps it's just as well that we know each other, Phillip," the Russian said after a moment, his use of Greer's first name a calculated touch. The implicit threat underscored by the quartet of men who emerged from their concealment behind the Mercedes, spreading out to flank Greer and Roth. Hard, muscled, *mafiya* types, in the intelligence officer's estimation. "Less chance that we might. . .misunderstand one another."

"No chance."

A shrug. "As you prefer. Mr. Norris has requested political asylum in the Russian Federation—something about domestic surveillance here in the UK. . .I don't know the details. I am only the messenger."

Another thunderclap punctuated his words, the rain continuing to fall—lighter now, yet steady. The sky ink-black above their heads, shrouding the airport in gloom.

Once, these fields had borne witness to young men in Spitfires and Hurricanes, climbing into that very sky to defend their country against unspeakable evil. The men, the planes were gone. . .but the evil remained. A different form, a different face, but the threat never so real.

"If Mr. Norris desired asylum," Greer said quietly, "he should have applied through proper channels. But he hasn't, and there's no asylum here. You're not leaving—none of you are. Deliver that message, *messenger.*"

Another smile, this time directed at where Roth stood, a few paces behind Greer and to his left. Sizing up the former Royal Marine.

"Who is going to stop us. . .you?"

5:08 P.M.
Embassy of the Russian Federation
Kensington Palace Gardens, London

"Then tell him that it's *important!*" Valeriy Kudrin swore, glancing angrily up at the clock on the wall of his office. It was his second call in the last five minutes, and thus far, the *rezident* was running into a brick wall with the ambassador's head of security.

"Mikhail Yevgenyevich is at dinner with his wife and the Canadian ambassador," the bodyguard replied coolly. "He left explicit instructions not to be disturbed, but I will convey your message once they have finished."

"Listen to me very carefully," Kudrin began once again, acid in his voice. "I do not care if the ambassador is at dinner with the Prime Minister *himself*. If you do not get him for me at once, your next assignment will find you pulling private security in Damascus. Do you understand?"

There was a brief pause, and then a mumbled apology from the man. "One moment."

It made one wonder how he had risen to such a high level without realizing that one did not trifle with the security services, Kudrin mused—forcing a smile to calm himself as he waited. It wasn't a mistake the bodyguard would make a second time.

On the wall, the moments ticked by, Kudrin's office quiet enough to hear the movements of the clock's hand. And then a man's voice came on the line.

"Mikhail Yevgenyevich," Kudrin greeted warmly, "I am deeply sorry to have disturbed you. . ."

5:09 P.M.
Biggin Hill Airport
Bromley, UK

"I mean," the Russian continued, taking a step closer to Greer, his cheeks wet with rain, "I know you've closed the airport. But. . .money can unlock many doors in this country. Perhaps it can even unlock the sky? Are you really going to stop us?"

"If necessary," the old spook replied, his eyes never leaving Vasiliev's face. Sensing his men, spreading out further. *Flanking.*

So this is where I die, he thought. All those years, running counter-intel against the Soviets in Eastern Europe—he'd rarely feared death. And now, here he was. . .preparing to meet his end in the fields of Kent. The world had changed, after all.

Just not in the way Ashworth expected. The thought brought an ironic smile to his lips as he braced himself, feeling Roth tense at his side. They would go down together.

And then, as if in a dream, he heard the sirens—saw the pair of Armed Response Vehicles swing out into the open around the edge of the hangars, lights flashing through the rain.

A woman in the bulky, wolf-grey tactical uniform of the Met's CT-SFO teams emerging from the lead ARV—her rifle already up as she advanced, flanked by her fellow officers.

The easily recognizable, ambulance-like silhouette of an armored Jankel Guardian crossing the airfield fifty meters out to take up a blocking position on the runway—operators spilling out of the back, weapons leveled. The distinctive outline of a sniper rifle in one officer's hands.

Greer turned back to Vasiliev, meeting the man's eyes. "Checkmate, Alexei."

The Russian took a step back, a strangely enigmatic smile playing across his features as he spread his hands, raising them in accordance with the woman's barked order. "No, Phillip. . .only 'check.'"

5:14 P.M.
Embassy of the Russian Federation
Kensington Palace Gardens, London

The ticking of the clock was enough to drive a man mad. Valeriy Kudrin swore softly to himself, shaking his head, the sound of his own voice somehow alien in the quiet.

Waiting. It was a helpless feeling, all the more so since he'd been tasked with the execution of another man's plan—not his own. An unaccustomed subordination for the *rezident.*

He could only hope that the confidence Moscow seemed to repose in Alexei Mikhailovich was well-placed. Working in the security services, one always heard stories about men like Vasiliev. Men who remembered the old days.

Who had survived the chaos of the interregnum in the '90s, strangely unscathed.

Kudrin rose from his chair, walking over to the window of his office, gazing out from the chancellery over Perks' Field to the southwest, toward Kensington Palace itself.

From this vantage point, one could often see the royal helicopters landing on the field below, their occupants hurried toward the palace under escort. Heavy escort now, in the wake of the Balmoral attacks.

Attacks in which Russia had itself had an unknowing hand, the *resident* thought. Hoping in that moment that the stories of Vasiliev were true.

He glanced back toward the clock on the wall. They would all know, soon enough.

5:17 P.M.
Biggin Hill Airport
Bromley, UK

"You are being placed under arrest on charges of violating the Official Secrets Act."

A death knell in the woman's voice, ringing again and again in Norris' ears—a pair of uniformed CO-19 officers gripping him tightly under the arms as they pulled him to his feet, a light rain still falling on his upturned face.

"No, no, no," he stammered, his body shuddering as he twisted his head around to stare at Vasiliev—standing there a few feet away. "You can't *do* this—you can't let them take me. *You promised.*"

But there was no help to be found there, no sympathy in the Russian's face. Only *contempt*.

So always to traitors. . .

"He can't help you now," Greer observed, raising his voice to be heard, the wail of the police sirens providing a discordant accompaniment to the now-distant rumble of thunder. The storm was passing, ever so slowly, its fury spent. "He can't even help himself. Place this man under arrest as well, Sergeant."

"On what charge?" Vasiliev asked, that curiously unsettling smile still playing at his lips. *What was his game?*

The uncertainty nettled Greer. "You're an FSB intelligence officer, operating in the UK under a false passport. I think that should about cover it. Cuff him, Sergeant Thomas."

The policewoman moved to comply, but the Russian backed away, holding up a hand.

"Please, may I?" he asked, mindful of the officers' weapons on he and his men—gesturing to the inner pocket of his soaked sports jacket.

She nodded cautiously, her hand resting on the pistol grip of her H&K G36—her eyes never leaving Vasiliev's face as he produced a passport, handing it over. "I believe you'll find everything to be in order. . .I'm not sure what Mr. Greer has been told, but I'm here in the UK officially, as a diplomat of the Russian Federation. And as such, I possess diplomatic immunity."

The Russian was lying. It was that simple. *There was just no way. . .*

He saw the policewoman begin to nod, and the smile faded from Greer's face. *No.*

She handed the passport over, and Greer began to leaf through it—his breath catching in his throat. *Impossible.*

And yet, if it were a fake, it was a high-quality one. The kind of thing the FSB were so very good at. Always had been.

But was there time. . .

"But he has the drive!"

It was a panicked, angry cry, bursting from Norris' lips as he struggled against the officers holding him back. *Betrayal.*

"A drive?" Vasiliev asked, spreading his hands in a gesture of innocence as the officers dragged Norris off to the waiting Guardian. "I don't know of what he speaks."

He glanced back to see armed CO-19 officers escorting a young man off the plane, his hands cuffed behind him. "If you would accept a piece of advice, Mr. Greer, from a friend—"

"You're not a friend," Greer responded coldly. *What is he playing at? Buying time? For what?*

A shrug. "From an adversary, then. Tread carefully around Roman Igorevich—his father is a very, very powerful man. In both Russia and here, in the UK. Very wealthy, with many business holdings in this country. I would be cautious about trifling with his son."

Greer nodded, his eyes boring into Vasiliev. "I'm sure you would be. But I'll hazard the risk. Sergeant Thomas!"

"Sir?" the policewoman asked, her hand still resting on the grip of her rifle.

"Clear the plane—take everyone into temporary custody, until we've located the drive to which Mr. Norris refers."

"Right away, sir." She toggled her lip mike, speaking brusquely into it. "Rogers, Mittal, move in on the plane and clear it. Husain, maintain overwatch on the long gun."

"Sergeant!" Greer swiveled to see one of the CO-19 officers approaching, a mobile phone in his outstretched hand. "A call for you—London."

He exchanged an uncertain glance with Roth, watching with a growing sense of disquiet as she moved fifteen feet away, taking the call.

It was impossible to hear the conversation at that distance, but the anger and confusion was clearly visible on her broad, open face the longer she listened.

What was happening? Even as he watched, she shoved the phone back in the pocket of her tactical vest, issuing orders into her lip mike. Her voice indistinct, but the effect. . .immediately visible as the armored Guardian began to back off from its blocking position on the runway. The officers near the jet, removing the cuffs from Roman Igorevich. Backing away, their weapons now lowered.

He looked over to see Vasiliev smile, the sight enraging him beyond words. *With the certainty of what had been done.*

"What's going on here, Sergeant?" Greer demanded, the anger boiling up within him as she returned to where they stood.

"My team has received orders to stand down," she responded, her voice clear and professional. All emotion, now suppressed, somewhere deep inside. "The plane is to be allowed to depart—with its full complement."

Disaster. Greer just stared at her for what seemed like an eternity, unable to process her words. The fury, spilling over.

"On *whose* authority?"

"Scotland Yard. That was Commissioner Harington herself on the phone, sir." *The head of the Met.* "And I've been ordered to give you an escort back to Thames House. Immediately."

We all fall down. And he could hear Ashworth's voice, echoing once again through the chambers of his mind. *"I won't hear of you antagonizing the Russians further."*

"You don't understand the stakes here, Sergeant. If these men are allowed to leave this country, people will *die.*"

She shook her head, resolution clear in her eyes. "I have my orders, sir. And respectfully, you do as well."

There was no moving her. Anymore than one might have moved a stone wall. He turned to meet Vasiliev's smile, easy and mocking. "It appears that you won't be hosting me after all, Phillip. A pity. Perhaps another time. If you are ever in Russia. . ."

The Russian bowed slightly before turning away to walk back toward the business jet, flanked as ever by his *mafiya* escort. And all Greer could see was the death images of Dmitri Pavlovich Litvinov, lying slumped on the floor of his Hounslow flat, his body distended in death—neck twisted to one side at a grossly unnatural angle.

And he knew he had looked into the eyes of his killer.

"Sergeant Thomas," Greer began quietly, a murderous glint visible in his eyes, just behind the thick glasses. "Give me your sidearm."

"What are you doing, sir?" Roth's voice, faint and indistinct. *So very far away.*

"That was an order, Sergeant Thomas." His own voice sounded alien in this moment, tinged by an unfamiliar desperation. "Give me your weapon. *Do it now!*"

"I'm sorry, sir, but I can't do that."

And he felt an officer's hand on his arm—holding him back as they stood there, watching the Russians board the business jet, one by one. Disappearing from view within the aircraft's fuselage. Each one of them, another nail biting deep into the lid of a coffin.

He was still standing there, his eyes hard and cold, twenty minutes later as the Embraer Legacy 4500 taxiied out onto the main runway, gathering speed as it raced down the apron like one of those fighter planes from so very long ago. Rising into the cloudy skies to the north-east. Disappearing from sight.

And through it all, a single name continued to ring through Greer's mind. Merciless. Unforgiving.

Ashworth.

Part II

(Two weeks later)

Chapter 21

1:30 A.M. Central European Summer Time, July 28th
A hotel room
Paris, France

It had been a week since the e-mail had arrived, Grigoriy Kolesnikov thought, padding back across the soft carpet of the hotel room to where the laptop sat open on the wood of the bureau.

An e-mail from a dead man. *Said bin Mohammed Lahcen.*

He had been playing around the edges of Gamal Belkaïd's criminal network since receiving the folder, but he hadn't anticipated that the man himself would reach out.

Even less that it would be done in such an. . .unsubtle manner. He had clearly discovered the money in Lahcen's accounts, but he had to know that whoever had been paying Lahcen would also know of his death.

Yet he had apparently chosen to probe anyway. *See what would happen.*

Moscow had taken several days to deliberate on their response, an abrogation of his own field authority that nettled Kolesnikov.

But in the end, they had made the decision to send him in. *With back-up.* Such as it was.

He tabbed to the e-mail client, tapping his finger impatiently against the bureau top. *Eight hours.*

And no response. Had he—had *Moscow*—waited too long? Had Belkaïd been spooked by their own non-response?

And yet the FSB's agents-in-place within the world of European organized crime reported no signs of any such moves taking place. And a player of

Belkaïd's influence would have left signs.

Kolesnikov yawned, covering his mouth with the back of his hand. He'd spent longer nights, many of them, partying with women in Moscow's club scene back in his early twenties, but he was no longer in his twenties, and the demands of sleep were somehow far more pressing than they had once been.

A weary smile touched his lips at the memory. Back then, the women had often mistaken him for a "Forbes"—a youthful member of Russia's *nouveau riche*—but those who had come to share his bed had learned the truth.

That *power* could exist, separate from wealth. And was its own aphrodisiac.

A sudden *ping* from the laptop drew his attention back to the screen, a new message showing in the client.

A single word, displayed on-screen as he opened the message. *Agreed.*

It was on.

5:03 A.M.
A farmhouse
Outside Liège, Belgium

The door of the shed groaned as Harry pushed it open, stepping out into the humid, still air of the morning. He took a few steps before stooping over—hands on his knees, breathing deeply, drinking it into his lungs as though he could somehow purge himself of the odors that had surrounded him for the previous seven hours—the pungent smell of bleach that clung to him like a garment, permeating his clothing and even his very hair.

He needed a shower, badly, but he knew even that wasn't going to be enough. This was the kind of smell that stayed with you. *The smell of death.*

Or at least its close cousin. *Triacetone triperoxide.* Or TATP, as it was known in the community parlance.

The explosive used by terrorists in the London bombings a decade before. . .and countless times since.

The explosive he'd spent the better part of the last week "cooking" several batches of in this farm shed.

He dropped down to one knee, staring up at the oak trees surrounding the small Belgian farmstead—the light of the moon filtering through the leaves, outlining their gnarly branches.

The trees were ancient—they had been here when the Wehrmacht had steamrolled through this country in 1940. When the army of the Kaiserreich had smashed its way into neutral Belgium in 1914.

Perhaps even when Napoleon had been here? It wasn't impossible—the farmhouse was certainly that old.

He looked up to see Aryn emerge from the shed behind him, stripping off his gloves. The young man looked exhausted—neither of them had slept, a dangerous state in which to be handling a substance as volatile as TATP.

Dangers he had purposely done precious little to mitigate, Harry reminded himself, drawing in another deep breath of night air as Aryn collapsed to the grass beside him. An explosion could set them back weeks.

Perhaps more.

He was rolling the dice with his own life, and he knew it all too well, knew the consequences of a miscalculation. There wouldn't be enough of his body left for Western intelligence agencies to even identify.

Harold Nichols would simply. . .cease to exist. And perhaps it would be far better that way.

"You doing all right, brother?" he asked, hearing Aryn cough spasmodically beside him, the young man's body convulsing.

Aryn nodded, his face just visible in the morning darkness. "Yeah, that stuff just gets in your throat." He grinned wryly. "I could use a drink."

There was surprise and disapproval in Harry's eyes, and it must have showed, because the younger man shook his head. "Oh, I don't drink anymore. . .I know it's *haram.* But I used to, back before I went to prison, and sometimes the thirst is still there."

He went quiet for a long moment, gazing off into the darkness of the woods. "It's going to be worth it all in the end, though, isn't it? When we feast together in those gardens?"

"*Insh'allah,*" Harry whispered quietly. "Beneath which rivers flow. . ."

"I still think of what they did to her," Aryn said after a moment, his voice filled with pain. "How my mother died. . .alone, surrounded by the unbelievers. How I couldn't be there for her, at the end."

"You were there for her when she needed you," Harry responded, placing a hand on Aryn's shoulder.

"Do you believe that?" There was a raw earnestness in the question.

"As Allah is my witness. And now, after so many years of care, He has relieved you of your obligations to your family. As He knows best."

The young man nodded slowly. "So that I can at last fulfill my obligations to the jihad."

"*Alhamdullilah.* For He is the best of planners." The words had barely left Harry's lips when he heard the sound of vehicle engines in the distance—the harsh glow of headlights flickering through the trees. *Coming toward them.*

Harry scrambled to his feet, drawing the CZ P-10 Belkaïd had given him from the holster on his belt. Bringing it up to low ready, a round already chambered.

"Get inside the house," he warned, glancing back over his shoulder at Aryn, "and wake the others."

If this was the Belgian security services, they wouldn't last long, he thought—wincing in pain as he vaulted the low stone wall that ran along the edge of the entrance road toward the barn—collapsing in its shadow, his back to the wall, the pistol clutched in his hands.

And he would die first. Irony of ironies.

He was still crouched there moments later, when three SUVs rolled into the farmyard—lights reflecting off the white stucco of the farmhouse. Men spilling out of them, rough voices, raised in a mixture of French—and Arabic.

Harry rose from his crouch, the weapon still held loosely in his right hand as he turned to see Gamal Belkaïd dismount from the nearest SUV, less than ten feet away.

"*Salaam alaikum*, my brother."

6:14 A.M. British Summer Time
The terraced house
Abbey Road, London

The flat was quiet in the morning—the only sound the faint *snick* of scissors biting into paper. Julian Marsh removed the clipping from the sheet of newsprint, tossing the previous day's *Telegraph* to the floor beside his desk as his eyes scanned once more over the article, taking in the relevant passages.

Andrei Vladimirovich Dubovsky, 61. . . .former member of Russian intelligence. . . prominent businessman. . .found drowned while vacationing in Azerbaijan.

Roughly the same age as the rest, the former director-general thought grimly, opening the drawer of his desk and placing the clipping on top, the latest in a growing collection.

The right age to have been recruited by British intelligence in the waning years of the Cold War. Maintained and groomed for ever-building prominence as they rose through the ranks—as the old world was exchanged for the new. *And back for the old.* His own words to Ashworth, ringing once more in his ears.

And now they were dead. Dead, "disappeared", or in prison, swept up in a new "anti-corruption" initiative that, as ever, seemed to come nowhere near the Russian President's acolytes.

He had no doubt there were others, if his suspicions came anywhere near the truth. Younger, lower-profile members of Russian society and government—off the radar too far to warrant a news piece. But just as surely damned to the same fate.

There had been nothing from Greer since that morning, two weeks prior. Just *silence*, telling Marsh all that he needed to know.

That they had failed. Their best efforts, nowhere near good enough.

It wasn't the first time in his career that he'd been forced to face such a reality, but somehow now, sitting here in this empty flat. . .it hit home far more painfully than ever before.

Always in the past there had been the distraction of new crises to confront, the constant pressures of the intelligence business combining to keep one facing forward. *Let the dead bury their dead.*

Now. . .there was only this. A signal note of failure, to punctuate the end of a long career.

Marsh closed the drawer and rose, walking over to the window and pushing back the curtains to either side to let in the first rays of the morning sun. *A new dawn.*

And so many who hadn't lived to see it. . .

7:31 A.M.
The farmhouse
Outside Liège, Belgium

"You're taking a risk here," Harry observed quietly, once Belkaïd had finished—the small group of them gathered around the farmhouse's massive oaken dinner table. He felt Yassin's eyes on him—only too aware of the rift which remained unhealed between them since he'd been decoyed into Belkaïd's trap. "A risk we don't need to take. If I am right—if Lahcen was in the pay of the security services, we're never going to walk back out of there."

"If you're afraid, then I'm willing to take your place," Marwan spoke up from the other end of the table, the hostility only too visible in his dark eyes.

"If I were afraid," Harry responded, an amused smile creasing his lips, "I wouldn't have spent the last week working with unstable explosives while you remained in Liège. But *that* was a necessary risk."

"As is this," Belkaïd said, cutting off Marwan's angry retort with an upraised hand. "Men don't give money in exchange for nothing. We need to know what Said bin Muhammed exchanged for his money. And the only way to do that now is to meet with those who gave it to him. If they are security services, we will know before going in."

"How?"

Belkaïd responded to Harry's question with a searching glance, then, "Why don't you join me outside? Both of you."

The cloying, humid air of mid-summer already hung heavy in the air when they emerged into the farmhouse's rude courtyard—flanked by Belkaïd's armed bodyguards as the black market trafficker moved to the back of the nearest SUV, throwing open the rear door and extracting a large, hardened polymer case from within.

Unsnapping the latches with a practiced motion, he threw open the lid. . .revealing within the various components of a large quadcopter UAV, disassembled for transport.

Harry heard Marwan's sharp intake of breath, knew in that dangerous moment just where the young man's thoughts had gone. The *potential* of what lay before them.

"You wondered, perhaps, how I maintain my security?" Belkaïd asked, smiling at them. The smile of a man in control. "For meetings like this one—like our exchange with the drug smugglers in the Ardennes?"

So he had, Harry thought. The reason for Belkaïd's confidence in his security becoming suddenly apparent.

"This is the answer. The latest in commercial drone technology, the Guardian was designed for Western oil companies who need to. . .maintain surveillance over their oil fields in places where they might be vulnerable to attack. To sabotage. It boasts a payload of eight kilos, and a flight time of more than ninety minutes, when burdened only by the camera system. And above five hundred feet, the Guardian is noiseless. If anyone is waiting for us at the meet tomorrow night, we will know."

9:08 A.M. Eastern Daylight Time
CIA Headquarters
Langley, Virginia

Kranemeyer flipped open the cover sheet of the transfer request, scanning down the list of names before him, each with its brief, attached bio.

There was no reason to linger—his decision had been made, even before the request had been placed on his desk. His review, a formality—nothing more.

He reached over and retrieved a pen, scrawling his signature quickly across the bottom.

"Approved," he said, looking up into the obsidian-black eyes of the former Marine standing in front of his desk. "You'll have the men you want."

Jack Richards nodded, his hand extended as Kranemeyer handed back the clipboard. "Thank you. They're good men, all of them—they'll make a fine team."

"I'm counting on it," the DCS replied, leaning back in his chair. "How long before you'll be able to go operational?"

"Two-three months, max, I should think."

"That long?" Kranemeyer raised an eyebrow. "There's only so long we can sustain our current op-tempo with a team down, Jack. You know that. And the missions aren't going away."

"It takes time to train a team to operate together," Richards countered, not backing down an inch. "Even if they're all experienced officers—if they haven't worked together, if they don't know how the guy next to them is going to handle himself in the field—you don't *have* a team. And if you don't. . .you're going to lose people out there."

Kranemeyer smiled as the Texan paused, seemingly exhausted by the flow of words. It was an impressive effort for the usually taciturn officer. *He was growing into the role.* As Kranemeyer had known he would.

Being a leader meant more than just commanding men in battle. It meant protecting them—not just from the enemy, but from pressure exerted from above. And Richards was up for that job.

"It's your team," the DCS observed quietly, rising from his chair to clasp the Texan's hand. "Go make it happen."

The door closed behind Richards as Kranemeyer once again took his seat, absently rubbing the fabric covering the knee of his prosthesis as his eyes returned to the screen of his computer, and the notes for the upcoming House Intelligence Committee hearings, now only five days away.

Leadership. It *was* about protecting your people.

Whatever that took.

4:56 P.M. British Summer Time
HMP Belmarsh
Thamesmead, Southeast London

The lights. They were exhausting after so many hours. . .countless hours—days?—since he'd first been brought into this room.

Simon Norris lifted his manacled wrists from the table, placing his hands over his eyes in a desperate effort to shut them out, but it was futile. *Madness.*

That's what he was being driven to—or *perhaps*—perhaps he was already there. Had been there, before all of this. His betrayals themselves. . .acts of insanity.

He heard a metallic *click* as the door opened behind him, the lights dimming as a new presence entered the room. He didn't open his eyes, waiting in painful silence as the footsteps rounded the table.

"Nikolai Andreyevich," Phillip Greer's voice announced, harsh and unforgiving—Norris' eyes opening to find a glossy, 8x10 photograph placed on the table before him. The face of a young man not ten years his senior, staring back at him. "Andrei Vladimirovich."

Another photograph, another face.

"Ekaterina Ivanovna." A woman, this time, somewhere approaching middle age—kindly eyes looking out at the camera. Kindly eyes, somehow full of reproach.

Norris closed his eyes again, his manacled hands clasped in front of him—his head bowed, the tears beginning to flow down as his body shook in silent, pathetic sobs.

"Look at them!" Greer bellowed, his usually measured voice suddenly filling the narrow confines of the room. "They're dead—all of them. Because of *you*."

And so they were, he thought, beginning the litany once again as Norris wept. "Konstantin Grigorevich. . ."

Name after name, running together. Faces, blurring like ghosts in the mist. Men and women, now dead or disappeared—vanished forever into a prison network which had lost none of its ominous terror since the bad old days.

The worst single disaster in the history of British intelligence, perpetrated by the pathetic, sniveling figure before him. Something less than a man—and yet no less dangerous, for all that.

It could be so easy to underestimate your opponents—so easy to forget that even the weak, the impotent, could deal death blows.

Vauxhall Cross had made an effort to get their people out, but they didn't begin to possess the resources necessary for an operation of that magnitude. He had stood in their operations room, waiting and watching as British officers in Kaliningrad waited for an asset who never materialized.

A woman, a television presenter for a Russian news network who simply. . .ceased to exist, from that night forward. Her seat on-screen, filled without a word of explanation.

Terror. That's what was being spread, emanating outward from each victim like a mutating virus.

There would be no more walk-ins—no more casual recruitments, not in the wake of this devastation. The knowledge that there was no protection for those found spying for the British. That to do so, was as good as a death sentence.

British intelligence was blind now in Russia, and would be for a generation. Perhaps longer.

He had come to interrogate Norris, but he found himself unable to master his emotions for the effort—rage and sadness playing in Greer's eyes behind those thick glasses. He threw the rest of the photographs on the table before the chained man. . .the now-anonymous images spreading out like a macabre fan as he walked out, closing the door behind him.

Let him keep company with the ghosts, a while longer.

6:39 P.M. Central European Summer Time
Port de Lille
Lille, France

It felt as though he were walking into a trap, Grigory Stephanovich Kolesnikov thought, looking up at the massive heaps of coal, gravel, and ballast stone mounded up on the quay on both sides of him as he walked out toward the sluggish waters of the Deûle, the rest of the port of Lille stretching out along the banks of the river to the west—the sound of cranes and trucks backing up a discordant clangor in the distant.

The taxi had let him out nearly two kilometers from the port, an easy walk in the late afternoon sun. A chance to stretch his legs after the last few days' confinement in the hotel room—waiting on Moscow. Waiting on Belkaïd.

He was waiting no more.

His suit jacket was out of place here in the rugged atmosphere of the port, the young man thought—glancing down at the grey fabric—the stylish black dress shirt beneath the jacket. The gold chain bearing his icon of Our Lady of Vladimir visible in its open throat.

But it was a calculated impression. At times, it suited one to be underestimated.

Times like this one, the young FSB officer thought, catching sight of the small knot of men tucked in between two towering heaps of dark coal, gathered around their motorcycles.

And there they were.

"He is known to us," the burly, close-to-middle-aged leader of the bikers acknowledged, nodding his head grudgingly.

The man had identified himself simply as "Maxim", but Kolesnikov had seen his file. Knew the man's history probably better than he knew it himself—from his first imprisonment in the old days of the USSR, to his rise to prominence as a captain in the Night Wolves, the Russian motorcycle club which had grown out of those waning years of the Cold War. Each step along the way, recorded in the tattoos that sleeved the biker's arms, and covered most of the rest of his body. In the colors of his cut. And his name wasn't Maxim.

"Is that going to be a problem?" Kolesnikov asked quietly, glancing from Maxim around at the half-dozen bikers clustered around them, most of them leaning on the handlebars of their Harley Davidsons. These men weren't here of their own free will—the Night Wolves answered to Moscow, only slightly less directly than he did.

And he didn't know what, exactly, had brought them here—it was rare to see the Night Wolves this far from Eastern Europe. But they were all here now, serving the same master. Or so he hoped.

"Maxim" shook his head slowly, running a pair of weathered fingers over his wisp-thin, silvery mustache. The rest of the older man's hair hidden under a black skullcap bearing the image of Iosif Vissarionovich Stalin. "Gamal Belkaïd is a man it would be unwise to underestimate. And we have had. . .business dealings with his network in the past. But our orders were clear."

He smiled—a contemptuous, patronizing smile bordering on a sneer as his eyes swept over Kolesnikov's slight frame. "Have no fear, friend. . .we will keep you safe."

Kolesnikov smiled back, pretending to ignore the implied insult.

"*Spasiba, tovarisch.*" He looked around at the group. "Are you all armed?"

"Maxim" raised a suggestive eyebrow. "What do *you* think?"

Kolesnikov glanced coldly back at him. "In the future, Nikolai Timofeyevich," he said, watching the man's eyes open suddenly wide at the use of his *real* name and patronymic, "you would do well not to answer my questions with questions. Am I understood?"

Another grudging nod. "You are."

"Good," Kolesnikov smiled. "Then we will rendezvous tomorrow night in

Mons, and proceed to the meeting together."

"How will you get there?" One of the bikers asked from Kolesnikov's left and the FSB officer looked over to see the man sitting there, his long, curly hair flowing back over the colors of his cut as he leaned over the ape hangers of his Harley. "Ride? On what?"

He made an obscene gesture and began to laugh loudly, the other bikers joining in.

Kolesnikov turned quickly toward the man, closing the distance in two swift strides—reaching him almost before the laugh had died away—lashing out with a vicious kick that connected with the man's kneecap. Unbalancing him, a scream of pain escaping the biker's lips, his eyes opening wide with fear as the FSB officer shoved him, hard.

The Harley tipped over, carrying the biker with it as it crashed sideways to the gravel of the port, accompanied by the satisfying *crunch* of bone. Incoherent, sobbing screams filled the air as Kolesnikov reached for the handlebars, pulling the Harley off the broken body of its former owner. Throwing his own leg easily over the saddle.

He turned toward Nikolai Timofeyevich and the rest of the bikers, taking in the shock, fear, and anger playing across their rough features. *Good.*

"Now," he said, the smile never leaving his lips as he casually brushed a fleck of dust from his black shirt, "I believe I *am* understood."

6:54 P.M.
The farm
Outside Liège, Belgium

Harry set the bucket back down gently, his arms and shoulders weary from the day's exertion, eyeing the trace amounts of white, crystalline powder remaining around the bucket's rim. A weird smell, something akin to grapefruit, filling his nostrils.

TATP. Enough explosive—just there—to kill him, if he didn't exert the utmost care.

Him. Or someone else, he thought, glancing from the bucket over to where Marwan stood a few feet away, mixing together the hydrogen peroxide with the acetone.

The look in the young man's eyes when Belkaïd had unveiled the drone had been a dangerous one—both of them clearly grasping in that moment its potential for a use far more dangerous than that for which the black market trafficker was employing it.

And if they did. . .there was no sense in dwelling on that. He only had to stop Marwan. Ensure that his ideas died with him.

"I need a break," Harry announced suddenly, rising to his feet from beside the bucket—his muscles protesting against the day's exertion. He was growing stronger with each passing week, but still nowhere near where he needed to be. And the constant presence of the chemicals filling his lungs wasn't helping. "This stuff gets to you after a while."

Marwan acknowledged his words with a curt nod—he wasn't the most sociable of lab partners, the hostilities of their first acquaintance still simmering there beneath the surface.

"You likely should as well," Harry offered. "Your senses need to be razor-sharp working with these materials. If they're not—*boom!*"

He pantomimed an explosion with his hands, smiling at the younger man's reaction. "See? That's what I mean. You need a break, *habibi.*"

"I'll be fine," Marwan replied, a sharp edge to his voice as he turned away from Harry. "I'll take one after a bit. But you go on ahead."

"All right." Harry turned back with his hand on the door. "Once you finish that, empty the rest of the powder into the drum."

"You're sure?" He hadn't allowed anyone else to do it for the last week, making sure to be the only one handling the explosives in their most delicate state.

A nod. "Just be careful with it, okay?"

The sun was already beginning to sink beneath the trees when Harry emerged from the shop, taking deep breaths of the humid air as he made his way toward the farmhouse—glancing back toward the shop even as he did so.

It was so hard to calculate what would be a safe distance. The explosive power of TATP, ever imprecise.

He saw one of Belkaïd's men posted up along the entry road—a rifle leaning against the stone wall beside him. The trafficker himself had long departed, but he had left them with extra security.

Reza was standing near the farmhouse's old well—a rough, circular parapet of stone crumbling from age and disuse. He shifted away guiltily at Harry's approach, only then revealing that he wasn't alone—Nora adjusting her *hijab* about her face as she pulled away from him.

"*Salaam alaikum,*" Harry said as he came up, pretending not to notice the intimacy of their posture—the color flushing the young woman's cheeks.

"*Wa' alaikum as-salaam,*" Reza murmured uneasily, his glance shifting from Harry to Nora, seeming unable to look either one of them in the eye. "I should probably go check in on Marwan."

"I just left him," Harry replied evenly. "He's fine."

A quick, nervous nod. "I know, but I had told him that I would come help—he's probably wondering where I am."

And there was nothing more to be said, Harry realized, a dark fear gnawing at his heart as he watched the young man turn away toward the shed. Unable to say anything more to stop him. His fate now in God's hands.

Insh'allah.

"Are you all right, sister?" he asked quietly, looking over into her face, shadowed by the overhanging trees. Nora was beautiful, no one could deny that—a beauty dimmed only by the unfathomable sadness, ever-present in her eyes.

She nodded wordlessly, seeming—like Reza—to avoid his eyes.

"If there is a problem," he began once more, pressing gently. "If Reza has not respected your—"

"*No,*" she responded fiercely, the words coming out with sudden passion. "Reza is *everything* to me. He was there for me when no one else was—there to show me the way. Without him, I would never have found the true path."

"*Alhamdullilah,*" Harry whispered, smiling at her and receiving a smile in return. One of the first real smiles he had seen from her.

"You know that you need a shower, *non?*" she asked, her nose wrinkling at his closeness to her. "That. . .stuff stinks."

"One of the prices we pay," Harry replied, smiling easily, "that our world itself may be cleansed. It will take more than a shower to remove this smell."

"You were right, Ibrahim," a new voice interjected—Harry turning to find that Marwan had come up on them quietly. "I needed a break."

The young Algerian lifted his hands up in front of his face, the fingers visibly trembling. "I went to add the powder to the drum like you said. . .couldn't do it, they were shaking so badly."

Harry just stared at him, that dark fear within suddenly very real. The knowledge of just how his plans had gone astray, only too clear. "Then. . .you just left it for later?"

A shake of the head, driving home that fear like an icy dagger. *Disaster.* "No—Reza came in and I asked him to do it. He's fresh, he should be—"

It was a sentence Marwan would never finish—their world exploding into fire in that moment, the shockwave rippling outward from the epicenter of the blast as the shed which had been their workshop disintegrated, flying bits of rubble peppering Harry's body—a seven-inch splinter of wood stabbing through his jeans like a knife, burying itself in the meat of his thigh.

He ended up on the ground, Nora pressed to the earth beneath him— dazed, his ears ringing with the blast as he sheltered her with his body.

Her eyes were wide with shock and fear as she stared up at him—her *hijab* coming loose to reveal her blonde hair. He rolled off her, raising himself to one knee as he stared at the devastated remains of the workshop fifty meters away, nearly leveled by the force of the explosion.

Flames licking at what little remained of the wooden beams outlining where the structure had once stood. He heard Nora scream Reza's name, reached out to seize her as she tried to run toward the flames.

She swung into him—her fists beating against his chest, hot tears running down her cheeks as he held her close.

And as he looked over her shoulder into the consuming flames, he found to his surprise that a tear was making its way down his own weathered cheek—testament to a grief, all too real.

Loss.

Chapter 22

The farmhouse
Outside Liège, Belgium

There had to have been at least thirty emergency vehicles clustered around the burnt-out ruins of the farmhouse and its outbuildings, Anaïs Brunet thought as she dismounted from a Eurocopter Dauphin emblazoned with the familiar DGSE emblem—a globe, sheltered within the wings of a bird of prey.

Partout où nécessité fait loi. Wherever necessity makes law.

She ducked her head, feeling the rotor wash whip at the jacket of her pantsuit as she and her bodyguard moved together across the open field toward the remains of the dwelling. It had been ten hours since the call had come in from their counterparts in Brussels, a call taken by the DGSE's duty officer.

Reports of a massive explosion on the outskirts of Liège—passing motorists dialing 101 to report a fireball off the roadway, just visible through the trees.

Early forensic reports had indicated TATP—one of the most common homemade explosives favored by terrorist groups.

She saw Danloy and one of his VSSE lieutenants standing on the periphery of the police line and made her way over to them.

"*Bonjour*," Danloy greeted, extending a hand as she reached him. "I was surprised to learn that you were coming in person, Anaïs. Surely a subordinate would have been—"

"Insufficient," she replied, cutting him off with a hard look. There needed to be someone on-scene who knew the details of LYSANDER's operation. And there was no way she was going to ask Césaire to expose himself like this. "What are we looking at here, Christian?"

"A bomb-making operation gone wrong, most likely. At least based on the preliminary forensics." The administrator-general seemed delighted by the prospect, which was perhaps not without reason. Better for the bomb-makers to blow themselves up here, out in the countryside, than in the city center of Brussels. And yet. . .

"Were the bomb-makers killed in the blast?" she asked, glancing around her at the devastation. There *was* one ambulance among the emergency vehicles, but it sat unattended—away from the center of activity.

Danloy's face clouded. "We have recovered human. . .tissue from the epicenter of the blast,that shed off to the side of the main house. But no vehicles were found on the property when we arrived, and we have reason to believe the farmhouse itself was torched separately."

"By other members of the cell, seeking to cover their tracks before they fled."

"*Oui*. Presumably. What are your. . .other sources telling you, Anaïs?"

She glanced around them, taking note of the nearest Belgian police officer, nearly fifteen feet away.

"Nothing," Brunet said finally, reaching up to brush her hair back from her face. "We've heard nothing from LYSANDER in a couple weeks. We have to presume that he's being watched too closely to transmit a message."

"Or he's already dead." Danloy's voice was cold, but he wasn't wrong. It was a possibility they had to consider. And had been.

"Or he's already dead," she agreed, inclining her head toward the smoldering wreckage. "We will want access to the tissue samples your technicians recovered—to run a DNA match against our officer."

9:08 A.M.
The warehouse
Liège, Belgium

"How could something like this have happened? Answer me that, why don't you?" Belkaïd was furious, pacing back and forth—almost beside himself with anger and fear. Both at the threat of exposure, and, he suspected, the timing,

Harry thought, with their meeting with Lahcen's mysterious "contact" in Charleroi less than twelve hours away.

"You might as well ask how could it not!" he snapped back, grief and rage finally finding their voice. The knowledge of his own actions, weighing him down. *But it wasn't supposed to have been Reza.* "I warned you that the compound was extremely unstable—I suggested we move the drums off the property the moment they were filled. I was *overruled*."

He pulled up just short of adding *"by you."* The arms trafficker had—not at all without reason—been concerned that the drums could blow up in-transit, on the open road, compromising their operation before it could even get underway. So now here they were.

With Belgian and French security services swarming over the ruins of the isolated farmstead.

"And now my brother is dead." Struggling to master his own raging emotions, Harry glanced over to the laptop sitting on the desk a few feet away, its screen displaying the streaming video feed from a thousand feet over the smoldering farmhouse.

At some point, deep down he still hadn't been able to process that it was by his own hand that Reza had died. That *he*—and he alone—was responsible. He closed his eyes, wrestling with the memories. The strange, inexplicable *guilt*.

"I'd also pull in the drone," he observed, this time more quietly. "It's only a matter of time before someone notices that something is in the sky which doesn't belong there—starts asking questions."

Belkaïd turned, glaring at him for a long moment as if there was an angry retort poised there on his lips, but he left it unspoken, turning toward the man seated before the laptop. "Get word out to the truck—tell them to bring it down."

It was impossible for him to even know why he had said that—why he hadn't simply allowed Belkaïd to make his own mistakes. *Bring them all crashing down.*

Just another mistake of his own, he mused as the man rose, leaving the room to place the call. Now too many to count.

"Where do we go from here?" he heard Aryn ask, a cold chill permeating his body as the young man rose to his feet at the other side of the small warehouse office. Their *mission*, still clearly uppermost in his mind. "The explosives with which we'd planned to carry out our attack are gone."

"My *brother* is gone!" Yassin exploded, the words coming out in a choking sob as he finally found his voice, the young man's cheeks wet with tears.

"As is my mother," his older friend retorted, not giving an inch. "It doesn't alter our responsibility to follow in the way of the Prophet, to play our part in Allah's struggle."

"Aryn is right," Harry interjected, mastering himself with a final effort. Knowing he had to take control of this. *Now or never.* "Our brother died a *shahid.* He would want us to honor his memory by continuing his mission. The only question is how to do it."

He found Driss looking at him—the young Moroccan's eyes shifting between him and the now-abandoned laptop. "What about the drone?"

Devastation. Harry stole a glance at Marwan, but he seemed as surprised by the question as anyone else. "What?" he demanded, refocusing his attention on Driss. "What do you mean?"

"Couldn't drones like the ones we're using for surveillance—couldn't they be armed for an attack? Think of it, brother, we would turn the crusaders' weapons against them, bring home to *them* the very terror they have sowed in Muslim lands."

"It wouldn't work," Harry responded, striving to inject his voice with a note of confidence which was completely unfelt. "You would need military-grade high explosives to work with the limited payload of the system. Those were hard enough to come by in *Sham.* Here? Impossible."

Or so he hoped, recognizing in the young Moroccan's eyes that this was an idea that wasn't going to die.

"But what if—"

"None of this matters right now," Belkaïd said, cutting Driss off. "What matters is our meeting with Lahcen's contact. We leave for Charleroi in three hours."

11:23 A.M. Eastern Daylight Time
A diner
Potomac Falls, Virginia

"Seriously? You haven't found anything *yet*?" Melody Lawlor asked, stabbing once more at her salad, the irritable motion betraying the anxiety there, just below the surface. *Threatening to break through.* "I thought you said you had this covered. You promised me that—"

"I do," Ian Cahill responded, leaning back against the faded red faux leather of the booth. The diner had seen better days, that was for sure, but there was something comforting about it, for all that. *Americana.* A reminder of what the world had been like when he was a boy.

So much *simpler.*

"The food here is awful," she said finally, a look of disgust on her face as she laid down her fork.

"The burgers aren't," Cahill observed, replacing the remains of his on his plate and dusting the crumbs from his fingertips. "And no one recognizes either of us here, which is far more important than the food. You need to be taking this seriously."

She half-rolled her eyes, murmuring an obscenity beneath her breath. "I'm the one who has to live with this, day in and day out, and you think you have to *remind* me?"

"I do," Cahill replied, suppressing a curse of his own as he favored the young woman with a baleful glare. "Are you still sleeping with him?"

Her fork paused in mid-air, half-way to her mouth. "I don't see how that's—"

"Answer the *question*," the political operative spat, losing his patience—his voice coming out far louder than he had intended. His head suddenly coming up to find a middle-aged waitress standing at his elbow, eyeing him with a look of weary disapproval. "More coffee?"

"Yes, please," he said more calmly, gesturing to his cup. He waited until she had filled it and moved on a few booths down before he pressed the question once more. "So?"

"As little as possible," she managed finally, refusing to look him in the eye. "The last few weeks, only when I can't put him off."

He swore, his worst fears confirmed in that moment. "We've talked about this—you can't be doing anything that would cause him to suspect. To think that *anything* has changed."

"That's easy for you to say," she fired back, her eyes flashing fire. Her salad, now long-forgotten. "You're not the one who has to put on an act, every day, pretending to love someone."

"You never had any problem before."

She just looked at him. "I'm not a prostitute, Ian."

"Of course you're not." *Prostitutes were far more honest*, Cahill thought. The strictly transactional nature of the relationship. . .far more clear.

Not that Coftey wasn't old enough to know better. "Still, what has changed, really?"

"He scares me." She wasn't lying—he could see the fear in her eyes, cracking through the too-old-for-her-years D.C. exterior. She had finally encountered something she didn't recognize, and had no idea how to handle it.

"He should," he responded coldly. "And *always* should have. If you ever thought Roy Coftey was just an oversexed good old boy who could be trifled with without consequence, you were a little fool."

The expression on her face was as though he had slapped her. Perhaps he should have. *Long ago.*

"And that's why you need to handle him carefully," Cahill pressed, leaning forward and covering her hand with his own. "These people are *dangerous.*"

"I thought you said you didn't know anything about them," she replied, pulling her hand away—suddenly wary.

"I don't. But I know who's not talking, all of a sudden." Cahill's eyes grew hard. "And that. . .tells me plenty."

5:57 P.M. Central European Summer Time
An abandoned industrial site
Charleroi, Belgium

Charleroi had once been the capital of *le pays noir*, Grigoriy Stepanovich Kolesnikov mused, glancing around him at the desolation of the colliery—the heavy grass and weeds growing through the rotting ties of the deserted railway tracks not fifty meters to his west. *The black country.*

The vast coal mining operations that had fueled the Belgian economy for more than a century, his intel packet from Moscow had noted, until deposits had begun to run out in the second half of the 20th Century and Wallonia had spiraled into decline—a deep economic depression that some observers likened to the American Detroit.

He had seen it on the ride over, he thought, shutting off the big Harley's throbbing engine and dismounting. The desolation, palpable in the small villages one passed through—in abandoned buildings like these, scattered across the landscape.

The vaunted West, buckling under a mere *taste* of the pain they had inflicted upon his own country.

Soon, they would know far more than a taste. And the promise of that made even working with the likes of Gamal Belkaïd palatable. *Just barely.*

He removed his helmet, hanging it over the handlebars of the Harley as he turned to Nikolai Timofeyevich. "Have your men spread out—there along the rails—one up there near the entry road. I want you to stay here with me."

The Night Wolves' leader nodded, relaying the orders to his men as he drew a compact Smith & Wesson semiautomatic from its holster in the small of his back, beneath his cut.

"And keep your weapons holstered," Kolesnikov admonished sternly, shooting him a warning look. "I don't want this to escalate unnecessarily."

Something he wouldn't have even had to say if he were working with professionals, he realized, watching as the biker grudgingly reholstered his weapon—wishing, not for the first time, that he had some of the men from *Spetsgruppa A* he'd served beside in the Ukraine two years before. *Put one of them up on the top of that coal elevator with a long rifle. . .*

But there was no point in wasting time wishing for that which was out of reach. No profit in it. Kolesnikov turned back toward the Harley, noticing for the first time the icon of Gregory of Nazianzus mounted above the headlight.

As though the bike was meant for me, he thought, a smile crossing his lips at the familiar image of the saint for whom he'd been named. *Fate.*

"You crushed his ribs, you know that," Nikolai Timofeyevich announced behind him, clearly referencing the bike's previous owner.

"What of it?" Kolesnikov asked, turning to face the biker—his gaze cold and appraising.

"One of the ribs punctured a lung—he's struggling, may not make the night unless we were to take him to hospital."

And that was out of the question, and he could tell from the look in the older man's eyes that he didn't need the reminder. He simply needed to make his point—to lay the guilt at Kolesnikov's feet, as it were.

"He was a good man."

"A good man, perhaps," the FSB officer replied, leaning back against the saddle of the Harley—his body utterly relaxed, his eyes never leaving Nikolai's face, "but one who failed you utterly in the time of testing."

"Testing?"

"Of course," Kolesnikov said, his gaze still unwavering. "Why do you think God brought me here, if not to test your faith."

6:05 P.M.
A van
Seven kilometers to the southwest, along the banks of the Sambre

"And there they are," Harry observed, rising from his seat in the back of the van, watching as the Guardian drone described its slow orbit more than a thousand feet above the decaying ruins of the colliery, its cameras focused in on the small group of men gathered by their bikes along the train track.

They looked like members of a motorcycle gang—all except for one man leaning against a Harley in the rough center of the outspread men, his suit clearly distinguishing him from the rest.

Their principal, that much was evident. *But who was it? What did they want?*

Questions he had no answers to, like so many over the course of his career in intelligence. Moving—*fighting*—in a world of shadows.

"Do you see anyone else moving into the area?" Gamal Belkaïd asked, his hand resting on the drone operator's shoulder as the man manipulated the UAV's videogame-like controller—bringing the cameras out once more to pan around the vicinity.

"Nothing yet."

Belkaïd seemed to consider the answer for a long moment, the pale glow of the electronics strangely illuminating his swarthy face in the darkness of the van. "All right—we give it ten minutes, and then we go in."

5:14 P.M. British Summer Time
HMP Belmarsh
Thamesmead, Southeast London

"There's no way he could have gotten the names," Norris spat desperately, anguish showing in his eyes. "Not from me—the drive was encrypted. I took *precautions!*"

The earnestness was almost pathetic, Phillip Greer thought, regarding the traitor with a cold, unsympathetic stare across the metal table. As though he expected that he could genuinely convince anyone that he hadn't *intended* to betray his country, that this was all simply some kind of terrible mistake.

"You have to believe me, I didn't *want* him to have those files."

"Unless you were safe out of the country along with them, you mean," Greer returned evenly, leaning back in his chair. "You would have gladly given them up, all those men and women. . .so long as it meant that you were free. But he tricked you, didn't he? He took what he wanted and left you here to rot."

"Yes, but there's no way he could have gotten into them without *me*," Norris shot back. "I didn't write the key down, anywhere—not even in my flat. You have a leak, somewhere else—this wasn't my doing, you *must* believe that."

"He asked you for proof of the drive's contents, surely?" Greer's voice was quiet, his eyes impassive behind the thick glasses. Every fiber of his body yearned to reach across the table and strangle this *man* where he sat, but he suppressed the urge.

A quick, almost jerky nod—as if Greer were going somewhere Norris' own psyche had refused to *allow* him to go.

"I pulled the files up for him—on the computer."

"And you would have had to enter the key to do so. His computer or yours?"

Norris hesitated, pain and fear flickering across his pale face before he raised his manacled hands in a gesture of surrender. His voice barely above a whisper. *"His."*

"And there you have it."

6:17 P.M. Central European Summer Time
The abandoned industrial site
Charleroi, Belgium

The two cars pulled into the empty yard of the colliery not more than eighty meters from the nearest of the bikers—Harry's eyes flickering up to the looming coal elevator a hundred and fifty meters to the west as he pushed the passenger door of the sedan open, stepping out.

If there were someone up there—and he wouldn't have failed to post someone there, if he were running this op from the other side—he'd have a clear field of fire.

Even with the Guardian providing overwatch. . .he still wasn't comfortable with any of this. He felt the CZ's bulge against his hip, beneath the light jacket—his gaze shifting over to where Belkaïd's men were emerging from the second vehicle, the foremost man retrieving a folding-stocked Chinese AK knock-off from behind the seat of the car—extending it back against his shoulder.

His mate appeared a moment later, carrying a similar Type 56-2, a second magazine taped to the first.

It wasn't a reassuring sight—he'd seen plenty of the trafficker's men over the previous couple weeks. In a fight, they'd more than likely ensure that their principals got cut down in the crossfire.

Blue on blue. Friendly fire. And just as dead, for all that.

Trading glances with Marwan, Harry moved into position behind Belkaïd and to the right, letting the young Algerian take the left flank as they walked out into the open—toward the small knot of bikers, clustered near the railroad tracks.

The distance closing with each stride—Harry's eyes scanning the terrain, the abandoned buildings of the colliery, alert for threats in every shadowed corner—every potential sniper's perch.

But there were far too many such places. Belkaïd had gone against his advice, even in this—now it remained to be seen whether they would all pay the price.

Like Reza. Harry's face tightened, knowing he couldn't allow himself to deal with that now. His. . .friend's death, still far too surreal. For there was no other word to describe Reza. A friendship built upon lies, but a friendship, nevertheless.

Twenty meters now. "*Salaam alaikum,*" a voice greeted them unexpectedly, bringing them up short.

The man Harry had seen on the Guardian's cameras detaching himself from the bikers who surrounded him—his arms outstretched as he came forward to greet them.

"You are a follower of the Prophet?" Belkaïd asked, clearly nonplussed. His voice wary.

A smile. The man was young—perhaps four or five years Harry's junior, young and expensively dressed, his urbane appearance a sharp contrast with the rugged bikers that formed his escort.

But a man to be reckoned with—a lethal edge, barely concealed there beneath the polished facade. It might take another killer to recognize the killer in his eyes, but it was there, all the same—clear to Harry as though it had been engraven on his forehead.

He shook his head. "*Non,* but I believe any good relationship must begin with respect."

The voice was Russian, Harry thought—his ear honed through long experience, even though the man's French was nearly without flaw.

Russian, and. . .so very *familiar,* he realized with a sudden start—his eyes narrowing as they focused in on the younger man.

"You may call me 'Grigoriy'," he heard the man say, the words suddenly transporting him back to Baghdad, the late winter of '07, with a pair of Russian intelligence officers standing before him in the nearly deserted hotel restaurant of the Palestine, across the Tigris from the Green Zone.

A younger version of this man—then only in his mid-twenties. *And Alexei Vasiliev.*

5:25 P.M. British Summer Time
HMP Belmarsh
Thamesmead, Southeast London

"One final question," Phillip Greer announced, closing the last of the folders before him and stacking it atop the others. Looking across the table at the weary, disconsolate figure sitting across from him, hands manacled in front of him.

Norris had been awake for a long time—day and night losing all meaning in this place. Less than three weeks and the normally lean analyst had already lost weight, his face sunken and white.

"Was Alec MacCallum involved in your plotting with Arthur Colville?"

Or did you set him up, Greer thought, leaving the second part of his question deliberately unasked. His team had already reopened the investigation, uncovering "irregularities" they had missed the first time around, so certain they had their man.

Certitude. Certain damnation, in this business—a trap, so easy to fall into. He knew he would never forgive himself for any of this, to the end of his life.

"What can you give me if I answer your questions?" Norris asked, raising his head to look at Greer. Still clinging to whatever little scraps of leverage he had left—like a man falling off a cliff, desperately clawing to grasp any possible ledge on the way down. "If I would be willing to testify?"

But every ledge was crumbling to powder, and the fall. . .was bottomless, even if he didn't know it yet.

"Nothing," the CI spook replied flatly, reaching up with a single finger to push his glasses higher on the bridge of his nose. "But it might be as close as you'll come to redemption, this side of hell."

A long pause, before Norris bowed his head, unable to look Greer in the eye. His hands clasped before him, as if in prayer. *Surrender.*

"He's innocent."

6:26 P.M. Central European Summer Time
The abandoned industrial site
Charleroi, Belgium

Harry felt an icy fist close around his heart, his mind racing—seeking an exit and finding each of them closed off in turn. Knowing he was a dead man if the recognition were mutual.

It had been nearly a decade, a decade that had changed and aged him far more than he could ever have imagined, and even yet. . .it wasn't impossible that the memory would still be there, as strong for the Russian as it was for himself.

For that meeting had proved the beginning of a confrontation which hadn't marked the highest point in either of their careers. A confrontation which had ended in an exchange of gunfire, a man's life forever changed by the Russian's bullets. Grigoriy's own life, nearly ending at Harry's hand—a rifle grenade falling just short of its target on that desolate road in Anbar.

But there was nowhere to run, nothing for it but to face it down—to walk straight into the fire, as he had so many times before in his life. The CZ seeming to tremble beneath his jacket as he heard Belkaïd respond, "Who are you, and what did you want with Said?"

"Who I am," the younger man responded, "is far less important than what I am prepared to offer. I had a deal with your colleague, and while I regret his untimely death. . .I see no reason for my deal to die with him."

A deal. Between a jihadist—and Russian intelligence, Harry thought, his pulse quickening. The chill in his heart growing ever colder. For he was as sure as he had ever been of anything that "Grigoriy" was still with the FSB, now as then, back there in Iraq.

"What kind of deal?"

"We may not share the same God," Grigoriy went on, reminding Harry ever more of his mentor in that moment. *Alexei, you taught him well.* "But we share the same enemy. And that will have to be enough. You desire war against the West? I'm here to help you wage it."

Chapter 23

It had been a long day, Armand Césaire thought, eyeing regretfully the as-yet-untouched glass of wine that sat about a foot away from the laptop at one end of the long conference table.

A day which had begun far too soon with the call not long after one in the morning from his counterparts at the Belgian security services, the explosion outside Liège filtering its way through their chain of command—triggering alarms as it went.

"*Certainement.* I understand that, director," he nodded, Brunet's face visible on the screen of the laptop—the camera aimed at his own face. "But I am afraid that the political pressures here may be growing far too strong."

He had spent nearly the entire day at the VSSE's headquarters, a small, nondescript building on the other side of the city. Watching as the mood turned away from initial alarm to cold resolution. In a city—a *country*—already rocked by repeated jihadist attacks, they would not let this happen again.

No matter what it took.

And so now here he was, sitting in a hastily-cleared conference room in the building from which his legend indicated he worked on a daily basis, explaining the situation to his real superiors back in Paris.

"Danloy mentioned nothing of this when I was with him earlier this morning."

"I am not entirely sure it is the decision of the *administrateur général*," Césaire returned flatly. "Yesterday this was the sole province of security professionals. Today, it has become the domain of the media."

And they had both been in this business long enough to know what that meant.

"In light of the greater perceived eminence of the threat, OCAM has raised the threat level to three and the Belgians are pushing to put direct, physical surveillance on Gamal Belkaïd and any other members of the Molenbeek cell which can be located. Perhaps even move on the cell directly, to take them down."

Disaster. The end of all their plans.

"This was intended to be a long-term operation, Armand," Brunet replied after a long moment. "An in-depth penetration of the jihadist networks in Belgium. If they take the cell down now, we lose that. And if they establish direct surveillance. . .we risk losing our officer."

And this is why we should never have read in a foreign service, Césaire wanted to say, his dark features an impassive mask, concealing the emotions roiling beneath its surface. LYSANDER's face, still vivid in his mind's eye. If his fellow officer died now, it would be his responsibility and his alone. *Before God.*

"I know, *madame le directeur*. But you will have to convince Danloy. And his masters."

8:09 P.M.
The van
European Route E42, Wallonia, Belgium

"I can give you what you need. Whatever *you need. You need only to ask."*

And the reasons for Lahcen's confidence seemed suddenly clear, Harry thought, staring out the window of the van into the gathering darkness as they merged with traffic, flowing eastbound along the E42.

No wonder he had seemed assured of his ability to procure heavier weapons—with the support, whether he knew it or not, of Russian intelligence.

Destabilization. The ultimate goal of all "active measures", no doubt Russia's agenda in this, as in so many of its other operations in Europe stretching back across the decades.

But even so. . .to think of the Kremlin going so far as to finance and supply terrorists within Western Europe—that staggered him. The threat here, far more dangerous than he had even begun to suspect.

Far more difficult to handle.

He was in over his head and he knew it, just as surely as he knew there was no way out. *No exit.*

Just as surely as he knew, as the van sped on into the night, that if he couldn't find one, people were going to die. *Far too many of them.*

Chapter 24

"No," Harry heard himself say, raising his voice over the murmur of voices surrounding him. "The risks are far too great."

The murmur died away suddenly, every eye in the small office suddenly focused on him. Gamal Belkaïd's gaze locking with his own.

"I disagree."

"You have no way of knowing who you're even dealing with here," Harry spat back. "You can't begin to think that you'll be able to control every situation as carefully as you did tonight. And what happens when you can't? What then? One slip, and we all end up in prison. *All of us.*"

"Does that thought frighten you, Ibrahim?" Belkaïd extended the clenched fist of his right hand sideways toward Harry, skin stretched tight over bone, revealing the small tattoo, five dots arranged in a pattern like that on a die, inked into the leathery skin.

Un homme entre quatre murs—the man between four walls. *The prisoner.*

Somewhere, at some point, Belkaïd had done hard time. Not surprising for someone in his line of work—one didn't become a crime boss starting at the top. *And even so. . .*

"It does," Harry replied, staring him in the eye. "In Syria, all those months, the thought of dying on the battlefield held no terrors for me. The thought of being *taken*, of it all ending in the dungeon of a *nusayri* prison, prevented from ever giving my life in martyrdom—*that* terrified me. We're so close to

350

being able to launch an attack, here in the West. To jeopardize all that, for the illusory aid of a *kuffar*, is utter folly."

"But are we?" Marwan's voice, pulling Harry's attention away from Belkaïd.

"Are we what?"

"Are we really 'so close'?" There was a skeptical light in the young man's eyes, the danger only too evident as he once more maneuvered for position. "Two days ago, we had explosives, but no target. Then those explosives killed Reza—nearly killed me, as well. And now we have no explosives, or target either. That doesn't seem 'close' to me."

"God has provided us with the men," Harry replied, his tone a stern rebuke. Wishing for the thousandth time that the explosion had done its intended work. "He will also provide the means, *insh'allah*."

"Perhaps He *has*," the young Algerian returned evenly, refusing to back down. The implication of his words only too clear, an unanswerable challenge.

"I am making inquiries," Belkaïd said, before Harry could respond, "throughout my own networks. If this 'Grigoriy' is truly *mafiya*, they will know. And then we will act."

And you'll find the legend has been back-stopped from here to the Volga, Harry thought, recognizing the determination in the trafficker's eyes. The futility of arguing against it. *Because that's how Russian intelligence works. . .*

9:49 A.M.
Place Charles de Gaulle
Paris, France

"We marched into this city, triumphant, when this arch was nothing more than its foundations." Kolesnikov glanced at his phone, checking the fitness app as he stooped down in the welcome shadow of the *Arc de Triomphe*, recalling his mentor's words on their first visit to Paris together, more than a decade before. Remembering the passion, the fire in the older man's voice. *The pride.* *"Russian troops, encamped upon the* Champs-Élysées. *A vanquished Talleyrand, handing over the key to Paris to Tsar Alexander. An abdicated Bonaparte, melting away into exile on Elba. The zenith of Russian power in the West."*

Vasiliev had always loved his history.

It was that rare, defiant pride that had drawn him to the older man from the beginning, he remembered, rubbing sweaty palms against the legs of his jogging shorts. Pride in a humbled, but once-great nation. A Russia which could be *made* great once again.

"We dictated terms to the great powers of Europe that April, at the point of a thousand bayonets. And one day, we will do so again."

Perhaps that began here, Kolesnikov thought, straightening—his heart still beating fast from the run.

He had made the hand-off in a shopping mall on the western bank of the Seine, his written report on the previous night's meet—a report he'd spent the entire night awake typing up—encrypted and passed along to a cut-out who would in turn deliver it to an officer working under official cover at the Embassy of the Russian Federation on the Boulevard Lannes.

His assessment of the men they were dealing with. Gamal Belkaïd. . .and the others, the men Belkaïd had chosen to bring with him.

There was something familiar about the elder of the pair, an uncanny feeling of recognition that Kolesnikov couldn't seem to shake, no matter how hard he tried.

Perhaps it was just the smell—the ghastly odor that clung about both of them like a garment. A smell he remembered vividly from Syria, six months before, gathering intelligence in the ruins of an *Ahrar al-Sham* camp along with a contingent of Russian "mercenaries." *TATP.*

Belkaïd wasn't waiting. He'd been cooking his own explosives—linked to the explosion outside of Liège which was still featuring prominently in the news cycle, perhaps?

It meant he was going to have to handle them carefully, if his mission here was to have its desired impact. He glanced up once again at the arch, Vasiliev's words running once more through his head.

One day.

7:34 A.M. Eastern Daylight Time
Vienna, Virginia

The house was quiet. Painfully so, Roy Coftey thought, leaning heavily against the counter as he brought the cup of coffee to his lips.

Melody had been gone all week, visiting an old college friend in New Hampshire. *Or so she'd said.*

The doubt emerged unbidden, in his mind almost before he was aware of thinking it. But she'd been distant these last few weeks—ever since returning from Oklahoma, really. They'd had sex. . .three times, was it? *No more than four.* And even in those intimate moments of union, she had seemed withdrawn, as though she were withholding something from him—as never before.

He took another sip of the steaming coffee, glancing down at the phone in his other hand, scrolling absently through her social media accounts, looking for any sign that she was where she said she was. She had posted a picture the night before, of her and her friend, captioning it, *"So great to see this girl again #memories"*

But it was an old picture, of the two of them together in Paris, back during college, standing at the foot of the Eiffel Tower.

Why an old picture? It was a question he couldn't shake, no matter how foolish it made him feel, as though he were some kind of jealous lover. . .

Perhaps because that's exactly what he was.

He left the phone on the counter, taking the coffee with him as he padded barefoot back to the master bedroom, pulling open the drawer of the nightstand on his side of the bed—withdrawing his old Vietnam-era M1911 and laying the big pistol to one side as he rummaged through the drawer's contents.

He found the small square velvet box tucked in the back, beneath a jumble of papers—the light coming in through the open shades of the bedroom glinting off a diamond set in gold as he opened the lid.

He'd taken Jessie's wedding ring to a jeweler two months before—asked them to take the old diamond and place it in a modern setting, the centerpiece of a far more expensive ring than he could ever have afforded back in those days as a newly minted SF officer.

Since then. . .he'd just been waiting for the right moment. To give it to the only woman who had ever truly begun to fill the void Jessie had left.

In his heart—not just in his bed.

And now, sitting on the edge of the bed looking down at the new setting, the velvet box perched delicately between the fingers of his big hand—the

M1911 lying forgotten on the sheets beside him—Roy Coftey began to wonder if it had all been a mistake.

2:30 P.M. Central European Summer Time
DGSE Headquarters
Paris, France

"I am sorry," Christian Donlay responded, his face impassive on the screen at the head of the conference table. "But what you are asking is simply impossible."

"I am asking," Anaïs Brunet responded, favoring the camera with an icy glare, "for you to keep your word—to honor the agreement we reached when you were first read in on this operation, not even three weeks ago. We *had* an understanding, Christian."

"Circumstances have changed."

"You knew we were tracking an active terror cell three weeks ago. That remains the case today. Nothing, substantively, has changed. In fact—one could argue that with the loss of a significant amount of explosives and even personnel, their potential operational capability has been degraded."

On-screen, the Belgian intelligence chief went quiet for a moment. "I am going to be utterly frank with you, Anaïs."

"*S'il vous plaît.*"

"You and I do not serve at our own pleasure, *non?* We act at the behest of the political leadership in our respective countries. Three weeks ago, you and I knew of the Molenbeek cell, but our political leadership did not. Now they do—and that makes all the difference in the world, even if the operational realities were to remain unchanged."

He wasn't wrong, Brunet thought. But that didn't make the reality of this any easier. Or change the responsibility she bore.

"You have to be *seen* to be doing something," she responded flatly. "Even if it means endangering the life of our officer."

Danloy murmured something just off-mike that sounded like an exasperated curse. "Your officer may no longer be alive—you know this as well as I do. You've heard nothing from him since the explosion, have you?"

"That doesn't mean anything, in itself," Brunet countered, refusing to back down. "The cell will be working to minimize their exposure right now, in the wake of the explosion. I wouldn't have expected LYSANDER to make contact under the circumstances."

"What *do* you expect of your officer?" There was heat in Danloy's voice, a hard edge.

"This has to be about more than one bomb, Christian," she exclaimed, the tension in her voice rising to match his. "This is about our best chance to effect a long-term penetration of jihadist networks in Western Europe. Give us time to re-establish contact with LYSANDER. Then we can more properly assess the situation."

"Respectfully, Anaïs, for the last day the Belgian media has featured nothing but 'expert' analysis of the damage such an explosion could have done if it had been set off in Brussels. And people are panicked. One bomb *is* one too many. I can give you twenty-four hours, no more. After that, we'll have to proceed to place physical surveillance on Gamal Belkaïd and anyone else of the Molenbeek cell who can be located."

It wasn't enough. Brunet shook her head. "That may not be—"

"Twenty-four hours, Anaïs."

4:30 P.M.
An apartment building
Liège, Belgium

"It still doesn't seem real." The young man's voice was numb, scarce above a whisper. He stirred idly at the long-dissolved sugar in his tea, seeming scarce conscious of the movement of his own hand. "It feels as though I should expect him to walk back through that door, any moment now."

"I know." It wasn't even a lie, Harry thought, turning away from the open window of the apartment toward where Yassin sat, scarce a breath of air stirring the faded, dirty curtains. That was the worst of it. He'd killed so many men, over the years, and Reza Harrak had deserved it no less than any of them.

But the detachment he'd enjoyed back then was. . .strangely absent.

It was different when you had come to *know* the man in those quiet, intimate moments which formed the inevitable foundation of brotherhood.

In another life, they could have been friends—*no*, that was evasion. In *this* life, they *had* been friends.

In another life, that friendship might even have endured.

Harry stared down into the glass of tea in his hand, finding in it no relief from the nearly claustrophobic heat of the late afternoon. The familiar taste of spearmint permeating his mouth.

It wasn't the first time he'd killed such a man, but always before there had been a team there for him when he'd come back in from the cold—there to help re-orient him, get his head back in the right place. Re-tasked, pressing on. *Next mission.*

Now? There was no one—the line between friend and enemy blurring irreparably, leaving him standing here alone, hands stained with the blood of his brother. *Cain.*

"Your brother was a good man," he said finally, unable to find other words to express the way he felt. Taking another sip of the tea. "I regret that I could not have known him for longer. . .but such was not the will of Allah."

"And this was?" Yassin demanded, a raw edge creeping into his voice. Bitterness and grief, intermixed.

"What else could it have been?" There was a seductive comfort in fatalism, Harry mused. *A freedom from agency.* "All our lives are ordered by God, and we die only in the time and the place appointed us."

Like Carol. It was a comfort he would have desired for himself, if he could have come to a place of believing in it.

"But what purpose could there possibly *be* in Reza's death?" Yassin spat, tears shining in his dark eyes as he rose angrily to his feet, a grimace of pain passing across his face. The wound he had received there on the Outremeuse, so nearly healed—yet still causing him pain in unexpected moments.

What purpose?

That familiar, unanswerable question. The very question he had himself asked, so many times over the months, the only answer a mocking echo in the void. *Or so it seemed.*

"That's not for us to know," he said finally, collecting himself with an effort. "None of us are going to live to see the end of this war, brother. I learned that on the battlefields of *Sham.* It has to be enough for us to know that Reza died no less a martyr in that shed than if he had given his life in an attack on the West. A noble sacrifice, in the cause of God."

"*Insh'allah.*" There was acceptance in Yassin's voice, grudging, but inevitable. The acceptance of one who had been raised for generations to believe it was the truth. *Fate.*

"How is Nora faring with all of. . .this?" Harry asked, realizing suddenly that he hadn't seen the young woman since shortly after their return to Liège.

Yassin shook his head. "I don't know. Belkaïd sent her to stay with his sister, across the city. I haven't spoken to her since."

"I should go see her."

7:57 P.M. Moscow Time
A dacha
Rublyovka, Moscow Oblast

"You did good work in England, *tovarisch.*" Igor Zakirov smiled, extending a tumbler of brandy toward Vasiliev. "Or so I have been told. Unofficially, of course."

Of course. Alexei accepted the tumbler with a smile, the crystal poised delicately between his long fingers. Officially, a man like Zakirov no longer occupied any place in the FSB's intelligence hierarchy.

Unofficially. . .the influence of the *siloviki,* high-ranking "former" intelligence officers like Igor Petrovich, was far-reaching and undiminished by their transition to private life.

"I hope I was not too. . .harsh on your son," Vasiliev said, taking a seat across from his old friend in the library of the dacha, looking around him at the thousands of volumes covering the towering shelves. Unsure, suddenly, in the presence of the man himself, whether he might not have transgressed too far.

"Roman? *Nichevo,*" Zakirov smiled, shaking his massive head. *It does not matter.* "He could use someone like you in his life. I fear I have been too lenient with him. . .he is given to excess, like so many of our young people these days. They don't understand what life was like back when you and I were coming up—how hard we had to *fight* for everything we achieved."

Everything we earned, Vasiliev thought, aware of just how ironic that idea was in the context of the system under which they had become men.

But however beautiful it might have seemed to a political philosopher, the First Chief Directorate had had no place for *"each according to his need."*

In that world, only the strong survived—or *thrived*, as he and Igor Petrovich had done. The weak. . .remained only to be trampled underfoot, as they ever had been throughout the history of humanity. Their rightful *place*.

It was as though the visage of Dmitri Pavlovich Litvinov flickered across his mind's eye in that moment, the way he had looked, hanging there in his London flat, the chair kicked away beneath his dangling feet. The life slowly leaving his body with each desperate, tormented breath. Sometimes the weak survived far longer than they had any right. But they all found their place in the end. *Sometimes with help.*

"Speaking of sons," Zakirov said, easing himself back in his chair, "I commend you on the accomplishments of your protégé, no less than your own. He's turned into a fine officer."

"Grigoriy?" A smile touched Vasiliev's thin lips. He'd mentored many young officers over the years, as the old world was changed for the new, but really only one of them deserved the name "son." *Grigoriy Stepanovich Kolesnikov.* "I told you to give him time, didn't I, Igor?"

A nod, a smile spreading across his old colleague's face to match his own. "He was exceedingly raw, in those days, even you must admit."

"An uncut diamond."

6:05 P.M. Central European Summer Time
Amercoeur District
Liège, Belgium

The shadows were lengthening down the narrow city streets as Harry stopped in front of the open gate, glancing in at the narrow opening sandwiched between a turn-of-the-previous century brick townhouse on the left, and a squat building with modern siding on the right.

There were no overt signs of security, but perhaps Belkaïd's reputation was simply formidable enough to assure his family's safety. *Or perhaps he was simply missing something.*

That latter, more likely, Harry thought as he stepped through the entrance, finding himself in a small, cobblestoned courtyard filled with plants.

The fronds of a potted palm brushing against his bearded face as he pushed past it, making his way toward the door of a third house that sat back, perhaps fifteen meters off the street.

Fifteen meters of space that someone had, with painstaking care, turned into a garden—flowers everywhere, a carpet of red begonias surrounding a young planetree in the center of the courtyard. More palms, scattered across the cobblestones. Clustered pots of aloe vera atop a picnic table not far from the door.

It reminded him, with a pang, of his own grandmother. Of the love with which she had always tended her plants. Love evident here, in this strangest of places.

He lifted his hand and knocked, the sound awkwardly loud in this place— removed as it seemed from the bustle of the street.

A few moments, barely audible footsteps, and then a woman's voice. "Yes?"

"It's Ibrahim," he announced, the false name, by now, seeming far more natural than his own.

A moment's pause and the bolt slid back, the door coming open to reveal a slight, leathery-faced woman perhaps eight or nine years Belkaïd's senior standing in the opening, her form cloaked in a dark *abaya*, a loose *hijab* wrapped hastily about her hair.

"*Salaam alaikum.*"

"*Wa' alaikum as-salaam.* Gamal said to expect you," she said flatly, her voice devoid of emotion, containing neither approval nor disapproval. "I've made tea."

6:12 P.M.
The hotel
Paris, France

Grigoriy walked over to the window of his hotel room, gazing out toward the Eiffel Tower in the distance for a long moment before drawing the curtains, walking back toward the bed.

Still nothing from Moscow—no official response to his report on the meet with Belkaïd. Perhaps he should have known better than to expect one. He had been at this business for over a decade, and it seemed as though the Centre's responsiveness only became more lethargic with every advance in communications technology.

The Night Wolves were gone, though, and of that he was glad. Any explicit tie to the *Rodina* was a hazard, given his strictly non-official status here in Paris, but his superiors had believed they would help sell his *mafiya* cover with Belkaïd.

Perhaps they had, but they had posed a risk, even so. The Centre was not all-knowing, or all-wise.

Which was just as well for him, the FSB officer thought, unzipping his laptop case and retrieving the holstered Smith & Wesson M&P Compact from within, along with the loaded magazines of 9mm Parabellum.

Maxim's gun. Left behind, at his insistence, when the bikers had departed. The man hadn't argued with him—had no way of knowing the Centre's policies against arming their officers in Europe.

But what they didn't know, wouldn't hurt them. A smile played at his lips as he shoved one of the magazines into the butt of the pistol, racking the slide back with a smooth, practiced motion.

And that was another thing Vasiliev would have said.

6:15 P.M.
Amercoeur District
Liège, Belgium

Harry leaned back into the threadbare cushions of the couch, listening to the sounds of the woman bustling about in the kitchen, glancing around at the sparse furnishings of the small home. He didn't quite know what he had expected, but this was something. . .less than he had imagined Belkaïd would provide for his family.

"You may call me Ghaniyah," she announced, returning with a tray bearing three tall glasses and a silver teapot with steam escaping from its spout. "Nora will be out in a few minutes."

The name meant *beautiful woman*, Harry thought, smiling up at her with a murmured *mash'allah*. And perhaps she had been so, once. But the years had not been kind.

But then, life and time left few without their marks.

She poured the steaming tea into the foremost glass, extending it toward him—and he noticed only then that two of the fingers of her right hand were missing from above the knuckle, the sleeve of her *abaya* falling away with the movement to reveal deep lacerations scarring the flesh of her wrist. Old scars, weathered by years.

Wounds.

He lifted the glass to his lips, savoring once again the characteristically strong spearmint of Maghrebi tea as the older woman settled into the chair across from him, regarding him with a penetrating gaze.

It was a long moment before she spoke, and then, unexpectedly, "I understand that you are the *mujahid*."

He nodded quietly, unsure of his ground.

"Good."

It wasn't the reaction he had expected, and yet. . .he remained silent, watching her face. Waiting for her to continue.

"Gamal has become distracted over the years," she said, wrapping both hands around her own glass of tea—resting it and them contemplatively on her lap. "His 'business interests' have consumed far too much of his focus— he's allowed himself to forget."

"Forget what?" Harry asked quietly, gauging her reaction. He had to be careful not to press too far, but there was something here—something important. All thoughts of Nora, his original purpose for the visit, forgotten in this moment.

"Our *suffering*," the woman spat, her dark eyes flashing with a sudden intensity. Her gaze shifted toward a small, framed black-and-white photograph sitting on an end table at one end of the couch.

It was an old, weathered picture of a family, taken somewhere in Northern Africa, judging by the architecture of the building in the backdrop.

A husband and wife and their teenaged son. And standing before them, in the foreground of the picture, a young girl—not quite yet in her teens, clasping the hand of another boy more than a few years younger. *Her and Gamal?*

"My father," she began slowly, her voice trembling with emotion as if the memory were still fresh, "was a shopkeeper in Algiers at the time of the revolution. They came to suspect him of having driven a car for the FLN during the bombing campaigns, and one night when I was thirteen the French paratroopers came to take him away. My older brother Youcef tried to stop them and they shot him in the head, left him to bleed out on the floor of our kitchen. My mother was raped—*I* was raped—that, I suppose, I have in common with Nora, if little else. We didn't see my father again for nine months, and when he returned, he was a broken man. He died before Algeria could ever become free."

"Nora?" Harry asked, taken off-guard by her words. "She was. . .?"

"You didn't know?" the older woman asked, favoring him with a skeptical glance. "But you wouldn't, would you?"

He fell silent for a moment, accepting the implicit rebuke. "It wasn't. . .it wasn't Reza, was it?"

A snort. "Reza *saved* her, as I have understood it. But that's now a part of her past, as it is of mine. And now here you are, come to remind my brother of his obligations, long overdue."

"*Insh'allah.*"

It was growing dark by the time Harry left the small house on the Rue Denis Sotiau, making his way out once more into the garden—Nora showing him to the gate. The two of them, alone for the first time all evening—though he had no doubt Ghaniyah Belkaïd was still watching from a window.

He stooped down on one knee, brushing back the leaves of an overhanging dwarf palm to reveal the African violets nestled beneath, their rich hue vivid even in the gathering twilight.

It surprised him that there was enough sun for them, in this small courtyard, but here they were, flourishing. Evidence of love. *In the presence of death.*

For there had been death in the older woman's eyes—memories of wounds never healed, a life which might have been, ripped away from her in the flower of youth. A pain which now sought only to be assuaged in destruction. *And, perhaps, these flowers.*

Contradictions. Ever the nature of man. Trying to reconcile them all would drive you mad.

"*Mash'allah,*" he whispered, rising once more to stand by Nora's side. "She has put so much work into these flowers. . .it is beautiful."

She nodded as he turned to face her, self-consciously tucking a loose strand of blonde hair up under her *hijab*. "She's a good woman. The love she has showed me. . ."

And love was a seductive thing, Harry realized, painful memories of his own, rising to the fore. It drew you in—*held* you in its power. Until it was far too late.

"You should leave," he said suddenly, his eyes locking with hers. "Go back to the university. There's nothing here for you, anymore."

Leave now, before I bring everything crashing down around all of us, he thought, not daring to speak the words. To warn of the darkness to come.

She started to respond, surprise visible in her features, but he shook his head, holding up a hand to cut her off. "This isn't a woman's war, little sister. Think about it."

And then he was gone, vanishing through the gate into the lonely street beyond. *Into the night.*

6:32 P.M.
Gare de Liège-Guillemins
Liège, Belgium

Twenty-four hours. And too much of that, already come and gone, Armand Césaire thought, stepping from the carriage of the Thalys train onto the platform of Liège's massive railway station.

It wasn't going to be enough. He knew that. Director Brunet knew it. Likely enough, the Belgians even knew it.

But it wasn't their officer in harm's way. And maybe even that wouldn't have made any difference. They weren't about to risk another bomb going off in Brussels—their citizens, crying out for protection the government seemed powerless to afford.

Anything but that. Even if someone had to die, along the way.

It was the reality of what he had warned Brunet, weeks before. The kinetic nature of this new threat, forcing everyone's hand—rendering all but unworkable the patient, thorough spycraft of an earlier age. Operations, forced to the harvest long before they could ripen. *Develop.*

Césaire sighed, the exhaustion showing in the lines of his dark face as the intelligence officer pushed his way through the crowds of commuters exiting the station. There had been so many mistakes in this operation—that all of them had been forced on him, from above, was small consolation.

Daniel was still his responsibility, morally speaking. The one last vestige of morality that had not escaped him in decades of this sordid business. *Honor.*

He would go to the funeral, if there was to be one. Look his survivors in the eye, tell them what they needed to hear.

A brave man was owed that much.

But this brave man wasn't dead just yet, despite their superiors' best efforts. And it was up to him to ensure that their recklessness didn't end in disaster.

Césaire glanced at his watch as he made his way out onto the street. He would leave the emergency signals tonight, in the

locations he and Daniel had agreed upon following their meeting in the Place Poelart, more than three weeks before.

And then, he would wait. *And pray.*

6:57 P.M.
Pont de Fragnée
Liège, Belgium

The night was quiet, reflected blue light from the bridge above shimmering off the waters of the Meuse, only a few meters away from his outstretched feet.

Harry leaned back into the concrete wall, looking up at the naked girders of the first arch, stretching out across the water. The lights above reflecting briefly off the darkened screen of the burner phone in his hand.

How had he gotten here? It was a question he'd asked himself a thousand times, and the answers weren't getting any better as he went along.

But he had run as far as he dared. To keep running would jeopardize far more lives than he had any desire to risk. Any *right*.

It was time to come in out of the cold.

He reached down, powering on the burner—finding himself hesitating, even in this moment. The costs of his chosen course of action, all too apparent.

But like so many other moments in his life. . .this decision was *necessary*. Nothing else for it.

No choice at all, really. *A singular course.*

He ran a hand across his beard, staring at the phone for another long moment before he began to enter a number from memory—a fragment of his past. A lifetime ago, now. Or so it seemed.

He could only hope it hadn't been changed.

Moment of truth.

Taking a deep breath, he pressed *SEND*, bringing the phone up to his ear, the glow of its screen casting strange shadows across his face. Waiting as it rang once, then twice. Then, a woman's voice, clipped. *Professional.* The duty officer, no doubt. "*Allô?*"

"Listen to me," Harry began, "very carefully. . ."

Chapter 25

7:37 A.M. Central European Summer Time, July 31ˢᵗ
DGSE Headquarters
Paris, France

". . .details of an attack being plotted by Gamal Belkaïd. I will divulge this information only in person, to a French intelligence officer and a French intelligence officer alone. Your Belgian counterparts are compromised. Have such an officer meet me beneath the Pont de Fragnée on the east bank of river Meuse, tomorrow night at this time."

"That doesn't give us much time," Anaïs Brunet heard the duty officer respond, her disembodied voice coming through clear over the recording.

"To set up a full surveillance operation?" the strangely distorted voice of the caller asked in French. "*Non.* But to send a single officer. . .it's all the time you could need. If you send more, I will see them. And I will disappear."

One could hear the voice of the duty officer attempting to say something further in reply, but the line was no longer open—the recording ending with a startling abruptness.

"Is that everything?" Brunet asked, glancing up.

"*Oui,*" the duty officer herself responded from the other end of the conference table, visibly taking a deep, weary breath. She hadn't left since the call. "I did my best to keep him on the phone, *madame le directeur*, but I was unable—"

"He knew we would be tracking him," Brunet replied. "There was nothing more you could have done. What *did* we get?"

"The call was placed from Liège." Césaire's supervisory officer, Albert

Godard, took the question, putting on his glasses to look down the table at Brunet. "Somewhere near the Pont de Fragnée itself—within a mile radius. We weren't able to get closer, given the time."

"And what does the audio itself give us?"

"We've run voiceprint analysis, but it seems that the caller was using some kind of voice distortion app. If we are able to isolate which app was used, we may be able to reverse-engineer the audio, but that's going to be a lengthy process. We—"

"The point, Albert. *S'il vous plaît.*"

"His French is relatively fluent, but not native, in our assessment. Without hearing it naturally, it's impossible to analyze any possible accent."

"There's no possibility that this is an attempt by LYSANDER to make emergency contact?" It was beyond unlikely, and Godard looked surprised that she had even asked the question.

"Not in our estimation, *madame.* That would mean that he had disclosed his status to a third party, and the odds he would take such a risk. . ."

"Then how did this man obtain the number he used?" That was the question that had been troubling them all, ever since the call came in. "It's not as though he called a publicly available number—this is an emergency contact line for assets and officers in the field. If this is not someone who has worked with us in the past, he knows someone who has. Do we have any assets out there unaccounted for?"

Silence fell across the conference room, uneasy looks flickering back and forth between the DGSE officers present as each of them slowly shook their head. "Your thoughts, Daniel?" Brunet asked, turning to the CIA station chief, leaning back in the chair to her right.

The American was rumpled this morning, without a tie for the first time she could remember, his eyes bloodshot. A mug of coffee, sitting unattended beside his briefing papers.

"I can run the audio by Langley, if you want, but. . .I think you have a serious problem, no matter his identity. There's someone, presumably in Belkaïd's organization, presumably *not* your officer, who nevertheless knows your internal communication protocols well enough to contact your headquarters and reach the duty officer directly. And he's telling you that the partners you've been sharing intel with have themselves been compromised."

"What do you make of that assertion?"

Daniel Vukovic shook his head. "He could easily be lying—working an angle. Tell me, what would be the first thing you would do after receiving a communication of this sort?"

Brunet paused for a moment, looking the American in the eye. *There were many things, but...* "We would try to pull surveillance footage from the area surrounding the call, look for any known actors. But that would require the cooperation of local authorities, and—"

"He's just firewalled you off from reaching out for any such cooperation," Vukovic replied, nodding. "If he knows your comms protocols, I suspect he knows that as well."

Silence fell over the conference room for a long moment before General Gauthier cleared his throat, voicing the question in everyone's mind. "But what if he *is* telling the truth?"

"That's the catch-22 in which he's placed you," Vukovic acknowledged, glancing down the length of the table to where the former Legionnaire sat. "Information you can't validate or disprove, but at the same time, far too important not to be taken seriously. Because if he's telling the truth, LYSANDER is in grave danger—if not already compromised."

An impossible dilemma. But one that demanded a decision, without delay. Brunet closed her briefing folder, looking down the table till her eyes met Godard's. "Contact Césaire. At once."

8:01 A.M.
VSSE Headquarters
Brussels, Belgium

"*Goedemorgen*, Jan."

Jan Vertens glanced over at his coworker, returning the greeting with a slight nod as he pulled out his desk chair, its casters groaning in protest. He'd ordered a new chair three weeks before and it had yet to arrive, while this one continued its slow, inexorable destruction of his lower back.

He let out a heavy sigh as he sank into it, reaching down to power on his computer's tower. Middle age was getting to him. A dead end. *Just like this job.*

"What's on for today?" he asked over the wall of the cubicle, only half-interested in the response as he reached down, rummaging in his messenger bag. Most days, it seemed as though it was paperwork. He didn't know why he was still in this job, really. He'd been a police officer, once upon a time—before deciding that the street was no place to grow old and transitioning over to the State Security Service.

He'd have been better served by staying on the street.

"We're staging to provide support for a surveillance operation in Liège," came his colleague's unexpected answer, bringing Jan's head up in sudden attention. "Targeting Gamal Belkaïd."

The Belgian intelligence officer froze at the sound of the name, his breath seeming to catch in his throat. "The Algerian black marketer? Why?"

He'd first heard the man's name years before, during his time on the Brussels force. A minor player, then, just beginning to muscle his way in on the Belgian underworld. He could never have imagined then that he would end up working for the man. Funneling him information, for a price. A price that was buying his own future, a future for he and Rana, away from all of this.

It was a long moment before his colleague responded, a moment seemingly stretching out into an eternity. Then, "No idea. They haven't told us much, yet. All very hush-hush."

3:15 A.M. Eastern Daylight Time
Dover Air Force Base
Dover, Delaware

He'd been here so many times, Jack Richards thought, staring out through the windshield of the Nissan toward the lights of the runways—the dark, hulking shape of the just-arrived C-130 clearly visible in their glare. The sound of an orchestra playing Frederick the Great's *Symphony in D Major* coming through the car's speakers around him.

So very many times. Leaving. Coming home. Coming here to escort back someone else who. . .had made it home only in a coffin.

And times like this, picking up a friend who'd gone themselves. He spotted the lone figure advancing toward the car in the early morning shadows when they were still fifty meters out, his hand stealing toward the butt of the Glock holstered inside his waistband.

Another twenty meters, though, and he recognized the man, his familiar stride as he covered the ground, a light backpack slung easily over his shoulder.

His hand eased away from the gun as he reached up, unlocking the Nissan's doors.

"Welcome back," he said simply, a moment later, turning down the music as Thomas Parker opened the door and slid into the passenger seat beside him—throwing his backpack unceremoniously into the back seat.

"Thanks," the New Yorker replied, glancing over with a weary, ironic smile. "It was a good trip. The travel brochures don't lie—Niger is beautiful this time of year."

Then, more seriously, the humor vanishing from his voice as quick as it had come, "We'll be back there, before you know it. Things. . .aren't good."

They never were, Richards thought, putting the Nissan into drive—beginning to navigate his way back off the Air Force base. Like a firefighter, no one ever bothered sending them where things were good.

Or if they did. . .things were about to get worse, for someone. *Firefighter. Arsonist.* It was a thin line, at times. Sometimes, they just made things worse, despite their best efforts. *Like the Sinai.*

"I was sorry to hear about Mitt," Thomas said after a moment, seeming to divine his thoughts. "Tough break."

"He'll be okay," Richards replied, thinking of the last time he had visited Nakamura in the hospital at Bethesda, two weeks before. "Supposed to be coming home tomorrow. Long road back, but he's going to pull through. Donna was with him last time I stopped in."

"She's a good woman."

"None better." You had to be to stay with any man long in this business. The kind of woman who would have survived out on the frontier, a century before, Richards often thought. Rare breed.

"Sounded like the Sinai turned into a real mess," his friend observed as they exited the base, turning south onto Route 1.

"You heard right," came the Texan's short response, his eyes on the road. "Congressional hearings, coming up late next week. Kranemeyer's been called to testify."

Thomas swore softly. "What's he going to tell them?"

"The truth, I imagine. That it was a clean strike, everything by the book."

The future textbook case for how horribly things could go wrong even when you did everything right, he thought, but didn't add. It wasn't how he'd expected his career with the Agency to be remembered. . .not that he'd expected it to be remembered at all. *A failure, in itself.*

"I hear you were tapped to take Mitt's place."

A nod. "I asked for you, Granby, and Ardolino, and Kranemeyer approved the request."

There was a bemused look in the New Yorker's eyes. "So you're putting the band back together, huh?"

"On a mission from God," Richards replied, a rare smile creasing his swarthy face. "Or the seventh floor."

Thomas laughed. "Close enough for government work."

There was a long pause, the flat farm fields of Delaware flashing past as the car sped south through the night.

Then, "Any further updates on Harry? Any word where he might have ended up, after Scotland?"

Richards' smile vanished, his obsidian-black eyes narrowing into glittering points as they focused on the road ahead. The red tail-lights of another car, appearing off on the horizon.

"No," he said finally. "He's a fugitive now, after everything in the UK. . .if he's smart, he won't be putting his head up anytime soon."

"That can't last."

"I know." The Texan went quiet for another long moment, the closing strains of the old Prussian's symphony filling up the silence. "I don't know what happened to him, what. . .*broke*, somewhere inside. Wish I did. But that's the past, like it or not. And we have a job to do."

"Copy that."

9:32 A.M., Central European Summer Time
Rue Hors-Château
Liège, Belgium

Harry shut the door of the sedan behind him as he stepped out onto the street, waiting on the curb as Belkaïd's bodyguard finished speaking to the driver— his eyes flickering across the street to the towering red baroque facade of the

Church of Our Lady of Immaculate Conception looming there above them, mute stone saints staring down upon them from their carved niches in the stonework.

Staring down in judgment, or so it seemed, in this moment. Belkaïd's call had come unexpectedly, forty minutes before, followed quickly by his bodyguard—despatched to retrieve Harry and bring him to the trafficker's own residence. No reason given, clearly Belkaïd felt no need to provide one.

And so here they were, standing in the historic center of the old city of Liège. The heart of Walloon culture, centuries-old. A few more hurried words, and the car pulled away, the bodyguard coming over to motion Harry into the arch of the building's doorway. *Up we go.*

Belkaïd's apartment was on the third floor—the *entire* floor, from what Harry understood, glancing over at the bodyguard as the man entered a passcode for the elevator access—his sidearm printing against the thin fabric of his shirt as he bent over, tapping in the code.

8-5-5-7, Harry thought, filing the number away for future use—wondering at the significance of it. *None*, if the trafficker was savvy. He didn't know just how careful Belkaïd was when it came to such details—it was an area where even some of the best allowed themselves to be tripped up. The human impulse, almost impossible to overcome. For him, as much as anyone else.

Was this about last night? Had he been followed from Ghaniyah's apartment to the Pont de Fragnée? Was it just that his lengthy absence from the warehouse and apartment building had been noted, his very disappearance from their radar causing questions? He had intended to take the phone and plant it in Marwan's room as an insurance policy, but he hadn't gotten that far—leaving it instead disassembled and hidden in an old box of cereal in their apartment's pantry—something left over from the previous occupants.

The elevator shuddered to a stop and the bodyguard entered the passcode once more, the doors sliding open. The man extended his hand, not a trace of a smile in his eyes as he gestured for Harry to lead the way into the hallway. "After you."

9:35 A.M.
VSSE Headquarters
Brussels

"This is highly irregular, Anaïs," Christian Danloy responded, glancing up from his briefing notes toward his counterpart's face on the teleconferencing screen. "I'm afraid, if you're going to ask me to push back my timeline, you're going to have to provide me with a reason for doing so."

He could see the DGSE director hesitate, clearly choosing her words carefully. *What* was *going on here?* "There have been developments in the situation. . .I'm afraid that's all I'm able to divulge, Christian."

"You've heard from your officer, then?"

"Not exactly, no," Brunet acknowledged, glancing at someone off-camera.

"Then I must insist that the timeline stands. Please, understand what I am dealing with here. We have a terrorist cell here in my country, potentially on the very brink of going active. . .and you're asking me to refrain from surveilling them. This is madness."

"Twelve more hours, Christian. That's all I'm asking for."

"Then surely you can tell me *why*. I am not being unreasonable here, Anaïs! If you have intelligence this specific affecting the national security of Belgium it is imperative that you share it with me. It is—"

"If you will excuse me, *madame le directeur*," he heard another voice interject, a man's face coming up just then in a split-screen with Brunet. "It's been a long time, Christian."

It took Danloy a moment to place the man, but then he remembered. *Daniel Vukovic.* Two decades earlier, they had both served as liaison officers for their respective agencies at the NATO Headquarters in Brussels. It had only been nine months—Vukovic had been finishing out his tour, on his way elsewhere at the bidding of the CIA—but Daniel had introduced him to the woman who would later become his wife. His *ex*, now—but it had seemed like a good idea to everyone at the time.

"Indeed it has, Daniel. This is something of a surprise, though I remember now there were reports you had taken over for Kassner at Paris Station."

A smile. "You're well-informed, Christian, as ever. We don't have a lot of time here, so I'm going to cut straight to the point. Given the CIA's interest in the success of this operation long-term, we would appreciate your cooperation in this. . .extension of your timeline. The Agency would be grateful."

Do us this favor now, Danloy thought, the subtext of the American's words only too clear, *and we'll do you one later*. A "marker," as Vukovic would have called it, to be redeemed at a future date.

And being able to call in a favor from one of the world's most powerful intelligence agencies. . .offers in this business didn't get much more seductive. *But if it ended up meaning bodies in the streets of Brussels. . .*

It felt like a Faustian bargain, with his old friend playing the role of Mephistopheles. And yet irresistible, for all that.

He shook his head, a sharp, incredulous laugh escaping his lips. "You're honestly telling me that the CIA has greater access to matters pertaining to the national security of Belgium than the State Security Service itself? *C'est incroyable.*"

He understood, of course. *Limitless money, the sinews of war.* Money bought access. And no one in this business had "limitless money" quite like the Americans. But understanding didn't make this pill any less bitter.

"All right, then," he said finally, glancing around him at his subordinates as he spread his hands in a gesture of surrender. "You have your extension— our surveillance will be deferred until tomorrow morning, at this time. But no longer."

9:39 A.M.
Rue Hors-Château
Liège, Belgium

"Please, Ibrahim. . .have a seat," Belkaïd announced, gesturing to a leather armchair in the apartment's living room. "I appreciate you coming, even though the notice was short. I'll be with you in a moment."

"Of course," Harry responded guardedly, glancing around him. The contrast between the trafficker's living quarters and those of his sister couldn't possibly have been more stark.

This was the home of a man to whom money was no object. A man who valued luxury—opulence, even. And yet his sister. . .

Belkaïd was still padding around barefoot, dressed in sweatpants and an old off-white wifebeater, as if he had just recently risen from bed. *A calculated ploy to allow himself to be underestimated? Or simply. . .what it was?*

The older man re-emerged from the back room bearing a laptop—placing it on the coffee table in front of his plush sofa, sinking back into its cushions.

"Please," he offered, gesturing to a crystal bowl of fruit which sat on the table between them, "help yourself."

It was the kind of invitation one didn't just refuse. Harry reached out, taking an apple from the bowl. Turning it in his hand as he withdrew his knife—the only weapon left to him—and began to peel back the skin, watching for any imperfections that would indicate the fruit had been tampered with. *Nothing.*

Out of the corner of his eye, he saw the bodyguard react, stiffening at the sight of the blade, and apparently Belkaïd felt it as well, for he turned to the man. "You may leave us now."

A nod, and the man was gone, leaving through the door from which they had entered—the apple's firm flesh giving way as Harry's knife sunk in, slicing quick to the heart.

"That's the knife you used to kill Hakim, isn't it," Belkaïd observed, crossing one leg over another as he leaned back into the sofa. A curious smile playing across his face.

Harry nodded, slowly, his eyes never leaving the Algerian's. The knife slowing, juice running along the blade as he pulled it back out the other side of the apple. "And Said bin Muhammad."

"And perhaps even me, eventually?" The older man's voice was casual, disinterested, almost. Bored. *Dangerous.*

"That depends," Harry replied, recognizing that to show weakness in this moment could be fatal, "on whether you've done anything to deserve it."

Another quiet smile. "In some men's eyes, I suppose I have done many such things. It all depends on what side you're on."

Warning.

"I stand with the Lord of the Dawn," Harry responded quietly, the knife now motionless in his right hand. "His 'side' is my own. And truly Allah loves those who fight in His Cause in battle array, as though they were a single structure, joined firmly."

"A single structure," Belkaïd mused thoughtfully, running a hand over his greying beard. "But that's never been our reality, has it, Ibrahim? We've been fragmented, turned against each other—manipulated by the West for their own ends, until brother killed brother."

The tragedy of the Arab world. Divided against itself for centuries.

"I understand that you met my sister yesterday," the Algerian went on, not waiting for a response. "What did you think of her?"

9:43 A.M.
DGSE Headquarters
Brussels, Belgium

"Unacceptable," Anaïs Brunet spat, waiting only until the screens darkened, indicating the Belgians had gone off-line. "Just what did you think you were doing there, Daniel, undermining the relationship of French intelligence with our Belgian counterparts in such a manner?"

"I was buying us time, Anaïs," the CIA man replied, his gaze unwavering as his eyes locked with hers. *Unrepentant.* He knew exactly what he had just done—established his own service as arbiter in this, as so much else. "Time to get your officer out of harm's way."

"That wasn't the way to handle it." You didn't simply run roughshod over the norms of inter-agency cooperation—not without serious, long-term consequences. The next time there was a joint operation, the Belgians would be uncertain with whom they *really* ought to deal. The French, or the Americans.

And she had seen the suppressed anger in Danloy's face. He had felt it, no less than her. The VSSE might have been a small agency, but it was one of the world's oldest, with an institutional pride that matched their long history.

The American might have gained his point for this moment, but it would rankle nevertheless. And repairing the relationship would involve far more effort than Brunet wanted to think about.

"You're right, Anaïs," Vukovic responded, rising to his feet. "It wasn't. The way to handle this would have been for me to go to Danloy in the beginning—use my personal relationship with him to smooth the way for a truly joint operation. Or, perhaps, simply establish surveillance from the outset, instead of risking the life of an officer."

That would have been Vukovic's preference, certainly. His preference for technical means of intelligence gathering was well known.

"But here we are," he said finally, still holding her stare. "So make the most of it. Get your officer *out*—while you still can. Because it only gets more dangerous from here."

And then he was gone, the door of the conference room closing behind him. *Americans.*

9:44 A.M.
Rue Hors-Château
Liège, Belgium

"A remarkably strong woman," Harry replied, truthfully enough. "A *survivor.*"

"Ah, she told you then." There was pain and sadness in Belkaïd's eyes as Harry answered his question with a simple nod of the head. "Ghani has always been a rock. Even as a child."

He paused, his eyes growing reflective. "You know, I can't remember that day—no matter how hard I try. I was five, then, but I don't remember a thing—not the screams or the gunshots. Or my brother, laying dead on the floor. I don't remember my brother at all, really, just the shadows of a face, here and there. Fragments. I only knew my father as he returned, broken in body and spirit. And I was too young, of course, to understand the brutality my mother and sister had been subjected to."

Trauma. It was a strange thing, Harry thought, watching Belkaïd closely, but seeing no signs of deception in the older man's face. Some things, it seared into one's memory as if with a brand. Others. . .it were as though the brand had scorched away reality itself, leaving behind only a gaping hole. The knowledge of *loss.*

"Ghani accuses me, at times, of having forgotten. . .but the truth is far more bitter. I never *knew.*" There was an agony there, in the words, a desperate yearning to understand the unspeakable. To *share* it. "And perhaps I have. . .allowed other things to get in the way, over the years. No longer."

He reached out a hand, opening the screen of the laptop and turning it to face Harry. The pictures on-screen were of a massive soccer stadium, open to the summer sun, packed with screaming fans by the tens of thousands.

"The *Stade de France*," Belkaïd replied, answering Harry's unspoken question. "In a week's time, it will host the final qualifying match for the World Cup, determining whether France's team will go on to the Cup itself. The President of France himself will be in attendance. And that's when we'll strike."

It was audacious. Even an unsuccessful attack could be devastating. *And yet.* "This has already been tried," Harry replied, recalling another jihadist attack in Paris. Not so very long ago. "You'll never get in."

A smile, as if it were a concern he had already thought of and dismissed long ago. *How long had he been thinking of this?* "But *we* don't need to get in. Driss is right. Now that we have a supplier able to obtain military-grade plastic explosives for us, we can simply use the UAVs. Fly a pair of them into the stadium, directly to President Albéric's box. Should take no more than ninety seconds to cross the open space from the roof to the box—the first explosion will take out the security glass of the skybox, opening a path for the second UAV to fly straight in. Boom."

He spread his hands in a pantomime of the explosion, smiling widely. "Everyone dead. What do you think?"

"It's a good plan," Harry acknowledged, struggling to keep his inner turmoil off his face, his mind racing. The DGSE would have to be warned, no matter the risk. He resisted the urge to glance at his wristwatch. Tonight's meeting couldn't arrive quickly enough. "If you think we can really trust this Russian to provide the plastique. But it's a good plan."

"Good," the older man replied, his dark eyes suddenly turning hard and cold as he stared across the room into Harry's face. "Then why have you betrayed us?"

9:47 A.M.
A hotel
Liège, Belgium

There was still nothing at the dead-drops, Armand Césaire thought, running a hand over his scalp, tousling the tight silver hair. No sign that Daniel had even seen his signals, let alone made an effort to respond to them. They were running short of time, and *now*. . .his masters on the Boulevard Mortier had added another tasking.

This *meeting*, on the Pont de Fragnée, with—they had no idea whom. He shook his head. *Madness*. They were risking exposure sending him in like this—bringing it all crashing down about their heads.

It should have been given to another officer, that's what he'd told Godard. Someone firewalled off from LYSANDER. Someone who couldn't talk.

He paused, as if realizing only then what he was preparing himself mentally for. The possibility of being *taken*.

It had been years. Africa, the last time he had truly found himself in physical danger. Sitting in a stopped car at a rebel checkpoint, somewhere in the Congo. Looking down the muzzle of a battered old AK-47 held in the trembling hands of a man young enough to be his son. Young and scared, screaming at the top of his lungs as if he could somehow find courage in the volume—the rifle's muzzle waving back and forth.

He'd talked his way out of that one—eventually—but he was enough of an old hand to know. Sooner or later, the day came that you couldn't talk your way through.

And that day was the day of your death.

9:53 A.M.
Rue Hors-Château
Liège, Belgium

"What do you mean?" Harry stared across the room back at Belkaïd, time itself seeming to slow down. His fingers tightening imperceptibly around the hilt of the switchblade, certain in this moment that the Algerian was himself armed. *He must be.*

Could he cross the room in the time it would take the older man to draw and fire? *Probably*. Plunge the knife in deep, finding the heart beneath layers of fat and muscle. But the consequences for failure. . .

"Do you take me for a fool?" Belkaïd snarled, contempt filling his voice. "Perhaps you do. I *warned* you that I had sources within the Belgian security services—that if you were a plant, I would know."

Someone had talked, Harry thought, knowing in this moment that he was a dead man. The DGSE had disregarded his warning—shared intelligence once more with their counterparts in Brussels. And it was going to be the death of him.

"I heard from my sources an hour ago," the older man continued, not waiting for a response, "and you know what they told me? They told me that I am being placed under *surveillance. Now!* Of all times."

"Are you serious?" Harry exclaimed incredulously, seizing his opportunity. The classic playbook, old as time. *Admit nothing. Deny everything. Go on the attack.* "Is this some kind of joke? I *killed* a man for you, Gamal. A man who by Islamic law did not deserve to die, and I shot him dead to prove myself to you—to cement our alliance. To *ensure* that this attack could go forward. Would I have done that—would I have killed a man if I were a plant, an officer of the *kaffir* security services?"

Doubt. Written clear in Belkaïd's eyes. *Drive it home.* "You knew it was a test any Western spy would fail—that's why you gave it to me. We both knew that. *And I didn't fail.* And now you want to question my loyalty—why? Because you've been told that the police are placing you under surveillance? You are a *criminal*, Gamal. Stop acting so paranoid—this is a part of the game, you know this."

"But why *now?* I've conducted my business affairs in this country for years, I've been investigated many times. But this—this is different." There was still skepticism in the man's voice, but he had his attention now, he was listening—open to being talked down.

"Think about it," Harry replied, folding the blade of the knife back into its hilt—dropping it casually into his lap. The halves of the apple, poised nearly forgotten in his left hand. "You've seen it on the news—there's nothing there the last couple days except the explosion. They know we're here now. They're going to put eyes on any criminal who might be involved—anyone big enough to supply the needs of the righteous. You, my brother, *are.*"

Chapter 26

5:09 P.M.
DGSE Headquarters
Paris, France

"Is there no way we can move officers into position to cover Césaire at the meeting?" Anaïs Brunet asked, looking up from her notes. The faces which looked back at her were haggard—weary. Most of them hadn't left the crisis room for hours.

She had just returned from her own office a few minutes before. There were other tasks she had to handle as director—other operations in play, as all-consuming as this had seemed to be, the last few days.

"It's a risk," Godard replied, pursing his lips into a thin line. "We have other officers in the area—moved them in from Brussels to support the operation this morning. But when it comes to putting them on the streets, we have to move cautiously—the caller warned us that if we sent more than a single officer to the meeting, he would know. That might easily have been a bluff, but the question: are we prepared to take the risk that it's not?"

And the answer to that was *no*, as Brunet knew as well as anyone else at the table. The pressures of their timeline didn't permit anything which might scuttle this meet even before it began. They might not be given another chance.

But it had to be asked. "What are the odds, Albert? In your professional opinion."

"That's very hard to say. The location he's chosen. . .its access is very limited." He threw up a map of the area on the big screen, showing the location of the Pont de Fragnée, sitting just to the south of a triangular-shaped peninsula, jutting out like a dagger into the Meuse. "You can reach the site by either crossing the bridge itself from the west, the Pont Gramme from the north, or the Pont de Fétinne from the northeast. Otherwise, you're coming straight up the Quai Gloesener from the south. It's all much too exposed—our officers would have to be placed too far out to reach Césaire if a problem were to develop."

It felt as though that were by design, Brunet thought, shaking her head. Unable to lose the feeling that something was wrong here. *Very wrong.*

"Ultimately, the caller was right," Godard continued. "Give us a week? We could probably do this. Twenty-four hours? Not a chance. And he knows it."

"All right then. How long will we have sat coverage?"

That was their remaining trump card—their only way to surveil the meeting without putting officers in the streets or petitioning the Belgians to allow a drone to be put up in their airspace.

"The satellite will arrive on-station in an hour twenty—just shortly before Césaire will be due to arrive at the bridge. The window will remain open for forty minutes thereafter. We should be able to see anyone coming and going there on the southeast bank of Meuse. If anything goes wrong—we'll know."

Too late. But they would know.

"All right," she said, knowing that it lay with her to make the final call. "Send him in."

11:29 A.M. Eastern Daylight Time
Liberty Crossing Intelligence Campus
McLean, Virginia

". . .where top intelligence officials are scheduled to testify in the next week concerning the decision to prosecute the failed drone strike in the Sinai against Umar ibn Hassan. Here with us this morning to discuss the upcoming hearings, we have former CIA counterterrorism official and current contributor, Lucas Cordair. Good morning, Lucas."

"Good morning, Nancy," Lawrence Bell heard Cordair respond as he reached for the remote, favoring the image on-screen with a dour look in the split-second before it went dark.

He'd been a good man, in his day, but Bell had little use for those who went on to find a second career on the talking head circuit. Speculating about things they were no longer read in on, offering their opinion as an authority on events they no longer knew anything more about than the average American on the street.

It wasn't a path he would ever have chosen for himself, no matter how good the money. Not that he was going to have such a choice.

The DNI frowned, adjusting the glasses on his nose as he leaned forward once more, going over his hand-written notes one more time, making sure they were all in order for the hearing—that there were no discrepancies, nothing that might trip him up in his upcoming testimony before Congress. *Just days away, now.*

"Are you sure you want to do this, Laurie?" his wife had asked before he'd headed out the door this very morning. *"For it all to end—everything you've done, all the years you've been in Washington. . .to go out like this. It's not right."*

And it wasn't, he thought, a nauseous feeling seeming to settle in the pit of his stomach. The medication wearing off, once again—it didn't seem to last nearly as long as it had when the doctor had first prescribed it, at the beginning of his treatment.

But they'd both been in Washington long enough to know that "right" had nothing to do with any of this. There was only what was necessary, and that was what he was prepared to do.

He smiled quietly, fighting back the nausea to focus on his work. She was the only one who had ever called him "Laurie". . .

5:37 P.M. Central European Summer Time
Erasmus Station, Anderlecht
Brussels, Belgium

"We believe Gamal Belkaïd to have become involved in a terrorist plot of a nature yet to be ascertained. This marks a departure from what we had believed to be the exclusively criminal focus of his organization. . ."

Danloy's words still rang in Jan Vertens' ears as the Belgian intelligence officer disembarked from the metro train, finding himself swept up in the crowd of commuters moving quickly toward the station's exits—toward home at the end of a long day at work.

He knew his face must have gone pale in that moment—hoped no one at the meeting had noticed, or at least that they would think it nothing more than the normal surprise one might feel at such news.

"What is our source for this new intelligence?" one of his branch supervisors had asked skeptically, directing her question to Danloy.

"The DGSE," had been the *administrateur général's* reply. *"They have an officer inside Belkaïd's organization, reporting back to them on the activities of this growing cell. But it's not enough—we need our own eyes on this. The security of our own country is, after all, at stake."*

Vertens adjusted the strap of his messenger bag, making his way out toward his parked car—realizing his palms were slick with sweat. He would never have gotten involved with Belkaïd if he'd had the slightest idea that he was connected to terrorism, and yet now. . .he saw no way out.

If he had only waited until after the meeting to place the call. He could have feigned ignorance. But he had *reacted*, taken off-guard by the first word of the proposed surveillance—reaching out to contact his usual cut-out for the Algerian at the first opportunity.

And now he was trapped. He collapsed into the driver's seat of his aging Renault, staring out through the windscreen back toward the station. Noting absently that it was in need of cleaning.

He knew Belkaïd would now expect him to call again with an update on the situation, giving his report on what had taken place at the meeting.

But this was different, now. This wasn't about money anymore—petty crime, smuggled electronics. This was about life.

And death.

6:14 P.M.
The warehouse
Liège, Belgium

It could work, Harry reflected, staring thoughtfully at the large Guardian drone sitting there on the folding table in the center of the room. That was the problem.

"I'll need to have the specifications of the Presidential skybox," he said finally, glancing over at Belkaïd. "The materials used in its construction—the thickness of the glass. Once I have that, I'll be able to appropriately size the charge. Assuming, of course, that the Russians come through for us, *insh'allah*."

The truth was that there was no ballistic glass in the world that would withstand the direct application of plastique—but this might buy a little time. Perhaps even trip some alarms, if the French security services realized someone was making inquiries of such delicacy.

"Leave the Russians to me," the older man replied grimly, favoring Harry with a penetrating look. *Searching*. He wasn't in the clear just yet—he'd talked Belkaïd down, but the paranoia remained intact. Ever there, just beneath the surface.

He knew without looking at his watch that he should have already left for his meet on the banks of the Meuse. But there was no way to break away, not now—even if he'd wanted to. And he no longer did, not after the realization that the DGSE had disregarded his warnings—passed along the information from the call to their counterparts in Brussels. And, by extension, Belkaïd's own agent-in-place.

It wasn't that their help was any less essential. . .if anything, it was far more so after learning of the scope of the Algerian's plans. But he couldn't trust them to keep him alive—not now.

He'd risked his life so many times before, but if he died now. . .it would all be for nothing. Their chance of stopping this cell, dying right along with him. Belkaïd would simply move on, to another plot—another target.

Until he had finally obtained vengeance for Algiers. For all that had been done to him—to his family, nearly six decades ago. For all he *could not* remember.

"*Mash'allah*," he heard Marwan breathe, the excitement—the *fanaticism*—clear in the younger man's voice as he gazed at the drone on the table. Harry's eyes darkening into steel-blue orbs as he watched him trace his hand over the large quad-copter's body. *If only the explosion had done its work. . .*

He could have talked Reza down, but not Marwan, he could have—*no*, that was madness, he realized, recognizing that he had grown far too emotionally attached. He couldn't have reasoned with the college student any more than he could reason with Yassin. Or Driss. *Or Aryn.* There was only one way this ended for all them, if he could bring himself to it.

Driss. He looked up to see the young Moroccan smile as Marwan continued speaking, "Your idea, brother—it was genius. There is no way they will be able to stop us."

The French weren't going to be able to save him now. To intervene, before it came to the end of this. It was up to him. And he was going to have to kill them all.

7:17 P.M.
Pont de Fragnée
Liège, Belgium

Thirty minutes late. Armand Césaire glanced at his watch for the second time in as many minutes, looking north and south along the Meuse.

There was no sign of his contact, no sign whatsoever. A few boats, proceeding up and down the river in the gathering twilight. Traffic, flowing across the Pont de Fragnée itself, just above his head.

But no foot traffic that he had been able to see—no one approaching the place where he waited, in the shadows of the bridge. It occurred to him to wish for a cigarette, something—anything—to pass the time, but Claire had cured him of that habit a couple decades before. *Bad for his health*, she had said. Like the rest of his life wasn't?

He shook his head. The stress of this job would kill him long before tobacco ever got the chance. He had no illusions about that.

"What are you seeing?" a voice in his ear asked. *Godard.* A reminder that Paris was monitoring this situation. . .actively.

"*Rien du tout*," he replied. *Nothing at all.* "There's no sign of him."

He heard a curse of frustration from the other end of the line, then Godard replied, "You only have another eight minutes before the satellite window closes. Once it's gone, we can't guarantee your safety."

You couldn't guarantee my safety before, you desk-bound fool, Césaire thought, shoving both hands in the pockets of his slacks he scanned the opposite riverbank once more.

"Once the window closes, you are to leave, Armand. Do you understand?"

"*Oui. Certainement.*"

8:03 P.M.
The hotel
Paris, France

Grigoriy Stepanovich Kolesnikov smiled, looking over the e-mail one final time before erasing it from the Drafts folder. *It was on.*

The meeting with Belkaïd had left him uncertain whether the trafficker actually intended to follow through, but he had. And he had a wish list.

And a target.

That latter, yet unknown, but judging from the equipment the Algerian had requested, it was going to be big. And it was going to happen here.

Kolesnikov picked up his glass of Pinot Noir and walked over to the window, pushing back the curtain with his free hand to stare out at the Parisian night. The thousand shimmering lights of the Eiffel Tower, a flaming torch glistening high in the night sky. *The City of Lights.*

Burning so brightly but seeming, even yet, incapable of dispelling the darkness, slowly settling over it all.

And it seemed as though he could somehow make out the black flag of jihad in the darkness of the sky, out beyond the tower, the white lettering bearing its blasphemous boast. *For there is no God but Allah. . .*

He raised a hand to his chest, touching almost unconsciously the icon of Our Lady of Vladimir beneath the fabric of his shirt. *Forgive me.*

But there was nothing to be forgiven, as his head knew, even if his heart at times wavered. His eyes darkening as he gazed out into the night, taking another sip of his wine.

This city had once been a center of the Christian faith, a beacon—shining as brightly as the garlands wreathing the Eiffel this night. *Now?* The West had crumbled into moral decay and an unbelief far more complete than the Communist state could ever have dreamed of.

They had been entrusted with the Word of God, with the protection of His church. They had failed, and in their failing, attempted to drag Russia down into the mire right along with them.

Now all that remained was to cleanse it with fire. To ensure that they could never again humiliate the *Rodina* as they had once. That Russia would once again be seen for what it was—the true defender of the faith, the world leader its history so richly deserved.

Fire. That's what men like Belkaïd were. A torch, in the hands of those who wielded them. The French President had barely won re-election in a bruising campaign against his National Front opponent five months prior. After an attack of this scale, here in Paris. . .the government itself would be lucky to survive.

To the death of the Fifth Republic, Kolesnikov thought, raising his glass to the night in a mock toast. He drained the glass, reaching forward to close the curtains with a rough gesture as he turned back toward the bed and the laptop, waiting for him to begin encoding his report to Moscow.

It would all begin here.

8:29 P.M.
Mont-de-Mans Air Base
Landes Department, France

The sun was sinking quickly into the western sky, sending a last few rays filtering across the airbase's runways—glinting off the delta wing of a parked Dassault Rafale as Sergeant Nathalie Jobert stood on the open balcony of the control tower, her left hand resting on the concrete parapet. Her dark eyes scanning the gathering darkness, ears straining to catch the slightest sound.

A useless endeavor, as she should have known by now. Glatigny's senses were much sharper than her own, she thought, feeling the golden eagle stir restlessly on her gauntleted right arm—its own, far keener eyes probing the dusk.

He was full-grown now, the largest of the three raised from a single clutch, each of them named after one of the fictional French paratroopers from Jean Larteguy's 1960 classic *The Centurions.*

Glatigny, Esclavier, and Raspéguy.

A smile touched her lips in the darkness. She could still remember the first time she had laid eyes on Glatigny, eighteen months earlier—a barely feathered ball of white fluff, tearing at raw meat on top of a wrecked drone.

Now. . .he had grown into a bird worthy of the nobility of his namesake, a scion of one of France's old families.

A defender of France. Glatigny's wings stirred in the night, a keening cry escaping the eagle's lips as she let the jesses slip free, the bird launching itself from her arm like a rocket, streaking across the runway toward the fading western sun.

Jobert reached up with her free right hand, bringing down her NODs over her eyes. And then, only then, in the pale-green glow of the night-vision, could she see what Glatigny had seen. A small quadcopter, coming in from the west, still half a kilometer or more out, penetrating the base's airspace.

But not for long. Even as she watched, the raptor circled, gaining altitude before diving into the UAV like a falling meteor, its leather-and-kevlar-mittened talons extended to seize the quadcopter, unbalancing it and knocking it off course.

She continued watching, but by now this had become a matter of course—an exercise she had witnessed a hundred times before as Glatigny brought the drone down to earth, crashing amidst a wreckage of snapped and mangled plastic.

But this was one of the first times they had attempted it in low-light conditions and, just as she had assured her superiors, it had made no difference in the end result.

Une victoire écrasante. A crushing victory.

9:34 P.M.
Pont de Fragnée
Liège, Belgium

He had waited as long as he dared. Far longer than his superiors back in Paris would have tolerated, had they known. Armand Césaire stood there for a moment longer, his form illuminated by the glow of the overhead streetlight, gazing up at the gilt statues towering far above him here at the eastern end of the bridge—a pair of angels, playing upon the trumpet.

Guardian angels? Something in him hoped so—hope against hope, hope against the experience of decades.

A hope he knew wouldn't die until this was over. Until he saw Daniel again—alive or dead.

But it was time to leave. Whatever this had been. . .whatever intelligence Paris thought they would gain from this mysterious caller, it had been all for nothing. A dry hole, like so many other promising intelligence coups through the years.

Whatever salvation there was to be found here, it would be found in their own officer, nowhere else. *If he was still alive.*

Time to check his signals. Once again.

Chapter 27

9:45 A.M. Central European Summer Time, August 1ˢᵗ
Liège, Belgium

"You're going to need at least two vans," Harry observed, leaning back into the front seat of the SUV as the vehicle came to a stop in morning traffic, winding their way through the streets of Liège. "Perhaps three."

"Why?" Belkaïd had picked him up in his personal vehicle for the trip to the warehouse this morning. *An olive branch after the events of the previous day? Or a trick designed to lull him into relaxing?*

"You don't want both of your drone operators to be in the same vehicle— if they are, and anything goes wrong. . ." He paused as they began moving again, the implication of his words obvious. "They ought to be utility vans, preferably from *Électricité de France*—something that won't draw attention near the stadium. Uniforms, even, if you can manage it—so that there can be activity around the vehicle which will give it the appearance of legitimacy."

The way he had done it, on a hundred surveillance ops over the years. He paused, realizing again just how easy it was, despite it all, to slip into the old ways of thinking. To view this through the familiar, if now distorted lens of *just another mission*. And yet Belkaïd was no fool—he would recognize bad advice if he was given it. "And we're going to need to train—Yassin and Driss seem to think that flying these drones will be like playing a videogame, but it's not that simple. It takes skill."

"You've done it?" the older man asked, and he could feel Belkaïd's eyes on him from the back seat, watching him closely.

A nod. *In Afghanistan*, Harry thought, glancing into the SUV's side mirror.

Still there. And Yemen. And a dozen other places, around the world—putting up a handheld UAV to conduct reconnaissance for an Agency operation.

"My friends and I back in Germany used to take quadcopters into the *Schwarzwald,*" he said, referencing the Black Forest, "and race them between the trees. An obstacle course and a race, all in one."

He smiled. "I was never very good—but the adrenaline rush of those afternoons. . .it gave me purpose in those days, before I found the true faith."

"Do you believe they can learn? In time?" Harry looked back to see a concerned look on the older man's face—glancing, even as he did so, through the rear windshield. *Still there.* Closer now.

"Mohammed," he began, turning to the driver, ignoring Belkaïd's question, "take the next right."

The man looked at him in surprise, taken off-guard by the sudden order. *"Do it now."*

He hesitated a split-second longer, distracted by Belkaïd's surprised query from the back seat, but then he put the wheel over, swinging the SUV into a narrow side street lined with parked vehicles, offering scarcely enough room for two cars to pass.

"What's going on?" Belkaïd demanded, leaning forward—his hand entering his jacket. *Going for his gun.* "This isn't the way to the warehouse."

"We've had a car behind us for seven blocks," Harry responded coolly, his eyes fixed on the rear-view mirror. *Waiting.* And there it was, the same off-white sedan he had been watching for the last ten minutes.

It didn't stop, didn't turn, but there was a hesitation there—a visible slowing of the vehicle as if its occupants were looking down the street to ascertain their position—relay it to another follow car. An easy mistake, but fatal.

Got you.

10:03 A.M.
An apartment in Anderlecht
Brussels, Belgium

The mid-morning sun was already filtering in through the window when Jan Vertens woke, finding himself already sweaty beneath the thin sheet covering his body. He felt the woman stir in the bed beside him and he smiled, reaching out to trace his fingers over the smooth curve of her back, leaning down to bestow a kiss on her bare shoulder. "*Goedemorgen, liefje,*" he whispered, hearing her murmur a sleepy reply. *Love.*

That was what had brought them together, a lonely middle-aged Belgian divorcee and a younger single mother from Egypt. An agnostic and a Copt. *Opposites.* And yet. . .somehow exactly what each of them had needed at that moment in their lives. *If he had met her earlier. . .*

Perhaps he would have gone a different path. Avoided the mistakes he had made along the way—mistakes which had kept him awake half the night, staring up at the ceiling of their bedroom.

Rana stretched out her arms, her dark hair splayed out against the pillow as she turned over, looking into his eyes. Throughout the week, they went their separate ways, to their separate jobs—but this morning, they had for themselves. *Together.*

"Do you think you can take Youssef to his football camp this afternoon?" she whispered, running her fingers through the hair of his chest.

"*Natuurlijk,*" he replied, reaching out to draw her in close for a kiss. He always enjoyed the time he spent with her son, but today. . .today anything that kept his mind off his work—his *mistakes*—would do.

Anything.

10:34 A.M.
Rue Hors-Château
Liège, Belgium

"How could you know they were there?" Belkaïd demanded, almost as soon as the door had closed behind them, closing off the corridor without. They hadn't gone on to the warehouse as planned, opting instead to circle back through the streets of Liège to the Algerian's apartment, predictably picking up at least one—possibly two—more tail cars along the way.

"The better question," Harry spat, his voice low as he turned on the older man, "is how you could *not?* Weren't you even looking for them? You warned me yesterday that surveillance was being contemplated—I kept my eyes open."

"Even so—"

"And keep your voice down," Harry interjected, cutting Belkaïd off. "You don't know who may be listening. Not now."

As if to punctuate his words, in that very moment he heard a door close, somewhere deeper in the apartment—a chill striking through his heart. *Was a member of the Belgian surveillance team still here? More than one?*

If they were, keeping them alive would be an almost impossible challenge, Harry thought—glancing at Belkaïd's face to see if he had heard the sound.

Everything blown in this moment. To hell and gone. And perhaps that would all be for the best.

But Belkaïd gave no sign, an intent look in his dark eyes as he asked another question, this time in a much lower voice, about the surveillance Harry had picked up.

"We're going to have to shift our base of operations," Harry replied, his face grim, his own hand lingering near his waistband and his holstered CZ. "Somewhere out in the country, preferably. Perhaps even across the border, into France itself."

He backed toward the kitchen, trying to draw Belkaïd out of the entry hall, but without success—hearing suddenly a small, feminine gasp from off to his right.

Turning to find Nora standing there in the hall leading back, presumably, to the bedrooms—her hand up to her mouth, her blonde hair flowing free over her shoulders. She was still in pajamas, having all too clearly spent the night. *With Belkaïd.*

"Please, Nora," Belkaïd said imperturbably, "make Ibrahim some tea. I have calls to make."

"I should put something on," she murmured, a stricken look on her face—unable to look Harry in the face.

"You're fine," the older man replied flatly, pushing past her into the hall. "Make the tea—I will need to remain undisturbed. And Ibrahim? I will be careful, in what I say."

Harry felt the girl slip past him into the kitchen, his eyes following Belkaïd down the hall toward the back of the extensive apartment. It was an old story, what had happened here—but being old made it no less tragic.

He thought of Ghaniyah Belkaïd, wondered if she had known of her brother's intentions when she sent the girl over. She had to have marked her absence, in time. Her words, still echoing in his ears, the memory of trauma still fresh in her voice. *I was raped—that, I suppose, I have in common with Nora.*

And now here they were again.

Harry moved into the living room of the apartment, leaving Nora alone in the kitchen as he began a methodical sweep for listening devices—probing behind every piece of furniture, checking the light fixtures. Nothing out of place. *Yet.*

He was still on his knees, examining the electrical outlet behind the sofa, when Nora emerged from the kitchen nearly twenty minutes later—bearing a tall thin glass of tea.

She handed him the drink without a word, still unable to meet his eyes—turning away as if to retreat back into the kitchen. He seized her wrist before she could move out of reach, their eyes locking as she finally looked up into his face. *Fear. Guilt.* Playing across her delicate Gallic features.

"Sit," he instructed simply, motioning her to the sofa as he himself took his seat on it, a few feet away. Raising the glass to his lips.

Harry suppressed a grimace at the first sip—the tea was far too sweet, even by the generous standards of the Maghreb, overpowering the taste of the mint. An outsider, trying to mimick the traditions of a culture she had adopted as her own, but to which she remained an alien. The tea, an ironic metaphor for her faith as she sat now across from him—never looking less a Muslim than in this moment.

"I'm sorry," she began, her face distorted in an agony of uncertainty. "I didn't mean for this to. . .I mean—"

"You should have left, as I warned you," he said soberly, overcome by his own sense of responsibility. *There had to be a way, even yet. . .*

To save her.

"If you need money to get home," he began, setting aside the tea to reach into his pocket, "I can give you enough to get you on your way. I—"

"No," she shook her head, something desperate in her voice. "I *can't* leave. Not now."

"Why?" Harry asked, reaching out for her hand and taking it in his own—feeling her shrink away from his touch. "What's left for you here? Reza is dead, you're only a distraction to those who remain. And Belkaïd isn't going to be satisfied with one night."

The words were cruel, but he had learned long ago that some cruelties were *necessary*. To save a life.

He watched a tear slide down her bare cheek, but she made no effort to reach up, to wipe it away. "You don't understand," she whispered numbly, an edge of bitterness creeping into her voice. "Reza was there for me when no one else was—when no one else could understand, not even my parents. He showed me how Islam valued—*protected*—women in a way the West no longer did. He brought me to the light."

"*Alhamdullilah.*" He forced a smile, knowing he had to tread with care. His tone quickly becoming sober once more. "But men are still men. And even among the Caliphate itself, I found men who would take advantage of a woman. A sister, even. I can't protect you from them."

She raised her hand then, brushing away the tear with a quick, angry gesture. "I'm not asking for your protection."

"What, then?"

And there were no more tears. Just the measured tones of a woman who knew what she wanted. And was prepared to do anything to get it. Even if it meant sharing the bed of a man like Belkaïd.

"A chance to give my life in this war. You were wrong, you know—wrong to say that it was no place for me. There is no other place, not now, not after all I've done." She paused, her eyes shining with a strange fire as they locked with his own. "Reza didn't just show me the light. He showed me why it was worth dying for."

2:04 P.M.
Médiacité
Liège, Belgium

Heat radiated off the pavement as Daniel Mahrez crossed the street toward the massive Médiacité mall, its distinctive wave-glass roof shimmering in the summer sun.

He'd been a teenager when it opened, not that many years ago. *A lifetime, now.*

LYSANDER's eyes flickered from one side to another, alert for more than just the traffic. Knowing all too well the dangers of this moment—the reasons he hadn't dared make contact with his handler over the last several weeks.

Belkaïd was becoming ever more paranoid with each passing day. As a trained intelligence officer, he knew the signs. Recognized the tightrope he was walking on here. *And al-Almani. . .*

Daniel suppressed a grimace. There was something about that man—something far more dangerous than even Belkaïd. And now the two of them together. . .and this *plan.*

He had left the counter-signal for Césaire thirty minutes earlier. Now it remained only to leave the drop—a micro-drive containing an audio recording of what he knew of the plot—in the designated location, inside the mall's cinema.

Daniel marked a man in a tracksuit crossing the street behind him, behind and to the right, the man's reflection visible in the glass doors of the mall ahead. Another man, in shirt and jeans, perhaps fifteen meters to the left. There was no sign that the two men were together—connected even—but even as he reached the door, he saw one of them glance over at the other. *Or did he?* It was almost impossible to tell, the flicker of a glance in a mirror—his own mind playing tricks on him. *Had Belkaïd put a team on him?* Did he suspect?

Calm down, he told himself, knowing it would do him no good to lose his head. Not now. There was nothing for it but to press forward—see what came.

Daniel ducked as a toy helicopter buzzed through the air past his head, hearing a child's delighted laugh as he glanced quickly over toward a kiosk in the middle of the mall's concourse, finding the kiosk's owner instructing the child of a passer-by in the manipulation of the controls. The kid was no more than seven, a couple years older than his own Saphir.

A shadow passed across the French intelligence officer's face as he used the moment's distraction to glance behind him. *Still there.* He hadn't seen his son in two months. And if he put a foot wrong now. . .he never would again.

Neither of the two men appeared to be North African, but not all of Belkaïd's crew were—he'd been around them long enough to know that.

And *they* were following him, that much was undeniable now—fifteen minutes in. There would be no chance to make the drop, not now. Even going into the cinema could excite their suspicions—something he and Césaire should have thought of when setting this up, the advantages of the darkness and privacy outweighing all other considerations.

He tightened his grip on the bag of spices he had purchased in a shop here on the second floor of the mall, resisting the urge to wipe his sweaty palms against his pants as he made his way toward the escalators down. *And the exit.*

He'd have to ditch the drive on the way out. Try again, another time.

2:23 P.M.
VSSE Headquarters
Brussels, Belgium

". . .exiting the mall now—we're still with the target."

"*Goed*," Christian Danloy responded, circling the table in the center of the room—listening to the report from one of the half-dozen surveillance teams they now had spread out over the city of Liège, tracking Belkaïd's people. The members of the Molenbeek cell identified by the DGSE. "Stay on him. Did he do anything other than buy spices at the shop?"

"*Nee.*"

"All right, then," the VSSE chief said, breaking off the connection as he glanced around him at the gathered officers. "File a warrant to access the mall CCTV footage in and around that shop. If any other members of the cell have frequented it over the last month, we need to know. Let me know when it's done."

3:41 P.M.
Parc Astrid, Anderlecht
Brussels, Belgium

The shrill blast of a whistle broke through the humid summer air, a man's voice barking out sharp commands as a couple dozen young players ages eleven and below spread out across the stadium's field, awaiting their coach's next signal.

Youssef was lucky to get in this camp, Jan Vertens thought idly, glancing up from the game on his phone—recognizing the coach as one of R.S.C. Anderlecht's top footballers.

Perhaps he might even play for the club himself some day—if he stuck with it. Kids often didn't, even kids as dedicated and earnest as Youssef. A year gone by and he thought of him almost as his own son. *Perhaps. . .*

Vertens leaned back into his seat in the bleachers, tapped the screen again, once, twice, watching the brightly-colored blocks cascade down into a new position. He certainly hadn't intended to be a policeman as a kid. He—

His phone began to pulse with an incoming call just then, a strange number displayed on the screen. He stared at it for a long moment, frozen, as if entranced—as if he suddenly found himself holding a poisonous snake in his hand.

Willing it to stop. *To go to voicemail.* Anything to delay the inevitable. But having such a message on his phone. . .

He pressed *Accept*, lifting the phone to his ear with a trembling hand. *"Ja?"*

"I've been waiting on your call, Jan. Is a football camp really so much more important than the obligations between the two of us?"

A chill ran through his body. He knew the voice, even if he had heard it so very rarely over the years. *Gamal Belkaïd.*

And he knew where he was.

"What are you *thinking*?" Vertens demanded, finding his voice. "Calling me like this—on my personal *phone.*"

He realized suddenly that he was speaking far too loudly—other parents beginning to look at him strangely. He flushed red, rising from his seat and shuffling along the seats toward the exit.

"If you didn't want me to call you, Jan," the black market trafficker replied calmly, "you should have made contact before this. What did you learn?"

Silence. He made his way out of the bright sunlight and into the darkened corridors of the stadium, his mind racing. He couldn't betray the French asset—couldn't endanger a man's life like that. Couldn't—

"Don't trifle with me, Jan," Belkaïd said after a long moment of dead silence. "You're there with the boy, aren't you?"

"Ja. Waarom?" Why. But he knew why, his heart congealing into an icy fist in the pit of his stomach.

"A couple of my men are there as well. They may, perhaps, be even closer to him than you are yourself."

"Don't you *dare* harm him!" Vertens exploded, his voice trembling with fear and rage—his eyes measuring the distance back down the corridor. *Could he make it in time?*

"It's you who will harm him, Jan. Think carefully about what you say next."

Vertens closed his eyes, leaning against the wall—his free hand clenching and unclenching spasmodically, a thousand unspoken curses passing across his lips. *There was no choice.*

He took a long, deep breath, knowing what he had to do. Struggling to steady his voice as he spoke again. "You have a mole. . ."

Chapter 28

5:34 P.M.
The apartment
Liège, Belgium

"When I was raped, I thought my life was over. My boyfriend left me, refused to believe that I hadn't in some way brought it on myself. Perhaps he was right, even, I don't know—I was so far from the truth then. I was already taking drugs. . .thought I would just lock myself in my chambre *and end myself. And then there was Reza."*

But of course, Harry thought, lifting the spoon to his lips—the fiery taste of red pepper spreading throughout his mouth as he tested the *muhammara*. Not enough lemon, he realized, moving away from the counter to rummage in the apartment's refrigerator.

Reza. Generous and impulsive as ever, stepping in where no one else saw a need—where no one else *cared*. Like he had when Harry had first arrived in Molenbeek, half-dead.

Both of the brothers had welcomed him into their apartment, but it had been Reza who had recognized the need that day at the mosque—Harry nearly collapsing into him as they rose together from Friday prayers. Insisted on taking him to the hospital—then back to their own apartment when Harry explained why a hospital was impossible.

That he would have found Nora in her lowest moment of despair—would have helped her get back on her feet—was so like him. The sad ghost of a smile passed across Harry's face. *And now he was dead.*

"This meant everything *to Reza,"* she had continued, her bright blue eyes

burning with passion. *"He would talk so often of the way Muslims in the Middle East were oppressed by America, by the West, in an effort to* force *them to change—to no longer shelter their women from the kind of violence which had left its scars on me."*

And he had listened, as she continued, knowing the reality was so very different—knowing that he couldn't *trust* her enough to save her. Knowing then how it would end, for her, like all the rest.

"How could I betray him by leaving—now, when we're so close? When we finally have a chance to show the world the pain they've so carelessly inflicted everywhere else? To show them how it feels.*"*

He'd realized something then, watching her—something he should have picked up about her behavior long before. *"You said you had done drugs, once. . .have you touched them, recently?"*

"No," she'd answered quickly. *Far too quickly.* And he knew then how Belkaïd had seduced her. A temptation beyond any personal charm of his own—too strong for her to resist.

"How's it going, *habibi?"* Harry's head came up from stirring the *muhammara* into a thick red paste to find Aryn standing in the doorway, eyeing the food.

"Good," he responded absently, the young man's appearance pulling his mind from his thoughts. He reached out, tearing off a hunk of bread from the loaf on the counter, ladling the dip onto it. "I think this is almost ready to eat, if you want to try it? There was a man in *Sham*, who taught me how to make this. We rarely had the vegetables there to do it, but a few occasions. . .*mash'allah.*"

5:42 P.M.
VSSE Headquarters
Brussels, Belgium

"Hold up, hold up," one of the targeting officers announced, raising his finger to point to one of the screens, a traffic camera covering the street in front of the towering apartment building they had identified as providing residences for the majority—if not all—of the Molenbeek cell members, and more than a few of Belkaïd's own men. "We have activity on the street."

Christian Danloy hurried over to look where he was pointing, watching as four SUVs pulled in off the street, one right after the other—men piling out almost before they had come to a stop.

"What's going on?" The *administrateur général*'s eyes narrowed, watching the scene unfold before them—the men spreading out as if to form a perimeter. "That's Belkaïd himself—why weren't we alerted that he was inbound?"

"His follow team lost him fifteen minutes ago," came the infuriating reply. "Heavy traffic—they weren't able to make up the difference and re-acquire him. We need eyes in the sky."

And they had known that, but tasking it and working through the legal issues had been other matters entirely. Danloy stood there, watching as a small group of men closed around Belkaïd, disappearing into the building itself—the rest remaining, as if on guard, without.

"What do we have on the inside in terms of audio/visual surveillance?" he demanded, glancing around at his team. "Talk to me."

"*Vergeef mij, meneer,*" his lead officer responded, shaking his head. *Forgive me.* "We've not been able to get officers inside, not yet—the neighborhood. . .it's difficult to do so unobtrusively."

"*Het maakt niet uit,*" Danloy replied, his eyes fixed on the cameras. *It doesn't matter.* Not now.

And yet somehow, as he watched the men on-screen, he knew. It mattered very much indeed.

"Find out who we have in the area—move them to cover the apartments. *Snel.*"

Quickly.

5:46 P.M.
The apartments
Liège, Belgium

"It seems hard to believe," Aryn said thoughtfully, his mouth full of bread and *muhammara,* chewing slowly and with evident relish as he spoke.

"What?" Harry scooped more of the dip onto his own bread, remembering another kitchen in another apartment—it didn't seem so long ago—cooking dinner for himself and Mehreen Crawford. But that had been before it had all fallen apart. . .*fallen?*

No. That implied an accident. Something unintentional. But there could have been nothing more intentional than the way he had destroyed them both.

"That we could be this close," the young man replied, something almost. . .reverential about his tone. "All those years, as I took care of my mother—I followed the news coming out of Iraq, Afghanistan, then Syria. And I wanted nothing more in this world than to be a part of it. To finally take *action.* And it's finally almost here."

He crammed the rest of the bread in his mouth, bringing an unbidden smile to Harry's face as it bulged out against his bearded cheek. "We're doing this, Ibrahim. We're actually *doing* this!"

"*Insh'allah,*" Harry whispered, the smile vanishing as quick as it had come. "Be careful what you say, brother."

He hadn't told the other cell members about the surveillance yet—Belkaïd had, for reasons known only to himself, insisted that he wait. But he had swept the apartment for listening devices, and found nothing. They were in the clear, if only for the moment.

"But how could *this* be anything other than the will of God?" Aryn exclaimed, seeming incredulous. "How could—"

Whatever he might have been about to say next was forever lost as the sound of splintering wood announced the flimsy outer door of the apartment being kicked open—the sound of booted feet against the tile, moving toward them.

Harry saw Aryn's eyes darting around wildly, looking for a weapon—*any* weapon—torn between his instincts for fight or flight. He left his own pistol where it was, in its holster inside his waistband, beneath the loose shirt. If this *was* the police, he wasn't getting shot. *Not if he could help it.*

Aryn's eyes fell on the knife block, his hand whipping out to seize a steak knife even as Gamal Belkaïd appeared in the doorway of the kitchen, flanked by two of his men. Their pistols already drawn, muzzles sweeping the kitchen.

Down the hall, Harry could hear another crash as one of the bedroom doors was kicked in—a cry of surprise from Driss. *Or Marwan.* Yassin was in the shower, the sound of the running water filtering its way through the adjoining wall.

"What is the meaning of this, Gamal?" he demanded, finding his voice finally. "What are you even *thinking*, risking coming in here like this, when you know they're watching?"

Belkaïd transfixed him with a murderous glance, a gaze that seemed to pierce to Harry's very soul. "Perhaps you know, Ibrahim. Perhaps you've always known."

"What are you saying?" Aryn asked, staring open-mouthed into the muzzles of the guns. The knife dropped, uselessly at his feet.

"I'm saying," Belkaïd replied coldly, turning on the younger man, "that one of you is a Western *spy*."

5:51 P.M.
Médiacité
Liège, Belgium

The fifth row from the front, third chair in, Armand Césaire thought, his gaze flickering around the nearly-deserted cinema to make sure what few eyes remained were focused on the screen before stooping down in the semi-darkness, examining the bottom of the theater chair's metal frame. The drive should be somewhere here. . .

He had seen the flag an hour before—the acknowledgment that LYSANDER had *finally* seen his signals and would be making a drop. And this was the first of the drop sites.

But nothing except metal met Césaire's probing fingers. *Nothing.*

He felt a cold chill run through him, as if seized by some premonition of evil. And he left the theater, just as quickly as he had come.

Paris would need to be informed.

5:53 P.M.
The apartments
Liège, Belgium

Harry shook his head, staring incredulously at Belkaïd as his men hustled Driss and Marwan into the cramped kitchen of the apartment—roughly shoving them forward into the middle of the room. Followed a moment or two later by a dripping Yassin, a towel wrapped hastily around his midsection.

"We've already been down this road, Gamal, you and I—yesterday," he said quietly, keeping his hands away from his sides. *Easily visible.* "And now your paranoia has endangered us all. If the Belgian surveillance picked up you and your men coming in here like this, with *weapons.* . ."

"It's not paranoia when you *know*, Ibrahim," Belkaïd said harshly, their eyes locking across the room. "And now I do, thanks to my source in the security services. The French DGSE has a spy in our midst."

The French. That call, again, Harry realized, proving his undoing. *No good deed.* At least he'd had the chance to plant the phone—wiped to clean off any stray prints and slipped beneath Marwan's mattress. The SIM card and battery removed but lying only inches away, the call still logged, easily retrievable.

He saw the surprise in the young men's eyes, the sudden suspicion— glances flickering back and forth. *Fear.*

His eyes locked with Marwan's across the room, recognizing a bitter animosity in the young man's face. *Danger.*

He started to speak, but the younger man beat him to the punch, taking a step forward into the center of the room—seeming to ignore the guns leveled at them.

"It's you, isn't it?" he demanded, looking straight at Harry. "You, who have betrayed us. You came to us, said that you had fought in Syria—but no one you claim to have served with seems to have survived. No one who could support your claims—or deny them. And from the very *beginning*, at every turn you tried to delay, to obstruct—to prevent us from carrying out an attack here."

The truth. Always the worst enemy of the spy. It was impossible not to wonder where, exactly, he had slipped up. What it was which had betrayed him. No—*killed* him. His eyes never left Marwan's face as he reached up, slowly and deliberately beginning to unbutton his shirt—each small, almost imperceptible gesture breathing defiance.

Harry shrugged the shirt back off his shoulders, letting it fall unheeded to the floor. Standing there before them, stripped to the waist, the pistol now visible in its holster inside his waistband. The pair of ugly, purplish pockmarks decorating his upper abdomen stark against the ghostly pallor of his flesh. *Memories of that dark night in Aberdeen.* Only the most recent of his scars.

"Go on, boy," he said, his hands outstretched toward Marwan, "show us the wounds *you* have received in the struggle of God."

5:55 P.M.
VSSE Headquarters
Brussels, Belgium

"They haven't moved," Christian Danloy breathed, watching the CCTV closely. The fanned-out group of men spread out around the apartment building's main entrance, just standing there—a few of them smoking, but alert. *Waiting.* For what?

That was the question none of them had the answer to. "How long before we have officers on-scene?"

"Another five minutes," came the infuriating response. "Twenty before we get a full team together—we're having to pull officers off the warehouse, off Belkaïd's apartment and—"

"Just do it," the VSSE chief replied. "Get them there, and move them into position—if you can, without alerting them to our presence in the neighborhood."

5:56 P.M.
The apartments
Liège, Belgium

Harry saw the look in the young man's eyes, saw him recoil onto the defensive. Knew, in that moment, that he had him. *Move in for the kill.*

"This afternoon," he began, his eyes going cold and hard, "you went out— where were you going?"

"You know," Marwan retorted angrily, "I went to Médiacité, to buy spices. For *you.*"

Harry shook his head. "No, 'brother.' I asked you to get them only after you'd already told me you were going out. So, where were you going?"

And that was a lie—he *had* asked him to go out, to give him time to plant the phone—but only the two of them knew that. The irrefutable lie. *Always the best kind.*

"And what about the other night?" he continued, keeping him off-balance, pressing the counterattack home with a merciless intensity. "Again, with no explanation, you had to 'go out.' What about Reza's death? I left you with instructions for transferring the compound—the next thing I know, you're standing beside me and he's *dead.*"

And there was fear there now, that emotion so easily confused with *guilt.* "But that was *your* bomb!"

"And I warned *everyone,*" Harry retorted, his voice filled with the soulless intensity of a man with nothing left to lose, "that it was dangerous. That it had to be handled with the utmost of care. And you didn't—you pushed him on, to his death."

You couldn't care about your own survival if you wanted to *live.* A contradiction, in the eyes of anyone who had never been here. Who had never looked Death in the face. Who didn't know that it was *caring* that killed you.

"What did you think—that you would pick us off, one by one?" His own play, turned back on Marwan. *Projection.* That was what a psychologist would have called it, but that didn't mean it didn't work. "That you could weaken us and bring us down?"

"No, no," Marwan replied, his face betraying confusion and fear—his eyes flickering between Harry and Belkaïd's men. "Nothing like that. I didn't—"

"You killed Reza?" Yassin demanded, finding his voice unexpectedly, his voice filling with grief and rage. "You drew a gun on Ibrahim in the beginning, threatened to kill him there in the boxing club. Risked bringing the police down on all of us, even then. Is that what you *wanted?* Did you—"

"*Enough!*" Belkaïd spat, barking an order to his men—the muzzle of a gun thrust suddenly into Yassin's face checking his attempt to charge forward, seize Marwan by the throat. "All of you. We're not going to get to the bottom of anything like this."

"And you don't have the time, Gamal," Harry replied, his voice even. *In control.* "Not here, not now. Suspect me if you must, investigate this fool's accusations to their fullest, but right now—we need to *leave.* Before the security services come and find us here, all of us together, holding each other at gunpoint."

Belkaïd seemed to hesitate for a long moment, searching Harry's face for any sign of duplicity. Of *betrayal*. Then he nodded. "You're right."

"And before your men leave," Harry continued, turning back to look Belkaïd in the eye as several of his bodyguards began to shepherd them from the room with barked curses and rough shoves, "make sure they go through everyone's room and belongings. *Thoroughly*."

6:07 P.M.
DGSE Headquarters
Paris, France

"Are you certain, Armand? It wasn't there?" Anaïs Brunet swore softly to herself as she heard Césaire repeat his assertion, in the negative. This was getting out of control. Perhaps it had been, long before this. Perhaps Vukovic had even been right, from the beginning, in his insistence that they maintain their dependence on technical collection, instead of risking an officer in the field.

"I don't understand it," the case officer went on after a long moment. "He should have proceeded straight from leaving the signal to the cinema—made the drop at once. One, but not the other. *Cela n'a pas de sens.*"

It makes no sense. *Unless LYSANDER had been compromised en route*, as they both knew.

An aide entered the room just then, and Brunet pressed the "mute" button on the microphone before her as the woman began speaking quietly into her ear, her face changing as she listened.

"*Certainement*," she said finally, "have it transferred through to this room. *Merci.*"

Gauthier, sitting a few feet away down the table, shot her a quizzical look. The general looked weary, a mirror, she was certain, of her own exhaustion. She hadn't been back to the apartment which served as her Paris residence in nearly thirty hours.

Both of them, running on fumes.

"Thank you for the report, Armand," she said, unmuting the microphone once more as the aide left the room. "Please keep us apprised of developments. Paris out."

"What's going on?" Gauthier asked then, waiting until Césaire had signed off.

"An update from Brussels, apparently," Brunet replied, reaching for the remote beside her briefing notes and aiming it at the television screen on the far wall. The face of the VSSE administrator-general materializing on-screen a moment later.

"*Bonsoir*, Christian. What do you have for us?"

From the moment he began speaking, she knew that her greeting had been a lie. There was nothing "good" about this evening. . .

6:31 P.M.
Liège, Belgium

"They're still back there," Harry announced quietly, glancing behind him through the tinted windows of the SUV. They had been driving south for twenty-five minutes, out of Liège, following east along the banks of the Ourthe as it flowed west into the Meuse.

There were two of Belkaïd's men in the vehicle with them—one of them sitting only a foot away from Harry on the back seat of SUV, his hand on the butt of his holstered pistol—plus the driver. Driss occupying the front passenger seat. Neither of them were bound—presumably to avoid undue questions if they were stopped—but there was the gun.

Easy enough to take, if it came to that. If it were expedient—and it wasn't. He had to play the long game here, had to see this through.

He had wanted to go with Marwan, to keep the younger man off balance, to prevent him from gaining Belkaïd's ear further—but that had proved impossible, with the younger man being herded away from him as they split up into multiple vehicles, taking multiple routes out of the city.

Belkaïd had at least possessed the instincts to do that. Offer their surveillance as many targets as possible—count on them not having the manpower to follow up on them all.

But *somehow*, even so. . .they'd drawn a short straw.

He saw the driver react, startled, at his announcement—something of fear and defiance passing across the man's face, seeming instinctively to depress the accelerator, the SUV lurching into a higher gear.

"*Don't* react," Harry said through clenched teeth, his eyes meeting the driver's in the rear-view mirror. "If you react, you'll give them a reason to stop us. And I don't think you want that, *mon frere*," he said, addressing himself to the bodyguard beside him in the back seat, "unless that pistol is licensed."

"Why do you care?" the man spat, and Harry could smell the fear, the rancid odor of sweat coming off the man's body.

"Because it's not true what he said," he replied simply. "I would have given my life for the Caliphate, but I survived its fall. Survived when I should have *died.*"

The best lie was always the truth, Harry thought, looking steadily into the man's eyes. *His story.* So many times through his life—living on when he should have died, face-down in a ditch. When better men had taken a bullet, right beside him.

"This is my *one* chance to redeem myself. To finish what I began. And I will let nothing stand in our way." He cleared his throat, gazing forward once more at the driver—catching sight of a blue street sign bearing the words *Chênée-Centre* as they rolled out onto the bridge. "Take the next left—follow the road along the banks of the Vesdre to the west."

7:06 P.M.
DGSE Headquarters
Paris, France

"It's him, it's Daniel," Brunet whispered, a raw edge in her voice as she stared at the CCTV footage. Recognizing, even in the low-resolution imagery, the familiar figure of their officer being hustled into the back of a darkened SUV. *Shoved?*

It was impossible to tell, from this distance, whether he was going willingly or being coerced—but one thing *was* clear. Gamal Belkaïd was shifting his base of operations. *Suddenly.*

Gauthier nodded, and she saw the same recognition of their reality. This was trouble.

"*C'est vrai,* Christian?" she blazed, unmuting the microphone on the table before her. "You've blown this operation wide open. How could your people be *this* incompetent?"

On-screen, she saw Danloy take a deep breath, clearly measuring his own words. "We don't know this, Anaïs, not yet, *si'l vous plait*. It remains possible that—"

"*Non*," she fired back, venom permeating her voice. *Righteous fury.* "You can't possibly believe this. Less than twelve hours since you first put surveillance on Gamal Belkaïd, and he's already in the wind. He *knows*, Christian, he has to know."

Brunet paused, bridling her anger as she glared at the figure on-screen. "Tell me you at least still have them."

There was a long moment's pause. *Too long.* "*Je suis désolé*, Anaïs. *C'est ma faute.* The follow teams lost track of them outside the city."

Chapter 29

6:03 A.M., Central European Summer Time, August 2nd
Somewhere in northern France

Deja vu. It felt as though they were beginning, all over again—like climbing out of a well, only to lose one's footing once more, stone and mortar giving way beneath one's hand. That heart-stopping moment, just before the fall.

"I have told you all this before, Gamal," Harry said wearily, staring across the table into Belkaïd's dark, unyielding eyes. His hands were cuffed behind him—his body bound to the frame of the wooden chair. He hadn't slept in over twenty-four hours, and he now had no idea where they were—somewhere in northern France, most likely, but he and Driss had been hooded shortly after their successful crossing of the border. "Why would I lie?"

"To protect yourself?" Belkaïd asked, his face impassive. "That's usually why men lie."

Harry shook his head. "If I wanted to protect myself, if the betrayal Marwan accuses me of were true, I would have killed you there in your own apartment. The knife was in my hand."

"I had a gun."

"And I have been in battle."

Belkaïd seemed to consider that response for a long moment, as if he was once again re-assessing the man in front of him. "You believe you could have done that?"

"Had Allah willed," Harry responded evenly, only too aware of how this could escalate. He'd been hearing the screams, coming from some other part

413

of the house, for hours—but so far, he'd only been knocked about. "But He ordained instead that we should *both* live, brother—that we should live to carry out His war against the West."

"Nora tells me that you tried to send her away," the older man said, changing tack suddenly—as if looking to catch Harry off-guard. "Tried to convince her to leave us, go back to her family. Why?"

You tried to save someone, and ended up only damning yourself. Another piece of evidence, in Belkaïd's case against him—the weight, bearing him down beneath the surface, legs kicking desperately against the water in the effort to rise.

Your mind, screaming that it was already too late. Only your body, still refusing to give up. *To die.*

"She is a distraction," he replied, injecting as much calm into his voice as he could muster. "To you, now, Gamal, as she was to Reza before."

He saw Belkaïd flinch, knew the dangerous ground he was treading on—but knew he had to sell this, even if it meant offense. *And it surely would.*

"Wherever there is a woman, there will always be a man willing to take advantage of her."

Belkaïd's eyes flashed fire, and a cuff from the bodyguard's hand caught Harry in the side of the cheek, rocking the chair back on its legs—nearly going over.

Harry recovered, working his jaw muscles as if to make sure they were still functional as he opened his eyes, staring back across the table at the Algerian. "Have me beaten, if you like. . .but the truth will remain the truth. And *sharia* will remain *sharia.* I spoke to her because I perceived the temptation she was already becoming to you, to others—even more so after Reza's death. There is no place for a woman in the day of battle, and I saw only trouble in her continued presence among us."

The silence hung heavy between them in the empty room for a long moment.

Then Belkaïd nodded, slowly. With almost palpable reluctance.

"I believe you. You're telling the truth." His gaze flicked over to the bodyguard, standing once again a few feet away, chewing on a snack bar. "Unlock his cuffs and untie him. Give him something to eat and drink. And then you will come with me, Ibrahim. . .I have something to show you."

6:37 A.M.
VSSE Headquarters
Brussels, Belgium

Devastation. That was the only word that Christian Danloy could think of to describe the scene on the screens before him.

It had taken twenty minutes circling the apartment building with the quadcopter UAV before they'd found it—a window in the one of the target apartments that wasn't curtained off.

"Are you seeing this, Anaïs?"

"*Oui,*" the DGSE head responded, her voice still icy. *Unforgiving.*

And what they were seeing was the remains of an apartment which had been torn apart—utterly demolished in an effort to find. . .something, it was hard to say what—curtains torn down from the window to reveal the chaos within, a mattress ripped to shreds and left wedged awkwardly in the doorway of the bedroom—a nightstand smashed to kindling.

"Is the rest of the apartment like this? The others?"

"We've not been able to ascertain that. . .can't get an angle with the drone—the only way we learn more is to get a warrant, send officers into the building itself to investigate."

"*Non.*" Brunet's voice was clear, firm. "Do that, and you'll confirm whatever they suspect. The intelligence value you gain will be nothing compared to the value of the intelligence they'll glean from your presence."

"Then where do we go from here?"

"*Je ne sais pas.*"

I don't know.

6:41 A.M.
A house
Northern France

The house had been abandoned, for a very long time, Harry realized—glancing around at the walls stripped bare, the floors devoid of furniture.

It had probably been built sometime in the '70s, judging by what he could tell of the architecture. Built, lived in for decades, and then. . .abandoned.

Hard to say when Belkaïd had acquired the property. Or if he had, even.

He set down his glass of water as the Algerian motioned for him to follow—leading him down a long, dimly-lit hallway toward the back of the house, the bodyguard following behind.

There were steps there, leading down into the basement, and Belkaïd motioned for Harry to take the lead, down into the darkness.

Was it a trap? If so, he was already inside it, Harry thought, hesitating for only a moment before beginning to descend the steps—the old, threadbare carpet rough against his bare feet.

If Belkaïd wanted to blow out his brains, he could do so just as easily here as below.

A light met his eyes as he reached the bottom of the steps, his toes meeting concrete, cool and damp—the bright glare of an industrial light bursting through the doorway of a nearby room.

And then he heard it, the low moans of a man sobbing in well-nigh unbearable pain. The sequel to the screams he'd listened to earlier.

A drenched Marwan sat shivering uncontrollably in the center of the room, lashed tightly to the frame of a metal chair with electrical cords—his face bruised and bloodied, three of the fingers of his right hand mangled beyond recognition.

He'd been a boxer when they first met, Harry remembered, his eyes narrowing pitilessly as he entered the room, glancing from Marwan to his torturers. But he'd never fight again—not with those hands.

His eyes flickered over to a table sitting in one corner of the basement room, catching sight of the phone lying on the table a few feet away from the hand of Belkaïd's man.

So they had *found it.* Just as he'd intended them to.

It was hard not to feel some kind of. . .sympathy, in this moment, looking at the young man before him in the chair. *Helpless.* Sobbing uncontrollably through his pain, tears and mucus running down his trembling cheeks. Little more than a fragile husk of the man he had once been. *Before the pain began.*

But it was only a scant fraction of the pain he had dreamed of *inflicting.* Harry's face hardened into a mask, remembering the excitement he'd seen in Marwan's eyes the day of the bombing in Berlin—every time they talked of their own plans since. The passion of a true believer. *A fanatic.*

The kind of man he'd sacrificed everything to stop, all through the years. No different than any of them. No more deserving of pity.

He'd corrupted the other members of the Molenbeek cell and dragged them down with him into the pit, and. . .and then Harry realized that the attention of the man sitting at the table wasn't on the phone at all, but on the laptop computer before him.

Marwan's laptop.

He was fiddling with the external speaker, as if struggling to produce more sound from it.

"Do you have it?" Belkaïd's voice, from behind him, somehow chilling him to the bone. *A premonition of evil.*

"*Oui,*" the man replied, still playing with the computer. "I believe I have recovered the deleted files from the hard drive. . .they may be corrupted, but we should be able to access them."

Harry glanced from the table back to Marwan, to Belkaïd, feeling a stab of uncertainty go through him—suddenly realizing this was about more than the phone. *Much more.*

The man at the computer leaned back in his seat just then, depressing a key on the laptop before him—a stream of broken audio pouring from the speakers at full volume.

A man's voice, low but recognizable. Speaking French. *Marwan.*

"*I apologize for not making contact before now. . .*" his next words were lost in a haze of white noise, clearly the result of the file corruption. "*. . .things have escalated over the last few days, and the cell is now planning to go active, within the week.*"

Harry felt as though the blood had drained from his face, staring in mute shock at the savagely mutilated form of the man in the chair before him. *His fellow intelligence officer.*

"*They're planning an attack. . .next Saturday, on the Stade. . .we have to shut them down,* immédiatement. *We. . .*"

More white noise, as Harry looked up to find Belkaïd smiling at him.

"You were right, brother, after all. We found our spy."

10:03 A.M.
Palais de l'Élysée
Paris, France

"*Mon Dieu. . .*" the French president breathed thoughtfully, shaking his head as he glanced over the hastily prepared briefing before him. "Who authorized this operation?"

"I did, *mon presidente*," Brunet replied, gazing steadily into Denis Albéric's eyes. They were both from the same generation, as strange as that seemed, in this moment. A generation which had grown up under De Gaulle in the late '60s, in the era when France had reasserted itself once more on the world stage.

*L'Europe, depuis l'Atlantique jusqu'à l'Oural. . .*Europe, from the Atlantic to the Urals, as De Gaulle had famously put it. A Europe which would decide the destiny of the world.

But Destiny had proved a far more fickle mistress, as any Frenchman should have expected.

Her father had been a fairly low-ranking deputy in the *Ministère de la Défense*. Albéric's, a colonel in the French Army—a paratroop officer.

But here they both were. . .with Destiny taking a hand once more.

"This was a joint operation set up with the cooperation of *les Américains*," she continued evenly, glancing over at her DGSI counterpart, sitting in another chair a few feet away, "and run out of Alliance Base."

"And you believe that your officer has now been compromised?" Albéric mused, tenting his fingers before him as he seemed to consider her words.

"We have to consider that possibility. His last signal indicated that he had intelligence of an imminent attack—and now he's gone dark. He missed the drop, and we have CCTV footage of him getting into a van not far from Liège's Outremeuse district. After that—nothing."

"And the DGSI was never read in on any of this?" Raoul Dubois demanded, finally finding his voice. "*Pour quoi?*"

Why.

"Few even at the DGSE knew, Raoul," she replied, meeting the DGSI chief's gaze with a composed stare of her own. She'd gotten a few hours of sleep before coming here, but they were precious little enough. "A handful of operations personnel—a few of us at the top. We were minimizing risk."

"It would not appear as though you succeeded."

She ignored Dubois' jab with a mighty effort, refocusing her attention on the president, even as Albéric cleared his throat.

"And you're telling me that this terrorist cell may have now crossed the border into France?"

"It's a contingency we must be prepared for, *mon presidente*. Two of the target vehicles were on a southwest heading from Liège when the VSSE lost track of them."

"You have a number of public appearances coming up over the course of the next week," she continued, ticking them off on her fingers, "your visit with flood victims in Orléans, your visit to Pozières for the memorial, your appearance at the qualifying game for the World Cup at the *Stade de France*. . .you're going to be exposed, in public. *Vulnerable*."

"I am always vulnerable, *madame le directeur*. I am the President of the Republic. I can't hide from that."

"*Bien sûr que non.*" *Of course not.* "I am only suggesting that you minimize your exposure until we in the security services," she glanced over at Dubois, "can better ascertain the threat."

There was a long pause—uncertainty and a measure of fear playing across Denis Albéric's features as he weighed out her proposal, glancing back and forth between his two intelligence chiefs. Seeking reassurance and finding none.

But even as she watched, something of a grim resolution seemed to settle over the president's countenance.

"*Non*," he replied finally, a sharp edge creeping into his voice. "I will not alter my schedule, or fail to keep my commitments to the people of France. I have a job to do. As do both of you."

11:03 A.M.
The safehouse
Ardennes Department, France

"I simply can't believe it." The words seemed distant and far-away, penetrating through into his mind as if spoken in a dream.

Harry glanced over to see Yassin's face distorted in anger and pain, anguish in his eyes. Their own differences, seemingly buried by the tide of new grief. Of betrayal.

"I *trusted* him—loved him as a brother. And he betrayed us. He *killed* Reza."

No, Harry thought, scarce daring even to think the words, *he didn't. That was me. Because I've betrayed you too.*

And he had failed to recognize an *ally,* until it was far too late for both of them.

Had the signs been there, all along, just waiting for him to recognize them? To realize the truth?

Haunting, *damning* questions, but deep down. . .he knew the truth. There had been no "signs." They had both played their parts to perfection, to the very last—both of them blind, unknowing. Inextricably entwined in a grotesque *danse macabre* that had been bound to claim one of them or the other, at the last.

Or so he would tell himself, long after this was over. *Again and again.* When the ghosts came to visit in the night.

But Marwan wasn't dead—*yet.*

He stared down into the cup of coffee in his hands, his mind once again turning over the dilemma facing him. *Looking for an exit.* Something—*anything.*

But each door he found was sealed off, each exit blocked. Marwan wouldn't make it five hundred meters in his current condition—even assuming they knew the country and he didn't. And more of Belkaïd's men had arrived the hour before, all of them armed—he had to assume they would have a perimeter flung out, even in the light summer rain now falling outside.

No way out. Except forward, as ever—even though he knew what that would mean this time. The price they would both have to pay.

". . .I just think," he heard Yassin say, realizing only then that he had been talking this whole time. *How long had it been?* "I was the one who first met Marwan. I introduced him to Reza—to *you.* You even warned me then that he could be French intelligence, and I refused to listen."

Tears welled up in his eyes as he stared at Harry. Tears of sorrow and wrath. "If I had only listened. . .my brother might still be alive."

Harry set down his cup on the bare counter of the kitchen, beckoning to Yassin with his hand—wrapping an arm around the younger man's shoulders as he broke down, the tears flowing freely. Hot, angry tears running down his cheeks.

"I. . .I would have killed him, Ibrahim," he sobbed, lost in his own grief. "I still should—it should be mine, by right. My *duty*."

"*Insh'allah*," Harry whispered quietly, suppressing the emotions roiling within himself—an inner revulsion that left him nearly nauseous, his hand resting on Yassin's upper back, only inches from his neck.

A moment, and he could have snapped it—like breaking a rotten branch—Yassin dead before the realization of the betrayal had even made it to his brain.

The man who had once saved his life, dead at his feet. As he would be, sooner or later. Only one way out of this, for any of them.

And it was so tempting to do it—*now*, before he could think, before he could pull himself back from that precipice. End it all, right here—right now. *The void, beckoning to him.*

But Aryn appeared in the doorway of the kitchen in that moment, his dark eyes meeting Harry's. "Belkaïd wants you. Downstairs."

It was a long moment before Harry responded, knowing in his gut that this was it—the moment of truth. His decision already made, and even yet. . .

"I'll be there."

11:09 A.M.
Médiacité
Liège, Belgium

He shouldn't have been here. Deep down, Armand Césaire knew that. Even his presence represented a potential compromise. But he had to *know*.

Médiacité's head of security had given him access after he'd presented his credentials—he had no jurisdiction here, in Belgium, and they both knew that, but in the present environment. . .the man had simply asked him if it was connected to the explosion outside the city, and he'd declined to respond, in that way that confirmed the man's suspicions more firmly than if he'd spoken the words.

And now here they were, reviewing the security footage from the afternoon prior—a lengthy, painstaking process that might lead absolutely nowhere, as Césaire knew all too well. LYSANDER might not even have made it as far as the mall.

But it was a starting point. And he had precious few of those.

He reached up, pushing aside his glasses to rub the bridge of his nose—shaking his head wearily. Something was wrong, he knew that much, instincts honed by decades of intelligence work warning of danger.

He had to find a way to get to Daniel—to *find* him, in the midst of this chaos. If it wasn't already too late.

His eyes narrowed then, focusing in on one screen of the CCTV imagery—a vaguely familiar figure captured approaching the main entrance of the mall. *Daniel Mahrez.*

"This man," he announced, indicating his undercover with a forefinger. "Let's follow him."

Ten minutes later, after identifying another man in the footage as a Belgian intelligence officer—a man he'd been introduced to at VSSE Headquarters only days prior—Césaire knew what had happened, a sad sense of irony twisting like a knife in his stomach.

The VSSE had put surveillance on LYSANDER without knowing his identity—and he knew that if he could pick up their people from the CCTV cameras, then Daniel had seen them too. *But he hadn't known who they were. . .*

And he'd bolted—there, on the very cusp of making contact once more. Of providing them with the details of whatever this. . .*attack* was which he had warned of in his signal.

Césaire's face twisted into a sad, bitter grimace, something deep inside telling him that they were already far past the point of no return. That this mistake had been fatal.

Oh, the irony. . .

11:20 A.M.
The safehouse
Ardennes Department, France

Harry knew from the moment he saw the tripod-mounted cellphone camera—the tarpaulins now draping the walls—what was to come.

He'd stood in so many of these rooms before—analyzed so many videos—and yet. . .he'd never actually *been* there. In the moment when it happened.

Marwan—*whatever his name truly was*—was, if possible, even bloodier and more disfigured than when he'd last laid eyes upon him, sagging limply against the bonds holding him to the chair, his hair matted with blood, one eye swollen closed. It struck Harry in that moment just how *young* he was—but that had been the purpose, after all, hadn't it? Young enough to infiltrate himself into a cell of young radicals in Molenbeek, to present himself as one of *them*.

And he'd done it—fooling everyone until the very last, when Harry's phone call to French intelligence had compromised them both. Each of them denouncing the other in an effort, not just to survive, but to *weaken* the enemy.

Harry suppressed a shudder at the memory of that fateful moment in the Liège apartment, the moment when the tables had turned—the savage *triumph* he'd felt then. A triumph turned to ashes in his mouth. He had won when he should have lost, lived when he should have died. *Once again.*

For *losing* would have left an officer in place with a team, a network to rely upon—someone who could have stopped all of this. Not someone alone, out in the cold.

It was the kind of mistake that could cause a man to go out back and blow out his own brains. His blood an atonement for his sins.

But there was no atonement to be found here, Harry realized, his gaze flickering around the room—taking in the positions of Belkaïd's men, a couple of them armed with AKs, positioned just out of the camera's frame. No *redemption.* Nothing but the knowledge of what was about to happen. Of what he must do.

Marwan stirred as Harry entered the room, murmuring a vile curse in French, turning his head ever so slightly to spit on the floor—blood and

423

phlegm landing on the plastic dropsheet.

"He's confessed," Gamal Belkaïd smiled, his eyes meeting Harry's. "To everything. . .to betraying his brothers—to betraying his faith."

Marwan coughed up more blood, spitting out a defiant *"non"*, his remaining open eye simmering with hatred as he stared toward them. "You're the ones who have betrayed Islam—you're not Muslims, you're animals. You are of the *Khawarij,* apostates, all of you."

And here they were once again, Harry thought, remembering Ismail Bessimi's words, standing there in that muddy North Yorkshire lane—his hand on the shoulder of a young man about to take his own life. Reciting the words of their own Prophet back to him, warning of those who would come— men just like these around them, men who would pervert doctrine for their own ends. *"And in the day of reckoning, they will rise with the Dajjal."*

A false messiah. *For false believers.*

But Marwan wasn't done, his voice rising with what remained of his strength. "You kill the innocent, you kill *everyone*—you break every law of warfare the Prophet ever gave us, and you use his words as a cover for your crimes. You—"

Belkaïd's fist caught him in the side of the head and he reeled, the flow of words suddenly cut short. A baleful light in the older man's eyes as he pulled back, rubbing his knuckles.

"Enough." He seemed on the verge of saying something else, then thought better of it, picking up a long, wicked knife from the table behind him and turning it over in his hand—extending it hilt-first to Harry.

"Take this," he said, his eyes filled with a dark, implacable fury, "and take his head."

No. It was all Harry could do not to recoil physically from the knife, a wave of nausea threatening to overwhelm him. But there could be no delay— no *hesitation*—in this moment, everyone's eyes focused on both of them.

He reached out, taking the knife from Belkaïd's hand, accepting a dark black balaclava from one of his guards and pulling it on over his head, down until his eyes stared out through the slits of the ski mask. Moving into position behind Marwan's battered and bloodied figure as the camera began to roll.

"You have invaded the lands of the *Ummah*," he began simply, staring out at the camera. Seeing his. . .*friends* from Molenbeek standing there, just off to one side. Yassin and Driss, the pair who had stopped Marwan from shooting him there in the boxing club. . .it seemed so long ago. Aryn, standing a few feet away. *All that remained.* "You have sent your spies among us, trying to sow discord, to turn the faithful against one another."

Harry felt his voice tremble ever so slightly, the knife hilt cold in his sweat-slick hand. This wasn't possible—it wasn't happening.

But it was. There was a part of him, even yet, which wanted to take the knife and lash out—disable a guard, perhaps even kill Belkaïd himself. But as he'd learned so long ago. . .you couldn't save the world.

"So in the name of Allah," he continued, wrapping a hand around Marwan's throat—pulling his head back, "I give you back your spy."

Chapter 30

4:03 A.M. Central European Summer Time, August 3rd
The Boulevard Mortier
Paris, France

Fifteen hundred euros was a lot of money for a boy from the *banlieus*. *A lot of money*, Bilel ben Samadi thought, his thighs burning as he pedaled the bike down the Paris boulevard, his gaze flickering back and forth at the shadowed spaces between the streetlights. It had been a long ride from the public housing where he lived in Aulnay-sous-Bois, but the money was just too good. *Impossible to turn down.*

The fourteen-year-old had never seen the man before in his life, but his friend Yacine had bought drugs from him in the past. And he'd been willing to give him a third of the money up-front.

All he had to do was deliver a backpack—drop it off on the street, really, in front of the GPS address displayed on the brightly-lit screen of his phone mounted to his handlebars in front of him.

It was hard to know what was *in* the backpack—it wasn't heavy, maybe five kilos at most.

A long wall ran along the perimeter of the street to his right, a faint chill running through Bilel's body as he took in the razor-wire surmounting its top. The bollards blocking off the curb from vehicle access, and ahead—an entrance in the wall which almost appeared. . .fortified.

What was this place? The fourteen-year-old slowed, taking his foot off the bike's pedal—the worn sole of his battered tennis shoe scraping against the asphalt. *Police, perhaps? If so. . .*

His older brother and their cousin from Belgium had been stopped by the police two years before, stopped and searched as a suspect in the robbery of a small market in the *banlieu*.

His brother Salim had gotten away, but their cousin had struggled against them, and been beaten, severely. He was still in a wheelchair, would likely never leave it, according to the doctors. The former soccer player, reduced to a flabby husk of his former self.

The memory was almost enough to make the teenager turn the bike around, but. . .*no*. It was far too much money to be tossed away so lightly, particularly after he had ridden so far.

His mother would think he had stolen it, but. . .perhaps, if he only gave her a little, here and there. *Bien sûr.* Of course. *That might work.*

Unstrapping the backpack from his shoulders and hefting it in one hand, he gripped the handlebars of his bike once more, pedaling rapidly toward the entrance. *Drop the bag, and race off.*

Maybe before anyone even saw him. Before the police—*if it was the police*—could react.

He was fifty feet away when the *gendarme* appeared, his uniformed figure cloaked in the shadows of the entrance—a hoarse shout breaking through the humid early morning air, even as the long gun in the man's hand came up, the familiar outline of a rifle aimed at his head. *"Halt!"*

Too late. The fourteen-year-old panicked, flinging the backpack away from him with a reflexive gesture as he skidded almost to a stop—the bike swaying beneath him as he struggled to turn, to reclaim his speed. The voice of the *gendarme* ringing again and again in his ears.

The backpack skidding across the rough asphalt to a resting place near the curb, not far from the entrance.

Bilel turned his head back toward the east, nearly standing up on the bike as his tired legs began to pump the pedals once more.

The teenager would never hear the rippling burst of gunfire that killed him, the 5.56mm rounds ripping into his back, tearing through muscle and tissue as they exited his chest, dropping him in his tracks.

He went down hard, falling in a mangled heap of bike and boy on the asphalt boulevard. Dead, before he hit the ground.

Long before the street itself flooded with light, uniformed officers everywhere as they cordoned off the area around the entrance to DGSE Headquarters. Marking out a cautious stand-off distance from his body.

And the backpack.

5:30 A.M.
The safehouse
Ardennes Department, France

There were moments, over the years, that stayed with a man. Seared into the memory—a crimson stain.

Harry pulled back the kitchen chair, listening to it scrape across the kitchen floor, nearly the only sound in the house at this hour. The low murmur of voices filtering through the open window from without, where Belkaïd's men stood post.

There had been no sleep for him, the previous night—no rest to be found at all. Marwan's face, haunting him whenever he closed his eyes.

The Romans had believed that the spirit of a man slain would haunt the place—and the instrument—of his death, forever seeking a rest which could only be found in the blood of the guilty. *Di Manes.*

He didn't know that he believed it, but it was hard to find a better explanation for what he had experienced, all through the years. *The faces.* Each one of them, more indelible than the last.

And Marwan had died far more horribly than any man deserved to die—the knife, nowhere near sharp enough for the work. *And that had been deliberate*, Harry thought, remembering the look on Belkaïd's face. A purposeful cruelty.

Revenge, in some way, for his own family? For his sister—for that day he couldn't remember, in Algiers?

Impossible to know. Even more impossible to forgive. Because he'd recognized himself in Marwan's eyes in those final, fateful moments. Knew what it was like to know your cover was blown past any chance of redemption.

Harry lifted the cup of coffee to his lips, taking a long sip of the steaming liquid. Feeling the heat rush down his throat, a fire filling him from the inside. That could have been him in that chair.

Might be, even yet.

Harry looked up from his coffee to see Gamal Belkaïd standing in the doorway of the kitchen, dressed—as a couple days earlier—in a wifebeater and sweatpants.

"Bonjour," the Algerian announced, a quiet smile playing across the older man's face. *Satisfaction.* No doubt it *was* a good morning to him.

A quick, reflexive nod by way of reply. *"Bonjour."*

"We are supposed to have clear skies today," Belkaïd said, moving over to the window and gazing critically out at the early morning twilight, the sun just beginning to filter through the treeline thirty meters to the west of the house. "Should be a good day to begin giving your people flight time on the drones. *Insh'allah.*"

Harry's head came up. "You're still going ahead with it?"

"Of course." Belkaïd looked at him as though there had never been a question of doing anything else.

"But the recording. . .Marwan gave us up. He gave them *everything*, Gamal. If we go ahead, if we carry out this attack—they're going to be waiting for us."

Buy time. That's all he could do now—give himself time to come up with a *plan*. Force Belkaïd to recalibrate.

But the older man shook his head. "No, he didn't. He may have made the recording, but he didn't deliver it. If he had, we'd already be dead. They would never wait."

A smile. "We're in the clear, brother."

"Alhamdullilah," Harry murmured, unsure for once if his face matched his words. *Praise be to God.* And the worst of it was that Belkaïd was right.

He took another sip of his coffee, looking over to find Belkaïd regarding him curiously.

"What did you say to him?" the older man asked, his dark eyes transfixing Harry. "There at the last. I was watching the video, and. . .you said something to him. What was it?"

Harry froze, the cup of coffee poised half-way between his lips and the table—Belkaïd's words carrying him back once more to that basement room, the morning before.

"Jazakallah khair," he'd whispered, his lips only inches from the young officer's ear. Feeling Marwan's body react in that final moment—stiffening

against the hand around his throat. *May God reward you goodness.*

An acknowledgment that he died at the hands of a friend—that his death would *not* be for nothing.

One last mercy for the damned.

"I told him," Harry replied, his face a mask, "that I would see him burning. In the fires of hell."

6:03 A.M.
Life Style Fitness Liège
Liège, Belgium

The strains of Jef Gilson's *Modalité pour Mimi* filled Césaire's ears as his feet hit a steady rhythm on the treadmill, the sound of the big band's trumpets through his earbuds driving the remaining tendrils of sleep from his brain.

Gilson had been one of the greats of his own childhood, and the music took him back, to his youth. To his early years with the *Deuxième Bureau.*

To a simpler time? No, not really. Not when he reflected on how hard those years had been—the discrimination he had faced when he had first joined France's foreign intelligence service.

Like he'd told Daniel, standing there in the Place Poelart in the heart of Brussels. On the dark afternoon when he'd convinced him to go back under.

"We've both risked our lives in the service of a country that had marginalized us, viewed us as something less than citizens of France, each in our own time—in the belief that one day, that would change. That we could, by our sacrifice, bring such change."

Had it? He wanted to believe it had, certainly, that everything he had done had been worth something. Perhaps that was it—the *desire* to believe. Overriding all else.

His music cut out suddenly, in the middle of the song, and he pulled the phone out of his pocket to see a familiar number displayed on-screen. He turned off the treadmill, wiping the sweat from his forehead with a small towel as he raised the phone to his ear.

"Allô ?"

He listened for a long moment, feeling the blood drain from his face—his eyes staring unseeing at the far wall of the gym. *No.* It wasn't possible.

But it *was*. And Césaire murmured a low, bitter curse which went unheard in Paris, knowing, in that moment, the truth.

He had failed.

8:39 A.M.
DGSE Headquarters
Paris, France

"*. . .so in the name of Allah. . .I give you back your spy.* Allahu akbar!"

The first time Anaïs Brunet had watched the video, she had flinched when the knife went in, blood spurting from Daniel Mahrez's throat as he slowly died.

Now she simply watched, stone-faced, as the executioner sawed back and forth, blood spattering Daniel's clothes and the plastic drop cloths spread out beneath him.

Watched, the rage burning inside her building to a barely-suppressed fury, until it was over—the masked jihadist presenting the severed head of their officer to the camera.

"How did they know?" she demanded quietly when the screen went black. The one question none of them had the answer to.

Somewhere, somehow, they had slipped up. . .or been betrayed, or. . .the possibilities were truly endless.

"What do we have on the identity of the courier?" Brunet asked then, brushing aside her briefing papers to reveal the photo of the boy now laying out on a cold slab in a Paris morgue. *So very young.*

He reminded her strangely of her own nephew, Guillaume, just past his twelfth birthday.

"Nothing yet," Albert Godard replied, glancing down the conference table. "He carried no identification whatsoever. . .we can assume that he was likely from the *banlieus*, but that is only an assumption. It's likely that identifying him will be a long process, and even once we do—it's hard to say whether we'll learn who tasked him with delivering the. . .the head to our door."

Dead ends. "What about the officer who shot him?"

"*Aspirant* Brémond has been suspended pending a judicial review of the incident, and has already been interviewed about the details by our officers. He's still here, in the building, though, if you would like to speak to him yourself."

"*Non*," Brunet shook her head. "That won't be necessary."

The man's initial after action report was already in her briefing notes, and it revealed next to nothing. And he would be fine, legally speaking—the *gendarmerie* operated under far looser restrictions on firearms use than the regular Paris police. Particularly those officers tasked with protecting sensitive sites like the DGSE. The CCTV footage alone would exonerate him from any wrongdoing.

How he would cope with having killed a boy. . .that was another question, and one he would have to answer for himself.

Probably no better than she would deal with losing an officer. She inclined her head toward the now-darkened screen. "The man in the video—the executioner—what do we have? Is this Abu Musab l-Almani?"

"*C'est possible*," Godard nodded, clicking a button to bring the man's image up on-screen once more, a baleful masked figure, frozen in time. "We don't have any confirmed photos to compare against, but it would fit with what Daniel had told us of his leadership role in the cell."

"We are going to find him," she began, her face itself a frozen mask as she stared into the figure's eyes, "and we are going to *kill* him."

Godard shook his head, his voice rising in protest. "*Madame le directeur*, it would perhaps be wiser—"

"I said, 'kill him', Albert," came the ice-cold response as Brunet turned to glare at her subordinate. "There is ample *précédent*, surely."

"*Oui*, but—"

"No, Albert, there will be no 'buts.' We will have our vengeance, come what may. However long that takes." Brunet paused. "Have we informed Daniel's family yet?"

"*Non*. Once we do that, we have to be prepared for the news to go public. We're not there yet. And when we do. . .Césaire has requested that he be allowed to serve as the notifying officer."

3:23 P.M.
Ardennes Department
France

"Look out, *habibi*, you're going to wreck us! Bring it up, bring it up!"

On-screen, the quadcopter seemed to jerk upwards briefly before the sound of an impact came over the speakers with a sickening *thud*, the camera tumbling into a spinning blur, offering a brief glimpse of the tree branch above as it tumbled to the earth, somewhere off in the woods.

A general laugh arose, echoing through the clearing as Aryn stared down, shame-faced, at the controller in his hands—the screen of the laptop on the tailgate of the light utility vehicle sitting in front of them.

"It's about four hundred meters out," Harry observed grimly, not joining in the laughter—his thumbs guiding the controller's joysticks as he brought his own quadcopter back around to hover over the downed drone. "South-by-southwest. You're going to need to be more careful, brother—if something like this happens on the day of the operation. . ."

He allowed his voice to trail off, the rebuke made clear. The laughter, dying away suddenly. The young man's face flushing scarlet. "I'm sorry, this is just taking a while to—"

"It's all right, Aryn," Belkaïd said, casting a curious glance in Harry's direction. "That's why we're here, today. And that's why you're starting off on these, instead of the larger drones we will use in the attack."

"You will retrieve it," he added, gesturing for one of his own men to accompany Aryn into the woods, "and we will begin again."

He came over to Harry a few moments thereafter, as Aryn and the guard disappeared into the woods—as the rest of the group dispersed around the clearing, taking a break. Driss kicking a soccer ball back and forth with Yassin.

Only one of Belkaïd's bodyguards remained, hovering at his shoulder, a dour Algerian perhaps a few years older than Harry, known to him only as "Faouzi."

Back in Liège, he had been one of the black marketer's regular drone pilots—brought in now to help oversee their training. His personal motivations. . .unknown, but presumably Belkaïd wouldn't have allowed him to accompany them from the city if he'd had any doubts of his loyalty. Or his dedication.

"This was your idea, after all," the older man said after a moment, his voice low, too low to carry to the rest. "You said they would need the practice, and you were right. You're being too hard on them."

"And you're not being hard *enough!*" Harry snapped back, the anger which had been building up within him for the last twenty-four hours finding an outlet. *Channeled*, as ever, into his cover. This was wrong, all of it. The laughter, the ease with which everyone had simply. . .moved on. Past the death of a man far better than any of them. *Even himself.* "We cannot have any more mistakes, Gamal, we cannot afford them. Not now. Not when we are *this close.*"

"You think you want this more than I do?" Belkaïd smiled, a rich irony playing across the older man's features, glancing at Faouzi. "*C'est impossible.* You came to know our faith, but you will never understand what it was like to grow up as a Muslim under French dominion. To know, no matter what you did, that you would never be good enough. *Good enough* for the society of those who had murdered and raped your own family. Those are feelings you will never—*can* never—understand. I've waited years for this."

Harry held his gaze for a long moment before nodding. "You're right, of course. *Je suis désolé.*"

I am sorry.

A nod was Belkaïd's only reply. "The French president's father," he began unexpectedly, staring off into the trees—the sun beating down hard upon them both, "Francois Albéric, was a paratrooper. In Algiers."

And there you have it. This was *personal*, for the older man. A motivation like no religion could ever touch. *Or dissuade.* Harry turned toward him, the question on his lips. "Was he. . .?"

Was he one of them? he thought, unable to finish the question, to bring himself to speak the words. *On that day?*

Belkaïd just looked at him, knowing exactly what was left unsaid. "Does it matter?"

And Harry remembered Stephen Flaharty, sitting there with him in the car, that night on the M-1 Motorway, justifying his own actions to Harry—to himself, perhaps most of all. "*You may never get the man who shot your brother in the sights of your rifle, so you shoot the sod next to him and tell yourself it's justice.*"

Or that 'sod's' son, in this case.

And no, it didn't. *Didn't matter at all.*

4:11 P.M.
Rue Hors-Château
Liège, Belgium

This could get messy, Sergeant Benoît Renier thought, his knee pressed against the metal of the van's floor as he went over the building schematics one last time.

"We're going to need to reach the apartment itself within ninety seconds of initial breach," he stated soberly, looking up from the screen of the tablet into the eyes of his fellow operators, forming the *Group Diane* assault team. "Take everyone inside down before they can mount a resistance. Before they even know we're *here. Begrijpt u?*"

Do you understand?

The men around him nodded, their eyes staring back at him through the slits in their black balaclavas. They were all professionals, like himself—they knew how this was to be done.

"Welaan!" Very well.

He reached up, pulling his own mask down over the lower half of his face—keying his radio to signal to the other team that they were in position. "Blue Element, be prepared to block all egress from the target building. And you know the target's face. If you see him, take him down. Alive, if you can. *Ga nu, ga nu!"*

Go now.

And the doors of the van were flung open, Renier's eyes taking in the familiar red facade of the Church of Our Lady of Immaculate Conception across the street as his boots met the pavement—his weapon already coming up—the sound of shuffling feet as the breach team moved toward the door, bringing their ram to bear.

Time to do this.

4:32 P.M.
VSSE Headquarters
Brussels, Belgium

". . .*suis vraiment désolé*, Anaïs," Christian Danloy intoned, his face shadowed as he stared into the camera. *I am terribly sorry.* There were no words to express how he had felt watching the video, hours earlier—no way to make amends for what the actions of his agency had, apparently, precipitated.

"Spare me your apologies, Christian," his counterpart returned, her face like a flint. "Just tell me what is now being done about it."

"*Group Diane* is in the field," Danloy replied, collecting himself. "Twenty minutes ago, they conducted a simultaneous assault on three of the most common locations associated with Gamal Belkaïd and his 'business associates,' including his own residence in the Rue Hors-Château. There have been at least fifteen arrests, and we believe that we will soon have information leading to his location."

"'Soon'? So he wasn't at any of the sites you raided?"

"*Non.*"

Brunet seemed to consider his words for a long moment, then asked, "Our intelligence indicates that Belkaïd has an older sister, Ghaniyah, living there in Liège. Have you taken her into custody?"

Danloy suppressed a curse with a mighty effort, running a hand across the lower half of his face. "She's gone as well—when they bolted from the city two nights ago, we had to mobilize all available assets, and we pulled her surveillance team to join in the effort. By the time we returned. . .she was gone."

5:34 P.M.
The apartment in Anderlecht
Brussels, Belgium

"The French officer is dead, executed by the members of the cell he had infiltrated. Somehow, they believe our actions compromised his cover." It had been all he could do to control his reaction to the news, Jan Vertens thought, burying his head in his hands as he sank into the cushions of the couch, his mind still screaming out against the reality.

Of what he had done. Of the *consequences* of what he had done. Deadly consequences, the like of which could never be undone.

And then had come the video—an hour or two later, streamed to them from their counterparts in Paris. The gruesome footage, the stuff of every intelligence officer's worst nightmares in this War on Terror.

And he had been *responsible* for it.

There was no way he could live with that, the middle-aged man told himself, tears spilling from his eyes to run down his cheeks as he reached up to wipe them away angrily. *Futilely.*

And yet what could he *possibly* have expected? He had known what Belkaïd would do with the information—there was no way he could claim ignorance. *Or innocence.*

He might as well have taken that knife and cut the Frenchman's head off himself. The blood was on his hands, all the same.

He opened his eyes to look at the Walther P99Q lying on the low table in front of the couch. *The gun he had carried in his final years as a police officer.*

After transitioning to the VSSE, he'd sought and secured permission to own the weapon. To protect himself, he'd said, against anyone from his days on the street who might want revenge.

It was loaded now—nine rounds of 9mm Parabellum in the magazine, another in the chamber. Rana would be home soon, bringing Youssef with her from his after-school football practice.

A sad, bitter smile crossed his face as he thought of them—of how he had *betrayed* them, as much as any of his fellow officers. Their life together had been so perfect, *would* have been perfect, if only he hadn't been such a fool.

But there was only one thing he could do now, even knowing it offered no atonement. Knowing it would only bring them more pain. But perhaps no one would ever need to know *why*. And there was that.

He reached forward, picking up the Walther in a hand that was now trembling almost uncontrollably—his fingers feeling wooden, lifeless as he raised the weapon, placing its muzzle in his mouth. Biting down as if to steel his resolve—the taste of metal against his tongue.

His thumb, pressing tremulously against the trigger. *Taking up slack.*

A moment later, a single gunshot shattered the silence of the empty apartment.

Chapter 31

5:31 A.M., Central European Summer Time, August 4th
Marseille-Fos Port
Marseille, France

The container ship loomed large in the night, riding at anchor within the breakwater, dwarfing the men standing on the pier beside it.

Grigoriy Stepanovich Kolesnikov smiled to himself, hands resting easily on his hips as he looked up the steep sides of the *Enrico Delgada.*

She—for his grandfather had been a sailor in the Red Fleet, and had lived long enough to impress upon a young Grigoriy that all ships were "she"—was officially registered in Liberia, but he had it on good authority that her owning corporation was nothing but a shell, with the actual owners residing in St. Petersburg.

And her next port of call was supposed to have been Latakia, on the Syrian coast.

"My business associates and I," he began, raising his voice above the whining and gnashing of the crane's gears in the air high above him as he glanced over at the harbour master, "are grateful for your cooperation, *Monsieur* Delacroix."

The Frenchman nodded nervously, not meeting Kolesnikov's eyes as the crane slowly lifted the single container from the deck of the *Enrico Delgada,* the heavy container seeming to tremble and sway in the night above them, as it moved back over the pier, toward the waiting flatbed semi-trailer. He knew what was at stake here. *Or thought he did.*

The FSB officer smiled in amusement, knowing the truth. *The harbour master had no idea.*

"It would not have been impossible for us to pay import duties," he added smoothly, as if to salve the man's conscience, "but it seemed so much simpler to pay you."

Another quick nod. "You *have* seen to everything, haven't you? The cameras?"

"*Bien sûr.*" Of course. "It will all be taken care of, *monsieur.*"

"Good," Kolesnikov smiled, a predatory glint in his eyes. He didn't need to know the details of how it would be done, only that it would be. And it wasn't the first time Moscow had done business with *Monsieur* Delacroix. He was *theirs*, whether he knew it or not. "Any misunderstanding would have been. . .regrettable."

Message sent. He leaned back, watching as the crane brought the container into position high above the semi, lowering it with a steady hum that echoed out over the water. Unlike the man beside him, he knew what it contained.

Arms. Weapons and explosives, originally intended to arm pro-Assad militia fighters in Syria, to assist them in finishing off the last remnants of the rebellion.

Now diverted here—at least one container of the shipment. It was far more armament than Gamal Belkaïd had requested. Far too much, really, for any one cell—but there would be others. Of that Kolesnikov was sure.

But after tonight, the hardest part—getting the weapons into the country—would be behind him.

Then there would be time to simply. . .watch it all burn.

6:03 A.M.
The safehouse
Ardennes Department, France

". . .*Al-Ḥamdu Lillāhi Rabbi Al-'Ālamīna,*" Harry whispered, his arms crossed in front of his chest as he stood in the living room of the safehouse, his prayer mat stretched out on the floor before him—hearing the voices of his brothers around him, repeating his words in rusty, halting Arabic. *Praise be to Allah, Lord of Worlds.*

He thought of Ismail Bessimi in that moment, his mind drifting as he recited the opening chapter of the *Qur'an* from memory. The way the old imam had looked at him, that day in Leeds, reproaching him for his single-minded quest for vengeance. *"Those who seek to take that which belongs to the Lord of worlds. . .do so at their peril."*

And he'd been right, Harry thought, mouthing the words, *"Ar-Raḥmāni Ar-Raḥīmi.Māliki Yawmi Ad-Dīni. . ."*

The Beneficent, the Merciful. Master of the Day of Judgment.

But there had been another day. And he could remember the look in Bessimi's eyes then, as he lay dying in the mud and gravel of a Leeds alley. *"The time has come. . .for a hunter. Promise me you won't fail."*

Had he kept that promise? It was hard to know, looking back. Rahman had died at his hand, as had Tarik Abdul Muhammad. But was that success, or only another kind of failure? *"Īyāka Na`budu Wa 'Īyāka Nasta`īnu. . ."*

Thee alone we worship, Thee alone we ask for help.

It hadn't felt like *success*, standing there that night on the docks, looking down at Tarik's broken, lifeless corpse. And yet, the alternative. . .had been unthinkable. *Much like now.*

"Ihdinā Aṣ-Ṣirāṭa Al-Mustaqīma. . ."

Show us the straight path.

And he felt a strange intensity build within him as he repeated the words, realizing that it wasn't just repetition, this time. That these words *were* a prayer. A prayer he *meant*—like he had meant no prayer in a very long time.

Show me.

11:03 A.M.
DGSE Headquarters
Paris, France

"Then you talk to him, Raoul," Anaïs Brunet snapped back, her eyes flashing as she glared down the table at her counterpart from the DGSI. "You convince him that this is real, that he should take appropriate measures. *Quoi?* He isn't listening to you either, is he?"

Raoul Dubois didn't flinch at the onslaught, merely shook his head in reply. *He wasn't.* "Albéric believes that this is his duty, that this is his place, at the head of the Republic. That to shirk it would be—"

"Politically disastrous," Brunet observed shrewdly, not giving him an inch.

Dubois responded with a Gallic shrug, his hands spread out before him. She had the feeling it was a gesture he had perfected over his decades as a government official. "That's one interpretation of his decision, surely. But that's unimportant, really. What matters is that he's not going to adjust his schedule to accomodate your concerns—or mine."

"What can be done?" That was, after all, Dubois' responsibility—not her own, at least on the short-term. Albéric's trip to Rome was still a month and a half away, and he wasn't scheduled to leave the borders of France before then. Within them. . .he was out of her jurisdiction.

"I have spoken to *Commissaire* Leseur," Dubois responded, referencing the head of the GSPR, the unit charged with the President's physical security. "Suggested that she do her best to harden the security around the President's public appearances."

"The *Stade de France* holds eighty thousand people, Raoul. How, precisely, does one 'harden' *that*?"

"We will have to find a way."

11:57 A.M.
Mont-de-Mans Air Base
Landes Department, France

"Ma cherie. . ." Sergeant Nathalie Jobert sighed heavily, the mobile phone cupped against her ear as she considered her next words. Raising a daughter had not gotten any easier over the years, particularly after Jean-Louis' abrupt exit from their lives. *Not that he had ever been much help.*

But now that Cécile was in her teens. . .she was so different than Nathalie had herself been at that age. Far more beautiful—she favored her father—and yet *withdrawn*. And no more willing to listen to her mother than most daughters. "Be careful around him," she said finally. "I know you think he's fond of you, but. . .you don't know him well."

She could almost hear her daughter's eyes rolling back in her head.

"You don't understand. Pierre and I—"

A knock came at the door of Jobert's temporary office in that moment—her daughter's next words lost as she covered the receiver, calling out, *"Oui?"*

"Commandant Coulon wishes to see you in his office. At once."

441

She acknowledged the order briefly, before turning her attention back to her daughter. "Cécile, I am going to have to call you back. I have to—"

"Work." The word came out bitter and sullen, but Nathalie chose to ignore the tone. A problem that would have to be dealt with, at another time. *"Oui."*

Five minutes later, she was standing before *Commandant* Maurice Coulon, the commanding officer of their small unit. A veteran of counter-insurgency operations in the Mahgreb, Coulon was a short fireplug of a man, shorter even than Jobert—but one glance at his face would have cured anyone of the inclination to underestimate him—a long white scar running the length of his cheek standing out pale against his swarthy cheek. A shrapnel wound, legacy of an insurgent mortar round which had burst far too close.

"Have a seat, Sergeant," he instructed, gesturing to a chair drawn up in front of his desk. *"S'il vous plaît."*

"Merci."

"You'll be leaving for Paris tomorrow," he said, the announcement taking Jobert by surprise. "And taking Glatigny with you, along with your support team."

To say that the news was unexpected was an understatement. *"Pour quoi, mon commandant?"*

"You and your team will be helping provide security at the *Stade de France* for the final qualifying match for the World Cup, at the request of the GSPR."

Her eyes opened wide. *"Le Groupe de sécurité de la présidence—"*

"Oui," Coulon replied, cutting her short. "President Albéric will be attending the game. Help keep him safe."

12:09 P.M.
VSSE Headquarters
Brussels, Belgium

"And there was no note?" Christian Donlay asked, looking up from the photos spread out on the desk before him, his face visibly pale.

"Nee," the police officer replied simply. "We found nothing that would give us any idea why *Meneer* Vertens would have committed suicide. But there

seems little room for doubt that the wound was self-inflicted."

"You were there?" Donlay asked, only half-hearing the man as he stared down at the photos, seeing the distant, vacant stare in Jan Vertens' lifeless eyes. In an intelligence service as small and close-knit as the VSSE, you knew *everyone*, and he had known Jan well. *Or thought he did.*

"*Ja.* I was on the scene late last night."

"I appreciate you coming to make this report, *Inspecteur*," Donlay said, taking a deep, trembling breath. "You have our thanks."

He waited until the police officer had left the office before he let it out, his hands shaking ever so slightly as he shuffled the photos together, covering up the ghastly wound where the bullet had blown out the back of Vertens' head. First the explosion outside Liège, then the savage execution of the French officer, and now. . .*this.*

Were they connected? Was *any* of it connected? *And could they even begin to manage the fallout if they* were. . .

1:34 P.M.
Ardennes Department
France

Show me the way. Harry's thumbs moved carefully over the controller, his eyes fastened intently on the screen of the laptop as he guided the UAV through the trees, steadily increasing the throttle, edging in on the other quadcopter, being piloted by Driss.

He knew the way now—perhaps he had *known*, all along. What he must do, if he was given the opening.

And now there was no more waiting—the opening must be *made.* They would be leaving here in a few short hours, heading to a rendezvous with the Russians—to take delivery of the weapons, apparently.

They might return here, they might not. A chance he couldn't take. He cast a quick, sidelong glance at the young Moroccan, knowing he had to do this carefully—that there would be a video recording of whatever he did.

He forced a smile to his face, a false laugh breaking from his lips as he hailed the younger man. "Want to race, *habibi*?"

Driss looked back over his shoulder, taking his eyes off the screen for a long moment, even as Harry brought the quadcopter alongside. "I don't know, man, I think we—"

The high-pitched, grinding sound of rotors biting deep into plastic erupted suddenly from both sets of laptop speakers, Harry's eyes darting back to the screen in feigned shock just in time to watch as his quadcopter staggered off-course, now uncontrollable—its video feed blurring as it fell, crashing to the forest floor below.

A flurry of curses breaking from the young Moroccan's lips confirming that his drone had suffered the same fate from the collision. "What were you *thinking*? You knew we needed to be careful, that we couldn't—"

"Allah reproaches my pride," Harry said, looking over to meet Gamal Belkaïd's eyes. "I *was* too hard on Aryn yesterday, and now God reminds me that such accidents could happen to anyone. I am sorry, brother."

He saw Aryn nod in acceptance, turned his attention back to Driss. "It was my fault, *habibi*. Come, let's go retrieve our drones."

7:54 A.M. Eastern Daylight Time
CIA Headquarters
Langley, Virginia

". . .in so doing, I believed that I was carrying out the orders I had been given by DNI Bell." Bernard Kranemeyer's hand paused, fingers poised above the keyboard as he stared at the words on-screen, the prepared notes of his testimony before Congress. *The lie.*

It was hard to think that that's where this was going to end, in perjured testimony before the representatives of the people.

The people. Kranemeyer leaned back in his chair, a reflective look in his dark eyes. It was unlikely that they would ever know the truth—even less likely that they would care if they did.

But that was the weakness of democracy, wasn't it? When the people no longer knew the truth. . .or *cared* to.

And he would play his own part in keeping them from it. *For better or worse.*

He had begun to type out the next sentence, the click of the keys resounding beneath his thick fingers, when the phone on his desk began to ring, insistently.

"Kranemeyer," he answered simply, resenting the intrusion on his thoughts. He *needed* to finish this—the hearings were almost upon them.

"Sir, I need to speak with you," Carter's voice replied, alarm bells going off in Kranemeyer's brain at the words. *Ron knew better than to call him "sir."*

"Yes? What is it, Ron? I'm in the middle of preparing my testimony."

"I'm sorry, sir, but this can't wait. It's about the video the French sent over yesterday."

"Yes, I saw it. Gruesome stuff, terribly hard to lose an officer like that—"

"It's not that—the DGSE asked us to run voice analysis, match against our databases."

"And?"

"And we have a problem."

"I'll be down."

2:03 P.M. Central European Summer Time
Ardennes Department
France

"Let's just make sure we don't crash into each other on the day of the attack, okay, *habibi?*" Driss laughed, seeming to have recovered his good humor as he and Harry picked their way deeper into the woods, the GPS beacons of the downed drones beckoning them on. The sun, filtering down upon them through the trees above.

"It still seems impossible to think that we're really doing it," the young Moroccan went on, his voice growing thoughtful. "You know how it is, Ibrahim, when you've dreamed of something so long. . .a woman, perhaps. And then you finally *have* her, and you almost can't believe it."

The moment when fantasy meets reality. Rarely as idyllic as the younger man imagined, Harry reflected, moving a few steps behind Driss—his eyes flickering through the trees and underbrush surrounding them. Hearing the sound of birds in limbs above, singing their summer song. Things looked so very *different* down here, but they had to be at least six hundred meters away from the staging area in the clearing now. It couldn't be much farther.

He recognized a dead oak off to the left in that moment—shattered by lightning and slowly decaying, its branches breaking and falling to the forest floor. And somewhere in front, he could hear the faint gurgle of water. *Almost there.*

They were on the precipice of the ravine almost before even Harry realized it, Driss recoiling from the brink—an almost involuntary obscenity escaping his lips—staring down into the flowing waters of the small creek which ran beneath them, large, water-smoothed rocks breaking from its surface. The ravine wasn't very broad—no more than seven meters, if that, but it was at least five meters deep. *And there were the rocks.*

"How are we going to get around?" he demanded, glancing up and down the stream. "I had no idea this was here."

But I did, Harry thought, moving in close behind him—his hand descending firmly on his young friend's shoulder, seizing his arm. There was no time to react, no time to shout—just the look of confusion passing across Driss' face in the split-second before he lost his footing, Harry's forceful shove propelling him out over the stream.

A scream escaping his lips, cut short suddenly as he hit the rocks, landing on his back—his arms splayed out helplessly in the water.

He was still moaning in pain when Harry reached him five minutes later, wading out into the stream to get to his body. Taking in the look of agony and confusion in the boy's eyes as he looked up to see Harry standing over him.

"Pour quoi?" Driss managed, weakly, as Harry took a knee in the stream beside him—seeing his own pain reflected in Harry's eyes. *Why?*

It was a question he couldn't bring himself to answer. He looked so. . .*harmless*, laying there. *So innocent.* But there was no room for mercy, not here. Not now.

"*Shhhh*," Harry whispered, gripping his hand firmly—as if to comfort him in these final moments. And then he reached up and took him by the shoulder, dragging his helpless, broken body off the rock and into the deeper pool of water just downstream—hands on his chest, forcing his head below the surface.

Watching through the distorted lens of the water as Driss' face convulsed in the agonies of death, bubbles escaping his lips as he struggled for air, flailing weakly against Harry's hands.

And the tears began to stream down Harry's own cheeks, tears of pain. *Of regret.*

By the time the body went limp beneath his hands, floating listlessly below the surface, he was weeping openly and unashamed, the young Moroccan's face flickering before his eyes as it had appeared so many times before. *So full of life.* Of hope.

He dragged Driss' lifeless corpse from the stream with an effort, silent, bitter sobs wracking his body as he knelt down beside him in the gravel of the bank, shadowed by the overhang of the ravine above. Staring up into the sky, the rays of summer sun streaming through the trees. *A perfect day.*

The injustice of it all. It seemed as if the birds had stopped their singing, hushed in the presence of death. His hand, groping blindly for the cellphone in his pants pocket—scarce able to see the screen as he pulled it open, dialing a number.

"Gamal," he began, his voice choked with scarcely feigned sorrow as the other end was picked up, "Gamal, there's been a terrible accident. You must come quickly. . ."

8:09 A.M. Eastern Daylight Time
CIA Headquarters
Langley, Virginia

"*. . . In the name of Allah, I give you back your spy. Allahu akbar!*" Carter paused the audio, running it back. Kranemeyer's eyes narrowing as they focused in on the screen. The video playing out once again in all its macabre, gruesome tragedy.

Neither man flinched as the knife went in, bright red blood spurting from the arteries of the neck. The last anguished agony of the doomed man, picked up all too clearly on the microphone.

They'd watched far too many of these, for far too many years. Too many years at war, but this. . .this wasn't *war*, Kranemeyer thought. This was butchery, pure and simple.

"What am I watching for, Ron?" he asked finally, watching with cold, hard eyes as the masked jihadist took a step toward the camera, holding the severed head in his left hand, the bloody knife in his right.

"May God's judgment so fall on all such traitors."

"You don't recognize the voice?" Carter asked grimly, tension written in the lines of his dark face. "I didn't either, at first. But the machine is smarter than both of us, put together. It's Nichols."

Chapter 32

8:13 A.M. Eastern Standard Time
CIA Headquarters
Langley, Virginia

Kranemeyer just stared at him, the color draining away from his face. "You can't be *serious*," he spat, the words coming out in a hiss.

Carter pursed his lips. "I wish I wasn't. But the algorithms are returning an 87% match between our file recordings of Nichols and the voice of this man the French believe to be Ibrahim Abu Musab Al-Almani. The odds of that being a coincidence. . ."

Were a statistical long shot, as Kranemeyer knew well. *And yet it was impossible.* To think of one of their *own*, having gone over to the enemy. Nichols always had been something of a rare breed, adapting himself to the faith, the culture, of the Global War on Terror's primary antagonists with an ease few Agency hands ever mastered.

But that had been his *job*—then. A long way from taking that final step of *becoming* the enemy. A very long way.

And yet, if he closed his eyes, he could once more see the photos of the carnage there on the docks of Aberdeen, the burned-out hulk of a vehicle destroyed by a suicide vest—the mangled bodies of the dead.

He had gone farther that night than any of those who knew him could ever have imagined. And perhaps they'd underestimated him, all along.

"Who else knows about this?" Kranemeyer asked suddenly, shooting the analyst a sharp glance. "Were you. . .?"

He let the question hang there, meaningfully, in the air between them, seeing the recognition in Carter's eyes.

"No, I wasn't the one who did the original audio analysis," Carter returned flatly, meeting Kranemeyer's gaze. "It's already been filed. I couldn't suppress it if you asked me too—even if I was willing to go back out on that limb, and I'm not. Not on this. Too many people already know."

"But not the French?"

"Not yet."

2:19 P.M. Central European Summer Time
Ardennes Department
France

"Leave him," Gamal Belkaïd announced finally, gazing down at Driss' broken body.

Harry heard Yassin's sharp intake of breath, felt something even within himself protest at the injustice of this. Even knowing his own part in all this, all too well.

The part of Cain.

"No," he heard himself say, scarcely knowing what prompted the words. "He was our *brother*, Gamal. We're not going to leave him here, for the dogs and the birds. He deserves a proper burial, in accordance with Islam."

He staggered to his feet, his cheeks shining with tears. Taking a step closer to Belkaïd, heedless of the man's bodyguards—a blind, unreasoning anger filling his body. There came a moment when you became lost in your own deception, when you could no longer tell black from white, white from black.

When right and wrong became little but names.

Perhaps all that had been drowned in the waters along with Driss, perhaps. . .it had died long ago. He no longer knew.

"And what if you do?" Belkaïd countered, his eyes transfixing Harry. *Did he know? How could he?* "And they *find* him—find a buried body, where they could have simply found the victim of an accident?"

"By the time anyone would find him, we'll all be dead." And he believed that, too, with the assurance of a man who had accepted his fate. *So long ago.*

He stood there, his shoes sinking in the soft, damp earth on the edge of the stream, holding Belkaïd's gaze—watching the conflicting emotions play over the older man's face. Feeling Yassin move up in support, standing at his own shoulder.

Standing with the murderer, if he'd only known. Irony of ironies.

A moment more, and Belkaïd relented, nodding, "All right, then. Bury him, best you can. Pray over him. And then get ready to leave. We can't stay here any longer."

Harry stood there, watching as the older man turned to leave—picking his way through the mud and gravel of the riverbank along with his bodyguards as he retraced his path back out of the ravine.

He was almost out of sight when Harry saw Belkaïd reach down and pluck his phone from the back pocket of his jeans, raising it to his ear to answer a call.

And what is that about? Harry's eyes narrowed as he stared after the Algerian. But he was too far away. And he had a duty to perform, he thought, staring down into Driss' empty eyes.

A final duty. . .to a *brother.*

"You get his feet," he said, motioning to Aryn as he stooped down by the head, lolled lifelessly to one side. "Yassin, help me lift his shoulders."

2:23 P.M.
Northbound on European Route E17
Marne Department

"What do you mean?" Grigoriy Kolesnikov demanded, staring out through the windshield of the semi-trailer as it sped north, only a handful of clouds in the sky above—doing nothing to provide shade from the merciless summer sun. The air-conditioning in the semi's cab was broken—something his local contact had failed to tell him in advance, and it had to be at least forty degrees Celsius in the cab, with the window now rolled up to allow him to hear the voice on the other end of the phone.

"Exactly what I said, *monsieur,*" Gamal Belkaïd replied, a strange edge in the older man's voice. He was rattled, Kolesnikov thought. *But why?* "We cannot make the rendezvous tonight to take delivery of your agricultural equipment. It will have to wait. *Vous comprenez?*"

"Has something taken place?" the Russian asked, warning bells exploding in his brain. *If Belkaïd had been compromised. . .*

"Non," the Algerian responded. *Almost certainly a lie.* "I simply must ask you to postpone the delivery. A day, only."

It was in moments like this that *you* had to make a decision—on your own authority—no turning to the Centre for approval. For sanction.

He never felt more alive than at such times. *On his own.*

It was an attitude which might not guarantee rapid promotion up through the ranks of the *Rodina's* hide-bound intelligence bureaucracies—anymore than it had for his mentor—but he would *live* while he could. And leave his mark on the world, even from the shadows.

"Very well," he replied, finally, deliberately having let the silence build between them for a long moment. "I can give you a day. Nothing more."

10:05 A.M. Eastern Daylight Time
The Russell Senate Office Building
Washington, D.C.

". . .what do you see as the outcome of these hearings, Congressman Imler?"

"The truth, I hope," the man on-screen replied, visibly straightening to his full height—what there was of it. Hank Imler *was* a small man, Roy Coftey thought, gazing at the image on the television. Small man, small mind, as he knew from years of having served with him in the same party. Only thing large about him was his ego—an ego his position as ranking member of the House Permanent Select Committee on Intelligence—HPSCI—had only inflated. "The Sinai affair illustrates the remarkable disparity between this President's rhetoric and his actual actions, behind closed doors. When Richard Norton was elected, I had hoped that this might mark a turning point, that perhaps we might finally see the dawning of a new age of transparency in the national security sphere. Instead, all we have is another president in the tradition of Republican presidents post-9/11, using the blanket of 'national security' as a cover for their actions."

Hank had hoped for nothing of the sort, Coftey mused ironically, watching the eyes of the man on the television as the camera zoomed in for a close-up. He'd been in the meetings, after all, watched the reaction of his fellow Democratic leaders to Norton's surprise victory. The only man in the room to whom it hadn't come as a surprise.

Because he had engineered it.

And what had that wrought, in the end? Hancock's treason had required his removal, but Norton. . .his administration was proving more chaotic than anyone could have expected. The pity, it seemed, was that they *both* couldn't have lost.

But Imler had harbored no hopes of "turning points" or "dawnings of a new age," whatever he might claim now. Rather he and his compatriots had gotten to work planning their opposition—their "resistance", as they'd melodramatically styled it—to the new administration from Day One.

"What a clown," Coftey observed aloud even as Melody entered from the outer office, a folder in her hands.

"Who, Imler?" she asked, glancing briefly at the screen as she set a sheaf of print-outs on his desk. "Here's the research Sheila was able to come up with on SB 367—you asked to see it as soon as he had it ready."

He nodded absently, the fate of wild burros on state lands in the West the furthest thing from his mind as he stared at the screen.

"Imler. Between he and Tony," he replied, referencing the HPSCI chairman, Antonio Tamariz, "these hearings are going to be such a joke."

Coftey let out a short, barking laugh. "Just when you think HPSCI had no more credibility left to lose. . ."

She didn't join in the laugh, and he glanced at her, feeling once more that strange. . .distance between the two of them, a distance he still couldn't explain, as though she had built up a wall within, that he was unable to breach.

He cleared his throat, finishing his thought lamely. "I guess we'll find out tomorrow."

1:09 P.M.
CIA Headquarters
Langley, Virginia

There was a long moment of silence in the office on the seventh floor as David Lay processed Kranemeyer's announcement, his face pale and drawn—looking as though he had been slapped, the DCS thought, watching his boss with a critical eye.

453

He still hadn't recovered from his daughter's death—that was the reality of it, as harsh as it sounded. And yet he stayed on, having returned to his post as DCIA after only a short leave of absence, a leave precipitated more by his injuries than his grief. *For better or worse.*

"How can you be *sure*?" Lay asked after another long pause, a strange tremor creeping into his voice.

"I'm not. But Carter and the team which conducted the original audio analysis have expressed 'high confidence' in their assessment."

Lay nodded, letting out a heavy sigh as he settled back into his chair. He had been such a big man at one time, Kranemeyer reflected, but looking at him now, he seemed small. . .*shrunken.*

He had yet to regain the weight he'd lost after the bombing—after he'd been shot. Grief, taking an even greater toll.

"Then I suppose we have no other choice," he said finally, seeming to have reached his decision. "We'll have to tell the French—tell them the truth, the whole truth, or. . .at least most of it."

He murmured a low curse, shaking his head. "First the British, now the French. Just how many more bridges is Nichols going to burn for us before this nightmare is over? Reach out to Vukovic there at Paris Station—have him deliver the news to Brunet. Daniel's a good man, one of the best deputies I ever had on station—he'll know how to handle it. Authorize him to offer whatever level of help the DGSE and their counterparts in Brussels will accept."

"Respectfully, David," Kranemeyer replied, looking his old colleague in the eye, "I think that's the wrong decision. If we give the French this, we have no guarantee that it won't find its way to the media. *None.* We're already looking down the barrel of legislation aimed at gutting the intelligence community's ability to carry out our mission. I'm scheduled to appear before the House Select Committee in *public* hearings tomorrow. We can't—"

"You don't have any guarantees, one way or the other," Lay shot back, his eyes suddenly blazing to life. "Nichols left a trail of bodies across the United Kingdom in his effort to kill Tarik Abdul Muhammad, and the only thing that kept *that* off the networks was the UK's rigorous control of the press and their government's embarrassment over the whole affair. And now he's showed up in Belgium, where he appears to have. . .somehow become part of a jihadist cell."

"We don't believe he's actually a part of the cell," Kranemeyer said quietly. "There was an earlier piece of audio the French asked us to look at—a phone call from someone within Gamal Belkaïd's network, claiming knowledge of an imminent attack. The voice was digitally distorted, but Carter went back after this audio analysis was done, and he believes they're the same voice."

"With what confidence?" Lay asked, favoring Kranemeyer with a shrewd glance.

"Low-to-medium," the DCS admitted. "But Carter is always a cautious one. I knew Nichols a long time, David—whatever else he was, he was always a patriot. That he would have gone over to the other side. . .I find it very hard to believe."

"As do I," Lay replied heavily. "And I knew him longer than you. But tell me. . .as long as you've known him, could you ever have predicted his actions of the last eight months?"

And the answer to that was *no*, as both men knew.

"It's immaterial anyway," the DCIA said, not waiting for an answer to a question which had, in any case, been rhetorical. "He's on video, *beheading* a French officer—there's nothing we can do to minimize that or make it go away. Tell the French what they need to know—perhaps they can succeed where the Brits failed and take him down. Save us all a world of hurt."

There was a curious tinge of bitterness in those last words, grief and anger intermixed.

"Is that what this is about? Taking him down?" Kranemeyer shook his head. "Because if it *is*. . .you're just going to take all of us down with him."

"No, that's what *he* is going to do if no one stops him!" Lay spat, his face flushing with anger. "Do you not understand the stakes here?"

"I believe I do," the DCS replied calmly. "We're talking about willingly handing over to a foreign intelligence agency extremely sensitive information that would constitute a massive scandal if it were ever to become public, at the very time we're immersed in a political fight for our lives. From where I sit, that looks very much like loading a gun and placing it in one's own mouth."

Lay swore again in exasperation. "And what's your alternative?"

"I think we need to take a step back," Kranemeyer said, rising to his feet. "Regroup. Face down one storm at a time. Nichols can wait—HPSCI can't, and won't. We need to *survive* right now, David, even if that means sweeping something like this under the rug. I can't do it myself, not given those who already know—but *you can.* And you need to."

"And if the French find out we knew, somehow, later?" There was indecision in Lay's eyes, and Kranemeyer pressed his advantage, driving it home.

"Then we cross that bridge when we come to it. *If* we ever come to it. One storm at a time, David. One storm at a time. . ."

8:04 P.M. Central European Summer Time
Chateau-Thierry
Aisne Department, France

One could just make out the flowing waters of the Marne in the gathering twilight as the sedan sped out across the span, a last few rays of sunlight striking Harry in the face as he rested his hand on the open window, leaning back into the seat as Belkaïd's man drove. They'd been in the car for several hours, driving southwest across France toward. . .another safehouse, apparently. A back-up location where Belkaïd had decided to move their base of operations after the "accident."

The end of a beautiful summer day. That's what it had been, he supposed, remembering the singing of the birds in the Ardennes woods. The way they had all gone silent, in the moment of death. As if they *knew.*

The blood cries out from the ground. Disturbing all of nature in its wake, silencing every song.

Where was this all going to end? He knew the answer to that, the truth of what he had told Belkaïd. *Death.*

And yet just how far could he bring himself to go? Each of these. . .*murders*—for that's what they were—tearing at his very soul. First Reza, now Driss. *Marwan,* most of all—the only innocent.

He had allowed himself to get too close, to bond far too closely with these young men. He'd let his guard down, in his time of weakness—the wounds laying him low, leaving him desperate for help. For a *reason* to live.

And somehow, perversely, they had become that reason. . .despite himself. Despite all he knew. Finding that rarest, most intimate of things, a *family,* for the first time in so long.

But now. . .now it fell to him to tear that family apart, piece by piece. *Burn it all down.*

He closed his eyes, hearing the persistent beep from the back seat of the mobile game Yassin was playing on his phone. Like any other kid in his early twenties, amusing the boredom of the drive away.

Forcing himself to remember how it had felt to be forced to take Marwan's life—how they had all rejoiced in his agony, every last one of them, in his screams in those final moments before the knife severed his vocal cords.

When Harry opened his eyes once more, his face had hardened into an implacable mask.

Set it ablaze. . .

9:25 P.M.
DSGSE Headquarters
Paris, France

The remains of Anaïs Brunet's dinner had grown long cold on the cafeteria tray resting neglected to one side of her desk. Her brow furrowed as she worked over the latest reports from the Belgians.

Danloy's people were canvassing south across Wallonia through the Ardennes toward the French border—seeking any information on the passage of the vehicles they had lost days before, but it was a cold trail and the VSSE simply didn't have the manpower to pull it off.

Their counterparts in the *Police Fédérale* had gone to work rounding up Belkaïd's known associates in Liège, but that had, likewise, yet to produce results.

And were unlikely to, she thought. The odds that a man like Belkaïd would have confided his plans for a terrorist attack in low-ranking members of his broader criminal organization were extremely low indeed.

As for the possibility that they had already crossed the border into France. . .Dubois assured her that he was pursuing every possible lead. And that was where it had to end—she had no statutory authority to assist with intelligence collection within the borders of the Republic, as helpless as that made her feel, knowing what could be coming.

Which left her with the man in the video. *Ibrahim Abu Musab al-*

Almani—whatever his real name was, or had been, before Syria.

A light flashed on her desk and she reached over, pressing a button to hear her secretary's voice. "*Madame le directeur*, there is a man to see you. He—"

"*Oui*," Brunet replied shortly, not waiting to hear anything further. "Send him in."

The door opened a moment later to admit a small, slightly built man in his mid-forties, dressed in jeans and a light sports jacket.

"*Monsieur* Vautrin," she began, gesturing to a chair in front of her desk. "Have a seat, *si'l vous plait.*"

He took it without a word, crossing one leg over the other—hands clasped in his lap. Staring at her with dove-gray eyes, deceptively soft—almost feminine. He was the kind of man who could have been lost in any crowd, his face one you would forget within minutes of seeing it.

Just another man. So easy to have underestimated him, if she hadn't been so familiar with his file.

"I trust your drive here was uneventful," she began, almost apologetically. "I regret not having reached you until after you left the Fort."

He shrugged. "*Ça ne fait rien.*" It doesn't matter. "My wife is used to this—my son is in his second year of *université*, and has even less to do with me than he did as an adolescent."

An ironic smile creased his face as though that had seemed impossible. *Once.*

A wife and a child. And the facade completes itself, Brunet mused, finding it difficult, somehow, to reconcile the placid family man before her with the reality of what she knew. For Emile Vautrin was no ordinary man.

In the late '90s, he'd been a para with the 8e RPIMa—the storied 8th Marine Parachute Infantry Regiment—playing cat-and-mouse games with Serbian armor to force them into the open where they could be destroyed by NATO airpower. A dangerous game, but he and his fellow paras had played it and won.

From there he had gone to *Cote D'Ivoire* as part of Operation Unicorn, before finding himself in the late '00s serving with the ISAF coalition in Afghanistan. And he'd been there on that late August day in the Uzbin Valley when the French had found themselves in the middle of a Taliban ambush.

Brunet had seen the classified after-action reports following Uzbin—knew the reality of what had happened in that valley, whatever the French government had chosen to tell the public. And she also knew that, if not for Vautrin's battlefield leadership, they would have suffered even heavier casualties.

Which was why when he'd been transitioned back to France, to convalesce from his wounds, the DGSE had reached out, recruiting him for a role in the *Division Action*, the direct action arm of the service, based out of the old Fort Noisy-le-Sec in Seine-Saint-Denis, the eastern suburbs of Paris.

And that's where he had remained, ever since, taking the fight directly to the enemies of France around the world with a lethality no one who passed the slight, unassuming man on the street would have ever dreamed he could possess.

All of which made him perfect for his job.

She turned her monitor around until it faced him, the video of Daniel Mahrez's. . .death displayed on-screen. "I want you to watch something. The man in the chair is—*was*—one of ours."

And she sat there, shuddering despite herself at the sound of Daniel's agony—watching Vautrin's face, the softness vanishing from his eyes as the video continued.

He waited until it had finished, the curtain falling on the final macabre act of the play before he turned to face her. "What is it that you want from me?"

"I want you to identify his executioner. *Find* him. And then kill him."

Chapter 33

8:57 A.M. Central European Summer Time, August 5th
DGSE Headquarters
Paris, France

"This way, *monsieur*." Daniel Vukovic reached up, pinning his visitor badge to the breast pocket of his shirt as the young woman guided him along the corridor, pausing finally outside a door marked *Crisis Room 4*.

She knocked briefly, and then opened the door, holding it open as he entered, his eyes meeting Brunet's at the end of the long conference table.

"Good morning, Daniel, you're just in time. Please, have a seat."

He took the indicated chair, smiling briefly in thanks as an aide handed over his briefing folder. Heavily redacted compared to the one Brunet held, no doubt, but that was the way of cooperation between allies. His own, anything but full—as he had so recently been reminded.

The screen at the other end of the table was still dark, unexpectedly so. "We're still waiting on Danloy," Brunet said, as if in answer to his unspoken question. "Tell me, Daniel. . .was your Agency able to find any matches on the voice from the beheading video?"

He had been expecting the question, but somehow she still managed to take him off-guard. A fresh reminder to *never* underestimate this woman.

Vukovic lifted his head to look her in the eye. "No. We found nothing. I'm sorry."

9:35 A.M.
Saint-Denis, Seine-Saint-Denis
Suburbs of Paris

"And there it is," Harry breathed, bending down to tie a shoelace which wasn't loose—Yassin jogging in place beside him as both men stared through the trees lining the Rue Ahmed Boughera El Ouafi, the massive outline of the *Stade de France* looming against the skyline, barely a couple hundred meters in front of them.

The target. Harry felt his pulse quicken at the sight, old instincts rising once more to the fore. It was hard to suppress them, even now. The feeling that he was back in the game, that this was yet another mission. Another target, like so many, all through the years.

It was at his insistence that they were here, in the commune of Saint-Denis, conducting a pre-mission reconnaissance of the stadium. He, Yassin, Aryn, and. . .a minder, Belkaïd's drone pilot, Faouzi. The only one of them yet who had flown the actual Guardian drones they would use in the attack, given how abruptly their training in the Ardennes had been cut short by Driss' death.

His murder.

"We'd better keep moving," he said, straightening—his eyes never still as he scanned their environment. There were no cameras visible, but it was so hard to ever be sure, these days. Miniaturization technology advancing by leaps and bounds with each passing year—light-years beyond anything he had faced when he had first entered the field, shortly before 9/11.

Nothing like tech to make a man feel old, he thought, his shoes pounding against the pavement once again as he set the pace, hard and punishing, his lungs protesting against the exertion—his side still not fully healed from its wounds.

But he was almost there. *Almost back.* And his time for recovery was running out.

His mind passed to Belkaïd and all thoughts of his injury passed away, his face darkening in the mid-morning sun, rivulets of sweat staining his thin shirt. For the needs of this "mission"—the need, in reality, to prove his own commitment to the Algerian—only formed a part of his reason for this morning trip in from their new-found base on the outskirts of Coulommiers, about an hour east of Paris.

The rendezvous with the Russians to take delivery of the promised weapons would be happening within the hour, and he wanted to be as far away from another meeting with "Grigoriy" as he could possibly get. *Was it recognition he had glimpsed in the Russian's eyes, there in the yard of the abandoned colliery, the week before?*

Impossible to know. Iraq had been years ago—a lot of water under that particular bridge. But if he had recognized the FSB man from a single encounter. . .

It was a risk he couldn't afford to take.

10:21 A.M.
The Fountainebleau Forest, near Le Bois du Mée
Seine-et-Marne Department, France

It was hot, even in the shade—the cover of the trees overhead offering little protection from the humidity of the French summer. Grigoriy Kolesnikov stirred restlessly against the wheel of the parked semi-trailer, staring down the desolate side road. Off in the distance, one could just make out the traffic passing on the main highway, a car every minute or two—sometimes a handful together.

Busy enough. He raised a hand to wipe the sweat from his brow, the gesture lifting his shirt to expose the holstered M&P Compact on his hip.

He would far rather have been back in Russia in the summer, enjoying himself in the capital in those few short, halcyon months before the Moscow cold returned once more, inevitable as death.

But there was the mission, and that came first, as ever. He saw the car, then, turning off onto their road.

He reached up, hammering his left fist against the door of the articulated cabin, the noise of the movie stopping abruptly from within, followed almost immediately by the sound of Maxim's phone hitting the truck's dash.

"Wake up, Nikolai Timofeyevich," Kolesnikov ordered brusquely, glancing up as the biker's head came popping out the open window of the cabin. "We have company."

Quite a bit of company, he thought, eyeing the end of the road as a second and then a third car joined the first, all three vehicles shimmering in the lines of heat rising off the pavement as they approached.

Here's hoping Maxim was up to this job. He hadn't wanted to be saddled with the Night Wolves again, but the discovery that their leader had been a truck driver—that he retained an active C license in the EU—had been all the Centre needed to hear.

The lead cars slid to a stop fifty meters away, Kolesnikov's eyes narrowing as they fanned out to block both lanes of traffic. *Treachery?* It seemed unlikely—this was a gift, after all.

And perhaps, for that reason, itself suspect.

He lowered his hand to his waist, not far from the holstered semiautomatic—glancing back over his shoulder to where their bikes were parked, almost out of sight beneath the trees. Maybe a thirty-meter run. He'd take his chances, if it came to that.

If Maxim didn't make it. . .*pity*.

As Kolesnikov watched, Gamal Belkaïd emerged from the third, furthermost car—walking forward along the road, flanked by his bodyguards. An impressive figure, even at his age—exuding that aura of command which all true leaders have.

That *presence*, which brooks no disobedience. It would be almost a shame to have to kill him when all this was over, the Russian reflected. But he'd promised himself that he would. *For Sasha*.

For all the memories of a brother torn from him, by criminals like this man.

"*Salaam alaikum*, Grigoriy," the Algerian greeted him as they approached, reaching out to embrace him—his arms wrapping around Kolesnikov's shoulders, the two men kissing briefly on both cheeks.

The kiss of Judas, Kolesnikov thought, briefly tapping the icon of Our Lady of Vladimir beneath his sweat-stained shirt as they disengaged. There was no justice in this moment, but there would be. *Soon enough*. At his own hand.

The Algerian smiled, his dark eyes scanning the semi-trailer. "Is this everything?"

A nod, as Kolesnikov scanned the faces of the men Belkaïd had brought with him. They weren't the same men who had accompanied the Algerian to the colliery.

"You can look for yourself," he said, turning to lead the way to the back of the trailer, Belkaïd following behind. Reaching up to unlatch the door—rolling it up to reveal the contents.

The Algerian ordered one of his men up into the trailer to inspect the shipment, standing back with Kolesnikov as the man picked his way through the footlockers of weapons and explosives.

"The men who came with you to the colliery," the Russian said finally, unable to ignore longer the feeling that had been gnawing at him for days. "They're not with you today."

He saw Belkaïd stiffen momentarily at the implicit question, before recovering. "My organization is a large one, as I'm sure you understand. I have many men."

But he was lying now, as his initial reaction had made clear. *Interesting.* And there was a reason he had asked the question. . .

"The older man," Kolesnikov went on after a moment's pause. "I know him, from somewhere. . .I couldn't place it."

And now he had Belkaïd's attention. *"C'est vrai?"*

"Oui. Somewhere, before, our paths have crossed. I don't know where." It had been there, just *gnawing* at him ever since the meet at the colliery. Like an itch he couldn't scratch.

"He has told me that he was in Syria," Belkaïd offered, a moment later. "Perhaps you might have encountered him there?"

"Perhaps."

10:34 A.M.
Seine-Saint-Denis
Suburbs of Paris

". . .we're going to need to launch the drones outside the city, get them up to altitude before making our way in toward the stadium," Harry said, drawing a circle on the tablet's screen with his stylus. "Perhaps *here.* Or here. If we're discovered at launch, it's all over—but their extended flight time should give us plenty of room to launch on approach."

He lifted the tablet in one hand, holding it up so that Aryn and Yassin could see the screen from the back seat. Hearing their murmurs of assent—

Faouzi's dark eyes on him from the driver's seat as he went on, outlining the plan.

Just like so many times before—standing in the ready room at Langley, sketching out a rude map in the dirt outside a FOB in Afghanistan. It was all so very familiar, preparing to lead men—*mujahideen*—into battle.

And it was a good plan, he had to admit. Nearly flawless. Or would have been, if he hadn't been there. If they weren't already several men down.

"We can drop you here," he continued, meeting Yassin's eyes in the rear-view mirror, "near the stadium, before proceeding to our control point with the vans. . .here."

"What about Nora?"

*What about her. . .*Harry went silent for a long moment, the SUV's engine throbbing gently under the hood in front of him, cold, conditioned air blowing over his face. She was back, as of last night, along with Ghaniyah—both of them brought to the house in Coulommiers by Belkaïd's guards.

She had shared Gamal's bed, once again. And she was going to take part in the attack, no matter what he or anyone else had to say about it. *Case closed.*

He cleared his throat, only too aware that he had to answer the question. "She'll be with me."

11:07 A.M.
Vélizy – Villacoublay Air Base
Thirteen kilometers southwest of Paris

"Sergeant Nathalie Jobert, reporting for duty as ordered, *madame*," Jobert announced, drawing herself up at attention, her right hand snapping off a crisp salute

A smile creased the face of the middle-aged woman behind the desk as she rose, rounding the front of the desk to offer Jobert her hand. "There is no need for these formalities, sergeant, *si'l vous plait*. I have not held a commission in the *Armée de l'Air* for nearly two decades. Now, I am simply a *commissaire*, tasked with protecting the President of France. Marion Leseur, but you may address me as 'Marion.'"

Simply, Jobert thought, struck by the woman's calm, authoritative demeanor. Leseur possessed none of the trappings of authority that she had become accustomed to in her own career in the French military, but there was a confident assurance in her voice, her bearing, that left one with no doubt as to who was in charge.

"Please, have a seat," the *commissaire* continued, waving to a chair. "Lieutenant-Colonel Deneuve was kind enough to offer me the use of his office for this, our first meeting."

"Merci," the French Air Force sergeant responded, taking the proffered seat.

"You've been briefed on the security situation surrounding the upcoming game at the *Stade de France?*" Leseur asked, going on when Jobert nodded. "In addition to the crowd of nearly seventy thousand, we are expecting a significant protester presence, as part of the ongoing anti-drone protests."

"Still?" Jobert shook her head. It had been weeks, but still they continued, harassing diplomats outside the American embassy in Paris—beleaguering the residences of high-ranking French ministers, pressing for an official condemnation of American actions in the Sinai.

Leseur nodded grimly. "They don't seem to be going anywhere, at least as long as President Albéric maintains our ongoing cooperation with American forces in Syria. They've been a presence at all of the president's engagements for the last month. It creates a. . .challenging environment for my officers, as I'm sure you can understand. And now we have a credible terrorist threat to deal with as well."

Jobert flinched palpably, knowing her reaction had been visible in her eyes—*that* hadn't been part of her briefing, and she suspected Leseur knew it.

"*Oui,*" the older woman went on grimly, almost subconsciously smoothing a crease out of the leg of her dark pantsuit, her eyes never leaving the younger woman's face. "And that is where you come in. You. . .and your eagle."

11:14 A.M.
The Fountainebleau Forest
Seine-et-Marne Department, France

Freedom. At one with the wind, the road. *The machine.* There was something exhilarating in it all, Kolesnikov thought, feeling the slipstream tug at him as he tucked his body into the turn, accelerating past a small sedan—deliberately close, hearing the sound of their horn behind him as he sped up the road, a wild grin on his face.

Outlaw. That's what he was, for all the training the Centre had instilled in him. For all they had tried to rein him in. They had trained him, and then handed him over to Vasiliev. And *that* is where he had truly learned to be a spy.

When he had learned that the secret of surviving in the field was knowing when to follow the rules—and when to *break* them.

The fields of France flew past, an emerald-and-tan blur as the Harley Davidson's big engine powered him up the A6, toward Paris. *Toward his destiny.* Passing a brown sign for the *Château de Vaux-le-Vicomte* as he slid the bike into the next lane over, in front of a semi-trailer.

Another few days, and this would all be over. The French president, dead. This country in flames, tearing itself apart along fault lines which had been allowed to slowly widen for generations. *A new revolution?* Perhaps.

The Fifth Republic had stood for long enough. Time to bring it all down.

8:05 A.M. Eastern Daylight Time
CIA Headquarters
Langley, Virginia

It was quiet in this wing of the New Headquarters Building, this early in the morning, Bernard Kranemeyer realized, glancing around him at the artifacts of the OSS Exhibit, the CIA Museum's only permanent display.

So many relics from those early days of their history—years in which every action could have made or unmade the nascent agency, rendered them vulnerable to the political sharks which had circled even then, sensing blood in the water. Eyeing covetously the turf these cowboys had carved out for themselves.

But Bill Donovan had looked out for his people—ensured that they would survive, go on beyond their wartime role to the brave new world which lay beyond.

Even if that new world would hold no place for him.

There had still been a handful of old OSS hands remaining at Langley when he had himself come to the Agency, almost a decade before—a small knot of men and women, in their eighties, so far past retirement that one wondered if they even remembered what it had looked like.

Still there, serving their country. Despite all they had seen. Stark testimony that idealism actually *could* survive six decades at Langley.

But how strong would you have to have been, going in? Kranemeyer wondered absently. Far stronger than himself, that much was clear.

He paused by a familiar exhibit, a hand-written letter under glass, written on the letterhead of one Adolf Hitler.

The letter of a young father, an OSS officer named Dick Helms, to his three-year-old son on Victory in Europe Day.

"Dear Dennis," it began in a strong, flowing hand, the words so familiar that Kranemeyer could have quoted them from memory. *Had*, more than once.

"The man who might have written on this card three short years ago when you were born once controlled Europe. Today he's dead, his memory despised, his country in ruins. He had a fear of intellectual honesty, a thirst for power, he was a force for evil in the world—his passing, his defeat, a boon to mankind, but thousands died that it might be so. The price for ridding society of bad is always high. Love, Daddy"

Helms had known what he was talking about, Kranemeyer thought. Known, and gone on to head the Agency for seven long years, in the heart of the Cold War. *Paying the price.*

Because it was ever there, just waiting to be paid, by each and every generation which came through these doors.

And what am I doing today? Kranemeyer asked himself, glancing around as though he had hoped to find the answers written somewhere in these relics. *Paying the price, or deferring it? Shifting the blame to the shoulders of another man?* Surviving, *true enough, but at what cost?*

"I had wondered who was in here, so early," a woman's voice began, breaking in upon his thoughts, and he looked up to see the familiar visage of the museum's curator, her face framed by the shadows as she stepped from the fuselage of an old OSS transport which served as an entryway to this part of the exhibit—her short, golden hair glinting in the overhead lights. "I should have known."

Kranemeyer smiled. "Just getting my bearings, Toni. Trying to prepare, to ground myself."

She nodded her understanding, a sober look in her eyes. Everyone at the Agency had been bracing for this, ever since the first images came back from the Sinai. Knew what it could mean. "Have you found what you need, sir?"

"I'm not sure," he replied thoughtfully, looking away—his eyes gliding once more over the Helms letter. "Perhaps guidance is too much to ask of ghosts."

Another nod. "It's going to be a long day."

3:07 P.M. Central European Summer Time
Fort Noisy-le-Sec
Seine-Saint-Denis, suburbs of Paris

There was silence in the small room when the video finished playing for the second time. As Emile Vautrin glanced around at the faces of his team—three men, and two women. All of them prior French military—one of them a Legionnaire—all now working for the *Division Action*. Assassins, to put it baldly, and he saw no reason not to do so. Unlike their allies across the Channel, the French had never quailed from direct action.

"This man," he said, extending a long, delicate index finger toward the frozen, masked image on-screen, "is our new target. We know him only by the *nom de guerre* Ibrahim Abu Musab al-Almani, a returned fighter from Syria. He is believed to be a German convert to Islam—a Caucasian, not an Arab. And that's about all we know, or think we know."

"That's not very much," Bérénice Lefebvre observed, a cold, skeptical look in her dark eyes. They'd met five years before, on an operation into the Algerian Maghreb, and it had been her bullet which had killed their target— her status as a woman getting her in closer than any of the rest of them could have ever dreamed.

"*Non,*" Vautrin acknowledged. "It's not. But that's our starting point. And we won't rest until we've identified him. Until we've found him. Until he's dead."

10:45 A.M. Eastern Daylight Time
Capitol Hill
Washington, D.C.

". . .the committee will come to order," Antonio Tamariz intoned, glancing briefly up at the battery of press cameras surrounding him before returning to his prepared notes. "I would like to welcome our witnesses, Director of National Intelligence Lawrence Bell, and Director of the National Clandestine Service Bernard Kranemeyer. Thank you both for being here today."

Kranemeyer nodded, almost imperceptibly, a grim smile frozen on his lips—his coal-black eyes unreadable. He felt Bell lean back in the chair beside him, envied the man his ease. Then again, this was far more his "battlefield" than it was Kranemeyer's. The place where political blood was shed, where victims were to be sacrificed to appease the gods.

One wondered what they would read from his liver, Kranemeyer thought unamusedly, his eyes meeting those of the chairman.

"Before we begin," Tamariz continued, a pompous, grating edge to the voice of the congressman from Arizona, "I would like to remind our members—and witnesses—that this is an open hearing. I recognize the challenge of discussing sensitive national security issues in public, however, as part of this committee's investigation into June's tragedy in the Sinai, I consider it critical to ensure that the public has access to credible, unclassified fact."

And what will they do with it, once they have it? Kranemeyer found himself asking, a cynical half-smile playing behind the mask. *Do they even care? Is anyone even watching?*

There was no delusion more common in this city than the belief that their every waking moment was of vital importance to the nation. That people out there, in fly-over country, clung to their every word.

Nothing could have been further from the truth. Most of them, simply didn't care. They had better things to do with their lives. *Leave them to it.*

". . .at this time, I will ask the witnesses to stand and raise their right hands."

Kranemeyer heard Bell's chair slide back beside him, pushed himself to his own feet, balancing against the prosthesis as he raised his right hand, palm facing outward, toward Tamariz. The chairman meeting his gaze for a brief moment, before looking away.

"Do you solemnly swear or affirm, that the testimony you will give to this committee will be the truth, the whole truth, and nothing but the truth, so help you God?"

"I do," Kranemeyer replied, unblinking, taking his seat once more at the chairman's nod. A saying from long ago running over and again through his mind.

"My tongue has sworn; the mind I have has sworn no oath. . ."

5:07 P.M. Central European Summer Time
The new safehouse
Coulommiers, France

"I think these will work," Harry announced, emerging from the back of the second utility van now parked in the vacant lot behind the Coulommiers safehouse. They weren't *Électricité de France*—the plain white vans bore no markings at all, but they were unobtrusive enough. The type of vehicle even a trained eye might see and forget, without a second thought. "They're the right size—we just need to build some kind of simple platform in the back of each to support the control laptop. Nothing elaborate—it could even be wood."

"Can't you simply hold the computers?" Gamal Belkaïd asked, motioning to one of his men to close the doors as Harry stepped down.

Harry shook his head. "You saw our results in the Ardennes—and that was with smaller, unloaded drones. We really need more practice, at least for Aryn—another couple weeks, optimally. But we have less than two days. At the very least, we have to have a stable operating platform. Without it. . ."

He pantomimed a crash. "All this, for nothing."

"I'll have my men get to work."

"Tell me, Ibrahim," Belkaïd began, as they walked back toward the house together, "what do you think of our chances?"

"They are as Allah wills," Harry replied simply, glancing over at the older man. "Our fate is in His hands, and His alone."

Belkaïd emitted a short, barking laugh. "If I had been content to leave my fate in the hands of God, I would have spent far more time in prison than—"

"Do *not* blaspheme!" Harry spat, his blue eyes turning steely as he turned on the Algerian. "You endanger us all. Do you *want* us to fail?"

"Of course not, don't be absurd. I am sacrificing everything for this. Everything I have built, all through the years—for this moment of vengeance. Of *justice.*"

"Then don't tempt the Lord of Worlds with your impiety." He held Belkaïd's gaze for a long moment before subsiding, answering the man's question. "Quite good, I believe, as long as we can get the drones in the air without being detected. A launch from the forest of Montmorency is, I think, our best option—if you believe the loaded drones will have the range."

A nod. "*Oui.* They should. It's not more than eleven or twelve kilometers, at the most. Faouzi will go with you, as part of your team. To fly the drone."

Harry pulled up short, unsure whether he had heard Belkaïd properly. He and Aryn had been the designated "pilots," since the loss of Driss.

"I don't understand, I—"

"You are the only one of all of us who has seen combat, Ibrahim," the Algerian replied, not looking back. "You're wasted behind a computer. I want you there, at the gates, engaging the security teams. Cause as much chaos as you can."

"*Insh'allah,*" Harry responded, his mind racing to process what he had just been told. *This changed things.*

He was still working through it when Belkaïd paused on the step just ahead of him, his hand on the back door of the house. "The Russian—the one who calls himself 'Grigoriy'—he believes that he has met you before."

Harry froze, taken off-guard, looking steadily into the Algerian's dark, glittering eyes. "*C'est vrai?*"

"He couldn't remember just where—Syria, perhaps. Do you not remember him?"

"There were foreign advisors in our camps in *Sham,*" Harry replied, choosing his words carefully. Knowing how thin the ice had just become beneath his feet. "Russians among them. It is possible. But no. . .I don't remember him at all."

11:09 A.M. Eastern Daylight Time
Capitol Hill
Washington, D.C.

". . .the final death toll, as reported by the Egyptian government, stands at over thirty souls, Mr. Kranemeyer. Civilians, women and children, executed by your hand—on the orders of this administration. In light of the results, can you still say that the decision taken to execute the strike was justified?"

"I can," Kranemeyer replied calmly, gazing across the room at Hank Imler, remembering Coftey's words about the congressman from Nevada. "Based on the intelligence we possessed at the time of the strike—the prosecution of the target was in strict accordance with the Law of War."

"You're not going to be Hank's target, Barney," Roy Coftey had said, a grim look in his eye, *"that's the President. You're just going to be the nearest proxy. And if crucifying you is the quickest way to crucify Norton, then that's what he'll do, without a blessed thought for the broader consequences. He's a small man, with a mind to match—too small to see the big picture, out beyond the end of his political nose."*

But they were prepared for that.

"And let us not forget," Kranemeyer continued, pre-empting Imler's quick response, "despite the media focus on the admitted failure to eliminate the primary target, Umar ibn Hassan, three prominent Islamic State leaders *were* confirmed among the dead—the entire senior leadership of *Wilayat Sayna*, wiped out in a single blow."

And Umar ibn Hassan had stepped in to take their place, establishing himself—unchallenged—as the caliph's personal representative in the Sinai, Kranemeyer thought, but didn't add.

The Agency had been set up, if the truth be told, but truth wasn't the purpose of these hearings. It never was.

Congressman Imler shook his head, leaning in closer to his microphone as though he feared the press cameras wouldn't pick up his every word. "And that's sufficient justification, in your view, for all of this. . .carnage?" he asked, pausing dramatically. "For the decision you took to end innocent life."

Kranemeyer began to respond, but Bell cleared his throat beside him, cutting in. "If you might excuse my intrusion, Mr. Chairman, the ranking member seems to be laboring under the mistaken belief that the final decision to prosecute the strike against Umar ibn Hassan was Director Kranemeyer's. It was, in fact, mine."

The faces of Tamariz and Imler were a study in contrast in that moment. . .the chairman's face flushed with chagrin as he stammered out a response, the ranking member's triumphant, leaning back in his seat to enjoy his counterpart's confusion.

And he saw what Tamariz's game had been in that moment. *Contain the fallout. Shift the blame onto the intelligence community itself, away from their political masters. Isolate it far enough away from the President, that he—and by extension, the party—couldn't be directly implicated. At least in the eyes of the general public. The voters.*

Kranemeyer had been far enough down the food chain for the plan to work. The Director of National Intelligence. . .wasn't.

And his mind returned to that afternoon in the DNI's office in Liberty Crossing, the hard look in Bell's eyes as he'd stared across the desk. The look of a man who had already made up his mind.

"Let me take the fall on this one, Barney. It's for the best, trust me."

"But it was *my decision, sir,"* Kranemeyer had responded. *"We both know that. By all rights—"*

"Right has nothing to do with it. Nothing to do with anything in this town." Bell had paused, as if choosing his next words very carefully. *"We both know what you did—I imagine we both wish it could be undone, knowing what we know now. Do things over again, make the right call. But that's not going to happen. Pandora doesn't go back in the box. The only thing for us to do is figure out how best to manage the fallout. And the best way to do that is for me take responsibility."*

"It'll be the end of your career."

A shrug. *"It'll be the end of someone's. Might as well be mine. The Agency still needs you."*

"But, sir—"

"I'll be dead in five months, Barney. Maybe less—that's what the doctor has given me." There was nothing of bitterness in the DNI's voice—just a calm acceptance of his fate. *"Cancer. They found it far too late to do anything about it. . .it's everywhere."*

"I'm sorry." The words had seemed as insufficient, as meaningless, as ever, and Bell had shaken his head.

"Don't be. Just let me do this one last thing for my country. Let me fall on my sword."

"Is—is this representation of events accurate, Mr. Kranemeyer?" Antonio Tamariz demanded, his voice bringing him back to the present. A desperate look in the chairman's eyes. The look of a man who has just found the ground shifting beneath his feet—opening up to swallow him whole.

"It is," Kranemeyer nodded calmly, not a trace of hesitation in his voice.

The mind I have has sworn no oath. . .

5:36 P.M. Central European Summer Time
The safehouse
Coulommiers, France

"We can put the first van here," Harry said, circling a point on the satellite map with the mouse cursor, "on the Rue de Brennus. And the second with Aryn and Yassin, here, farther north—along the Rue de l'Olympisme. Once the drones have hit their target, there's going to be panic in the stadium, a flood of people trying to get out, to get away. And that's when we'll abandon the vans and make our way out onto the Avenue Jules Rimet, in front of the stadium itself—two separate teams of *shahid*, targeting Gates C & E. The terror of the crowd will be to our advantage—hinder the efforts of the French security services to reach us, to *stop* us."

It should have seemed strange to talk so calmly of one's own death, Harry thought, glancing around the small room at the eager faces surrounding him—but it was something he had done so many times over the years.

And every single time, he had walked away in the end—alive, even if only just barely.

No more. This was the end of the road. *One final sacrifice.*

There was an irony in the thought. . .his chosen end, not that dissimilar from the would-be martyrs who now huddled around him, straining for a glimpse of the laptop's screen. They still sought redemption in their deaths— he knew better than to harbor any such hope.

But the end was the same, for all that. *Blood and fire.*

"Why wouldn't we just pack the vans with explosives?" Aryn asked quietly, looking up from his seat a few feet away. "Drive them into the crowd as they exit the gates."

"Impossible to get close enough," Harry replied, repressing a shudder at the young man's words. This was the same Aryn who had stayed at his mother's side in her waning months, caring for her. *Loving her.* And regretting every last moment that her illness prevented him from joining the jihad.

"You could see the anti-vehicle barricades stacked near the main gate this morning, ready to be moved into position. With President Albéric attending the game, the security presence will be intensified. It will take all the confusion of the attack to even get close enough on foot."

"Why not separate the attacks even farther," Gamal Belkaïd asked, speaking up after studying the laptop for a few moments. A frown on his face. "Move the second van up to the Rue du Mondial, hit the G or H gates."

Because that would be too far away for me to move to intervene, was the thought that went through Harry's mind, but he didn't give voice to it, looking up to meet Belkaïd's gaze. "We only have a few men, Gamal—unless you are prepared to commit more of your own personnel to the attack. We need to be in position to support each other, if possible. To sell ourselves dearly."

Belkaïd seemed to consider the proposal for a long, painful moment before shaking his head. *"Non,"* he said finally, "if I reach out further in my organization, I risk finding those who would be less. . .committed. Unwilling to martyr themselves for their faith."

Like yourself. It was another thought which went unsaid—there had never been the slightest hint that Belkaïd would himself seek martyrdom in this operation. An irony so old as to be worn out from overuse—it was never men like Belkaïd who ended up on the front lines, wearing an s-vest.

War and death, revolution—*jihad*—the province of young men, as they had ever been. Only the names, the purported causes, changing with the passing of the years. Fresh labels for the oldest of scams.

"Do what you can," Belkaïd continued, thoughtfully, turning to leave the room, "with what you have."

11:42 A.M. Eastern Daylight Time
The Russell Senate Office Building
Washington, D.C.

". . .to reach the obvious conclusion. . .the President deliberately misled the American people to bolster his foreign policy credentials. . ."

The low hum of voices from the television greeted Melody Lawlor's ears as she pushed open the door to Coftey's inner office—not bothering to knock. The senator wasn't there, anyway, he was out to lunch with. . .one of the junior senators on the Select Committee, she didn't remember the man's name.

Her heels sank in the carpet as she walked over to his desk, the geography of the room so familiar to her that she could have made the journey blindfolded—the navy blue couch off to one side by the door, well-used, of that she had no doubt.

A shadow box, containing his decorations from Vietnam hung above the couch, along with a picture of himself from his first Senate run—decades before.

There was a fireplace across the room, a large Xiang Zhang painting of the 1889 Oklahoma Land Rush framed above its mantel. *A reminder of home*, she thought ironically. Coftey had spent far more time in D.C. than Oklahoma over the last thirty-plus years.

She circled the desk, depositing the folder neatly in front of Coftey's chair—the continuing murmur from the television over to one side of the fireplace drawing her attention in that moment.

". . .and what was the initial basis upon which you based your assessment of Umar ibn Hassan's presence at the target location, Mr. Kranemeyer?"

"That's not a question I can answer in open session, ma'am," she heard a strangely familiar voice respond as the camera panned away from Representative Claire Nitikman, re-focusing on a broad-shouldered man seated behind the microphones. "I can only state that the intelligence community had 'high confidence' in the accuracy of our assessment, a confidence shared by multiple involved agencies."

"A misplaced confidence, clearly. . ." Nitikman responded, but Melody was no longer listening, the world around her seeming to fade away as she focused in on the man's face. *Remembering.*

Coftey's friend in Chandler—that *voice*, ominous as death, filtering to her through the thin walls of the farmhouse, replying to the senator's comment about Haskel and Shapiro. *"We do not discuss that.* Ever. *"*

And here he was again. . .before Congress.

She was trembling by the time she reached the outer office, almost slamming Coftey's door behind her—her face ashen as she retreated to her own desk, rummaging in her purse for the burner.

Her first attempt to swipe the phone's pattern lock failed, and she swore, glancing toward the door as if expecting the senator to return at any moment.

Another try, and it unlocked, her thumbs flying across the screen as she tapped out a brief message. *Turn on your TV. The hearing. It's him.*

She paused, her thumb hovering over the SEND button—knowing that this was the final point of no return. The moment when none of this could ever be undone.

Or perhaps she had passed that point, long ago. It was so hard to tell, looking back.

Another low curse escaped her lips, and she jammed her thumb into the screen with a violent gesture. *Sent.*

6:03 P.M. Central European Summer Time
The offices of the Consortium Stade de France
Paris, France

"Non. C'est impossible." The man shook his head, a stubborn, immoveable expression on his broad, plain face.

"I am sorry if I conveyed the impression that this was a choice I was offering you, *Monsieur* Aubert," Marion Leseur replied, returning his look with a hard stare of her own. "I have the power to implement these measures of my own accord—and I will do what is necessary to protect my principal. Informing you is a courtesy, that is all."

The CEO's curse was low, but clearly audible, a frown furrowing his brow as he stared across the desk at her. *"Pardon, madame.* But you *must* understand the implications of what you are proposing. To use mobile jammers to shut down communications in a two-kilometer radius surrounding the stadium—

for the duration of the event—as I said: *impossible.*"

"*Pour quoi?*"

Aubert sighed heavily, running a hand through his thinning hair as he rose, pacing back and forth behind his desk. "We will have over sixty thousand people in that stadium Saturday—most of them below the age of thirty-five. Do you have children, *Madame* Leseur?"

She shook her head. In fact, she did have one son—a recent *université* graduate now pursuing an engineering career in Toulouse—but she saw no reason to discuss her personal life here, with this corporate executive.

He snorted. "I do—two daughters, both in *université*. I couldn't separate them from their phones if my life depended on it. And at an event like this, people will be taking photos throughout the game, sharing them on social media—messaging their friends. And if they cannot do so at an event they have paid for. . ."

A shrug, as he spread his hands toward her. "There will be massive outrage—outrage directed, not at your own agency, of course, but at my company. We will take the blame, for your decision."

He paused, seeming to contemplate his decision for a long moment. "I am afraid that we here at the *Consortium* will have to request that President Albéric absent himself from the game. It would be our honor to host him, but if this is the price. . .it is too high. *Je suis désolé.* Please, convey this message to him."

2:03 P.M. Eastern Daylight Time
Capitol Hill
Washington, D.C.

Once, Kranemeyer thought, camera flashes going off in his face as he hustled through the halls of the Capitol Building back toward the HPSCI hearing room, any photos taken of him would have been carefully redacted to remove the faces of he and his fellow Delta operators. Their unit's existence, one of the government's multitude of open secrets. Their identities, one of its most jealously guarded.

Blacker than black.

Those had been the days. Now, with reporters attempting to jam microphones into his face as he walked—cameras everywhere—his face was going to be appearing everywhere, on every 24/7 cable news program, at least for the few days until they settled upon the next distraction.

And the Internet. . .it was forever.

No going back.

The committee members were themselves returning from lunch as Kranemeyer took his seat once more beside Bell, exchanging a simple, professional nod with the older man. The hours of media attention had been grueling for both of them.

Returning. . .but the chairman was himself nowhere to be seen, Kranemeyer realized, his eyes briefly scanning the room for Tamariz.

A moment later, as if in answer to his thought, the Republican congressman from Arizona put in an appearance from a side entrance, a sheaf of papers tucked under his arm—an aide at his side as he walked, the two of them carrying on a low, animated conversation in the few moments before Tamariz dismissed the young woman.

The chairman took his seat, re-opening the hearings with a few brief, perfunctory words.

"It has come to my attention," he continued, cutting off the ranking member as Imler attempted to seize the moment and the microphone, "since the revelations of this morning's session, that this committee is already in possession of sworn written testimony from Stewart Arntz, an attorney with the CIA's Office of General Counsel, who was called upon to provide legal guidance on the QUICKSAND strike, and has given us a detailed account of how events unfolded."

Kranemeyer didn't look at Bell, his pulse involuntarily quickening. They had discussed this possibility, but even so. . .

"Allow me to quote from Mr. Arntz's testimony. . .'the final decision to execute the strike was taken by Director Kranemeyer while the DNI had absented himself from the room. When Director Bell returned, he appeared surprised. . .'"

There was barely restrained triumph glittering in Tamariz's dark eyes.

"He goes on," he continued, gesturing with his hand to the sheaf of paper before him, "but I think that much is sufficient to point to the apparent contradiction we find ourselves faced with, between the written testimony of

Mr. Arntz, and the claims which have been made before this committee this morning."

The room seemed to go quiet in that moment, all eyes—every camera—focusing on the two directors. "Can you explain this?"

There was a dangerous moment's hesitation on Bell's part before he responded, but when he did, his voice was clear and unwavering.

"There is no contradiction, Mr. Tamariz, however it might appear," the DNI replied calmly. "My instructions to Director Kranemeyer, over the days leading up to the execution of QUICKSAND, were clear and unequivocal. If the moment came, and our preconditions were met, the strike was to be launched. The moment came, and those preconditions had been met. . ."

7:37 P.M.
The safehouse
Coulommiers, France

They had done a good job, Harry thought, circling the drone on the table—eyeing its payload of plastic explosives with a critical glance.

It was a job he had hoped to be tasked with, given his "background" in Syria. A simple adjustment here or there to the wiring, even to the weight distribution of the *plastique* itself, might have been enough to spike Belkaïd's cannons. But the crime boss had, instead, entrusted it to a pair of his men. . .and the work they had done was impressive.

"*Mash'allah*," he breathed, glancing over with a smile to where Faouzi stood by the door, a Chinese-made Type 56 AK clone in his hands. *Standing guard*.

The man didn't return the smile, his eyes unwavering—as if he somehow expected to divine Harry's thoughts.

Good luck. Harry cast another glance back at the drones, his eyes sweeping over at the sturdy black fuselage. There *might* be just a chance—tomorrow, when they took them out to test them for the first time. A simple collision, like the ones he had arranged before. . .could take both of them out of action. *Delay*. It would be risky, but even so. . .

"It will be a beautiful day, brother," he smiled once again, moving to the door—placing a hand on Faouzi's shoulder as he passed

The Algerian's hand came up with unexpected swiftness, seizing Harry's wrist in a firm grasp—their eyes locking as Harry assessed the threat, reading the intensity written in the man's swarthy face.

"Do you think truly that this is going to be *enough*?" Faouzi demanded, his dark eyes radiating fire. *Hate.* "That it could *ever* be enough, for what has been done to us?"

Harry just stared at him, his eyes cold as ice—holding the stare until the Algerian released his grip on his wrist.

"Non," he replied then, his own hand falling to his side. "This isn't the end, but only the beginning, my brother. Others will take us as their example."

"Will they, though?" There was the bitterness of the skeptic in the man's voice. Bitterness and sorrow. "My son went to visit family in the *banlieues* of Paris two years ago on summer vacation. He was sixteen at the time. He and a cousin were stopped by the French police—wrong place, wrong time, a robbery had happened, *apparemment,* and you had two young Muslim men in the area. Both of them ran—the cousin got away, but my son. . ."

The man paused, his voice suddenly choked with emotion. "They caught him, and they beat him—with their batons. He. . .he will never walk again, will never leave his chair, without help. My only son. And no one did anything. I—his *father*—did nothing."

Harry placed his hand once more on the man's shoulder, squeezing it fiercely. "Two more days, brother. . .and that will no longer be the case."

Chapter 34

1:35 A.M. Central European Summer Time, August 6ᵗʰ
The safehouse
Coulommiers, France

The house was quiet, the kitchen dark when Harry entered it, the only sound the faint murmur of the television from down the hall, the room where the drones still sat, out on the big table.

When he had looked in, an hour or two before, the new guard had been watching *Die Hard,* his own rifle cradled in his lap, fingers curled loosely around the pistol grip. There had been a contented, even amused smile on his face, watching Bruce Willis take down one German terrorist after another.

Everyone is the hero, Harry thought, moving to the cabinets. *In their own story.*

John Patrick Flynn had told him that once, on one of their first missions together overseas. *Wisdom.* Like so much else the older man had passed along in those early years at the CIA, becoming far more than a mentor to Harry. *Almost a father.*

What would he say now? To see how things had ended for his protégé, now on the run and out of time.

Impossible to say.

Harry reached up, pulling a tin down from an upper shelf—the distinctive aroma of cardamom filling his nostrils as he scooped the loose leaf black tea into a ball-shaped diffuser. Flynn had been gone for years, dead after a lengthy battle with cancer, having finally, after a career in the CIA which had spanned from Vietnam to Afghanistan 2.0, found the one enemy even he couldn't beat.

483

Perhaps he was at rest now. *Perhaps.* It had been rare for the the old CIA hand to discuss anything of his own personal life.

At any rate, Belkaïd's guard was far from asleep, Harry thought, bringing his attention back to the present as he brought the water to a boil—rendering any attempt to get to the drones. . .perilous, at best.

He had few doubts that he could overpower the man, even in the still-weakened condition he found himself in post-Scotland. But could he do it quietly enough to avoid bringing the house down on him?

That was a much harder question, and he had to face the reality that disabling the drones wasn't enough, in itself. Even without them, they would still have the weapons—the explosives, Russian intelligence had provided them.

Russian intelligence. Harry dropped the ball into the steaming water, closing his eyes as he remembered the way Gamal Belkaïd had looked at him. So Grigoriy *had* remembered him. Perhaps not as vividly as he himself remembered those days in Iraq—but the memory was there, nevertheless, no less dangerous for lying dormant. He would have to—

"Unable to sleep?" a woman's voice asked, and he turned, the steeping glass of tea in his hand to find Ghaniyah Belkaïd standing there in the doorway of the kitchen, her figure cloaked in the formless folds of her *abaya.*

He nodded, truthfully enough. There had been far too much on his mind, too many questions, too many riddles left yet unsolved. "There's just so much yet to be done, so much we have to account for—to plan for."

He smiled ruefully at her. "I wish it wasn't tomorrow. We really need more time."

"You will succeed," the older woman responded, her worn, leathery face lit with an unaccustomed passion as she dropped into a kitchen chair, her elbow resting on the table as she regarded him. "You *must* succeed. Everything depends on it—*everything.*"

He turned away from her wordlessly, pouring a second glass of the warm water and dropping the diffuser into it before crossing the room to set down before her the first glass he had prepared.

"May God bless you," she said, a smile creasing her aging countenance as she looked up at him. "For *all* you have done."

He shook his head. "I have done nothing—I am but the slave of God."

Her hands appeared from within the folds of fabric, reaching over for a packet of sugar and tearing it open. "You are more than a slave. You are the reason for all of this, even if you have yet to realize it."

The words hit him with the force of a physical blow, the certainty with which she spoke them—forcing him to turn back, to look at her.

"My brother," Ghaniyah continued, dumping the sugar into her tea before looking up at him calmly, "left Algeria behind decades ago—he was too young to have remembered what was *done*. Too consumed with money, to care. And then you came into our lives—reminded Gamal of the demands of his honor and his faith. Showed him the *way*."

"Insh'allah," Harry breathed, scarce able to keep his voice from trembling as he regarded her, sitting there across from him—a quiet, almost matronly figure.

Was it even possible that she was right? That all of this had, in fact, been set in motion by his own actions.

The brothers in Molenbeek, hanging out with their friends at the boxing club—talking jihad on the Internet forums—but talk had been all it was. . .until he had arrived in their midst.

Gamal Belkaïd, running his drugs, his counterfeit electronics, his women—a criminal, perhaps even a facilitator of terrorists, but little more—until he had gutted Lahcen like a fish there in the Outremeuse, bringing the crime boss in to investigate, to clean up the mess.

Marwan, most of all.

The smallest of stones, rolling down a mountainside, colliding with others—gathering momentum, building force—until it was unstoppable, crushing everything in its path.

Avalanche.

9:06 P.M. Eastern Daylight Time
An apartment
Washington, D.C.

Kranemeyer had been expecting the knock at the door ever since the phone call three hours earlier.

"Come in," he called in response, brushing the final scraps of his takeout to one side of his plate as he reached over for the remote, pausing the film.

He could hear the door open, the sound of heavy footsteps against wood in the brief moments before the figure of Roy Coftey appeared in the entryway. "Getting a little careless, leaving the door unlocked, aren't you, Barney?"

Kranemeyer inclined his head toward the Sig-Sauer P226 lying on the end table a few inches away from his fingertips and shrugged. "It wasn't open long. Have a seat."

The senator rounded the kitchen counter to step down into the apartment's living room, stopping short at the sight of Kranemeyer sitting there in the wheelchair—an involuntary expression of surprise on his face.

"What?" Kranemeyer asked, quiet amusement in his voice. *It never failed.*

Coftey shook his head, covering his confusion with a short laugh. "I'm sorry, it's—I just—"

"It's all right, Roy," the DCS said, the smile making its way out onto his face. "Everyone does it. . .even those who know. It's just not something that crosses their mind. Doesn't, unless you have to live with it."

He raised himself up in the chair, the stump of his leg brushing against the edge as he shifted position, gesturing Coftey to the sofa. "Please, sit down."

"I was out today while you were up on the Hill," the senator said, regarding Kranemeyer with a canny look as he took his seat, "but I caught the highlights."

"How did I do?"

"You weren't comfortable, the camera could tell that much, but no professional ever is, under those lights." Coftey shrugged. "Listen to CNN, Fox, MSNBC. . .they're all reading something different into your facial expressions. But that's what talking heads are gonna do—talk. If they had anything relevant, they wouldn't be trying to decipher your ugly mug."

Kranemeyer laughed at that, a harsh, mirthless sound.

"The only reaction that's worthwhile is that of the White House, and between you and Lawrence. . .you put the fear of God into them." Coftey cast a glance toward the window, the D.C. night beyond. "Tamariz is probably there now, trying to plan out their next move for tomorrow's round of hearings, not that they have any good ones. Lawrence will be gone by the end of next week, that much is sure. Likely branded, in media sources friendly to the President, as a holdover from the Hancock administration who never truly had Norton's policies at heart. A member of the so-called 'Deep State.'"

The scapegoat, Kranemeyer thought. *Led away into the wilderness, carrying with him the sins of the administration.*

A slate washed clean. *Go and sin no more.*

There was bitter irony in the realization, even though it was what they had planned. *Prepared for.* That a good man's career would end this way, in disgrace.

"But it wasn't his call, was it, Barney?"

Coftey's question came so suddenly, so unexpectedly, that Kranemeyer simply stared at him, unsure if he'd heard the senator correctly. "What did you say?"

"It wasn't Bell's decision to pull that trigger, was it?"

8:57 A.M. Central European Summer Time
DGSE Headquarters
Paris, France

". . .a couple, out hiking with their dog in the Ardennes Department near Bogny-sur-Meuse, came across the body in a shallow grave late yesterday and called the police," Albert Godard said, his eyes never leaving the notes on the screen of the computer before him. "It took some hours for photos of the corpse to make their way up to our counterparts at the DGSI—*after* word of the body's discovery had already leaked to the media—but we got word from them two hours ago, with a positive identification. It's one of the members of the Molenbeek cell. . .a 23-year-old Moroccan named Idriss Benslimane."

Anaïs Brunet took a deep breath, processing the reality of the news. *They were in the country.*

Confirmation of what they had all feared following Belkaïd's flight from Liège. "What killed him?"

Godard shook his head. "We don't know, yet—won't have an official cause of death from the coroner for several days, but there was blunt force trauma to the back of his head, and water was found in his lungs—we believe he was drowned, perhaps in the small stream which lies less than a quarter of a kilometer from where he was hastily buried."

Brunet grimaced. It made no sense. *None*, whatsoever. But this world rarely did.

"You said that this was already in the press, *non?*"

"*Oui.* The discovery of the body—not its identification, *naturellement.*"

"Let's ensure that it remains that way."

9:26 A.M.
The forest east of Villeneuve-le-Comte
Seine-et-Marne Department, France

It was a near-perfect morning, Harry thought, gazing around him as Belkaïd's men unloaded the drones from the back of the van, setting up the controls and getting them ready for flight. Cool, at least by the standards of a French summer, and slightly overcast—providing relief from the intensity of the sun, the birds singing in the nearby woods.

The beauty of the morn marred only by the reality of what they were here to do—and his own lack of sleep.

The field in which they found themselves was one of the few open spaces in several kilometers of forest, an abandoned house lying nearly a hundred meters behind them to the south, a thick hedgerow walling them off from the view of passing cars on the road, fifty or sixty meters west of their current position.

It had taken less than a twenty-minute drive from the safehouse to reach this spot, and several of the Algerian's "employees" were already fanned out toward the driveway, pulling security.

Inside the vans, the laptops were already being set up on the makeshift wooden platforms which had been built for them—the drones' software coming on-line. This was as close to a dress rehearsal as they were going to get.

A dress rehearsal, for a play which would never see the stage. Not if he had anything to do with it.

Only Belkaïd himself was absent—had said he'd be along in an hour, maybe less. Business to take care of, apparently.

It was enough. He wasn't going to need long, not to do what he needed to do.

A single flight, and that would be enough to crash. . .at least one of the drones, perhaps both. That would be enough to postpone the attack, buy himself more time.

And what will you do with that time, once you have it? A nagging, insistent voice from within asked. *Anything? Anything at all?*

Just another question with no answer—he'd been putting off the inevitable for far too long, each effort to confront it costing him another tattered piece of his soul.

Every man might well have been the hero in his own story—but he had become the villain in his. *Reza. Driss. Marwan.* All of them dead at his hand. *Only the beginning.*

And how were they any different, from all the rest? The voice asked. *All the men you have killed, all through the years? No less deserving.*

But I knew them, he felt himself reply, fighting back against the voice's insistence. And that was it, at the heart of this. Killing a man wasn't about right or wrong—it was about your ability to disassociate yourself from his humanity.

And he was losing his ability to do that—*had been*, ever since Hamid Zakiri, only his rage at Davood's murder carrying him through the final act.

But now, as then. . .he had no other choice. *Not really.* He stooped down beside one of the large quadcopters, running his hand along the black central fuselage, barking a quick order to one of the Algerians to hand him the controller. Time to get them in the air.

Time to do this. He felt the smooth plastic of the controller beneath his fingers, felt Yassin's eyes on him as he stepped up, into the back of the van— powering the laptop on. Just a few moments, and laptop and UAV would sync, each device recognizing the other. Another minute, and it would be in the air.

And then he heard Faouzi's voice from without the van, rough, shouting. "Shut everything down, pack it back up. *Yalla, yalla!*"

Quickly.

"What's going on, brother?" Harry demanded, leaping down from the van to confront the Algerian, coming face-to-face with the man, standing there— a cellphone pressed to his ear.

"It's Belkaïd," came the reply, as Faouzi covered the phone with his hand.

"He's ordered us to return to the safehouse. At once."

Disaster.

"*Pour quoi?*" Harry demanded. There had to be some reason—if this attack were to succeed, this rehearsal was essential.

"He says it's all over the news. They found the body. . ."

10:13 A.M.
Palais de l'Élysée
Paris, France

"*Non,*" President Denis Albéric responded firmly, shaking his head as he paced the room, his suit jacket discarded over the back of his chair—hands resting on his hips. "I am sorry, but I simply will not do this."

"But, *mon presidente,*" Anaïs Brunet began, trading a look with her colleagues around the table, "given the potential severity of the threat. . ."

"I would advise against it," the GSPR head spoke up, her clear, authoritative voice cutting across the room. Brunet had always admired Leseur's no-nonsense, at times almost brusque, approach—never more than today. "With the *Consortium* refusing to make the requested concessions to meet our security requirements, the task of protecting you has become—"

"Your requests were unreasonable, *madame le commissaire,*" Albéric interjected, cutting her off, "and everyone sitting here at this table knows it. There was no way the *Consortium* could be expected to comply with such measures."

"You have entrusted me with your personal security, *mon presidente,*" Leseur retorted, not backing an inch. "With respect, I do not view any measures necessary to keep you safe as 'unreasonable.'"

"But *are* they necessary? *C'est vrai?*" Albéric stopped his pacing, glaring back at the table. "Tell me, Raoul—do *you* have any intelligence indicating a specific threat to the *Stade de France?*"

"*Non,*" Dubois replied, reluctance in the voice of the DGSI chief, "but as we now have reason to believe that the terrorists have crossed the border into France itself, we must—"

"And you, *madame le directeur?*"

Brunet shook her head slowly. "No specific threat to the stadium itself."

"Commissaire?"

"I can only act on the intelligence provided by my counterparts in the security services, *mon presidente*," Marion Leseur replied, her eyes still filled with cold resolution. "The GSPR does not itself collect or analyze intelligence. Based on what I have been provided, I believe the threat to be—"

Albéric didn't wait for her to finish. "Then none of you, truly, have anything new—anything which would justify a decision on my part to cancel my attendance."

"The presence of Gamal Belkaïd within this country—"

"Then *find* him. I stood before you," he began, looking around him at their faces, "not four days ago—in this very room—and gave you my decision. It stands. I will be attending the World Cup qualifier at the *Stade de France* tomorrow night, as planned."

12:31 P.M. Moscow Time
FSB Headquarters
Lubyanka Square, Moscow

The man at the the desk appeared slight, almost gaunt in the light streaming in through the large window behind him, the room itself nearly swallowing him up—his hair silver and thinning, betraying an age one never could have guessed from his plain, unremarkable face.

His eyes, though, were what people remembered about him, their irises a curious shade of brown, almost amber. Eyes like those of Iosif Vissarionovich, some said—and he did nothing to discourage such talk. His origins, as simple as those of Stalin himself—though he had been born in the old Perm Oblast, not far from the banks of the Kama. The son of a factory foreman. Humble beginnings, but it was what a man *made* of his beginnings that counted, and he had made much of his.

It had been a long road from that crowded, stinking, tenement in Perm, but one which had led, ultimately, to where he found himself today. One of the most powerful men in the new Russia, with the ear—and more importantly, the secrets—of the *most* powerful.

Dmitri Andreyevich Mironov reached forward, picking up the classified memo from the desk before him, holding it poised delicately between the long, thin fingers of a classically-trained pianist, his eyes scanning the Cyrillic, though he knew already what it said. Had read the brief message three times since it had arrived, transmitted over secure channels from Paris.

Everything is in order. Another day will decide the issue.

Simple, professional. *To the point.* Just the way the Centre had trained him. A good man.

After a moment more, the FSB director stood, extending the memo wordlessly to the man occupying the lone chair in front of his desk. Turning his back on him to move to the window, staring out over Lubyanka Square, toward the familiar shape of the Solovetsky Stone, resting barely a hundred meters from the facade of the FSB's headquarters—a stark, desolate rock monument raised in commemoration of those who had fallen in the prison camps, the gulags of the Soviet Union. *"To the victims of the Communist Terror. . ."*

An eyesore, Mironov thought, a contemptuous sneer curling at his lips. He'd sent no one to those camps himself—his remit, like that of the man sitting before his desk, had always been foreign, not domestic, intelligence collection. But he knew those who had, and they had been good men. *Professionals*. Doing their duty to their country.

To have such a monument, standing in the very shadow of their old headquarters—it was more than an insult, it was a public slap in the face. *Humiliation.*

"But what does this mean?" a voice asked from behind him, and Mironov turned, regarding the man with a grim smile.

"It means, Alexei Mikhailovich, that you were right, and I was wrong."

There was caution in the man's ice-blue eyes, a moment's hesitation before Vasiliev answered the smile with one of his own.

"In what way?"

"Your protégé. . .years ago, you believed in him, when few others did. When some, like myself, believed him far too young for the trust you reposed in him. You told us we were old men, who had forgotten our own youth. The mistakes, and the triumphs."

Mironov's smile warmed at the memory. "It's been years since then. But tomorrow, all your trust will be validated. . ."

7:54 A.M. Eastern Daylight Time
The apartment
Washington, D.C.

A worn face looked back at Bernard Kranemeyer from the mirror as he draped the necktie around the back of his neck, adjusting it briefly before bringing it up in the beginnings of a half Windsor.

Coftey had left after only a few hours, but his words had stayed behind, ominous and foreboding. Costing Kranemeyer his already tenuous claim on sleep.

"Be careful going down this road, Barney. These hearings aren't about getting at the truth—they never are—but that doesn't mean the truth won't be used against you, if it ever comes out."

"How did you know?" It was a question he'd had to ask, despite himself. He didn't like placing himself further in Coftey's debt, though, he had to confess, perjury was a relatively minor charge compared to what the senator already knew.

A short laugh. *"I know Lawrence. And I know you—one of the few who do, so you're likely safe. Before yesterday, few people in this town even knew your name."*

Would that it could have remained so, the DCS thought grimly, bringing the knot of the tie in tight against his throat. But the gods of democracy present had demanded a sacrifice.

Transparency. . .

2:06 P.M. Central European Summer Time
The safehouse
Coulommiers, France

". . .and in so doing, have jeopardized our chances of success in tomorrow's attack!" Harry spat angrily, glaring across the room at Gamal Belkaïd, his voice rising with each word.

"And if you had listened to me, none of this would have happened to begin with," the Algerian fired back, his hands resting on the tabletop as he leaned forward, his eyes flashing.

Harry began to respond, but stopped, glaring around at those surrounding them. "Give us the room. *Yalla!*"

Yassin and Aryn moved to obey immediately, Faouzi and the other two bodyguards hesitating until Belkaïd gave his assent with a quick, angry nod.

The two men, just looking at each other as those around them filed out—the door closing finally, with an audible *click*.

Alone. Harry could feel the bulge of the CZ on his hip, beneath the shirt—wanted nothing more but to draw and fire it. Two rounds, right between the eyes, nearly impossible to miss at this distance.

Two hollowpoint bullets, mushrooming through Belkaïd's brain. *Exiting out the back of his head.*

But the pistol stayed in its holster, a hard look in Harry's eyes as he glared at the Algerian. "Do you have any idea what you've *done?*"

"I have done what was—"

"I saw this happen so many times in *Sham*," Harry went on, cutting him off. Stalking restlessly back and forth along the one end of the room, his eyes flashing cold daggers at Belkaïd. "Young men, fresh recruits, handed a rifle and a couple mags. . .thrown right into the front line against the *safawi* regime of Damascus. No training, no preparation. It was a sin to waste such lives, given to us by Allah, but at the very least we *had* more men. You do not, and yet you are prepared to risk their lives with almost no preparation. *Que fais-vous?*"

What are you doing?

The older man shook his head. "*Non.* What has happened is not my fault, Ibrahim, no matter how much you would like to make it so. It is yours. I warned you that if you buried him and his body was discovered, the police would assume he had been murdered. And so it has happened."

"And you would have left a brother's body to the vultures and the dogs," Harry replied, subsiding after a long moment. "Do they know who he was?"

"The media is still reporting it as an unidentified body. But we cannot take that risk. Enough, Ibrahim," the Algerian said, raising his hand to stop Harry just as he started to speak. "I have made my decision. . .until tomorrow afternoon, no one will leave this house. The risk, thanks to your actions, is now too great. As to the ultimate success of our mission, that—as you once told me—rests in the hands of Allah."

11:07 A.M. Eastern Daylight Time
Capitol Hill
Washington, D.C.

It had been clear the moment they walked in, Kranemeyer reflected, a seemingly attentive mask plastered on his face as he stared across the room at the ranking member.

Hank Imler had arrived for the second day of the hearings loaded for bear. Where he had gotten all of his information, was impossible to say. Perhaps he truly had been paying attention to his briefings.

". . .has now, in the wake of your abortive strike, established himself as the Emir of the Islamic State's Sinai province. That doesn't sound like success to me, Mr. Bell, nor, I think, to anyone else in the room. It sounds as though Umar ibn Hassan's position has been strengthened, not weakened, by the intelligence community's actions."

And so it had. But the question—or statement, rather, for there were few questions this morning—had been directed to Bell, not himself.

"With due respect, Mr. Imler," Bell replied, taking a long, deep breath before replying, "when you decapitate the leadership of a network, someone is always going to 'benefit' from your action. If Umar ibn Hassan had been killed in the strike along with the others, it would have been someone else. It's not something which can favor prominently in our calculus."

"And the position which you reference as 'strengthened', Mr. Imler," Kranemeyer interjected, "is itself growing weaker by the day, as the United States continues to liaise with its Egyptian partners to place pressure on the remnants of *Wilayat Sayna*."

He regretted the words the moment they were out of his mouth, Imler's attention immediately re-focusing on him. *Why had he spoken?* Perhaps it was because Bell seemed worn this morning, less sure of himself—the cancer exacting its inevitable toll.

Move out and draw fire.

"Your Egyptian partners?" the ranking member asked, somehow seeming incredulous. "And have these partnerships actually survived the events of the last two months?"

"The intelligence community's partnerships are ones which have been developed and nurtured over the course of decades," Bell replied for them both, meeting Imler's gaze. "They are resilient enough to weather more damaging circumstances than this."

"'Than this?'" Kranemeyer saw the look in the ranking member's eyes, knew the DNI had made a misstep. "So you would acknowledge that this administration's decision to prosecute the strike against Umar ibn Hassan *was* damaging to America's foreign partnerships in the region?"

11:24 A.M.
The White House
Washington, D.C.

". . .with due respect, Mr. Imler, the question you've asked me is a political one, and thus not one which I am able to comment upon in this context."

President Norton swore under his breath, his eyes fixed on the television screen—glaring at the image of DNI Lawrence Bell as if he expected the man to somehow sense his gaze. *Quail under it.*

"This is turning into a disaster," he announced, muting the television with a gesture of frustration—looking back at the man who stood a few feet away. Dennis Froelich, his chief of staff.

"We always knew the hearings would be a risk, Mr. President," Froelich responded, shaking his head. "But given the public outcry which followed the strike. . .we had few other options. We—"

"*Don't* lecture me on what our options were, Dennis," Norton spat, the words coming out through clenched teeth. "I know why we made the choice we did, and I know that Tamariz assured us—me, personally—that he had the situation under control. That the responsibility for the decision to take the strike could be confined to the intelligence community. That this was, in fact, the perfect opportunity to use the Clandestine Service's incompetence to re-open our attempt to pass the intelligence bill through Congress. *None* of that has proved to be true. None of it, Dennis."

Norton lapsed into silence, staring at the screen. It had seemed so clear, once. So certain—viewing the presidency from without. It was a clarity which seemed to be slipping ever further away from him with each day spent in this job.

He knew what he had been elected to do, knew what he had said he *would* do. And yet it seemed that each day required some compromise, some. . .alteration of those plans, as if ideological purity was itself ill-adapted for governing a nation.

It was maddening, the helplessness. The President of the United States was supposed to be the most powerful man in the world—*was* the most powerful man in the world, in so many ways—and yet when it came to pursuing the agenda for which he had been elected, he so often found his hands tied, hamstrung by the very checks and balances of the government he was trying to restore.

The Founders' system of meticulously divided governance had been fine when it first began, the President thought, his face shadowed as he stared at the screen. Now? It only hampered the task of setting things *right*.

But there were some things still within his control, and he *would* control what he could. "Dennis?" he asked, a hard look coming across his face.

"Yes, Mr. President?"

"Contact the ODNI. I want Bell's resignation on my desk by Monday."

5:23 P.M. Central European Summer Time
Avenue Henri Delaunay, Saint-Denis,
Suburbs of Paris

They were already setting up the vehicle barricades, Sergeant Nathalie Jobert realized, moving quickly past uniformed police officers as she made her way down the street toward the command trailer which served as the GSPR's tactical operations center, or "TOC" as it was commonly referred to in military parlance. Her own uniform had been traded in for civilian clothes, part of Leseur's effort not to draw attention to the GSPR personnel in the day leading up to the event—the late afternoon sun burning into her bare arms.

Just to her south, the stadium itself rose into the sky, a looming presence.

The vehicle barricades—and the permanent bollards behind them, closer in to the *Stade de France* itself—would serve to prevent any disaster like that which had happened at the Christmas market in Nantes in 2014, a man ramming his vehicle into the crowds gathered at the gates. But aside from that. . .the situation was a security nightmare, Jobert thought, raising her hand to knock on the door of the command trailer.

There would be tens of thousands of people everywhere, flooding the area, funneled through the security checkpoints at each of the stadium's gates. Each of them, a painfully vulnerable target.

But the safety of the crowd was, strictly speaking, the responsibility of the *gendarmes*, Jobert reflected, the door of the trailer opening as a middle-aged man wearing a holstered pistol on his hip ushered her into the darkened interior. *Their* responsibility was President Albéric—and that was more than enough.

Commissaire Leseur stood in front of a bank of screens which lined one wall of the trailer, the hum of the air-conditioning—working overtime to keep the electronics cool in the Paris heat—muffling the sound of her voice as she spoke to the analyst at her side.

She turned, seeing the Air Force sergeant standing there. *"Bonsoir,* sergeant. What have you found?"

"I believe I have located a vantage point from which my eagle and I can conduct operations, *madame commissaire."* Jobert turned toward the digital satellite map thrown up on one of the big screens. Picking out a big, flat-roofed building to the west of the stadium itself, just across the Avenue Jules Rimet. She had passed it on the street less than five minutes before, the blue *"Decathlon"* sign ornamenting its facade marking the building distinctly. "Can you get me roof access?"

Leseur took a brief look before nodding. *"Oui. Certainement."*

7:02 P.M.
DGSI Headquarters
Levallois-Peret, Paris

"Oui, si'l vous plait. Merci." Raoul Dubois nodded, managing a tight, joyless smile as he picked up his tray and strode back across the cafeteria in the basement of the towering modern glass-and-steel building on the Rue de Villiers which housed the headquarters of France's internal security agency.

Most Friday nights, he would have been home by now—or perhaps out at dinner, with his wife and some of their friends.

But he had woken, nearly fourteen hours before, to the news of the discovery of Idriss Benslimane's body, bringing with it the near-certainty of Gamal Belkaïd's presence within the borders of France. Which meant that Brunet's problem had now become his.

He had considered her plan to infiltrate an officer into the jihadist underworld of Molenbeek inexcusably hazardous from the first he'd heard of it. The kind of risk that a careerist like himself would never have even considered, had he been read in at the beginning.

But even he could never have anticipated the disaster this had. . .somehow, become.

He let out a heavy sigh, picking at his *coq au vin*. It wasn't that Gamal Belkaïd hadn't crossed their radar in the past—he had, many times. As a criminal.

Not a terrorist.

It was impossible to know, in this moment, what had flipped the switch. Perhaps it was just a natural consequence of France and her neighbors having accepted the presence of so many. . ."others" within their borders, over the decades.

Those who would never become truly *French*, no matter how many decades they and their children spent taking up space. Their inability to assimilate, leading first to crime—then to terrorism. And perhaps the path Gamal Belkaïd had followed really *was* that simple.

A path leading them all. . .where, precisely? They still didn't know, and that was the question he and his officers had spent the day, without success, attempting to answer.

Futility.

The DGSI head took another bite, savoring the taste of the wine-soaked chicken—almost startled when he heard the scrape of the chair across from him being pulled out, looking up into the face of one of his deputies.

"Pardon, monsieur le directeur," the younger man began, excusing himself, "but we have a development."

"C'est vrai?" If so, it would be their first of the day, Dubois thought, gazing skeptically across the table at the younger man—his fork poised half-way between plate and mouth, a few drops of juice falling unheeded from the meat to the table.

"Local authorities in the Ardennes received a tip from a woman outside

Nouzonville who remembered seeing SUVs like those used by Belkaïd in his departure from Liège—coming and going over the course of several days this past week along a desolate country road to the northwest of the town."

Dubois shook his head in exasperation, jamming the bite of chicken into his mouth with a frustrated gesture. *"C'est n'importe quoi. . .*there are many such vehicles."

A nod. *"Certainement.* But we looked at the road on our satellite imagery, and found an isolated house. . .it's only half a kilometer from the woods where Benslimane's body was found. And there are still vehicles outside."

He stopped chewing, then—just staring at the man, waiting for him to continue. Something of a chill prickling at the hairs on his neck. *Could it be?*

"Have they gone in?"

A shake of the head. *"Non.* Given the sensitivity, the local police want GIGN to handle the operation, and Place Beauvau agrees with their assessment. They say it's your decision."

Convenient. Dubois suppressed a smile at the younger man's use of the familiar metonym for the Ministry of the Interior, located four kilometers to the southeast, on the *Place Beauvau,* in the 8th arrondissement.

His superiors.

But they were leaving the decision to strike, or not to strike, to him—which could only ever mean one thing: they wanted him to bear the responsibility, if it proved to be the wrong call.

Enough. It wasn't as though they could afford to let this go. "Send them in."

Chapter 35

2:35 A.M. Central European Summer Time, August 7th
The safehouse
Coulommiers, France

"He screamed when I shot him, Harry. It was a good sound." A muffled, choking sound in the semi-darkness, the broken form of Hamid Zakiri lying before him, sprawled on the floor. Framed in the sights of the Colt.

His own voice, remorseless—his finger tightening around the pistol's trigger. "Burn. . ."

But when the trigger broke, it was Carol's face which appeared beneath, her body shattered by the bullet, blood staining his hands. No harm.

The pistol falling from his nerveless fingers to clatter against the pavement as he stooped down by her body, scooping her up in his arms—a soundless scream escaping his lips.

Her face seeming to transform, even as he lifted her body—lights washing over them in ghoulish, alternating hues. . .red, white, and blue.

Until he was looking down into the youthful face of Aydin Shinwari, lifeless eyes staring back into his own—a small red hole in the center of the boy's forehead. Painfully neat, masking the devastation which lay beyond.

"He meant nothing to you, did he?" He heard a woman's voice demand from behind him, a voice in the darkness. "Just another pawn, in your bloody great game. A piece to be played. Like you have me."

And he turned to confront her, just as the gun in Mehreen's hand spat fire— a hot brand lancing into his side. Another shot, and he was falling, falling down. . .the cold, wet pavement meeting his own body. The severed head of

Marwan, staring down at him from above—laughing, a hideous, macabre visage, distorted by pain.

Laughing, mocking, growing closer and closer, eyes staring wide, until—

Harry came awake in that moment, sitting bolt upright from his blankets on the floor—his heart beating so fast it seemed it might burst from his chest, sweat running in rivulets down his skin—his fingers clawing for the holstered CZ which lay only inches from the huddled blankets forming his pillow.

His vision only then, as his fingers closed around its grip, clearing to reveal the darkened room around him—the familiar figure of Yassin lying on the sofa a few feet from him, the outline of the open door, not ten feet away.

Familiar. Everything in its place. Everything as it should be—the ghosts banished to their respective hells. But *no. . .*nothing was as it should be, he realized, his hands balling spasmodically into clenched, whitened fists. *Nothing.*

Nor could it ever be. It felt as if he were going mad, his eyes drifting inexorably back to the pistol—his hands, moving as if of their own accord to withdraw it from its holster, the textured polymer cool beneath his fingers.

Thumb hitting the magazine release, he slid the mag out, hefting it in his hand. Feeling its weight. *Fifteen rounds of 9mm Parabellum.* One in the chamber.

Enough to kill everyone in the house, if he moved quickly—used the advantage of surprise, the confusion of sleep. Enough to kill *himself.*

Do it, Marwan's voice—or was it the mocking voice of the demon— whispered in his ear. *Avenge me.*

Kill yourself. Kill them all in their sleep. Kill. . .

The magazine slid back into its well with an audible *click*, as if sealing his decision. *Do it now.*

"Ibrahim?" a questioning voice asked from the darkness, and he almost thought it was his dream once more. . .but the demons knew his real name.

He turned to see Yassin staring at him through the darkness—half-raised on one elbow on the sofa. "What's wrong?"

It seemed an eternity before he could find the words to reply, though it was probably only a few seconds before he slid the CZ back into its holster, smiling back at his friend. *The crisis, past.*

"Nothing, brother—get your sleep while you can. Tonight, we will sleep in *jannah*. In the arms of the virgins. . ."

3:27 A.M.
Outside Nouvonville
Ardennes Department, France

They had been lying in the field for over three hours, Maurice Navier thought, adjusting his shoulder once more against the buttstock of the PGM Hécate II anti-materiel rifle, slowly sweeping the house with the night-scope. *Nothing.*

No signs of life. No movement from the house, not a flicker of activity around the pair of SUVs parked to the side. The GIGN sniper shifted uncomfortably once more, knowing the assault team was out there somewhere—moving in on the house, preparing for the final breach. And he had to be prepared to cover it.

He would have far rather brought his lighter Accuracy International sniper rifle, but the commander had been insistent—if anyone tried to get away, they needed to be able to stop their vehicles. So the Hécate it was. . .

Navier pulled his eyes off the scope for a brief moment, staring out through the darkness toward the house, past the massive muzzle brake at the end of the Hécate's long barrel which reduced the 12.7mm rifle's felt recoil to little more than that of a standard 7.62mm NATO. Listening, but there was nothing he could hear beyond the night song of the birds in the woods behind them to the west—the gentle hum of crickets in the humid summer night. The even rhythm of his spotter's breath, lying just a few feet to his left. *In and out.*

There was a crackle of static in the *gendarme's* earpiece then, the hushed voice of the assault team leader issuing his final orders. *Get ready.*

He could make out the assaulters now, materializing out of the night near the house—stacking up by the door.

There was no warning in his ear when the moment arrived, everything now communicated through hand signals—only the distant *thud* of the ram slamming into the door reaching his ears. Men disappearing within the house as the door crashed inward.

Navier's hand curled around the rifle's pistol grip, bringing the stock back snug against his shoulder as he focused in on the vehicles—settling the nightscope's reticle on the hood of the first SUV, center-mass on the engine block.

When the explosion came, he was taken completely off-guard. . .

9:54 A.M.
DGSE Headquarters
Paris, France

If they had needed confirmation of the severity of the threat posed by Gamal Belkaïd, Anaïs Brunet mused, glancing down at the images displayed on the screen of her laptop, the DGSI's overnight raid on the suspected safehouse near Nouvonville had surely provided it.

If in a far grimmer manner than any of them had hoped, as the blast-scorched, blood-stained inner walls of the safehouse bore testament.

". . .triggered a small IED in the dwelling's kitchen," she heard Dubois announce, his voice a flat monotone, "killing two *gendarmes* and wounding four more."

Brunet winced. The death toll had gone up since the initial report, which had mentioned only the one officer.

"*Je suis désolé,* Raoul. Brave men."

On-screen, Dubois nodded, accepting her condolences with a look of weary resignation. "As you will already have been informed, no one was there. Either they had already left the area, or they fled after the discovery of Benslimane's body. But it was not entirely a dry hole. If you'll look at the photos we sent over, Anaïs, we were able to obtain confirmation that the film made of Daniel Mahrez's execution *was* made in the basement of the house. And we found a trove of litter and other paraphernalia left behind when Belkaïd and his people made their exit, including a laptop computer. We're working to determine what intelligence can be derived from. . ."

Dubois' monologue continued, but Brunet was no longer listening, her attention drawn to where Albert Godard sat off to her left, an expression of unusual animation on his face as he stared at his laptop, his eyes suddenly darting up to meet her gaze. "*Excusez-moi, madame le directeur. . .*"

"*Qu'est-ce que c'est,* Albert?" *What is it?*

"It's the laptop," he explained quietly, feeling every eye in the room, suddenly on him. "It's the one we gave LYSANDER."

11:34 A.M.
The safehouse
Coulommiers, France

". . .unconfirmed reports of an explosion and fire outside the Ardennes town of Nouvonville early this morning, accompanied by a massive police presence. At this time, we. . ."

Belkaïd swore beneath his breath, his eyes fixed on the newscast playing out across the laptop's screen.

He didn't look over at Harry, didn't need to. Each man knew what the other was thinking—or thought they knew.

But it was Aryn who spoke first, leaning against the doorway. "We knew this was going to come, once they found Driss' body. It was only a matter of time."

"We need to leave," Belkaïd announced, tension pervading the older man's voice. "Within the next few hours."

"You're coming with us?" Harry asked, surprised at his words. There had been no indication that he had ever intended to be part of the attack.

"Non," Belkaïd replied, shaking his head. "Only so far as Montmorency. I have a residence, an hour southwest of Paris. I will go there and await the results, with my sister."

Oh, yes. He remembered it having been mentioned, around the warehouse in Liège. . .somewhere in the Eure-et-Loir *department*, near a town called Béville-le-Comte, he thought.

"They will come for you there, after what we have done."

"Let them," the older man replied, a stolid, defiant look in his dark eyes. "They will have no proof, and even if they do. . ."

He clenched his fist, raising it to display the old tattoo. *The man between four walls.* "I have been in their prisons once before—I am not afraid of going back."

It may not be prison. It was another thought best left unsaid. Unlike their rule-bound allies across the Channel, the French had rarely been squeamish about utilizing more. . ."direct" methods of dealing with those they wished to put out of the way.

Assassination. Often carried out by the DGSE's very own *Division Action,* running its operations out of Fort Noisy-le-Sec in Seine-Saint-Denis. He had worked with some of their officers over the years, knew their reputation was. . .hard-earned.

Wouldn't have wanted to find himself in their cross-hairs.

He left Belkaïd a moment later, heading down the hallway back toward the room where their gear had been stowed—some of the Algerian's men, working the entire previous day to rig the vests with the explosives the Russian had provided. Explosives, laced with scrap metal and ball bearings, embedded in the *plastique.*

Devastation.

Like so many times before. He would be wearing one of these, just as he had back in Leeds, running his deadly bluff against Conor Hale. *Bluff?* No, for he had been deadly serious that day. Hell-bent on achieving his mission. *No matter the cost.*

Harry reached out, running a hand over the vest, noting the carefully concealed wires, running to the detonator tucked in the pocket. The sheets of explosive had been molded thin enough for the vests to be concealed under even a light windbreaker, though even that would be conspicuous in the August heat. *No help for it.*

His fingers found the wire, tugged at it gently—testing its strength. It would be so simple to disable the vests, conceal the damage, until it was far too late. *Until. . .*

"Ibrahim."

11:41 A.M.
Saint-Marguerite
Marseille, France

It was a quiet neighborhood. *Peaceful,* Armand Césaire thought, raising his hand once more to knock on the door.

Just the sort of a place where a man would want to raise his family.

The house itself was small, constructed from stark concrete block, its roof red—so characteristic of this part of Marseille, its white shutters now faded by the passage of time, their paint chipping to reveal the bare paint beneath.

He was standing at the top of the second flight of outside stairs leading to the main entry—*exposed*, the intelligence officer within him noted. His presence, painfully visible to anyone passing through the neighborhood.

Still nothing. Césaire glanced through the window of the door, unable to descry anything of the interior—the bright late-morning sun reflecting off the glass.

And then he heard footsteps, and the voice of a small child, from somewhere within.

"I want my son to know a better world—a better France *than my parents knew, than I have known. I want to help create that world."*

A world he hadn't himself lived to see, if it were even possible. Césaire winced, remembered Daniel's words on that last night in Paris, the two of them, having dinner together one final time before he went under as "Marwan Abdellaoui."

He hadn't had the heart to tell him that a "better world" was beyond the ability of any one man to create. That France. . .was never likely to change, no matter how many young Muslims might lay down their lives for the tri-color.

Daniel Mahrez's own ancestors—hard-bitten desert fighters from France's colonial posessions fighting in the ranks of the French *1re Armée*—had once, after all, liberated this very city from the Nazis. . .and won nothing for it but a bloody war in their own homeland, a scant decade later.

But being a case officer wasn't about telling the truth. So he had told the young man what he needed to hear, and sent him off. *To his death.*

A death the whole country would learn of, soon enough. It had surprised them all that the video hadn't been released on the Internet yet, but the decision had finally been made to notify his family. Brunct's call, he imagined, like as not. Which is why he was here, standing at this door in Marseille.

He heard the sound of a bolt being slid back—the door opening but a crack, the face of an older woman staring out at him, her face framed by the light cloth of a *hijab*, dark, suspicious eyes emanating from deep, weathered sockets.

"*Madame* Hania Mahrez? Is she at home?"

"*Oui,*" the woman nodded, "*ma belle-fille.*"

Daughter-in-law. So this was Daniel's mother, Césaire realized, a pang striking at his very heart. "May I come in for a moment? I am a colleague of Daniel's."

Was.

"*S'il vous plaît.*"

11:43 A.M.
The safehouse
Coulommiers, France

The sound of the voice sent a chill shuddering down Harry's spine, turning to find Nora standing there in the doorway, watching him. His opportunity for sabotage, slipping away in that moment.

"Yassin tells me that I'll be going as part of your group," she observed, her eyes watching his face closely, "not his. *Pour quoi?*"

She began to close the door behind her, as if wanting this conversation to remain private, but he shook his head, motioning for her to leave it open to the hall without—it would not do for a man like himself to be found alone with a woman, no matter what Belkaïd might himself have done with her. Even this was borderline, according to the tenets of the faith as he would have learned them in the Salafist mosques of Germany.

"Yassin still feels great affection for you, on account of his brother's love," he began, his own voice cold and aloof. "If he was with you in those final moments. . .it might unman him, cause him to lose sight of his purpose."

He saw the flash of anger in her eyes, raised a hand to cut her off. "You weaken us, sister. . .by your very presence, you cause us to lose strength. I have told you before that you should leave, go home—this jihad is not yours."

"This jihad belongs to everyone who has the faith to believe in it," she retorted, moving in closer to him. Picking up one of the suicide vests and lifting it up, against her chest. "If women were not meant to fight. . .why does one find them among the companions of the Prophet? Why did Nusaybah bint Ka'ab so nearly give her life, fighting by his side?"

Nusaybah, Harry thought, remembering the hadiths well. She had been one of Muhammad's earliest converts, and when the Muslim army had scattered before an enemy charge at the battle of Uhud, she had been one of only ten fighters who held their ground, fighting like demons, shielding their beloved prophet from his enemies, offering their own lives for his.

By the time the army rallied, she had received thirteen wounds and was fainting from loss of blood. *And truly Allah loves those who fight in His Cause in battle array. . .*

"This *is* my jihad," she said softly, sensing his hesitation, his weakness. Her hand, almost touching his. "I know what the French have done—what they did to me, what they did to Ghaniyah and her family in *Algérie*. And they are not *my* people anymore."

She had chosen her course, he realized, his head low, not meeting her eyes. That was all there was to it. And he would have to kill her for it. *Just like all the rest.*

If he was capable of it.

"You and I," Nora went on, as if still somehow seeking to persuade him, "are so very alike."

He doubted that very much, but he could hear the earnestness in her voice. The *tenderness.* And she wasn't done. "Neither one of us was born for this fight. We could have walked away from it, continued to drown ourselves in the meaningless existence of the West. We could have, and didn't, we chose the truth. . .and that's what makes our sacrifice important. It will finally force them—all of them—to *look* at what they have done. At what they have allowed to be done, in their name."

"It isn't, though," he responded quietly, finally looking her in the eye.

"Quoi?"

"Our sacrifice. It isn't any more important than that of anyone else—all of us, the same in the sight of Allah." He turned away, then, moving to the door. "Remember that, sister. And be ready."

12:03 P.M.
Saint-Marguerite
Marseille, France

"He was my only son," the older woman spat, more anger than sorrow in her voice as she glared daggers at Césaire. A natural reaction. *Shock.*

"He was a good man," he replied, a heavy sigh escaping his lips as he looked across at her, his hands folded helplessly in his lap.

They were about the same age, Daniel's mother and himself, driving home the realization as never before. . .that Daniel could have been his son. They had both seen the same France, if through different eyes. All it had done, all it could have been.

And yet here they both were, testament to a world changed so very much less than anyone might have wished.

"It was my honor to call him a friend," he went on, searching for words. He had never been any good at this. He was only here because of his promise.

"You were no *friend* of Daniel's," his mother responded, the words coming out in a low, venomous hiss, her hands distractedly smoothing the folds of her *abaya*. He began to reply, but stopped himself—knowing that there was no way to counter the accusation. That she was *right*, more than not.

A friend would have told him the truth.

"How did he die?" Hania asked, wiping the tears away from her bare cheek, clearly struggling to maintain her composure, to stave off the anger consuming her mother-in-law. Daniel's wife couldn't have been more than twenty-six—twenty-seven?—a dark-haired, slightly-built woman, more plain than pretty. But the way Daniel had glowed when speaking of her. . .

"The terrorist cell he had been tasked with infiltrating. . ." he began, choosing his words carefully, questioning how much detail to go into. *What to say.*

The little boy—Saphir, she had called him—had been packed off to the neighbor's house within minutes of his arrival, fear in his little face. *A premonition of evil.*

"They executed him," he said finally, unable to find a better way to say it. Ignoring the pulse of the phone in his pocket, an unnecessary distraction. *Not now.* "We believe they found out who he was. . .somehow, we don't know how."

"How did he die?" she repeated, her voice brittle—running her hands nervously along the legs of her jeans, one leg crossed over the other at the knee. Visually, the two women couldn't have been more different, but there was something of the desert in them both, an edge of resilience, bearing up under the pain.

"*Quoi?*" he asked, now unsure he had understood her question.

"*How* did they kill him?" There was pain in her eyes, shining through the tears, but there was no mistaking her resolve to know the truth. *No matter how brutal.*

"He was beheaded." He heard a deep, soul-rending groan escape the mother's lips, saw Hania tremble, controlling herself with an effort.

No doubt asking herself how she was going to break any of this to their son.

"Then. . .there is no body?"

"*Non.* Not that we have found, yet, at least. It has been several days," he admitted, feeling the phone pulse once again. Ignoring it further would be imprudent, he realized, retrieving it from the inner pocket of his jacket and glancing briefly at its screen—recognizing Godard's prefix.

"*Pardon*," he said, glancing between the women—embarrassed by the interruption. "I am afraid I must take this. It is—"

"Just leave us," Hania said, her voice nearly breaking as she rose to show him out. *"Si'l vous plait."*

"He was a good man," he repeated as she ushered him to the door of the small home, seeming at a loss for words of comfort, "and he always spoke fondly of you, and of Saphir. He loved you both, very much. I promise you that we—that *I*—will not rest until his death is avenged."

Césaire saw from her eyes that she did not believe him—*could not* allow herself to believe him. Cold comfort, in any case. Not another word passing between them as she showed him out onto the stairs, closing the door behind him.

An anguished cry breaking from somewhere within the house as he made his way down the first flight of stairs, a dam bursting beneath the weight of sorrow.

It felt as if his mission here had been a failure, but there could have been no other outcome. And he had kept his word.

Making his way out onto the street, he answered the phone as it began to ring once more. *"Quoi?"* he demanded angrily, his own pent-up emotions now flowing free.

"Vous êtes où?" Godard's voice, as he had expected. *Where are you?*

"With the Mahrez family, as ordered. In Marseille. I was with them when you called."

"We need you back in Paris," his supervisor replied, a strange tension in the man's voice. "As soon as possible—a police helicopter will pick you up at the *aéroport.* LYSANDER's laptop has been found. . ."

Chapter 36

1:47 P.M.
The safehouse
Coulommiers, France

Loose hair fell away from Harry's face as he guided the clippers across his cheek, trimming his beard down to a half-inch, removing the scraggly excess which had built up over the last few weeks.

Purifying himself. Preparing his own body for death, in accordance with the teachings of the *sunnah*. Some of the younger men were going the whole way and shaving their faces clean, but that wasn't a step he was prepared to take. Even this. . .was dangerously close to how he might have looked in whatever jacket photos the French would have on hand.

It wouldn't matter, he told himself, once he was dead. *Nothing would.*

He turned off the clippers, placing them to one side of the sink as he turned the faucet on hot, water splashing into his cupped hands. Harry raised them up, smoothing them over his cheeks—droplets of water dripping down from what remained of his beard as he stared into the mirror, barely recognizing the man who stared back at him.

A stranger. In far more ways than one.

How long he had stood there when the knock came at the bathroom, Aryn's voice demanding, "Ibrahim?" he didn't know, but the sound jarred him back to the present. The realities of what remained for him to do.

"Your turn, *habibi*," he smiled as he opened the door, clapping Aryn on the back as he pushed past him into the hall.

"*Mash'allah,*" Yassin exclaimed, humor twinkling in his dark eyes as Harry

512

joined the rest of the group in the main room of the residence. "*So* beautiful."

Harry laughed, cuffing the younger man as he ran a hand over the remains of his beard. "Control yourself, brother."

The laughter sounded false, at least to his own ears—a mockery of the betrayal to come.

"Here, take these," he heard Faouzi say, nudging him in the arm with an elbow. He looked down into the Algerian's outstretched hand, seeing a dozen or more small, off-white pills.

"Are these what I. . ."

"Captagon," Belkaïd announced from across the room, nodding. "You no doubt remember them from *Sham*."

Harry nodded slowly, his eyes never leaving the older man's face. *Fenethylline.* A compound of amphetamine and theophylline, it had long been a drug of choice among jihadists—a powerful stimulant that kept a man alert, sent him into battle riding a euphoric high, fear stripped away.

Youth, adrenaline, religion, and drugs—a potent cocktail for belief in one's own immortality. *Power.*

"It's important that you all take them before tonight's attack," Belkaïd continued, glancing around at the men assembled before him—a smile touching his lips as his eyes settled on Nora, standing off to one side. "They will calm you, keep you alert. Ensure that you do not hesitate, in those final moments before death."

No second thoughts. Harry saw Yassin nod, popping one of the tablets into his own mouth and chewing. He'd no doubt take a couple more over the course of the next few hours, smothering any pain from the still-healing wound he had received from Lahcen's men back there on the Outremeuse.

"*Non,*" Harry responded, pushing away Faouzi's hand. "Not for me."

The movement caught Belkaïd's attention. "*Pour quoi?*"

"When I was an unbeliever—far from the light of God—I did drugs," he replied, his eyes hard, unyielding. "That was something I left behind me in Germany. . .I will never go back."

10:03 A.M. Eastern Daylight Time
The apartment
Washington, D.C.

". . .sources within the White House have confirmed to Fox News that DNI Lawrence Bell has formally tendered his resignation, after accepting responsibility for June's drone strike in the Sinai, which failed to kill its target, Umar ibn Hassan."

Sources. Bernard Kranemeyer snorted, leaning against the counter in his boxer shorts and a light t-shirt, a cup of coffee in his hand. With Fox the administration's outlet of choice for any and all "leaks" which furthered their own narratives, the "source" for that information was like as not Norton himself. Or his chief of staff. They'd want to put it out themselves, ensure their spin was placed on it.

And it was done, at least for now. The hearings would continue, into the next week, but the scapegoat had been chosen—was already being led out into the wilderness.

It was a strangely empty feeling, the inevitability of it all. The feeling of defeat, even though he and Bell had executed their plan without difficulty. *No one should have been sacrificed.*

But that wasn't their reality. And this wasn't about victory—or what was *right.* This was about surviving, another day.

Might not be much more than a day, at that—even with Bell's seppuku, the rumblings of a reintroduction of the Intelligence Bill hadn't stopped swirling. The administration, flailing in the throes of self-inflicted wounds, still struggling to find a way to turn events to the service of their own agenda.

This fight. . .far from over. But this battle, at least, had been won—for this moment. Thanks to one man's sacrifice.

His expression lost in his coal-black eyes, Kranemeyer raised the cup of coffee in a toast as an image of Lawrence Bell appeared on-screen, accompanying the talking heads' ongoing prattle.

To a brave American.

10:34 A.M.
Fort Washington Park
Fort Washington, MD

He knew she was there before she spoke—something of her footsteps against the brick giving her away, a familiar cadence.

"You pick the strangest places for us to meet."

"I pick places neither your colleagues nor mine are ever likely to frequent," Ian Cahill replied, resting his elbows easily on the brick parapet, his eyes scanning out over the descending slope toward the waters of the Potomac, sparkling bright in the early morning sun. "It's the safest that way, for the both of us."

The former White House chief of staff looked back to see Coftey's secretary step over the large concrete semi-circle which once served as a swivel rail, enabling the fort's massive Rodman guns to be traversed back and forth—commanding the river below.

Melody's low heel caught on the concrete, and she let out a low curse, regaining her balance with an effort before joining him at the parapet. "It's a beautiful view. . .I had no idea this place was here."

"Most people in D.C. don't," he observed, the irony in his voice going unnoticed. This fort had stood in protection of the capital for two hundred years, and most of the people whom it had protected were never even aware of its existence.

Would never have known, unless one day the ships of an enemy had sailed up the Potomac. . .and this fort was all that stood in their way.

"The message you sent me," he went on after a long moment, turning to face her, his left arm still resting on the wall, "you're certain?"

She swallowed hard, nodding. If she hadn't understood the stakes before—and he was somehow sure she hadn't—she was beginning to. And she was frightened.

For good reason.

"It's him," she replied, "the voice, the face. . .I'm sure of it. Bernard Kranemeyer is the man who was at Coftey's ranch on the night of the Fourth. I'm certain."

"Good," Cahill responded, his eyes grave as he looked at her, "because we can't be making any mistakes about that sort of thing. Not now."

Another nod.

"It would explain everything," he relented, turning his gaze back to the river. "Those who were willing to talk, but knew nothing. Those who wouldn't, but did. The Director of the Clandestine Service is a formidable man, as is Senator Coftey. Together, they're a force to be reckoned with. But now they're vulnerable, and don't yet know it. Which only leaves the question: just how far are you prepared to go?"

5:39 P.M. Central European Summer Time
DGSE Headquarters
Paris, France

"Have you tried his wife's birthday?" Césaire asked, running dark fingers through his curly silver hair. He had only arrived at the headquarters building on the Boulevard Mortier twenty minutes before, after an extremely long flight from the southern coast of France.

A flight full of regret and self-recrimination. Surely there had been a better way to handle things with Daniel's family, a way which could have left them less. . .devastated. *Non.* That was absurd. There was nothing he could have said or done that could have made it better. Only done his *job* in the first place, protected the younger officer as he should have.

"Certainement," the young technical officer replied, with a backward glance over his shoulder which implied Césaire took him for a fool. "It was one of the first passcodes we tried after receiving the laptop four hours ago. We may have to brute-force it."

"How long will that take?" Albert Godard asked, leaning against the door of the room.

The younger man shrugged expansively. *"C'est difficile à dire*
. . .for an alphanumeric passcode like this one, could be eighteen-twenty hours, perhaps more. We *will* get in, though—you have my word."

Godard and Césaire exchanged glances before the supervisor shook his head. "We may not have that kind of time."

The older intelligence officer swore softly, kneading his brow with the fingers of his right hand. His mind racing, straining to come up with a solution. There had to be an *answer* here. . .something obvious, he was missing.

The training centre. . .naturellement!

"He often spoke proudly of the day he finished training," Césaire exclaimed, his face suddenly animated, his eyes flashing as he looked across at Godard, "and officially became a member of the secret service. Do we know what date that would have been?"

"I'm not sure. . ."

"It would have been three years ago," Césaire went on, not waiting for an answer, "a spring course, I believe. . .sometime in April."

Godard nodded quickly, turning to the workstation computer in front of the technical officer. *"Excusez-moi."*

A handful of keystrokes later, and he looked up. *"Oui.* The 25th of April."

"Do it," Césaire ordered, finding his pulse beating quicker as he rested a hand on the back of the technical officer's chair. *Was it possible that they would learn what he had been trying to tell them? What had gotten him killed?*

Another moment, and the officer shook his head. *Nothing. Come on.*

"He was trained at the centre in Perpignan—add that to the date."

Again, the sound of the technical officer's fingers clattering against the keys, the keystrokes sounding unnaturally loud in the stillness of the room. And again, the shake of the head.

"Non."

6:15 P.M.
Saint-Denis, Seine-Saint-Denis,
Paris, France

The game wouldn't begin for the better part of another couple hours, but the crowds were already streaming into the stadium—men and women elbowing and jostling their way past Grigoriy Stepanovich Kolesnikov as he stood there at the corner of the Rue de Brennus and the Avenue Jules Rimet.

It went against all protocol for him to be here, visiting the scene in advance of the attack, but he'd had to *see it*, for himself. And he had seen few surveillance cameras covering the streets of Saint-Denis on his way in, though he felt certain that the entrances to the stadium itself were blanketed.

Would need to be, for security teams to even begin to screen the volume. *So many people.*

So many of whom would be dead or injured by the time this night was over. The Russian intelligence officer smiled—he shouldn't allow himself to think of this attack in terms of body count, they would be lucky to even rival Bataclan, and only then if Belkaïd's martyrs got very, very lucky in the chaos at the gates.

But terrorism was never about body count. It was about *fear.* And every one of these thousands who filed past him toward the lettered gates of the *Stade de France* was going to know fear by the time this night ended.

The assassination of their head of state, before their very eyes. . .gunfire and even more bombings filling the night as men and women poured uncontrollably from the stadium following the attack. Likely more people would be trampled than killed by the explosives he had supplied to Belkaïd.

And what would happen after, as an already-destabilized France reacted to the chaos. . .another quiet smile lit up Litvinov's face as he turned away, melting into the crowd.

Another barrier to Russia's ascendancy in Europe, removed. *Glory.*

5:26 P.M. British Summer Time
HMP Belmarsh
Thamesmead, Southeast London

". . .and if you will just sign here, please. . .yes, and also here. . ."

Julian Marsh looked away as Alec MacCallum took the pen, his former colleague's hand seeming to tremble as he scrawled his signature across the forms, pausing only briefly to ask another question of the female officer. The very last formalities, prior to his release.

He would leave here a free man, Her Majesty's government dropping all charges against him in the wake of Norris' confession.

A free man but a shattered one, Marsh thought, noting the pallor of the man's face, the unsteadiness of his hand. For a careerist like MacCallum—a man who had given so much of his life to the Service—the very suspicion of treason had been worse than any death sentence.

He was gaunt now, the street clothes Marsh had brought hanging loosely on his body—his eyes ringed with loss of sleep. A shell of the once-confident branch head who had run G Branch for so much of Marsh's own tenure at Thames House.

"Thanks for coming out here today, sir," MacCallum said a few minutes later, as they made their way out past uniformed guards to the carpark, his voice hesitant, uncertain. Barely above a whisper.

"Julian," the former director-general corrected gently, searching for words. "We're not at Thames House anymore."

And weren't going to be, either of them, ever again. That hardest of truths. A door closing, forever.

"I should have believed you," he continued after a moment, the sun burning down upon them as they walked out through the rows of parked vehicles, heat radiating up from the asphalt. "You deserved that much."

No response, and he shook his head. "Mehreen, Darren, all of the chaos with the Americans, and then Colville. . .it was a time of great uncertainty, and my faith in you wavered. Forgive me."

Another long, painful pause. "You did what you felt best. . .Julian. For the good of the Service. I don't blame you." MacCallum stopped short, his voice faltering. "There were moments in. . .*there*, I hardly believed myself innocent, given all the evidence. Hardly could have expected you to have done so."

"That doesn't change a thing," Marsh replied grimly. "I had a duty to my *officers*, as well as the Service. And you were one of my best."

Were. All of that, now behind them both. They reached the silver Vauxhall just then, and Marsh opened the back door for his colleague, catching the shock in MacCallum's eyes as he recognized Phillip Greer sitting behind the wheel. One could feel the hesitation with which he closed the door, the uncertainty. Recognizing in the head of CI the man who had, more than perhaps anyone else besides Norris, been responsible for his confinement.

A tense silence reigning in the car as Marsh opened his own door, sliding in on the passenger seat. Then Greer reached forward to shift the car into drive, glancing in his rear-view mirror at MacCallum as he pulled out of the space.

"I'm sorry."

A weary shake of the head served as MacCallum's answer, weary and saddened. "I told you that you had the wrong man."

Greer nodded soberly. "You did. I don't apologize for not believing you—there was no reason to. But I apologize for not looking closer, for not *finding* those reasons. That was my job, and I failed."

And that failure had destroyed a man's career, as they all knew. As MacCallum grasped without bothering to ask. The charges might have been dropped, but he'd never work for the Service again. He'd have to find some way to start over—find a new career, more than half-way through his life.

It wasn't an enviable lot.

"At least you got him," Alec MacCallum observed finally, as Greer pulled out onto the A2016, merging with traffic. "You found the mole."

And so they had, Marsh reflected, knowing what MacCallum did not. His eyes growing hard as he stared at the road ahead. *But not in time.*

6:33 P.M. Central European Summer Time
Saint-Denis, Seine-Saint-Denis,
Paris, France

Sergeant Nathalie Jobert wiped away sweat from her forehead with the back of a gloved hand as she scanned the crowd toward the stadium through her binoculars. There had been a warning of possible protesters in the final GSPR briefing—remnants of the crowd which had besieged the US Embassy in the early weeks of July, protesting against American drone policy in the Middle East—but there was no sign of them, yet. The Parisian summer had seemed to sap their fervor as the weeks went by, all but the most dedicated melting away—back into the streets.

Here, now—she could understand why. The late afternoon sun still beating down with a fierce intensity, the bare roof offering no cover—no relief from the oppressive, baking heat.

Too hot for Glatigny to spend long on the roof—she wouldn't be bringing the eagle's carrier up for a while yet, in fact, she would be going back down herself in twenty minutes.

But it was as good a vantage point as she could have hoped for, the swelling sides of *Stade de France* itself rising to the west—her view to the east unobstructed out across the Seine, the runways of Le Bourget just barely visible nearly six kilometers away.

She lowered the binoculars, exchanging a tight-lipped smile with the young airman who had been tasked to work as her assistant. "This is going to work, Jacques. Now, just to hope we are not needed, *non*?"

He simply nodded quickly, his nerves showing on his face as Jobert checked her watch. Another couple hours before President Albéric arrived on site. . .

Not very long.

7:48 P.M.
Montmorency Forest, Val d'Oise
North of Paris

Paradise. It almost seemed as if they might already have entered *jannah*, Harry thought, drinking in the cool of the shade, dappled sunlight filtering through the leaves of the chestnut trees above to strike his face.

Arms folded easily across his chest as he scanned the open field out toward the pond—watching as Yassin, Aryn, and a younger enforcer named Abdelatif kicked a soccer ball back and forth across the grass. Idling away their remaining time before launch.

It reminded him strangely of a picnic—a barbecue back home, though it had been years since the last one he'd bothered to attend. The younger guys, out back playing touch football as meat sizzled on the grill.

A hundred meters away, Nora strolled aimlessly over by the pond, her hair uncovered for the first time since he had seen her in Reza's bed there in Molenbeek, striving now to look as non-Muslim as possible.

It came naturally to her.

Of their little band of *shahid,* only Faouzi seemed determined not to enjoy his last few hours on earth. . .a scowl plastered across the older man's face as he sprawled in the grass—leaning up against the nearmost van's rear tire, whittling away at a scrap piece of wood with a penknife. A carving he would never finish.

Perhaps he was thinking of his crippled son. Or his coming vengeance. *Likely both.*

They were not alone in this part of the forest—there had been at least four or five groups of passerby in the hour since they had arrived, but it was about as secluded as they were likely to get, this close to Paris.

No one had given them more than a passing glance. There would be no salvation coming from that direction—no heroic bystander, coming to the rescue. *"If you see something, say something."*

He had thought it might be possible to place a call—even now—to the French police, but their cellphones had been stripped and destroyed back in Coulommiers, just before their departure. All that remained to them, the presumably encrypted radios they would use to coordinate the attack, down to the very last second.

"It is nearly time, brother," Gamal Belkaïd said, a smile on the older man's face as he came up to Harry. "The moment we have all dreamed of for so long."

Harry nodded, suppressing the bile that seemed to rise in his throat at the words. *This* was *really happening.*

"*Insh'allah,*" he replied simply. "We are in God's hands now, as ever before."

A nod. "Call your men in. . .it's time to give them their final instructions."

8:05 P.M.
DGSE Headquarters
Paris, France

The tension in the small office in the basement of the Boulevard Mortier headquarters building had become nearly unbearable—silence broken only by murmured suggestions, followed by the rapid-fire *click* of keys, answered always with the technical officer's crestfallen, almost sullen *"Non."*

Armand Césaire kneaded his brow with the fingertips of both hands, wishing for all the world that he could lock himself away in a room for an hour, with only his classic jazz to keep him company. Perhaps something from Jo Maka. . .music had always helped him think, relax—process hard problems. But his phone, with all his music, was securely locked away, several floors up.

He let out a heavy sigh, burying his head in his hands as he struggled to think of what they could possibly be missing, what they might have overlooked. Some *aspect* of Daniel Mahrez's life they hadn't considered, they hadn't known. . .some. . .

Wait. What had he just thought? Of Daniel Mahrez's life. . .but of course!

"Je suis imbécile!" he exclaimed, punctuating his words with a curse. *Of course.* Godard looked over at him with a start, the supervisor's eyes betraying bewilderment at the sudden outburst.

"He wouldn't have used anything connected to his *real* life," Césaire explained, the words pouring out of him in a rush as he cursed himself for this oversight, brought on by lack of sleep, the emotion of the day. "It would have been based in his *legend*. I need everything we worked up to backstop Marwan Abdellaoui. And I need it now."

8:07 P.M.
The Montmorency Forest, Val D'oise
North of Paris

". . .in another thirty minutes, we'll launch the drones," Harry said, looking around into the faces of the jihadists surrounding him. *His men*, perverse as that seemed, "and bring them to an altitude of two hundred feet ASL, placing them in a pre-programmed orbit over the densest part of the forest. That's where they'll stay, as we make our way into Saint-Denis itself. . .we have no good way of knowing how long it will take us to work our way through traffic into our launch positions for the final attack, and we don't need the quadcopters drawing attention to themselves during that delay. With the President in play, the security presence will no doubt be heavy."

"The drones should have enough battery life to account for the delay," Gamal Belkaïd interjected, picking up where Harry had left off. "But we will want to minimize it as much as possible, to preclude unforeseen difficulties. As soon as the drivers reach their destinations, they will make contact with each other, and hand off comms to the pilots, who will then bring the UAVs out of orbit and in toward the *Stade de France*, while the assault teams go ahead and move into position at the gates. Once the French President has been slain, the pilots will then drive the vans in as close as is possible to the crowds fleeing the stadium, and then detonate the explosives in both vehicles."

Harry's head came up at those last words, knowing that surprise—if not outright consternation—must be visible in his eyes. "I did not understand that—"

"It was a good plan, Ibrahim," the older man returned with a smile. "But even the best of plans can be improved—and we had unused explosives. I had my men rig the bodywork of both vans yesterday afternoon. The carnage should be. . .devastating."

"Alhamdullilah," Harry whispered, forcing the words past this throat with a painful effort. *Praise be to God.*

So *that* was what they'd been doing after their return from the abortive test flight—while he'd been arguing with Belkaïd, trying to sort out a way to yet disable the drones themselves. *The folly of it all.*

He'd allowed his vision to narrow to a singular focus, ignoring all else.

And now people were going to die. . .

8:23 P.M.
Saint-Denis, Seine-Saint-Denis
Paris, France

There he is, Sergeant Jobert thought, adjusting the binoculars to her eyes as she focused in on the figure of the French President, stepping out of the limousine—pausing briefly to wave to the crowd before the phalanx of Leseur's officers closed back upon their principal, hurrying him in through the gates of the *Stade de France*—out of earshot of those few protesters who had actually shown up—perhaps forty of them, at most, waving their signs and cardboard mock-ups of American Predator drones, chanting over and again in French, *"Drones kill kids."*

"Roland Actual, this is Baligant-1," she heard over her earpiece, the voice of one of the GSPR snipers positioned—like herself—on a nearby rooftop. "We have the principal on location, entering the *Stade* itself now—losing visual. No visible threats."

Nothing. If there was going to be an attack, this was when they had expected it to come—the moment when he was most exposed, the crowds at their peak. Jobert raised her eyes to the sky, glimpsing the majestic, regal form of Glatigny in the distance, soaring above the stadium. The massive raptor ever alert, ever watchful.

"Magnifique," she murmured, struck by the same awe she ever felt watching him fly. The effortless grace with which he mounted to the heavens.

Perhaps this would be a quiet evening, after all.

8:29 P.M.
The Montmorency Forest, Val D'oise
North of Paris

Even two hundred feet up, you could hear the hum of the quadcopters' rotors. A vague, indistinct sound—but very much *there*, if you knew what you were listening for.

Harry took another look at his computer screen, marking the positions of both drones on the tracking software, confirming that they had entered their preset orbits over the forest.

Time to move.

"May God be praised," he said, forcing a smile as he dismounted from the van. "We are fully operational, my brothers. *Allahu akbar!*"

"*Allahu akbar!*" the answering shout went up, the passion—the fire—visible in the eyes of the men surrounding him.

Nora didn't join in the cry, taught like any good Muslim woman not to raise her voice in the company of men, but the fire was there, all the same. *She was in this*. No second thoughts, no hesitation.

Aryn reached out, and Harry drew him into a fierce embrace—hugging him tight, feeling the bulk of the suicide vest beneath his loose shirt. "Till *jannah*, brother."

"Till *jannah*."

Yassin was next, his eyes shining with tears as they embraced. "I *knew*, brother—from the moment I met you—I knew my life had forever changed."

So it had, Harry thought, only too aware of the irony as he hugged the man who had saved his life in that boxing club in Molenbeek. *From Marwan*, irony of ironies, compounding upon each other.

All their lives, changing in those moments. *Forever*. "Go with God," he managed, the words seeming to struggle to emerge from his throat. He clapped Yassin on the back as they disengaged, stepping back from his friend. "Till *jannah*."

"*Ameen.*"

8:49 P.M.
DGSE Headquarters
Paris, France

"They're planning an attack. . .next Saturday. . ."

Armand Césaire heard a low curse break from Brunet's lips, his own face twisting into a grimace as they all listened to the audio fade into a distorted mass of static, the corruption of the recovered file proving fatal.

"We have to shut them down, immédiatement,*"* he heard the voice of his damned officer say, uttering the words which had condemned him to death. The last message he had never lived to deliver. Perhaps even the one he had tried to leave for them in that *cinema* in Liège, before becoming spooked by Danloy's officers. *"We—"*

More static, the face of Daniel's mother and the wife rising before him in this moment. The *sorrow*, the pain.

"We need to know what he said," he heard the director announce, her voice cold as ice—clearly unaffected by the personal dimension of what they were hearing.

A part of him hated Brunet for it, a greater part recognizing that this *was* her job. To remain detached, above all else. Focused on the mission—*their mission.*

We are all pawns, he thought, reminding himself of what he had ever known. *In the service of the Republic.*

"I am sorry, *madame le directeur,*" the young technical officer replied, looking back over his shoulder at her. "I will do what I can, but the recovery process is very difficult for a file this corrupted. It appears that it has already been deleted and recovered once, then deleted again. And now to recover it again. . .it is not impossible, but it will be difficult to get any more than I've recovered already."

He had tried to cover his tracks, Césaire realized, envisioning the scene all too clearly in his head. *Tried and failed.*

"I don't need an explanation," Brunet responded, resting a hand briefly on the technical officer's shoulder. Looking down into his eyes. "I need results. Get to work. Albert—flash Leseur. Tell her the attack was to be today, have her put her people on alert."

9:01 P.M.
Saint-Denis
Paris, France

It should have taken barely thirty minutes to drive from the forest to the stadium, on a normal day. But this was no normal day—the district around the *Stade de France* choked with traffic—and they were still on the other side of the Seine, having driven farther toward Le Bourget than strictly necessary, in order to approach the stadium from the east.

Harry leaned back in the driver's seat, glancing at the GPS mounted to the windshield, giving him the van's updated ETA on their target. *7:13*.

This was going to cut it close, even on flight time, if they waited to launch until they were in position. . .giving the quadcopters barely ten minutes of battery power left when they reached the stadium.

A part of him hoped they didn't make it—that they came crashing down, out of power, somewhere short of the target.

But he knew better than to harbor such thoughts. Hope was a mirage, a phantasm clung to by those who couldn't bring themselves to face the truth.

The truth of what he was going to have to do—to set this *right*. His hand slipped from the steering wheel to his lap, feeling the bulge of the knife tucked into his waistband, on his left side, beneath the jacket. The compact CZ, in its holster on his right.

The pistol would have been more certain—but he had no suppressor for it. . .a last resort, at best. Particularly in these initial moments. It would have to be the knife.

His gaze shifted to the rear-view mirror, taking in the sight of Nora, sitting behind him on the bench seats lining each side of the back of the utility van—a *tasbih* in her hands, the beads running self-consciously through her fingers as she recited the names of God beneath her breath. *Who had taught her that?*

Reza, most likely. As Reza had taught her everything—rescuing her, nurturing her. Giving her life new meaning, new purpose in the wake of loss.

Bringing her down a path that would lead to the loss of it all.

"This is our turn," Faouzi announced from his position at the laptop, clearly keeping track of their progress himself as Harry swung the utility van out into heavy traffic on the Rue Francis de Pressensé, a tree-shaded street choked with vehicles. "Only half a kilometer or so to the river."

Almost there. He glimpsed a smile cross Nora's face at the words, trying and failing to answer it with one of his own. Knowing that it was almost time.

And that he would have to kill her first.

9:09 P.M.
The Stade de France
Saint-Denis, Seine-Saint-Denis

"Understood," Marion Leseur responded, the phone pressed against her ear as she made her way through the back corridors of the stadium. "*Oui. Certainement.* I am on my way to him now."

Another moment's pause, as she listened. "Can you give me nothing more specific, Anaïs? He is going to want specifics."

"I have given you all I have," she heard Brunet respond, "and I know it's not much. It is even possible that the compromise of our officer may have caused them to scrap their plans altogether. This could all be for nothing— but we *cannot* rely on that. I will keep you apprised of any further developments."

"*Merci,*" Leseur returned shortly, spying one of her men near the door of the presidential box as she returned the phone to the inner pocket of her suit. "We may have a potential threat against our principal—pass the word to your men and be prepared to move out. I will need to speak with the President."

9:11 P.M.

Out on the pitch of the Stade de France, Kylian Mbappé sent the ball flying toward the opposing team's goal with a precisely-executed scissor kick, the sweat on the footballer's dark face visible as he ran, the roar of the crowd drowning out all else. . .

Chapter 37

"We have arrived," Harry heard Faouzi announce into his radio, a glance into the rear-view mirror showing him the Algerian's face as he pulled the white utility van to a stop along the side of the Rue de Brennus, beneath the shade of an elm—the very edge of the circular stadium roof just visible in the distance, like a glimpse of an alien craft come in for a landing.

Aryn, Yassin, and their driver had—according to their earlier transmission—reached their destination farther north along the Rue de l'Olympisme nearly five minutes before.

Reached it, and begun waiting. Timing, coordination was everything—the lesson drilled into them over the course of the previous week.

"*Oui.* Initiating. . .taking the vehicle off autopilot, programming a new course, heading one-four-nine."

In his mind's eye, Harry could see Aryn running through the same procedure. . .both UAVs coming out of their programmed orbit—moving south at a lumbering, burdened seventy kilometers an hour.

It had begun.

He pushed open the door of the van, and stepped out onto the pavement—the knife enclosed in his fist as he scanned his surroundings for a brief moment, marking the positions of nearby pedestrians, passing cars. Knowing that his zipped-up jacket, the bulk of the explosive vest beneath, made him conspicuous in the August heat.

Time was precious. In more ways than one.

529

A few short, hurried steps and he was at the back of the van, giving a short rap against the back door panel. *All clear.*

A moment passed, then two—irreplaceable seconds ticking by, his palms growing slick with sweat. Fingers clenching and unclenching around the hilt of the knife. *Come on.*

Just as he was about to reach up and wrench the door open, he heard the scrape of metal against metal—felt the door being pushed outward, Nora's face appearing in the opening.

She smiled, a wan, nervous smile—handing him the cut-down, short-barreled AK-103 he was to conceal under his jacket.

"Keep it," Harry replied shortly, catching her off-guard. "Take my hand."

Tucking the rifle against her side, she accepted his hand to help her down from the van, moving hesitantly in the heavy vest. There was something in her eyes. . .something of *hesitation*—was she having second thoughts? A change of heart?

But there was no time. No chance for repentance. Those exits passed, for all of them, so very long ago.

His right hand coming up, moving fast—even as she relinquished her hold on his left, turning to close the door behind her.

Her eyes opening wide in surprise, her lips parting in a scream that would never be uttered as the knife went in, deep into her neck, his hand clamped over her mouth as he slammed her back into the door of the van with his own body, driving the blade home. His left hand wrapping around the AK's receiver, controlling the weapon.

Bright red arterial blood spurting out over his hand, the sleeve of his jacket.

Nora's eyes, only inches away from his own—filled with shock and fear, her face distorting in agony as she struggled beneath him, growing weaker with every passing second—the life draining from their depths. *Forgive me.*

"What's going on?" he heard Faouzi demand, clearly having heard the sound of the struggle. Footsteps, against the bare metal of the van's floor—moving the few short steps to the door.

He moved to withdraw the blade from her neck, the flesh seeking to close around it—to hold it fast—even as the opposite door came open, the Algerian crouched in the opening, shock playing across his face.

Out of time. The knife refused to give, the shock in Faouzi's eyes changing to anger—his hand moving toward his gun.

Harry brought the Kalashnikov up in his left hand, slamming it butt-first into the older man's face.

Caught off-balance, resting on his heels, Faouzi crashed backward onto the floor of the van—the half-drawn pistol clattering away from him as Harry tore the knife away with one final desperate wrench, letting Nora's body crumple to the pavement.

His hand seizing hold of the door, levering himself into the back of the van just as the Algerian rose, reaching out for the headset he had taken off at the sound of the struggle, left abandoned on the laptop keyboard.

Attempting to scream a warning.

Harry's hand closed around the headset's cord, ripping it out of the laptop's USB port even as Faouzi reached it, the tip of his knife raking along the man's forearm.

The Algerian screamed, a sound full of pain and hate, lashing out, heedless of the knife—driving Harry back against the side of the van—neither man able to stand aright in the confines of the vehicle.

"All that time," he spat, taking advantage of the opening to hammer home another punishing blow to Harry's ribs, "you were one of *them*."

9:17 P.M.
The Stade de France

"Look," President Denis Albéric began, taking Leseur's arm and guiding her away from the group, to a quieter corner of the room, "I comprehend your position, Marion. And I appreciate your concern for my welfare. But this is an important night for me—look around you, at these people. All of them, are important to me. Do you understand?"

There had to have been at least fifty people in the massive skybox, *Commissaire* Leseur thought, her eyes following the direction of Albéric's gesture. Not counting the serving-staff or her own security personnel, strategically positioned throughout the room.

There had been fifty-five names on the guest list, all of them carefully vetted by her people. CEOs, foreign diplomats—high-ranking members of Albéric's government, even a few *députés* from the opposition.

All of them milling around—talking, sipping champagne, sparing only the occasional glance at the game proceeding on the pitch below. The game wasn't why any of them were here, it was about the *prestige* of being here.

"Oui," she nodded briefly, resigning herself to his decision. He wasn't going to be moved now, any more than he had been in the debates leading up to this night.

And perhaps it was all for the best—the windows of the skybox itself were constructed of heavy, impact-resistant glass that would stop most anything short of an artillery shell. Her guards, posted at every exit.

He was likely as secure here as he could be anywhere else. "I understand."

9:18 P.M.
Saint-Denis, Seine-Saint-Denis

One of them. The words seemed to ring, over and again through his head as he struggled to keep his feet—pain shooting through his body, the impact reawakening the wounds he had suffered on the docks of Aberdeen.

The wounds which had nearly taken his life, which had brought him to this place. Here, at the end of it all.

One of them. One of the Western security services. Of the police. Of those who had crippled the Algerian's son.

He could smell the hate, the thirst for vengeance, on the man's breath as he closed in—recognized that deadly passion. *So familiar.* So destructive, as he had learned to his own sorrow. His head was swimming with pain, his brain refusing to process what was happening. *But he still had the knife.* Some elusive part of his subconscious clinging to it, like a drowning man to a scrap of wood.

"You betrayed all of us, didn't you?" the Algerian demanded, his face only inches away from Harry's, eyes filled with anguish and rage as he forced the knife hand back, fighting to control it—that deadly blade glittering in the fading rays of sun streaming in through the front windshield of the van, falling upon the faces of the struggling men.

He wasn't going to last long—not like this, Harry thought, fighting through the pain, struggling to think clearly as he fought back, resisting Faouzi's attempts to wrest the knife from him. He'd underestimated the Algerian. . .or perhaps overestimated himself. Perhaps it would have even been better to have taken the proffered Captagon, the drugs coursing through the man's body fueling his rage—giving him an undeniable edge.

Fighting to maintain his balance, Harry pulled his head back, smashing his forehead into the older man's face—the impact leaving his head swirling, a curse breaking from Faouzi's lips as he staggered back, taken off-guard. *Leaving himself open.*

Harry pushed himself off the side of the van, seizing the opportunity— the knife flickering out, into the Algerian's side, its blade sinking deep into the man's unguarded armpit, seeking the axillary artery.

Faouzi screamed in pain, a pain too sharp to be masked by the drugs. His eyes wide, blood flowing freely from the wound, staining his shirt as Harry pulled the knife back out, delivering a vicious elbow strike to the point of the man's chin—rocking him back.

He went down—hard—crashing into the crude wooden platform, his outstretched arm knocking the laptop to the floor as he fell to lie motionless, seemingly unconscious. . .the only movement the steadily widening pool of blood issuing from the wound beneath his arm.

He would bleed out long before he ever woke up, Harry realized, breathing heavily as he staggered to one side—wiping the blade of the knife against the dark fabric of his jeans. *Still alive.*

It came as almost something of a shock—the realization of his own survival. His breath coming in huge gasps as he collapsed against the side of the van—forcing himself to focus, to work past the pain now throbbing through his body.

How long had the fight even lasted? It seemed like an eternity, and yet when he glanced at his watch, barely three minutes had elapsed since he had stepped from the driver's seat of the van, since Nora. . .

Nora.

9:20 P.M.
Groslay
Eight kilometers north of the Stade de France

At six hundred feet ASL the pair of Guardian UAVs were almost undetectable from the ground—all but invisible against the darkening sky, spaced nearly seven hundred meters apart, the sound of their whirring rotors lost in the air as they moved south. Following their pre-programmed course toward Seine Saint-Denis and the Stade itself to the waypoint where, two kilometers out, their operators would once again resume direct control.

Seven minutes.

9:21 P.M.
Saint-Denis, Seine-Saint-Denis

Harry folded the knife back in upon itself, his gaze torn between the laptop lying by the floor by Faouzi's body, offering control of the UAV. . .and the knowledge that she was still laying there, exposed in the street. A peril to him, in every passing moment.

Another six minutes, and the drones would reach their target, but the risk. . .

There was no choice.

He tucked the knife back into his pocket, pushing open the door to step back out once more into the gathering shadows of the Paris night. Cars passed, their lights reflecting off the side panels of the van, the noise of their engines nearly drowning out the laughter of pedestrians from just down the street, but if anyone had noticed the body of the woman huddled there in a heap at the rear of the white van. . .no one had cared.

Her face was pale in the twilight, eyes wide, her face still distorted in that mixture of agony and surprise which had been her last emotion on this earth. Her head lolling helplessly to one side as he slipped his hands underneath her arms—trying and failing to lift her, the dead weight too much for him in his exhaustion and pain.

You're getting too old for this, a voice within reminded him. *Hard truth.* And then he saw them—a group of young men, moving down the sidewalk toward him from back in the direction of the Seine—dressed in footballer jerseys, their laughter giving them away in the semi-darkness.

Too close.

9:23 P.M.
DGSE Headquarters
Paris, France

"They're planning an attack," Césaire heard Daniel Mahrez's voice announce for what seemed like the hundredth time in the last half hour. Over and over again, as the DGSE technical officers worked with the recovered file, trying to restore the corrupted seconds of audio.

The voice of a dead man, crying out a warning from beyond the grave.

". . .with weapons supplied by a. . ." Césaire's head came up, a glimmer of hope appearing in his eyes, even as the audio faded once more to static. *That was new.*

If they could recover that much, perhaps. . .

"It's set f. . .next Saturday, on the. . ."

The next word was there, but it was indistinct, almost lost in a haze of white noise—the technical officers skipping the audio back five seconds to listen again.

"It's set f. . .next Saturday, on the St. . ."

Was it "*Stud*"? But that made no sense. *"Quoi?"* he heard one of the officers demand, equally puzzled—playing it back one more time.

And then he heard it, the sound of the word driving an icy dagger into his heart—his hand reaching out instinctively for the phone on the desk of the technical officer before him. Fearing it was perhaps already too late.

"Stade. . ."

Chapter 38

". . .*c'est impossible*. . .you'll see. He'll come through for us, always does. . .he needs to start soon, if he's going to be of any use. . ."

Snatches of conversation, drifting through the open window of the utility van as Harry hunched down in the driver's seat doing his best to remain inconspicuous as the group of football fans moved by, passing along the sidewalk on their way to the station. Hoping they wouldn't have taken note of the van's sudden movement, rolling backward in neutral until it concealed Nora's body beneath its own.

Or he hoped it had. There hadn't been time for anything else. He shifted from the seat as they passed, his breathing still ragged and heavy, into the back of the van—stooping down by Faouzi's body to pick up the laptop. Seeing the blank stare of the man he had murdered, the man who had spoken so passionately about his crippled son. *Who had*—he closed his eyes briefly, shoving away those thoughts with an effort, forcing himself to focus. He had to.

Three minutes, he thought, glancing at his watch. He was running out of time—the case slick with blood, one hinge of the laptop's screen hanging drunkenly loose as he lifted it, a broken piece of plastic falling to the metal floor of the van.

Damaged in the fall. A knot formed briefly in his stomach at the thought that it could have been damaged beyond repair, but the computer came back to life as his fingers moved over the touchpad—picking up the controller as he brought the UAV control program up on-screen.

There. He could see the camera feed, the view over Paris in the darkening sky. . .the UAVs' positions marked in the split-screen Map View as they moved in from the north. But something was wrong.

It took him a moment, his brain still fogged with pain, to sort out what had gone wrong. Perhaps a control had been jammed during the fight, perhaps the software had malfunctioned, somehow.

But the drone he controlled—his only hope of catching up to the other one, of *stopping* it—was lagging nearly half a kilometer behind.

9:25 P.M.
The rooftop

Maybe it was going to be a quiet night after all, Sergeant Jobert thought, the fiery red glow of the dying sun bathing the rooftop in light as she raised her gloved arm toward the heavens—Glatigny's wings sweeping across her face as the golden eagle sprung once more into the sky, rocketing upward.

The sudden roar of the crowd from the *Stade* clearly audible across the street, an unearthly, swelling sound, tens of thousands of voices raised as one—as if in applause for the raptor's flight.

She watched him go, soaring into the western sky—out toward those towering clouds tinted blood-red by the setting sun. There was something ominous in the sight, a sudden chill running through her body—but she was at a loss to account for the feeling, bringing up the binoculars to track the eagle's flight.

Another few minutes, and the twilight which had already enfolded the lower streets would enclose them as well, she thought—rendering the binoculars useless.

She swept them around right from where she stood at the edge of the roof, aiming them north, across the Seine. And then she saw it, in the fading twilight. . .a pair of small dots, one a fair distance back from the other, moving in across the sky.

Moving fast.

9:26 P.M.
Saint-Denis, Seine-Saint-Denis

Harry's thumb rocked forward against the control lever, the quadcopter tilting forward, once again picking up airspeed. *98Km/h.* He spared a momentary glance at the map display, marking the distance between the drones. *Two hundred meters and closing.*

And just out from the Seine, he realized, noting the body of water below, at the very edge of the camera lens. He could just see the other UAV now, its black, metallic fuselage glinting in the fading sunlight as it crossed the river, heading toward the stadium.

One-twenty. One-fifteen. . .

"Come on," he whispered, more of a prayer than anything—as close to a prayer as he could bring himself to come. He just needed to close the gap, ensure that *both* drones would be caught within the blast radius when he triggered the device. Forty meters would be optimal, to ensure that the lead UAV would be shredded by the explosion, not merely knocked from the sky.

And with it, their dreams of jihad—their hopes of assassinating the President of France. . .

In his mind's eye, he could see Aryn, hunched over a similar laptop in a van not half-a-kilometer distant, only now taking over manual control of the drone, preparing to guide it in on its final run.

Seventy-five meters. Sixty. Just a few seconds more, just—

The impact came without warning, so suddenly that Harry felt it almost as a physical blow, the video feed from the UAV's camera blurring as the heavy quadcopter careened sideways, its gyros fighting to stabilize itself—to prevent it from falling out of the sky.

And then he saw it, out of the corner of the camera's lens. *The flash of feathered wings. . .*

The rooftop

"Oui. Certainement," Sergeant Jobert replied over her headset radio, hearing Leseur's voice in her ear—her heart in her throat as she stared up into the sky, unable to do anything now but watch it unfold. *Fate.*

Glatigny had engaged the UAVs, just as he'd been trained, but both quadcopters were large, nearly twice the size of those they had used in the golden eagle's training. And he had gone after the rearmost drone, leaving the lead vehicle to continue, unimpeded.

"They're still inbound," she spat into the radio, a tinge of fear coloring her voice as she watched the second drone level out, perhaps four hundred feet off the deck. Hearing Leseur relay an order to her snipers over the earpiece. *Weapons-free.*

The Stade de France

". . .as you can understand, *messieurs*, your support is vital," President Denis Albéric said, a champagne flute poised delicately between his fingers as he glanced around into the faces of the small knot of men surrounding him, "if this policy is to be a success. If—"

A hand on his shoulder cut him off, as he looked back into the face of a bodyguard—one of Leseur's GSPR officers.

"*Excusez-moi, mon presidente,*" the man began, an urgency in his voice, barely veiled by the apology, "but I need you to come with me. *Immédiatement.*"

Not again. Leseur was truly elevating what his American counterpart had once called "security theater", to an art form. He attempted to shake off the man's hand with an impatient gesture, but found its grip on his shoulder was like iron.

"What do you think—"

"*Immédiatement,*" the man repeated, and behind him, toward the door, he could see Leseur—a pistol drawn in her hand, beckoning toward them both.

"*Mon presidente!*"

9:28 P.M.
Saint-Denis, Seine-Saint-Denis

Seventy-five meters, Harry noted, a leaden weight seeming to settle on his chest as he pressed the controller's joystick all the way forward with his thumb—glimpsing the other UAV, still out in front, just beginning to sweep out over the massive elliptical roof of the *Stade* itself.

He had fallen back when knocked off course by the eagle's attack, but made up much of the time difference in the lost altitude—Aryn's drone only just then beginning its own descent.

It was still possible, he thought, his eyes glued to the screen, the palms of his hands sweaty as the UAV responded to his controls, pushing the upper limits of its speed. *101Km/h.* Knowing that both vehicles had to be near the end of their battery life, that the increased strain he was putting it under would only sap that faster.

But there were only seconds left. The roof beneath his own quadcopter now, the Presidential skybox just visible across the pitch. *Fifty meters.*

He felt the turbulence just then, the camera shaking ever so slightly—his left thumb jamming the stick hard up and to the left, sweeping the quadcopter into a sharp vertical ascent even as the eagle passed by beneath, missing the UAV by scant inches.

And they were both out over the pitch now, within sight of the spectators—if anyone was looking up. *Forty-five meters.*

The lead UAV looming large in his camera now as the gap narrowed. *Forty meters.*

Thirty-five. No more time. His finger reached out, depressing the button.

And the screen went white. . .

The rooftop

A curse broke from Jobert's lips as an explosion erupted from within the stadium, a violent flash of fiery light, visible through the glass of the massive roof.

Failure. All the months, the years of training—and they had *failed.* Her eyes searching the sky in vain for any sign of Glatigny, hoping against hope, but knowing the truth—having seen him in those last moments, in a final dive toward his targets.

That the eagle had been consumed in the explosion. . .along with how many others?

The Stade

Out on the pitch, players froze in shock as the sky lit up above them with the fire of the noonday sun, debris and shards of broken glass from the roof raining down, pelting player and spectator alike.

There was a moment's unearthly silence as the shockwaves of the explosion died away—and then the screams began. Tens of thousands of men, women, and children, pushing and shoving their way out of their seats, through the stands. Without order, without reason—without purpose, save one. *Get out.*

The skybox

The bullet-resistant glass of the skybox buckled under the force of the explosion, barely fifty meters out from its face, but it refused to break—holding firm. The only internal damage appearing to be a table of refreshments, overturned when a heavyset Republican senator from Provence had attempted to throw himself behind it.

Marion Leseur raised herself up on one knee, looking over to where the president lay, pinned under the body of the GSPR officer who had thrown him to the floor at the moment of detonation, sheltering him with his body—Albéric's eyes visible over the man's shoulder, wide and filled with fear. *Terror.*

"Get him up and let's move," she spat, raising her voice to carry above the rising panic. Fifty, nearly sixty people in the room—the powerful, a few moments before. All of them now helpless, frightened, seeking a way out, looking for salvation. But she was responsible for *one.*

And she needed to get him out, before it was too late. Before another attack came.

She brass-checked her Sig-Sauer SP 2022 briefly as her officers lifted Albéric to his feet—forming a protective formation around him as they hustled him to the door, other officers fanned out, keeping the rest of the dignitaries at bay. Beyond practice, she hadn't had to so much as draw her weapon in years, but its bulk felt comforting in her hand as she pushed the door open—gesturing for the officers without to take point down the long corridor, their FN P90 submachine guns already unslung.

Move.

The hurried phalanx of officers were perhaps twenty meters down the corridor, almost to the stairs, when the phone in Leseur's pocket began to pulse, a familiar number displayed on-screen.

The DGSE.

"Allô?"

It was Anaïs Brunet's voice on the other end, as terse as ever. *Urgent.* No greeting, no preamble. "We've just come into possession of new intelligence, Marion. The *Stade* is the target. Tonight. You—"

Leseur shook her head, overcome by the irony of it all. Pausing as she began to descend the stairs to cast another glance back down the long, empty corridor toward the skybox they had so recently evacuated.

"We know."

9:30 P.M.
Saint-Denis, Seine-Saint-Denis

Harry stared at the screen for a long moment, the controller fallen to the floor of the van—his hands trembling, all the energy seeming to have drained from his body in the last few moments since the explosion. *He had succeeded. . .or had he?*

It had been so close. . .

Another question without an answer, and he knew he couldn't afford to wait for one. Not with so much still hanging in the balance.

He rose, stripping off his outer jacket and the explosive vest in quick, frenzied movements—the fabric of the undershirt beneath soaked with sweat, a sharp, searing pain shooting through his abdomen as he pulled the shirt from the waistband of his pants, down over the holstered CZ in an attempt to conceal it.

Another moment to collect himself, and he took a crouching step toward the door, realizing only then that his shoes were soaked in Faouzi's blood, the viscous fluid seeping into his socks—the Algerian's body still lying there, barely a foot away, that same reproachful, contemptuous look still visible on the dead man's face as he gazed up sightlessly at his murderer.

But there was no time to consider any of that, not now. *Later.* When the demons came in the night. *With a new face.*

He pushed open the back door of the van as he stepped out, leaving it open—blood dripping to the pavement. Knowing the hardest part of this was yet ahead.

They would know they had failed, would already be moving into position for the second phase. And he had to be there, to stop them.

The end of the road.

Chapter 39

Anaïs Brunet's face seemed to be drained of color by the time she set down the phone—the television on the far wall of her office already changed to breaking news of the attack on the *Stade*, with live replay of the stadium in the moments leading up to the blast, and hosts openly speculating about Albéric's status.

They had failed. That was the truth of it, pure and simple. Their—*her*—plan to infiltrate the Islamist networks of Molenbeek, to bring them down before they could strike. . .couldn't possibly have failed more spectacularly.

Ending in an attack in the suburbs of Paris itself, targeting the President of France. It was incomprehensible.

Albéric's salvation—if he was, in fact, saved—due to little more than a freak accident, a premature detonation of the explosives. But he wasn't out of the area yet—and GIGN's response team was another fifteen minutes out, the gendarmes tasked to perimeter security, overwhelmed by the crowd now pouring, uncontrolled, from the *Stade* into the streets.

It was the perfect scenario for a double-tap strike, Brunet thought, as everyone involved—likely including the terrorists—knew. But there was so *little* she could do, her hands tied by the limits of the DGSE's remit.

Unless there might be chatter they could access—some warning of further attacks. She reached for the phone on her desk, lifting it from its cradle, even as some movement—something—drew her eyes back to the screen.

And that was when she saw the second explosion, rising from somewhere along the Avenue Jules Rimet. . .

9:34 P.M.
Avenue Jules Rimet
Saint-Denis, Seine-Saint-Denis

Harry knew what the sound was the moment it struck his ears, the familiar muffled *crump* of high explosives audible above the thousand voices surrounding him as he passed the *Stade*'s Gate B—pushing his way through the swelling crowd. The briefest of flashes, lighting up the twilight.

Someone had detonated their vest. Already. *Before he could get to them.* Had it been Belkaïd's young enforcer, Abdelatif?

Yassin?

It bothered him just how much he hoped *not*—hoped, despite all this—despite everything he knew, despite *reason* itself, that his young friend was still alive. Hope against hope, hope against the knowledge of what was still to come. *Damnation.*

He ducked under the yellow awnings of *La 3ème Mi-temps* brasserie, picking his way among toppled, broken chairs as the mob continued to flood past—the screams of panic and fear growing louder in the wake of the explosion.

How many, already dead? he wondered, pain throbbing through his stomach as a man was shoved into him in the press. He had witnessed scenes like this before, in Iraq—an s-vest detonated in the middle of a crowded market.

Seen the aftermath. . .men and women torn to shreds by the blast. *Children.* He remembered the body of one little girl, no more than seven, lying in the dirt of the market—eyes wide as she stared up at the sky, her face perfect, unscarred.

Everything below the waist. . .mangled meat, scarce even recognizable as part of a human body. She would have bled out in seconds.

And that was going to happen here—*had* already happened—if he didn't get to them first. If he didn't *kill* them.

Van first. The VBIED had to be taken out of play before Aryn could bring it in any closer to the *Stade*. Before he could detonate it, and himself with it.

Both of them had to be stopped, no, killed—*killed*, a voice in Harry's brain repeated, as if trying to convince himself of its truth. Of a reality he'd spent far too long avoiding.

He shoved a middle-aged man aside, the man's shout of protest lost in the cacophony as he waded back out into the street, crossing the Rue Tournoi des 5 Nations—pushing against the flow of the crowd, seeing the desperation, the fear in every passing face. One more city block—just one more.

Fear you could have prevented, the voice said, distracting him, a hollow sound, echoing in the dark recesses of his mind. *You brought this on them. You. No one else.*

Madness. His world, narrowing to a singular focus. A single word, repeating itself over and over again through his brain as he forced his way along, struggling to make headway, to even stay aright in the press.

Kill. Kill. Kill. . .

9:37 P.M.
The Stade de France

Chaos. That's all she was seeing, Marion Leseur thought, glancing at the screens in the security hub of the *Stade*, buried deep in the basement of the stadium. Cameras covering the streets without, tens of thousands of blurred images in the darkness—pushing, fighting and clawing their way back toward the Seine.

And they were trapped—helpless. Taking the president out into that chaos would be insane, one suicide bomber having already detonated a vest outside the E Gate. God only knew how many more of them, out there somewhere.

And with the UAV threat, an air evac—a helicopter setting down on the football pitch to take Albéric on-board—was equally out of the question. A single such drone, coming within range as the helicopter took off. . .*devastation.*

All that remained was for them to hold their ground, to wait it out. *Weather the storm.*

"What is the latest from General Darroussin?" she demanded, referencing GIGN's commander.

"Response teams are still eight minutes out," came the response from an officer standing a few feet away, monitoring activity on the screens. "The *Police Nationale* have a QRF less than a kilometer away, but they're struggling to make their way through the crowd."

As would GIGN, when they arrived. *Eight minutes.* Such a short time, on any normal day.

Such an eternity, now.

GSPR officers were posted by each door—more without, setting up tactical positions, barricades—file cabinets and office furniture, dragged out into the corridors leading to the hub.

She glanced over to where the president sat, a few feet away, collapsed in a rolling office chair—a half-empty bottle of water held in his trembling hands.

He looked shrunken, somehow—huddled there in the chair, the armpits of his suit stained dark with sweat.

"I really. . .I really didn't think it would—that it *could*—happen," Albéric stammered, his voice hushed, seeming to speak to everyone and no one at the same time. His eyes darting fearfully around the room. "I didn't think. . ."

"Madame commissaire," one of her officers announced, looking up from the workstation as he removed his comms headset, "we've just received word from the *Police Nationale* of a strange van, along the Rue de l'Olympisme. The driver is identified by bystanders as a young Arab male, and was apparently trying to drive in closer to the stadium after the explosions when another driver trying to get out rammed into him in a head-on collision. Officers have not yet made an approach, but—"

"Are they armed?"

A quick nod. *"Oui."*

"Tell them to secure a perimeter and take it down," Leseur replied brusquely, her tone brooking no disagreement. As head of the GSPR, she was not, technically, in the police officers' chain of command, but that didn't matter. Nothing mattered, right now—except preventing another bombing. *"Immédiatement."*

She saw the hesitation in the man's eyes, saw him pause before relaying the order. "If they do not secure the van, and it turns out to be full of explosives, hundreds in that crowd will die. *Do it now.*"

9:39 P.M.
Rue de l'Olympisme
Saint-Denis, Seine-Saint-Denis

It felt as though he had run a marathon in the last ten minutes, the scant two blocks back toward the van turned into a writhing sea of thousands upon thousands of people, a tide of humanity, sweeping out toward the river.

Offering no mercy for the fallen, Harry thought, remembering the face of one woman who had lost her footing, barely ten yards in front of him. The anguished look of terror on her face as she'd gone down, trampled beneath the feet of the crowd—her cry for help washed away in the clamor of voices. She'd been dead by the time he reached her—that same look of terror still fixed on her bruised face.

You can't save the world. A hard truth, he'd had to learn so very long ago. Perhaps he'd learned it too well.

He pushed his way past a middle-aged man in a football jersey, hearing him call out desperately in French for his young son, lost somewhere in the mob. The anguish in the man's voice, driving a dagger into Harry's heart.

You did this to him. The voice, echoing again and again in his mind. *Relentless.* Unsparing.

And this time he recognized it—knew the sound. Knew to which of his demons it belonged. *Marwan.*

"I could have stopped them," the voice continued, remorselessly. *"Could have prevented. . .all of this. But you stopped me, didn't you? Didn't you?"*

Harry shook his head, struggling to clear his thoughts—to keep his focus as he stepped over a knee-high concrete vehicle barrier, put in place before the event to mark the security perimeter. *The van had to be close now, it had to be—*

He moved to his right, onto the sidewalk, pushing through the crowd past a silver SUV parked up against the curb. He felt people move back against him, as if repelled by some invisible force—the sharp point of someone's elbow slamming inadvertently into his side.

Pain. Lights flashing through his brain as he collapsed back against the side of the vehicle—struggling to keep his feet, nausea overwhelming him.

It felt for a moment as though he might black out, but he pushed himself aright, staggering to the back of the SUV—his right hand pressed against his side, his left supporting himself against the vehicle.

And then he saw it—the thin line of gendarmes with riot shields—struggling to turn back the crowd, to form a frail perimeter. *Around the van.*

Even from this distance—nearly fifty meters away—he could guess what had happened. A driver, attempting to escape the area around the *Stade*, ramming into Aryn as he pulled out of his parking space—the van swerving in an effort to get out of the way at the last moment, taking the impact nearly head-on, crumpling in the front—the driver's side door. Deploying the airbags.

No sign of the driver.

He forced his way through the crowd, ignoring the pain—the exhaustion pervading his body. Moving forward until he found himself in the front—pressed against the line of police, his hand on a gendarme's shield.

"The driver," Harry shouted, a warning in his voice as he stared across the shield into the young officer's eyes, "he has a bomb! I saw him arm it, I—"

He saw the look of incomprehension on the gendarme's face, his words swept away in the roar of voices around them. Started to repeat them, to push in closer, heedless of his own danger.

And then he heard it, from somewhere up the street, the crowd's panic reaching new heights. The familiar crackle of a rifle on full-automatic. . .

9:41 P.M.
Stade de France

"We have a shooter," the officer by the screens of the security hub announced suddenly, drawing Marion Leseur's attention to the cameras covering the Rue d'Olympisme—picking out in the semi-darkness a masked figure kneeling before one of the storefronts, a rifle in his hand—shooting indiscriminately into the crowd.

The GSPR *commissaire* swore loudly, adjusting her headset radio and keying the microphone. "Perimeter teams, we need a twenty on the gunman. Does anyone have the solution?"

A moment passed, her radio crackling with static as one by one the GSPR snipers checked in. Their answers, coming as one—a curious finality in the words.

"Non."

9:42 P.M.
Ambassade d'Auvergne
Paris

". . .and your daughter? How is she enjoying university?" Daniel Vukovic heard his wife ask, daubing his lips with his napkin as he leaned back into his chair, glancing around the crowded restaurant.

The woman across from him beamed in reply. "Very well—she wants to be a journalist."

Vukovic cleared his throat, casting an ironic glance at her husband. "Going over to the dark side? Come, Phillip. . .how you could allow such a thing?"

Phillip Blake, the British Secret Intelligence Service's chief of station in Paris, just shook his head, smiling. "'Allow'? You don't have daughters, do you, Daniel?"

"You have me there," the CIA station chief replied, returning the smile as he took another sip of his pinot noir.

This had been a good night—a rare moment of relaxation, for both he and Blake. Their final dinner together, before Blake rotated out of Paris—back to Vauxhall Cross after two years in France. Two years in which Vukovic could have asked for no better ally, their partnership unusually strong, even by Anglo-American standards.

"To faithful friends, and a job well done," he said, saluting Blake with his glass. "It's been an honor."

"Here, here," the SIS man replied, raising his own glass in the toast. "Another few years, Daniel, and you might have even convinced me that you Americans weren't half bad."

That brought a laugh, and Vukovic returned his attention briefly to his plate, taking another bite of the minced duck. "I truly regret losing you here, Phillip. It has been—"

He broke off in mid-sentence as the phone within the pocket of his jacket began to vibrate insistently, taking it out to glance at the screen. *Paris Station.*

"Excuse me, Phillip, I have to take this. I—"

And it was only then that he realized that his counterpart was likewise glancing at his phone—their eyes locking across the table with the mutual, unspoken recognition of just what that meant.

This was bad.

9:43 P.M.
Rue de l'Olympisme
Saint-Denis, Seine-Saint-Denis

Chaos. Harry leaned back, pressing himself flat against the wall of the building on the left side of the street, watching the seething mass of humanity before him—caught between the fragile, wavering line of gendarmes and the gunman.

Yassin.

Some people had sought cover when the shooting started, others simply tried to run, finding themselves hemmed in by the police—their desire to keep people away from the potential VBIED inadvertently aiding the shooter. Turning the street into a slaughterhouse. *Like shooting fish in a barrel.*

He knew where he was now, though, scarce ten meters up the street—tucked into the alcove of the building Harry was himself now pressed against.

A good position, Harry had to concede—the compact CZ out in his hand, tucked against his thigh as he worked his way up along the wall—out of the line of sight of almost any of the nearby roofs, and any snipers the French might have pre-positioned as part of their security preparations in advance of the game.

Another ragged burst of fire struck his ears, followed by more screams. And then a pause. Yassin—no, the *gunman*, he had to think of him as the gunman, nothing more—had to be on his second magazine by now, maybe third. He couldn't have had more than five with him, could he? But there was no use in waiting to find out.

Harry's head came up above the concrete wall as he edged his way forward—catching a distorted view of the masked gunman through the spider-veined glass of the storefront. Down on one knee, in a stable firing position. The cut-down AK in his hands, clearly visible, silhouetted in the embers of the dying sun.

Reloading.

There was no time to hesitate, and yet he felt as if rooted to the spot—

overcome, in these final moments, by a strange reluctance. *Do it. Do it* now.

And he could see Nora's face before his eyes—the way she had looked in those final moments before her death, the bewilderment still playing across her features.

The venom in Faouzi's voice, as he'd spat out the words—damning him as a traitor.

Faiths betrayed.

He pushed those thoughts away with an effort, slipping off the CZ's safety as he rounded the corner, hammer back on a full chamber—catching Yassin in the act of rocking a mag back into the AK-103's well, pulling back the charging handle.

He saw the surprise at his sudden appearance, the rifle's barrel coming up instinctively.

A smile crossing his own face, as he hailed his young friend, lifting his voice above the chaos of the street surrounding them. "Brother!"

The Kalashnikov's barrel wavered, lowering almost imperceptibly—confusion there in Yassin's eyes, behind the balaclava mask. "Ibrahim, what's. . .I mean, why, I—"

9:45 P.M.

It felt as if someone was beating on his skull with a hammer, Aryn thought, pushing himself aright on the floor of the van—a hand clasped to the back of his head as he fumbled with the airbags billowing above him.

What had happened? And then he remembered, turning out into the street, still struggling to process what had happened to the drones—seeing the oncoming car, a moment too late. An impact which had thrown him from his seat, thrown the detonator. . .*where was it?*

He reached out, his hand groping in the darkness beneath the seat. And then he heard the voices—barking out orders of authority. *Moving closer. . .*

9:46 P.M.

The opening was there, and he took it—the compact CZ coming up in his outstretched hand, recognition entering the young man's eyes for a brief, terrifying second before the trigger broke beneath Harry's finger, fire blossoming from the pistol's muzzle.

Once, twice. *Double-tap.* The rifle falling from Yassin's hands, clattering against the concrete as he reeled backward, struggling to stay aright even as Harry shot him a third time, high in the chest.

He went down hard, crumpling to the ground in a half-sitting position against the storefront—staring up at the eaves above, desperation and fear in his eyes, visible in the dim light. Clawing desperately at something in his pocket. *The detonator.*

Harry kicked the AK further out of his reach, stooping down on one knee by the body of his young friend—seizing his wrist in an iron grasp.

"It wouldn't do you any good," he said gently, looking down into the eyes of the man who had once saved his life, "even if you could reach it. You remember when we embraced there in the park at Montmorency, saying farewell?"

Remember? It seemed a lifetime ago. *An eternity.* Scarce an hour.

"I pulled the wires then," he continued, watching the disbelief fill Yassin's eyes—anger distorting the face behind the mask. It had been simple enough to do—a snapped wire, perhaps two, the connection broken with a quick jerk. "You were never going to be able to trigger that vest."

The lips of the mask parted in a bitter curse, eyes filled with bewilderment and hatred gazing back into his own as he knelt there, the pistol still leveled in his hand. Harry reached up, his fingers twisting in the fabric of the balaclava and pulling it off with a rough gesture.

Forcing himself to look into the face of the man with whom he'd shared so many meals, spent so many mornings in prayer. *Bread and salt.* The man he had *betrayed*, in the end. Along with all the rest.

Yassin's head lolled back with the forceful motion, his strength clearly spent, not even the Captagon serving to keep him in the fight—the front of his jacket stained dark with blood. A fit of coughing seizing hold of him as he tried to respond—nearly collapsing if Harry hadn't caught him, supporting him against the wall. Holding him aright.

"You were one of them," he spat weakly, coughing up flecks of blood— clearly shot through the lung. "All along, you were one of *them*."

Harry nodded, not sure himself if it was even true. *Any of it.* "From the very beginning."

Another curse, impotent rage flaring in the young man's eyes—but even now, it seemed impossible for him to pull the trigger. To *finish* the job.

He was no threat now—it would be so simple to just walk away. *Leave him.* To die, to be found. . .as God willed.

Out of his hands.

Just take the vest and go, he thought, reaching within Yassin's jacket with his free hand, beginning to undo the clasps of the explosive vest.

The explosion came without warning, a massive detonation, lighting up the night sky, the shockwave washing around the corner of the building and over both Harry and Yassin. And Harry knew, before he even lifted his eyes to see the flames rising from the pyre in the middle of the Rue de l'Olympisme, what had happened.

The van. Somehow, some *way*, the gendarmes had failed. Their failure, a reflection of his own. A *consequence* of his own.

Marwan's face, flashing before his eyes—the way he had looked, in those final moments of his life, the blade tight against his throat.

The demon's voice, once again, murmuring its taunting, reproachful refrain. *"I could have stopped them. Could have saved, all these lives. But you stopped me. You stopped me. You stopped. . ."*

And he knew then, in a moment of soul-rending clarity, what he must do. Walking away wasn't enough. It would *never* be enough.

He wrapped an arm around Yassin's shoulders, drawing him close—hot tears running down Harry's face as he jammed the muzzle of the CZ into the young man's ribs.

And he pulled the trigger, again and again—the shots muffled by their bodies—feeling as though his own heart was being ripped out with each muted report, until finally the CZ's slide locked back and all fell silent once more.

Yassin's head resting on Harry's shoulder as the light slowly faded from his eyes, the two of them huddled there in the semi-darkness—the dying man. . .and the man already dead.

Chapter 40

3:48 P.M. Eastern Daylight Time
The apartment
Washington, D.C.

"Are you watching this, Barney?"

"I am," Kranemeyer replied simply, the phone pressed to his ear as he stared at the television screen, the news breaking from France having dominated CNN's coverage for the last ten minutes.

"It's horrific. . .over seventy thousand people in that stadium at the time of attack, according to the BBC. God only knows how many were trampled in the attempt to get out."

"Too many," came Kranemeyer's answer, his voice heavy. "I've already placed a call to Langley. Likely headed in, after a shower and a shave."

"No rest for the wicked?" he heard Coftey ask, irony in the senator's voice.

Never. And the war goes on, the DCS thought, a distant look in his coal-black eyes. The cold, unmelodic refrain of his life. *No end to it in sight.*

"We need to talk, Roy. About where this all goes from here."

There was a long moment's silence, then, "I know. We do. Name the time and the place."

"It'll have to be another time," Kranemeyer said, watching as the CNN ticker ran an updated death toll from the bombings in Paris. *Seventy-nine.* Almost certainly far too low. "And another place. Today just got busy."

3:53 P.M.
Dawsonville, Maryland

"Just put the chips and soda down over on the island, Jack," the middle-aged woman announced, glancing up from the stove as Richards materialized in her kitchen, grocery bags hanging from his right arm, a 12-pack of Pepsi in each hand, "right there by the beer. Glad you could make the drive up."

"Wouldn't have missed it, Donna," Richards replied, the ghost of a smile passing across his face as he looked at her. Donna Mellinger was a rare breed—one of the kindest women he had ever met, even if that kindness was often hidden behind a rough, hardened exterior. Perhaps not that much different from his own. "Long as I was Stateside."

She nodded, brushing a strand of blonde hair out of her eyes as she reached for a pair of oven mitts lying off to one side on the counter. She knew that score—had *lived* it for a lot of years. Her husband had been infantry, 3rd ID, Rock of the Marne, and his third tour to Iraq had been one too many.

"Mitt's out back," she went on, as she extracted something that looked like a pie from the oven, "at the grill with a couple of the guys. He'll be glad to see you."

"How's he doing?"

She set the pie down on the counter, turned to look at him. "He's all right."

There was a volume of emotion in those three simple words, as much hidden as disclosed.

"So he's told me."

A long, heavy sigh escaped her lips, something of resignation set in the lines of her weathered face. She was older than Mitt, by several years—and the years had taken their toll. "It's going to be a while before we're back out on our Harleys together."

That brought a smile to Richards' face.

It was how she and Nakamura had met, years before—after the death of her husband in Anbar. Their love of the open road bringing them together, forging a relationship that had now lasted half a decade. They'd never married, but what they shared. . .it was stronger than many who had.

"They released him from the hospital too early," she went on after a moment, and he could see the worry in her eyes—the mask cracking ever so slightly. "He ought to still be there, with what he's gone through."

Richards shook his head. "That's the VA for you."

"You were there with him when it happened, weren't you?" And that was a question she'd been wanting to ask for weeks, he knew—had seen it in her face the couple times he'd visited at Bethesda. But she wasn't going to ask in front of Mitt.

He simply nodded. Remembering that hellish day in the Sinai following the drone strike—the desert heat beating down on all of them . The lull following the firefight, broken by the *crack* of a single rifle shot. *Sniper.*

Nakamura, collapsing face-down in the sand.

"Not much more I can say. Still think there ought to have been something I could have done," he replied, the words coming hard, as words always did for him, "to have prevented it."

He had been the team's designated marksman, after all. *The weight of responsibility*, always resting heavy on his shoulders. Even heavier now, since he'd been entrusted with Mitt's team.

She reached out, her hand on his arm. A quiet smile of assurance passing across her face. *The mask falling back in place.* "You brought him home, Jack. That's all that matters. Now go out back, and let him show you his grill."

He caught sight of Nakamura, seated in a deck chair on the back patio by the oblong-shaped Green Egg grill as he stepped through the sliding door and back out into the August heat, closing the door behind him. A Hispanic man in a Ranger Up t-shirt and cargo shorts, standing a few feet away—lifting up the grill's heavy lid, steam billowing out around him as he examined the meat within.

Donna hadn't been exaggerating—Mitt was pale, paler than Richards ever remembered seeing him, and his arms had lost their accustomed muscle tone. He looked bad.

But his eyes lit up when he saw the big Texan emerge from the house, setting his beer on the table as he rose to greet him.

"Good to see you back on your feet, brother," Richards said, wrapping an arm around the smaller man's shoulders as he gripped his hand fiercely. "You're still as ugly as sin, but I suppose modern medicine has its limits."

His former team lead laughed, slapping him on the back—lacking something of the force of the old Nakamura. But the spirit remained. "Look who's talking. Glad you could make it up here, Jack. The other guys are running late, but they'll be with us soon."

Richards glanced over his shoulder to the steaks sizzling on the grill, making eye contact with the other man. "Make sure mine doesn't moo when I put a knife to it."

"You heathen," Nakamura laughed, shaking his head as he returned to his seat. "Some days I don't know how we're still friends. Jack, this is Hector Quiroz, an old friend of mine from the 2/75. We were in the 'Stan together."

"Good to meet you, man," Quiroz said, switching the big fork to his other hand and reaching over to clasp Richards' hand. "Mitt's the only reason I came home from over there. Any friend of his. . ."

Richards nodded, gripping his hand firmly. That's how it went in this world. Your brother's brother, your own.

He glimpsed Nakamura out of the corner of his eye, shaking his head. "I did my job, nothing more. You held your own."

"That's debatable. I understand you've been in the sandbox a time or two together as well," Quiroz went on, his attention turning back to Richards as he closed the Egg's lid. He shook his head. "Mitt's like me—he doesn't know when to quit."

"You're still in the Regiment?" Richards asked, favoring the man with a keen look. He had to be careful how much he said here, as did Nakamura—though he had no doubt that he *had* been careful. He'd always been good at that.

Quiroz laughed, wiping the sweat from his brow with the back of his hand. "Nah. I ETS'd five years ago—spent a couple years trying to settle down, found civilian life didn't agree with me or the wife, either one. Finally went to work for a private mil/intel firm called the Svalinn Security Group. It's run by a former—"

"I know who runs it," Richards replied, his voice suddenly as cold as ice. "I think it's best that—"

"Mitt!" He turned at the sound of Donna's voice, seeing her standing there in the open door, anger and fear written in her eyes. "You all need to see this. There's been an attack, in Paris. . ."

11:53 P.M. Central European Summer Time
A house outside Béville-le-Comte
Eure-et-Loire Department, France

Four guards. He had counted them, carefully—maintaining surveillance on the secluded property over the last couple hours, since the arrival of Gamal and Ghaniyah Belkaïd.

Grigoriy Stepanovich Kolesnikov leaned back in the seat of his car, touching the icon of Our Lady of Vladimir beneath his shirt as he murmured a brief prayer.

Reaching over for the pistol case that lay beside him on the seat, unsnapping the latches to reveal the Smith & Wesson M&P Compact nestled within.

This was going to be close. Even with the edge of surprise that he would gain in the confusion of Belkaïd's men recognizing him. . .he stood a very good chance of never walking back out of that house alive.

The Centre would never have approved, he thought, a mirthless smile crossing his face. Even with the overall failure of Belkaïd's attack on the *Stade*, the survival of the French President—who was due to appear on television in twenty minutes—they would have viewed eliminating him as far too risky.

But he. . .he had known from the moment he had first laid eyes on the Algerian's file. *That it would end like this.* One way or the other.

"For you, Sasha," he whispered, hefting the pistol briefly in his hand before leaning forward in the driver's seat to tuck it into the holster on his hip. The two spare mags going into the inside pocket of his suit jacket. *For all the years we could have known.*

And it seemed almost as if he could see his brother's face before him—no, not *face* but *faces*—a bewildering, dizzying collage of images, passing before him in rapid succession. *A life in fast-forward.*

Sasha, his hockey stick raised in his upraised fist following a goal—a cheer of defiance ripping from his throat as he glanced up at his little brother in the stands. The *pride* they had shared in that moment. Countless such afternoons on the ice.

But there had been other moments. . .and he could see Sasha the way he looked when he had visited him in prison, a decade before. The last time the two of them had ever stood in the same room.

His brother had been pale, strung-out, and haggard—a shell of his former self. Only the defiance remained, turned, like everything else in what remained of his life, into the service of his addiction.

A mockery of the man—the *hero*—he had once revered, the older brother who had taken on the role of a father in his life.

Until men like Gamal Belkaïd had taken that away from all of them. Everything that *could* have been.

He had taken the excuses, the endless defiant denials that day, until he could take no more—lashing back out at his brother, rage taking the place of tears so feebly dammed.

Feeling his brother's defiance rise to meet him, anger flashing in those worn-out eyes. *Hate.*

And they had parted that day, never to meet again. He was out, Grigoriy knew that much—had been in and out five or six times over the intervening years—but he'd never gone to see him again. That afternoon in the prison, confirming to him that the man who had spent nearly a decade and a half drifting in and out of prisons in Moscow Oblast was not his brother.

That man was long since dead. Killed by heroin, and the men who made their wealth from its trade.

Enough. He swore softly beneath his breath, cursing the past and all its memories. There would be time enough for them on another day.

He reached forward and turned the key in the ignition, the Peugeot's lights illuminating the desolate stretch of roadway. The drive leading to Belkaïd's residence, barely half-a-kilometer away.

It was time. . .

12:01 A.M., August 8th
Southbound on the N10 near Rambouillet
Yvelines Department, France

Walk away. Just turn your back and walk away from all this. Run.

But running was what had brought him to this place, Harry thought—catching a brief glimpse of his own face in the rear-view mirror of the stolen Opel, stark and pale, every sunken hollow illuminated in the headlights of a car accelerating past him into the right-hand lane as they sped south through the night.

Or was it vengeance? His own quest for revenge in the wake of Vegas, driving him onward, into madness. One domino, crashing into another, and another, and another. *And another.* Until the cascade became unstoppable, and not even the force which had set them in motion could suffice to avert disaster.

We all fall down.

Marwan's voice, a darker whispering in his ear. *"Avenge me. You took my life to save your own—now avenge my death."*

"No," Harry murmured, scarce aware that he had spoken aloud—his eyes fixed on the highway ahead, a high retaining wall mounting up on his right, the dark mass of woods surrounding the Etang D'or looming across the oncoming lanes of traffic to his left—shadowy and threatening. "I killed you to save countless lives, not just mine. It *had* to be done. There was no other choice."

The old lie. And he could still feel the agony, the horror of that moment— the feeling of the blood-slick blade in his hand.

The triumphant look in the eyes of all that had surrounded them. *Driss. Aryn. Faouzi. Nora. Yassin. . .*

"But you didn't, did you? Those people died anyway, trampled to death in their flight from the Stade. *Because you couldn't pull the trigger when it mattered. When it would have made a* difference. *"*

Yassin's body, shuddering against him in the semi-darkness there outside the stadium—jerking spasmodically as each round smashed its way through his flesh.

A last act of expiation, arriving far too late. When it no longer mattered. When *nothing* mattered, any more.

Any more than this would.

"I did everything I could," he spat back, anger in his voice—some last shredded vestige of his sanity protesting against the madness of this. *An argument with a ghost.* "All that *anyone* could have done."

"No," he could hear the demon reply, remorseless, unrelenting, *"enough with the lies. You did nothing. Until it was too late. Because you loved them. They took you in, cared for you when there was no one else. When you* had *no one else. And you loved them for it."*

He fell silent, unable to find the words to reply, unable to deny the truth. The knowledge that had come to him there in the street before the *Stade*, Yassin's dying body huddled against his own—that then, if never before, he had slain his brother.

And the Lord set a mark upon Cain. . .

"You took my life to save your own," the voice repeated, *"now give your life to kill the man who destroyed us both. Kill Gamal Belkaïd. Kill* yourself. *And come and be at peace. At peace. . ."*

And he could see Belkaïd standing there in the bright lights of that basement room, extending the knife in his outstretched hand. The compact C75 seeming to shudder beneath his blood-drenched undershirt. *Come and be at peace.*

He had a single magazine left. Fifteen rounds.

It would have to be enough. He glimpsed a road sign in the headlights of the Opel, giving the distances to Chartres. To Etampes. *To Orleans.* Nearly ninety kilometers to that last.

His own destination, not nearly so far. At the bottom of the sign, in white, there was a fourth listing. *Ablis. 9.*

He would keep left onto the D910 there, sweeping west-southwest toward the little rural commune of Béville-le-Comte. And the residence of Gamal Belkaïd.

Twenty-five minutes.

12:11 A.M.
The Palais de l'Élysée
Paris, France

Denis Albéric took a deep breath, endeavoring to collect himself as he faced into the cameras, hearing the technician count down the moments until they were live, on national television.

He tented his hands before him on the desk, only to realize they were still trembling, the sounds of the explosions still seeming to ring in his ears. The screams of fear and terror as thousands tried to flee from the *Stade*.

He could still hear all of it, *feel* every moment—the panic which had overwhelmed him.

One hundred and sixty-five dead. As of now, a number expected to rise—almost all of them in either the stampede, or the subsequent bombings. The explosions above the stadium itself, remarkably enough, causing only a handful of minor injuries among the footballers out on the pitch.

And there had been another VBIED discovered, abandoned, parked out on the Rue de Brennus, its interior spattered in blood, resembling an abattoir—two bodies found within and nearby. A young woman and an older man, both stabbed to death.

But its bomb had not gone off, whatever the reason, and that was an unlooked-for mercy.

"Quatre. . .trois. . .deux. . .un. . ."

"My dear compatriots," Albéric began, aware his voice was shaking, even now, ever so slightly, "as you are no doubt already aware, this evening there was a savage terrorist attack on the *Stade de France* in *Seine-Saint-Denis*. I was myself the target of the attack, but as you can see, they failed in their objective. The reports of my death which spread across foreign media earlier this night, are false. However, many of my fellow citizens were not so fortunate, and the reported numbers of dead and injured are still climbing. *C'est une tragédie.*"

He took a deep breath in the effort to calm himself before continuing. "We have, on my authority, mobilized all available forces to neutralize any remaining terrorists and prevent further attacks. I have also asked for military reinforcements, which are now moving into the Paris area. In a few moments, I will be meeting with my cabinet, to proclaim a state of emergency throughout the territory of France, and to once again, as we have before in times of such tragedy, close the borders of the Republic. We must ensure that those who have committed these crimes do not escape justice. Faced with terror, France must be strong. . ."

12:13 A.M.
The house outside Béville-le-Comte
Eure-et-Loire Department, France

". . .there is indeed reason to be afraid. There is dread, but we stand in the face of this dread, a nation that knows how to defend itself. . ."

On-screen, President Albéric continued to stare into the cameras, his voice emanating through the television's speakers into the darkness of the room, but no one was listening.

The form of Ghaniyah Belkaïd lay sprawled face-down in the carpet only a few feet away, nearly hidden by the voluminous folds of her *abaya*, her face turned sideways, one sightless eye staring out across the floor, both carpet and *abaya* now wet with her blood.

Something of resignation on that aged, leathery face—now frozen in death. She had known they had failed, before the end. Known, and accepted it, like she had accepted so much of life, from the earliest horrors she had known as a young woman in Algiers. The French paras in the streets—one of them, the father of the man whose face now stared down on her death.

". . .and I ask that, despite tonight's tragedy, you keep all your trust in what we can do, with the security forces, to protect our nation from further such terrorist acts. *Vive la Republique! Vive la France!*"

Somewhere, off in some other part of the house, another gunshot punctuated the words.

12:15 A.M.
DGSE Headquarters
Paris, France

"Based on the videos released in the last couple hours, we have reason to believe that the attacks earlier tonight received foreign support, perhaps from the remnants of *Daesh*, likely through the work of this man," Anaïs Brunet continued, pulling up a balaclava-masked visage on-screen, "Ibrahim Abu Musab al-Almani. We do not know if he survived the operation against the *Stade*, but we have to assume that he did, until we have proof to the contrary. Finding this man, and Gamal Belkaïd, is of paramount importance. We must not fail."

Once again, she left unsaid—unnecessary given the self-reproach she saw mirrored in the eyes of everyone gathered around the conference table. They had all spent the night coming to terms with the consequences of their failure. No reason to throw it in their faces.

"Our counterparts at the DGSI," she went on, after a moment's pause, "are focused on the domestic aspect—continuing to run down any and all information on Belkaïd's known associates within France, while we will focus on the foreign aspect, namely al-Almani."

"And to that end"—she gestured to where Daniel Vukovic sat, a few feet away—"the Americans have offered to make available any and all resources which may prove necessary to bring these men to justice."

Vukovic nodded, glancing around the table. His face grave, yet strangely unreadable. "Anything my agency can do to help. We stand together."

12:21 A.M.
The house outside Béville-le-Comte
Eure-et-Loire Department, France

Voices. In the next room, a low murmur of noise in the stillness of the house.

Harry pushed forward through the darkness, the compact CZ up in both hands, hammer back on a loaded chamber, its muzzle leading the way—the familiar, flickering glow of a television screen coming into view as he neared the open doorway leading into the living room.

He recognized it as a news channel, the hosts continuing to talk, unregarded, on-screen as his weapon swept the corners of the room—his eyes only then falling upon the crumpled form in the middle of the floor. *Ghaniyah Belkaïd.*

The pair of bodies in the drive, each man shot twice to the head, had been his first indication that something was wrong—very wrong—that someone else had beaten him here. But the house was dark and quiet, this wasn't a GIGN raid. Wasn't the way they would have played this.

Her right hand was splayed out, away from her side, the stumps of her missing fingers clearly visible. A strange look of resignation on her face, as if she had seen Death coming for her. As if she had *known.*

He could remember the first time he had met her, in that little apartment on the Rue Denis Sotiau. Sharing a cup of Maghrebi tea as she told him of Algiers, of the horror her family had suffered there.

"I understand you are the mujahid.*"*

The flower garden. Beauty in the midst of the darkness. An attempt at healing.

But it hadn't been enough.

"My brother has forgotten our suffering. . ."

And where was her brother now? Was he even still alive?Or was he dead too, lying in a broken heap like his sister, a bullet hole disfiguring his forehead. Harry stooped down by her body—pushing away the folds of cloth around her broken face, pressing the fingers of his free hand against her carotid artery. No pulse, as he expected, but the flesh was still warm.

The killer was still here, he realized, suddenly aware of his own vulnerability—rising from his crouch, pistol in hand.

Moving back to the doorway. *Leave*, a voice in his head whispered, but he was no longer listening to it. The *other* voice, guiding him now—the voice of the ghost, driving him onward. *Marwan.*

His decision made, back there on that desolate stretch of highway between Rabouillet and Ablis. He knew how this would end.

The only way it ever could have ended.

Another guard lay dead in the hallway as he made his way carefully down it, his footfalls soft against the thick rug. Another low murmur of voices striking his ears as he neared the back of the house—and this time, he knew it wasn't a television, words floating to him through the still night air.

". . .men like you, who destroyed my brother. Whom the West used, in their attempt to destroy my country. . .men just like you, who grew wealthy even as they traded in human lives."

Be sure your sins will find you out. As his own had, certain as fate. It took him a long moment to place the voice, but then he knew.

The pistol raised, he stepped into the open doorway of the office—taking in the sight of Gamal Belkaïd sitting propped up in a chair to the left of the desk, blood trickling down his face from a gash on his forehead, the right knee of his pants torn and soaked with blood. It looked as though he'd been shot through the kneecap.

And between the two of them, pacing back and forth before the desk— *the Russian*. A pistol clutched in his right hand.

"Grigoriy," Harry announced quietly, summoning up the name out of the past. *Memories of Iraq*, streaming to the fore. Of standing on that road in Anbar, the sun beating down from above—bodies scattered all around.

The FSB officer's head snapped back around, finding himself staring down the barrel of Harry's pistol. *Once again.* "*You.*"

He spat the single word as a curse, rage and disbelief mixing until they were indistinguishable.

"Ibrahim, what are you doing here?" he heard Belkaïd demand, confusion in the Algerian's voice. Harry ignored him, focusing on the Russian, the face framed in the sights of his pistol, pale in the semi-darkness.

"I *knew* I knew you from somewhere before," the Russian intelligence officer spat, his voice bitter. "I knew it."

"Anbar Province," Harry said quietly, supplying the missing information. "Winter of '07. You were in-country as the the No. 2 of Alexei Mikhailovich. His protégé, or so it seemed at the time."

And he could see the pride in the young man's eyes, at the memory. Pride, and defiance at the sudden realization, the recognition, breaking through.

"And *you* were CIA!"

Harry simply nodded. "I was, then. I'm no one now."

"What is going on, Ibrahim?" Belkaïd demanded once again, his voice rising, drenched in pain. His words punctuated with curses in French and Arabic. "Enough with the talking, this man came here to kill me."

"So did I," Harry replied coldly, his eyes never leaving the young Russian's face. *The pistol.*

"Drop the gun, Grigoriy."

"What is the meaning of this, Ibrahim—what—"

The Russian started to laugh, a harsh, mirthless sound, shaking his head helplessly as he glanced between Harry and Belkaïd. *Still retaining his grip on the pistol.*

"Don't you see, you *fool?* He was playing you all along—"

"Drop the gun on the floor, and kick it over here. Do it *now.*"

"He convinced you that he was one of you, one of your *mujahideen.*" There were tears in Grigoriy's eyes now, his body shaking with laughter, a mad laughter in the face of death. *The irony of it all.* "And all the while, he betrayed you. Sold you out. Destroyed you from within. If you want to know why you failed. . .he stands before you."

The look in Belkaïd's eyes was one of utter disbelief, his mind struggling to process the Russian's words through the pain. "B-b-but that's *impossible.* I watched him, I was there when he beheaded a French agent, I—"

The FSB officer shook his head. "Then you know how good he is."

"The gun, Grigoriy—"

The pistol came up in the Russian's hand, a blur of motion—fire blossoming from the barrel into the darkness of the room. Harry's own finger, reflexively curling around the CZ's trigger—taking up slack, the two shots so close together they sounded almost as one.

He saw Gamal Belkaïd collapse in the chair, shot through the head, his brains spattering over the nearby bookcase. Saw his own bullet strike Grigoriy high in the chest, the FSB officer's weapon coming up and around even as he stumbled back toward the desk.

And Harry shot him again, the CZ recoiling back into his palm, the report deafening in the confines of the room—leaving his ears ringing.

The Russian went down, slumped on the rug in front of the desk—the pistol clattering to the bare wood, a few feet away.

He looked up at Harry, still standing there in the doorway, making no move to retrieve his weapon. An ironic smile, twisting at his lips.

"I just had to kill him, you see," he coughed weakly, his shoulders shaking ever so slightly with the same mad laughter. "For my brother. No matter what happened after, I had to be the *one*. And I was tired of hearing him talk. I should have shot you."

Harry nodded slowly, taking a cautious step into the room—his weapon still trained on the FSB officer's face. "You should have. But you didn't. And now we're going to talk about the role the Centre played in all of this—the orders from Moscow which led you to place weapons in the hands of a Belgian terror cell. And once you've told me your story, I'll patch you up and you can tell it all again to the DGSI."

The Russian just smiled, coughing once again, and Harry edged into the room, moving toward the pistol lying there on the floor between them. He had to secure it, before he could do anything else. Put it out of his reach—*permanently.*

"So you think I'll talk?" He seemed amused by that, that same ironic smile, still playing at the corners of his mouth. "I was trained in a hard school."

"I think all men talk, no matter their school." And this one was talking too much, Harry realized, even as his foot closed down on the Smith & Wesson lying there on the floor, kicking it away—some warning light piercing through the weariness, the fatigue. *Too late.*

He felt the impact of Grigoriy's kick, catching him off-balance—sweeping his legs out from under him as he crashed down hard to the floor—losing his grasp on the CZ, groping for it, in the semi-darkness.

And then the Russian was on top of him, hammer blows crashing into his unprotected side, nearly doubling him up—pain shooting through his weary, tortured body as he struggled to fight back.

Knowing that it was a fight he would lose, the Russian's fingers closing around his throat in a deathly grip. The younger man, the stronger of the two of them, even with his wounds.

So this is how it ends. It was strange how abstract that seemed, his mind seeming to accept the inevitability of his fate, even as his body fought against it. His vision blurring as he struggled for air, the world around him narrowing to a faint pinprick of light.

This is how it was always going to end.

And he felt something cool beneath his fingers, scarce even aware of how they had found their way to his belt—the faint *snick* of the switchblade opening sounding loud in his ears, as if he was hearing it in an empty room.

He closed his eyes, fighting for breath as he brought his arm up, the blade describing a half-arc in the darkness as he summoned up his last reserves of strength, driving it deep into the Russian's ribs.

The hands around his throat relaxed instantly—a violent scream reverberating through the room as the FSB officer rolled backward—clutching at the knife, struggling to pull it from his body. Blood spurting from around the hilt.

And he was free, his oxygen-starved lungs gasping for breath as he pushed himself to his hands and knees, struggling to rise. Every fiber of his body crying out in protest. *In pain.*

His vision clearing as he looked around for his gun. *Finish this.*

Looked for it, and found it even as Grigoriy's hand closed around the pistol's grip—his mind measuring the distance even as the weapon came up. *Too far.*

The first shot went wild, fired off-hand as the Russian clutched at his stomach, and Harry didn't wait for the second—plunging backward into the darkness of the hall, nearly going down.

Pain searing like fire through his veins as he pushed himself aright, madness seizing hold. *Flight.*

Madness? Or the remnants of a sanity he'd thought long since abandoned? He was unarmed now, defenseless—long past the end of his tether.

He had to get out of here. *Run.* His hand propping himself up against the wall as he pushed himself along, making for the door—and into the summer night beyond.

Hearing the Russian's bellow of anger and pain behind him, the sound of another shot crashing out through the house—then another, the shots going wild in the darkness.

Harry's shoulder hit the door with a crash, knocking it open as he staggered out into the night—gazing up at the stars as they seemed to revolve above him. The woods nearby, reaching out for him, beckoning.

Come and be at peace.

Epilogue

4:07 P.M. Central European Summer Time, August 29th (three weeks later)
DGSE Headquarters
Paris, France

It was quiet in the office, the only sound the gentle tapping of Anaïs Brunet's pen against the wooden surface of her desk. A look of intense concentration on her face as she stared at the computer print-out lying on the desk before her.

Where are you?

But the balaclava-masked face of Ibrahim Abu Musab al-Almani held no more answers for her now than ever it had—the vaguely steel-blue eyes staring back at her from the photograph with a hard, enigmatic gaze.

He might even be dead, by now—though he hadn't been among the bodies recovered at the *Stade*. All those had been Maghrebi Arabs, with the exception of the young woman, identified as Nora Bercot, a native of Provence—a student at the *Universite Libre de Bruxelles* in Belgium.

Perhaps he had been the first suicide bomber there on the Avenue Jules Rimet, but she doubted that, very much. He had been too far up in the hierarchy of this group to have sacrificed himself in such a manner. A *planner*, not a foot soldier. Like Gamal Belkaïd.

Belkaïd. He *was* dead, along with his sister and a handful of his criminal network, all of them officially killed in a GIGN raid on one of his residences, in the Eure-et-Loire *department*, in the countryside outside the small commune of Béville-le-Comte. *Shot while resisting arrest.*

The truth. . .was more complicated. The truth that they didn't *know* the

571

truth. That Belkaïd had been dead two days before GIGN arrived on-site, the sudden flurry of chatter among the former black marketeer's associates enabling them to hone in on his possible location. Found propped up in his chair in the home's small office, his brains blown out by a single 9mm round to the forehead.

There had been a struggle, clearly—far more rounds fired within the confines of the office than could be accounted for by the almost execution-style killing of Belkaïd. Heavy blood stains on the rug before the desk that didn't match the Algerian's blood type.

But his killer. . .was nowhere to be found. An enigma, wrapped in a mystery.

Dead, nevertheless—however he had met his fate. One of the two architects of the *Stade* attack, removed from the earth. Which left them with the elusive al-Almani.

"We will find you," Brunet whispered, as much to herself as to the photograph—thinking of Emile Vautrin and his small *Division Action* unit out at Fort Noisy-le-Sec. "No matter how long it takes. . .we will find you."

7:42 P.M. Moscow Time
Chkalovsky Airport
Shchyolkovo, Moscow Oblast

The sun was setting over the airport as the aging Cessna Citation taxiied to a stop on the tarmac, the business jet's fuselage glowing in the last rays of the evening.

Alexei Mikhailovich Vasiliev leaned back into the door of the Mercedes, his face a mask as he stared out toward the jet—watching as its door opened and the stairs unfolded—men in suits maneuvering a stretcher down the steps. FSB officers, like himself—like everyone else gathered around the small convoy of vehicles gathered here in this small corner of the airport, awaiting the jet's arrival. Like the man on the stretcher.

And he was home. He felt himself release a breath he didn't realize he had been holding—moving forward to meet the party as they wheeled the stretcher toward the waiting vehicles, taking in his first sight of his. . .son, was the only word that sufficed in this moment, an unaccustomed emotion nearly overwhelming Vasiliev as he stared down into Kolesnikov's deathly pale face.

The young man looked worse than Vasiliev had even expected, the list of injuries that had made their way back from the *rezidentura* in Paris devastating enough.

He'd been shot twice, once through the lung—shot and stabbed, the blade missing his liver by scant centimeters. The details of the incident, remaining unclear, even now—but one thing was certain. He had come very close to death. *Even now. . .*the future remained uncertain.

"Grisha," Vasiliev exclaimed fiercely as he seized Kolesnikov's hand, using the diminutive of his young friend's name, heedless of their fellow officers all around, "my son, I had feared to never see you again."

A moment passed, and then he felt the answering squeeze against his hand—saw a weak smile edge its way across the pale face. "And. . .yet here I am. I'm not dead just yet."

"Who did this to you?" Vasiliev demanded, his eyes growing cold as ice. The one question none of the reports had answered, a cloud growing across Kolesnikov's face in the semi-darkness as he seemed to consider it.

"A ghost," he replied finally, his voice a weak rasp. Almost lost amidst the whine of the idling turbines. "A ghost from our past. . ."

6:57 P.M. Central European Summer Time
Chateau du Fleckenstein
Vosges Mountains, France

". . .and our first historical records of the castle come in 1174, when Gottfried of Fleckenstein was a member of Frederick Barbarossa's imperial court." Muriel Lecanuet announced, repeating the familiar litany as she looked around into the faces of the American college students surrounding her.

She had worked as a tour guide here at the castle for twenty years, and knew the history of the place by heart. "The castle is built into a sandstone outcropping nearly a hundred meters long, sitting more than three hundred meters above sea level, and offering a commanding view of the valley below, out toward the River Sauer, enabling its owners to control the line of communication between Alsace and Lorraine, while protecting Haguenau, then the site of an imperial palace. The family expanded the castle many times over the centuries, with the stair tower we're currently standing atop, part of renovations dating from the 16th Century, around the time that Strasbourg architect Daniel Specklin described it *Chateau du Fleckenstein* as 'the ideal castle.' A century later, the French soldiers of Louis XIV, the Sun King, took the citadel. . ."

Even as she spoke, she found her eyes drifting to the periphery of the group, catching sight of a lone figure just standing there, near the edge of the tower—looking out over the wooded Alsatian mountainside at the foot of the cliff, toward the border with Germany, barely six hundred meters away.

The man had arrived perhaps an hour before the tour group, a worn, haggard figure. *Jet lag?* Perhaps, but there was. . .something about him, something she couldn't place her finger on. Something different from the tens of thousands of tourists she saw pass through the castle every year.

He turned then to meet her gaze, as if he had felt her eyes on him—and she looked away hastily. *Why had she done that?* It was a question she found impossible to answer, something in those forbidding gunmetal-blue eyes chilling her to the bone.

"French soldiers?" Lecanuet heard one of the college students ask. "But we're in France."

"Not at the time," she replied, grateful for the distraction. "You see, back then the political situation in Europe was. . ."

When she looked back, a few moments later, the man was no longer standing there. Her eyes flickering around the confines of the tower, back toward the staircase—in an effort to locate the tall, lonely figure, but to no avail. He was gone. Simply. . .*vanished.*

As though he had never been there at all.

The End

An author lives by word-of-mouth recommendations. If you enjoyed this story, please consider leaving a customer review(even if only a few lines) on Amazon. It would be greatly helpful and much appreciated.

If you would like to contact me personally, drop me a line at Stephen@stephenwrites.com.

Coming Soon. . .
A New Novel from Stephen England

He's survived. . .but at what cost?

Haunted by demons of regret in the wake of the Paris attacks and pursued by the French security services, bent on avenging their fallen officer, Harry Nichols moves further east, into the heart of Europe, seeking to lose himself in the chaos of the Syrian diaspora. *To disappear.*

There's no going back. No second chances. Any prayer of redemption, dying along with Daniel Mahrez on the dirty floor of that basement in the Ardennes.

And as the Western democracies of central Europe struggle to contend with unrest precipitated by mass migration, and old evils rear their heads once more. . .a spy on the run could prove useful to the right people.

Or even the wrong ones.

Look for *Soon Dies the Day*, the fifth full-length volume of Stephen England's bestselling *Shadow Warriors* series, coming soon.

For news and release information, visit www.stephenwrites.com and sign up for the mailing list.

Stay in touch and up-to-the-minute with book news through social media.

On Facebook: https://www.facebook.com/stephenenglandauthor

Join the Facebook group to discuss the series with other fans:
Stephen England's Shadow Warriors

On Twitter: https://twitter.com/stephenmengland

Author's Note

The ending of each new book feels like the close of yet another marathon, and that's particularly true of *Presence of Mine Enemies*, a story which originated from the germ of an idea which occurred to me as *Embrace the Fire* was in its final edits.

It's taken me longer to reach the end of this particular stage of the journey than I had imagined when first setting out, but I've rarely been more pleased with the result, despite the unexpected (even to me) twists and turns it took along the way.

The dangers of undercover work as presented in this novel are based in reality, and though the specific circumstances of Nichols' situation caused me to go well beyond the pale of what would ever be tolerated in legitimate police or intelligence work—at least in the West—the perils of emotional entanglement with those one is intended to investigate, or subvert, are real. And that's even with the safety of a traditional law enforcement/intel network backing up an undercover officer.

I'm indebted to my colleague Steven Hildreth, Jr. for recommending Jay Dobyns' *No Angel* and William Queen's *Under and Alone*, a pair of memoirs written by federal agents involved in penetrating American outlaw motorcycle gangs as undercover officers. Those books were invaluable in helping me understand the kind of emotions that Nichols would experience as he, unexpectedly, found himself on the inside of a terror cell.

It's been eight years since the first debut of the *Shadow Warriors* series, and its subject, international terrorism, is sadly as relevant today as it was then—even with the collapse of the Caliphate in Syria. As for Nichols. . .his story remains far from over, and I look forward to sharing much more of it with you all.

Thanks go out, as ever, to my fantastic artist, Louis Vaney, for the work he did on the cover for this book—his ability to take a rough vision and create compelling art from it remains unmatched.

To the members of the *Presence of Mine Enemies* beta reader team: Bodo Pfündl, Paula Tyler, Joanne Elmore, and Joe Walsh. Your feedback on the unproofed manuscript was invaluable in turning this into a polished endproduct, and I am deeply grateful for the time you took.

To my colleagues in this at-times lonely business, who I am honored to call friends, Robert Bidinotto, Ian Graham, Nate Granzow, Matt Fulton, and the aforementioned Steven Hildreth, Jr., gentlemen whose advice and encouragement has always been appreciated. I encourage any fan of this series to check out their work—fine authors, all.

To my friends in the military and intelligence communities, who must remain uncredited, with thanks for all the guidance you've provided throughout the years. I take full responsibility for any mistakes which remain, along with whatever liberties I've taken with reality in the name of artistic license.

Special thanks goes out to the staff of London's Army & Navy Club—the "Rag"—for their willingness to answer countless questions about their club and the room in which Marsh and Ashworth met.

And most of all, as ever, my thanks to all of my readers, whose passion for Nichols' story over these years has been such an encouragement in those moments when writer's block had set in.

May God bless you all, and may God continue to bless America.